LITTLE SPARRW

For anyone that reads to escape, and is far too broke for therapy,
I got you.

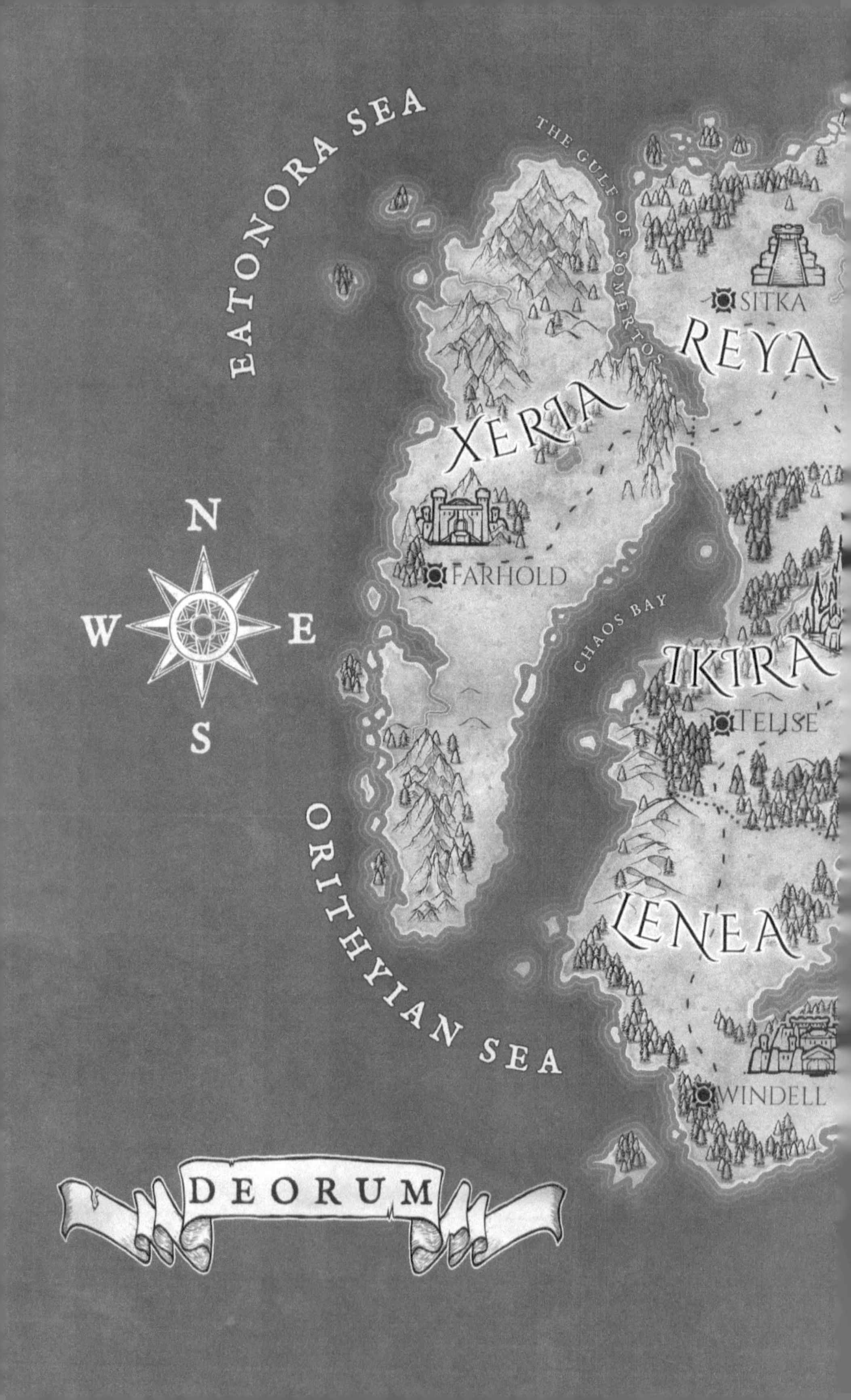

EATONORA SEA
THE GULF OF SOMERTOS
REYA
SITKA
XERIA
FARHOLD
N
W E
S
CHAOS BAY
IKIRA
TELISE
ORITHYIAN SEA
LENEA
WINDELL
DEORUM

THE PERICIUS SEA
ELEMETUM'S GULF
LIOS
ENDERIA
HANRA'S BAY
KENDELEN
TAROS
THE WASTES
THE SEA OF TIMEA
LEGEND
CAPITAL
BRIDGE
KINGDOM BORDER
TRADE ROUTE

PROLOGUE

It is not clear which came first, Light, or Dark, but come they did.

Opposite sides of the same coin, these two divine forces collided, forming the realm as we have come to know it; Adysium. They built the skies and the seas, stoking them until stars shone and rivers ran, mountains formed and plains expanded.

When they were done moulding the nothingness into something, they merged, in one final show of power, and from their union the beings we now know as Divinities came into existence.

Over the millennia these gods and goddesses grew tired of their paradise, tired of each other. Some chose to leave, opening gateways in hopes of discovering new realms to explore, others stayed. Two in particular, siblings Akros; the God of Chaos and Ades, the Goddess of Order, sought to test their strengths against one another by seeing who could create the finest being.

Ades looked within herself, and to the other divinities of Adysium, for inspiration, designing a being in their image. She created woman first. Soft as a spring breeze, but strong like a tempest. Beautiful like the first glimpse of sunlight, but deep as an ocean abyss.

Meanwhile Akros desired something different, something magnificent. As a result, he created beasts; creatures of all kinds. Some were small and silent, others huge and frightening. He was so impressed with his creations, at the vast differences from one to another, that he couldn't wait to show his peers.

When he presented his beasts to his fellow gods and goddesses, Ades was fascinated and praised him for a job well done, but the others seemed more interested in his sister's creations. Not one to be outdone, he insisted Ades had cheated, that she'd had assistance from the other divinities. She denied this, of course, but Akros would not hear it, demanding they try again in front of each other so there could be no tampering.

In the end, Ades agreed, if only to stop her brother's whining. The others gathered to watch. Ades once again went first, this time in the image of Akros himself. She created a man to compliment her woman. This man was strong as the oldest tree, but versatile like leaves at seasons change. He was fierce like some of Akros' beasts, and brave like the divinities who'd left Adysium in search of the unknown. Together, she named her creations Mortals.

Akros was filled with anger as the onlookers cheered for his sister yet again. He stared at this lesser reflection of himself, and his jealousy only grew. It spread through him like an infection, tainting his magic as he tried to create what she had, but better. A man with more strength. A man that her weak mortals would cower from. Beings so impressive that the others would have no choice but to acknowledge Akros as the stronger of the two. He would be the winner.

In his haste and blind rage, he created beings that took on his desired traits; extreme strength, fear inciting appearances, might that Ades' mortals could not combat, but like Akros, they too became tainted. Forged from rage, jealousy, and hatred, Akros created what the others would name Monsters.

Akros tried to tame his monstrous creations, but could not. The others laughed at him, turning once again back to Ades and her mortals. Akros stormed away in shame and anger, swearing to make his sister pay for her slight against him.

He waited a thousand years before making true of this threat. Biding his time, he waited for mortals to expand their numbers, to begin carving out life and purpose for themselves. All the while, he was whispering in the ears of any divinity that would listen, sowing the seeds of entitlement, convincing them they should be worshipped by these lowly creatures that were made in their image. These things with no power, no intelligence of their own.

After gathering enough allies, he began enslaving any mortals that wandered into his territory. His allies did the same, and helped keep Ades distracted, knowing she would not allow her beloved creatures to be treated as such. More and more divinities saw the benefits of having mortal servants and began taking their own to do with as they wished. By the time Ades discovered what her brother had done, thousands of mortals were already enslaved.

She demanded that all who had imprisoned mortals release them at once, but some had grown accustomed to having servants at their beck and call, and ignored her pleas. Ades refused to give in and gathered allies of her own; gods and goddesses who, like her, saw mortals as more than cattle, as children to be nurtured and taught, not enslaved and imprisoned. Many mortals joined Ades in the fight for their freedom, but some sided with Akros. They saw the divinities as beings they ought to worship and serve, so they pledged themselves to Akros, and in doing so, they too were tainted. Soon, Adysium was in an all out war.

For three hundred years, mortals and divinities alike fought in The Great War, siding with either Akros or Ades. With no end in sight, Ades knew that even if they won this war, Akros would never see mortals as more than slaves, nor would many of the others. As long as they walked this realm, mortal kind would never be safe. So, on the final day, along with the help of gods and goddesses such as Zalnea, Ikeara, Xeria, Lereya, Elios, Taros, Thadea, and others, Ades threw open a gateway to another realm, banishing Akros and his allies from Adysium, locking it behind them.

Such a feat was not without consequences. Ades couldn't simply banish Akros and a select few divinities. In order to banish one, she had to banish all, including those who'd sided with her. To close the door and ensure those she'd banished remained so, she had no choice but to forfeit her divine essence, sealing the realm and protecting the mortals who dwelled within it.

However, she feared one day her essence would fade, and those she'd exiled would find the strength to reopen the gateway and wreak havoc on the realm once more. So she gave mortals one final gift, in hopes it would help protect them should the gate ever be reopened.

The morning of that final day, before they were forced from the realm they cherished, Ades and some of her closest divine allies each gave a piece of their power to their strongest mortal warriors. In what became known as The Blessing, the warriors that fought on the front lines were gifted a magic that was strong enough to survive, even when the divinities were no longer around to stoke it.

These mortals became known as the Gifted.

When the war had ended, the divinities banished, and all other magic thought to be wiped from the realm, the mortals slowly rebuilt and recovered.

Free from their cages, mortals explored Adysium once again.

To those who have been deemed worthy, we bestow the Divine Giftings to help you prosper and protect your people. They are yours to do with as you wish. However, take care as we are watching, we are waiting.

– Unknown.

CHAPTER ONE

Sitting in a crowded tavern full of middle-class nobles and off duty workers, I gripped my tankard of ale. My gaze swept across the room, observing the patrons as they socialised and drank to their heart's content. Every time an ale maid passed, they'd dip into their seemingly endless coin pouches to order another round of refreshments.

Their pouches were not as endless as the ones hoarded by the highest standing lords and ladies of Kendelen, but I'd be hard pressed to find such prestige in a place like this, and that suited me just fine. In my stained britches, dirty boots, and dark cloak, I'd draw too much attention in the type of establishments the upper class frequented.

This tavern, with its dim lighting, nondescript walls, and private booths, catered to those with more than enough coin for me to have a fruitful night. With a mix of workmen drinking away their days, lesser noblewomen seeking to escape from the frills and expectancies, and lesser noblemen favouring frivolity of a more relaxed kind, this place, these patrons; I could work with.

From my carefully chosen vantage point at a shadowy corner table, I could assess the entire room. I would remain undisturbed, provided I continued to order tankards of ale that I discreetly spilt on the already sticky floor as I scouted for my next target.

The usual options presented themselves; the vain ladies in wait, hoping to snag themselves a husband if they wore enough kohl on their eyelids and wiggled their hips seductively enough, and the arrogant nobleman here to gamble their 'hard-earned' coin away. That is, if you considered being born into the right household, hard work.

There were a few city guards, whom I usually avoided. Not because I doubted my skill, but on the off chance one of them was a Parapure. It wasn't unusual for the magically gifted half-bloods to become soldiers or guards. In fact, it was expected.

There were the wealthy patrons that were well connected and always carried sizeable sums of coin on them, and lastly, were the middle-class workers; bookkeepers, hunters, medicae, and so on. The type of professions that made enough coin to fit in at a place like this but were never treated as equal to the nobility. Despite my attire, I blended in well enough with the middle-class workers.

I hid a smirk as a provocatively dressed woman sidled up to a group of noblemen. The men were already silently contending with each other for the dominant role of the group. She clearly knew what she was doing and had already singled out the likely leader among them. It was always entertaining to watch the game unfold. Both the man and the woman subtly sized each other up, whilst acting as if they weren't simply calculating how much they stood to gain from the other.

The woman proved quite the distraction for most of the men, even some women, as she swaggered past. I took that as my cue to begin. Weaving my way through the establishment, my hand slipped in and out from pocket to pouch, pouch to purse, in a solo dance of underhanded stealth. The patrons were none the wiser. They never were.

After a successful evening, I was on my way out when a nobleman also appeared to be exiting the tavern, stumbling from a little too much ale. His cropped blonde hair was flawlessly styled, and his clothing was of the finest material available in Taros, telling me he was considerably wealthy. Unusual for someone of his affluence to visit a place such as this. That alone was tempting enough for any thief on a good day, but when the two capital guards swaggered out behind him, I simply couldn't resist the opportunity to see what sort of protection the people of Kendelen's taxes bought them.

The act itself was easily accomplished. Like the rest of the clueless patrons I'd successfully stolen from tonight, the blonde nobleman was none the wiser. The guards, however, *just* so happened to be glancing my way as I slowly lifted the man's coin pouch from his pocket.

"YOU THERE! STOP!" The first burly guard called after me, followed by a string of curses when he realised I was ignoring his demand.

Unable to stop the small smile that graced my lips, I took off down the cobblestoned alley, mindful of the two men now taking chase. I'd needed that last mark, every coin counted when it came to buying our freedom, but I could have lifted it without drawing their attention. Perhaps it was arrogance, perhaps it was stupidity, but I never liked to go too long without testing our city's defences. After all, these were the guards I'd have to outrun or outsmart if they ever caught me for real.

So here I was, sprinting through the backstreets of Kendelen with two of the *city's finest* on my tail. You would think they'd have better things to do than take pursuit of an Impure thief so late at night.

To my surprise, losing them took a few more turns than I'd care to admit, along with some of the acrobatic manoeuvres Butcher had ensured I could do in my sleep. Still, they soon lost my trail. Perched atop one of the spacious houses that resided on this side of the river, I watched them grumble and turn back before I deemed it safe to return home unfollowed. They'd clearly increased their training since I'd last had to escape one of them. Perhaps the newly appointed captain of the guard I'd heard talk of had something to do with it. Supposedly the youngest ever appointed to the honoured position. I made a mental note to find out more about the man as I navigated my way through the streets, unhurried now that I wasn't running for my life.

By this time of night, the streets were quiet, save for the occasional drunkard wandering home from their local tavern. I slowed as I crossed the Sepa Bridge, which acted as a clear divide between the slums of the capital and the higher classes. I stopped, leaning on the railing and looking out across the river. It was always so peaceful in the dark, lit only by the moon high above and the reflection of the castle's watchtowers.

Those towers were lit every night without fail. Once, a necessity. Used during The Great War to communicate with other watch points and cities. Now, nothing but an outdated tradition. Letting out a sigh, I pulled back and made my way to our ramshackle hut, if you could even call it that.

When I entered, Sierra was, unsurprisingly, waiting up for me, still seated in her rolling chair. A thick wooden seat atop a four-wheeled frame made up the contraption known, for short, as a roller. It helped her move about without someone having to carry her. If we were wealthy, we could hire servants and a lectica to carry her around or purchase one of the more skillfully designed rollers that could handle rougher terrain.

Her shoulder length, jet black hair was loose to prepare for bed, in contrast to my long, muddy brown waves. Given my occupation, I should really cut it, but I'd never been able to. Our hair was not the only difference between us. We had similar facial features, like our noses and mouths, but Sierra's eyes were a crystalline blue, whereas mine were an emerald green. Her skin was paler than mine, but I attributed that to the fact that she spent less time in the sun than I did.

Giving her a guilty grin, I plopped myself down at the table.

"You're up late," I said cheerfully.

"You know I worry," she mumbled. *I really did.*

Sierra made sure I never forgot how much she cared. She didn't approve of the methods I used to keep us fed and sheltered, but knew I had little choice in the matter. She just didn't want me to get hurt. We were all we had.

"You have nothing to worry about. Besides, it is temporary. Just until we can earn enough coin to get to Reya. Then we can start over." I explained for what felt like the thousandth time.

Despite her constant worrying, despite our differences, I loved my sister with all I had. She rolled her eyes, as she always did when I mentioned Reya, the kingdom named after the Goddess of Healing, Lereya, and home to the Gifted Healeti. They could heal almost any ailment and injury.

Usually, she was the calm, sweet, level-headed one, and I was the stubborn, wild one. On this topic, however, she was stubborn as an ox, unwilling to fathom the idea of us successfully travelling to the land of the Healeti, where they could mend Sierra's legs and she could walk again. We could start over. She would be free from that divinity damned roller, and I would be free from The Butcher.

She finally sighed, shaking her head. "We should get some sleep. Camilla said to meet her at first light."

"Of course she did." I groaned. Divinities forbid we meet at a normal hour and I actually get a lie-in.

Camilla was my boss of sorts. Well, that might be too loose a term. Camilla runs the Kendelen Circus, having inherited it after her husband unexpectedly passed. She'd managed to build it into an attraction people travelled across the continent to see. She was *also* The Butcher, the biggest crime lord in the capital, with ties to every city in our kingdom, Taros, and even some of the other kingdoms. Lastly, she was our legal guardian. Well, she was no longer mine, but unfortunately Sierra was still 'under her care.'

She'd taken us in when we'd lost our parents. Not exactly a motherly figure, but she had given us a roof over our heads when no one else would. Sierra was only three years old when both our parents died in a house fire. I was six. That fire was responsible for Sierra's inability to walk. A burning wooden beam had broken her legs in several places, crushing her. With no other family, we'd become orphans; one crippled, and one way too mouthy for her own good.

Only the wealthiest families could afford to send their children to school, so the orphans like us, and even the children of poorer families, only had two options. Find someone to teach you their trade, in the hopes of one day being taken on as an apprentice, or steal the resources you needed to survive. Camilla stood nothing to gain by sending us to the streamlined schools, so she offered us shelter and food in exchange for child labour and her own special kind of training. I'd become her spy, her thief, having taken to it quickly. It helped that very few had suspected a six-year-old girl of any foul play. Sierra was her bookkeeper, having excelled in literacy and mathematics even from a young age. I'd often find her with her head in a book, much to my chagrin.

At least by night, that's what we did. By day, we were a part of her crew. I was 'The Masked Flyer', an aerial-acrobatic act that would fly through the air, completing all kinds of stunts. Masked, of course. We couldn't risk my identity being exposed if anyone ever caught me spying and traced that back to the circus. Meanwhile, Sierra managed Camilla's finances. Both the on and *off* the books kind.

It's not that I wasn't grateful for Camilla's generosity, however, said generosity only went so far. She gave us only what we needed to survive. She paid us for our work, but only the bare minimum. Just enough to pay *her* for the food and shelter she provided now that we were older. Even if we tried to leave and work for someone else, most people in the slums knew better than to cross her. No one would hire us for fear of incurring her wrath, leaving us with little chance of getting out from under her thumb, especially with Sierra still under the age of twenty.

Personally, I think twenty is far too old to not be considered an adult, especially when you've been looking out for yourself since the age of six, but Pures ran the continent, so they made the rules. Aging much slower than us lowly Impures, and living for far longer, Pures aren't considered fully mature until the age of twenty. Something to do with their magic causes their aging to slow once they hit twenty, which apparently means the rest of us non-gifted mortals have to follow the same rules.

One more year, and we would be free to leave, which is why my pick-pocketing had gotten more reckless as of late. We needed the extra coin, and I wasn't yet willing to stoop to other methods of attaining what we needed.

I shuddered, thinking of the girls I'd seen at some of the establishments Camilla invested in. They were often too young, barely past their first blood, and while they pasted on pretty smiles for the grotesque men paying for their services, their eyes had lost their light. I prayed neither Sierra nor I ever lost ours.

Shaking my head at my spiralling thoughts, I helped Sierra to her cot and placed her roller beside it, turning off the lantern, and getting into my own cot. I really should have slept, like Sierra suggested, but it was always nights like these that sleep eluded me. When my mind wandered and entertained crazy ideas of what our life could be like if I ever got us out.

There was an entire world out there to see, entire kingdoms. Six, to be exact, and that's just on this continent; Deorum. Each one is ruled by a Gifted *Pure.*

A large portion of Deorum's population still worshipped the Divinities, usually those involved with the Deos Credentes. An equally sized portion of people no longer revered the divine beings that had not been seen since The Great War, however, everyone certainly believed they'd once walked among us. There was no other explanation for the magic bestowed upon the soldiers that fought on the front lines to free mortals from enslavement four thousand years ago.

The descendants of those soldiers, including the current royals of the six kingdoms, possess unique abilities; Giftings, granted by the Divinities that fought alongside the mortals. Our kingdom's namesake, Taros; Goddess of Justice herself, granted the ancestors of our current ruling family magic that came to be known as the Kineti Gifting. The Navarre family has remained in power and governed our kingdom for hundreds of years. Our king, Hadrian Navarre, is a powerful Kineti. Specifically, a Teleki, with the ability to move objects with his mind.

The six Giftings; Kineti, Incrementi, Virbi, Animi, Healeti, and Elementi, tell us which God or Goddess *granted* the magic that now runs through the veins of the Pure, and that Gifting, determines their *Specialty;* the specific power they possess.

I have never seen King Hadrian in action, but it is said to leave you in awe of his raw power. His son, Prince Valor, takes after him, having inherited his father's magic, while his daughter, Princess Calliope, inherited her mothers. Queen Odette was an Incrementi.

For unknown reasons, when two Pures procreate, their children can only ever inherit one parent's Gifting. Probably nature's way of preventing any one person from having *too* much power. Because of that, outside of politically arranged marriages, the royal Pures rarely wed other royal lines in order to maintain their specific Gifting's legacy. Instead, opting for a marriage between themselves and a higher noble Pure who shares the same Gifting, but descends from a different bloodline.

No one knows for sure know why the specific families that we now call the monarchs of Deorum were chosen to rule, especially as so many soldiers fought on the front lines, from so many bloodlines. All of whom were given Giftings, during what is now known as The Blessing, becoming the first ever Pures.

It's most commonly assumed that not long after receiving their new abilities, the soldiers turned on each other, seeking more power. The royals we now serve today are most likely descended from the families that came out triumphant all those centuries ago. The victors divided the continent and named each territory after the God or Goddess of their new Gifting.

There is very little recorded of anything before The Blessing. Despite this, plenty still pray to the old Divinities, even though no one has heard even a whisper from a single one in the four thousand years since they disappeared. I, for one, believe the Divinities still live, but if they are still watching, I don't believe they particularly care what we do, and are therefore not a reliable source of comfort.

All of these unique Giftings and different lands, just waiting to be explored. We will go to the Healeti of Reya first. Sierra was too young to remember being able to walk and has long since lost hope of ever experiencing it, but I haven't. I want her to have the best life possible. So, we will start there, then maybe we will go to Terra, where Turfs worked the earth. Sierra would love that. It didn't matter to me where we went. All that mattered was that Sierra was happy, and we were free. I would do whatever I had to, sacrifice whatever I had to, so I could at least give her that. After she is healed, we can go wherever we want, see whatever we want, and be whoever we want. No more stealing.

I dreamt of faraway lands that night, like most other nights these days, faraway lands and a better life for both of us.

CHAPTER TWO

I awoke the next morning, leaving breakfast for Sierra on her bedside table as quietly as I could. Dressed in a plain tunic, I pulled my cloak over my head to protect myself from the early morning chill and left without disturbing her.

Butcher was seated in a lavish chair that matched the rest of her study's aesthetic; dark woods, decadent furnishings, and extravagant displays of wealth. Her blonde hair was pulled back into a formal-looking bun and her signature pearls adorned her neck. She wore heavy kohl eyeliner and a deep red lip stain. How she always appeared so elegant before the sun had even finished rising was beyond me.

I stopped in front of her desk, silently waiting as she took her time finishing whatever document she was probably not at all that interested in. Butcher knew the value of silence and the power one could wield with it. She finally looked up and nodded for me to sit.

"I have a new assignment for you, Adira. A big one." I ignored the small trickle of unease that always accompanied those words when they came from her.

Big assignments usually involved crossing more lines than I was comfortable with and the stakes were often high. They'd been getting higher and higher as of late.

"What kind of assignment?" I queried. She watched me akin to how I imagined a hawk watched its prey. I knew that look. Whatever this assignment was, it was important to her. Very important. Usually not a good sign for me.

"It's no secret that you are my preferred asset for these types of jobs, Adira. After all, I ensured you had the best training possible, at my own expense." Yes, she had, whether I'd wanted it or not. She never let me forget it either. There's a reason I was known in certain circles as 'The Shadow of Kendelen.'

I had a very vast and unique skill set. I spoke multiple languages, was highly trained in stealth, espionage, poisons, and more. I was expected to be in perfect shape, physically capable of outrunning or outmanoeuvring the best this city offered. Butcher had forced me to study politics, war, history, and all the other boring stuff that Sierra loved learning about.

I'd been poked, prodded, and pushed until my instructors had honed me into the perfect spy. There was only one area in which I was lacking. They forbade me from learning to fight. Something about it being unbecoming of a lady. I suspected it had more to do with the fact that if I'd had *that* weapon in my arsenal, I'd have found a way to use it against Butcher or my tutors. She couldn't leave her best asset *entirely* defenceless, though. So, they taught me the art of archery, along with some defensive manoeuvres. Always focusing on escaping, not overcoming. I had to be faster and smarter because if it came down to a physical fight, I would always lose. Which is also why they'd trained me to withstand torture.

If anyone caught me, she couldn't very well have me revealing her secrets. From a young age, I'd been exposed to every form of torture they could put me through without killing me. Butcher delighted in overseeing these particular lessons herself. They taught me to withstand physical pain and to keep my mouth shut.

Throughout all that training, though, I was always forbidden from learning any steel weapons or offensive combat. Making it in my best interest to be the best at what I did and under no circumstances get caught. I'd attempted to learn some basic hand to hand combat on my own, but my technique had left much to be desired without a tutor.

I would never forget the time I'd begged one of the older orphan boys, Terieus, to teach me some manoeuvres. I finally won him over, and we began meeting three times a week to train. Butcher eventually found out, as she always did, and the very next day, the royal guards arrested the boy for treason. He was never seen again, and I'd never dared ask anyone else to help me.

"Which is why," she continued, pulling me back from my drifting thoughts, "You're the only person I trust with this."

"What is the assignment, Butcher?"

She smiled that predatory smile of hers, the one that only appeared when the pay-out was sizeable.

"You will be on a need-to-know basis. Right now, all you need to know is that a powerful person has an interest in the royal court's current comings and goings. They have paid handsomely to have someone infiltrate the King's court and report back." I blinked. *Infiltrate the King's court?* Was she mad? Had she been inhaling too much of the pungent rosewater fragrance she seemed to bathe in? It would be considered treason if I were caught. The punishment for which was execution. No trial, and no jury. If I were captured, or worse, Sierra would be stuck here. She couldn't work like I could. She was valuable, but she could never make enough coin to leave on her own. I couldn't risk it.

"I'm honoured you would trust me with such an assignment, Mistress," I said carefully, using her preferred title, "but I must politely decline. The stakes are too high."

She frowned at my response. "They are only high if you get caught, which you will not."

"It's the royal court? They strung the last spy who tried to get into that place up at the castle gates without their head. I can't do that to Sierra. I'm sorry." She stared at me for a minute before taking a deep breath and speaking again, landing a blow I hadn't seen coming.

"I know you've been pocketing extra coin, Adira. I know you plan to take your sister to The Sana." The Sana was the most renowned institute in Reya, where only the best Healeti and even medicae, Impure but highly skilled healers, honed their craft. I stiffened. I had been *so* careful to hide it from her, but I should have known she would eventually find out.

"Butcher—" She held up a hand to silence whatever excuse I was about to come up with.

"This assignment would give you the means to do so. You would have enough coin to get her to Reya, and then some." I took a shallow breath.

This was why Butcher was the best at what she did. She was ruthless when it came to discovering your deepest desires, the lengths you'd be willing to go to for them, and finally, a way to exploit that for her own gain. I wondered how long she'd known about my plans. How long she'd waited for the right time to use it against me. At the rate I was going, it would take another year at least to garner the kind of coin we'd need to get to the Healeti, but this? To risk my life *and* Sierra's?

"I appreciate that, Mistress. I really do, but I still can't do it. I will find the money some other way. I can't risk it. I'm sorry." She looked like she might curse me to Heknos himself, God of the Underworld; Infernis, but as quickly as it had appeared, the anger vanished from her face, and she nodded calmly at me.

"Very well. As disappointed as I am with your initial response, you may take some time to reconsider. I will send for you again soon."

"Alright." I conceded. "But my answer will remain the same."

She waved her hand like a queen dismissing a servant. "Yes, yes, just consider it, child. Don't make hasty decisions. I taught you better. Think it over. I know you will make the right choice." Her tone, her threat, was clear.

I knew a dismissal when I heard one, so I nodded and rose from my chair, exiting the room. Only once I was a block away did I let myself loose a breath. Infiltrate the divinity damned royal court? I shook my head. It was absurd. I'd be lying if I said the asking price wasn't tempting, but no matter how well it paid, it was a fool's errand.

My meeting with Butcher had run shorter than expected, so I spent the remainder of the morning meandering through the markets, exploring the different vendors and their wares. When I spotted the robed men and women in the centre of the square, I made sure to give them a wide berth. Those unfortunate enough to make eye contact, or simply stray too close to the Deos Credentes disciples, would be accosted with talk of prayer, devotion, and how benevolent the divinities were. The Divine Believers were the second pillar of Taros, and a majority of the continent. Most kingdoms had their own sect of believers, that essentially governed alongside the ruling families. Even the royals had little sway over the Credentes, being that they were supposedly 'holier-than-though' worshippers of the divinities and are therefore above mortal restraints. I didn't particularly feel like being converted today, or any day really, so I avoided them.

I ended up spending a little of the extra coin I'd *made* last night to purchase a small rose pendant for Sierra. She loved flowers, and though I knew I should save the money, I could never resist getting her small things here and there to brighten her day.

For the most part, Sierra was a happy, incredibly intelligent, and sweet girl, but I noticed the way she sometimes struggled to smile, when she'd grow distant. Those days broke my heart. That was happening more often as she got older and really longed for the things she couldn't do in that damned roller. She certainly didn't need fixing, but if it were possible to reduce those smile-less days, and give her the ability to walk like the rest of us? I'd do everything I could to make that happen. She deserved that much.

She reminded me of my mother, at least what few memories I could recall of her. Gentle and warm. Sierra was too little to remember much about our parents. Including the way our mother lit up the room when she entered. I remembered people naturally gravitating toward her. Sierra had the same magnetic effect on people, but she always seemed completely oblivious, assuming people stared because of the roller. I knew that wasn't the case. She just had that *thing*, that warmth our mother had. Me? I imagined I was a lot like my father, as helpless to Sierra's gentle charm as he was to my mother's. I also remembered the way he would look at her, like she completely enamoured him, as if he might blink and she would disappear.

I had long since forgotten what my parents did for work. I remembered my mother being home with us a lot though, and I liked to picture my father as something brave, such as a huntsman. He was the loud to my mother's quiet. He was the troublemaker, always making us laugh until our stomachs ached, while mother chided us, hiding her own laugh behind her apron. Thinking of them stirred up mixed feelings. Happiness at the warm memories, pangs of loss, and a dull sorrow that they weren't here to raise Sierra right. I was no doubt messing up the whole parenting thing.

A hand attempting to slip into my pocket interrupted the morbid turn my thoughts were taking. I gripped the culprit's wrist, yanking it out roughly as I spun, coming face-to-face with the wincing blue eyes of Raphael Morrighan.

"Ow!" He grunted as I rolled my eyes, dropping his wrist.

"One of these days, you're going to lose that hand." I grumbled. He rubbed his wrist, grinning at me sheepishly. His blonde curly hair falling across his eyes before he tucked it back behind his ear.

"That's why I need you to practice on Adi."

Groaning, I turned and kept walking. Unfortunately, he had no trouble matching my strides with his long legs.

"What have I told you about calling me that?"

"Hmmm, let's see." He held up a hand and started ticking off an invisible list on his fingers. "Stop calling me that, you weasel! Call me that again, Morrighan, and you'll regret it." He put a hand to his chest and dramatically sighed as he imitated my voice, "Raaaafffff."

I couldn't help the small smile that appeared as I shook my head at his horrible impression. "Nothing better to do today than practice your pick-pocketing?"

"We can't all be as good at it as you." He grinned and slung a casual arm around my shoulder. "Old man Jotters gave me the day off."

Raphael was an orphan, like me. He would have been in the same boat as me too, still in debt to Butcher, if not for an old blacksmith who'd lost his only son and needed someone to take over his business one day. Jotters had offered to take Raf on as his apprentice. Butcher had agreed and sold him for a much lower price than she'd normally consider.

Since then, he'd been living the life all orphans dreamed of. He was probably one of my only genuine friends, aside from Sierra. It's difficult to make many friends when you're a spy and they arrested the last person you befriended for treason, never to be seen again. Trust didn't exactly come easily. So Raf was it. A friend and occasionally more.

We had an unspoken understanding. I don't think either of us planned for it to happen the way it did, but one night a little over a year ago, after one too many ales and a bad day, we'd stumbled back to his loft, and I hadn't left until the sun had risen. We'd agreed it was just to relieve stress and find a bit of pleasure when one of us needed it.

No love, no interfering with our friendship, and both of us had other partners over the years. Raf more so than me, but mostly because I had higher standards than he did. He was a shameless flirt when given the opportunity. It was easy with Raf. In another life, we may have fallen in love. Childhood sweethearts, they'd have called us.

If things had been different, if I didn't have Sierra to think of, if Butcher wasn't set on keeping me under her thumb as long as she could, it would have been possible to picture that future with him. However, that was not the hand the divinities had dealt for me or him. We knew eventually we would say goodbye for the last time, so we made use of the time we had.

He nudged me gently. "Earth to, Adi. Am I that boring?"

"As a general rule? Yes." I grinned. "If you're not busy, I have a bit of time before I need to set up for today's show?" I bit my lip when I met his eyes, a movement he tracked and immediately honed in on.

He smiled and silently escorted me to his loft, where I let him distract me from today's problems, and even tomorrow's. Just for a while. It wouldn't last, but it was enough.

Crouched on the rooftop of one of the old slum houses, I was still pissed at Butcher's ludicrous offer. I was good, but I wasn't *that* good. I may as well sign my execution warrant if I agreed to take on that job. Movement from the building across from me drew my attention away from my thoughts and back to the task at hand. It had been a week since she had offered me the job and she'd been frosty ever since. Giving me the worst assignments, and keeping me busy, away from the circus and Sierra.

My current assignment was akin to searching for a needle in a haystack. Butcher suspected one of her informants had been flipped and was feeding her dodgy information. She believed a rival crime lord had paid them off. One that had been slowly growing bolder, encroaching on her turf. She couldn't prove it though and was concerned there could be more than one rat in her crew. So, she'd tasked me with the lovely job of tailing each of her informants until she was satisfied they weren't betraying her.

Informants were paid handsomely for their information and their ability to evade watchful eyes. After all, their income relied on them being seen as reputable sources, with intel difficult to obtain. If the information they provided was common knowledge or easily gained, it wouldn't be very valuable. This made my job of tailing the sneaky, and often slimy, men a frustrating inconvenience.

The man I found myself squatted on the roof to watch was finally on the move. He glanced around the street cautiously. I lowered myself so I was flush with the roof. Once he'd deemed it clear, he scurried off down the path, keeping to the shadows. I smiled a little, pulling my neck gaiter up and obscuring the bottom half of my face before following him.

It was easy to track him from this high up, despite the darkness and his evasive skills, thanks to how close together the houses in this area of the city were. We were in the slums, after all. Overpopulation issues had forced the Impure residents to build their houses within close proximity of each other and were often two stories high if people could afford it, housing multiple generations of the same family.

The man scurried on, moving quickly and quietly. I frowned as he crossed the Sepa Bridge, entering into noble territory. Having run out of rooftops,

I climbed down and followed on foot. I raised my hood to be on the safe side, waiting for him to cross completely before pursuing. Noblemen were occasionally known to hire informants from this side of the bridge. Usually, to dig up nefarious dirt on their fellow Lords and Ladies. House politics never ceased to amaze me. If I had the wealth and privilege these nobles possessed, I certainly wouldn't waste my time secretly fighting with each other.

The man I'd been following went by the name Trench. Something to do with the supposed difficulty of obtaining the information he coveted. As far as I knew, he rarely did business across the bridge, nor did he associate with any of the nobles. Yet, here he was, coming to a stop at what appeared to be a dressmaker's shop. I ducked into an alley as Trench paused and glanced around again before knocking lightly on the door. I peeked around the corner to see a small, plump woman poke her head out. When she saw Trench, she hurried him inside and locked the door.

I left the safety of the alley and snuck around the side, checking for any unlocked windows or doors. No luck. I huffed quietly, glancing up and grinning as I spotted the chimney. This building likely doubled up as a shop downstairs, living quarters upstairs. I scaled the wall using a drainpipe, making my way across the roof before carefully climbing into the chimney. Luckily, this one was wide enough for me to fit into. Light came in to view as I inched closer to the fireplace's opening. Thankfully, the air tonight was warm. It was unlikely they'd light it, so I stopped just above and listened.

CHAPTER THREE

"Well?" A woman's voice questioned. "Did you do it?"

"Yes, my lady. As requested, I passed along the information you gave me." I recognised the second voice as Trench's.

A shadow moved came into view as someone moved closer to the fireplace, and I tensed.

"Good. That'll teach that Butcher Bitch."

I raised my eyebrows. Few knew that the infamous 'Butcher' was a woman. Camilla's alias was necessary for obvious reasons; maintaining her anonymity and keeping her personal affairs separate from her criminal ones. It was also beneficial if people didn't know she was a woman. People took you a lot more seriously when they thought you were a man.

Taros was more progressive than some other kingdoms, but it still had its issues. In the criminal world especially, to be as successful as she was, you had to demand respect. Men are handed respect simply for being born male, but women have to prove themselves tenfold to garner even a smidgen of the respect instinctively given to a man of lesser skill and value.

So Camilla took up the masculine alias *The Butcher*. Coined thanks to her inclination for removing the tongues, and various other body parts, of those she mistrusts or those that betray her. She calls it *muting*. Very few knew Butcher's true identity, and almost all that do are muted. That this woman knew The Butcher's gender was interesting.

"There is still the matter of payment, my lady?" Trench said, ignoring her comment.

The woman scoffed, and the shadow disappeared from sight. It had been her standing in front of the fireplace then.

"Yes, yes." The telltale sound of a coin pouch being placed in someone's hand reached me even from here. "You'll get the rest when she has learned her lesson. No one beds my husband and gets away with it."

My eyes widened slightly, and it was an effort not to laugh. Butcher had slept with this woman's husband, and she had gone to all these lengths just to get back at her? Divinities.

Trench cleared his throat. "Do you have any further information for me?"

"Tell her a new shipment of weapons for the royal guard is being delivered tomorrow morning at dawn. No doubt she won't pass up the opportunity to steal such a large cache."

"Is your information verified?" He asked carefully.

The woman was quiet for a moment, no doubt glaring at Trench for having the audacity to question her, if the awkward shuffling of feet was any indication.

"Of course. The shipment is very real, and the security is dismal. However, if the royal guards receive a tip that someone is preparing to steal their arms and secretly beef up their security, well, that's just the risk one takes in this business." The smile in her voice was clear. "You may go. Let me know when you have passed on the intel."

His footsteps faded, making their way downstairs. The woman followed, shutting the door behind them. I waited a few moments to make sure she didn't return, before carefully dropping to the ground in a crouch and climbing out of the fireplace. I was in a feminine-looking study, decorated with finer ornaments and soft pastel colours. Carefully dusting myself off first, rather than trail soot through the room, I glanced around. I needed to find out who this woman was, better yet, who her husband was. I walked over to the desk, searching the draws and ledgers. Everything related to the dress shop downstairs. Nothing personal. There had to be another study or room where they kept their personal notations.

I tiptoed to the door as I heard footsteps ascending the stairs. Cursing under my breath, I quickly pressed myself against the wall beside the door. The woman opened the door and walked in, muttering something to herself about a 'wretched whore' and 'getting what's coming to her' as she made her way to the desk, I watched her feet closely, timing my own steps towards the door with hers. Her footfalls masked the sound of mine as I ducked out of the room and into the dim hallway.

Creeping down the hall, I stopped in front of the closest door and listened. I couldn't hear anything, so I carefully tried the knob, easing the door open to find a bedroom. I slipped inside, closing the door just as silently as I had opened it. Rifling quickly through the draws and checking under the bed, I kept an ear out for approaching steps. I frowned as I surveyed the room, finding nothing of use. Onto the next one, then.

The next room was more promising. It was a whiskey room. If a man was to do business from his home, it would be in a room such as this. I picked up the first document on the desk and skimmed the words. There was a signature at the bottom. Quentin Lenture.

It was an effort not to scrunch the paper up in my hand as I recognised the name. Lenture was the very crime lord Butcher suspected of flipping her informants. She would have known exactly who he was when she entered his bed. It also explained why there was very little documentation here for me to find. Lenture was a pro. He knew how to hide information. He most likely kept ledgers away from his home and personal life. What kind of goose chase was she sending me on?

The click of a door handle told me I was about to have company. I swiftly put the document back in its exact place before hurrying to the window, stepping onto the ledge, and shuffling to the side, out of view.

Footsteps approached, and large hands rested on the windowsill. I held my breath as Quentin Lenture himself looked out at his city view. I waited for what felt like an age before he closed the window and turned away. I breathed out, closing my eyes for a second before looking down. There were thugs circling the building now. They must have arrived with Mr. Lenture, but thanks to the darkness, and the unlikelihood of someone being precariously perched on their boss's windowsill, they hadn't glanced up yet.

I reached into my cloak pocket and checked my supplies. *Let's hope there's only two of them.* I placed a small dart into a thin, hollow piece of wood and raised it to my lips. I waited until there was only one thug in sight, about halfway along this stretch of wall, before I took aim.

I blew into the dart-stick, hitting my mark right in the neck. He cursed as his hand flew up, but by the time he reached his neck, he was already hitting the ground. He'd have a headache tomorrow, but other than that, the darts were nonlethal. Nothing more than a potent sleeping elixir. I was grateful this building's exterior was made of old, sturdy bricks that had aged and chipped, making it easier for me to climb down and hurry past the fallen guard. Peering round the corner, I could see two more men. Probably at least one more on the other side. *Dammit.*

I looked back at the unconscious thug before assessing my surroundings. The neighbouring wall was too smooth to scale and there was too big of a gap between this building and the surrounding ones for me to climb back up and jump to safety. It wouldn't be long before the other guards circled around or noticed their friend was missing.

Groaning quietly, I pressed up against the building, using the shadows as best I could. I removed my cloak and pulled my neck gaiter up a little higher before letting out a sharp whistle. Sure enough, one of the thugs from the front came to investigate. He got a few strides around the corner before he spotted his sleeping friend. I raised the dart-stick again, waiting until just after he'd called out in alarm.

He quickly joined his companion on the ground. His cry had alerted the remaining thug and I once again pressed against the wall, right where it met the corner. This time, as the third man rounded the corner, I threw my cloak at him, wrapping it around his face and neck, moving behind him, and shoving him forward with a kick. He stumbled, keeping his footing until he tripped over something solid; his fellow thug.

The curses he let out had me chuckling silently as I took off down the street. I was in the clear as I moved toward an alley, until a solid iron ball smashed into the wall beside me, narrowly missing my face. I snapped my head in the direction it had come from, finding a man standing there with three iron pellets about the size of coins floating around him. A damned Kineti. This time it was me cursing as the pellet that had embedded into the wall shot back toward the man, joining the other three in their rotations.

I took off down the narrow alley, all too aware of the iron pellets shooting towards me. I hadn't expected Lenture to have any Gifted guards. At least the likelihood of this one being Pure was low. None of the Gifted would sully themselves with grunt work for an Impure gang boss.

He must be a Parapure, or Para; a half-breed that inherited some power from whichever parent had been a Pure Kineti. Kineti could either move objects with their minds, those were known as Teleki, like the king, or communicate within minds, Telepi. Paras always inherited a weaker version of their parents' Gifting. So thankfully, this Teleki most likely couldn't move just any objects with his mind, but he could apparently move iron ones. I bent backwards, my hands almost touching the ground, as a pellet shot over me, before looping around and shooting back toward me. From my upside-down position, I saw the other three coming from the opposite direction. *Shit.*

Timing was everything, so I waited until the pellets were only a few yards away before I let my hands make contact with the ground, placing me in a bend back position. I quickly raised my left leg and then my right, spreading them apart and timing my split perfectly, so the pellets flew past. Three smashed into the wall in front of me while the fourth collided with the Teleki's abdomen.

He grunted, not having expected me to dodge his attack, barely having time to stop his own iron pellet from smashing through him. My legs continued moving, and I completed the kickover, now standing with my back to him once more. A few lights came on, having been disturbed by the smashing brick. I smiled, spinning to face the Para Teleki and sprinted towards him. His eyes widened, clearly not expecting that either.

He braced himself, confident he could overpower me. He would have, if I'd actually attacked. Instead, I jumped to his right, pushing off a stack of crates and propelling myself to the left in a diagonal direction, briefly brushing against him as I twisted so I could push off the alley wall. I repeated this motion, moving upwards, leaping back and forth between the walls until I reached the rooftop. My legs strained, but I ignored their protests, quickly pulling myself up and risking a glance back at the man.

He was staring up at me in shock, having recollected his pellets and preparing to attack again. He couldn't launch them at me if he couldn't see me, so I simply raised my hand to my forehead and saluted him, before moving away from the edge and out of sight. I heard him take off, no doubt trying to get up to the roof himself and pursue, but I'd have disappeared into the darkness by the time he found a way up, along with his coin pouch.

After returning to Butcher's and filling her in, she had been unsurprised. Turns out, she had planned the entire thing for two reasons. The first was to gather genuine intel on Lenture's movements and the potential threat that his gang posed to our dealings. The second was just a 'punishment' for my attitude lately. She had slept with Mr. Lenture and ensured his wife Taniya found out, knowing how petty she could be. Then she'd set up the perfect opportunity for her to 'discover' that Trench was one of our informants and pay him off.

Now she had an angry wife feeding us information that actually revealed a lot more about Lenture's business dealings than Taniya knew. If I wasn't so annoyed at having wasted my week, I'd be impressed.

"Aw come on Adi, cheer up." Raf nudged my shoulder from his spot next to me, atop a hill overlooking the city, as we waited for the sun to rise.

I rolled my eyes. "Easy for you to say. You got out Raf."

"True, but soon you'll have enough coin to get out, too. I've been saving. If we combine what we have, you may even have enough now." His voice was serious when he said it, and I knew he really would give me everything he had, if it meant getting us out. I sighed, having had this conversation with him too many times.

"Raf, I won't take your money. You need that for yourself. Sierra and I will find another way to make up the extra coin."

"But–"

"Shh. No buts. You're missing the sunrise." I nodded toward the horizon, to where the sun was just peeking its head up. He rolled his eyes but followed my line of sight.

"One day you'll let me help you, Adira Nightfell. One day."

I smiled a little. "Keep dreaming buddy."

"Oh, I will," he said, grabbing me and pulling me on top of him, "also, who are you calling buddy?" He arched an eyebrow, ignoring the stray blonde curls that fell across his forehead.

I groaned. "Again, you're missing it."

He just smiled, not taking his eyes off of mine. "No, I'm not."

I swallowed. Up here in this spot of ours, where we'd never run into anyone else, it was easy to imagine a life with him. One where we lived far from here and didn't have anyone to answer to. One where I could let myself love Raf the way he deserved to be loved. But that wasn't my life, it wasn't our life. So, I averted my eyes.

"I have to get to the docks. The shipment should be unloaded by now, and I want to see the show."

I felt him chuckle softly beneath me before reaching up and tucking a stray strand of hair behind my ear. "Alright."

He rolled us over so he was on top. I gasped slightly, looking back at him. He smirked, placing a kiss on my forehead. Standing up, he offered me his hand. The rising sun created an outline of gold around the goofy orphan boy that had somehow grown into a man. As I took his hand, allowing him to pull me up, it made him appear ethereal and beautiful, as if blessed by Solissia herself, Goddess of the Sun. We walked arm in arm down the hill before parting ways. Him to go open the workshop for old Jotters, me to watch the chaos that was about to unfold down at the docks.

Taniya had, in fact, been telling the truth. The royal guard was expecting a shipment of weapons. Butcher, not being one to back down from a challenge, despite the tip off and heightened security, had lifted the weapons before the ship had reached the docks. She'd had Tolemas head up the operation. With crews on smaller boats, they'd snuck onto the larger vessel, just long enough for them to swap out the crates and hightail it out of there.

There was a reason Butcher had the monopoly on crime in Kendelen. She ran her criminal empire from the heart of the city's underground, known as The Cavum. Home to Kendelen's most infamous fights, black market products, shady business deals, and criminals themselves. She had a tight-knit, talented crew. They were loyal, despite the fact that almost none of them had seen their boss's face. Some for fear of getting muted, some out of respect for The Butcher's brutality, and others simply for the coin. I was unfortunately among the select few that had seen her face and was unwillingly a member of her inner circle.

I hadn't been involved in the theft, but I still had a job to do today. I could spare a few minutes to watch the entertainment unfold, though. Thanks to Taniya's tip off, guards were swarming the docks and the market square. The night vendors were packing up as the dawn vendors opened shop. Taniya had set up a stall with a perfect view of the loading dock.

I smiled to myself as I meandered through the square, monitoring the guards, and pretending to browse the wares on offer as I lifted a few coins and trinkets from the oblivious market goers. They were loading the crates onto wagons for transport back to the castle, when a street urchin tapped the guard overseeing the operation on the shoulder. He muttered something to the guard before scurrying off. He stiffened and called out for the men carrying the crate closest to him to halt. They did so, like the obedient dogs they were.

The guard walked over, instructing someone to bring him a pry bar. Prying open the crate, he found no weapons, but it wasn't empty either.

Inside each crate were a handful of dresses. Their maker easily identifiable by the same emblem she had proudly displayed on her market stall a few yards away. Within minutes, Taniya was being shackled and led back to the castle for further investigation, despite her protests and cries of outrage.

Almost feeling bad for the woman, I left the markets and headed to Quentin Lenture's official place of business. Not the dressmaker shop, but a warehouse building. I didn't go through the front door, instead sneaking past the hired thugs, through the back cargo entrance, and up to his office. He really needed to fire his security.

CHAPTER FOUR

By the time Quentin entered the room, I had my cloak on, hood up, and neck gaiter secured. I didn't turn from the window as he closed the door.

"Who the Hek are you?" He said, in a noble accent that wasn't as polished as he thought. Street intonation was hard to disguise if you knew what to listen for.

"Someone with a message," I said, still not turning around.

"A message from who?"

"In about sixty seconds, one of your men will come to inform you that the royal guard has arrested your wife." I finally turned to meet his eyes.

He laughed. "Arrested? Nonsense." I simply smiled and waited. He frowned as the awkward silence stretched out. "Listen—" a knock on the door interrupted him. He let out a frustrated sigh before opening it, careful not to expose his back to me. If only the men I was sent to deal with knew the infamous Shadow of Kendelen posed no physical threat to them. "What?"

"It's your wife, boss. She's been arrested by the royal guard and taken into custody. They say she swapped out their weapons shipment for... dresses."

Lenture tensed slightly before closing the door and turning to face me again. "You're her, aren't you? The Butcher's Shadow?"

I shrugged. "I prefer *The Shadow of Kendelen*. Has a bit more flair, you know?"

His brow furrowed. "What does she want?"

"You know what she wants."

"Be reasonable." He argued. "There's enough room for both of us."

I reached into my pocket. He flinched, no doubt fearing I had a concealed weapon. It always amused me to see men of his size and reputation cower in the face of a twenty-two-year-old woman in a cloak. Butcher really had done a brilliant job associating my alias with fear and mystery. He relaxed when he noted it was simply a rolled-up piece of paper.

"Sign this, agreeing to give The Butcher sixty percent of any income you make on their territory, and perhaps we can make something work."

He scoffed. "Forty percent? You're mad. She's mad."

"That's the deal. A generous one at that. Accept, and your wife's name will be cleared."

He hesitated. "I can find another wife."

I smiled. "Reject the generous offer, and not only will they try your wife for treason, but her link to you will be revealed and your business exposed. You have two hours to sign and drop it off at the location noted on the back."

He practically growled. "I don't take kindly to threats."

I placed the scroll down onto a table nearby before I stepped up onto the windowsill, glancing back at him over my shoulder.

"It's no threat, Mr. Lenture. It's an assurance." With that, I glanced down and smiled. I leapt from the building, landing in a horse-drawn hay wagon that promptly rode off down the street, as Quentin Lenture watched from his window. Despite my gaiter, I blew him a kiss as I rounded the corner. If he were smart enough, to his credit, I believed he was, then he'd immediately search the room to see if I had taken or disturbed anything else.

When he did, he'd find a small, round object. A pure, unmarked, black coin. My calling card, so to speak. Most didn't know my face, but as my reputation had grown and the nickname 'Shadow of Kendelen' had been conceived, Butcher decided she could benefit from the notoriety. Hence the black coins. It was now widely known that they were a message from me and, in turn, The Butcher. If she wanted it to be clear who was responsible, I was to leave a coin.

We came to a halt, and I hopped out, rounding the wagon and dropping a few marks into the driver's waiting palm. He nodded and continued on, whilst I headed to the circus to prepare for tonight's show.

"Oya, Sparrow!" I looked up at the nickname given to me by some of the crew when I'd first joined the circus, coined for my affinity with aerial skills and my quick feet. Somehow it had stuck. Tolemas, especially, had even taken to calling me his *Little Sparrow*. I glanced over in the direction the shout had come from and spotted the circus strong man waving me over.

Straightening from the stretch I'd been doing, I picked up my flask of water and approached him.

"Tolemas." I nodded. "How many times have I told you that 'Oya' is not an acceptable greeting?"

He grinned down at me, easily double my size. He was a brute of a man, and I truly wasn't sure if that was thanks to his Virbi Parapure status, or if he just had some kind of giant ancestry in his lineage. Paras were usually the result of a Pure procreating with an Impure.

In Tolemas' case, he'd inherited his Pure Virbi father's strength, albeit a more of a diluted version than a full-blooded Gifted would possess, like the Teleki I'd faced in the alley, but still impressive. Virbi were either gifted with extreme strength, making them a Forti, or they had skin that was invulnerable to all materials, the only exception being silver, and they were known as Argenti. Tolemas was a Para Forti.

Thanks to something in the Impure parent's biology, Paras were never as strong as their Pure mother or father, but Tolemas could still easily take on over ten mortal men at once without breaking a sweat. The only part of his act that was in any way an illusion was perhaps the oil they lacquered him up with before his shows.

His massive height? *Real*. His corded, rippling muscles? *Real*. His ridiculous moustache that curled up at the ends? *Real*, and his favourite form of facial hair. Even his dark brown, almost black, eyes were real. He was certainly the most intimidating man I had ever seen, even knowing he was a complete softy on the inside. He has known me the longest out of all the crew here. If anyone were to ask me who my family was now, I would think of Sierra, Tolemas, and Raf.

"Aye, it's acceptable to everyone but you, Little Sparrow." He reached down to ruffle my hair, but I quickly sidestepped and frowning up at him, holding back the smile that wanted to reveal itself. I only lasted a few seconds before the frown slipped and I grinned up at the big oaf. I couldn't help it.

"I'm supposed to be getting ready for the show, so are you," I said, giving him a pointed look.

"We all know you could do this show blindfolded, with one arm tied behind your back, kiddo. You can spare a few minutes to chat with a wise man."

I chuckled. "Fair enough." I sat down and watched as his shadow enveloped me, marvelling at the way his midnight skin made me look as light as the frost of the morning. I imagined that was how Sierra looked with her ivory pale skin standing next to my golden tan. He sat beside me and leaned back, his face losing its humour. "What is it, old man?"

"There's talk around The Cavum of a big job that Butcher is coveting," he said, ignoring my jab about his age. We always referred to Camilla as The Butcher when in public, even though we both knew who she was. Tolemas was, like me, one of the rare few that knew her identity and had kept their tongue intact. "No one knows what it entails, but it doesn't sound good. We all know you'll be her first pick. I want you to turn her down. Whatever she offers you, Adira, turn it down, you hear me?"

The sudden urgency in his voice, and his use of my name rather than nickname, took me back. Tolemas sometimes took part in the underground fights held in The Cavum and often became privy to information he probably shouldn't have. I could only assume that was how he'd heard about the job.

"What have you heard, Tolemas?" I questioned, since even I only knew the bare minimum, but he just shook his head.

He had that look that told me I'd sooner get information from a brick wall, which was ironic since he could break through a brick wall with no effort at all.

"Just turn down the job when she offers it," he said, standing up.

I stood with him. "I already have. You don't need to worry." He gave me a smile, and just like that, it replaced the weird warning that had been splayed across his features with the happy, mammoth of a man I knew so well.

"Ah, well, I knew there must be *some* common sense bouncing around in that thick skull of yours." He joked, reaching down in another attempt to mess up the hair I'd painstakingly styled for tonight's show.

I promptly dodged his touch once again, inciting a chuckle from him as he headed off toward Butcher's study. I didn't have a chance to ponder his ominous behaviour as the bell rang, signalling for me to get into position. I glanced around, seeking Sierra. She was seated on her roller with the ledgers in her lap. She always met with Butcher right before the show began, to give current numbers of the attendance and the profits made so far. Grinning at me, she placed a hand over the rose pendant now hanging from her neck. I beamed, winking at her as I went behind one of the many curtained entry-ways surrounding the stage.

The show passed by in a blur. Tolemas wasn't exaggerating earlier. I knew this show back to front and inside out.

Despite having seen behind the curtain and knowing all the tricks and illusions, I never failed to be entranced by the beauty that was Kendelen's Circus. In fact, I think it made me appreciate it even more. Every act put in so much blood, sweat, and tears, me included, to ensure the performance was the best it could be, that customers left the tent in awe of the fantastical feats they had witnessed.

When my time came, I climbed the tall ladder, reaching the highest plat-form, and ensuring my mask was firmly attached. The room went dark, and the crowd seemed to take a simultaneous breath, preparing for what might come next.

The orchestra began playing a tune of adventures and thrills. That was my cue. I grinned as I took a run up and launched into the air, free-falling for what felt like minutes, when in reality it had only been a few seconds before my hands gripped the trapeze. From then, everything happened in perfectly timed execution. I flew, spinning and whirling flawlessly. My costume glit-tered in the torchlight, my heart thudded in my chest, and every time I made a leap the audience gasped in either fear or wonder. This was my addiction. Nothing felt as exhilarating as this, and I wasn't sure anything would ever get close.

As usual, aside from Butcher herself, I was one of the last to leave for the evening. After taking a cold bath, I changed back into my tunic and cloak. Finally, out of excuses for loitering any longer. I always lingered after a show, trying to work off the adrenaline still coursing through me. Walking towards Butcher's study, I figured it best to get this over with sooner rather than later. I needed to clarify that I was not taking on this assignment and hopefully put an end to her frostiness. She could give it to one of her other spies. There were others she had taken in at a young age, just like me. They were highly trained, not as skilled, but better than most.

I knocked twice on her door and waited to be invited in.

"Enter." Her sultry voice called from behind the door. I did as I was told, stepping inside and closing it behind me. "Ah good. I was hoping you would come to see me instead of me having to send a messenger."

She took a large drag of her cigar as she casually sat back in her seat. "I take it you have rethought your stance on the assignment?"

"I have considered it. While I really appreciate the generous offer, I won't be taking on the assignment. I can't risk leaving Sierra alone. I'm sure the others will be more than eager to accept."

She stared at me as if my response shocked her, as if she did not know me, as if she had truly thought I would agree to such a risky operation.

"Adira, you are the best. Our benefactor has specifically requested our best and they will accept nothing less." Her voice took on an odd tone, one I hadn't heard from her before. It was colder than usual. The assignments she'd been sending me on lately had been getting riskier and riskier, but she had always given me and the others the autonomy to accept or decline.

"No one knows my identity. If they are dead set on using me specifically, you can send one of the others. Send Mavil. Tell the benefactor she is me. I don't mind."

She slammed her fist on the desk in an unexpected burst of anger. The sudden movement caused me to jump the slightest bit. "They will know. You need to get over your fears, girl. This job is practically made for you. I have given you everything you have. You would be nothing without me. You *will* accept this job."

My eyes widened slightly in disbelief. She had never forced me to take a job, encouraged me to? Sure. Made it hard to say no to? Yes. But she had never tried to force me to accept one before. "I said no, Camilla."

"I am no longer asking." She still had that odd tone to her voice, one that I couldn't place.

I frowned and shook my head. "If that is how you feel, Camilla, then I am sorry, but I am not doing it. If that means you no longer have use for me," I swallowed back the fear that thought evoked, "then so be it." I held my breath for what felt like an eternity.

She smirked, a glint in her eye that told me she knew something I didn't. She still had a hand to deal, in a game I hadn't realised we were playing.

"Oh, no, *Little Sparrow*." She spat the nickname with such menace. "It's not that easy." She chuckled low, and my stomach sank. "You will do this assignment for me or, Khollios forbid, something may happen to darling Sierra. Perhaps something already has?"

It wasn't just her casual mention of Khollios, the God of Punishment, that had my chest spiking, an arrow of icy fear slicing its way through. It was the look in her eyes, her voice, the curve of her mouth. I knew with certainty that whatever was going on; she was not playing a game anymore. She was certain she had already won.

Without another second wasted, I took off in a sprint toward our hut. As fast as I was, I wasn't quick enough to miss her cackle and say, "I will see you soon, Adira."

Surely it was an idle threat? She wouldn't hurt Sierra. No one who knew her could ever even *think* about harming her. Still, something in me urged me to go faster. Against all my instincts, all my training, I allowed the panic to take root as I passed unlit streets, vaulting over any obstacles in my way.

I spotted our little shack, the window glowing with lantern light, and relief instantly poured through me. She would be home and waiting to discuss today's show like we always did, or asleep in her chair, having drifted off, waiting for me to get home. In the morning, she would blame me for her stiff back. Camilla was just trying to scare me.

I burst through the door anyway, panting heavily. Sierra's roller was the first thing I saw and the relief I felt was like an immense wave of pressure being lifted. Until I looked up and my blood went cold.

The hut was empty.

CHAPTER FIVE

MY EYES DARTED TO her cot, then around the rest of the room. Fear and disbelief seized me tightly as my mind caught up. It gripped me so strongly; the panic wrapping around me like an unwanted embrace.

I spun as I called out for her. "Sierra?" No answer. "*Sierra?!*"

This wasn't happening. This *couldn't* be happening.

I took a steadying breath to calm my panicked thoughts. This wasn't helping. I paced the length of the hut. *Just breathe.* She wouldn't truly hurt Sierra. She's making a point. *Breathe.* I nodded to myself as I paced slowly, the fear thawing into determination.

It wasn't just anger that coursed through me as I stormed back out into the night and across the Sepa bridge. It was rage. Unbridled rage led me to Butcher's manor with no plan in mind other than getting to my sister. The guards at her gates either recognised me, were expecting me, or simply noted the look on my face and decided it wasn't worth the fight. They wisely parted without comment.

I walked inside, taking the steps of the grand marble staircase two at a time, aiming straight for her personal study. I walked in without an announcement, stopping dead at what I found. Just like that, the flames of anger that had been burning in me since I'd left the hut snuffed out into nothing but smoke as I took in the scene before me.

Butcher was lounging on her chaise by the fire, lounging and smiling like the damned cat that caught the canary. *Or the swallow.* But that wasn't what had me frozen in place. A few feet away from her, Sierra sat in a tall chair. My eyes swept up her body, stopping where the tip of a knife pressed into her neck. A droplet of blood trickled down to her clavicle, staining the rose pendant red. My eyes trailed up the arm of the person holding the knife and confusion swept through me. Standing there, one hand holding the hilt of the dagger, the other gripping the chair Sierra sat in, was Tolemas.

"What...?" I whispered.

Confusion weaved its way through my body like a serpens on the prowl, disbelief and denial soon joining it. Butcher, I could just believe, but Tolemas? I couldn't comprehend that kind of betrayal. Why would he warn me to turn her down if he knew this would happen? When I looked into my sister's eyes, at the pure fear they beheld, I knew I had to wrap my head around it. Either this was some terrible nightmare, or the closest thing we'd had to a father had betrayed us. Tears pricked my eyes, and I wasn't sure if they were from sorrow, anger, or both.

"Why?" My voice was louder, steadier, this time.

Tolemas didn't answer, he just stared at me, cold and uncaring.

"I gave you time to reconsider, Adira. You chose incorrectly and frankly, I am tired of waiting. So, here is how this is going to go. Our new business partner has requested *you* for this assignment and only you. So, *you* are who they are going to get," Butcher said, drawing my attention back to her.

I felt sick as I tore my eyes away from Tolemas and fixed my glare on her.

"I will do nothing while you have my sister restrained with a dagger to her throat. Let her go. She has nothing to do with this."

Butcher nodded to Tolemas, who pressed the tip of the dagger harder into Sierra's neck, causing her to cry out, tears now cascading down her rosy cheeks.

"Stop! Tolemas Stop!!" I screamed at him in horror, but he just stood there, unamused, unflinching.

Butcher sighed and rose from the chaise, moving to stand in front of me. "Let's try that again, shall we?"

"Let her go." I begged, defeat weighing heavy on my words.

"I will, once we settle exactly how this is going to go."

"I'll do your damned assignment. Just let her go."

"We have already established that, dear. As I said, our employer was very specific about their request. They wish for you to swear a blood oath."

She walked over to her desk, pulling out a thin parchment with a foreign symbol on it, and a dagger embellished with an emerald stone on the hilt. Ironically, almost the exact shade of my eyes.

"A blood oath? Blood oaths haven't been used for—their binding magic disappeared along with the divinities!?" Mortals had used blood oaths before and during, The Great War to bind a person to their promise. They were almost impossible to break. But, when the war ended, and the divinities had vanished, so too did any magic outside of the Giftings, blood sworn oaths included.

"Child, do you think I went to all the effort of getting you here under these circumstances, to argue with you about the legitimacy of a blood oath? You will swear to infiltrate King Hadrian's court and follow the commands given to you until the assignment is complete."

"Don't do it, Ira. *Don't.*" Sierra pleaded, using her own nickname for me.

"That is ridiculous. To pledge that would inherently promise to be in your servitude until the end of time. *No.*"

Her sigh was so dramatic it would put the entertainers from the theatre to shame.

"If you *don't* agree, Adira, your sister will have more than just a scar to show for your poor choices."

"Why is this job so important? Why do they want *me? Who even are they?!* Camilla, you can't do this. Some part of you must care for us, if not for me, then at least for Sierra. You raised us!" I pleaded again, already knowing my words were falling on deaf ears.

She snapped her fingers, and Tolemas replaced the knife with his hand, tightening it around Sierra's neck. His hand covered her entire neck, making her appear so small and fragile compared to him. His muscles flexed as he squeezed, and Sierra gasped for air.

"Stop!" He squeezed tighter and Sierra's face began turning red. "*No Please Stop! I'll do it! I'll do it!*"

Butcher nodded and Tolemas' grip relaxed, but he did not remove his hand.

"See, was that so hard?"

"A—Adira... don't..." Sierra rasped.

Heart aching, I stared at Sierra's tear-stained face as she caught her ragged breath. I was unaccustomed to this feeling of helplessness. I hadn't felt this useless since I was six years old, carrying an unconscious and bloodied Sierra down the road in search of help, as our home burned to ashes behind us.

"But I have some conditions." I forced out.

Butcher's grin made my stomach turn. "Glad to know you haven't forgotten everything I taught you. I am listening."

"Sierra is to be released and never harmed again. By you, anyone employed by you directly or otherwise, the same goes for whoever this divinity damned benefactor is. I will not swear servitude to you for an endless amount of time. I will swear to infiltrate the court as requested and report on whatever I am requested to, but only until you have the information you need, or until the next summer solstice, and I want double the original fee. Paid in advance."

A rich laugh escaped Butcher's throat as she eyed me. Almost proudly, she nodded. "Very well, however, we may need you to do more than report back. You will swear to report and follow the commands given, and in exchange, Sierra will remain safe, as long as you cooperate."

"I want to know who this benefactor is."

She smiled. "I am afraid that is out of the question."

"Bullshit. I will not agree to this without knowing who I am working for."

"You are working for me, Adira."

"And who are *you* working for, Butcher? Who's convinced you this ludicrous plan could possibly be successful?"

"A name is as much as I will give you." Her voice hardened with every word, her patience was wearing thin. "They go by Solis. After the Sun Goddess." *Solissia?*

"What kind of stupid alias is that? They're parading around as a goddess?"

"Enough!" She finally snapped. "I tire of your attitude, agree or Sierra dies."

I closed my eyes, forcing the pile of dread pooling in the pit of my stomach down as far as I could, and nodded. "Fine. Now let her go."

"You heard her, Tolemas, let Sierra go. You are dismissed."

Tolemas stepped back and exited the room without so much as a cursory glance in my direction. My heart cracked a little more. I hurried over to Sierra and hugged her tightly. She hugged me back just as hard.

"I'm so sorry," she whispered through her sobs, "I'm s-so sorry, Adira, I didn't know. I couldn't stop it."

"Shhh. Sierra, it's alright. It's okay. This isn't your fault. Everything is going to be alright."

Butcher cleared her throat. "I don't have all night, Adira. I can always call Tolemas back in."

I begrudgingly pulled away from Sierra, giving her hand a quick squeeze. I walked over and held out my hand, palm up. "Get it over with, then."

I listened as she went through the words I'd need to speak. She placed the parchment on her desk and moved my hand over it. She sliced a thin cut along my palm with the same knife Tolemas had threatened Sierra with, forcing my hand into a clenched fist. I tried not to wince as the blood trickled down my hand until droplets landed on the parchment.

"Begin." She ordered. I knew I shouldn't be doing this. She could betray me and go back on her word at any moment, but I was out of options. I could still see Tolemas's shadow cast under the door, waiting for another order. If I did this, Sierra could still be hurt, but if I didn't do this, she definitely would be. I took a breath and began as instructed.

"I, Adira Elia Bellator Nightfell, swear on my blood to honour this sacred oath before the eyes of the divinities. I swear to infiltrate King Hadrian's court." I looked at Butcher, pleading one last time with my eyes, but she simply she shook her head. "I swear to report back and follow any commands given by Camilla Stakov, until she deems the assignment complete, or the next summer solstice passes, at which point, I will be released from my oath. Until I am released, I am sworn to secrecy and will not speak a word of this oath to anyone unless I am permitted." I pulled my hand away from the parchment, ripping off a piece of my cloak and wrapping it around the wound.

Aside from the slight sting of the cut, I didn't feel any different. Not surprising, as this entire blood oath nonsense was ridiculous, and we all knew it. Butcher picked up the parchment and threw it into the fireplace, muttering something under her breath. I watched it burn, then winced as a sharp needle-like sensation burned through me.

I quickly lifted my shirt, exposing my mid-drift. On my right side, just above the V of my hips, was a tattoo. No, a brand. A replica of the foreign symbol that was etched onto the now burned parchment. A small elegant dagger, positioned diagonally with a drop of liquid falling from the very tip. *Blood.* A blood oath. *Shit. Double shit.*

Butcher leaned in to admire the mark, before I hastily pulled my shirt back down, not missing the surprised look on her face, one she quickly masked.

"The payment."

She nodded. "Ah, yes…" She made her way to her desk drawer, opened it, and pulled out a bag that thudded when she placed it on the table. I had never seen so many gold and silver coins in one place. She counted, offering half to me. "You will get the rest when the job is done."

I took the money, still seething but defeated, as I walked over to Sierra. I vaguely heard Butcher call for a lectica to be arranged for us; a carriage carried by servants. I shook my head.

"No. We want nothing from you."

I picked Sierra up just like I had on that night sixteen years ago. Thanks to the gruelling training I'd endured daily, along with Sierra's slight frame, I was strong enough. I tried to look as dignified as I could for both of us as I walked out of the room, past Tolemas, and down the steps. Butcher stood at the top of the staircase now.

"Report to me here at first light tomorrow morning, Adira."

I felt a pull in my chest at her words. It only lasted for a fraction of a second, but I felt it, and my heart sank. I didn't look back as I walked out into the brisk night air. Sierra said nothing, as we made our way home in the darkness.

Once I'd cleaned and bandaged Sierra's neck wound, I quickly started throwing her things into a satchel.

"Ira, what are you doing?"

"We have to hurry. She may already have someone watching. You're not going anywhere near her again. I will deal with this damned—" My mouth started to move, but the words 'blood oath' got caught in my throat. I couldn't say them. "—I will deal with everything else later, but right now, we need to get you somewhere safe. I have enough coin to keep you going for some time."

"I am not going anywhere without you, Adira."

I struggled to hide the panic that kept trying to claw its way into my words.

"You were in that room, Sierra. You know what I have to do! Even if by some miracle I don't get caught, that will mean putting on a façade. A different name, a different home. I won't be able to live here, and you aren't staying here alone. Please, Sierra, I cannot argue this with you right now. I just can't. Please."

She must have seen the desperation in my eyes or heard it in my voice, because she swallowed and nodded. "Alright, whatever you think is best." She reached out and squeezed my hand.

I forced a smile. "Are you ready?"

She looked around the tiny hut that was the only home she had ever known, then back to me. "I trust you."

I helped push her along in her roller, keeping us to the shadows, my eyes scanning the rooftops and alleyways for any of Butcher's spies. Sierra kept silent as I hurried her through the streets. When I reached our destination, I knocked on the door rapidly. It took a minute before Raf opened it in nothing but his undershorts, hair ruffled, as if I had woken him, or someone had just run their fingers through it, repeatedly.

"Adi? What's going on? Do you know what time it is—" he stopped himself as he took in my sister's bandaged neck, the drops of blood on her top and my no doubt panicked eyes. "—wait here." He shut the door, and I heard his footsteps retreating.

"Raphael? How can he help?" Sierra questioned.

"He will keep you safe, Sierra. You can stay with him until I can get us to Reya. He's the only person I trust with you."

Before Sierra could respond, Raf opened the door, now wearing pants at least. He also was not alone. Turns out, I was not far off with the whole someone running their fingers through his hair theory, as a rather agitated looking girl, about my age, stormed past, her eyes shooting daggers at Sierra and me on the way out.

"Come in, it's cold out." He stepped aside, looking completely unbothered by the woman's departure. Under normal circumstances, I would have found that highly amusing. I wheeled Sierra inside.

"I'll just be a minute, Sierra," I whispered, squeezing her arm before nodding for Raf to follow me to his kitchen.

Once he had closed the door and we were standing face to face, he remained quiet, waiting for me to talk. I opened my mouth to do just that, but I couldn't form the words. The events of the evening were catching up to me at rapid speed. My lip trembled. He took a step forward, and I swiftly shook my head, causing him to halt in his approach.

"Adira," he whispered, "I am here." Tears pricked my eyes, and I clenched them shut as if that would be enough to stop them from falling.

Raf waited a few more moments, letting me know he respected my desire for space. Then he closed the distance between us, enveloping me tightly in his powerful arms, knowing while I might want space, it is not what I needed. He always knew what I needed, even when I didn't.

Which only caused the floodgates to burst, and silent tears to spill down my cheeks. I gripped him tightly, letting him hold me. If only for a few minutes before I had to pull myself together, for Sierra's sake. For both of our sakes.

I did just that. I cried and slowly explained to him what had happened, leaving out the part about the blood oath. I told him about Tolemas's betrayal, Butcher's threat, and what I was being forced to do. He knew there were things I wasn't saying, but he remained silent, letting me talk. When I finished, Raf offered right away to care for Sierra, as I knew he would, saying she could stay as long as she needed. He would watch out for her.

Sierre had grown tired of waiting and slowly pushed open the door, rolling in. When I looked at her, it was an effort not to start crying again. When had I become so emotional? What in Taros's name was going on? Sierra could see I was struggling, so she turned to Raf and explained the things I couldn't. She told him about the blood oath, about this mysterious Solis. He tried to convince me there was something we could do about my oath, that we could run, that he would run with us. But I knew come first light whether or not I wanted them to, my legs would walk out that door, following the command uttered as we'd left the manor.

I spent the rest of the evening convincing Sierra that it would be fine, that I had overreacted out of shock earlier. Forcing bravado whilst explaining how this job would not be of high risk. That I was skilled enough to not get caught. I would get the information they needed, and quickly. Then we would depart for Reya with whatever we had. It would be fine. It had to be fine. She wasn't entirely sold by my faked nonchalance, however; she bought it enough to settle. I sat by her side, holding her hand and whispering stories of our parents into her ear as she drifted to sleep.

CHAPTER SIX

Long after she had gone to sleep on the makeshift bed Raf had made for her from his couch, he'd offered her his room but she was too embarrassed to be carried up the stairs, I quietly removed my hand from hers, walked over to the window, and peered out at the sky. It wouldn't be long before the first rays of light filtered through Raf's curtains. I didn't intend to be here when Sierra woke, on the off chance it was before then.

Feeling Raf's warmth behind me, I closed my eyes and breathed him in. His signature, calming, scent of coal and salt, wrapped around me. I had never been more grateful to have him in my life than I was at this moment. Divinities. I was becoming an emotional wreck. I opened my eyes and turned to face him.

He looked at me with sadness in his eyes as he whispered, "Why will you fight for everyone but yourself, Adira?" Instead of answering, I leaned up for what may be the last time, pressing my lips to his.

When I'd said one day, we would say goodbye for the last time, I hadn't considered that day would arrive so quickly. If they caught me, this really could be the last time. There was so much I should have said to him, thanked him for, but I didn't say any of it. I just pressed myself against his sculpted chest, solid from the days he'd spent slaving against metal and iron, and kissed him deeper.

His hands moved to my waist on instinct. Drawing me closer, he murmured, "Adi... don't kiss me like that."

"Like what?" I whispered, placing a kiss on his neck as my hands worked my way down the contours of his chest. He tensed ever so slightly, not in repulsion, but in conflict. I could practically feel him battling with himself.

"Like it might be the last time you do so," he whispered back, his voice tinged with slight desperation, gripping my waist even tighter.

I kissed up to his ear, my hands lingering near his waistband, as he sucked in a breath, before I finally pulled back, just far enough to look at him properly. The moon's glow highlighted his features. His jaw was hard set, but his eyes were on fire. A swirling mix of emotions splayed across his face. I could have lied to him the same way I had lied to Sierra, told him everything would be alright, but I didn't have that in me, and I was pretty sure he wouldn't buy it, anyway.

So, I did us both a favour and told him the truth. "I need you." I stepped back, unhooking my cloak so I could lift my tunic off and drop it to the floor. His eyes lingered on mine before trailing lower.

"I need this, Raphael, please." I begged.

My plea undid him, his eyes telling me the exact moment he'd given in. He'd always had a hard time saying no to me, particularly when I was only partially clothed. It was cruel of me to use that knowledge to my advantage now, but I hadn't lied when I'd told him I needed this, needed him. One last time before my life changed for good. I had a feeling he needed it almost as much as I did. He closed the gap between us once more, hoisting me up by the waist, forcing me to wrap my legs around him as he carried me up to the bedroom, quietly pushing the door shut behind us. I didn't fail to notice that the bed was made and unused.

"Then you can have me. *Sempre*," he said gruffly in the old tongue. *Always.* I ignored the unspoken confession in his words, as he laid me down, stripped me of the rest of my clothing, as well as his own, and dedicated the rest of the night to making me forget there was a world outside of this room.

I quietly dressed, as the sky lightened, the sun readying itself for the day, signalling the end of whatever fantasy I had conjured that didn't end with me leaving this bed, this loft, for divinities knows what awaited me at Butcher's manor.

'Report to me here, at first light tomorrow morning, Adira.'

I really tried to stay put, to ignore her words that replayed in my mind, telling myself the blood oath was a bunch of bullshit. But the closer it got to sunrise, the stronger the tug in my chest became. Morphing into a more forceful pull, and then to an all-out yank. I felt like I might burst as the pressure continued to build in my chest. The tattoo seared the skin beneath my shirt, as if I were being branded all over again. I took a step toward the door, then another, and the sensation slowly lessened.

The pulling calmed, but my heart sank. I glanced back at Raf sleeping peacefully, his blonde curls littered across his face. He needed a haircut. I was almost glad I'd be able to avoid the lecture I'd receive for leaving without waking him. Almost.

Sneaking quietly down the stairs, my gaze shifted to where Sierra slumbered, one hand wrapped around the rose pendant. My heart dropped further. I placed the carefully written letters, scribbled in the dimly lit loft after Raf had finally fallen asleep, on the dining table, silently slipping out into the early mists of the morning. I followed the invisible thread attached to my chest, leading me straight to Butcher's doorstep.

The pulling sensation refused to cease until I was standing in the exact spot she had spoken from last night, atop her staircase, and the bitch wasn't even here. The walk over had given my anger plenty of time to rise and build within me, begging for an excuse to erupt and free itself.

I had to remind myself to stay calm. Butcher hadn't gained her reputation, or control of the criminal underground, just for her looks. She was cunning, smart, and brutal. More so than I had realised, apparently. I was not having a good run with my judgement calls lately. If I was the sparrow, then she was the hawk, the lethal predator having cornered her prey. If I wanted to get out of this situation alive, I had to play this her way. I had to beat her with her own rules. I couldn't do that with blind rage.

So, I took the time she kept me waiting there like an imbecile, no doubt another power play, to calm my breathing. Pushing that anger down and honing it into a weapon of lethal determination. This was what I did. I was The Shadow of Kendelen. I was the best. I could play the long con. I could manipulate, steal, and bluff my way better than anyone else in this city. I would not fail, and when I succeeded, I'd make damned sure I brought Butcher, Solis, and anyone else who got in my way, down in the process, and I would not do so quietly. As the door to her study opened, I steeled myself.

"Come, Little Sparrow, we have much to discuss."

Sitting in Butcher's study, waiting for her to speak, was a new form of torture. She was really taking the power playing, silence wielding, thing too far. While she wasted both of our time with her little game, I took in every detail of the room, cataloguing it in my mind in case I should need it later.

"I hope we can put the nastiness of yesterday's events behind us." She finally opened with.

I looked at her, keeping the emotion off of my face as I replied. "Let's just get this over with. What is it you need me to do?"

She sighed in disappointment, still somehow managing to look not in the least bit remorseful.

"Very well. As you know, Solis needs an asset on the inside."

"Why?"

"So," she said, ignoring my question, "our first step is getting you in. Luckily, they appear to be well connected and have obtained an invitation to the royal banquet tonight." She lit the cigar nestled in its holder, happy to inhale the awful stuff, but Taros forbid she stained her fingers with it. She blew the air towards me, knowing full well I detested the smell.

I nodded. "That gets me in, but it doesn't get me even *close* to infiltrating the court. Who will I be posing as? A foreign noble visiting the court?"

"You will pose as a foreign lord's daughter, visiting for the first time from Xeria. It is important to catch their attention early, which is why you have graciously volunteered to do an aerial performance at the banquet."

The Kingdom of Xeria was named after the God of War, the same place Tolemas was from. The thought of him was like a painful jab to the chest, one that I promptly ignored.

"The act you perform tonight will be in honour of them, and your stay in their kingdom, so you must impress them. Convince the king he should house you for the spring." I nodded as I felt a tug in my chest.

The performance was one thing I was confident I would not fail at. Aerial art was my domain. The tricky part would be to prove more than an entertainer, but also not a threat to them. Luckily, it wasn't unusual for foreign nobles to visit a new kingdom and bring something from their homeland, or provide some kind of entertainment to honour of their hosts. She was right.

The slow approach was far more likely to prove fruitful, but was also a much more complicated game. I'd have to win over a lot more than one person. I'd have to gain their trust, and that would take a lot longer than I fancied.

We spent the next few hours going over the finer details. Memorising my backstory and my made-up family. Well, they weren't entirely made up; they existed, they just weren't *my* family. They were apparently in Solis's pocket, so if anyone should come sniffing, they had supposedly agreed to testify to my legitimacy. We also did a quick study on the royal family, whom I'd have to convince of my fake life.

Butcher, unsurprisingly, suggested I focus on gaining the King's attention, specifically in the context of a consort. Disgust aside, while I may need to charm the king on certain occasions, she put too much faith in my seductive abilities if she thought becoming his lover would somehow bewitch him into welcoming me into his inner circle. I would be better off playing nice with all the royals, and seeing where I may be of use to one of them. Best to keep my options open. It would be tedious, but it was my best shot at getting out of this alive.

There was a carriage waiting for me at the front of the manor by the time we finished studying. I raised my eyebrows.

"You need to appear wealthy and intriguing when you arrive at the inn we have arranged for you. I have already sent over your luggage, containing clothing and jewellery fit for Lady Elia Worthington." Butcher explained.

She had chosen one of my middle names as my alias, believing it would be harder for me to slip up with. Elia, Elle for short.

I nodded, allowing the coachman to open the carriage door for me as I climbed in.

"I will get messages to you. I expect prompt replies and for you to follow their instructions."

I looked at her with an annoyed expression. "Yes, you have made it abundantly clear I have little choice in the matter."

She smiled then, watching me closely. It was unnerving, the look in her eyes.

"Wear the red costume tonight. You will know which one. It is the King's favourite colour."

With that, she walked back inside; the doors swinging closed behind her. Luckily meaning she hadn't witnessed me jerking forward, not expecting the powerful pull at her words. This divinity damned oath.

Apparently, she put a bit more will and intent into that command, as it was by far the strongest pull I'd felt so far.

The carriage door shut, and it soon rolled into motion, weaving its way through the Kendelen. I watched through the gauzy curtain, concealing my face but still allowing me to see out of. I watched as we moved from the already upper-class area Butcher lived in, to the exclusive neighbourhoods reserved for the highest standing lords and ladies, as well as the dukes and duchesses of Taros and other kingdoms. The sun had risen fully now, and so began the start of most people's days.

The morning markets were in full swing, the local vendors keen to sell their wares to the highest bidder. I didn't miss the curious looks some courtiers shot my way as my carriage passed through. Butcher had spared no expense and had the carriage detailed in the Xerian colours, house sigil and all. A bear's claw. The symbol of strength and power.

The innkeepers themselves greeted me and I had to repress the urge to roll my eyes. Butcher had oversold Lady Elia's importance. No doubt on purpose to get tongues talking, making my act that much more difficult. I thanked the innkeepers after they saw me to my room, promptly locked the door, and began exploring the 'luggage' that had been sent ahead of me.

It was brimming with gowns of silk and satin, enough jewels to feed a small village, and shoes that reminded me of the stilt walkers. Twins in the circus, whose act involved walking on high wooden sticks covered by ridiculously long pants, as if they were their true legs. Hardly any of it was practical, but I suppose a lady of leisure and wealth would have no need for practical clothes. I would need to hide my own stash of tunics and cloaks for when I needed to explore undetected.

I laid out the costumes across the four-poster bed. This room was four times the size of the hut Sierra and I shared. I surveyed my options. There was only one red piece amongst the costumes, and it had me clenching my fist and cursing Butcher to Infernis and back. It was by far the most revealing item of clothing she had provided, aside from the lingerie I quickly shoved back in the trunk.

Groaning, I tried it on and risked a glance in the mirror. It showed more skin than I would like, but it fit my body perfectly and even I could admit, it looked good. Gripping my body, ruby red gems glittered in the lantern light, adorning the front of the costume and clinging to the silky material as securely as the outfit clung to my curves. Low cut at the front, it had symmetrical cutouts on each side. A delicate picture of fire and brimstone.

This outfit would certainly garner attention but would also make it difficult to play the sweet, trustworthy, and demure lady I had planned on becoming tonight. I didn't have time to curse Butcher a second time before I got to work on my hair and face.

By the time I'd finished, I barely recognised myself. I still looked like me, just a version that had lived a vastly different life. One that flaunted her assets instead of hiding them, one of privilege and mischief. My hair was bound in a beautiful crown braid, with a few loose strands framing my face. I lightly dusted my eyes with brown kohl, stained my lips a ruby red to match the costume, and sprinkled my cheekbones with a touch of powder that shimmered when the light hit them at just the right angle.

I wasn't sure how I was going to balance the appearance to the part I was to play. Intriguing, but not too unbecoming. Sweet, but not naïve. Intelligent, but not a threat.

If I hadn't just spent a painstaking amount of time on my face, I would have buried it into a pillow and screamed in frustration. That wouldn't do me any good, though, so I grabbed my cloak and fastened it around me, completely concealing the costume. I carefully folded the matching red skirt for after the performance into a satchel and headed downstairs to have my carriage readied. Once it was prepared and waiting, I pulled my hood up, minding my hair, and exited the inn, climbing in as gracefully as I could. My heart thumped as I neared the castle gates, crossing over the Sineti bridge that separated the castle from the rest of the city.

I had never been this close. It looked big from the markets, but up close? It was humongous, a startling stronghold of brick. They stopped us at the gate; the coachman handed over my invitation as the guards did a sweep of my carriage and luggage. I received a curious look from one guard as he checked inside, but he did not ask me to remove my hood. He simply stared, uncomfortably so, for far too long. I shifted to face him properly.

"Can I assist you with something, sir?" I said boldly, letting the slight irritation at being so rudely ogled seep into my voice.

He looked slightly taken aback as he fought to keep a smile from forming on his mouth. He was handsome. His dark hair slicked back and even through his uniform, I could see the bulge of his muscles. His eyes, whilst I couldn't make them out completely, appeared to be blue with flecks of brown. He still hadn't responded, so I wasn't embarrassed about assessing him, much more subtly than he had me. Even the way he carried himself exuded masculine confidence.

Finally, he spoke. "Apologies, my lady." His voice was smooth as silk as he bowed his head slightly. "Forgive me for staring. I was simply curious why a lady such as yourself would wear a hood inside her own carriage."

His explanation made sense, but I wasn't about to tell him that.

"Perhaps to avoid guards such as yourself staring?" I quipped back. This time, he *did* smile, making my traitorous stomach dip.

"You make a valid point." He conceded, retreating back down the step. "Enjoy your evening, miss."

He closed the carriage door and knocked on it, signalling to the coachman, who continued on through the gates. I quickly forgot about the interaction with the guard as I focused on my surroundings, noting every guard I could see stationed on the grounds and every viable escape route I could map. Once I had finished surveying for my safety, I took in the lavish castle and all its beauty.

Admiring the gardens, I couldn't help but think of Sierra, how she'd likely die in bliss surrounded by this many flowers. I wondered what she was doing and hoped she hadn't caused Raf too much strife. As I imagined how much she would enjoy having him around, I smiled a little. I mentally scolded myself for getting distracted. I couldn't afford to think of them now.

My name was no longer my own. I was Elia Worthington, only child to Lord Viktor and Lady Catlyn Worthington, hailing from the Kingdom of the Virbi, Xeria. I locked down the parts of me that were Adira, slipping on the mask of a courtesan as a warrior would their armour. After all, the battle had already begun.

CHAPTER SEVEN

THE ROYAL SERVANTS SHOWED me to my room for the night, more of a suite than anything. I deposited my things before they escorted me to the banquet hall to set up before the guests arrived. There were servants milling about, scrambling to get everything perfect, adding the finishing touches.

They directed me to an alcove housing a ladder that led to a tall platform, one I could use to remain hidden above in the silks before the guests entered the room and my performance began. A rather dramatic entrance tactic, if done properly, which should have the audience gazing up in surprise and, preferably, awe. It also, not so coincidentally, provided me with an early aerial view, giving me a chance to catalogue details like how many guards were stationed around the room, where the royal family would sit, and, therefore, the best angles for me to manoeuvre within in order to best capture their attentions. This performance was about more than just illusions and entertainment.

This would be my first move in the game of deception. My first manipulation to gauge how I would proceed for the rest of my time as Elia.

I watched as guests filed in, picking out the haves from the have nots. The King's inner circle was situated close to the dais. I began putting faces to names. His closest advisor and council representative for the Deos Credentes, Lord Chambersen, was standing close to the thrones, watching very much like I was, as people filled the room and chatted amongst themselves, anticipating the royals arrival.

There were guards posted around the room in lightweight armour of red and blue. The Navarre's house sigil, an open hand, palm facing out, was stamped onto their backs, as well as the top left of their breastplates. One guard, however, wore his sigil on the front of his breastplate, right in the centre. The position of the sigil, along with the gold trim, clearly marked the captain of the guard standing by the dais.

Killian Ambrosia stood alert but calm, assessing the room with a warrior's eye. He looked as young as they said, with his light tawny hair pulled into a bun, and his sword strapped to his side, but if he was a Pure like I expected, you could never be too certain of their age. The rest of the King's council were scattered around tables close by, as were the most prominent lords and ladies of the Navarre court. I appeared to be the only guest from a foreign kingdom in attendance, unless they weren't wearing their house sigil or colours, which would be unusual.

A bell sounded, and people came to attention. Anyone seated rose as the royal family made their highly anticipated entrance. Instead of entering through the same door as the guests had, they appeared atop a grand stair-case. My eyes fixed on our monarchs. King Hadrian stood tall and regal. He had aged well, appearing to be in his mid-forties, but from what I'd heard, he was nearing one hundred.

The ageing process for Pures was different to that of mortals. They *did* age, but it was much slower. There were records of Pures living for up to three hundred years. However, in most cases, the lifespan of someone with a Gifting was around two hundred.

The King's height, combined with his sandy blonde hair and brown eyes, painted a striking picture. He appeared relaxed, but alert, and there was a wisdom about him that told me deceiving him wouldn't be as simple as I had first hoped.

Beside him, arm linked through his, stood his wife, Queen Odette. She was as stunning as all the artworks of her portrayed. She wore a beautiful gown in deep fuchsia, her crown matching the King's, looking like it had been made for her, and only her. Her midnight hair was down but pulled back from her face. Her blue eyes appeared bored, almost cold looking. A beautiful sculpture of ice, one I couldn't shake the feeling I had seen before.

Everyone was hushed as they descended the staircase, followed by their children. Prince Valor and Princess Calliope. Pure rulers often decided to have children fairly late in their long lifespans. I suppose when you lived as long as they did, there was no rush. The prince was only twenty nine, and the princess was even younger. She only came of age a few years ago, making her the same age as me. My gaze shifted to them and my eyes widened a fraction. Standing beside the princess was the guard who had searched my carriage, the one I'd mouthed off at when he had stared for too long. Not a guard at all, but the damned Prince of Taros. I silently groaned. *Shit.*

Prince Valor was the spitting image of his mother, which explained why she had seemed so familiar. He looked like his mother, but he walked like his father, full of self-assurance and status. He smiled, but it was more restrained than the one he'd given me a brief glimpse of during our first interaction. Beside him walked Princess Calliope, who was a combination of her parents. With beautiful brown eyes like her father, but black hair like her mother. When she smiled, she appeared genuinely happy to be present.

Warm, like the spring. The two dark-haired heirs took their seats on either side of their parents.

The crowd knelt and remained bowed until the king waved his hand, signalling for them to rise and continue with the festivities. How long a king or queen kept their subjects waiting, said a lot about the type of ruler they were. King Hadrian had not abused his power like some, but he had waited those few extra seconds, before allowing them to rise.

The subjects took their seats, glasses were filled, and the chattering resumed.

That was my cue. I readjusted my position and nodded to the attendant, signalling for them to begin. The orchestra started to play a suspenseful tune as the torches were extinguished, leaving only a few lit around the edges of the room. A bright collection of them formed a spotlight of sorts right in front of the royal dais. The crowd hushed in surprise and glanced around. Even the king raised a brow.

That's when I leapt, tumbling down in a blur of red and black. No longer a sparrow, but a fire bird. I heard a few gasps as people spotted me hurtling towards the ground, coming to a sudden stop in a perfect split, each leg balanced on black silk. Facing the royals I was amused at the varying reactions; surprise, intrigue, boredom, and pleasant indifference. I bowed low, making eye contact with the prince as I went. I didn't miss the slight smirk tugging at the corner of his lips. He'd known who I was the entire time, then. I shifted my gaze to the princess, who looked excited. I winked and began my performance.

I was an elegant bird weaving my way through the air. I was the artwork, my body the canvas, and the silks my easel. My costume glimmered when the light hit it just right, casting beautiful shadows across the room. The crowd *oohed* and *ahhed* as I performed trick after trick.

A light sheen of sweat now coated my brows. I finished the performance in a similar fashion to how I'd started. With the silk wrapped around my waist, I tumbled down, my body splayed out in the shape of a star. Ending on the last beat of the drum, my back arched, head tipped back, and my hand stretched out toward the royals. The room was silent for a beat before applause erupted. Princess Calliope jumped to her feet, clapping rapidly, shortly followed by the king and prince in a much calmer manner. Lastly, and very slowly, the queen rose, deigning to honour me with a few bored claps.

Chest rising and falling, I gracefully untangled myself from the silks and gave the royals a proper curtsy. Father Chambersen, who looked violated at what he no doubt considered a very risque performance, stepped forward and introduced me.

"Lady Elia Worthington of Xeria, your Majesties. Only daughter of Lord Viktor Worthington, visiting our kingdom for the first time, she wished to perform in honour of the Navarre house."

Chambersen stepped back, having done his duty, leaving me kneeling before the crown. The king smiled.

"You may rise, Lady Worthington. Thank you for the beautiful performance. You have certainly honoured us." He chuckled warmly.

I stood, ignoring the fact that I was definitely underdressed in this outrageous costume.

"Thank you, Your Majesty, but the honour is truly mine. Thank you for welcoming me into your home—" I was cut off by the queen as if she had read my mind.

"Perhaps you should change into something more appropriate for this event, and we can chat then, dear."

"Of course, my apologies, Your Majesties. Please excuse me." I bowed my head slightly.

"I will show her to her rooms. This palace is a labyrinth!" Princess Calliope piped up.

"Calliope, a guard can surely show Lady Elia the way." The queen countered.

"Oh, let her go, Odette, it will be a wonderful opportunity for them to get to know each other briefly before they are both surrounded by the court." The king overruled. The queen simply nodded and turned to speak to one of her lady's maids.

The princess jumped up, linking her arm through mine, and leading me out of the ballroom. Guards instantly fell into formation around us.

"Thank you, Your Highness. You didn't have to do that," I said politely.

"Oh, please, call me Cali. Your Highness is so formal. And I should thank you. These things are so damned boring most of the time." She rolled her eyes. "Mother would have expected me to stay up there with her for far too long if you hadn't given me an excuse." She complained, and although I had already decided she would be the easiest family member to win over, I was still a little taken aback by her brazenness.

She had dropped all regal pretences and now appeared casual, still privileged and clearly a little oblivious to that fact, but kind nonetheless.

I laughed a little. "Glad to be of service, Your High—" I stopped short at the glare she threw my way "—Cali..." I corrected, and she smiled again.

"Where did you learn to do that? You were incredible!" The guards remained silent as she talked my ear off the entire way to my chambers.

Once we reached our destination, I quickly grabbed the satchel I'd prepared after arriving, leaving her in the sitting room while I went to the bedroom to change. Pulling out the red skirt that matched my costume, I hastily fastened it to my bodice. I grabbed the dagger I had hidden in my satchel and strapped it to my thigh. Next came the ridiculous high-heeled shoes I could only navigate thanks to years of balance training. I appraised myself in the mirror.

The top half of my outfit was still more revealing than I would like, but the skirt did a marvellous job of classing the whole thing up. It was the same bright red as the rest of the costume, but ruffled and long, fanning out at my waist and falling to the floor perfectly. I nodded, satisfied, and returned to the sitting room to find Cali rummaging through my small overnight trunk.

I frowned. She must not have heard me re-enter the room, as she was still searching when I cleared my throat, causing her to jump and spin around with a sheepish look on her face.

"… Can I help you with something, Cali?" It wasn't lost on me that this was the second time I had asked a member of the Navarre family that question tonight.

"Oh divinities. Okay, this isn't what it looks like, Elia, I swear. I just…" She blushed. "Truthfully? I wanted to see if you had any more outfits like the one you wore tonight and to find out who made them for you. They are stunning and Mother would *die* if she saw me in one. So naturally, I couldn't resist."

"Is there a reason you didn't just ask me?" I had to be careful, if I gave too much attitude she could have me thrown out, or at the very least, ensure the rest of her family wouldn't welcome me, but, if I showed too little, I would appear weak and uninteresting.

This is a girl unused to being challenged, clearly, one that lives for breaking rules, but knows she can usually get away with doing so.

"Honestly? While you were changing, I spotted the trunk, wondered if you had more outfits, and I just started looking. I'm so sorry. I know how this must look."

I gave her a forgiving smile, not quite buying the innocent act, but she didn't need to know that. I had taken precautions and hidden the few things that might seem unusual for Lady Worthington to have in her possession, having expected someone to search my room. Granted, I hadn't considered it would be the princess herself.

"You don't need to be sorry, it just caught me off guard, is all. I would be happy to have the tailor I used visit and design some outfits for you. He really is a master of his craft."

Her face lit up, and she clapped. "Brilliant! I will hold you to that. But for now, we better get back to the festivities before Mother has both our heads. Thank you, Elia."

I smiled back at her as we headed back towards the event. "Call me Elle."

She grinned and nodded. "Elle. I think you and I are going to get along just fine."

The excitement in her eyes was almost enough to make me feel bad for the deception. Almost.

As expected, upon entering, courtesans and courtiers alike swarmed the princess. I barely managed to slip out of the crowd and make my way over to a drinks station. I grabbed a glass of wine, taking a sip, and surveying the room. Any plans I may have had to win over the royal family with a timid

Lady Elia had gone out the door the second I had spoken to Prince Valor in the carriage. I hadn't known it was him, but that was even more damning. Confident and comfortable, Lady Elia it was.

I pasted an inquisitive smile on my face as I walked through the room curiously. I found my next move quickly; Lord Jameson Inkwell. One of the people Butcher had briefed me on when we were establishing my cover. He was easily distinguishable thanks to the swooning ladies that were whispering and casting glances his way as they passed by. The Inkwells were about as high standing as you could find in Taros, having maintained a close relationship with the Navarre family. Jameson himself was very good looking, and well aware of it. So, it came as no surprise when he leapt at the chance to help me as I 'accidentally' stumbled into him, gripping his arm to steady myself.

"Oh, my gosh! I am so sorry!" I blurted, my cheeks turning pink as I looked up at him, not letting go of his arm. *Damn,* he was tall and... familiar? He was incredibly tall actually, at least six foot five, with fair skin, a light smattering of freckles across his cheeks, cropped blonde hair and striking jade coloured eyes.

He smiled down at me. "It's quite alright, my lady. Are you hurt?"

"No, no. I am, however, a little clumsy. I could use a dance partner to ensure I don't trip and make a fool of myself again." I smiled back, meeting his eyes playfully. Still trying to place where I had seen him before. He looked surprised and intrigued as he put his hand over mine.

"What kind of gentleman would I be if I didn't help a lady in need?"

"Not a very noble one." I chuckled and let him lead me to the dance floor.

He laughed, and it was feathery light as he placed one hand on my waist, taking my hand in his free one, which was when I finally realised where I'd seen him before. Divinities. He was the nobleman whose pocket I'd nearly gotten arrested for picking at the tavern. The guards I'd assumed were off duty and, coincidentally, exiting the tavern after him, were probably a protection detail for the esteemed lord. That explained why they'd given pursuit so thoroughly, and why they were better trained than the ones I usually dealt with.

"So, do I get your name?" He asked, not showing any hint of recognition.

"Elia, but my friends call me Elle," I answered.

"And what shall I call you?" He raised a brow.

"Whatever you like, my lord," I said demurely, and he smirked.

"Interesting." He watched me the way a cat watches a mouse. *Hook, line, and sinker.*

I smiled as he spun me, letting out a small giggle as he did. Jameson looked as if he were about to say something else when he was interrupted by a tap on the shoulder. Peering behind him, I spotted Prince Valor. Exactly as I had planned.

CHAPTER EIGHT

WHEN FIRST LOOKING FOR a dance partner, I had been searching for three things: one; someone in the Prince's direct line of sight, two; someone he knew and three; someone he would enjoy interrupting.

Valor and Jameson were friends. I'd heard they liked to frequent taverns and were competitive in almost every aspect of their friendship. Swordplay, hunting, women, you name it. I was betting on the fact that whatever game the prince had started in that carriage would intrigue him enough to seek me out when he saw me with his friend. So I allowed him to, in a way that let him showcase his power.

"Mind if I cut in?" More of a statement than a question.

I felt, more than heard, the tiny groan that came from Jameson.

"You're the worst," he said, but he was smiling. He turned back to me.

"Well, Lady Elle, I hope I'll be seeing you around." Stepping back, he placed a kiss on my hand, before disappearing into the crowd, only for Valor to replace his now vacant spot.

I looked at him and raised my brow. "Shouldn't I be curtsying, Your Highness?"

"I'll let it slide, this once." He smiled and moved us to the music.

"How kind of you," I mused.

"So, Lady Elia, your first visit to Taros, have you enjoyed our kingdom thus far?"

"I have, immensely. You have a beautiful home." I couldn't quite get a read on him. He was being more formal than any of the others.

"We haven't had a visitor from Xeria in some time. I have heard of your family, but very little of you, I'm afraid." He was fishing, already suspicious. Not just a naïve princeling, then.

"My family is rather private, Your Highness. My father feared if he showcased me too much, I would be married off and moved somewhere far away." I chuckled, rolling my eyes. "His fears aren't entirely unfounded, but I would

like to see the world myself before I add someone else to the equation."
Letting him know I was available, but not there to trick him into asking for
my hand.

"That's an unusual stance for a lady of your status to take."

"Actually, you'll find a good many 'ladies of my status' share the same
view, but are simply too afraid to ask for it, or they are denied the opportunity." He was smart enough to see through any basic act, so I committed to
the confident lady he wouldn't have been expecting. "Do you usually make
a habit of posing as a guard, and searching ladies' carriages, Prince Valor?"
I questioned innocently, switching topics, although, from the amusement
flickering in his eyes, he saw nothing innocent about it.

"When unexpected guests from foreign kingdoms make an appearance?
Yes. Do you always wear a hood when inside?" He spun me.

"When I am in a foreign kingdom wanting to impress the royal family
with surprise and a show? Yes." I countered.

His lips turned up a bit. "Touché." I felt his arms relax a little, but that
could easily be a tactic meant to unarm me. He leaned in, indeed catching
me a little off guard, as his breath tickled my neck, and my stomach did that
stupid dip again. "I haven't figured you out yet, Lady Elia. But whatever you
are seeking, whatever the Xerian Queen hopes to gain from sending you here,
you will be thoroughly disappointed with the outcome." He stepped back
before I could respond, bowed, and departed.

I didn't allow the surprise to show as I made my way to a grazing table,
processing everything he'd just admitted. He had no reason to suspect I
would be working for the Queen of Xeria unless the two kingdoms were
currently at odds. I hadn't heard even a whisper of unrest between the two,
and I made it a point to keep up to date with the current political climate
of Taros. This assignment had just gotten a Hek of a lot harder. Of all the
kingdoms Taros could have had some sort of problem with, of course, it
would be Xeria.

I made a point of not approaching anyone else, allowing others to come
to me. A few ladies attempted conversation, mostly trying to get any tidbits
of gossip they could pass along to the rest, their efforts were unfruitful. The
men also tried their hands. I danced with a few and was as charming as one
would expect a lady to be, but still maintained that mystery, never giving
away too much information. People always craved what was withheld from
them, even when they normally wouldn't particularly care. The moment
something became challenging, it became a prize. So, the more people that
were left wondering about the elusive Lady Elia, the better chance I would
have at using them for information later.

It was past midnight as I made to exit the ballroom, when none other than
Captain of the Guard, Killian Ambrosia, *a somewhat ironic name*, stepped into
my path. He bowed his head.

"Lady Elia, the king would like a moment of your time."

Ignoring the slight jolt of panic that swept through me at the possibility of being caught so quickly, I nodded. "Of course, Captain, lead the way."

He began walking in the direction I had been heading, out of the event. The king and queen had left some time ago, right about the time the event became less formal, and the younger attendees relaxed. Princess Calliope included. Prince Valor appeared more relaxed at a first glance, but his eyes were sharp and his body was ready. The captain led me down a hallway, stopping at what looked like the door to a study.

"He is through there." *No kidding*, I thought, but I smiled, keeping my mouth shut and graciously entering the room. He shut the door behind me. The king sat at a mahogany desk, reading glasses on, his shirt unbuttoned a few times, and his sleeves rolled up. A very different picture from the one presented at the ball.

"Lady Elia, thank you for agreeing to speak with me. I know it's late, so I will keep it brief. Have a seat." He smiled warmly at me. Cali had the same smile.

I curtsied. "Of course, Your Majesty. It's not a problem." I took the seat opposite him.

"I just wanted to make sure your time in Taros has been pleasant thus far. I see you have already made acquaintance with my children, but you and I, unfortunately, did not have a chance to speak."

"I appreciate you asking. Yes, Taros is beautiful, so different from back home. Thank you so much for allowing me to visit. Both of your children were very welcoming." I mentally scoffed at the thought of Prince Valor being welcoming.

He watched me and smiled again, taking off his glasses. "Of course. Are your accommodations suitable?"

I nodded. "Yes, I am staying at the Inn on Westbrook Road. They have been very hospitable."

"My staff tell me you travelled alone? Only your coachman came with you, no guards?" He certainly knows a lot about me. Surely he doesn't personally look into every single visitor from a foreign kingdom?

"Should I have bought guards, Your Majesty? I didn't expect any threats to come whilst visiting. I am not of that high importance." Something in his eyes had me questioning whether there was some sort of threat he was concerned about. Why else would he have expected me to have guards?

"Perhaps, although with the way some of the other ladies were glaring at you during your dance with Lord Jameson, and then my son, I wouldn't be so sure." He chuckled. "But it is always better to be safe than sorry. I can provide you with guards for the rest of your stay. How long were you intending that to be?" He probed innocently.

"Until the season's end, if, of course, His Majesty permits me to stay that long."

"You are welcome to stay as long as you like, Elia." He took a sip of his drink, some dark spirit, by the looks of it. "Would you like a drink?"

"Oh, no, thank you. I had plenty tonight already." I smiled, sheepishly.

"Ah." He nodded. "I knew your father when I was younger, you know? Before he met your mother. You could say we were friends for a time." This could easily be some sort of test. If I played along and said my 'father' had mentioned him, which he surely would have if he was sending his daughter to an old friend's kingdom, then I risked exposing myself if what the king had said was, in fact, a trap meant to trick me into a lie.

"Really? Father doesn't talk much about the times before he met Mother. I would love to hear more about his younger days." I held my breath, waiting for his response.

He simply smiled and leant back. "I am sure we will have plenty of time to swap stories about your old man. In fact, why don't you come and stay with us at the palace?"

"Oh, no, I wouldn't want to impose, Your Majesty." I shook my head. "You have already been more than gracious."

"Nonsense." He waved his hand. "I could do no less for an old friend's daughter." *Had Butcher known of the King's ties to Lord Worthington? Is that why she had chosen this alias?*

"I don't know what to say. That would be incredible."

"Good, because I already sent my staff to collect your things from the Inn." I raised my eyebrows. Of course a king would be presumptuous enough to think no one could deny him.

"And what if I should decline your offer?" I questioned, allowing a bit of that confidence and sass to shine through, gauging his reaction to it.

He grinned. "I think you will find very few have an easy time denying me, Miss Worthington."

I didn't doubt it, but whether that was because he was a man to be feared, or because he was as kind as he appeared, remained to be seen.

"My daughter was actually the one to suggest it, if that makes you feel more comfortable. It seems you made quite the impression."

"Princess Calliope was the one who made the impression. She was very welcoming, and I am flattered she thought to suggest I stay."

"I'm glad. Well, I won't hold you up any longer. I hear you ladies need your beauty sleep. At least that's what my wife says." He shrugged like the concept made no sense to him. "I would love it if you joined my family for breakfast tomorrow? Give us all a chance to get to know each other better."

"I would be honoured." I stood right as the captain opened the door. How he knew we had finished our conversation was beyond me. "Thank you again for your hospitality." I curtsied again and turned, exiting the room.

I could feel the King's eyes on me long after I had left, possibly until the doors to his study were shut once more. The captain fell into step beside me.

"Allow me to escort you to your room, my lady."

"Oh, that's not necessary, thank you."

"I insist. What kind of gentleman would I be if I didn't help a lady in need?" He questioned, phrasing it the same way Jameson had. *Were all high standing Taros men given the same handbook?*

"Are all the ladies so lucky as to have the King's captain himself as their spy?" I said as I walked.

He easily matched my pace as he replied. "A mere coincidence. I happened to be nearby when you were conversing with Lord Inkwell."

"Mmm, how very convenient."

He smiled. "Why would I be spying on you, Lady Elia? Do you have information worth spying on for?"

"Everyone has information someone will find value in, but if you're asking regarding information that could harm your king or kingdom? No, I possess nothing that could be of value to the royal house."

"How convenient," he said, mimicking my earlier words. This man was a bloody parrot.

I stopped as we reached my chambers. Placing my hand on the doorknob, I turned to look at him. "Thank you for the escort, Captain Ambrosia. I hope you enjoy the rest of your evening."

"You too, Lady Elia." He bowed and stepped back. His green eyes were captivating, even as they portrayed no hint of what might go on inside that head of his.

I entered my rooms, shutting and locking the door, not missing the soft chuckle from him, as he no doubt heard the lock click into place.

I had achieved the first step in my plan tonight; get invited into their home, but not how I had expected to. It was far too easy, and the variance in behaviour tonight was far too odd. From the Queen's cold, barely there greeting, the King's unexpected welcome, and his supposed friendship with Lady Elia's father, the Princess's eagerness to befriend me, and the Prince's eagerness to do the exact opposite. Boy, would it would piss him off when he discovered I would be staying here. And lastly, the keen-eyed captain who, apparently, saw and heard much more than one would expect. Not to mention the apparent animosity between Taros and Xeria.

I would need to do some digging, but overall, the Navarre court was more suspicious than they should be of a nonconsequential, foreign lady on holiday. The invitation to stay, the offer of guards, both were no doubt less about my protection and more about keeping an eye on me. I'd have to find out why, and fast. I had a feeling I had stepped foot on a much larger playing field than expected, perhaps an entirely different game altogether.

I awoke to a knock on my door. Wrapping my robe around myself, I opened the door to find two lady's maids. I raised my eyebrows as they bowed their heads.

"Good morning, Lady Worthington. The princess assigned us to serve you for the duration of your stay here. My name is Lydia, and this is Tilly." A blonde girl around my age gestured to herself, then to another timid looking girl who appeared to be a few years younger, with red hair and freckled cheeks. She would turn heads as she grew older and more confident.

I opened my mouth to decline the unnecessary fuss, but promptly remembered I was supposed to be a noblewoman accustomed, and even expected, to be waited on. So instead of objecting, I smiled, nodded, and stepped aside.

"Of course, come in. And please, call me Elia."

They smiled politely and entered the room. Lydia spoke again. "Would you like me to run you a bath, Lady Elia? Breakfast isn't for another hour or so."

"That would be great, thank you." As uncomfortable as I was having someone else, let alone multiple someone else's, dress and prepare me, I let them. Then I headed to the hall for breakfast with the royal family. We passed Lord Jameson on the way. Poor Tilly practically collided with the man, apologising in pure terror of his retaliation. He simply steadied her, gave her a winning smile, and reassured her there was no harm done. He met my gaze as he continued on his way, giving me a playful wink.

As we reached the private dining room, I wondered what faces they would wear today. Would the queen still be icy? Would the king be as friendly? Would the princess be as bubbly, and the prince so obvious about his suspicions? I groaned softly to myself. I'd known this would not be easy, but I hadn't expected to be met with such varying reactions from the royal family members. I had expected to have to earn their attention, not be invited to dine with them after my first interaction.

Steeling myself, I nodded for the guards stationed at the doors to open them, giving a small wave to Tilly and Lydia as they departed, joining some other servants passing by. Walking in, I noted the atmosphere was a lot more casual than I would have expected. No crowns in sight, no formal wear. There was even—was the king in a robe? *Yep.* The ruler of Taros was sitting in front of me in a burgundy night robe, smiling warmly. What in the divinities' names?

"Good morning, Lady Elia. I'm so glad you could join us. Please sit, you're just in time. The food has just been served," King Hadrian said. I curtsied before glancing around at the rest of the room's occupants. There were minimal guards. The queen and princess were as I expected them to be. The former looked bored, unbothered by my presence, while the latter smiled that same smile as her father, and gestured to the seat next to her.

"Thank you, Your Majesty. I am honoured to have been invited." I took the seat Cali held for me and sat opposite Prince Valor. Face to face with him, he looked beyond pissed. Clearly, he hadn't been informed of my invitation. I smiled extra sweetly at him, before looking at the array of food on the table. Aside from the feast last night, which was obviously for an event, I had never seen so much food for a family meal. My mouth watered a little. This was heaven compared to the scraps Sierra and I prepared for ourselves in that ramshackle hut.

"Hadrian, you didn't mention we were to have a guest for breakfast. You should be dressed more appropriately." The ice queen scolded her husband.

"Oh come now, Odette. I hardly think Lady Elia will tattle on me." He winked at me while the queen rolled her eyes and simply began eating.

Seated with Cali on my left, that put the king to my right at the head of the table, Valor opposite me, still seething, and the queen at the other end of the table, opposite the king.

King Hadrian leaned closer and whispered, "You'll have to excuse my lovely wife. She is a tad grumpy in the mornings." My eyes widened, and I coughed lightly to hide my surprise, which he apparently found amusing, because he laughed. "Eat, Elia. The food will get cold." He sat back and ate his own meal.

"... Thank you, Your Majesty." I started eating, unable to comprehend the strangeness of this whole situation.

Here I was sitting in a *castle*, of all places, with the current ruling family of Taros. A Pure family. I'd likely never be in a room with this much power again. And yet, the king and queen squabbled like a normal married couple. Princess Cali was chatting away about some upcoming event, and Prince Valor was still skulking like a bratty teenager. It was so... normal.

Apparently, that line of thinking was cursing my luck because not a second after thinking it, the king took a sip from his chalice and began speaking to me.

"Elia, did your father ever tell you about the time he stole a pig from the loca—" he cut himself off and his eyes went wide. I glanced around the room but saw nothing amiss. By the time I glanced back at him, his face was red, his eyes wide, and he was gripping his throat. A red substance dripped from the corner of his mouth. *Blood*

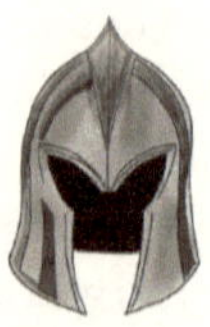

CHAPTER NINE

I JUMPED UP AS the queen screamed, and guards spilled into the room. The chalice spilled onto the floor. *Poison.* The king had been poisoned. I took a step forward. If I could get near that cup, I could identify which poison was used, and if there was an antidote. But in the time it took me to blink, I had a sword to my throat. I froze and followed it to the hand that was gripping it tightly, Prince Valor's hand.

They rushed the king from the room in a sea of guards, the princess and the queen hurrying along with them, shouting commands and clearing the halls.

I took a shallow breath. "What are you doing?"

"Do you take me for a fool? You arrive mysteriously without warning from Xeria, of all places. The *only* foreign visitor, the *only* person in this castle we do not know. You somehow weasel your way into dining with my family, and the next thing we know, our king has been poisoned?"

I gaped at him. "I did not do this! What motive would I have for killing the king? *Especially* in such an obvious way, as you've just pointed out. I'm not responsible."

He shook his head and stepped closer until we stood face to face. Gone was the playful man from last night, now I could see the barely restrained anger in his eyes. The tip of the sword pressed deeper into my neck, causing me to flinch, but I didn't back away.

"Guards. Lock her up. No food, no water. No one speaks to her without my permission."

"Your Highness, I can help. I am skilled with poisons and herbs. I was trained in Xeria. If you let me look, I can help," I said, knowing my knowledge on the subject could be seen as damning evidence against me, but I would have to be an imbecile to confess that to him if I *was*, in fact, guilty.

He gritted his teeth. "Get her out of my damned sight. *NOW*." He lowered the sword and walked over to the fallen cup, as two guards grabbed my arms on either side.

"No, I didn't do this!" I struggled. "Your Highness, you're making a mistake!" My pleas fell on deaf ears as the guards hauled my ass out of the room.

I stopped struggling, fairly certain I could manoeuvre my way out of their hold, but then what? It would only look more guilty, and I needed to stay here, needed to get useful information for Butcher. So, I let them lead me to their cells, down so many stairs, I was grateful for my strict training routine. They threw me in an empty cell and locked the door, exiting the way they came.

I glanced around. There were cells on either side of mine, dimly lit by torches. It was cold and smelt like the dead. I wrinkled my nose. Well, it wasn't the first cell I'd been locked in, but the smell was unpleasant, to say the least. I sighed before reluctantly sitting down, leaning my head against the wall and closing my eyes. *Perfect. Just perfect.* What the Hek are the odds that I arrive, and someone poisons the king? I can't fault the prince for thinking I was the culprit. It was framed perfectly. Was that a mere coincidence, or had someone seen me arrive and taken that as an opportunity? If so, why?

A scraping sound interrupted my thoughts. Opening my eyes, I glanced around.

"Hello?" I listened closely. I had passed a few occupied cells on the way in, but none seemed all that conscious.

"What's this? A new little birdy for the cage?" An old, croaky voice sounded to my left.

I peered into the darkness, trying to make anything out. It took a minute, but, as my eyes adjusted, I could just make out a small, cloaked figure huddled in the corner of my neighbouring cell.

It was a woman, but that was about as much as I could tell. She tilted her head to the left, watching me.

"Interesting. Do they know they've let a fox into the coop? I suppose they do or you wouldn't be locked up down here with the rats now, would you? But for the right crime? I think not."

She was babbling on like a madwoman, but her words had me tensing. Did they plant this woman here to goad a confession out of me?

"What are you talking about? I have committed no crimes. They have made a mistake."

She let out a hoarse laugh. "A joker, aren't you? No crimes? Child, the patrons of The Cavum would beg to differ."

Her reference to The Cavum did not bode well. Had someone leaked information? Had my alias been compromised?

"You have me confused with someone else. I am a lord's daughter visiting from Xeria. I don't have a clue what you're talking about."

"You've confused yourself for someone else, little bird. They clipped your wings, didn't they? Caged you. Oh, what a shock they will have when you learn to fly." She nodded to herself. *This woman was mad.*

I shook my head and stopped answering. She was clearly unhinged.

She chuckled again. "You slipped through the cracks. Slipped through the cracks and into the belly of the beast. What a delightful turn of events." The scraping noise reappeared, and I realised it was her nails, scratching on the concrete floor of her cell, as if she could somehow dig herself free out of sheer will.

I closed my eyes again. They would have to come for me soon, to interrogate me before they had me hung, to find out who sent me. I just had to wait, and then? Hope like Hek I could prove my innocence, or convince them to let me try.

I lost track of the time. It all seemed the same down here. Guards came and went, feeding some prisoners. Not me, of course, thanks to the prince's kind orders. Based on the regular meal times, I figured I had been here for at least two days, but I fell asleep at some point and with no light, I didn't know how much time had truly passed. I woke to the sound of a key turning in the lock of my cell. I opened my eyes to find two guards approaching me.

"Up," one said gruffly, "the prince requests your presence."

"Tell him I am busy, and shall endeavour to meet with him when I am free." I responded, sounding bored as I picked at my nails.

The guards weren't amused by my joke, and once again, manhandled me back up to civilisation. *Tough crowd.*

I now smelt almost as bad as the dungeon, and probably looked a mess. The guards dragged me to a meeting room of sorts and practically threw me inside, shutting the door.

I faced Prince Valor, Princess Cali, and Captain Ambrosia. The three of them wore different masks. The prince had reigned in his anger, but hatred was still burning in his eyes. Princess Cali looked unsure, and the red rings around her eyes told me she had been crying. Captain Ambrosia looked impassive, stood close to the two heirs, assessing and calculating.

I stood dusting off my dress, discarding etiquette at this point. I would bow to them once my name was cleared.

Prince Valor spoke first. "What poison did you administer?"

I sighed. "I did not poison the king. You have the wrong person."

"Bullshit. Tell us what you used, or we will find other, less pleasant ways, to make you talk." He nodded to the guard closest to me, who stepped forward.

"Brother, wait. We don't have any evidence yet." She looked at me. "Please, Elia, if... if you did this—if you know what poison it is, you need to tell us. Please, he is our father."

"Cali—" I tried.

"Don't call her that." The prince snapped. "Don't you dare speak as if you are a friend."

"Princess Calliope. I swear on Taros himself," the God of Strength, and our kingdom's namesake, "I did not poison the king. I hold no ill will towards any member of your family. You have the wrong person. I am truly sorry."

"What proof do you have? What reason can you give me to make me think you aren't guilty? I can't just take your word for it."

"When would I have had the time? I only arrived yesterday, was escorted to my room by the captain himself, and then in the morning, the lady's maids *you* sent woke me and escorted me to breakfast. I have no knowledge of where your kitchen is, nor was I unaccompanied at any point aside from when I slept."

"You had an opportunity when you met with the king last night in his private study," Ambrosia said, stepping forward, "perhaps you slipped something in then?"

I groaned. "That's ridiculous."

The prince frowned. "What were you doing meeting with my father so late at night, and alone at that?"

"I was just as surprised as you are now, when the captain informed me the king wanted to speak to me. All he did was welcome me, mention that he knew my father, and invite me to breakfast, I swear."

The royal heirs shared an unreadable glance. I could see that Valor had already decided I was guilty, and it looked like Cali *wanted* to believe I was innocent but was struggling to do so. Before they could condemn me anymore, I spoke again, looking at Valor.

"I wasn't lying earlier. I studied the art of poison in Xeria. Xeria values warriors, and I assume you know that. Warriors of all kinds. As a noble, Impure lady, I wasn't taught to fight, but they taught me other things that made me useful. They train us to perceive many distinct threats. Let me look at the poison, let me prove to you it wasn't me. I can find who did this." It was a risk, exposing that skill set. It probably wouldn't help convince them I wasn't working for the Queen of Xeria, but it seemed like the only way I could, at the very least, clear my name of *this* crime.

"Why would we do that? We know who did it. I'm looking right at her."

"Val." Cali's voice dropped. "The medicae can't identify the poison. If at the very least she can identify it, we have to make that the priority. We can deal with whether she did it when he is safe." They must not have a Remedi here. Not too surprising given the strenuous ties each of the six kingdoms had with each other, most would be like Taros, only having mortal trained healers, medicae.

"She's right Val. I will oversee it, and I won't let her out of my sight." I was a little surprised at the casual tone Ambrosia took with the prince, the kindness in his eyes.

Prince 'Val' closed his eyes and nodded. "Go... we don't know how much time we have." He opened them again and looked at me. "If you pull anything, you won't just be hung, Elia. I will oversee your punishment personally." There was a glint in his eyes that made it perfectly clear he was being sincere.

Apparently needing to get the point across further, a flick of his wrist had my feet lifting off the ground. I gasped. His Gifting. I'd never seen a Pure use their magic. I couldn't stop myself from rising into the air. My arms were pinned to my sides by my own sleeves and he was using my shoes to raise me into the air. As my clothing tightened around me, I swallowed.

"I understand. I am not deceiving you. Just let me prove it."

He relaxed his hand, and I dropped to the ground, *hard*. Wincing, I stood.

"Let's go." The captain walked out of the room, making it clear he had no problem turning his back to me, not perceiving me as a valid threat. *Rude.*

I hurried after him, back to the dining hall and over to the now dried liquid on the floor, thank the divinities they hadn't cleaned it up. They had cordoned the spill off and left the area untouched. Thankfully, the floor was hardwood, the liquid had dried but not soaked through. I bent down to examine it. Captain Ambrosia watched me closely, as did the royal children, who had followed, now standing by the door. I thought back to my training. There was no obvious odour, but the most effective poisons were often odourless and colourless.

"I need a parchment." The princess disappeared for a few moments before returning and hastily handing me the closest she could find.

"What other symptoms has the king exhibited? Aside from the red face and bleeding from the mouth?" I asked as I ripped the parchment, rubbing a piece against the dried spill, and swiping the other half around the edge of the chalice.

They seemed hesitant to answer me. "I need to know in order to determine which poison he ingested."

"He vomited and started convulsing. He's now in a catatonic state. No one has been able to wake him." Ambrosia supplied as I carried both pieces of parchments over to the closest candle. I lit them both on fire, watching closely as I ran through the mental list of poisons in my head.

The first piece burned as you'd expect, the flame remaining yellow as it devoured the paper. The second piece, however, burned slower, and the flame turned a deep red.

"Bellvenum. The assassin used bellvenum. Not in the liquid, but the rim of the chalice. Your medicae needs to mix the antidote with calabar and machineel. They need to hurry."

"Do you know how to make the antidote yourself?" Cali asked.

"Cali, we can't trust her! She could very well finish him off."

"We don't have a choice, Valor! Our poisons master is in Reya gathering supplies! None of the medicae knew what the poison was, but she identified it in *minutes*." I mentally tucked away that piece of information. Whoever did poison the king had to have known their poison master was away, meaning it had likely been an inside job.

I saw genuine pain in Valor's eyes, a twin to the pain in his sisters.

"I can help. Take me to him."

As we hurried to the royal wing, I rattled off a list of ingredients and supplies I would need to a guard, who took off to gather it all.

Queen Odette was sitting beside the King's bed, holding his hand like a lifeline, eyes puffy. She barely noticed us enter. The King's skin was pale and balmy. He was lucky to even still be alive. Bellvenum worked quickly. The guard hurried in with everything I had asked for, and I set to work brewing the antidote. The prince paced nearby, and the captain watched closely over my shoulder. Once I finished, I hurried over to the king, tipped his head back, and poured the liquid into his parted lips.

The entire room appeared to hold its breath. Everyone watched, waiting for either the King's heart to stop, or for him to open his eyes and declare everything right in the world. Neither of those things happened.

"Nothing is happening. What did you give him?" Valor demanded.

"It is happening. *LOOK*." The sweat on the King's face dissipated, colour slowly returning to his cheeks.

"Why isn't he waking?" Cali asked, worry in her voice.

"Everyone is different. It could take a few hours, days. He may be co-matose for longer. It depends on how much damage the poison was able to inflict."

"Get her out."

Captain Ambrosia grabbed my arm firmly, but not roughly, leading me out of the room. The queen hadn't said a word the entire time. Maybe she was in shock.

"Back to the cells, then?"

He looked down at me. "Not yet. For now, you'll be sequestered in your chambers. Until they decide what to do with you." *Guarded, no doubt.*

I sighed. It was better than the dungeon. I nodded and followed him to my room.

"I hope for your sake you aren't responsible, because if you are.... the prince has a lot of pent up rage."

"Noted." I shut the door in his face. *Bloody Hek.* Either The Fates were playing some sick joke on me, or I was the unluckiest spy ever.

I listened at the door, long enough to hear the captain order two guards to keep watch outside, before I made a beeline for the bathing chamber. I needed a long bath. Lady's maids be damned. I turned on the tap, running the water as hot as my skin could bear.

Only the wealthiest in Taros had baths with running, hot water available to them, as it involved having a heating room where you could store and heat the water, which then flowed through connected pipes and into your bath.

Most couldn't afford to have these installed, so having a hot bath usually meant heating water over a fire and manually carting it to your tub.

In the castle, however, there was at least one heating room on each floor, manned continuously by servants who kept the fires going and the water heated at all times. A luxury I planned on taking full advantage of. Undressing, I slipped in, breathing out as steam rose to the ceiling.

I recapped the events of the last few days in my head. I'd made it into the castle, which was unusual but not yet alarming, had received a mixture of responses to my presence, found out Xeria and Taros have some problems, that the prince is a royal pain in the ass, have been accused of attempting to assassinate the king, and then saved him. *Brilliant.* No big deal. Completely salvageable.

CHAPTER TEN

I closed my eyes and sank under the water. Maybe I'd drown in the tub and wouldn't have to deconstruct this mess. Right now, that sounded like a pretty good way to go. Before I could test just how long I could hold my breath, a noise drew my attention. I resurfaced, wiping the water from my eyes, and looked to the door. Only to find Prince Valor standing in the doorway, looking at me. I couldn't read his expression, but mine was certainly one of the 'what in the divinity damned world' category. I was so surprised to see him standing there at first that it took me a few seconds to remember I was, in fact, naked. I realised that minor detail at the same time he seemed to. His eyes left my face for just a second.

"Excuse me. It is highly inappropriate for you to be here." I sunk a little lower, no longer confident in the depth of this tub.

"Cover-up, and come out here," he simply said, before walking out and shutting the door.

I rolled my eyes, tempted to stay right where I was. I'd like to see him try to pull me out. Then I realised that he probably would if I didn't come out fast enough. I quickly got up, dried off, and wrapped my robe around myself, before following him.

He was standing by the fireplace, watching the flames dance. As unnecessary as I thought having servants waiting on nobles at all hours of the day was, I couldn't deny the perks of always having a warm room. He didn't look at me when I entered.

".... Is there a reason you're just standing there instead of either admitting you were wrong or dragging my ass to the noose?"

That caught his attention, and he looked me over.

"I would hardly call that covering up." I crossed my arms and said nothing. Butcher would be proud.

He sighed. "Look. I'm still not convinced that you had nothing to do with all of this. It's too much of a coincidence."

"This is a piss poor apology."

"*BUT*," he said, giving me an exasperated look, "my sister believes there's some truth to your claims of innocence... and... that we should give you a chance to prove it wasn't you."

"You mean me identifying the poison, making the antidote, and saving the King's life single-handedly wasn't enough proof for you?"

He didn't look amused. "No."

"Right, well, what tests would you like me to pass before I am deemed innocent, Your Highness?"

"I want you to find the true would-be assassin, if it isn't you."

"I may be adept at poisons, but I am still just a lady. I'm no inquisitor." It couldn't hurt to at least try playing dumb, like I hadn't already exposed myself.

He raised an eyebrow as if to say, 'that's what you're going with?'

I sighed. "Fine, but only because I don't seem to have much of a choice, and I really hope you have other people investigating."

"Of course we do." He walked over. "Do you think I'd risk the actual culprit getting away because I only assigned a girl, who may very well be the guilty one in question, to look into it? I am allowing you to investigate as a courtesy, but don't think I won't have you executed if you fail to produce another suspect in time."

"The culprit may have already gotten away while you were busy throwing accusations at me." I countered.

I really needed to work on controlling my attitude around this man. Something about him just irritated the inferno out of me. Apparently, the feeling was mutual. He opened his mouth to say something, but I cut him off before he could.

"And after the way you just burst into my bathing chamber, we *both* know I'm no 'girl,' Princeling."

His eyes simmered, and he stepped closer. "Princeling?"

I shrugged, not letting his nearness deter me.

He smirked. "You may be right, but that changes nothing."

"Of course it doesn't. Is there a reason we couldn't have this fun little chat tomorrow?"

"Not really."

I rolled my eyes but noticed his lingering on my neck.

My hand moved to the spot he seemed to be fixated on, snagging on the small nick from his sword.

"Guilty conscience?"

He didn't answer for a minute, studying my face instead. From this close, I could see the blue flecks of his eyes practically shimmering in the dim glow of the room. He studied me as closely as I studied him, and I couldn't quite grasp what he was thinking.

"Just imagining how much simpler my life would be if I had pressed harder." He replied, before stepping back and heading to my door.

"I'll see you at dawn. Try to be clothed this time." With that, he exited my room, the door slamming without him so much as lifting a finger, but not before I saw the guards exchange looks at his words.

What a jackass.

True to his word, by first light, Prince Valor was waltzing through my door without bothering to knock. What is it with people and their disregard for sleep? Would it kill them to start the day, I don't know, *after* the sun had truly risen?

I'd been half tempted to remain in my robe when he arrived, but thought better of it. I was, after all, supposed to be winning him over.

"Good morning, Your Highness."

"Let's go." He walked straight back out of the room. Charming.

I begrudgingly followed. "Where are we going?"

"The kitchen. You said the cup was poisoned, not the liquid itself?"

I nodded. "How many people knew your poison master was away? Follow up question, why on earth don't you have a backup or an apprentice?"

He looked surprised at my line of questioning. "We did, but he had an adverse reaction when completing his regular immunity training recently."

Often, poison masters were taste testers for the royal court, as well as simply experts in their field, meaning they needed to build up a tolerance of sorts. A common practice throughout wealthy houses.

"We couldn't save him, and with our current poison master already away, retrieving supplies we needed, there was no one else."

"How long ago did he die? Was it commonly known that the poison master was away at the time?"

He frowned slightly, following my line of thought and clearly not enjoying it.

"Five days after the master had left. Why? You think someone waited for our poison master to leave, then intentionally poisoned the apprentice to ensure no one could save the king?"

"If I were to poison someone? I would want to make sure it had the best chance of succeeding. It would be a smart move. Which poison did he die from?"

"The medicae couldn't identify it."

I gave him a look. "You didn't think that might be suspicious? That it might be linked to this?"

"Not with you, a blatantly obvious suspect right in front of us, no."

I let it drop as we entered the kitchen. At this time of the morning, I'd expected it to be empty, but a short, rotund man in a white apron was waiting for us. He must be the head cook.

"Pierre." Valor nodded in greeting. "This is Lady Worthington. She is assisting with my inquisition."

Pierre bowed low. "Your Highness, my lady. I wish we were meeting under different circumstances."

I smiled solemnly, requesting he walk me through how the breakfast was prepared, and where everything is stocked.

He led me over to where they stored all the plates, bowls, cups, and other cutlery. I surveyed the room, noting the closest entry to where I now stood. Someone could have snuck through the door to my left and gained access, but they'd had to have known which cup would be used for the king, since no one else was poisoned.

It was likely someone who served it or someone that had access to the chalice after they had assigned it to the king. Even if someone had somehow known which would be given to him beforehand, they'd have had a hard time going unnoticed. I turned to the prince.

"You need to put together a list of everyone who had access to the kitchen, and the meals the day before and the morning of. As well as all the staff, guards included, who were present in the dining hall while breakfast was happening. Then you need to question them all."

"We have already begun questioning those working in the kitchens. None of our guards would be responsible for something like this. They are *loyal* to the crown."

"People's loyalties can be swayed, Your Highness. Humour me, if nothing comes of it, then worst-case scenario, you have proven just how loyal they are."

He looked annoyed, opening his mouth to argue with me, but I spoke again before he could.

"I would like to see the deceased apprentice's body. Preferably, the source of his poisoning as well. Until you have completed your questioning of the staff, aside from trying to establish what killed him, and if it is in any way linked to the King's, I don't think there is much more information I can glean from here"

He looked surprised and then suspicious. For Ades sake, what now?

"You want to see his body? You realise he is dead? That he has been dead for days. It is not a pleasant sight or smell. It would be fairly unbecoming of a lady." I rolled my eyes. This pompous, patronising prince was certainly good at getting under my skin.

"Yes, well, whilst I would much rather spend my time doing something more 'becoming of a lady', the only thing I would like less than looking at a dead body, is being hung for an assassination attempt I did not commit."

He seemed to find that acceptable, but I could tell by the look in his eyes, he didn't think I could handle it. We said our goodbyes to Pierre and I let the prince escort me to the mortuary.

It was dimly lit, and the scent of death lingered in the air. I quickly switched to breathing through my mouth, even though the idea of tasting the stench was just as uncomfortable.

Valor ordered the servants to bring us to the body. Luckily, it hadn't yet been disposed of. Most likely thanks to no one successfully identifying the poison. The prince watched me closely, no doubt waiting for me to scream, vomit, or some other response he deemed appropriate for a lady to have.

As grossed out as I was, there was no way I would let him see an inch of discomfort from me.

I began my examination, thinking back to my training. Butcher had me trained by a poison master passing through from a foreign kingdom. She was certainly thorough with my training. Thanks to that, by the age of ten, I could identify the most commonly used poisons, and some rare ones. Unfortunately, that also meant I had seen my fair share of dead bodies and examinations. I was too young to give much thought as to where they'd acquired those bodies. Knowing what I do now, she probably poisoned them herself, just so I could practice. *Cold-hearted witch.*

I refocused, ignoring the Prince's stare as I worked, writing anything of note on a piece of parchment I borrowed from the servant on duty. Scanning the list I had compiled, as I'd suspected, it all pointed to bellvenum being the cause of death, but I was missing something. I knew it. Problem was, I'd checked for all the poisons I knew of in Deorum. Nothing was coming up. But maybe...

Glancing around, I smiled when I found what I was looking for. I mixed together a few of the herbs thankfully stocked here, until it formed a clear, gooey paste. Scooping it out of the bowl, I lathered it across the corpse's lips and waited.

"What on earth are you doing?" Valor questioned.

"Testing a theory." Picking up on the fact that I wouldn't elaborate further, he remained quiet as he watched me work. After waiting a minute, sure enough, the paste slowly changed colour.

"What does that mean?"

"It means it wasn't only bellvenum this boy ingested, there are also traces of a rare herb that isn't native to Deorum."

"Which means...?" He dragged out the question.

"It means I know how to wake your father."

Valor sent a servant to fetch Cali and meet us at the royal chambers while I gathered the herbs I'd need and mixed up the antidote.

Once we reached their chambers, he went in first, leaving me waiting outside. A few minutes later, my name was called, and the guards opened the doors, allowing me in. I stepped in to find the Valor, Cali, and Odette in the foyer. The princess immediately smothered me in a hug.

"You really think you can wake him up?" She asked hopefully.

"Can't... breathe..."

"Let the girl go, Calliope. You'll squeeze her to death," the queen said and Cali let go, blushing a little.

"Sorry, Elia."

"It's fine." I smiled a little. "I believe so." I held up the vial.

"How do you know it will work?" Valor asked, sceptical, as we made our way into the Royal Suite, and over to the King's sleeping form.

"You said that your medicae found no trace of poison, which limits the amount of poisons it could be. Very few leave no trace. I checked the apprentice for all the poisons I know of that fall into that category but came up empty, and the chalice only tested positive for bellvenum, which on its own isn't known for the comatose effects Hadrian is suffering from."

"Get to the point, Elia."

It was an effort not to glare at the pompous prince, only the watching eyes of his mother and sister kept me in check.

"There is one poison I know of that shows no trace until a person is deceased. It is rare and not found in Deorum, but it would explain why, when I tested the chalice, it didn't register. It only shows up on dead tissue. When I tested the apprentice, I got a positive reading for cadzium. That is why your father hasn't woken up. Both bellvenum *and* cadzium were used."

"We can hardly trust you. You are still a stranger."

"Oh, get over yourself, Val," Cali said, rolling her eyes. "What exactly do you want her to do to earn your trust? Walk across coals?"

"Sorry, I don't just blindly put all of my faith in anyone that gives me even the slightest bit of affection."

"Enough, children. Valor, Elia's explanation makes sense. The herbs you described to me before she entered, the ones she used in her antidote, are non-lethal and will not harm your father more than he's already been harmed. Cease your bickering so we can save him."

He bit back whatever he was going to say, sighed, and nodded. "Sorry, Mother." *What a mother's boy.*

Cali also murmured a soft, "Sorry." I took that as my cue to approach and administer the antidote.

I gently tilted the King's head back, tipping the contents of the vial down his throat, before stepping back a few respectful paces.

"How long does it take?" Valor asked.

"It should only be a minute or two before we will know if it worked."

We all watched silently in anticipation. *Please work.*

"There!" Cali exclaimed. "His finger moved!"

"That could have just been him moving in his sleep," Valor said.

"It wasn't! I saw it. It was intentional."

"You think everything is intentional?"

A groan quickly silenced the room. "Honestly, children, must you bicker so loudly?"

I breathed a sigh of relief. Valor smiled a little. Cali didn't hold back her tears as she hurled herself at her father, and the queen looked relieved.

I stepped back again, quietly leaving, as the entire family embraced each other. As I retreated, the king caught my eye and gave me a soft smile mouthing, 'thank you.' I nodded, returning his smile before shutting the doors behind me.

Escorted by guards, I returned to my rooms, ran myself a bath, and washed away the smell of death that still lingered on my skin.

I was dressed in a fluffy robe, staring at my reflection in the beautiful vanity mirror I was now sitting at, and mentally complaining about how difficult it was going to be to win Valor over, when a knock sounded on my door.

CHAPTER ELEVEN

Opening it, I found Lydia waiting.

"Oh, Lydia, hello."

She bowed her head and smiled apologetically. "Lady Elia, the princess has requested your presence for lunch. May I help prepare you?"

I nodded, stepping aside. "That would be great, thank you."

"Of course." She smiled, entering, and immediately selecting some options for me to wear.

"Rumour is, you discovered which poison was used on the king and helped save him." She commented, as I perused the outfits she had selected.

"Word spreads fast around here, doesn't it?"

"Oh, yes, especially particularly scandalous gossip."

I chuckled, selecting a dress. "And what scandalous gossip is circulating at the moment?" I sat at the vanity and let her attempt to tame the nest I called my hair.

"Well, there are rumours that Lord Vestisy is having an affair with the baker's daughter, who is half his age!" She prattled on, completely oblivious to whenever I casually slipped in questions about the castle layout, the royal court, the royals themselves, and anything else that might be useful to know.

"And of course, there's you."

"Me?" That caught my interest. I couldn't wait to hear what outrageous things people were saying about Lady Elia.

"You're quite the mystery, my lady. People say you showed up out of nowhere. Some are saying you're here to be married off to the prince. Everyone is placing bets on what your Specialty is." I raised my eyebrows.

The Worthingtons were a noble house, but as far as I knew, they weren't Pure. They may have some Para's in their bloodline, but they certainly weren't Pure. That would have made for a terrible cover if someone asked me to demonstrate my magic. People must be ignoring my family name and assuming I have a Gifting. How else could I be eligible for the prince?

"I bet I am a big favourite with the ladies of this court, then?"

She bit her lip nervously, clearly unsure if I would take out any anger at what she may say next on her. I am sure plenty of the nobles regularly did so.

"Relax Lydia, I don't bite. You can tell me." She hesitated, but ultimately her eagerness to gossip won the battle.

"You're quite right. I think a few of the ladies are jealous. They can't find any dirt on you, because you arrived so mysteriously, and the prince danced with you at the banquet, and Lord Jameson! *Then* you *left* the event with Captain Ambrosia..." She babbled.

People were paying attention. For the wrong reasons, though, it was still interesting to hear what outsiders noted and what they didn't.

"I heard Lady Josette say there was no way any of them would touch you because you're Impure and not even a proper noble. That you are only here because your parents tired of you."

I chuckled. "Josette Huntingwell, I presume?" I'd done my research. I knew the prominent ladies of the Navarre court. Josette was a Kineti, specialising as a Teleki like Prince Valor, and was favoured for an arranged marriage with the man. Apparently, and unsurprisingly, she was a jealous woman.

Lydia nodded. "I don't like to speak ill of people, but Lady Josette is.... difficult."

I smirked. "I can only imagine."

Lydia helped me into the dress that I considered too fancy for lunch, but Lydia assured me it was not. Looking in the mirror, I was once again surprised at how regal I appeared. If I didn't know better, I'd say Lydia had some higher power of her own to make me look like this.

The dress was a light blue in honour of the Navarre family colours. It had long shoulder-less sleeves that fanned out at the ends, and a bodice that cinched in at my waist before it, too, fanned out slightly.

"You look stunning, Lady Elia." She beamed at me before notifying the guards that we were ready.

I followed her out, expecting to see the same guards from earlier, instead I faced the captain. He bowed his head.

"Lady Elia, ready?"

I raised my eyebrows, surprised at his politeness given recent events. "Yes, thank you, Captain Ambrosia."

We started walking, his steps timed with mine, even if it meant him purposefully walking slowly.

"What happened to my other guards?"

"I am in the process of assigning you personal guards, per the king's request. However, I wanted to escort you to your lunch so I could speak to you myself."

"Speak to me about what?"

"I wanted to thank you for what you did for the king and apologise for our treatment of you."

I raised my eyebrows. "How much does it pain you to say those words?"

He gave me a striking grin, but didn't answer my question.

"Valor informed me you saw the kitchens and inspected Arnold's body this morning." *Arnold.* I hadn't asked his name. I was always taught not to. Taught not to let anything stand a chance at allowing emotions to become involved and therefore jeopardise the job. "Did you find anything else of note?"

"You mean besides the poison used to put the king to sleep? I'm sure the prince already filled you in."

"He has, but I asked if you noticed anything *else*, not what you told him you found."

He was smart to assume I wouldn't tell Valor everything, but I was no fool, either. I'd seen the way the two of them interacted, and Lydia had let slip enough for me to know that the prince and the captain were close. This was likely a ploy, one of them playing the snarky unlikeable one, and the other a friendly shoulder to confess to.

"You mean like how, why, or who poisoned the apprentice and the king?"

He nodded.

"When I have sound evidence for any theories I might have, you and the prince will be informed. I am unfamiliar with this court. It may take some time."

"Naturally. However, you do not have an abundance of time, Lady Elia."

"Thank you for stating the obvious, Captain."

He chuckled. "I meant no offence."

"Mhmm, of course you didn't." We came to a stop at a closed door with two guards posted outside.

"Where are we?"

"The princess's guest dining room."

The captain led me into a room that was as lavish as I'd expected. Beautifully decorated, but also somehow maintaining that homey feel. Giving off a warmth, much like the one the princess herself gave when she smiled at you.

The woman in question was seated on a chaise lounge. Once she spotted us, she jumped up, smiling. "Elle! I'm glad you came. In all honesty, I thought you might not."

I curtsied. "Why would you think that?"

She bit her lip. "After all the nastiness, I wouldn't blame you for not wanting to talk to me."

I smiled a bit. "It may be a little awkward, but I don't blame you, Cali. Your father almost died. You reacted how most would, but even then, you were still kind." *Unlike your brother.* The unspoken words hung in the air between us.

"Ah, you mustn't take my brother's words to heart. He means well, he just.... has trouble communicating that to people he doesn't know."

A scoff sounded from the Captain's direction, causing her gaze to fix on him. She raised an eyebrow.

"Do you have something you would like to add, Killian?" Her voice held a challenge.

His lips twitched with a barely restrained smile.

"You and I both know that is a vast understatement."

She cracked a grin, her eyes on his the whole time. It was subtle, likely unnoticeable to most people, but I was not most people. Their body language changed. The Captain's eyes softened, focusing intently on her, and she shifted, facing him more directly as her smile morphed from polite to charming. *Interesting.*

"Yes, well, that is why we are here, to balance out his prickliness."

He chuckled. The type of lighthearted one I imagined I wouldn't have heard if the princess weren't in the room. "Touché."

I remained silent, watching them watch each other for a second too long before remembering I was in the room.

Cali flushed bright pink when her eyes landed on me again, and she cleared her throat.

"We are being rude. Val told me you haven't eaten breakfast? You must be starved. Here, have a seat."

I hadn't thought my eating habits would be a concern of his, but I didn't voice that. I simply took a seat.

She turned back to the captain. "You can leave now, Killian. Thank you for escorting Elle here." He gave her a look that said, not likely.

"I am not leaving you unguarded, Cal." She rolled her eyes.

"Ridiculous, what is she going to do?"

Her blatant disregard at me posing any threat was mildly offensive. The dagger strapped to my thigh certainly suggested otherwise. But she didn't know that, and I needed it to stay that way. Best she remains thinking I am just an innocent lady caught in a mess.

"Queen's orders. You are not to be left alone with Lady Elia."

"Oh, nonsense. Since when do you answer to my mother?"

"Since your father was recently poisoned, Calliope." His voice was stern, leaving no room to budge. I guess that meant I hadn't won the queen over yet.

"You realise I am sitting right here? I can hear both of you. It's alright Cali, I can understand the precaution. He is just following orders."

"Like Hek." My eyes widened a bit at the Princess's terse words. "You can wait outside with the other guards." She started shooing him away like a pest, actually shooing.

He groaned. "Cal."

"Nope. Get out, Killian. You know very well I can take care of myself."
Could she? In what capacity? Was she trained?

Ladies did not train, it was unbecoming. Or at least, that's what they were told if they ever questioned the backwards logic that decided women did not deserve the right to protect themselves. That was the men's job, at least here in Taros. I couldn't speak for other kingdoms. I'd heard Xeria and Ikira trained their women, the Gifted ones at least, but I imagined the other kingdoms were very much the same as Taros.

He looked like he wanted to fight more, but ultimately, she won.

"I will be right outside, and I will check in on you regularly. If I hear even a whisper of something that doesn't sound right, I will kick down your door."

She mimicked him before shoving him out the door and shutting it in his face.

I covered my mouth to stifle my laughter. She turned to me, looking exasperated.

"I swear to the divinities, the men in this castle are outright infuriating!"

The look on her face was hilarious and I let a laugh slip, removing my hand.

"I can agree with that."

She shook her head and sat down. "I'm truly sorry about that."

"It's fine. That was pretty tame compared to your brother in all honesty."

She smiled apologetically, but refrained from saying anything else, as the servants' entry opened, and the staff brought in our lunch.

"Thank you." She smiled politely, making eye contact with each of the servants, seeming to genuinely mean it. She went to dig in as soon as they'd left, but I stopped her.

"Wait." I stood, and she looked at me questioningly.

"Two members of your court have been poisoned recently, and the culprit is still at large. Let me check it first?"

Her eyes widened, and her face paled. "You think the assassin is still here? That they might target one of us next?"

"You can never be too sure, not until we have found them."

She nodded. "Are you... how do you know it won't hurt you if it *is* poisoned?"

"I received training in Xeria. They don't allow the Impure women to fight like the Virbi Pure and Para women, but they teach us other skills, ways to be useful. I was particularly good at poison studies."

"Before you do, let me call Killian in. Just in case." She stood, moving to the door, where she exchanged a few hushed words with the captain before they both re-entered.

"Lady Elia, you do not need to do that. If something were to happen to you—we should have a servant test it."

"I am no more expendable than any of the servants, Captain." Both he and Cali looked surprised at my words, but I knew they'd had the desired effect when respect shone proudly in Cali's eyes and begrudgingly in Ambrosia's.

I knew it was unlikely the princess would be targeted so soon, but not impossible if someone was trying to pick off the royal family. I also had more of the antidotes I'd made up for the king, hidden in my corset as a precaution.

I checked the food carefully, scenting it first, then tasting. It was clear. I nodded to them.

"It's okay. I can't detect anything unusual."

Cali breathed out, sitting back down. "Divinities, that was stressful."

I smiled a bit, taking my seat again.

The captain watched me for a minute before looking back at Cali. "I suppose I still can't convince you to let me stay?"

"For divinities sakes, Killian. She just risked her life to make sure I wasn't poisoned. I think she has proven herself trustworthy."

He sighed. "Fine." He shot me a look that said he was still sceptical before closing the door behind him.

"They say *women* hold grudges." She complained, eliciting another chuckle out of me.

"How long have you and the captain been seeing each other?"

She coughed, quickly taking a sip of water as she scrambled for how to respond.

"I — What? You're mistaken."

I smiled a bit and waited. I had to give it to Butcher. The silence thing really was useful. It didn't take long for her to cave, followed by a groan.

"We haven't... we aren't together, we just—"

"Have a mutual interest in each other that hasn't been pursued because?"

"—I am a princess that is expected to marry another royal, not a captain. It would only hurt us both to pretend we could ever be more than what we are now." She finished.

"Even though you're not in line for the throne? Isn't that one perk of being the youngest royal? You have more autonomy to choose?"

She smiled sadly. "We do not have as much freedom as one might think."

Her circumstance reminded me of Raf and I. Both of us were in the same boat, unable to be more than we were because, ultimately, it would not end the way we wanted. Albeit a much less privileged version, but the two scenarios were eerily similar.

I reached over and squeezed her hand. "I'm sorry. It's hard to want someone you know you have no future with."

She looked at me. "Is there someone back home?"

I smiled a bit. "Sort of. We just weren't fated to be together, I suppose. But we still enjoyed what little time we had. It's complicated, but I thought it was worth it as long as we didn't let it go further."

"How though? How do you save yourself from the heartbreak? How can you stop yourself from loving him?" She asked, looking at the door.

"By living in a constant state of denial, I guess?" I offered, and she laughed softly.

"Perhaps."

I shrugged and finished my food. "So, not that I am complaining about dining with a princess, but is there a reason for this privilege?"

She looked back at me, and any trace of the sadness she had been feeling was gone.

"I wanted to talk about everything that has happened since you arrived. I don't think you poisoned my father, and that was before you helped me just now."

"I'm glad to hear that, because I didn't do it."

"I know, or at least, I believe you. Do I think you're being entirely honest with us? No."

Her confession caught me off guard, and I went to respond, but she held up a hand, silencing me. *This* was the girl I had expected. A princess, born and bred, taught to command a room, and know the power her status affords her. A stark contrast to the girl from a minute ago, the girl she let most of the world freely see.

"*But,* I believe whatever it is you *are* hiding, you will tell me when you feel you can. When I have earned your trust."

Guilt spiked like a hot iron to the chest. She knew that something was off, like her brother did, but trusted my intentions anyway. The two of them were smarter than they were given credit for.

"Cali…"

"It's alright, Elia, you don't need to tell me. You arrived and my family immediately hurled horrible accusations at you, then tossed you in a dungeon. I wouldn't trust us either, but I hope you give me a chance to earn it."

"Of course, but only if you do the same for me in return." I smiled a bit. "Friendship goes both ways."

"I like the sound of that." She smiled back. "Now that we have all the serious stuff out of the way, you haven't had a chance to get to know many people since arriving, given all the drama. There is a party tomorrow night to celebrate Father's recovery. I was hoping you would come?" She gave me a look that encompassed the physical manifestation of puppy dog eyes, and I couldn't help but smile.

"What kind of party?"

"Just the younger nobles. The older lords and ladies won't be present. Pleaseeee, Elia? You will have fun, I promise!"

I chuckled. "I'll see. You might be convinced of my innocence, but your bother and mother don't seem to be. I need to clear my name."

"I will talk to them about that, but I understand. If you change your mind, please let me know."

I smiled and nodded. "Of course."

CHAPTER TWELVE

WE SPENT THE REST of the meal getting better acquainted before Cali had duties to attend, and I headed back to my chambers, this time unescorted which was a pleasant change. She was a hard one to pin down; she seemed overly bubbly and trustworthy, even naïve, but there was a keenness to her gaze, to the way she spoke, that told me she was much more than she let on. I'd need to keep an eye on the Taros princess.

A group of servants passed by, and I smiled politely at them, then again at the guards posted outside my door. It wasn't until I was safely alone that I dared opened my palm and glance at the piece of paper one of them had slipped into my hand.

Time for an update, Little Sparrow.

Groaning, I closed my eyes. Just what I needed. There were guards stationed at my door, meaning I had to wait until nightfall, before attempting to scale down the walls unseen.

It felt like Lunos, God of the Moon himself, was intentionally taking his time chasing Solis away as the hours ticked by, but eventually darkness fell, and I changed from the beautiful dress to a dark tunic and cloak.

Making sure my door was locked, I moved to the window, opening it quietly, and leaning out to judge the distance. If I fell, it would definitely kill me. Luckily, they'd made the castle with thick bricks that were old and not without time's marks. There were enough ledges and footholds for me to scale my way down easily enough. I would just have to stick to the shadows. The hard part would be getting back in. Climbing up is a Hek of a lot harder than climbing down, but I had limited options.

I pulled my hood over my head and silently climbed out the window, scaling down the wall without issue. I had memorised the guard patrols after the first few nights, so sneaking out was easier than it should have been. The Navarre family needed to up their security, but I certainly wasn't complaining.

I made my way through the upper-class neighbourhoods until I got to Butcher's manor. Still keeping to the shadows, I snuck in through the back entrance and made my way up to her study, where Tolemas was guarding the door. My heart sank. I had intentionally avoided thinking about him, about his role in all of this, it was too painful, and that was what Butcher wanted. She wanted me to react, to hurt. I would not give her any more of me. I steeled myself and stopped in front of him.

"She is expecting me," I said calmly, no hint of emotion in my voice.

"Little Sparrow—"

"*Don't.*" I couldn't help the bite in my voice. "N*ever* call me that again. Either let me in or you can tell her why I left instead of seeing her as she requested." I didn't look at him as I spoke, not wanting to see whatever emotions were in his eyes, if any at all.

He did nothing for a few seconds, but then he sighed quietly and opened the door. I walked in, and he shut it behind me. Seated at her desk, Butcher was flipping through a ledger.

"The circus misses you. Mavil is nowhere near as skilled an aerialist as you, my dear."

I sat down in the chair opposite her. "Do you want a debrief, or is this about something else?"

She sighed. "I hope you aren't speaking to your hosts like that, or no one will believe you are an esteemed lady, Adira." I simply folded my arms and looked at her, unimpressed. "Yes, a debrief would be a good start."

That's exactly what I gave her. I told her everything that had occurred, watching her closely as I did.

"Did you have any idea that there may be tensions between Xeria and Taros when you picked my alias?"

"I did," she said, taking a sip of her tea. I wanted to rip the cup out of her hand and throw it at the wall.

"And you didn't think that was relevant information for me to have? You didn't think that could cause problems?"

"Oh, no, I knew it would cause problems." I looked at her in disbelief. Was she just trying to get me killed? Was this whole Solis thing nothing but a complete farce designed to punish me, getting me executed for betraying her, just like she had done to the boy who'd dared teach me to defend myself? "But I trusted your ability to navigate them. I trained you for exactly that, Adira. I knew you could overcome the problems and that when you did, the royal family would trust you with much more certainty."

"That was a bloody big gamble. What if I *hadn't* been able to? What if the two kingdoms were in serious disagreements and I was at risk?"

"There is always risk in our line of work, child. You know this. Enough about Xeria. You seem to have won the princess over, it was smart, offering to test her food. The captain seems cautious, but not hostile towards you. You might use his feelings for the princess to sway his opinion of you. The king should be more than thankful to you for saving his life. That leaves the queen and the prince."

"I have barely interacted with the queen, and the prince is a non-starter. He has decided already. There is no point trying to befriend him."

"The prince we can worry about at a later time. I want you to focus on the queen. You need to get into her good graces."

"There hasn't been an opportunity."

"You leave that to me. Just be ready when the opportunity arises."

"How could you possibly have any sway over that? What aren't you telling me?" It appeared I had worn down her patience. Her lips twitched in anger as she carefully placed her tea on the table before fixing an impassive stare on me.

"Kneel." She commanded, and her words hit my chest like a tonne of bricks. They forced me out of my chair and onto my knees. I flinched, trying to fight them as I strained against the command, but the blood oath did not budge. The Butcher rose from her desk and walked around to stand in front of me, a queen in all but a crown.

"Have you forgotten your place, child? Have you lost sight of who holds your strings? You are what you are because of *me*. I have given you *everything*, and I can just as easily take it away." I opened my mouth to retort, but she held up a hand. "Be silent." Again, her words tugged, and my lips slammed shut, leaving me shaking with rage.

"I will forgive your attitude this time, since it sounds as if you have had a tough couple of days. But consider carefully how you behave the next time we see each other, Adira. I will not be so forgiving then."

I steadied my breathing and nodded slightly, anger still clear on my face, but surrender in my eyes.

"Good. Now you will do what I said. Get close to the queen," my chest tugged again, "by whatever means necessary. You will find some things that may help back in your chambers when you return. Be wary of the prince, but if you don't see a point in befriending him right now, I trust your judgement. Rise, have your voice back."

I stood fighting against the part of myself that wanted to draw my dagger and slit her throat. Only the knowledge that she would have a redundancy plan in place should something happen to her kept me at bay. I couldn't risk Sierra.

"Is that all?"

"Yes, oh, but you should stop in and see — what's his name? Oh yes, Rafael. He misses you, I hear. You seem a little uptight, Adira. From what I've heard, he's your go-to boy toy these days?" I stiffened, but the tug never came. She smirked.

She knew. She knew where Sierra was. She knew about my relationship with Raf, and she was using it to put me in my place for my insubordination, knowing I'd see it for the threat it was.

That bitch.

I dug my nails into my palms and left, ignoring her *advice* to stop in and see Raf, I couldn't see face him or Sierra right now. Angry tears stung my eyes, but I refused to let them fall. I would not let her break me. When she was done with me, I wouldn't be the same person. I couldn't decide if that was good or bad, but whatever, or whoever, I became, she would not be weak, she would not bend, and divinities help anyone who gets in her way

The next day, I was finding it increasingly difficult to investigate this assassin with constant babysitters; the guards Killian had following me everywhere, so I decided I would attend the party Cali had mentioned. Hopefully, I'd be able to gather intel there.

The princess had been delighted when I'd informed her I would be attending, insisting on coordinating outfits. It was a big statement to make when one of us was royalty and the other wasn't. She wore a beautiful gown of contrasting blue, with an iridescent cape of light turquoise, golden shoulder cuffs, a belt, and lines trailing up her bodice. If she was light, I was dark, wearing a black strapless gown, dipping low at the front, flowing down in a gradient effect, as the black transformed to a dark blue, then a turquoise. The same shade Cali wore.

The event was a very different affair than the one a few nights ago. There was a lot more alcohol, the music was more upbeat, and the dancing was what some might call scandalous, at least for the royal court to be taking part in. Everyone dressed formally, but that was the only formal thing about the night. Cali was practically jumping with excitement as we entered, eliciting many, many stares.

"Let's grab a drink! It is a celebration, after all."

I chuckled and let her lead me to a servant with a tray. Cali promptly picked up a glass and downed the contents before grabbing another glass. I laughed, grabbing one of my own.

"Oh no. As the princess, it is my civil duty to ensure all guests have a good time. Bottoms up, my dear Elia."

I rolled my eyes and downed the drink before also grabbing another. It didn't take long for people to approach. I enjoyed watching them vie for the princesses' attention, whilst also trying to figure me out. Cali remained close to me and included me in every conversation, much to the distaste of the jealous nobles. After getting a feel for the court politics at play for a while, and listening out for any information I could use, I excused myself to get some air.

Grabbing a glass, I made my way to the balcony, looking out over the city. I took a breath, glancing towards the slums of the capital, towards Raf's home.

He'd be having dinner with Sierra, making her laugh, taking care of her, and getting nothing in return while I was up here dancing, laughing and drinking with royalty. I felt sick. Closing my eyes, I shut down those thoughts. This was for Sierra. I wasn't hurting anyone; I was just gathering intel.

"Not enjoying the party?" A velvety voice questioned as someone joined me on the balcony. I turned, finding Lord Jameson.

"No, it's not that. The party is great. I just wanted to admire the view." I smiled softly, curtsying. "It's nice to see you again, Lord Inkwell."

"Not as nice as it is to see you again. Although I prefer you in red." He slowly inspected my gown before returning his gaze to my face, telling me he'd likely had more than just the two glasses he was holding in his hands. I chuckled.

"You flatter me." I smiled as he approached.

"Of course. Would you like a drink, Lady Elle?"

"Well, it would be rude to decline such a generous offer from a lord, wouldn't it?"

"Why yes, it would." He handed me the glass, which I took, smiling gratefully, subtly sniffing it before taking a sip.

"Thank you. How about you? Why aren't you in there enjoying the party?"

"I followed a beautiful lady and ended up out here."

I rolled my eyes, smiling. "How often does that line work?"

"Every time," he said, stepping closer to me, looking me in the eye. "Although I have a feeling you may defy the odds." *So forward.*

"I hear that a lot." I smirked.

His grin was stunning. "You're very intriguing, Elia. Do you hear that a lot?"

I shrugged, turning away and leaning into the balcony railing, gazing back out to the city. "Not as often as I should."

"Cali won't stop chattering about you. I find myself curious."

I groaned. "Well, you know what they say about curiosity..."

Now it was his turn to chuckle. "You are a little too similar to the princess, I think."

I smiled. "What a lovely compliment."

"Concerning indeed. The two of you will make a dangerous pair. The prince must be pulling his hair out."

"It would be deserved." That caused a bigger laugh from the lord.

"Oh, I like you. You are going to make an excellent addition to court."

"I am only visiting," I said, straightening and turning to him once more.

"Ah, so the rumours about you being betrothed to the prince are untrue?" He smirked.

"You know very well that they are, Lord Inkwell."

He smiled. "And what about what I don't know? I don't see a ring, but that doesn't mean you don't have a nice nobleman back in Xeria."

"Are you asking if I am available, my lord?"

"If I am?" He asked, stepping closer.

I leaned in. If either of us moved an inch or two, our lips would touch.

"I would say... I am available to the right sort of man." I stepped back, turning away from him.

"And what sort of man is that, my lady?"

"Thank you for the drink." Without looking back, I re-entered the party, walking back over to where Cali still stood, all too aware of Jameson's lingering gaze. Better to let him think he had a chance. It never ceased to amaze me how much a man would reveal to a woman he was interested in. A small part of me even enjoyed the flirting, though I knew I shouldn't.

"Elle! There you are!" Cali exclaimed.

I laughed a bit. "How many drinks have you had since I've been gone?"

"Definitely not enough!" She grabbed a drink for each of us as if proving her point.

We continued to laugh, drink, and socialise. I thanked the divinities for blessing me with a somewhat decent tolerance for liquor, better than the princesses, apparently. But she could afford to let loose with Killian watching her every move. Her brother also tracked us throughout the room whenever he wasn't indulging himself in drinks, and the never-ending line of women vying for a position in his lap.

I could admit I'd definitely had more to drink than I should have, but it was necessary to convince them of who I was. A noble lord's daughter, interested in seeing this new place and having a good time. Not a threat. At least that's how I'd tried to justify it in my head.

I blamed the alcohol for the situation I'd now found myself in. Somehow, we had ended up in the same booth as Valor. I think Cali had wanted to talk to him, but how that had turned into me sitting closely beside him, while Cali danced with a nobleman, was lost on me. He seemed to have no interest in talking, so I simply ignored him and observed the rest of the party-goers.

It was late now, but the party remained in full swing. The music was sensual and carried a beat that was easy to follow. People danced and laughed, women tried to gain the attention of male suitors, and the men indulged them. Honestly, even the servants appeared amused by the drunken, relaxed state of the nobility. Everyone seemed to be having a good time, myself included.

CHAPTER THIRTEEN

Apparently, I'd jinxed myself because the next thing I knew, a woman in what I could tell was a very expensive dress, with an equally expensive air about her, was standing in front of me, giving me a death glare. Under normal circumstances, I would have paid more attention, but I was indeed enjoying myself, so I simply leaned a little to the side so I could peer around her.

In hindsight, I should have realised how close that brought me to Prince Valor. But again, I blamed the alcohol, as I didn't notice until I felt a hand on my leg. I glanced down at it, then to my left at the man himself, whom might I add, was not even looking at me. He was chatting to a nobleman on his other side, as his thumb began tracing small circles on my thigh. What in the divinities? Did he think I was someone else? I opened my mouth to speak, but another voice caught my attention; the woman who had been death glaring at me, and had increased her stare tenfold. It was quite impressive, actually.

"You must be Elia. The Xerian visitor?" Her voice was full of distaste. That's when I placed her. Lady Josette Huntingwell. The favourite to marry Prince Valor and become the next queen of Taros. She had styled her icy blonde hair to the extreme, her skin one shade above being too pale, she was no doubt one of the most beautiful people in the room. That explained the glare and the snotty air about her, she mistook me for her competition. I suppressed an eye roll and instead pasted on a bright smile.

"Yes, you're correct. And who might you be?" Her nostrils flared in annoyance at the thought of not being as well known as she thought she was.

"I'm Lady Josette Huntingwell. Surely you have heard of me?"

"I don't think so." I looked confused. "I'm sure you would have been mentioned, eventually. No matter, we are meeting now. It's a pleasure, however, could I trouble you by asking you to scoot a little to the right? I'm afraid you're blocking my view of the festivities."

I noticed then that the booth had gone so quiet you would hear a pin drop. The sound of someone coughing up their drink in surprise at my words was clear as a bell, but I didn't look to see who it was. Instead, I just looked at Josette expectantly. Her face was practically the same shade of red as my wine. She looked ready to launch herself at me, but something to my left had her eyes zeroing in like an Ozdros; a monstrous beast that dwelled in the forests on the outskirts of Kendelen. A predator at best, a nightmare at worst. I followed her gaze to the hand that was still on my leg, following it upwards and meeting Valor's gaze. He was already looking at me.

"Can I help you with something, Your Highness?" I said sweetly, just to piss Josette off.

He looked partly annoyed and partly amused. I suppose he was trying to decide who was more of a hindrance to his night. Lady Josette or me. I would certainly take offence if it was me.

"I don't know if you're capable."

"Oh, I think you'll find I'm *very* capable, Prince Valor." I grinned, ignoring Josette completely.

He raised an eyebrow and looked like he was about to call me out on my act, but just as I suspected, again much like an Ozdros, Josette pounced first.

"Your Highness, I was hoping we could talk? Privately," she said, with a pointed look at me. Everyone else immediately left the booth, obviously scared of her. Whether that was fear of her social status, or perhaps her Gifting, I couldn't be sure. I'd heard she was a strong Teleki, which is what made her a suitable candidate for the prince's hand. I, however, made no attempt at moving and waited for the prince's response. It seemed he had decided which of us was the lesser evil, because his hand visibly moved a fraction higher on my thigh.

"Maybe later, Josie. I actually have to discuss a few things with Elia. Would you mind closing the curtains on your way out?"

Oh boy. If looks could kill, I'd be hanging out with Heknos himself by now, but she couldn't risk looking like more of a brat in front of her potential future husband, so she reigned in her rage and gave him a tense smile.

"Of course, Val, come find me later." Her smile quickly morphed from tense to seductive, and even I could admit she was good at it. She left the booth, pulling the curtains across as she did. This would certainly get people talking.

Once the curtains had been closed, and we were alone, I shuffled away from him. He, however, clearly had different plans, because without lifting a finger, I was sliding right back to him. Before I could curse the pompous Teleki prince, he leaned in, closer than I would have liked. I could smell the ale on his breath, but it wasn't an unpleasant amount. Combined with whatever cologne he wore, it was actually quite intoxicating.

"Where do you think you're going?" I couldn't decide if he was drunk, irritated, or something else entirely as I looked into those pretty blue eyes.

Had I misjudged the entire situation? I was beginning to think I may have, given the look in the Prince's eyes. Surely I wasn't *that* drunk?

"Um, getting some personal space?"

His hand only slid further up. "You didn't seem to need personal space when Josette was around. Is that what you prefer? When people watch?" His words were thick with tension. I looked back at him, trying to determine what in the divinities' names was going on. There was no way he went from thinking I attempted to kill his father, to being interested in whatever *this* was.

"Only because it seemed like the most enjoyable way to piss her off. And it was."

My breath caught as his hand stopped, as high up as it could go before I would consider it somewhere other than my thigh. Thank Taros I had strapped my dagger to my right leg. He leaned in, his breath tickling my neck.

"Whatever game you're playing, Elia, I will figure it out. I see what you're trying to do with my sister. She might want to trust you, but I don't, and I won't. So remember this. If you step out of line, I will not hesitate to put you down. Not for a second." His grip tightened on my leg, his magic stopping me from moving away. I felt like I was being compressed from all sides as he used his ability to manipulate my clothing, tightening it around me like he had at the breakfast. The look in his eyes was one of lethal calm. He may have been tipsy, but he was in full control now, and he wanted me to know it.

"Do we understand each other?" I didn't let any fear show and instead gritted my teeth, fixing him with a glare that could almost rival Josette's.

"Yes." Suddenly, I could breathe again as he relaxed his hold and removed his hand from my thigh. I stood up, clenching one of my fists. "But let me *also* make something very clear, Your Highness." I spat his title like the insult I was starting to see it as. "If you threaten me again without proof or validity, you will not like the outcome. I do not take kindly to threats, especially from the likes of pompous, royal assholes like yourself."

Winning him over be damned. He'd made up his mind about me already. I wouldn't sit here and let him stroke his own ego. I turned to leave, but faster than I expected, he stood and pinned me to the wall, using his body this time. No magic. Inhaling sharply, I looked at him in surprise, then anger. He caged me in with his arms, his eyes flickering intensely, with an emotion I couldn't place.

"*Let. Me. Go.*" I gritted out, trying to push him away, but he didn't budge and my hands remained planted on his annoyingly firm chest.

"That sharp tongue of yours is going to get you into trouble, Elia," he said, not giving an inch.

I was about to unleash a barrage of unbecoming insults with said tongue when the curtains opened and the captain stepped in.

"Sorry to interrupt... whatever this is," he looked at us with a raised brow and cleared his throat before looking at Valor, "but your mother has sent for you Val, said it couldn't wait."

Valor let me go, and turned to Ambrosia, perfectly calm and collected. Not at all bothered by the fact that Killian must think we were in the middle of something intimate.

"Thanks, Killian, stay and watch over Cal?"

"Of course." He nodded and held the curtain open for Valor, who left without so much as a glance in my direction. *What a prick.* I clenched my fist. Ambrosia eyed my hand, then looked at me.

"I wouldn't." He too exited the booth.

Ugh, both of them. Absolute pricks. I grabbed a full glass of wine and downed it before exiting the booth, more than ready to retire to my room. Looking around, I saw Cali dancing and having a good time. If I went over there, she would try to convince me to stay, so I made my way through the crowd, slipping out of the party, and back to my rooms.

After crawling into bed, ready to sleep off tonight's events, I felt something crumple under my pillow. I reached under and pulled out a piece of parchment. I quickly scanned it, groaning softly at the words. Butcher's 'something to help with the queen' was apparently study notes. Lists of her favourite places, foods, things to avoid in front of her, even a map of her quarters. That was interesting, but it would have to wait until morning. It could *all* wait until morning. I needed some damned sleep. I hid the notes away and collapsed onto my pillow.

Shutting down my thoughts was easier than it should have been. Exhaustion helped. I closed my eyes, shutting out all of those intrusive thoughts, and allowed myself to drift to sleep.

The next day arrived far too quickly, and I woke to Lydia trying, and failing, to quietly tidy up before rousing me from my sleep.

"Oh, I'm so sorry, Lady Elia. I was trying to be quiet."

"Mm, that's okay," I said, stretching. "What time is it?"

"It is almost eleven."

"Oh, shit." I shot up, inciting a giggle from the maid.

"Don't worry, no one who attended the party has risen yet. I heard it was eventful."

I groaned, covering my face with my hands. I'd lost a lot of useful time today. I got up, and Lydia immediately went to run me a bath.

"People were talking about you and the princess all night!" She said, and I smiled a bit.

"Were they? What did they say?"

"Well, I heard you had a fight with Lady Josette over the prince, and that you won, because you got to spend time alone with him in a booth, not even any guards present!" Lydia exclaimed. I rolled my eyes.

"That's ridiculous."

"Which part?"

"Most of it." I chuckled. "Josette and I did not have a fight, we just finally met and I can tell you, I am not a fan. As for the prince, we spent some time together, but it wasn't nearly as scandalous as you're thinking."

I made my way to the bathroom, had a nice long bath, and let Lydia dress me appropriately before leaving my room, intending to check on the princess. Captain Ambrosia greeted me as he stood guard outside my chambers.

"Good morning, Captain. I thought you had better things to do than guard me?"

"Good morning, lady Elia. It appears I have some free time."

"Is Cali up? I thought I might check in and see how the rest of her night was?"

"Trust me, if you value your life, you do not wish to disturb the princess right now. Let's just say she is regretting the amount of liquor she consumed last night and is likely to take it out on whoever walks through her door." He warned, and I smiled a bit.

"Okay, well, maybe I can do some work then. Have you and the prince questioned all the staff and guards about the poisoning?"

"We have, yes."

"Any suspects?"

"No one of note. Everyone's accounts match up."

"I would like to speak to them. I might catch something you missed."

He raised his eyebrows. "I am trying not to be offended by that statement."

"I just meant that sometimes an outsider's view can be useful."

"That is true. Come with me."

"Don't you need to run it by the prince?" I said, already following him down the hall. He smirked.

"No, I do not." *Interesting.* I suppose he served the king and queen first. He led me down a few halls and then stopped.

"We have been keeping tabs on the staff that could have been involved to make sure there are no messages going in and out. They were all moved to rooms in this wing, with guards close by. I can come in with you when you question them."

"Actually, I would probably have a much better chance without the Captain of the Guard scaring everyone into silence."

He chuckled. "Again, you make a good point." He looked at me then, and I knew I'd made a mistake. "What is it you did back home in Xeria, Lady Elia?"

"Anything and everything they would let me, Captain." I smiled and entered the first room, shutting the door behind me, and cutting off any further questioning.

I made my way through the rooms and their occupants. Most feared talking to me at first, but it didn't take long for them to feel comfortable. It was amazing how simple it was to disarm people with the right words.

Killian had been right, nothing unusual had popped up. I took a brief break for lunch before returning to question the last few servants.

There were only three left to talk to, and I wasn't hopeful any of them would give me anything I didn't already know. My hope had not improved after I'd questioned the first two, and as I'd suspected, their stories all added up. I knocked and entered the last room, surprised to find Tilly kneeling beside her bed, praying of all things. She looked just as shocked to see me and quickly sat up.

"Lady Elia?"

It didn't look good for me that one of my lady's maids was currently a suspect. Cali had picked them out herself, though, which should absolve me.

"Hi Tilly, what have I told you about that formal title?" I smiled.

She bit her lip. "Sorry, Elle. It's... a hard habit to break..."

"Do you mind if I sit?"

"Oh, no, of course not. I'm sorry about the mess." She stood and organised a few loose things, tucking a strand of hair behind her ear. She was nervous, but she generally appeared that way.

"Come on, you clean my rooms. This is definitely not messy. Don't worry about it, honestly." I sat down.

"I didn't know you were under suspicion. Are you doing okay with all of this?"

"It's... unexpected, but I think I'm doing okay."

"Why do they suspect you? Were you working in the room? I didn't see you?"

"I was one of the staff bringing the food from the kitchen to the hall. I began feeling ill, so I asked my friend Kinley to cover for me while I went back to my room and slept it off."

Except she had been with me in the morning. She and Lydia prepared me for that same breakfast, and when I arrived the food had already been served, so she would have had to possess some unheard of Gifting in order to get there, and assist with delivering the food before I got to the room, or, she was lying.

I watched her as she spoke. She was fidgeting a little, playing with the hem of her dress, and struggling to hold eye contact. It was subtle, but it was there. Perhaps, if she had been serving another lady or royal, that story would have worked. They likely wouldn't have taken any notice of the maids serving them, but I had.

"Are you feeling better? I can arrange for you to have some time off if you need it?"

"Oh, no, I'm okay now. I think I just ate something that didn't agree with me." She smiled a little. "Thank you, though."

"Of course, I can't have my lady's maids being sick all over the place." I chuckled and stood.

If she had been in contact with bellvenum, she could have experienced side effects, especially with a dose the size of the one the king consumed. But why would she want to poison the king? She was working for someone else, or had some other motive.

"Rest up. I'm sorry to have bothered you. I just wanted to make sure you were okay in here."

"You really are nice, aren't you? It's not an act." She looked at me.

"I try to be. Everyone should be treated with respect unless proven to deserve otherwise. We are all mortal." I smiled softly.

She swallowed and nodded. "Thank you."

"Is there anything else you want to say, Tilly?" She looked at me, and she looked scared.

"I..."

"Tilly, I can help you, if you let me."

"I—can't... She won't let me."

"Who won't let you, Tilly?" She opened her mouth to speak, but then something changed in her eyes. The fear disappeared.

"What do you mean?" She smiled at me, and I frowned.

"You can talk to me. Who are you working for, Tilly?"

"The Crown of course." She looked confused. "Are you okay, Lady Elle?"

"Yes, sorry." I smiled. "I'll see you later." Killian was waiting when I exited the room.

"Who questioned Tilly?"

"Hello to you too, Elia. Valor did, why?"

"Were you present?"

"Not for that one, no. I was questioning the others. Why?"

Tilly said she was working for the crown. Valor had flung accusations at me right away. He questioned her, and yet found nothing amiss, even though something clearly is. He isn't stupid, he would have noticed. Cali also handpicked my maids for me. What if this was a coup? Are the heirs trying to take the throne early? If they were, who's saying the Captain of the Guard, one of the prince's best friends, and someone with a plain interest in the princess, isn't in on it as well?

"Just curious. Is the queen taking visitors? I'd like to check on the King's progress, and thank her for allowing me to stay."

It was clear he saw right through the subject change, but he let it slide.

"I'm not sure, but we can see. This way." He led me to the royal quarters. We stopped in front of a wall of royal guards. The royal guard, excluding the captain. He nodded to them, and they nodded back, respectfully.

"Stay here. I'll see if she will allow your visit."

"Sure, thank you." He entered the room and closed the door, careful not to reveal even a glimpse of what was inside.

CHAPTER FOURTEEN

I LOOKED AT THE guards, who looked at me with varying expressions. Some un-bothered, some curious, some intimidating. Overall, it was quite awkward. I busied myself subtly studying each of them, the weapons they carried, the formation they took. The door opened, saving us all from the weird silence. Ambrosia nodded.

"The queen will see you now." I nodded, the guards parted, and I stepped inside. Killian, however, stayed outside.

"Are you coming?"

"She requested I wait outside." I could tell by the hard set of his jaw he was unhappy about that request, but he couldn't disobey a direct order. So, he simply shut the doors, leaving me in what looked like a foyer.

"Alright then..." I looked around, expecting to see the queen, but she wasn't there.

"This way, Lady Elia." She called from a door to the right. I walked over and slowly pushed it open. The queen was sitting on a lounge chair, a cup of tea in her hand, looking every bit the regal leader that she was. Her hair was immaculate, and her dress was way too formal for her to be lounging around her own quarters in. I dropped into a low curtsy and stayed there. She let me remain there longer than the king had, which wasn't surprising.

"You may rise."

"Thank you for seeing me, Your Majesty. How is King Hadrian doing?" I asked as I rose.

"He is recovering well, thank you for asking."

"I am so glad to hear that. If there is anything I can do to help, please let me know."

"Is this why you asked for an audience with me? Instead of speaking to Killian, or perhaps one of my children? From what I hear, you have gotten quite close to my daughter."

"Your daughter is resting today, and your son, well, I am not a favourite of his."

"I can't imagine why," she said, taking a sip of her tea. I hadn't failed to notice that she still hadn't invited me to sit.

"If this is a bad time—"

"Say what you came here to say, Lady Worthington."

I pursed my lips. Alright then. "I believe I know who was involved in the poisoning of your husband, but I also believe she is not the sole person responsible, and that whoever is, has taken great lengths to keep that hidden."

"Why come to me instead?"

I could very well be signing my death sentence if I revealed to the queen that someone royal could be involved, but it could also be a way in with her.

"I wanted you to be the first person to know. You deserve to be updated any time there is a development."

"So, it's a matter of you trying to win my favour, then?"

Well, that makes my decision easier.

"If I was trying to win your favour, I wouldn't be disturbing you here with the information I could have passed on through a number of people. Nor would I be telling you that someone is protecting the servant who was hired, and I say hired because I am sure someone indeed hired her, or forced her, to do this on behalf of someone close to you. Someone a part of the royal court."

"You are aware that an accusation like this could land you in a cell?"

"I have already spent some time in your cells, Your Majesty, so if revisiting them is the price to pay for clearing my name and ensuring no one else is poisoned, then I will pay it. I understand you live in a world full of personal and political manipulations from all sides, so I felt you would prefer a straight, honest answer rather than what I think you want to hear. I hope that is enough to keep me out of those dungeons, but if not, then so be it." I bowed my head slightly.

She watched me, like a predator sizing up her prey. I didn't doubt she had her own claws. I would not be allowed in a room with her, unsupervised, if she did not.

"Sit." Masking my surprise and hesitation, I slowly sat opposite her. "You are more than you appear, aren't you?"

"I'm unsure what you mean, Your Highness."

She smiled at me. It was predatory, calculating, and amused. It was also the first genuine smile I'd seen from her.

"Of course, you don't. You think someone in my court is responsible for the assassination attempt on my husband? I believe you are right, and if anyone else is thinking the same thing, you are the only one who has had the gall to bring it to me."

"I'm sure the others are simply exploring other avenues first."

"Yes well, they are young and unaccustomed to betrayal, but not you." She looked into my eyes. "Isn't that right? You, my dear, have seen more betrayal than I would expect from someone your age. I can see it in your eyes, in the way you guard yourself."

I smiled a little. "I'm sure what I have experienced is nothing compared to a queen."

"Perhaps not, but I would say it makes you ideally suited to finding the traitor in our midst, wouldn't you?"

"Me? I am not sure I am qualified."

"Oh, come now. It's clear whoever your tutor was, they taught you well, Elia. A lady in appearance, and a serpens underneath. I have ladies like yourself in my employ. You know exactly how to use that pretty face of yours, don't you? That's how you got yourself here in the first place, is it not?"

I opened my mouth to speak, but she interjected. "Like calls to like." She watched me closely. "You see what my children are too arrogant, or too naïve, to see. You see the world for what it is. If all Xerian ladies were as well trained as you, we would certainly want to ally ourselves with your kingdom." That is interesting. Why would she bring up Xeria?

"I thought Xeria and Taros *were* allies? That all six kingdoms were, since the signing of the treaty at the end of The Great War?"

"So the history books say."

"Are you saying Taros isn't allied with Xeria? Or the other kingdoms?"

"I am saying alliances are fickle things, my dear. It only takes one loose thread to unravel the whole tapestry." Well, that was a weird way of avoiding the question.

"Never mind that now," she said, standing, "take me to this girl. I'd like to question her myself." I stood up as well.

"Alright, but as I said, I don't believe she was acting out of her own interests. She may not be completely at fault."

"We shall see, won't we?"

I wasn't sure which version of the queen I liked less, the quiet and cold one, or the one who spoke in riddles and smiled like she knew a secret you didn't. Either way, I was in this now.

The guards looked quite surprised to see me exiting by the queen's side, as did the captain. But when he questioned her, she simply told him to take us to the suspected servant's quarters and began walking, forcing the guards to fall into formation around us. *Us.* The queen and I.

If you'd told me a few weeks ago that I would be walking through the castle beside the queen, on our way to interrogate a potential assassin whose crime they'd accused me of, I would have laughed and advised you see a medicae. Yet here I was, feeling like maybe I should be the one to see one of the Impure healers. We stopped outside Tilly's room, and the queen ordered her guards to remain outside. I stayed by them until she looked at me pointedly.

"Not you, Elia. I want you present, to see what else you may uncover." I nodded and followed her inside, ignoring the look of disbelief and suspicion on Killian's face.

The queen shut the door and locked it, eliciting what sounded like a groan from a few of the guards outside. I had to hold back a smile. It seemed our queen did not make guarding her a simple task.

Tilly looked over and her eyes widened before she dropped to the floor in a bow.

"Your majesty."

"Matilda Erwing, if I'm not mistaken? You have worked as a maid in our home for about four years now, correct?"

"Y-Yes, Your Highness." She stuttered, keeping her head bowed low.

"You may stand," the queen said, walking over. Tilly was absolutely terrified.

"We just want to talk, Tilly," I said softly, "we aren't here to hurt you." Odette gave me a look that said *speak for yourself*, which was equally terrifying. Tilly stood but kept her head bowed.

"Anything I can do to help."

"Do you know much about gardening, Matilda?" Odette continued.

"Gardening, Your Highness?" She said, sounding as confused as I looked. "I—no, not really..."

Slowly pacing the length of the room, Odette glanced down at the floor. "The thing about gardening is, no matter how skilled you are, you will always get weeds. The difference between a talented gardener and an expert gardener is how they deal with them. Do they treat them with something and hope it kills them off? Do they pluck them out at the roots, to be sure?" She opened Tilly's window and glanced down.

"I... don't know, Your Majesty." Odette smiled then, and goosebumps pricked my skin. That smile was a viper's smile, a predator seconds away from pouncing.

"You pluck them from the roots dear, otherwise, you can never be sure how deep they go." Her finger twitched, and before either of us could react, a vine shot through the window, wrapping itself around Tilly, winding its way up her body like a serpens. The scream that escaped her mouth was one of pure terror. I breathed in sharply.

"Your Majesty, I don't think this is necessary." I tried, impressed my voice hadn't wavered. I'd never seen an Incrementi use their magic. The queen was a Flori, an incredibly strong one apparently, since she just grew a damned vine, had it climb the castle walls, and incapacitate Tilly, without so much as blinking. The Incrementi Gifting was bestowed by Lenea, Goddess of the Harvest.

"I think it's very necessary." A knock on the door sounded.

"YOUR MAJESTY?" Killian called.

"Everything is alright, Killian! Do not interrupt us again. That is an order!" My eyes widened. Fates, this woman was crazy. Said crazy lady, bent down to the floor.

"Brick is tricky sometimes." She ran her hand along it, searching, until she found a small crack, and smiled again. "This will do."

She removed something from her pocket, a seed maybe, dropping it into the small gap. She cupped both her hands over the tiny crack, and a dull glow emanated from her palms. Soon, a sprout appeared, growing until it formed a plant with a fully bloomed white flower.

I stepped back, recognising the plant colloquially referred to as Heknos Trace. A potent flower, incredibly rare. So rare, I only recognised it from the drawings I'd seen when studying poisons and their antidotes.

"You recognise this, Lady Elia? That is surprising."

There were mixed accounts of what effect Heknos Trace could have, but it's said to remove a person's free will. It doesn't show up on any poison test known to mortals. It's virtually untraceable, and often comes with amnesic effects, so you may not even remember taking it.

"I know enough poisonous flowers to identify one when I see it, yes, but I have never seen this one in person."

"Well, I am sure you will find this very interesting then." She glanced at Tilly, who still looked scared out of her mind. She had actually started sobbing. Guilt and fear coursed through my veins. I didn't know enough about Tilly's involvement to know if she deserved this brand of questioning, but even if I did, I doubted it would make me feel any more comfortable with the situation.

"P-please, Your Majesty, I will tell you anything you want to know."

"Oh, I know you will, dear."

She reached over to the plant and plucked the flower from its stem. Her palm glowed as she held the flower, the same way it had when she'd first used her magic to make it grow. Slowly, the petal, then the remaining bud and stem, broke down into a tiny powder. I took another step back. As little as touching or breathing the stuff in was enough for it to take effect.

I knew the second Incrementi Specialty, Immuni, was immune to poisons, but I hadn't read anything about Flori having the same resistance? I really should have paid more attention when learning about the Giftings of The Six.

"Is this really necessary, Your Majesty?" I asked one more time, for Tilly's sake. I would be lying if I said I wasn't curious about what would happen, but not curious enough to use Tilly as a test subject.

"Necessary? Possibly not, but I find this method a lot more efficient, and fun." She smiled, walking over to Tilly, who was struggling to break free of the vines.

I opened my mouth to demand she stop. I couldn't stand here in good conscience and watch this happen. I had to at least try to stop it, queen or not. Butcher's words suddenly rattled through my head, freezing me to the spot.

Get close to the queen by whatever means necessary

Panic shot through me as my mouth closed of its own accord, my body relaxed and a curious expression settled on my features. I tried to frown, to widen my eyes, to scream, but I couldn't do anything that would risk my chance at getting the queen to like me. I could only watch in horror as Odette softly blew the powdered flower, seeds and all, into Tilly's face, forcing her to inhale it. I refrained from breathing in myself, in fear of also coming into contact with it.

The queen chuckled, not a crazy, wicked chuckle, a genuine chuckle of joyful amusement when she beheld my expression. Divinities. What was wrong with this woman?

"Don't worry, Elia, I will not allow it near you. You can breathe."

I swallowed. Eventually, I had to breathe in, or I might very well pass out. I glanced over at Tilly, who had stopped struggling, her pupils now dilated.

"How do you feel, Matilda?"

"Lightheaded, like... like I've had too much wine." She giggled a little and appeared much more relaxed. She was conscious, but she looked drowsy.

"Excellent. Now tell me, did you poison my husband?"

"Yes." My eyes widened, and I watched Tilly closely. She looked fine, aside from the fact that I'd seen her struggling and crying seconds before. If I'd walked into this room right now, ignoring the vines, it would simply appear as if Tilly was happily engaged in a conversation with the queen.

"When?"

"Just before breakfast was served."

"How?"

"I laced his cup before handing it to another maid, who placed it in front of him."

"Why did you poison the king, Matilda?"

"Because she told me to." I frowned.

"Who told you to Tilly?" I cut in, taking a step forward.

"I don't know..."

"You don't know?"

"She didn't give me her name.."

"What name did she give you, Tilly?"

The queen regained control of the questioning.

"Did you see this woman's face? Can you describe her?"

"No... she... was very short, and wore a black cloak, with a sun sigil over her heart. Her hood completely concealed her face. She remained in the shadows."

"What did she give you in exchange for poisoning the king?"

"Nothing." She smiled, and my blood chilled.

"Nothing? So you attempted to assassinate your king for nothing in return?"

"Yes, I poisoned him because she told me to." What was going on, was this drug a hallucinogenic? Were her responses reliable?

"You can go now, Lady Elia. I will deal with the rest."

"Your Majesty, I think I should stay."

She didn't turn to face me, simply watching Tilly.

"It wasn't a request, Elia." She stroked Tilly's cheek and smiled when she shivered. "You are dismissed. Thank you for all that you have done today. The Crown is so grateful."

I couldn't argue with the dismissal. I physically could not argue more than I had, so I bowed my head a little. "It was my pleasure to assist in any way I could, Your Majesty. Thank you for trusting me to help."

I headed to the door, unlocked it, and stepped out. When I turned to shut it, I glimpsed Tilly and the queen. The vines had relaxed their hold, and Odette was standing so close to Tilly, as if in a lovers' embrace, as she whispered something in her ear. The vines slithered along Tilly's arms like serpens. Her eyes were closed, and there was a dazed smile on her face. Before I could see anything else, a vine shot up from the floor, slamming the door shut, causing me to jump slightly.

"Are you alright, Lady Elia?" Ambrosia said, watching me carefully.

"Yes, sorry, the door shutting so abruptly just startled me is all." I smiled sheepishly.

"Odette dismissed me, so I will head back to my chambers."

He nodded. "Tarryn, Hamish, escort Lady Elia back to her rooms, please."

Two men stepped forward, the same two guards who had been guarding me whenever Killian wasn't.

"Tarryn and Hamish will be your official personal guards for the duration of your stay."

I nodded to them both.

Hamish was tall and lean, with auburn hair, a freckled face, and an overall boyish look about him. Tarryn was shorter, but still a head or so taller than me. He was muscular, like he trained a lot, and appeared more reserved than Hamish. Hamish was the light to Tarryn's dark. Where Hamish's skin was fair, Tarryn's was golden-tanned like mine. Hamish's eyes were a forest green whereas Tarryn's were an ocean blue, and whilst Hamish's hair was wavy and down to his chin, Tarryn's was an elm-bark brown, cleanly cut and no longer than his ears. I hadn't really spoken to them before, but they'd never seemed rude or unhappy to be guarding me. I smiled politely at them and started walking. The smile remained on my face until I was safely in my room.

What in the divinities' names had I just witnessed? Perhaps when I told Butcher that the Taros queen was a literal lunatic, she would change her tactics and find another way for me to gather the intel she needed. I couldn't keep up with Odette's moods, and to see her power in person was unsettling, to say the least.

Taros give me strength.

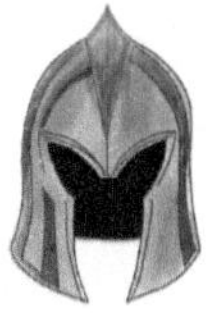

CHAPTER FIFTEEN

ONCE AGAIN, I HAD to wait for night to fall before I could risk sneaking out of the castle. I locked my door, changed, and then scaled down the walls like I had the first time. I needed to gather information, when I wasn't being tailed by guards, from reputable sources.

Pulling my hood back over my head, I made my way to the current location of The Cavum. Since Butcher's network was so vast, having a hand in almost every profitable criminal operation in Kendelen, that meant she was highly successful, but it also meant The Cavum was notorious, making it much easier for authorities to track if it remained in the same place.

To solve that problem, we changed the location regularly. There were stationary businesses and locations one could find if they knew the right people, but couldn't be trusted with The Cavum's whereabouts.

I was one of the very few that knew the schedule and locations of The Cavum for the next year. It moved monthly, unless there was a tipoff. Butcher forced me to memorise the locations and orders in which they'd be moved at the start of every year.

This month, it was using the basement of a small tavern in the slums as a front. I kicked the dirt off my boots before entering the small establishment. Leaving my hood on to obscure most of my face, I kept my head down as I approached the bar. It wasn't a busy night, and a few patrons gave me the once over but soon returned to their drinks. This establishment was known for shady dealings, so a woman in a cloak wasn't anything new.

The barkeep approached, but before they could ask what I'd be drinking, I placed a black coin down on the bar top. The barkeep paused before nodding, pouring me a tankard of ale and gesturing to a side door. I smiled a little, grabbing both the ale and the coin before walking over to the door and pushing it open. A dimly lit hallway led to another door manned by two burly looking guards playing cards. Apparently, it was a quiet night all round then. They took one look at the black coin that was rolling back and forth across my knuckles, and simply dipped their heads in deference, returning to their game.

This door opened to a staircase that led down to a huge underground basement. I removed my hood when I reached the men stood at the bottom of the stairs, the last layer of security upon entry. These two knew my face, as the lattermost entrance guards of The Cavum always did.

I remembered asking Butcher when I was younger if she was concerned about using the same group of guards. There were twelve in total that regularly manned the last entry point, all of whom knew my identity, along with Butcher's, and various other important members. She'd simply smiled and told me to ask one of them what was keeping them from betraying us.

I'd picked the friendliest looking one, a big man I knew as Phiggs. He'd often smile warmly at me and sometimes he'd even give me a treat when Butcher wasn't watching, but he'd never spoken a word to me. When I'd asked, he'd knelt down in front of me and lightly patted his throat. Frowning in confusion, I'd shaken my head, not understanding. He'd smiled a little sadly before opening his mouth and using his thumb to point at where his tongue *should* have been.

I'd stared in shock, first at his missing pointer finger, then at his tongue-less mouth, before glancing around at the other members of the inner circle security detail. They each nodded in confirmation. That's when I'd first learned about the outdated method of ensuring a spy's or informant's loyalty.

Butcher had taken it one step further, coining the term muting, and not only removing the tongue but also the pointer finger of each personal guard, and anyone else she deemed deserving of the brutal punishment. Even at seven years old, even I'd understood that one couldn't easily betray your secrets if they could not speak or write of them.

Phiggs wasn't on duty tonight. Loyle and Grayson nodded at me, opening the door. I made my way through the basement; They had cordoned it off into different sections. As always, the chief attraction was the fighting pits in the centre of the room. There were small stalls set up on the right side of the room with black market goods, a makeshift bar, some tables to the far left, and at the back were private booths for more covert dealings.

It only took a minute for me to find the person I'd come to see. I ordered another tankard before taking a seat opposite a broad-shouldered woman. She glanced up as I slid a tankard over to her, taking a sip of my own. Arching an eyebrow, causing her scarred face to scrunch up slightly, she took the drink and had a swig of her own.

Mallory Miller, or Mal as most called her, was an older woman looking somewhere in her mid-forties. She'd had a rough life and her appearance showed it. Deep wrinkles made her appear older than she was, combined with the nasty scar from a whip that stretched from her chin to just above her left ear. It clearly hadn't been treated properly if the jagged scar tissue was anything to go by. However, it was her eyes that warned you not to mess with Mal Miller.

One yellow eye and one black eye. Some would gasp when they saw her and proclaim she must have Sullied ancestry. Sullied was the name given to the mortals who were given magic by Akros, the God of Chaos, and the one responsible for the enslavement of mortals millennia ago.

The magic bestowed upon Akros's followers was dark, unlike that granted by Ades and her divine allies. As if to prove that true, those mortals that were gifted the dark magic always carried a sign. Marks suck as unusual blemishing, strange eye colours, elongated canines, and other anomalies.

When Ades banished Akros and all the divinities from Adysium, she found herself unable to cast out the mortals she loved so dearly, even those aligned with Akros. Instead, she dampened their magic as best she could. For thousands of years, Sullied were hunted and burned for their existence. Even those with no magic, anyone with unusual markings, had to go.

Eventually, Sullied were practically extinct. At the very least, the magic in their bloodlines had become dormant. The Sullied descendants with little to no magic became known as witches or heretics. It wasn't until the most recent millennium that the Sullied hunting ceased, but many in Deorum were still wary of the descendants, identifiable by their markings. Some even called for the burnings to be brought back.

Those were usually the same types that prayed endlessly to divinities that never answered. Sullied heritage or not, Mal was one of the best informants I knew. She had connections all over the kingdom and she was usually the first person I spoke to if I wanted intel from outside of Taros. Even Butcher didn't mess with Mal's business.

"Mal, it's been a while. You well?"

Her lips twisted into an amused half smile. "Kid, I ain't interested in hearing about ya life and I know ya ain't interested in mine. What can I do for ya?" Straight to the point, as always.

"Have you heard anything interesting of late?"

She leaned back and took another swig. "Depends."

I smiled a bit, placing a few coins on the table between us. She gave me a look, and I sighed before replacing them with an entire pouch. She opened it up, giving the contents a quick glance before nodding in approval and pocketing the pouch.

"What d'ya wanna know?" She stated more than asked.

"Whatever you've heard."

She considered this. "Same old lords and ladies squabbling. I heard Mr Lenture received a visit from the Shadow of Kendelen," she looked at me pointedly, "was fuming, I heard, but he's now joined the fold. That rebel movement appears to be spreading, gaining traction. Enough that they've given 'emselves a name."

I'd heard reports of a few minor attacks on villages close to Kendelen, claiming to have been executed by a ragtag rebel group. Everyone had assumed they were simply some disgruntled and misguided Impures who were sick of their lot and wanted more power. No one had taken them seriously.

"What have they decided to call themselves then?"

"They've gone with The Rise." She scoffed, but I frowned. The Rise? As in sunrise?

"Have they got a leader then? Someone responsible for this new revolt?"

"Goes by the name Solis." She rolled her eyes, clearly unimpressed by the nickname. "No one's laid eyes on 'em yet, but most assume they're a man. The smart ones assume they're a woman."

I blinked. The Rise? Solis? It made sense. Hadn't Tilly said the woman who'd asked her to poison the king had a sun sigil on their cloak? It all linked to Solissia.

Refocusing on Mal's words, I asked, "I take it you think they're a woman? Why?"

She shrugged. "Aside from the obvious reference to the *Goddess* of the Sun? Just a gut feeling. Her movements are smooth and precise. The attention to detail is impressive. She has a chokehold on her inner circle."

"Why do you say that?"

"Even my contacts haven't been able to get a verified rumour, let alone an actual glimpse of what Solis looks like, or any details about them. We don't know if they're male, female, tall, short, fat, thin, ugly, or beautiful. We don't know if they're cruel or kind, and we don't even really know what they want. If even my guys can't get the barest of details, I doubt anyone else can either. Meaning they've got a tight-knit, trusted inner circle, or they have such an expansive network of people below them, that it's virtually impossible for even those they command to gather information on 'em. Either way, they clearly run a tight ship. I just don't see any man remaining as anonymous as Solis has. Men are not subtle. They are flashy and stupid. It's all about grand shows of strength for them. This is a different kind of strategy, much more typical of a woman's mind."

I clenched my fist under the table. Butcher was working with the Heknos' damned rebels? Did she think I wouldn't figure that out? I had half a mind to storm over there and demand answers, but I knew that would get me nowhere. I needed more information before I made any rash moves.

"Anything else of note?"

"I heard the king is recovering from his assassination attempt. Shame." It was no secret she wasn't a fan of our ruling family. Although, she didn't seem to be a fan of royals in general.

"I don't suppose you've heard any whispers about who was responsible?"

"Maybe." I gave her a look, and she smiled a little. She loved to antagonise me. "Of course. Too many rumours. Some say he was steppin' out on his wife, so she tried to top him. Some say his son wanted the crown early. The mistress, the cook, the damned dog, all supposedly could have done it." She shook her head, clearly not believing any of those theories.

"And you? What do you think happened?"

She watched me carefully.

"It had to be an inside job. There's no way the king gets poisoned in his own dining chamber without someone close to him being involved. Although with the current political climate? Wouldn't put it past one of those neighbouring aristocratic knobs to try off him. Question is, how would a neighbouring kingdom buy the loyalty of someone so close to the king? That's an arduous task to accomplish." She'd come to all the same conclusions as me. It *had* to be someone close enough to the king to pull it off, or at least the person behind the attempt had to have paid *off* someone close to him.

I nodded and stood. "I trust if you hear anything else?"

She nodded, confirming she'd let me know if there were any developments. I turned to leave.

"Interesting timing, though, wouldn't you say?"

I glanced back at her. "How do you mean?"

"I heard a Xerian noblewoman arrived, entered the castle, and a day later the king had been poisoned."

"She'd have to be a fool to poison him when she'd be the easiest suspect." I replied.

"Mmm, that she would. Funnily enough, no one seems to talk about the fact that she's supposedly been in Taros for some time, yet no one saw her enter the kingdom, let alone Kendelen. One day, her carriage just showed up in town on its way to an inn. No one seems to know much about her either. It seems she has no ties to Taros."

"That is odd."

She met my eyes and grinned, dropping that line of questioning. "My money's on someone in his council of advisors or court. The family angle is too easy a leap. See who's recently been denied something by the king, or stands to benefit the most from him being out of action for a bit. I doubt it's a play for control of the crown, since his son would simply take his place in the event of his death. Someone is sending a message or they want the king out of action long enough to push whatever agenda they have through."

I nodded my thanks and left The Cavum, mulling over everything I had and hadn't learned tonight.

As if Lunos knew there was little worth shining for tonight, the sky matched my mood as I raced back to the castle with only the shadows as my shield.

As I had expected, the climb back up to my room was a bastard, but I snuck back in unseen, quickly swapping out my tunic and cloak for a pretty little nightgown. Switching outfits as well as personas.

The next morning, I was invited to breakfast with the royal family again. I was a tad nervous. Tilly was absent from my service this morning, as expected, leaving Lydia to prepare me on her own. I didn't ask if she knew anything was amiss, and she mentioned nothing.

They understandably held breakfast in an unfamiliar room this time, but my being allowed in was a positive sign. The guards escorted me in, and I curtsied, not dipping very low, before the king stopped me.

"None of that. You saved my life from what I hear, Elia. The bowing is unnecessary, at least when we are amongst family. Please, join us."

I smiled a little, but finished the curtsy. "I don't mind, Your Majesty."

"Please, call me Hadrian. You've earned that much."

"If you insist." I took my seat, and much like last time, I sat next to Cali, opposite Valor.

"I am happy to see you are doing well. Not to sound paranoid, but has," I paused, "someone checked everyone's food and drinks?" I bit my lip.

Hadrian snorted. "Yes, they have. I also hear that you tested Cali's food. Whilst I appreciate that immensely, your life is also valuable. I would prefer you let a servant do it next time."

Valor looked at me in surprise. Clearly, he hadn't heard about that.

"My life is no more valuable than anyone else's," I simply said.

"I beg to differ." He countered and started eating, letting everyone else also start. I watched closely, just to be sure he wasn't about to convulse again, before joining them. The conversations around the table were fairly normal. Valor was catching his father up on what he had missed. Odette and Cali discussed upcoming events, and I was minding my business, enjoying the meal, when Odette drew my attention.

"I'm sorry, Your Highness?"

She smiled a bit and said, "I'd like for you to join me after breakfast. I'd like to get to know you better, and Calliope tells me you brought little with you as far as clothing goes, so we can have you fitted by our tailor."

I wasn't sure how Cali would know that, more snooping probably..

"Oh, you don't have to do that, Your Highness." I didn't want to be alone with her.

"I insist, dear." *Great.*

I pasted on a smile. "Thank you, I'd be honoured."

Valor stood. "May I be excused? I have a fair bit of work to get done."

Hadrian nodded. "I will join you shortly." Valor nodded back and left the room.

Cali chuckled. "He so hates to be proven wrong."

"Wrong about what?" Hadrian asked.

"About Elle. He accused her of poisoning you and tossed her in the dungeons."

His eyes practically shot out of his head. "He did *what*?!"

"In his defence, Your Maje — Hadrian. It looked quite bad. He was just trying to protect his family. I don't harbour any hard feelings."

He groaned and rubbed his face. "He locked you in the cells? Divinities, I am so sorry, Elia."

"Really, it's fine, water under the bridge." I smiled a bit. "I just got a more in-depth tour of the castle," I said, trying to lighten the mood. "It was rather uneventful, aside from the crazy ramblings of the old lady in the cell next to mine." I took a bite of my food and noticed it had gone quiet. I looked up and found Hadrian looking at me strangely, Odette looking at me inquisitively, and Cali looking at them, confused.

"What?" Cali asked before I could.

"There are no women in those cells? Not currently." Hadrian answered first. I frowned. It was definitely an old crone I'd seen, but she'd worn a dark cloak with the hood up. Is it possible it was just a man with a feminine voice?

"Oh, I must have been mistaken..."

"You were probably in shock, dear. You had been through quite an ordeal by then." Odette offered.

"Yes... I must have been."

"Well, I truly am sorry, Elia. I will speak to my son," Hadrian said, standing. "I better get back to work. A man can't take a few days off without things falling apart." He winked and shared a look with his wife before exiting the room.

"I better go as well. I have lessons. Elle, can we catch up later?"

"Of course, that sounds great." I smiled, and she gave my arm a quick squeeze before also exiting, leaving me alone with the queen. *Shit.* I placed my fork down and looked at her. She was watching me closely.

"How did the rest of the questioning go? Did you find anything else of note?" I tried to be as nonchalant as possible about the entire ordeal.

"Not a lot more than what you heard." She answered.

"What is going to happen to Tilly?"

"She will be questioned more thoroughly, and offered a chance to help us. If she chooses not to, she will be executed for her crimes against The Crown."

"But... you heard her. It was someone else who put her up to it. It didn't sound like she did it willingly. Some things don't add up."

"Ah yes, but until we have further proof of that, or another suspect, she has admitted to poisoning the king and must be punished accordingly."

I pursed my lips.

"However, I agree that she certainly didn't come up with the idea to assassinate the king on her own. Someone else is involved, and I would like you to discover who."

"Me? Your majesty I am hardly qualified..."

"You've proven yourself to be resourceful, Elia. Tilly may have done the actual poisoning, but she cannot be the only traitor in our midst. I would like to know who helped her."

"I don't really know anyone here. I am unsure how I could pick them out."

"An outsider's perspective is precisely what we need. You have already proven yourself resourceful. I also have a plan that will most likely make things easier for you." *Oh, no.* I saw the look in her eyes, and without knowing exactly what it meant, I knew I would not enjoy it.

"A plan?" I said nervously, trying not to show how much that unsettled me, which only made her smile wider.

"Yes, if you are to get close to any would-be traitor, you need to be welcomed into court. As my daughter's friend, some would welcome you, but more would welcome my son's potential bride."

My jaw dropped. Did she say *bride*? She must have expected my stunned silence, and the objections I was about to voice, because she continued.

"Shocking, I know, but it is the perfect cover. Obviously, you will not actually be betrothed, but if people see you two together, if they see how close you are with Calliope, and they see me favouring you, say, for example, while dress shopping? It will take no time at all for assumptions to be made. At the end of it all, as far as the people know, it was simply a summer fling between their prince, and a visiting noblewoman. You will go back to your life in Xeria, most likely much better off for it. And in the meantime, you will have more opportunity to discover the traitors among us." The queen clearly enjoyed a good scheme. Usually, I did too. This one, however? Not so much.

"Valor will never agree to that. I am sure you know he is not my biggest fan."

"He won't be happy about it, but he will do as he is told. Hadrian is briefing him as we speak." She stood. Hadrian was on board with this? "Let's go get you fitted."

Oh, sure. Let us spend time together clothes shopping like you didn't just fake betroth me to your son, who hates me, so I could be your spy. Why not?

CHAPTER SIXTEEN

TRUE TO HER WORD, she did in fact have me fitted, purchasing an excessive amount of extravagant clothing for me, no doubt knowing that the servant workers would run and tell everyone the queen used her own coin to pamper me. Lady Josette would not be happy. By the time they had packed all the garments for the servants to lug back to my rooms, it was nearing lunch, and I was getting ready to make my leave.

"I hope we understand each other, Elia?" Odette said out of the blue.

I looked at her. "Understand each other, Your Majesty?"

"Yes, and your role here."

"My role?" I glanced around. "You mean pretending to be a potential candidate for the prince's hand?" I whispered, as any nervous noblewoman would.

"That, and the rest. I simply mean," she stepped closer, lowering her voice, and warning bells sounded in my head, "my family has been very generous to you. You are intelligent, and something tells me you know much more than you want anyone to know." I maintained my façade of innocent calm, staring into those unsettling blue eyes of hers. I'd forgotten that before I'd seen the unhinged side of her, I'd seen her as ice. *Cold and deadly.*

"Just remember, dear." She took my hand. "You are in my home. If you step out of line, I will put you down." The warning was eerily similar to Valor's during our dance.

"Of course. I won't betray your trust or waste the opportunity you have given me, Your Highness. I give you my word." Lady Elia's word, not Adira's. She smiled and squeezed my hand tightly, so tight, that her nails dug into my skin a little. I did not wince, getting the feeling that she would get more satisfaction from seeing me stay calm in the face of her threat, rather than cowering.

With that, she departed, taking her guards with her, leaving only Hamish behind.

He leaned in and whispered. "That woman is *so* creepy."

I laughed a little, trying to shake off the chill that had settled over me.

"I'd have to agree with you." I replied, and he shuddered.

"Where to now?"

I sighed. As much as I would like to avoid this confrontation, it is probably better to get it over with.

"To wherever Prince Valor is."

He chuckled at my expression. "I'm sure it won't be that bad."

"Clearly, you haven't interacted with him enough then." I complained as we started walking, eliciting another laugh from Hamish.

"If it makes you feel better, he's like that with most people."

"A little." I smiled, but came to an abrupt stop, narrowly avoiding colliding with someone.

"Sorry! I wasn't watching where I was going—Lord Jameson? Unexpectedly running into you is becoming a regular occurrence." I smiled a bit.

"Lady Elia, this is a timely surprise." He grinned and kissed my hand.

"Timely?" I asked, bobbing in a slight curtsey.

"Yes, I was hoping I would find you today. May we speak?" He glanced at Hamish, who stood there imposingly, then back at me. "Preferably in private?"

Hamish made no effort to move, and I smiled a bit.

"Hamish, would you mind giving us a minute?"

He nodded. "Call out if you need anything, my lady." He stepped far enough away that he was out of earshot, but could still see us.

Jameson smiled. "Walk with me? I assume you were heading towards Valor?"

I raised my eyebrows. "What makes you say that?"

"Because I just saw him, and he was in a bit of a state. I've only ever seen him this frazzled, when it is something pertaining to a certain foreign lady." The prince had clearly been told of his parents' plans. I ignored the fact that the thought of Valor having a tantrum brought me more joy than it should.

"I do not know what you mean," I said, causing him to grin.

"Mmm, I'm sure..." He linked my arm through his and lead us in the direction I'd been headed.

"Weren't you heading the opposite way?"

"Only to find you." He winked.

"Why?"

"You are straight to the point, huh?"

I smiled up at him, batting my eyelids a little, not entirely convinced I didn't look like a moron with something in their eye. He chuckled, which wasn't particularly reassuring.

"I wanted to ask if the rumours were true. I rarely pay much mind to them, but this one was intriguing."

"And what rumour might that be?"

He stopped in front of a door and held it open for me, encouraging me to enter.

Hamish took a step forward, but I waved him off and went through the doorway. Something about Jameson told me I could trust him enough to be in the room alone with him. He actually reminded me a little of Raf. They both had that boy-next-door air about them, despite being ridiculously attractive, and certainly *not* boys. I sat down on the couch, finding we were in a private sitting room, and watched the lord close the door, before turning to face me.

"The one about you being betrothed to the prince, which I know you already said was not the case, but..."

I arched my brow. Bloody Hek word spread fast, but then again, he may have heard it from the prince himself.

"You tell me, Jameson. You were just with the prince, were you not? What did he have to say about it?"

"In all honesty, I couldn't make out much other than cursing and your name." He smirked a bit and sat down next to me.

"Do I look like the kind of lady with enough status to marry a prince, Lord Jameson? I am a lesser lord's daughter. A foreign and Impure one at that."

He looked me in the eye, and what he said caught me completely off guard.

"You, Lady Elia, look like the type of woman men would go to war for." His eyes didn't leave mine, and he looked dead serious, no humour in his eyes to tell me he was just harmlessly flirting, even though that is exactly what it was. I rolled my eyes at him and smirked a bit.

"That is a wonderful line, Lord Jameson. One I am sure wins you hearts everywhere you go."

He smiled, losing the seriousness in his eyes. "No doubt it would, if I had ever used it. So tell me, Elia. Is it true?"

"Why are you so interested? Surely you can ask your friend."

He leaned forward, and I recognised how close we were, almost as close as when we had been when dancing.

"Because I'd like to hear directly from you, if my friend is now also my competition."

I breathed in a little. This man was brave. I had to give him that. "Competition? Lord Jameson—"

"Call me James," he said, tucking a strand of loose hair behind my ear.

"James," I said, "first, I am not a prize to be won, nor am I a game. I can tell you that there is no ring on my finger, but if you have questions about a betrothal, I suggest you ask the prince." I made to stand, but he stopped me, grabbing my waist, pulling me against him, and pressing his lips to mine. *Divinities.*

I began immediately regretting my decision to have flirted with him the last time I'd seen him. I pulled back, trying to be less annoyed at how good of a kisser he was. He looked at me, not moving to kiss me again, but looking very much like he wanted to.

"You're wrong," he said.

"Excuse me?"

"You are a game. But not the kind you think." He stroked my cheek. "There is just something about you... that I can't quite put my finger on." He ran his thumb across my bottom lip, and I involuntarily shivered. I couldn't blame the guy. I technically didn't exist, so no wonder he was having some trouble.

"I don't want you because you might be betrothed to the prince. I wanted you before that. The moment I saw you, actually." Putting an odd emphasis on the last bit.

"You want what you can't have. You aren't the only person who hears rumours. I know you and the prince like to compete for women."

"We do, but that's not what this is. For starters, Val has tried nothing with you, despite him knowing I was interested from the start." I figured now would not be a good time to mention the booth at the party. Granted, all that flirting was solely so he could threaten me, but still.

"Right, but until you heard there may be something going on with the prince and I, you were happy to keep harmlessly flirting, yet now, now you want to go all-in?"

"I'll admit it is very fun flirting with you like that, but this is more fun." He looked at my lips again. Honestly, he was being very conceited, but it wasn't coming across that way. It was hard not to be at ease. He simply was a massive flirt, and for whatever reason, decided I was his next target.

I leaned in a bit, my eyes flickering to his lips for a brief second, before moving back to his eyes.

"I owe you an apology." I whispered, noting his slight intake of breath.

"For what?" He inched even closer.

"For letting you flirt, for even flirting back a little." I placed a kiss on his cheek, barely missing his lips. I disentangled myself from his arms and took a step back before he could grab me again. "For that, I am sorry. You should find someone else who can give you what you want because, unfortunately, that isn't me."

"And why can't it be?" He watched me.

I smiled a bit and shook my head. "Is it truly that hard for you to believe a woman simply may not be interested in you?"

"Yes." He answered surely, and I laughed.

"Well, Lord Jameson, there is a first for everything." I winked, then exited the room.

"We'll see." He chuckled before the door closed, cutting off whatever else he may have said.

I breathed out. I'd be lying if I said I didn't think a night with Jameson Inkwell would be enjoyable, but this fake betrothal made that impossible. If I wanted people to think I could be engaged to Valor, I couldn't very well be seen flirting with his best friend. I looked around, not surprised to see Hamish standing guard right next to the door. I smiled.

"Sorry about that. Which way is Prince Valor again?"

He chuckled and shook his head.

"This way, my lady." He held out his arm, which I gratefully took, and we continued on to what I was certain would be a much less fun confrontation.

"Good luck," Hamish said with an annoyingly knowing smirk on his face as he took up his post outside Valor's study. I stuck my tongue out at him, then knocked on the door.

"Come in." It wasn't particularly welcoming, but it was better than I'd expected, telling me he didn't know it was me. I slowly opened it and stepped inside.

"Your Highness." I curtsied.

He was leaning over his desk, examining a map of sorts. A map he promptly covered once he noted who was standing in his doorway.

"Lady Elia," he said, watching me for a minute before sighing, "shut the door."

I did as he requested, glancing around his 'study'. It looked more like a war room. Maps, books of strategy, even weapons, piled up around the place.

"Sorry to bother you. Is this an alright time to talk?"

"It's as good as any," he said, pouring himself a glass of whiskey, grabbing a second glass and looking at me expectantly. I nodded. I'd need that drink just as much as he apparently did to get through this conversation. He poured me a glass and walked over to where I stood, holding it out.

"Thank you..." I said, taking it. He simply nodded and took a sip of his.

"So, was this your idea or hers?"

"Excuse me?"

"This insane idea for us to put on the charade of me courting you to be my potential bride." He rolled his eyes. "Was it your idea or hers?"

I groaned and sculled the rest of my drink before walking over to his desk, and pouring myself another.

"Trust me, this is the last thing I wanted. I have no interest in being in closer proximity to you than I have to be."

He scoffed. "Most girls would kill to be this close." Now it was my turn to roll my eyes.

"Yes, well, that has a lot more to do with your crown than your winning personality, Princeling."

"Stop calling me that. And I assure you, it's about much more than my crown sweetheart." His insinuation was clear.

I pulled a face. "Gross. Whatever you need to tell yourself."

"I know you're up to something. First the poisoning, weaselling your way into my family's good graces, and now, a convenient fake betrothal. What I can't figure out is why my parents would agree to it. I looked into your family.

You don't have enough standing to warrant a genuinely good match. You're not even a Pure."

Everything until now, I had expected. But I hadn't been prepared for his last comment, and my temper flared at his words.

Of course, that was his problem. Not that I was foreign, not that he didn't know me. It was that my social standing wasn't high enough. I was a weak Impure. He couldn't be seen sullying himself with the rabble.

"Yes, I'm Impure. How disgusted you must be to have to socialise with one."

In his defence, he looked like he regretted the words the second they were out, which only incensed me more.

"That's not what I meant…"

"I don't give a damn what you meant." I put my glass down, harder than I needed to. "Listen, I get it. You are royal, you are Pure. A divinity damned gift to the world, I'm sure. You are entitled and privileged, and I know you are unused to anyone calling you on your bullshit, but I am sick of it. I have been nothing but kind to your family." Hypocrisy aside, I was tired of whatever problem he had with me.

"I may have given you some attitude, but you deserved it. You threw me in a damned *dungeon*. So hear me when I say I did *not* plan this betrothal. You are the *last* person I would want to be engaged to, you pompous ass."

He looked at me in surprise. "Elia—" but I wasn't done.

"This is how it's going to go. I will play the good little lady when we are in public and act as if the thought of being with *you* doesn't make me want to pluck my eyelashes out, but in private, we can stay the Hek away from each other. Or, you can do us both a favour and convince your parents to call off this entire scheme." My face was slightly red from my outburst, but I didn't give him a chance to comment further as I stormed out of the room, startling Hamish, who had clearly been eavesdropping.

"Lady Elia!" I ignored Valor's protests, probably the first person to do so, and kept walking.

Hamish dutifully followed me. "Well, that sounded like it went well."

"Arrogant, prejudiced bastard," I muttered as I kept walking. Hamish knew better than to laugh, but I caught his lips twitch in amusement.

"Where are we going?"

"I don't know. I just need to be moving." He nodded and just walked with me, deciding the silence was probably better than trying to make conversation with me right now.

I didn't know where I was going until I ended up outside an empty training room. I was hardly dressed for any physical activity, but I really needed to work off some steam. After entering the room, I watched as Hamish took up a position against the wall. I suppose he was used to being silent when guarding nobles. I looked down at the dress I was wearing. *Screw it.* I took off the top layers of my skirt and twisted my hair up into a messy bun as I began stretching.

The rest was a blur of acrobatics and exercises. I ran through my full training regime as fast as I could manage and then repeated it. Acrobatics, core workouts, defensive manoeuvring.

CHAPTER SEVENTEEN

I SOON LOST TRACK of time. It wasn't until I heard a low whistle sound from the entrance that I realised I had blocked everything else out. I looked over, huffing, and found the king leaning against the doorframe with his arms crossed. Hamish was standing alert but looked comfortable. *How long had he been watching?*

"So, this is what they teach their ladies in Xeria, is it? Impressive. Perhaps I should have taken notes."

I flushed and shook my head before bowing. "Not exactly, Your Majesty."

"I can believe that. You certainly seem to have a diverse skill set, Elia."

"You never mentioned how you knew my father?" I changed the subject. "You are from Taros, and royalty at that. He was born and raised in Xeria, to a noble house, yes, but I can't think of a situation where you two would be friends."

"I suppose you wouldn't. Things are different now. But when I was a young man, the relationships between the six kingdoms were a lot stronger. It was common for the princes and princesses of their respective peoples to visit each kingdom. Learn about the different cultures, build relationships, and foster trade. I met your father on my tour of Xeria. I snuck out one night with a few of my confidants and we ended up in the same tavern as him. He snuck us out when the Royal Guard came sniffing, then showed us around your capital city, Farhold. After that, I requested he be my guide for the rest of my trip."

"That's quite the story."

He smiled. "I suppose it is. I was actually there when he met your mother."

"You said things are different now? Implying the relationships between the six kingdoms aren't as strong. Why?" He watched me, smiling a little at my blatant curiosity.

"Over time, the kingdoms grew apart. There were some minor conflicts that forced countries to take sides, and I suppose they never truly recovered."

"So Taros and Xeria chose different sides?"

"They did," he said, "I hope you know that does not put you in jeopardy with us."

"Me personally, maybe not, but Xeria?"

"That depends on your queen."

"Are you in talks with Queen Tira?"

"I noticed you didn't practice any offensive moves. Is that because you don't need the practice?" He switched the subject, much like I had whenever he was discussing Elia's family.

"No, it is because I never learned offensive moves. It is unbecoming of a noble Impure lady."

He raised his eyebrows. "And yet, you have been taught everything else?"

"My parents wanted me to have a diverse skill set should I ever need it. I imagine your daughter is even more educated than I am."

"I suppose you make a good point. Xeria is known for its warriors, so I am just surprised they did not train you as one."

"My family's standing probably has a lot to do with that. They train the Pures and the Paras, and then the lowest class daughters who choose to become soldiers or guards. But they expected those of us in the middle to be proper ladies, spending our time courting and finding a beneficial match for our family. I am lucky my parents were flexible enough to let me learn what I did."

He nodded slightly. "And yet, you don't seem all that happy about the match with my son?"

"If only it were a genuine match," I said to him pointedly, causing him to chuckle.

"Enjoy the rest of your afternoon, Elia." With that, he left the room, leaving me with a lot of information to mull over.

I returned to my chambers, bathed, and cleaned myself up. Then I stuck my head out of my room to find Tarryn had joined Hamish outside my door.

"What can we help you with, Lady Elia?" Hamish asked.

"Is there a library in this place?"

"Of course there's a library. This is a castle," Tarryn said, like I was an idiot. I rolled my eyes.

"Well then, could you please show me where it is?"

Hamish chuckled. "Of course, my lady."

"Hamish, I told you to stop using that title."

"Yes, but it is so much more fun seeing how it agitates you when I do."

I sighed. "You two are infuriating."

"Don't lump me in with him," Tarryn sounded offended, but his eyes smiled.

"I certainly will. I get the impression that you are both as bad as each other."

Hamish dramatically put his hand on his heart. "You wound us, my lady, or perhaps I should call you Princess." He smirked, knowing exactly how much that would irk me. I shot him a death glare but didn't deign to respond, and just started walking.

Tarryn cleared his throat. "The library is this way." He gestured in the opposite direction with a satisfied smile on his face. I groaned.

"Lead the way then," I said impatiently, but I was fighting a smile myself.

Hamish laughed and Tarryn looked amused as they did indeed lead me to the library.

It was massive, shelves spanning the entire lengths and height of the walls. Artwork in a few sparse places. It was beautiful. I made my way through the shelves. It would be easy to get lost in here if it weren't for the lanterns and even then, it was difficult. I found what appeared to be a history section. I grabbed 'A *Guide to The Six and their Kingdoms*' and '*Politics and Alliances of Deorum*' before moving on, searching for two more books on very specific topics.

I found a book about the Giftings fairly easily. It couldn't hurt to brush up on my knowledge on at least the Kineti and Incrementi.

The last book took a long time to find. It was deep in the library on a mostly empty shelf. The dust gathering along it told me no one had touched it for some time.

'*A Warrior's Sacred Promise.*'

I gathered the texts and made my way back to Hamish and Tarryn. I couldn't say what made me pause, but something had me stopping. Before I knew why, I heard a voice from around the corner.

"Were ya followed?" A gruff male voice said.

"No." Replied another firm voice. A woman.

"Good. D'ya have it?"

"Of course. Do you think I would risk meeting you if I didn't?"

"No need for your bloody sarcasm, woman. Just show it to me."

There was a rustling sound, like someone unwrapping an object.

"Divinities, sure ya weren't followed?" The man questioned again.

"Yes, you big oaf, stop questioning my capabilities."

"If you're caught, they could trace it back to us." He hissed.

"I'm not dumb enough to get caught, and you can tell the boss I said so."

I risked a peek around the corner. Both figures were cloaked and had their faces carefully hidden. I could see what looked like a dagger nestled in a cloth. That must be what the woman had unwrapped.

"Do you think it really does what they say?" She asked quietly.

"Don' know. All I know is the boss wants it." The woman nodded and wrapped the dagger back up. That's when I noted the hilt. An intricate design was carved into it, but what caught my attention was the symbol in the middle. I had seen it before. I held my breath as I glanced down at my hip and traced the shape of the tattoo.

There, in the middle of the hilt, was a dagger angled diagonally with a droplet of something falling from its tip. *Blood.* That dagger had the same symbol as my blood oath.

The man glanced around, and I quickly ducked back behind the row of shelves I was hiding in. I clenched my eyes shut. I'd glimpsed his eyes as he surveyed. Pure white, no irises. If I didn't know better, I would think him blind.

I heard what sounded like a cloak being lifted. The man was pocketing the dagger.

"Good job. Go dark until given further instruction. We need to keep this quiet, boss's orders."

I risked glancing around again in time to see the woman nod and hold a fist to her chest.

"To the Rise," she said, and he mimicked her motion.

"To the Rise." He nodded back, then turned and disappeared down another row of shelves. I took a step forward, I had to follow them. They were the only solid lead I'd found so far.

"What are you doing?"

I whirled around, coming face to face with Killian. I breathed out.

"You startled me."

He raised his eyebrows. "Is everything alright?"

"Yes, fine. This library is just a little creepy." I flushed, and he smiled a bit.

"You're not wrong. Well, sorry to have scared you. Hamish said you came this way. The princess has asked if you're free to have that catch up she supposedly mentioned this morning."

"Oh, of course. I just need to drop these books off in my room."

He scanned the titles of the books in my hand. "Interesting choices."

"Not particularly," I said and began walking back to where I'd left Hamish and Tarryn.

"We can have a servant deliver those to your rooms."

I would prefer to take them myself, not liking the idea of others knowing what I was reading and reporting it back to someone, but he was already suspicious. I gave him a grateful smile.

"That would be wonderful, thank you."

He nodded, and a servant came forward, taking the books from me.

I thanked them and they smiled politely before heading off to my rooms.

"The princess is in the gardens." He held out his arm. I took it and began walking with him. I would have to put what I'd just heard and seen to the back of my mind until I was alone. Hamish and Tarryn trailed at a respectful distance.

"I heard about the.... situation.... with you and Valor." Killian started carefully. I scoffed.

"That's a nice way of putting it."

"Yes, well, it was a rather unexpected turn of events for some. Namely Valor, even me."

"I already told him I was just as surprised as the rest of you. It was the Queen's idea, not mine."

"I know. That's what I'm curious about. Why exactly does she want you close?"

"Shouldn't you be asking her that?" It seems the king and queen had only told the others the bare minimum, but not the reasoning behind it. I wasn't about to tell them if they hadn't. That meant they didn't trust them, which is why I was in this mess.

"Yes, because the queen and I have such a chummy relationship." He quipped, and I chuckled at the image of the captain and the queen at high tea together.

"Fair enough, but I'm not at liberty to discuss the Queen's plans if she hasn't shared them with you. Just know I am almost as in the dark as you."

"Convenient that." He was a lot more polite than the prince, but his suspicion and scepticism were not subtle.

Luckily, Cali spotted us at that moment and called me over. Killian lowered his arm once we reached her, and bowed his head.

"Princess."

"Killian." She nodded, feigning disinterest and linking her arm through the spot his had occupied. "Thank you for finding Elle for me." She began leading us away, and I chuckled softly.

"Playing hard to get?"

"Shhh, he might hear you."

"He didn't." I smiled.

"Well, then yes and no," she said, "like I said, it's complicated."

"Right."

"Anyway, thanks for joining me. I needed to get outside after today's lessons kept me cooped up inside all day."

"No problem, I could use the fresh air too if I'm honest." I breathed in the distinct aromas filling the air. The garden was quite beautiful, neat and tame, but still beautiful.

"Good, because the other ladies are so boring, and I never know which of them is being genuine or just trying to climb their way up the social ladder. With you, it's much easier." *If only she knew.*

"Well, I'm glad to be of service."

"Also, I want the gossip. How did my brother take the news? Mother told me, oh I *wish* I could have seen his face."

"I'm glad someone finds this amusing."

"Oh, come on, it is hilarious! Plus, he's really not so bad when you get to know him. He's just... a little prickly."

I scoffed. "Prickly? I've seen cacti with fewer spikes than him." That made her laugh again and even I smiled. Her joy was infectious.

We spent the rest of the afternoon gossiping and giggling together in the grass. It was nearing dinner time, when I received a summons from the prince himself. I groaned, and Cali grinned.

"Say hello to brother dearest for me." She teased, and I rolled my eyes at her before standing, brushing myself off and heading to the room he had requested I meet him in. *This should be fun.*

Turns out, I was being summoned to one of the dining halls. It was busy at this time of the evening, with many people enjoying their dinners. This room was only for royals and the uppermost of nobles. It didn't take me long to spot the arrogant prince.

He was seated on a chaise with people surrounding him, vying for attention, both ladies and gentlemen. He was dressed in finery as usual, but something about his attire, or perhaps his posture, gave off a more casual impression.

The sleeves of his white tunic were rolled up to his elbows, exposing his forearms, both of which were resting along the back of the chaise as he conversed with his admirers. Sighing, I and made my way over, plastering a pleasant smile on my face. He no doubt chose this setting so I couldn't yell at him again. *Sneaky bastard.*

I finally got through the crowd, finding Jameson to Valor's right and none other than Lady Josette herself to his left. She was giggling uncontrollably, touching his arm as she did, and leaning in like whatever he'd said was the funniest thing she'd ever heard. *Gross.*

"Prince Valor." I smiled, announcing myself. "You requested my presence?"

He glanced over, giving me a breathtaking smile, one he would never truly direct at me. It was charming and gave the impression I had his full attention, much to the dismay of Lady Josette. I wouldn't be surprised if her claws were now digging into the Prince's arm.

"Lady Elia, yes. I'm so glad you came." He stood, placing a kiss on my hand. *Yeah, I'm sure you are.*

I blushed a little, averting my eyes briefly, before returning my gaze to his.

"Of course, it is an honour." *Double gross.* "What can I do for you, Your Highness?"

"You can have dinner with me." He grinned. He was a better actor than I'd thought.

"Oh, I'm sure Lady Elia has plans already," Josette said, shooting daggers at me now that Valor's back was to her. I glanced at her and smiled.

"Lady Jolene, was it? Wonderful to see you again." She gritted her teeth, and her eyes narrowed.

"It's Lady Josette." She seethed.

"Oh, right, my apologies! I'm so forgetful when things aren't particularly memorable."

I heard a muffled sound, and shifted my gaze in that direction, to find Jameson choking down a laugh.

"I beg your pardon?" Josette said, standing up.

I smiled sweetly, meeting her eyes. "Then beg."

The group of onlookers went silent, and Josette's fist clenched as she took a threating step forward.

"Easy, Josie, she meant no harm," James said, failing to hide the smile in his eyes.

I am sure the only thing that stopped her from letting me have it was our present company. I shouldn't have poked the bear, but I couldn't resist.

Valor took that as his cue to loop his arm through mine and begin leading me away "Yes to dinner?"

I turned my attention back to him and smiled. "I would love to." I placed my hand on his arm and glanced over my shoulder.

"It was so nice seeing you, Lord Jameson, Lady Jessica. I hope you have a lovely evening."

Valor pulled me away at a brisk pace after that. I smiled to myself as I caught a few gasps from those nearby.

"Did you enjoy that?" He muttered quietly, smiling the whole time. If anyone looked at us, it would simply appear as if Valor were whispering sweet nothings to me. So I blushed and said back equally hushed.

"Very much so."

He led us to a two-seater, rather intimately sized table that was far enough away from everyone else that no one would overhear us, but still on full display to the room.

Damn, there goes my plan of stabbing him with the nearest fork when he inevitably said something stupid. He dismissed Hamish and Tarryn, before pulling out a chair for me and I sat down. He took the seat opposite me.

"You shouldn't tease Josie. She has a lot of power here and would be better as an ally."

"Trust me 'Josie' and I would never have been friends, whether or not I teased her. But we aren't here to discuss your many admirers, so why don't you tell me why we *are* here?"

A servant appeared, pouring us each a glass of wine, which I greedily took a sip of. I was going to have a drinking problem by the end of my stay here.

"I figured this was a…. safer… place for us to finish our earlier conversation."

"Oh no, I'd say our earlier conversation is very much finished."

He sighed, and I could tell it pained him to say whatever he was about to say next.

"I am sorry for upsetting you, Elia. What I said about you know, being Pure… came out wrong. I didn't mean—"

"I really couldn't care less what you meant Princeling, don't worry about it."

He looked at me, pursed his lips, and seemed to decide he wouldn't win this battle right now.

"Mother thought it best that we get the ball rolling and start being seen in public settings together."

"Having dinner surrounded by strangers, very romantic."

His jaw ticked, the only sign of his irritation. To everyone else, he appeared to be happily in conversation with me. He had even reached over the table a little, touching the hand that was holding onto my wine glass like a lifeline.

"You are a very difficult person."

"Yes, well, I could say the same about you."

"Can we just have dinner and act like we don't despise each other so we can get out of here?"

"That I can do, although acting like I'm enjoying being here with you, is a big ask."

He ran his thumb across my knuckles. "So, do you really think that—" he paused as a servant bought out the first course. I smiled and thanked them. The prince waited until they were out of earshot. "Do you really think this plan will work? That you will find out who might not be loyal to the kingdom by posing as my current love interest?"

"Well, the story would be a lot more believable if you didn't outwardly enjoy all those women throwing themselves at you all the time." I didn't enjoy how jealous I sounded. I was *not* jealous, I was simply annoyed at how difficult he was making my life. "But yes, I believe it could work. People underestimate women a lot."

"Do you know much about court politics?"

"I know enough. Whatever I don't know, I will study up on."

He leaned back a bit and took a sip of his wine. He studied me, which could be for our audience's sake, or because he was searching for something. I couldn't discern what.

CHAPTER EIGHTEEN

Ignoring his stare, I started eating, taking a break in the conversation to observe the room. There were courtiers, courtesans, and there were also some advisors.

No guards were eating, but they were posted around the room. *One, three, five.* There were five guards standing by. An odd number to choose, usual formations involved guarding in pairs, so you'd expect an even number to be in the room.

"What are you thinking about?" Valor asked, and I glanced back at him.

"Oh, nothing interesting." I took another sip of wine. "Your sister said to say hello by the way."

"It's odd that she has taken such a quick liking to you. She rarely warms up to people that fast."

I raised my eyebrows. "Are we talking about the same princess?"

He chuckled a bit, and it almost could have been genuine. "Her and I are more alike than you'd think. We are siblings, after all."

"Yeah, about that. Are you sure? Because I honestly cannot understand how you two could be related. She is so nice and you are so.... not."

He rolled his eyes. "Because you're just a little ray of sunshine."

That brought a genuine smirk to my face, and I shook my head, taking a bite of my food before glancing around again.

One, three, five... I recounted. *Six.* There was one more guard on duty now. I double counted to make sure, but there was definitely one more. Maybe they realised they were short staffed?

I looked around the rest of the room and noticed the advisors had left, so had Jameson and Josette. The room was emptier than before but there were still people enjoying their meals or socialising.

"Well, this is fun." Valor commented dryly.

"How many guards should be posted in this room?" I was definitely being paranoid, but with what I'd overheard in the library, and now this, something just felt off.

He looked at me quizzically. "What? Why do you want to know that?"

"Just answer the question."

"For a room this size? At least one guard at each entryway," there were two entries or exits, "a guard in each corner," that would make six. I guess I really was reading into things too deeply, "and then one on either side of the room without a doorway." Two more, totalling eight.

"Is there a changeover due?"

He frowned, looking around at the guards. "Why are you asking?"

"Because you're short two..."

"Why would you even notice that?" He started counting, his brow furrowing further. "There isn't a changeover due, no. They probably just needed to utilise guards elsewhere."

"Maybe." I finished my drink and looked at him. He appeared calm, but he was still glancing around the room. The person most likely to be responsible for a royal assassination would be a known enemy of the crown, and whilst the kingdoms were clearly more at odds than I'd first thought, neither Hadrian nor Odette had mentioned suspecting the other kingdoms. After that, it would be a family member, one who stood to inherit something, like the crown.

Valor stood the most to gain if his father passed, but despite his obvious dislike of me, and how quickly he pointed the finger, he seemed to truly love his father, as his father did him. The whole family seemed to care deeply for each other, aside from Odette, who I was yet to figure out. I didn't know enough to rule out the royal family completely, so I had to look at all the likely culprits.

After them it could be anyone, however, because of the nature of the attempt, they would need access and knowledge that not simply anyone would possess. Knowledge and access that someone close to the king would have, someone like an advisor.

I don't know if I would have caught it, had I not been watching Valor so closely. Movement over his shoulder snagged my attention as a cloaked figure stepped out from the shadows with something in their hand. A knife. They raised their arm to throw it. My eyes widened, and without thinking, I practically leapt across the table, knocking us both over.

"What the Hek?!" Valor shouted in alarm. I heard people gasp in shock as the knife flew just above my head and embedded itself in the wall. That's when all Infernis broke loose.

From the shadows, more cloaked figures emerged. Two for every guard in the room, dressed in completely black cloaks with hoods pulled up, obscuring their faces. The only notable thing was a yellow symbol on the top left side of the cloak. The sun. A rising sun. Screams sounded, pulling me away from the details as people started dropping to the floor.

"Shit." Valor cursed, rolling us so he was on top of me. He flipped the table up, creating a shield of sorts. "Are you alright, Elia? Are you hurt?" His eyes rapidly swept over me. "We have to get to cover."

"I'm fine." I nodded. "I'm good, but they have all the exits blocked. How are we supposed to find cover?"

He looked around before withdrawing a short sword that had been strapped to his side. I should get one of those.

"Just stay behind me and do as I say. Understand?" He looked me in the eye, and I nodded, ignoring the slight condescension.

"Lead the way." I reached for the dagger I had strapped to my thigh and unsheathed it. His brows rose, but he shook his head and peeked around the corner of the table.

"There's still enough people. We can use the chaos to get to the nearest exit. Just stay behind me and call out if anything is coming from behind."

"Right." I crouched and let him take my hand.

"Now." We made a break for it, manoeuvring through the fleeing diners.

The cloaked figures were rounding them up. I almost tripped over more than one body, obviously they hadn't bothered to round *everyone* up. The guards that were left had either been surprised and were now engaged in combat, or they were trying to get to us. To the prince.

Some tried to protect the bystanders, but most knew their duty was to the prince. It made me sick. A cloaked figure stepped in front of Valor and smirked, but it was quickly wiped away when the prince engaged him.

I spun, putting my back to Valor's just in time to see another attack coming. *Shit.* I gripped my dagger, but I wasn't trained in combat. These cloaked figures moved like soldiers. They knew what they were doing. I could evade them, but wouldn't stand a chance in a one-on-one fight.

"Valor incoming from behind." He grunted as he blocked a blow from someone to his left. He was fighting three opponents now. They had narrowed in on us; I was on my own.

I glanced around for anything I might use, coming up empty-handed. I looked at the approaching figure, who grinned, exposing yellowing teeth. Up close, I could see a nasty scar on his right cheek.

"Well, who do we have here? Out on a date with the young prince? How sweet."

"I wouldn't call it a date," I said, my feet already shifting, ready to move.

He chuckled. "You look like you have fire, love. If you move out of the way, maybe I'll take you on a private date with a real man."

"Pass," I said, tensing to fight.

He shrugged. "Suit yourself." He raised his sword and swung it at me. Dropping low, I barely dodged the blow. I swiped my blade across his calf, causing him to hiss in pain. I just had to keep him distracted long enough for more guards to arrive. Someone must have sounded the alarm by now.

"You little bitch." He stepped back and swung again. This time he'd expected my dodge, but underestimated how fast I was. His sword nicked my shoulder, but I didn't let it slow me. I ducked again, and somersaulted to the left, causing him to follow me instead of going for the prince, as I had hoped.

"You aren't very quick, are you?"

He growled. "Your death won't be fast, you little whore. I'll make sure you suffer. Maybe I'll cut out that damned tongue of yours first." He came at me again, hard and fast. It was difficult to evade his movements, but I had just enough defensive training to apparently pull it off. It was all very similar to acrobatics.

Just keep moving.

I ducked, weaved, and flipped away from every thrust of his sword. He finally knocked the dagger out of my hand, and clocked me one in the jaw, but I wasn't any good with the blade anyway, and the hit to the jaw allowed me to knee him in the stomach hard enough to elicit a groan from him.

He was coming at me again. I leapt back, but I didn't consider the recently fallen body of one of his cloaked friends, and I stumbled forward. He took advantage of my slip, thrusting his sword into my stomach. I jerked back at the last second, preventing it from going in too far, but a fiery pain shot through me like a hot iron. I winced, falling back and landing on my backside as he advanced.

"Pig." I spat on the floor by his feet. If I was going to die here, I would not be polite about it.

He smirked and raised his sword, then he froze. His eyes widened, and he glanced down at his chest.

He fell to his knees in front of me, his sword clanging to the floor. Valor stood behind him, blood splattered on his clothes, and face. He ripped his sword out of my attacker's back and was at my side in an instant.

"Shit, Elia. Put pressure on it." He moved my hand over my wound and I hissed but held firm.

"I'm fine. Is the path clear?"

"Yes, but more are coming. The guards should have arrived by now. No one has sounded the alarm. Can you walk?"

"Yes." I pushed myself off the floor, wincing. "Let's go."

He looked concerned, but slid his arm around my waist and quickly led us to the doorway he had cleared a path to. I tried not to focus on all the bodies that we passed. Cloaks, guards, and nobles alike. Servants too. This was an organised attack. They knew how many people they'd need to successfully take the room. We made it through the door right as someone yelled out.

"THE PRINCE IS ESCAPING! DO NOT LET HIM GET AWAY!"

"Shit." Valor cursed again, and I almost laughed at him swearing in front of a lady. "This way." He led us down the hall to a statue of his father.

"I hardly think this will be enough for us to hide behind."

"Shhh." He reached around the statue and a click sounded as it shifted to the side, revealing a hidden door leading into darkness.

"Secret tunnel? Nice."

He shook his head. "Just get in, Elia, for divinities' sake."

I did as I was told for once and ducked inside. He followed me, using his Teleki abilities to slide the statue back into its place, and triggering the door to close, leaving me blind.

"Well, this is cosy," I said, and it was. Turns out, this wasn't so much of a tunnel as it was a small room. It was about the size of a storage closet.

"I didn't have time to get us to a proper tunnel. We will have to wait here until someone comes to find us. Once the threat has been neutralised, and they haven't found us, Killian will check the closest hiding spots to where we were. He knows about the tunnels and the rooms like this one."

"Well, that's reassuring." I could tell by his tone of voice he wasn't happy about hiding rather than fighting. But me being with him didn't give him much of a choice, apparently.

"Is there at least a light source in here?"

I could hear him moving along the wall. It sounded like he was running his hands over it, feeling for something. Then a lantern was lit. He looked over at me, still gripping my stomach.

"How badly are you hurt?" He stepped forward to inspect me.

"Not badly. I'll be fine. Just a scrape." I lied.

He gave me a look that said he didn't believe me for a second. "Elia, let me see."

"I'm fine, Valor." It was the first time I'd used his name without his title. But he didn't seem to mind at this point. He groaned.

"I saw the blood, and I can still see it all over your hands. Are you so stubborn that you'd prefer to bleed to death rather than let me inspect the wound?" Possibly.

I sighed, slowly removed my hand, and looked down at it. I lifted the bodice of my dress slightly to expose the wound. It was deeper than I had thought and was still bleeding. *Not good.*

He cursed again. "Bloody Hek, Elia, I'd hate to see what you'd consider as not fine." He leant forward and gently touched the area around the wound.

"You should see the other guy." I joked, which he did not find amusing. He took off his jacket, then his top.

"Um, what do you think you're doing?"

"Making a bandage for you?" He made a large tear in his shirt and then began wrapping the material around my waist, tight enough to hopefully compress the wound and slow the bleeding.

"I could have used some of my dress. There is a lot more material. Now you're shirtless." Which, if I was honest, was harder to ignore than I'd like in my current blood lacking state. He clearly wasn't just a prince, he must train regularly.

"You're welcome," he said, "Are you hurt anywhere else?" He looked me up and down.

"No, he nicked my shoulder, but that's barely a graze, and I'm sure there is probably a lovely bruise forming on my right cheek, but other than that I am fine."

He looked at me sceptically. "That's what you said about your literal stab wound."

"Fair point, but I'm not about to undress to prove mine. I am not injured anywhere else." I slid down and sat on the floor, breathing out.

"What the Infernis was that?" I asked, hopefully stopping whatever plan he had to check that I didn't have another hidden injury somewhere.

"An attack. A well planned one."

"Did you see the symbols on their cloaks?"

"The suns? Yes. It's that bloody rebel group."

"The Rise?"

He looked at me. "How do you know that name?"

"Some of the villagers were talking about it at the markets, but they made out like it was just some disgruntled citizens and not to be taken seriously?"

He scoffed. "That's a bit of an understatement. They've been causing problems as of late, but most of the instances have been non-violent. Disrupting trade routes, stealing. That sort of thing."

My mind went straight to the dagger I saw exchanged in the library.

"Well, this was not nonviolent. What if they attacked more than just the room we were in?"

"The bells would have rung if the castle itself was under attack. Someone would have definitely noticed if it was more than our room."

"Not if they took it as efficiently as they took the one we were in. It took seconds to take out most of the guards, multiple bystanders, and close in on you."

"No, they may have gotten in, but to get more than what they had in that room would have been virtually impossible. Someone would have noticed." His confidence in his guards was interesting, given how very close I came to being impaled, and the amount of blood that covered him.

"Does all of that blood belong to others?"

He glanced down at himself. "Most of it."

I crossed my arms at the hypocrisy but quickly regretted it, wincing at the pain in my stomach.

"I got a cut to my arm, but it has stopped bleeding."

"How would you know? You've had it covered up till now. Turn around and let me see." He did as instructed. He had quite a nasty gash on his arm. The bleeding had slowed, and it didn't look like it would scar, but given that we were in an old dusty alcove, it was probably best to at least cover it up.

I grabbed a leftover piece of his shirt and ripped it to the right size. I copied what he'd done and bandaged up his arm. He was quiet while I did, just watching me. His skin was warm and smooth to the touch, which was a good sign.

"There, hopefully that will prevent any infection." I carefully sat back down.

"Thank you," he said, following my lead and sitting down opposite me.

"... How long until they look for us?"

"Depends on how quickly someone notices the attack. Could be five minutes, could be five hours. Better get comfortable, Sunshine."

I sighed. Dinner with just him was bad enough, but now I was trapped in a dimly lit box with the man. The divinities really had a sick sense of humour.

CHAPTER NINETEEN

I DIDN'T KNOW HOW much time had passed. I'm sure it hadn't been that long, but it felt like hours. Sitting here with Valor was about as pleasant as I'd expected. He said nothing, just sat there with his eyes closed, looking serene. Meanwhile, I had catalogued the entire tiny room.

The walls were brick, there was dust everywhere, and a fair few cobwebs, telling me it hadn't been used for some time. However, this wasn't the only hidden room or tunnel in the castle. I would have to look into that. The awkward silence was slowly driving me mad. My stomach was still sore, and I had a feeling the blood had not slowed as much as it should have by this point. I was about to crack and break the silence, but he spoke first.

"Do you usually stare at people for this long?" He said without opening his eyes.

"How would you know if I'm staring?" I countered.

"You went quiet."

"I wasn't even talking."

"No, but you were tracing shapes on the ground, occasionally sighing dramatically, and even tapping your foot. You stopped doing those things, which tells me you focused on something specific, since I am the most interesting thing in this room." He shrugged and opened his eyes with a satisfied grin.

I immediately regretted wishing for anything other than silence. *Arrogant bastard.*

"Yes, well, I was wondering how many people know about this room. I wanted to know the odds of me killing you, leaving your body here, and getting away with it."

He chuckled, which was very off-putting. "You could try."

I rolled my eyes and didn't bother with another response.

"So, you have a tattoo? Unusual for a lady of your stature." For a second I was confused and then I realised, the brand from the blood oath, he must have gotten a glimpse when he bandaged my wound. *Crap.*

"How would you know what's usual for a lady of my stature?"

"Ah, well, I've seen my fair share of ladies without—"

"Okay nope, forget I asked." I needed to stop asking him questions.

He smiled a bit. "I didn't get a good look at yours, though. What is it?"

"That's none of your business."

"Oh, now you're shy?"

"I simply have no interest in being another lady whose body you discuss with apparently anyone."

"I'll show you mine if you show me yours."

I rolled my eyes. "I'm not interested in seeing anything of yours. In fact, I could do with seeing a little less." He must be cold without his shirt on, but he looked completely at ease.

"No? I am sure I could change your mind about that." *So cocky.*

"Doubtful."

"Perhaps you prefer James' company?"

That got my attention, and I glanced back at him. "That is also none of your business."

"It is, if we are to convince people we are an item. You can't be seen throwing yourself at another man."

I frowned.

"I do not throw myself at *any* man and even if I *had*, it is alright for you to indulge in the women throwing themselves at you, but not the other way around? That's a tad hypocritical, don't you think?"

"That's different. I am a prince. Ladies of the court are always going to vie for my attention."

"So, I suppose that makes it okay for *you* to flirt back, just not me?"

"I haven't flirted with any of them since mother told me her, or maybe your, plan."

"Mhmm, I'm sure."

"... James is my friend, but you shouldn't go there with him." *Divinities,* why was this his topic of conversation?

"And why exactly is that?" It suddenly became irrelevant that I'd already decided not to pursue anything with James.

"He just enjoys the chase. Once he beds you, he will probably forget about you."

"Have you considered maybe that's the same thing I want? After all, I am in a foreign kingdom that I will leave soon enough. Why not have some fun?"

His eyes widened slightly, and it took him a minute to respond.

"Is that what you want?" He tilted his head to the side and watched me. "Some fun, Sunshine?"

I pulled a face. "Don't call me that. And isn't that what everyone wants? Enjoyment?"

"If you are allowed to call me Princeling, I can certainly call you Sunshine."

I rolled my eyes. "It's not the same thing."

"Well, if it's enjoyment you're after," he leaned forward, one arm resting on his knee, "I'd say we still have time before anyone finds us." He wiggled his eyebrows.

I made a gagging sound. "I'd rather get stabbed again, thanks." That elicited a loud laugh.

"Shhhh!" I said. "If the attackers are still at large, they might hear you."

"I wouldn't worry about that. These walls are incredibly thick. Designed to keep sound in and remain undetected."

"Great, so no one will hear when I eventually cave and scream for someone to get me out of this small space with only you for company?"

"Nope."

"Excellent." I looked at him. "Do you think they would have killed you, or taken you hostage?"

"Their intent was to kill. At least the ones that were attacking me. It was obviously a message, not a strategic play to ransom me."

I nodded slightly. "... But what was the message? They slaughtered so many people."

"I suppose it's that they can get to us if they desire. It was a threat."

"What do they want, though? To overthrow your family and then what?"

"We believe it is a solely Impure uprising. People unhappy that the divinities did not deem them worthy and are without Giftings."

I scoffed. "Is that what you think? That the divinities chose you because you're *superior*?"

"No, but for whatever reason, my ancestors *were* chosen. That isn't something I can control."

"But why such a drastic rebellion and why now? From what I've seen, the Impure aren't treated too badly here."

"My father doesn't believe in such drastic divides between our people based on an event that occurred millennia ago. However, not everyone shares his opinion. It's taken years to get to this point. The Impure haven't always been treated well, here or in the other kingdoms."

He wasn't wrong. I knew our history, probably better than he did. Once the divinities had blessed mortals with abilities similar to their own and disappeared, it didn't take long for those with newfound powers to get greedy.

For a long time, Impures were treated like cattle. Forced into the very slavery they'd fought to escape. Some kingdoms would prefer we still lived by those rules. The laws in Taros are much more favourable to people like me, but there is still a divide.

"But again, the people of Taros aren't treated horribly. I mean, yes, it is difficult to earn the amount a Para or a Pure could, but they earn enough to get by comfortably, mostly. No different from if no one was Gifted."

"I'm surprised you see it that way, given how mad you got regarding my comment about you not being a Pure."

"You're an idiot for bringing that up. I, however, am not so prejudiced that I would say all Pures are bad, the same way some Pures say all Impures are useless. I can separate facts from personal experiences. Although, the name Impure itself really is fairly derogatory, wouldn't you agree?"

He shrugged. "You make a fair point, but I didn't create the word. It's how it has always been."

"Just because something has always been, doesn't mean it always should be." I crossed my arms, causing me to wince.

He frowned slightly. "How is your stomach?"

"Oh, fabulous."

He sighed and rose, moving so he was crouched in front of me. "Let me have a look."

"You just want a closer look at my tattoo."

He smiled a bit. "Stop being so stubborn, and just show me."

I sighed and removed my hand, slowly lifting the bottom of my bodice to reveal the makeshift bandage, completely stained red and soaked. The wound wasn't clotting.

"Divinities, Elia. Has it been bleeding this badly the entire time?"

"I'd say that's highly likely."

"Why didn't you say something?"

"Because there is nothing else we could do about it. You said we have to wait here." *And I may have been a little judgement impaired thanks to the blood loss.*

"We need to get you to a medicae."

"It's too dangerous, especially if they're after you."

"I'm sure they've been chased off by now." Before I could protest, he swept me up into his arms, causing me to gasp, then groan, in both surprise and pain.

"Put me down. I can walk."

"Stop being so stubborn. It will be much quicker this way." I didn't mention that my head was spinning, but I conceded he might be right. "I'm going to open the door and get you to the medicae wing. Try not to bleed out before we get there."

I simply gave him a thumbs up. He didn't look reassured, but he looked at the door and it slowly opened without so much as a gesture from him.

He glanced around and apparently deemed it clear as he started making his way down the hall. I could hear his heart beating against my head. It was oddly calming, and I let my eyes fall shut.

"Hey! *ELIA!* Open your eyes. You can't sleep right now."

"Mmm, watch me," I said, snuggling closer to his chest. Fates, I must be suffering from *severe* blood loss.

He groaned. "Heknos' Hounds Elia, look at me. You can sleep after the medicae see to you. Open your damned eyes, woman."

I sighed in frustration. "You are incredibly annoying, you know that?" I opened my eyes and looked at him. He shook his head, but had a look of relief on his face.

"So you keep reminding me. We are almost there, just hold out a little longer, Sunshine."

"Stop calling me that."

"No."

I groaned, not in pain but in exasperation. I only knew he was silently chuckling because I could feel his chest vibrating.

We reached the infirmary without incident, and I stayed conscious, just. It felt like the time my tutors had me try small doses of different drugs before attempting certain tricks so I could escape if anyone ever drugged me.

He burst through the doors, and I immediately noticed cots full of the injured. They were all from the attack. It seems some had survived. Everyone stopped and stared as we walked in. We must have made quite the spectacle. Their prince, shirtless, a little bloodied, carrying a lady in his arms who probably looked half-dead, and was also covered in blood. *Ugh, soon everyone would no doubt be talking about how heroic their prince is. Gross.*

"I need a medicae. *NOW.*" He commanded, and the room spurred into action. They placed me on a cot and a medicae attendant stepped forward to inspect Valor's arm.

"Not for me, for her. I am fine, tend to her."

I would have laughed if I wasn't in so much pain.

"Her wound isn't clotting. Could they have poisoned the weapon they used?" He questioned. *Shit, of course.* I should have considered that. It's not uncommon for dishonourable fighters to coat their blades in poison, designed to slow the clotting process.

"We have had a few others with similar signs. We have identified the poison, and have the antidote, Your Highness." A medicae announced as he walked over, stopping to bow, before moving to my side and undressing my makeshift bandage.

"Will she be alright?"

"We will do our best, Your Highness."

"You know I am right here. I can hear you."

Valor smiled a bit. "Yes, I am well aware."

A commotion from the doorway told me someone else had entered the room, which turned out to be multiple someones. The entire royal family, apparently. Cali rushed over and grabbed my hand.

"Oh divinities, Elle! What happened?!"

"Give her some space, Cali. Let the medicae help her." Valor warned.

I turned my head to look at her and noticed tears in her eyes. Either she was an excellent actor, or she was genuinely worried about me.

"We couldn't find either of you. We thought they took you." She wrapped her arms around her brother and hugged him tightly. I looked away, feeling like I was intruding on the moment.

I hissed as the medicae poured some kind of amber liquid over my wound.

"Apologies, my lady. We don't want to risk infection and we need to get you closed up quickly."

I nodded slightly. "Just do it." I noticed the king and queen standing nearby, talking to the attendant and glancing at me.

"We don't have time for a numbing agent. I'm afraid this will be quite painful."

"I said just do it. *Please.*"

He nodded slightly, and I felt Cali retake my hand in hers, squeezing softly.

Blinding pain is one of the last things I remember, before passing out as the medicae began stitching up my wound. I let out a scream and gripped Cali's hand. The last thing I saw before darkness swept in, was Valor turning away and leaving the infirmary. He'd done his duty by getting me here, and I suppose now he was happy to be free of my company again.

When I woke, it was not in the same room I had passed out in. I was no longer in the infirmary; I was in a bedroom. It was dimly lit, but I could tell by the feel of the silk sheets beneath me and the decorative carvings on the bedposts above that this was a room in the royal wing.

I went to sit up, but groaned at the pain in my stomach.

"Easy, you don't want to tear your stitches." I turned my head to see the king himself sitting at my bedside reading a book of all things.

"Your Majesty, I.... sorry you are not who I was expecting."

He closed the book and placed it on the bedside table.

"Perhaps you would have preferred my son?" He smiled.

"Divinities, no." He raised his eyebrows. "I mean—he's done enough for me." I bit my lip, aware that was not at all a good save. But his smile faded.

"Doing enough would have meant you never being wounded. I am terribly sorry, Elia."

"No, he protected me. He tried to get me out of there, but he was surrounded by a group of attackers, yet he still fought them off, and then killed the one responsible for my wound. Valor got me to safety and got me to the medicae in time. His actions saved my life." *Not that I'd say that to him.*

"And you also apparently saved him. He told me it was you who figured out something was amiss. That you spotted the assassin about to throw a dagger at him, and you pushed him out of the way. That is twice you have saved a member of the Navarre family, Elia, and we repay you by having you almost bleed out."

"Really, I'm fine. All patched up now and I am sure I will be out of this bed, back to annoying your son and entertaining your daughter in no time. How long have I been asleep for?"

He smiled a little. "About a week. I'd like for you to move into this wing of the castle. Where you are better protected." *A week?!*

"Oh, that's unnecessary, Your Majesty."

"Hadrian. And I believe it is. Some attackers got away. They know your face, and probably already know your name thanks to what my wife calls 'the gossip vine.' They could retaliate against you for saving Valor's life. Or they could target you if they think you are important to him."

It would mean I'd have to be more careful about how I acted if I was in closer proximity to the royal family, but it would help in gathering information.

"If you insist, Hadrian." I gave him half a smile, and he nodded.

"I do. And as the king, I command it." He winked, then stood. "I wanted to make sure you were okay and let you know there are a few people waiting outside for you. But say the word, and I will tell them to buzz off until you are up for visitors."

I laughed a little, then winced, putting my hand over my stomach.

"It's fine. I am sure Cali will go nuts if she doesn't see for herself that I am okay."

"You are most probably right, my dear. I am glad you're okay, Elia. Thank you for saving my son." He kissed my hand and then made his way out of the room. I'd somehow, unintentionally, saved a Navarre again and earned more good graces from the king.

If Butcher had known about this attack, I really was going to lose it the next time I saw her. I didn't have long to debate the ways I could make her suffer, because Cali burst into the room and ran over to my bed. It looked like she was about to launch herself at me, but at the last minute thought better of it and settled for a gentle hug, careful not to touch my injured side.

"Oh, Elia, you scared us half to death. There was blood *everywhere*."

"Slow down Cali. I'm fine." I smiled a bit. "The meda patched me up. I'll be good to go tomorrow."

"Like Hek you will." She sat on the end of my bed. "You're staying here until you're really better."

I groaned, but smiled at her. "Whatever you say, Your Highness." She rolled her eyes.

"OKAY, YOU CAN COME IN NOW!" She called out, and I raised my eyebrows.

"What?" She said indignantly. "I wanted to see you first."

"Who else is here?"

"Oh, you have quite the line of admirers, Lady Elia." She giggled, and I shook my head.

CHAPTER TWENTY

Hamish was the first one to appear, followed by Tarryn. Both appeared relieved to see me, but glum.

"What's wrong?" I asked as they approached.

"We're so sorry Elia," Hamish mumbled.

I frowned. "What do you have to be sorry for?"

"We weren't there..." He looked down, Tarryn looked straight ahead, shame clouding his features.

"Oh, divinities, don't be ridiculous. You weren't on duty. You have followed me around day and night. Guards *and* the prince surrounded me. Why would you have been there?"

Tarryn looked at me. "Regardless, we are sorry we weren't there to protect you. It will not happen again, Lady Elia, I swear it." The look in his eyes threw me. He was always serious, but I'd never seen him so determined.

"Really, it's alright, Tarryn, I appreciate it, but it's alright. That goes for you too, Hamish. I am glad you weren't there and in the line of fire."

Hamish sighed. "Agree to disagree, but I'm really glad you're okay. We will let you rest. We just wanted to apologise and see if you needed anything."

"No thank you, I am alright." He squeezed my hand and then nodded at Tarryn. "We will be just outside if you need anything."

I rolled my eyes.

"Stop being such a mother hen." I shooed them away, which seemed to lighten Hamish's mood because he smiled and exited with Tarryn.

Cali sighed next to me.

"What?"

"I wish my guards were that dreamy. Mine are old and boring. And absolutely no fun."

I laughed softly. "What about Captain Ambrosia? I am sure he'd happily be your personal guard." I wiggled my eyebrows.

She gasped. "Oh, hush!"

A knock drew my attention back to the doorway where Jameson was now standing.

"I hope I'm not interrupting?"

"No, not at all," Cali said, jumping up, "I was just leaving."

I raised my eyebrows. "You were?"

"Yes, Elia, as much as I'd like to stay and fuss over you, the castle *did* just get attacked. I have to see where else I can help." She practically scolded. *How convenient.*

"Mhmm."

She kissed me on the cheek and whispered. "Now *he's* dreamy." She winked, then left the room, shutting the door behind her. I rolled my eyes, and James chuckled as he made his way over.

"Subtlety was never one of her strong suits." He commented and took the seat next to my bed.

"No kidding," I said, causing him to smile.

"It's nice to see being nearly stabbed to death hasn't dampened your spirits."

I shrugged. "Could be worse."

He laughed a little.

"It could be. But I am still very glad to see you are mostly intact."

"I appreciate that, but you shouldn't be here, Jameson. People can't hear that you are the one consoling me in my bedchamber when I am supposed to be courted by your best friend."

"I won't stay long, and I came with Hamish, Tarryn, and Cali. As far as everyone else is concerned, I am just visiting like the rest of them. Besides, your prince isn't one of the visitors, so I don't think people will notice." I had wondered if he was one of the people waiting outside. I am not sure what I was really expecting.

He must have read my features because he said, "He's gone with Killian to track some attackers that got away."

I nodded. "Of course, I would expect nothing less."

He watched me. "If I were him, I'd have been by your side the entire time."

I sighed. "Because you're *such* a romantic at heart, my lord?"

He smiled. "For you, I could be." I rolled my eyes, and he chuckled.

"You gave everyone quite the scare, Elle. Have they had any luck discovering why they attacked? Or who was behind it?"

"Everyone keeps saying that as if I had a say in the matter. Trust me, when I thought I'd rather be stabbed than dine alone with the prince, I wasn't actually being serious." His lips quirked up in a half-smirk. "Before you make some comment about how dinner with you would be much better, or something like that, you can save yourself the trouble. As for the attackers, I'm not sure. I'm not exactly in the loop. Valor thinks the rebellion is grower bolder, and wanted to send a message that they can get to The Crown if they want to. "

"You're no fun."

"I can be very fun."

He stood. "I will be happy for you to show me when that stomach of yours is all healed. The only pain you'd feel with me is the kind you ask for." He winked.

I groaned. "Get out of here before I'm sick." I threw one of my pillows at him.

He laughed, caught it, and placed it beside me, before leaning in and kissing my forehead.

"Rest up, Lady Elia…. I'll be seeing you soon," he said.

"No, you won't!"

He smirked and left without responding, leaving me alone at last. I breathed out and closed my eyes. Of course, I'd get stabbed.

Well, if I am forced to be in bed, I may as well do something useful.

"Hamish!" I called, and he poked his head in.

"Yes, my lady?"

I rolled my eyes. "I had those books from the library taken to my rooms. Can you please ask the staff to bring them for me?"

He smiled. "Of course. I'll have them sent over now."

"Thank you."

He bowed slightly before closing the door again. Time to learn everything I could about the politics at play, the Navarre family's Giftings, and with any luck, some information on this damned blood oath and how to break it. Completely achievable.

I started with *An Updated History of the Deorum Giftings,* something a little more interesting than politics.

Skimming through, the book appeared to contain a few chapters on each of Deorum's Giftings. Detailing things such as descriptions, famous Pures and Paras, common professions, weaknesses, strengths, and so on. I started with the introduction, though, curious how they would sum up the magic we still only have a small understanding of.

Introduction

In the beginning, there were countless unique powers bestowed by the divinities themselves, upon the soldiers that battled on the front lines during The Great War. This magic became known as Giftings.

Those blessed with these Giftings became the first of a new class of mortal. It took them time to hone and gain an understanding of their new magic, even longer to explain it to others, eventually leading to the classification of Giftings that we still go by today.

Whilst there are many Giftings, from many of our divine allies, in this text we will explore solely those that are prominent in Deorum, those bestowed by the divinities known as The Six.

Chapter One: Understanding the Magic Behind the Giftings

To understand the capabilities and limitations of a Gifting, one must first understand how the magic works. If one possesses a Gifting, that tells us they have magic in their blood, however, it is not immediately accessible and it does not tell us what that magic can do. This is where we start to learn about Confirmations, Testings, and Specialties.

The Confirmation

A <u>Confirmation</u> is a ritual used to confirm whether a child has inherited any magic and, therefore, possesses a Gifting.

After much trial and error, mortals discovered a way to determine if a child has inherited a Gifting. This ritual must be completed before the child reaches the age of six, any later and the magic will become dormant, no longer revealing itself until The Testing is complete.

To complete a Confirmation, a priest must take a drop of the child's blood, then combine it with divine herbs, and add to flame. The concoction will ignite, and the colour of that spark will reveal the mortal's class.

Classes of Mortals

<u>Green Spark</u> = Pure, Gifted
<u>Blue Spark</u> = Parapure/ Para, a half blood with less powerful magic, but still classified as Gifted
<u>Red Spark</u> = Impure, a mortal with no magic in their blood, no Gifting.

Since I hadn't gone to school, I never had a Confirmation. If I had, my spark would have been red to showcase how very ordinary I was. I remember some of the other orphans would peek in the windows of the closest school, hoping to glimpse a Pure's Confirmation.

Royals are Confirmed at birth, but the rest of the population has theirs at the beginning of their education; first grade, starting at age five, just before the magic becomes dormant. Those of us that can't afford to go to school, are only Confirmed if we, or our parents, can somehow come up with an exuberant amount of coin to pay the priests of the Deos Credentes, since they are the only ones with access to the divine herbs.

Confirmations are done at the start of the school year, so they can separate the children into curriculums based on their class.

Those who spark as Pure or Para immediately undergo their Testing and spend the rest of their education training.

The Testing

The <u>Testing</u> is a trial used to unlock a Pure, or Parapure's, magic and reveal their Specialty.

In true divine fashion, the divinities decided the Gifted mortals that would inherit magic through blood and ancestry, rather than by their hands, should be challenged before unlocking the full scope of their power.

So, before they vanished, they created The Inbetween, a place known as Erro, that exists between the sealed mortal realm, Adysium, and the surrounding realms. The divinities cannot enter Adysium, but they can choose to enter or influence Erro, challenging the descendants of the mortals they revered so highly before allowing them to return to their realm with their magic unhindered.

Once again, a priest's involvement is required. They must administer divine herbs to the Pure or Para wishing to undertake their Testing, so they may enter Erro, where they will be tested and challenged, unlocking their power and discovering their Specialty.

Specialties

A <u>Specialty</u> is the term we use to describe the specific ability a Pure or Para can wield with their Gifting.

No two Giftings are alike, primarily because they were each given by a different divinity, and subsequently, have their own set of Specialties.

Once a mortal has completed their Testing and discovered what their Specialty is, they return to their realm and begin training to master it.

It is important to note, whilst there are many, a Pure will only be capable of specialising in, or wielding, one. They are born with that one Specialty and cannot choose or change.

Chapter Two: Giftings and Their Unique Specialties

The six Giftings of Deorum are as follows: Kineti, Incrementi, Virbi, Animi, Healeti, or Elementi.

All but the Elementi Gifting have two known Specialties, the Elementi have four. Therefore, in Deorum there are fourteen possible Specialties, some rarer than others.

On the following page we have constructed a table detailing each Gifting, the divinity responsible for the magic, the Specialties, what one can do with them, and which kingdom it is home to.

Divinity	Sigil & Gifting	Specialties	Kingdom
Elios God of Unity	Elementi	Breather = manipulates air Piro = manipulates fire Tear = manipulates water Turf = manipulates earth	Lios
Taros God of Strength	Kineti	Teleki = moves object with their mind Telepi = communicates within minds	Taros
Lereya Goddess of Healing	Healeti	Morti = kills and decays Remedi = heals and gives life	Reya
Ikeara Goddess of the Hunt	Animi	Imperi = communicates with animals Orati = controls an animals will	Ikira
Zalnea Goddess of the Harvest	Incrementi	Flori = controls plant life Immuni = immune to poisons	Lenea
Xeria God of War	Virbi	Argenti = skin invulnerable to all materials other than silver Forti = possesses extreme strength	Xeria

Moving on from the basic explanations, I started the Kineti chapter. I already knew a fair bit about this one, since it was the Gifting of Taros, given its name after the God of Strength.

Kineti

The Kineti Gifting, at its core, is one of the more mental abilities of The Six. However, it is not to be underestimated, as it can still pose a very physical threat.

Kineti can Specialise as either a **Teleki** or a **Telepi**. The first can move manufactured, or mortal made, objects with their minds. The latter can communicate within someone's mind, however, this ability is less common.

I scanned the pages for any information that I didn't already know. I thought about what I'd seen of Valor and Hadrian, both of whom were widely known as two of the strongest Teleki in all six kingdoms. At the bottom of the page, it appeared as though someone had added some text.

Reports of perhaps a new Kineti Specialty have been growing, supposedly possessing the ability to read thoughts. However, we have had so few of these claims prove true that it has not been acknowledged as an official specialisation — Library of the Lost.

There was no date or author.

Reading someone's thoughts? That sent a chill down my spine. If anyone here could read my thoughts, I'd be a dead woman walking.

I was distracted from my fear as I remembered something. During my first meeting with Hadrian, Killian had opened the door, ready to escort me out before I even knew our conversation was over. Could Hadrian and Killian have been communicating without me knowing? And did that mean one of them was a Telepi, or perhaps they possessed this new ability to read thoughts?

The king was thoroughly documented as a Teleki, and since you can only specialise in one ability, he couldn't *also* read thoughts, right? Perhaps Killian was a Telepi, or this new rumoured specialisation with no name? Come to think of it, I'd never seen him demonstrate his magic. Someone that could communicate with others, silently, and with no one knowing, would certainly make for a useful captain, general even.

I shook my head, disregarding the possibility of Killian having this un-known Specialty. Like I'd thought earlier, if anyone here could read my thoughts, I'd be hanging at the castle gates by now. Still, I made a mental note to figure out what Killian's Specialty was, and if he was a Telepi, as I suspected.

I flipped through to the chapter I'd been both hesitant and eager to read. *Incrementi*. The Gifting belonging to the Kingdom of Lenea, named after Goddess of the Harvest, Zalnea. Odette and Cali were both Flori.

Incrementi often choose professions such as farmers, horticulturists and apothecaries. The *Flori* can grow and foster plant life, whilst the *Immuni* are insusceptible to poisons and most drugs.

The people of Lenea are solitary people. They interact little with other nations, other than Reya, due to how close the Healeti and Incrementi magics are to each other. The Healeti need the herbs and plants that the Incrementi can create and vice versa.

I'd always thought it odd that Odette had married Hadrian. A strange pairing for such a reclusive kingdom to make.

I read through the rest of the related text, looking for anything else that might be useful. I couldn't find anything other than a mention of Flori being able to grow any plant if they had the right materials, which would include poisonous ones. So, theoretically, they could make their own hybrids. Is that what Odette had done? Is it how she had been immune to the Heknos Trace, even though she wasn't an Immuni?

Some things just weren't adding up with Tilly's confession. She'd said she hadn't seen the person's face, only that it was a short, cloaked woman wearing a sun sigil. That could realistically have been anyone. I find it very hard to believe Solis herself was in the castle, convincing a maid to poison the king, and not succeeding. Tilly's reasoning for going along with it also made no sense? Simply because she was told to? That's hardly believable.

Could the queen have been involved? She was obviously familiar with poison and manipulation. She most likely knew about the rebellion. Had she simply picked the rebellion symbol as a scapegoat? It made little sense for Solis, the supposed leader of the rebellion, to send me in to gather intel, if she already had someone on the inside, ready to poison the king. It made no sense.

This was going nowhere. This book would not assist me in finding the disloyal members of the court.

I skimmed through the rest of the chapters. Virbi hailed from the same kingdom as Lady Elia, Xeria.

The Virbi are proud, powerful people, with the most physical Gifting, applicable to both of their Specialties.

Forti; gifted with inhuman strength, and *Argenti*; possessing skin invulnerable to any weapon or material, with one exception: silver.

Tolemas was a Forti Para, but I'd never met an Argenti, Pure or Para.

The Healeti settled in Reya. Incredibly gifted healers, but also capable of destruction. The two Specialties of Healeti are *Remedi,* those that heal and give life, or *Morti,* those that destroy life. The second Healeti Specialty is rare, and often Morti children are seen as bad omens.

Supposedly, the cost of having a power that can take is that you cannot also give. My plans to get Sierra to Reya seemed so far out of reach now, but all I needed was to meet one Remedi. Once I was free of this Akros damned oath, I'd find one and convince them to help.

Soon, I was up to Taros's neighbouring kingdoms.

Ikira is home to the Animi. They specialise as either an *Orati,* with the ability to communicate with animals, or an *Imperi,* capable of making an animal's will their own. Imperi are harder to come by, with Animi more commonly specialising as Orati.

The second Specialties of Incrementi and Virbi were fairly evenly inherited, but for the other Giftings I'd read about so far, the second Specialty didn't follow the same rule. Telepi, Morti, and Imperi all seemed to be less common.

Whatever they were born with is what they were stuck with. The current rulers, King Rahmor and Queen Elsbeth, could both control fire.

They named the Elementi Specialties after the elements a person could wield. Fire manipulators were known as *Piros*, water manipulators; *Tears*, earth manipulators; *Turfs* and air manipulators were *Breathers*. For obvious reasons, Lios was one of the strongest warrior kingdoms.

Flipping the page, it appeared I was at the end of the book. But it looked like pages were missing, as if someone had torn them out. I trailed my hand along the inner spine of the book. Down at the very bottom, scribbled in the same writing I'd seen earlier, was a small symbol that had my blood running cold.

There, in the bottom right-hand corner, was a sketch of a dagger tilted diagonally, with a drop of something about to fall from the tip. The same symbol that was branded on my torso. The same symbol I'd seen on the hilt of the dagger the mysterious figures in the library had exchanged.

I moved my hand over the sketch and swallowed. I frantically searched the book again for any mention, any more drawings. Something, *anything* else, that might link to it, but found nothing.

Accepting defeat, I grabbed the last book I'd found in the library. '*A Warrior's Sacred Promise.*' Skimming through, it was mostly what I had expected. Discussing the vows warriors would make to their kingdoms, commanders, and even lovers. But it mentioned nothing magical. They appeared simply mortal promises. I stopped as a small paragraph caught my eye.

That was millennia ago. The war ended four thousand years ago and began three hundred years prior to that. If blood oaths were being used prior to that, then their magic hadn't come from a Gifting, it came from somewhere else? How in Heknos' Hounds had Butcher gotten her hands on that kind of power? More importantly, how could I break it?

To sever a blood oath would be to forfeit one's life. The magic binds a warrior's promise to their blood. If the oath is broken forcefully, it is akin to ripping the blood from one's body. The only way for a blood oath to be broken is for the one whom they made the promise to, to release the sworn party, or for the divinities themselves to intervene and remove the bindings.

I laughed bitterly. I wasn't sure which was more likely; Butcher releasing me, or the divinities intervening. My money was on the divinities.

I sighed and read the rest of the book, but found nothing particularly useful. No more familiar symbols or loopholes to be found, and no solution to my problem. I closed my eyes, trying to tame my frustration. I must have been more tired than I thought because the next thing I knew, I was waking up to something touching my face. My eyes flew open to find Odette sitting on my bed, stroking my cheek.

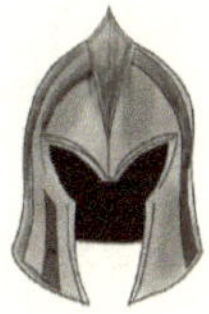

CHAPTER TWENTY-ONE

"Hello, Elia dear. How are you feeling?" She moved her hand from my cheek and instead began stroking my hair, looking at me with the same gleam of madness that I'd glimpsed when she had questioned Tilly.

"... I'm feeling much better. Thank you for asking." I tried to sit up, but she held me back down.

"Shhh, don't strain yourself, child. You still need rest." She glanced at the books beside me. "Curios."

"I appreciate you checking on me, Your Majesty, but really, I am fine."

"I have no doubt you will recover quickly." Her eyes bore into mine. "However, that is not the only reason I am here."

"Oh?"

"That is twice now you have saved a member of my family. Which leads me to believe I can trust you with this."

"Trust me with what, exactly?" The look on her face had my stomach dropping. Her eyes glinted with what I could only describe as pure sparks of insanity.

She smiled. "Tagget!"

My bedroom doors opened, and the queen's personal guard, Morrysin Tagget, wheeled in a large object. It was rectangular and covered in a drape of some sorts. I couldn't see what was beneath it.

"Thank you Tagget. Ensure we are not disturbed. By *anyone*. My husband included."

He nodded. "As you wish, Your Majesty." He exited the room, a lock clicking into place. There's a lock on the outside of this door? *Not good.*

"What is that?" I asked, even though I *really* did not want to know. Odette smiled again and stood, finally taking her hands off me.

She walked over to the object and pulled off the drape. My eyes widened. It was a cage, and it wasn't empty.

"Matilda, dear? Are you awake?"

The person, standing in the cage with their head bent forward as if they were sleeping standing up, moved, tilting their head back up, revealing a smiling Tilly. She wasn't asleep, apparently. She was just... stood there.

"Yes, Your Highness." She answered, straightening. Odette smiled sweetly at her, which was much more terrifying than any of the other expressions I'd seen her wear.

"Good, you have a visitor."

"Lady Elia? It's so nice of you to visit" She smiled brightly, no sign of fear or discomfort. I looked around the room, then back at Tilly. Visit? *What in Taros's name was going on?*

When I risked a glance at Odette, she nodded as if in permission.

I swallowed. "Tilly, what are you doing in there?"

"In where?"

"... In a cage?"

"What cage?"

She looked confused. *Crap.* "Have you been in here since you confessed to poisoning the king?"

"I confessed to poisoning the king?" She frowned, not looking alarmed, simply confused. I looked to Odette for an explanation. Her viper's smile was back in place.

"Did you know I was an Incrementi before coming here, Elia?" Odette asked.

"I did, Your Highness. You're one of the few current queens that doesn't have the same Gifting as her ruling King."

"Ah yes. Remember what I told you about alliances? Fickle things, so much so, that my father felt the need to strengthen his with Taros, therefore resulting in the union between Hadrian and myself."

"I have heard that the people of Lenea are rather solitary, not mixing with other kingdoms often."

"You heard correctly. Aside from Reya, my father rarely sees the need to mix with other kingdoms, but for whatever unknown reason, he felt the need to for my marriage, and so, here we are." I nodded slightly, wondering where she was going with this.

"See, there are a lot of misconceptions about those of us with the Incrementi Gifting. Such as, all of us being nature adoring nomads who can simply play with plants," she said, watching Tilly now, who was watching Odette, seemingly interested in the story, "but in fact, we can do so much more than that. Some of which you saw when I questioned Matilda here. We can grow..." She opened her palm, which contained a small seed. Her palm glowed softly, and the seed blossomed into a beautiful lily.

"We can also decay."

The petals darkened and shrivelled before crumpling in on themselves like the life had been sucked out of them. I breathed in. "Only plant matter, of course, but plant life is like mortal life in many ways." The sinking feeling in my stomach grew.

"Why can't she remember? Why doesn't she know she's in a cage?" It was an effort to keep the panic from my voice.

"Well, as you saw, I grew my own hybrid of Heknos Trace, with very specific qualities. Once she had ingested it, I was able to question her while her inhibitions were lowered, but I needed to know for certain if she was being honest. There are things about my people, and what we can do, that little to no outsiders are aware of. One of those things being, that regardless of where plant matter exists, if it is present we can control it."

I looked at Tilly in horror. Butcher's order prevented me from outright objecting, demanding she stop this, but even the oath couldn't prevent the horror I was sure she'd be able to see in my eyes.

"What did you do to her?"

"Oh, nothing horrible dear, don't worry. I simply used what was already inside her to create something that would assist in my questioning." She smiled almost proudly, and I was careful not to let my disgust show.

".... Like what?"

"Well, once the Heknos Trace had been absorbed into her bloodstream, I could access it. Control it. I simply moved it through her blood, up to her brain, and had it infiltrate her mind. As we speak, tiny little seeds and vines are controlling the signals that are being sent to and from dear Matilda's mind."

My eyes widened. "You can control her?" Every muscle in my body wanted to tense, but the oath fought it, willing my body to remain still, rather than jumping up and making a run for it as my instincts were screaming to.

"Is a demonstration in order? Oh, I do *so* miss being able to show people my abilities!" She practically squealed like a schoolgirl.

"Oh, no! I believe you, it's alright—"

"Shhh." She held up a hand, silencing me. She had that unhinged look in her eyes again. "You can see why we don't allow many to know the full extent of our magic. We would be highly sought after." She walked over to me, picked up the candle beside my bed, and walked back over to the cage, holding it through the bars.

"If you can control the right person, you can control everything. So we stick to ourselves. The brain is a beautiful, complex creature. I have spent many years studying it, learning to use my magic to this extent, but now that I understand it, I can determine what the mind processes and what it doesn't. Like pain, for example."

I stiffened as Tilly lifted her hand and moved it over the flame.

"Your Highness, this isn't necessary."

"Do not interrupt me, Elia," she said, the command clear in her voice. *Shit, double shit.*

Tilly's smile didn't falter as the flame burned her skin, turning it pink, then red. I could see the burn mark going deeper the longer she held her arm there, but she just held it there, smiling like nothing was wrong.

"See? She feels no pain." Odette removed the candle and stroked Tilly's cheek through the bars. "She is the perfect puppet."

I had to get out of this room.

"Why do that to her when she is going to be executed?"

"Oh, I only did it to make sure she wasn't hiding anything else, and to see if she could be of further use. The rest is for fun. I rarely get to use my magic for more than mere parlour tricks these days." She smiled forlornly, like one might over a forgotten love.

"So, you... can control her mind. Do you also control her memory?"

"Heknos Trace is an amnesiac, so by using properties of that, yes. I can't give her fresh memories, but I can make her forget recent periods of time."

"Is she... aware? Does she know what you're doing?" Odette looked impressed that I was asking such questions, as if she truly had expected me to make a run for it. I wasn't stupid enough to think I would get away with that, stomach wound or not. I had to bluff my way out of this.

"Yes." She smiled. "I entwined my plants with every part of her mind that I could reach. It takes a large level of skill and concentration to do such a thing, therefore I don't waste time shielding her from what I am doing. It doesn't matter as long as I am in control."

"It's terrifying, but impressive." Both things were true, one more so than the other. She would likely know if I pretended it was no big deal.

"I was hoping you could appreciate it for the skill that it is."

I nodded slightly. "Why show me this? If it is such a secret, it would surely be a risk to show me?"

"It is, but I trust after seeing it yourself that you would be smart enough not to betray me?" She tilted her head to the side as she watched me, and each time I looked at her eyes, she appeared less and less mortal. More reptilian. If I didn't know better, I'd say she was an Animi, some have been said to pick up traits of the animals they interact with, and she was certainly doing an excellent imitation of a serpens.

"Of course, I will tell no one. I am just surprised you would trust me with such a secret."

She smiled. "Well, I wanted to reward you for protecting my family, to show you I can protect you." The unspoken *'Or do this to you if you step out of line'* sat silently between us. It wasn't lost on me that she'd waited until I was weakened to reveal this to me.

"I understand," I said, and I did. The threat was perfectly clear. She had figured out I was more than I appeared, but rather than shut me out, she was going to continue to use me, just not without making sure I knew who I would be messing with. If I betrayed her or pissed her off, I would end up like Tilly. I swallowed, which seemed to satisfy her.

"Excellent, I am glad we agree." She opened the cage, stepped in, and kissed Tilly's forehead, prompting another smile. "You have been so well behaved." She stroked her cheek, the same way she had been stroking mine when I woke. *Divinities let this be a nightmare.*

"When is her execution date?" Please be soon. Put the poor girl out of her misery.

The queen shrugged. "Oh, it will come eventually, but why rush? She is such a useful girl. As I'm sure you know, having had her as your lady's maid."

"So you're.... she's your lady's maid? You've been having her tend to your needs?"

Odette's chuckle was vexing. "Oh, yes. She has been... very proficient at catering to *all* my needs." Her hand trailed down Tilly's arm and my eyes widened. Surely she didn't mean? I didn't know what to say. This was all insane. She was *insane.* Her eyes were still on Tilly, thank the divinities, so she couldn't see me trying to mask my look of terror.

"Mmm, this entire display has worn me out. I must retire to my bedchamber, where Matilda can do as you said and serve."

"Oh, I'm sorry you've exhausted yourself."

She waved a hand nonchalantly. "Tagget!" The lock was released, and he entered the room.

"Yes, Your Majesty?" The queen stepped back from Tilly, who was smiling lazily at her, and locked the cage again, replacing the drape.

"Take Matilda to my rooms and prepare her for me."

"Of course." He nodded and wheeled Tilly out. Odette turned back to me, and just like that, her eyes regained their sanity. Her movements became more like that of an actual person.

"Oh, I am so glad we could have this little chat, Elia." She grinned. "We are very thankful you have stumbled into our lives." She walked over and kissed my cheek. I never thought I'd be grateful for the blood oath, but at that second I was, it was the only thing that kept me from recoiling.

"Rest up, dear. I will see you soon." Then she just waltzed out the door humming to herself, *actually humming,* like absolutely nothing out of the ordinary had just happened.

The queen was not only a lunatic but also an extremely strong Incrementi, with an ability no one even knew about. This was bad. This was very bad.

I was stuck in that damned room for almost two weeks before the meda deemed it safe to remove my stitches. The royal family fussed over me like an infant. I was incredibly excited to go for a walk, with Hamish and Tarryn escorting me, of course.

I'd had frequent visitors while I was recovering. Cali being the most common one, spending a lot of time just making me laugh, or entertaining me with court gossip. James came by a few times, checking in and asking if I had any updates on the attack, but I told him off each time and sent him packing.

Hadrian came by every day to check on me, making sure I had everything I needed. It was... nice. A small part of me even enjoyed the fussing a little. I certainly didn't trust the royal family, but they had welcomed me in. Hadrian and Cali treated me like family. Hadrian was a lot like what I remembered my father to be like. It was nice to think of him and not feel sad.

I hadn't seen Odette again, nor had I seen Valor. Both of which I silently thanked the divinities for. I'd used my two weeks as best I could. Reading over the books I'd borrowed, combing over everything I knew about this assassination attempt and who could have been behind it.

My gut was still swaying me towards an inside job, but I was growing increasingly more sure that none of the royal family were behind it. Now that I had recovered, I planned on digging into the advisors and royal council.

When the Navarre's or James weren't visiting me, and I wasn't obsessing over my endless problems, Hamish or Tarryn would take turns sitting with me. Hamish would tell stories and jokes, essentially doing anything that would make me laugh, whilst Tarryn taught me to play chess. 'A *strategy game'* he'd called it.

So we played. Chess, card games, anything he deemed beneficial to the mind. Don't ask me why.

I stepped out into the garden with both of the men in question close on my heels. They were extra paranoid today, but I didn't care. Fresh air. Sunlight. Moving to a spacious area of grass, I sat down, closed my eyes, and slowly breathed in. The grass was freshly trimmed but still soft underneath me. An earthy scent hung in the air, reminding me of Sierra's gardening.

Laying with my eyes closed, the sun warming my cheeks, and the air still fresh enough that it had a little bite to it, I could almost pretend Sierra was here beside me, tending to the plants while I entertained her with ridiculous made up stories and memories from our childhood. I could feel the men giving me odd looks, but they wisely remained silent. I thought back to this morning, when I'd woken to a small letter on my bedside table. It was from Butcher. I'd just about had a heart attack. Anyone could have seen it.

Your report is overdue. Get it to me or I will pay a visit to your sister and your lovely gentleman caller.

If she knew to get a note to me, she knew about my injury and that I couldn't easily sneak out. Apparently, that was irrelevant. I sighed, trying and failing to sink further into the grass, praying the ground would simply open up and swallow me whole.

"How ladylike." I heard Hamish say. I promptly ignored him. I'd have to get a message to her, or somehow get there myself. I contemplated what I would have to report, the stakes so much higher now, knowing that whatever I passed on to Butcher would be given to the rebels.

I didn't sign up to be a pawn in a civil conflict. I didn't even know who I'd side with. That wasn't true. I wouldn't choose either if the options were Solis and Butcher, or an insane queen. Neither were people I would fight for willingly, but I may not have a choice. Would Butcher force me? The oath was to infiltrate the court and follow her commands, but she had me until the next summer solstice. Who knows what her end game really was, or just how heavily involved she was with this rebellion?

A shiver interrupted my thoughts as a shadow fell over me, blocking out the sun. I cracked open an eye to find Prince Valor standing above me, raising an eyebrow.

"How very unbecoming of a lady."

CHAPTER TWENTY-TWO

AN AMUSED SMILE GRACED his lips, eliciting a snigger from my left. I shot Hamish a glare before fixing it on Valor.

"If you would be so kind as to move, you are blocking the sun." I closed my eyes again.

Grass rustled, alerting me just before I felt his presence beside me. Sighing, I looked over to find him laying beside me, hands propped behind his head.

"Can I help you with something?"

"Not really. Just thought I would see what you enjoyed about this. It is quite relaxing, I suppose."

"Well, it *was*." Emphasis on the *was*.

He smirked. "Good to see the attack hasn't affected your charm."

"How would you know? You didn't see me afterwards." The unintentional bite to my words surprised even me.

He was quiet for a minute, searching for the right words. "I'm sorry for that. Killian and I were tracking some of the escaped attackers."

I propped myself up on my elbows. "Did you catch them?"

He shook his head. "No." He looked frustrated and even a little ashamed. "We lost them in The Wastes."

My eyes widened. "They fled to The Wastes? That would be suicide."

He nodded. "Apparently, they would prefer that to being captured."

Taros is one of the biggest kingdoms on the continent, but the Sineti River divided it into two. The northern part is controlled by the Navarre family. The southern is known as The Wastes. While technically under the Navarre's jurisdiction, the land is uninhabitable, barren and deadly.

They say it used to be green and habitable. No one knew what caused the decay. Some say it was the divinities, some say it was a witch's curse, but no one can find any record of what truly happened. Every attempt to survive out there has failed. They say to travel into The Wastes is to welcome Dykos, the Goddess of Death.

"Is it possible that the rebels survived?"

"We have sent scouts to check it out, but it's a death sentence." He shook his head, he wasn't happy to be risking their lives. "It's more likely they were afraid we would get information out of them if caught, so they chose to die with their secrets, rather than risk exposing them." Given the Queen's method of questioning, I'd say they had chosen a better ending for themselves.

I nodded a bit. "So, we have nothing?"

"We have another trail leading to The Cavum."

A foreign noblewoman wouldn't know about The Cavum, so as innocently as I could, I asked, "What's that?"

"It's Taros's largest criminal operation. They move around which makes it hard to track, but Mother questioned one of the few surviving attackers we caught. Now we know where it will be tonight. If there is a genuine rebellion brewing, The Cavum would be the first place to look. Killian and I will investigate it tonight." *Shit.* Butcher would have my ass if the crown prince and captain of the royal guard infiltrated The Cavum, and I didn't warn her.

"Won't you be too recognisable?"

"Not if we are careful."

"If it is a criminal underground, surely they are all familiar with your face, Valor."

"It's a risk we have to take. We can't lose this lead."

"Then send someone else. You and Killian can't go, they will surely recognise you."

"And who would you have me send?"

".... Send me." He looked at me like I'd lost it.

"You?"

"Yes, no one will suspect me. I know how to blend. I can get in and out without being noticed. If you and Killian walk in, they will attack you at best, kill you on sight at worst."

"Even if that's true, you are still recovering. You aren't trained to protect yourself or to fight off an attacker, you'd be a liability. I'm not sending you in."

"It could work out well for you, you could kill two birds. Get information, and have me removed."

He frowned. "That's not funny."

"Isn't that what you've been trying to do the entire time I've been here? Get rid of me?"

He sighed. "I may have judged you a little soon, but I would never send you into a death trap, Elia." He looked at me. "I apologise for not being there when you woke up."

His apology caught me off guard.

"... It's fine. I didn't expect you to be there."

"Well, I am sorry for that, too. I haven't made the best impression, and for that, I apologise. I shouldn't have treated you the way I did."

"Okay, you're starting to weird me out. Are you sure *you* didn't stumble into The Wastes, and come out with some mysterious illness that makes you... nice?" I shuddered and Hamish coughed out a laugh. Valor rolled his eyes.

"I probably deserved that. But either way," he met my eyes, "I meant what I said. If I could have been there when you woke, I would have."

How unsettling.

"... Alright."

"And you aren't coming tonight."

I groaned. Luckily, I had another person I could ask. Even if I detested the thought. I nodded a bit and stood up, brushing myself off. He sat up but remained there.

"Enjoy the rest of your day," I said.

"You too Sunshine," he said with a smirk. I rolled my eyes, heading back inside, a soft chuckle sounding as I did. Hamish and Tarryn dutifully stepped into position behind me.

I reached the Queen's chambers much quicker than I would have liked. I'd planned to avoid her at all costs, but Valor had forced my hand. I *needed* to go tonight. I couldn't scale the walls just yet, and I *had* to warn Butcher, preferably also preventing Valor from doing anything stupid.

I knocked, as Hamish and Tarryn took up places with the other guards. A servant opened the door and bowed her head.

"My lady, come in."

"Thank you." I entered, trying to ignore the feeling of dread in my stomach as the door shut.

"This way. I shall see if Her Highness is up for visitors."

I nodded, then at her instruction, waited outside the bedchamber as she entered and announced my presence. She returned a few minutes later, inviting me in, before stepping out herself.

"Thank you, again."

I steeled myself as I stepped into the room. Glancing around, I curtsied, immediately regretting my decision to come here. Odette was lounging on a decadent daybed by the window. She had a glass of wine in her hand and was in a very revealing robe, which appeared to have nothing underneath, and that wasn't even the worst of it.

Tilly sat at the foot of the bed. She was massaging the Queen's calves, dressed in a completely sheer night slip. She wore her wavy red hair down, bright red lip stain, and darkly coloured eyelids. She looked like a different person. I couldn't see her eyes, but I could only imagine what they would behold.

"Elia, It's so nice to see you up and about." Odette smiled and when I met her eyes briefly, she had that unhinged look in them again. I couldn't quite pin it down. They appeared vacant and yet not, present and yet far away. It was unsettling. Was using her magic so often driving her mad?

"Oh, I'm sorry." I averted my eyes. "I didn't realise you were... busy. I can return at a better time."

"Oh no, it's perfectly fine." She waved a hand. "Matilda doesn't mind. Do you, Matilda?"

I glanced at Tilly. Dread coiled in my stomach like a parasite.

Tilly glanced at me then. Her eyes were—she looked normal, like she was in full control and under no influence. So different from the look she'd worn the last time I'd seen her. She'd appeared drugged out of her mind in that cage, but now she appeared perfectly sober and sane. I wasn't sure if that was good or bad.

"Of course not. I always enjoy your company, Lady Elia. Would you like me to give you two some privacy, Odette?" She was calling the queen by her first name, not appropriate for just any lady's maid, but Odette didn't seem to mind.

"That is quite alright, Matilda, you carry on." Tilly nodded and continued her massaging. I swallowed. I had to convince Odette to let me go tonight.

I watched Tilly with what I hoped was a look of awe and not disgust.

"Incredible. How...?" Looking back to Odette, I must have appeared as impressed as I'd hoped, because pride shone in her eyes.

"With a lot of work. It's why I haven't been to see you, dear. It's very exhausting fine-tuning my work."

I walked over and took a seat by her daybed. "That's amazing. I've never seen anything so powerful. I hope you aren't overexerting yourself, though?" Concern laced my tone.

She smiled. "I may have overdone it a little, but it was worth it. I am recovering now."

"What exactly did you do?"

She lit up like an excited child showing off a new toy.

"Plants are living, meaning they can work on their own. I had to spend a lot of time correcting Matilda's mind."

"Correcting?"

"Yes, I have fixed her. Where before, she was dull, meek, and disobedient, she is now the perfect specimen. Beautiful, obedient, and loyal. As long as I tend to what now lives in her mind, and keep it maintained like any other garden, it will grow and behave the way I designed."

I repressed a shiver. "How did you achieve such a thing? It's equal to the power of a goddess." Delight shone in her eyes at the goddess comparison, causing nausea to rise in my stomach.

"As you know, I infiltrated her mind using a plant of my creation. Which allowed me to, without boring you with the details, retrain her mind. But as you saw, it is exhausting. So, I have spent a significant amount of time slowly improving her, recreating her. Once I'd successfully achieved that, the plant only needs to stay in place to ensure my alterations also stay in place. I don't need to be constantly controlling it. It is a living organism with a purpose I created for it. Therefore, it can operate autonomously. I simply have to prune and nurture it now and then."

"What have you rewritten her mind to think... or do, though? She seems like herself, yet not?"

Odette nodded. "She is still herself. I have simply altered her. She now knows that she answers to me. Her desire is to please me. When she does so, her mind is flooded with endorphins, depending on how pleased I am by her actions, of course. It creates a natural high, which has made her quite the willing subject. The allure of euphoria will do that to most people I suppose."

Divinities, she's turned her into a high functioning addict.

"Wow, that is—I have no words, Your Majesty."

"Would you like to see?" No. I really, really didn't. I honestly thought I might throw up. This was so wrong, and I had no clue how to stop it.

"Oh, no. That seems like too much trouble. I don't want to wear you out anymore. I actually came here to ask you about something else."

She grinned. "Not to worry, dear, now that I've done the hard work as long as I am close, it doesn't require much power. It is no trouble at all." She returned her attention to Tilly, and I steeled myself.

"Matilda, I would like for you to forget your name."

Tilly just smiled at Odette and continued massaging. I frowned.

"Ask her." She insisted. I hesitated, opening my mouth to politely decline, but what came out was an address to Tilly. This damned oath, I felt as if I were watching myself through a glass wall. Those were my words, my mouth, and my voice, but it wasn't me.

"What is your name?"

Tilly looked at me as confusion crossed her features.

"I.... don't know..... I—" she stopped massaging "—I don't know my name." Panic seeped into her features, and it took everything in me not to go to her, to try to comfort her.

"... That is incredible," I forced out. I hated myself, but the other version of me, the one driven by Butcher's command to win her over, simply stared in awe, even smiling a little. Odette grinned proudly.

"You might think that she *could* simply be a talented actress? That would be a reasonable assumption." She glanced at Matilda. "Remember your name, Matilda. It will please me greatly if you do."

Tilly looked at Odette, her eyes lighting up with relief and recognition, before they rolled back into her head and she fell to her knees, causing me to jump slightly in surprise. I looked to Odette who was watching with a satisfied smirk on her face. Tilly was panting as she slid down to the floor, letting her body relax completely.

"Is she okay?" This time I couldn't hide the concern, or the touch of horror, that was woven into my words. Apparently the oath had determined expressing concern an acceptable response that wouldn't jeopardise the queen's favour.

"Oh, she's very okay. I trained her mind to release endorphins when she knows she has satisfied me. I have taught her to recognise the signs of my pleasure. She will respond to verbal confirmation but also physical tells like a smile, a look or.... other things." Odette watched Tilly with something akin to hunger as she said the last bit. I refrained from imagining what 'other things' referred to.

"How big of a reaction I have determines how much pleasure she will feel, which is why she is so intent on keeping me happy. Her mind is desperate for that feeling. It's akin to experiencing a certain drug or extreme joy. She is more than okay. But I know what you're thinking; she could still be faking. Matilda, stop breathing."

I tensed as Tilly, indeed, now held her breath, her eyes still locked onto Odette's. Odette had an enormous smile on her face and was nodding encouragingly, which only made Tilly's smile grow as she tilted her head back in ecstasy. *Divinities.* Although she was losing air, although she was suffocating, at the same time she was feeling pleasure? She was enjoying dying!

"Oh no. This isn't necessary. I believe you," I said too quickly, stepping forward. I couldn't just watch her die. If I intervened, I'd risk blowing my cover, but what other choice did I have? Regardless of her crimes, she did not deserve this. I had to overcome this damned command. A girl's life was at stake!

Tilly's face was turning red. It felt like a minute had passed, and she was still holding her breath. I dug my nails into my palm. She wouldn't kill her, she wouldn't let her die after going to so much trouble, surely?

"Your Highness?" I asked, worry clear in my voice. "You can stop."

Tilly passed out, having run out of oxygen, but when she still did not breathe, panic filled me and I dropped to the ground beside her, feeling for her pulse. Odette simply giggled.

Giggled.

"You can breathe now, Matilda. Wake up and continue your duties. You have pleased me greatly."

Tilly immediately woke up. She stood, moving back to her earlier position, and began massaging the queen's legs again, a pleasant smile on her face and a glazed look in her eyes, despite her ragged breathing and lack of colour.

"Convinced now, Elia?"

I don't know how I managed it, but I laughed a bit. "I would be a fool if I wasn't. That was incredible. A power like that is terrifying, but..." I shook my head, "you are incredibly gifted, Your Majesty."

She smiled. "Thank you, but you didn't come here to praise me, child. What can I do for you?"

It took me a second to refocus on why I had come. I was struggling to take my eyes off of Tilly, in fear of her dropping dead at any second. I had to find a way to get her out of here.

"I saw Prince Valor today. He told me they had been tracking the attackers, and that one man you questioned gave you a lead. He said that he and Killian are planning to go to The Cavum tonight. I expressed my concerns to him, however, he wouldn't listen. I was hoping you would hear them?" She nodded for me to continue, taking a sip of her wine.

"If this truly is an underground crime syndicate, surely people will recognise the faces of the crown prince, and the Captain of the Guard together? It's not sound for Valor to go. I volunteered. I might not be a warrior, but as you've already determined, I'm excellent at gathering information. I can blend in and I know how to read people. You saw something in me, enough to share your secret. Let me repay the favour by ensuring your son does not take unnecessary risks, and by getting you the intel you need."

She watched me thoughtfully. "You make a good point regarding them being recognised together. It is quite an enormous risk."

"He could remain close, but the less noticeable he is, the better. It seems wiser to send less noticeable people in to look around. Let me prove I am worthy of your trust, Your Highness. I will not let you down." I bowed my head in respect.

She looked at Tilly. "Matilda, get dressed and fetch my son."

Tilly stood. "Yes, Your Majesty." She left the bedroom, presumably to cover up, and then seek the prince.

"I appreciate you coming to me, Elia. My son is young and untested. He lets his heart get the best of him sometimes, much like his father, which leads them to do heroic, but reckless, things. It will be best if you aren't here when I talk to him. He will be more than a little annoyed at you having come to me at all."

I nodded. "You are most likely right. I will return to my chambers. If you need me, simply send word."

She smiled warmly. "Thank you, Elia"

Taking the cue, I left as calmly as I could. I nodded at Hamish and Tarryn before making my way back to my room. I closed the door, ran straight to the bathroom and hurled the contents of my stomach up. Tears stung my eyes, and I clenched them shut. My breathing increased. *What I had just done? What had I let happen?*

CHAPTER TWENTY-THREE

I THREW UP AGAIN. *Fates,* I had to free Tilly. I couldn't panic. I had to keep my head. Taking a deep breath, I stood and leaned against the sink, splashing water onto my face. *I could do this. I had to for Sierra.* I couldn't lose sight of that.

A knock sounded. I quickly dried my face, went to the door, and opened it. Valor was standing there, his begrudgingly handsome face twisted in anger. *That was fast.* He stormed past me.

"Uh, *sure.* Come on in?"

He spun to face me, reaching over me to push the door shut, then backing me up against it.

"Where do you get off going to my mother behind my back?"

"At least buy me a drink first."

He gave me an unamused glare. Up this close I could see the fury in his eyes, mixed with something else. Whatever it was, it was charged and captivating.

"You were making a bad call."

"That is none of your business."

"You made it my business when you told me, Valor."

He scoffed. "Clearly, that was a mistake."

Yes, probably. "I am sorry, but I knew if I told you, you would have stopped me. I am trying to help. You could get yourself killed."

"Oh, this is for my wellbeing? Not your need to impress my mother?" He moved closer, we were practically pressed against each other now, and I took no satisfaction in how well our bodies seemed to fit.

"I don't need to impress your mother." I crossed my arms, putting some much needed distance. *Lie.*

He shook his head, looking down at me. "No?"

"No. I was just trying to protect you, the same way you protected me during the attack." That seemed to catch him a little off guard, as he opened his mouth, but nothing came out. He closed it and sighed, running a hand through his hair.

"You are infuriating."

I bit my lip. "I know."

He looked at my lips and then at my eyes. He said nothing, and the silence stretched out just a moment too long.

"Are you going to say something? Or just stare at me for another five minutes?"

He shook his head and stepped back. "Well, your plan partially worked. Mother wants you to come tonight, despite my arguments about you not being fully recovered."

"Why *partially*?"

"I am going in with you. Killian will wait outside."

Oh, joy. This just keeps getting better.

The woman staring back at me in the mirror was the perfect depiction of darkness. I donned a tight-fitting black bodice with pants and boots. I had a cloak fastened around my shoulders, my eyelids covered in kohl, and my lips stained in a maroon red. I'd pulled my hair back, with a few loose strands framing my face, and there were weapons fastened to my belt, well on display, although I couldn't really use any of them.

I embodied a woman who welcomed trouble. *Ironic.* It felt odd to be going out with no gaiter, but I needed to at least pretend I wasn't adept at covert operations.

Valor was waiting for me when I stepped into the hall, and I had to do a double-take. His pants and boots were dark like mine, but much more masculine. He wore a dark grey, loose tunic, with one too many buttons undone, and a singular blade sheathed to his side.

His hair was tousled a bit, a stark contrast to the usually neat and slicked back way that he favoured. He looked like your average, arrogant thief. When I looked at his face, he was also appraising my costume for the night.

"Ready?" I asked.

He said nothing as his eyes continued to take me in.

"Well?" I said, ignoring the way my body tensed as his gaze wandered, as if in anticipation.

He grumbled something inaudible, possibly a 'yes', and started walking. *Charming.*

We met Killian at the gates, holding the reins of a horse. One horse, apparently we'd be sharing. He nodded at me.

"Lady Elia. That look suits you."

I chuckled. "I enjoy the pants, but the rest is a bit much."

He smiled a little. "Glad to see you in good spirits after the attack."

I nodded. "Likewise."

"This is a stupid plan." Valor complained. It felt like it was the thousandth time he'd done so.

"Then don't come." I shrugged. He rolled his eyes, taking the reins from Killian.

"You two will take a horse to the location of tonight's fight. You shouldn't draw too much attention dressed the way you are. Most will assume you're a couple there to earn some coin betting on the contenders."

I nodded slightly.

"I'll follow close by and keep to the shadows," He glanced at Valor. "If the situation goes south, you know where to meet."

Valor nodded. We mounted, and rode into the heart of the Kendelen slums.

"Follow my lead when we get in, Elia. I can't have you screwing this up."

I rolled my eyes.

"The whole reason I am here is so *you* don't screw it up." I was there to do exactly what he was afraid of, *yet another lie.*

We dismounted and headed to the door. He casually slid his arm around my shoulder, and I watched as his demeanour changed. He appeared an arrogant delinquent, keen for a night of gambling and drinking. Me, his arm candy.

Standing at the door was none other than Tolemas himself. I kept my face neutral. I was banking on him seeing me at some point, so he could notify Butcher, but I didn't think he would be on door duty. They either knew we were coming, or something else was up.

"State ya' business." Tolemas crossed his muscular arms. The prince was in good shape, but Tolemas still looked like he could crush him with one hand.

"Same as everyone else. Here to win big, man." He grinned and lightly punched Tolemas's arm. Tolemas did not appear amused.

"Ya gotta pay to play."

"Of course," Valor said and pulled out a bag of coin, "is this enough for me and my lady?" He grinned. I giggled as one might when the man she was interested in referred to her as *his* lady.

Tolemas rolled his eyes, checked the bag, and stepped aside.

"'Ave a good night."

"Thanks, champ." Valor smiled and led us inside.

"Champ?" I muttered.

"That's how they talk here."

I almost laughed. *Bloody Hek.* I took in the room as we made our way to the bar. It looked as it had the last time I was here. They'd cordoned off a large square in the centre of the room, the fighting ring, where criminals bet and fought with only one rule; no weapons. Often bloody, and without honour, Tolemas always did well here.

There were curtained booths around the room. Some open, some closed. There were women serving food and drinks, all dressed in what I could only describe as bedchamber attire. Certainly not appropriate for the public.

Men would pluck one from her task and onto their laps without care, and the woman would let them. I glanced up to where I knew the high rollers watched. To where Butcher likely was. We reached the bar, and Valor ordered us both a tankard of ale. I took a sip, and he did the same, glancing around the room.

"Stay here. I'm going to scout the room. Do not go *anywhere*."

I rolled my eyes at his emphasis on 'anywhere.'

"Yes, father."

He shook his head walked away. I waited until he'd disappeared among the crowd before heading in the opposite direction. Someone stepped into my path, and I stopped glancing up.

"This way, Little Sparrow." I gritted my teeth, but Tolemas simply turned and started walking before I could tell him off for using the old nickname. I followed him up a familiar stairway leading to a curtained doorway. He held the curtain open, and I stepped in, taking off my hood.

"Adira, it is about time." Butcher purred from her seat across from me. I imagined her with a glass of wine in hand as she flipped through a ledger. I couldn't actually see her, thanks to the thick black mesh that divided the room in half. She used this mesh to conceal her identity when dealing with those she didn't trust. She had obviously just finished up a meeting, or was having one soon, if the dark wall was already in place, making it impossible to even glimpse an outline of her.

"I came as soon as I could. I'm not here alone and I don't have much time."

"Yes, Tolemas informed me you brought a date."

"Someone told the queen about tonight's fight. They have linked the rebel attack to The Cavum."

She sighed. "I knew that was a potential outcome."

"Did you know about the attack? I almost died. Someone *stabbed* me with a poisoned bloody blade."

"I knew about it, but did not sanction it. Solis also claims she was unaware until it was too late. The Rise has many followers who often have their own grudges against The Crown and act accordingly. Solis extends her apologies that you were injured in the crossfire."

I scoffed. "Tell her to control her damned people, or I can't do my job."

"Speaking of your job, report. Now." My chest tugged forcefully, and I hastily gave her my report of everything that had occurred since I last saw her. She certainly wasn't wasting time tonight, which I supposed was a good thing.

She'd taken particular interest when I'd told her about the situation with Odette, asking some follow-up questions.

"This is very good. The queen trusts you. The princess is naïve and clearly desperate for a friend. The king, for whatever reason, is treating you as family, and the prince, well, even he is warming to you."

"Weren't you listening? I would not call his behaviour towards me *warm*."

"You will see."

I shook my head.

"This is not what I signed up for. I won't be involved with this rebellion or the horrible shit going on in that castle. You didn't see what she did to that girl. This wasn't part of the deal."

"The deal was for you to follow my commands until I say otherwise, Adira."

"This is bullshit. I have done everything you asked, and then some! I took a *knife* to the *abdomen*."

I could tell by the tone of her voice that she was frowning. "You are being very disrespectful, Adira."

"Please. I've done more than what you asked. Let me and Sierra go. You don't need me."

I heard the sound of a glass being placed on a table and the atmosphere of the room changed to a deadly calm.

"What did I tell you about that attitude of yours, Adira? I warned you there would be consequences if you acted this way again."

"Camilla, *please*. You must have some tiny shred of sympathy for us. You are the closest thing Sierra knows to a mother. You were our family." A screwed up family, but still a family. Surely some part of her cared for us.

She sighed. "That was always your problem. You let your feelings get the better of you, no matter how hard we tried to beat it out of you. Enough of this. Your guest will notice you are missing soon. You will continue to gather any information you can and report back to me. I've had enough of the attitude. Do your job." My chest tugged, and I clenched my fist.

"Win the prince over. Make him trust you by any means necessary. He is the last puzzle piece. We will help where we can." *Tug.* "Now go, get out of my face."

I had no choice but to walk out, anger boiling through me like a hot spring. Tolemas watched, but said nothing as I walked back down the staircase.

Someone standing beside it caught my eye.

"Nice get up." Mal snorted as I surveyed the room, keeping an eye out for Valor.

"Gotta change it up once in a while."

"You know soon enough someone with half a brain will recognise your companion, right?"

"Yep, so unless there's a purpose to this little chat, I best go make the most of the time I've got."

"Something is happening, kid."

"Can you be more specific?"

She shook her head. "People are going to ground."

I frowned. "Who? Why?"

"Some of the big power players, those that are usually in the know, those closest to the borders. Murmurs of rebellion are getting louder and louder."

"You think people know what's coming?"

"All I'm sayin' is, keep your head down and your ears open. Whatever's brewin', it's not far off." She glanced around. "Your friend's coming back. You best be goin'."

I glanced over to see she was right. Valor was looking around and frowning.

"Cheers Mal."

I headed toward where Valor had left me, but not before I caught Mal say quietly.

"It's all connected, kid. The attempted assassination, the rebel attacks, the advisors' secret meetings, even whatever you're doing. I hope you know what you're gettin' yourself into." Advisors secret meetings? I'd have to question her about that another time.

I held back my resigned sigh as I reached Valor. I definitely didn't, and there was nothing I could do about it.

"There you are. Where the Hek did you go?" He demanded.

"Relax, I had to use the privy." He looked at me incredulously. "Did you find anything?"

"No, not yet. A meeting is supposed to take place in an hour. We have to blend until then." If he can go on unrecognised for that long. I nodded, taking a big swig of my drink.

"You better place a bet or people will notice. Back the little one."

He gave me a curious look as we walked over to the ring to inspect the upcoming fighters.

There was a mix of people. Men and women. No way to tell if any of them were Para. Certainly no Pures though, they wouldn't sully themselves by participating in an event with Impures. Whatever he observed was enough to convince him, apparently. He backed the man I'd suggested and won.

We made a show of excitement and eagerness, watching the bloodshed unfold. Placing some more bets, we drank, and we laughed. We even danced a little. Valor was touching me at all times, with either an arm around my shoulder or my waist. At one point, he pulled me onto his lap, which I made silently clear he would hear about when we were out of here.

"There." He nodded toward a man in a cloak who sat down in a booth. The man glanced around and my breathing hitched. His eyes were white. No pupils. It was the man from the library.

"Creepy," Valor said, "the rebel mother questioned, mentioned a man with white eyes. I didn't realise he meant... that."

I swallowed. "How unsettling."

"We need to get closer." We got up, and I giggled loudly as we made our way through the crowd, sitting down at a table much closer. "Now, we wait and see who else arrives."

A man and woman were the first to arrive. They looked eerily similar, both with darker skin and bright blue eyes. I'd hazard a guess that they were siblings, rather than a couple. They nodded to the white-eyed man but remained silent as they sat down.

An enormous man followed, with a scar that ran down the left side of his face and neck. Was it a prerequisite that all bad guys had facial scars? He had two short swords strapped to his back. Grinning, he shook the white-eyed man's hand before taking a seat beside him and ordering a tankard of ale.

A woman showed up next, dressed in what looked like lightweight armour. I couldn't discern any symbols or sigils that might give away where it came from. A cloaked man was the last arrival. He removed his hood and his blonde curls fell free.

I froze. I'd know that hair, those blue eyes, anywhere. Shaking hands and smiling at the white-eyed man was Raf. He took a seat with the others, and the curtain was pulled shut.

"Are you alright?" Valor asked, sensing my tension. I forced myself to calm down and nodded.

"We need a better visual. We need to get into that booth."

"That's impossible."

"It's not, but you have to trust me." I stood, but he caught me by the wrist. Rolling my eyes, I explained my plan.

"No way, it's too risky."

"I'm willing to take the risk. You said it yourself. We need this win. Trust me, Valor, please?" I looked at him, he looked back. He closed his eyes and released my wrist.

"First sign of danger. You get the Hek out of there. Do you understand?"

I nodded. "I'll be fine."

I walked to the *actual* privy this time, removing my cloak and pants, revealing the shortest skirt I had ever worn. I tightened my bodice, pushed up my cleavage, and undid my hair, letting it fall down my back. I looked like the women working tonight.

I stashed my clothes under the sink and went back out to the bar, aware of Valor tracking my every move. I slipped behind the bar, poured a few tankards, and approached the white-eyed man's booth. I quietly slipped in, and dutifully went about setting down the tankards of ale, as well as collecting the empty ones.

CHAPTER TWENTY-FOUR

M OST OF THE ROOM paid me no heed, but I saw Raf's eyes widen a fraction, and I saw the scarred man take in my outfit appreciatively.

"You all know why you are here. For one reason or another, you are all in a position to help the cause," the white-eyed man said.

"Why should we interfere? It sounds like you need us more than we need you." The armoured woman said in a thick accent I couldn't place. The blue-eyed siblings nodded their agreement.

"Because you're just as sick of your people being treated like the rest of us. Anyone who visits the capital might believe the lies The Crown so skilfully spreads, but you have all seen the truth. You know what happens to people like us outside the borders of Kendelen and in other lands." *People like us? Was he talking about Impures?*

"And you think we can change it? People have tried and failed. What makes you any different?" The scarred man questioned, even though his eyes hadn't left my ass.

"Solis is the difference. With them, we can win. You heard about the recent attack? That was but a minor example of their reach. A message telling The Crown we can still get to them, regardless of how many walls and soldiers they hide behind."

"We are yet to meet this Solis. I'd like to hear it from her," the woman said.

"Solis will not waste time meeting those that have not shown their loyalty."

"What do you need from us?" Raf asked, and I had to refrain from shouting at him.

"You all have a part to play. All that we ask is that you be ready to play it when the time comes. We will be in touch with each of you individually. Tonight was simply a chance for you to meet one another and have questions answered. And perhaps enjoy a few rounds of drinks." He chuckled. "The tab is on Solis and The Butcher."

"Now, that, I can get behind," the scarred man said, pulling me onto his lap, "are the staff also on offer?" He smirked down at me and I kept my face neutral.

The white-eyed man looked at me and shrugged. "I suppose the only way a woman would go near you is if we paid her." He waved his hand. "I've been instructed to see that you enjoy yourselves tonight, by any means necessary." *Well, that is not good.*

"Excellent. In that case, I've had enough business talk and would like to move on to the pleasurable part of the evening." His hand slid up my side.

"At least let her fetch us another round before you have your way with her." Raf chuckled. "A man could die of thirst otherwise."

"Mmm, you make a good point." He slapped my ass. "Be a darl and fetch us some pints, gorgeous."

I smiled politely at him and rose, exiting the booth. *Disgusting brute.*

I went back to the bar and refilled their glasses, glancing around. I took out a tiny vial, courtesy of Odette, and slipped it into one of the glasses. The siblings were leaving the booth when I reentered. The woman was engaged in conversation with the white-eyed man, and Raf was chatting to the scarred one. I walked over, placing the ales down, and was promptly placed back in the man's lap, much to my dismay. He picked up his pint.

"What excellent service." He grinned and took a swig. Raf picked his drink up, and leaning back, did the same. The woman rolled her eyes and left.

The white-eyed man simply smiled. "Enjoy your night gentlemen, if you need me I will be upstairs."

The scarred man raised his cup to him and Raf nodded in thanks as he left. Leaving just Raf, the scarred man, and me.

"Well, if you don't mind, kid. I'd like to see just how good the service is. In private."

"Oh, you don't like sharing, Borys?" Raf questioned.

"Not unless it's with women, I'm afraid." His calloused hand slid up my thigh as he took another swig.

Raf looked at me, and I shook my head the slightest bit and flicked my eyes to the exit. He seemed like he might argue, but I shook my head again, glancing at Borys's cup.

Raf understood. "That's a shame, perhaps next time. Let me know how she goes." He smirked and exited the booth. If I'd played this right, Valor would be too preoccupied with the fact that neither I nor Borys had left the booth to follow Raf.

Borys's hand slid further up my leg. "What's your name, love?"

"Whatever you want it to be, Sir," I said in as sultry a voice as I could manage, trailing my finger lightly down his chest. He chuckled.

"Oh, is that so?" His hand moved to my inner thigh, and he leaned in, placing a kiss on my neck.

I tilted my head to the side, trying to picture anything other than the current scene, and nodded.

"You can call me whatever you like."

"It doesn't really matter." He placed his pint down and put his now free hand over my breast and squeezed. "Exquisite."

I was grateful he couldn't see the grimace on my face or the rage no doubt burning in my eyes.

"Mmm." My hand pressed against his chest.

Valor stormed into the booth and drew his dagger, right as the drug I had laced Borys's drink with kicked in, his head falling forward onto my chest.

Valor's eyes were full of anger as he practically growled. "Get your hands off her. *Now*."

"Valor, relax," I said, grabbing Borys's hair and yanking his head back. "He's out cold."

Valor sheathed his dagger. "What the Hek are you doing?"

"What needed to be done to ensure we got the information we needed? Now, are you going to help me?"

He groaned and walked over. "You should have told me."

"Would you have allowed it?"

"Probably not." He admitted.

"Exactly. I wanted to tell you, but your mother ordered me not to. She knew you wouldn't risk me, but agreed this might be necessary."

I looked at him, and he sighed. "Can you support some of his weight? He's a big man."

"I should be able to. Help me get him up." We each took up a side and slung his arms around each of our shoulders.

"Ready?" I asked.

Valor nodded. "This better work."

"It will. Less talking, more walking." He shot me a glare before we began carrying him out. We smiled and laughed, acting like a group of drunken patrons, whose friend had indulged in a little too much liquor.

Tolemas was manning the door again. He held it open without a word as we slipped out into the night. I breathed out in relief, but it was short-lived. We still had to get him back to the castle.

"Killian should be around the bend. It's just a little further."

I nodded, and we carried him around the corner. The captain was indeed waiting, with raised eyebrows, once he saw we weren't alone.

"Get him back to the castle and into a cell. Inform Mother you have a prisoner for her to question. We will meet you back there."

Killian nodded and together, all three of us hoisted him up onto the horse before Killian joined him and took off towards the castle. I started walking back to where we had left our own horse, but Valor grabbed my waist and pinned me against the closest wall. *What was with him and walls?*

"Excuse me?"

"What you did in there was reckless and stupid," he said, looking into my eyes.

I sighed. "It was nothing you wouldn't have done if you'd had the opportunity, Valor. I was fine. It was your mother's idea."

"My mother doesn't care who gets hurt if it gets her the information, Elia! You could have been captured, or worse."

"But I wasn't."

"You could have been!"

"Why the Hek do you even care, Valor!?"

"BECAUSE I DO!" He breathed out and closed his eyes. "The last thing I need is news spreading of a foreign lady dying whilst in my care." For a second, I thought he might say something else.

I wanted to shake my head and yell at him for seeing me as a publicity problem waiting to happen, instead of a human being, but that pull in my chest wouldn't let me. *Win the Prince over.*

My voice softened as I sighed and placed a hand on his chest. "I am sorry. I didn't mean to worry you. Next time, I won't hide anything from you."

He opened his eyes and looked down at me, finally noting how close we were.

"Next time?"

I smiled a bit. "Oh, come on. We make a good team, don't we?"

He groaned. "You are impossible." But I saw the smile tugging at the edge of his lips.

I shrugged, biting my lip. "I heard you enjoyed a good challenge."

His gaze dropped to my mouth, eyes darkening as he watched me.

"Is that what you are? A challenge?"

I grinned and shrugged again.

He shook his head. "Come on, we have to get back."

He stepped back, and we continued on to our horse, riding back to the castle in a very different silence to the previous ride.

When we arrived back at the castle, Valor walked me to my room. On the way, I filled him in on everything I'd heard while in the booth. He was going to watch the questioning and see if they could use what I'd told him.

I nodded, said goodnight, and entered my room. I needed to get to Raf somehow, tonight may be the only good chance, while everyone was distracted with Borys. The question was, how? Hamish and Tarryn were still posted outside.

I walked to the balcony railing and looked down. They had removed my stitches, but the wound was still a little tender. I would like to avoid scaling walls if I could, but what other options did I have? Maybe I could convince Cali to help me sneak out if it was for a good enough reason. It would be a risk, but it was my best option.

I made my way to Cali's chambers, which were conveniently close now. I knocked and waited. She opened the door in her nightclothes.

"Elle, hey, come in." She stepped aside, and I smiled, entering.

"Thanks. Are you busy?"

"No, I was just reading. Is everything okay?" She said, shutting the door.

"Sort of. I was hoping to ask a favour, but I understand if you say no."

"Now I'm very curious. What's up?"

"... I need you to help me sneak out."

She raised her eyebrows. "Sneak out to where?"

I sighed and closed my eyes. "To see a man."

She squealed. "A MAN?!"

"SHHH!" I looked to the door where Hamish and Tarryn were inevitably on guard.

"Who?! Tell me everything!" At least she whisper-shouted this time.

"Do you remember our conversation about wanting people you can't have? About the man from back home?" Her eyes widened further, and she nodded. "I received a letter from him. He's here in Taros. I haven't been able to see him because it was too much of a risk if I hope to convince people your brother and I are..."

"Oh my Fates, why didn't you tell me?!"

I felt bad for lying to her, but what other choice did I have?

"I wasn't sure what you would think since I'm supposed to be 'betrothed' to your brother. I need to see him, if only to tell him I can't see him again, but Hamish and Tarryn follow me everywhere. It's impossible to get out undetected."

"Oh, I can help!" She walked over to her vanity and felt along the wall until she found a barely noticeable indentation. *Another tunnel?* Sure enough, a click sounded, and the wall shifted in on itself, exposing a long, dark, tunnel.

"James, Kil, Val and I would sneak around these tunnels when we were kids and then, when we got older, and wanted to sneak into town without our parents knowing." Based on the look on her face, I had a feeling she and Killian had also used these tunnels without Valor being present.

"Do they run throughout the castle?"

"Only through the old wings. They blocked the rest off. But there's an exit that leads to town. I can show you!"

"Are you sure?"

"Of course!" She grinned. "Let's go."

"Uh, do you want to put something warmer on?"

"Oh no, I'll be fine. These are warmer than they look."

I laughed a bit. "If you say so."

She lit a torch on the wall, grabbed it, and then my hand, practically pulling me down the tunnel. She was right. There were hallways branching off, and I made mental notes. We stopped at an old-looking iron gate. I could see it led to a garden.

"This opens up in the centre gardens. Are you able to find your man's lodgings from there?"

"Yes, I should be able to."

"Okay, I will light the torches that lead back to your room, so when you come back, you can find your way. I'll dismiss your guards for the night. I'll say we are having a sleepover or something." She hugged me then, and I hugged back.

"Thank you, Cali. It really means a lot."

"Of course, anything for romance." She winked and then nudged me forward. "Off you go. I expect to hear all the juicy details tomorrow!"

I laughed a little. "It's a date." I smiled, pushed open the gate, and started down the path.

I had to duck under thick branches and force my way through the hanging vines. Eventually, I emerged into the garden. The vines had fallen back into place when I turned around. You would never know there wasn't a wall behind them.

I looked around, gathering my bearings, before hurrying to Raf's loft. I didn't risk knocking in case it woke Sierra. I prayed she was asleep.

Taking a pin out of my hair and picking the lock, I opened the door, wincing at the small creaking noise it made. I carefully shut and relocked it. Thankfully, Sierra slept peacefully on the couch as I tiptoed up to Raf's bedroom and pushed open the door. He was already up, holding a—*was that a sword? When did he get a sword?*

He relaxed, lowering his weapon once he saw it was me.

"Divinities, Adira. You scared the shit out of me." He put the sword down and walked over, attempting to pull me into a hug. Before he could, I punched him square in the jaw. He winced slightly, clearly not having expected that, though I'm pretty sure it hurt me more than him. Then I threw my arms around him, hugging him tightly.

"You bloody idiot," I mumbled into his chest.

"You're giving me mixed signals here, Adi?" He hugged me back, just as tightly.

I stayed in his arms for a few moments before I pulled back.

"What in Ades name were you thinking, Raf? A rebel meeting?!"

"What were *you* doing there, Adira?"

"I asked you first."

He smiled a bit. "Sit with me and I'll explain? Please...?"

I sighed and followed him to his bed. We sat down and I looked at him expectantly.

"I thought you were in danger, Adira. Sierra heard talk from your old crew that Butcher had you, and was going to sell you to someone at that meeting. I had no idea what it was really for."

My eyes widened. "That's ridiculous."

"How is that more ridiculous than anything else that has happened?" *He had a point.*

"Why in Infernis is Sierra talking to anyone from Butcher's crew? They can't be trusted, she knows that."

"She hadn't heard from you, Adira. Neither of us had. She figured it was worth the risk to find out if you were still even alive." I sighed and closed my eyes.

"I told you in the letters that I—"

"Oh yeah, the letters. You mean the ones you left after sneaking out without a proper goodbye? Saying you wouldn't be able to contact us for a while, to look after each other, and if you haven't checked in after a few months, to board the first ship we can find and leave the continent without you? *Those* letters?" He seethed.

".... Yeah... those."

He shook his head. "How could you leave with only a damned letter, Adira? After everything?" It was rare that Raf got this angry with me, but I could tell by the hard set of his jaw that it was more than that. I'd hurt him.

"I had no choice, Raf. You would have tried to make me stay and I couldn't. I had to go, you know that."

He ran his fingers through his hair. I could see he was frustrated, part of him agreeing with me.

"What were you doing there tonight?"

"It's safer if you don't know."

"Dammit, Adira..."

"No, listen to me, Raf. I am sorry. I really am, but I just came here to tell you to stay the Hek away from the rebels, Butcher, the white-eyed man, all of it. It's too dangerous. I can't lose you or Sierra, or this whole thing will have been for nothing."

"Give me more than that, Adira."

"I can't."

"Can't or won't?"

"Does it matter?"

Pain entered his eyes as he looked at me. "Is that all you came for? Message received."

I sighed. "Raf...." I reached for him, but he moved away.

"If that is truly the only reason you came, then you should go. Before someone notices you're gone." He looked away from me and my heart ached. It was probably better this way. The less attached to me he was, the better. He would still protect Sierra, no matter how mad he was. So I stood and stepped back.

"... Stay away from them, Raf. I mean it."

"Yeah, I heard you the first time."

I swallowed back the pain. "I'm sorry." I stepped out of his bedroom, shutting the door. My eyes were closed as I willed myself to leave.

"Ira?" A sleepy voice said. My eyes shot to the bottom of the staircase, finding Sierra clutching the pendant I'd bought her. Seeing her awake and sitting there like that undid me.

I hurried down the steps, embracing her tightly.

CHAPTER TWENTY-FIVE

She hugged me back just as tight, tighter even. "How long are you staying?"

"I have to leave in a minute," I said, breathing her in. She smelt like her, and something else. Something familiar, but I couldn't put my finger on it. Roses maybe? Had she been gardening?

She simply nodded, leaning back a little. "I've missed you. I thought—I heard that you..."

I shook my head. "Listen to me, okay?" I put my hand on her cheek. "Believe nothing you hear from Butcher's crew, okay? Or Butcher. I will make sure if anything happens to me, a message is sent to you, but unless you get that message, you know I am okay. Do not trust any of them."

She nodded a bit. "I'm sorry. I didn't mean to endanger Raf." She looked down, seeming every bit the little girl she would always be to me, even though she was practically a grown woman now. My little sister, who would cry if she harmed a fly.

"Shh, it's alright. He's okay." I hugged her again.

She hugged me back, burying her face into my shirt.

"I need you to be strong for me alright, Squirt?" It had been a long time since I'd called her that. Long enough that I could feel her pulling a face against my chest, which made me smile.

"I will."

I pulled back and kissed her forehead. "I know you will." I smiled softly. "I have to go. I love you more than anything. It's you and me against it all, right?"

"Right." She nodded. "I love you too, Adira."

I stepped back. "This will all be over before you know it." I winked and walked out the door, unable to shake the feeling that it might be one of the last times I did so.

I kept to the shadows as I made my way back to the gardens, trying desperately to forget the look on Raf's face when he'd turned away from me or how it made me feel. I told myself it was better this way, over and over, until hopefully, I could believe it.

Once I was back in the tunnels, I followed the torches Cali had lit. Luckily, none had gone out. When I got to the final one, I noticed a crown carved above the doorway. I guess it marked the rooms in the royal wing? I felt along the wall until I found the odd piece and pressed it. The wall shifted.

I stepped into the bedchamber beyond. Only it wasn't mine. *Shit.* I went to step back into the tunnel, which was the moment Valor exited his bathroom in nothing but a towel, immediately spotting me. His eyes widened.

"Elia?" His eyes flicked from the tunnel, to me, and back again. *That sneaky little...* I was going to kill Cali.

"... I can explain?"

He crossed his arms, drawing my attention to his chest. His very well sculpted chest that still housed a few droplets from his recent bath.

"Enlighten me."

"This is apparently Cali's idea of a prank."

He raised his eyebrows. "Cali's?"

"She wanted to show me the tunnels. She apparently thought it would be funny to get me lost down there. Eventually, I found a torch lit path and followed it. I thought it would lead back to her chambers or mine." Sometimes, I was alarmed at how quickly I could lie through my teeth.

"You two were playing in the tunnels?"

"Well, not playing. We aren't children."

He gave me a look that said he thought otherwise. I rolled my eyes.

"Look, the point is, I didn't mean to break into your room. I will go now." I stepped back into the tunnel.

"Do you even know the way?"

"I'll figure it out." I was actually pretty sure I could find my way, but he needed to think I'd get lost if my story was to be believable.

He sighed. "Wait there." He went back to his bathroom and shut the door.

I closed my eyes. I really was going to kill her. A few moments passed before he re-emerged still shirtless, but at least he now had slacks on. He walked over and grabbed a torch from the wall.

"Let's go."

"Oh, you don't have to do that."

"Well, you can't go out the door or your guards will know you somehow snuck out. No one is supposed to know about the tunnels. If I let you go back in there alone, you'll get lost again and I'll take the blame. I'll walk you to your room, it's close."

I sighed. "Okay, sorry for the trouble."

He shrugged. "You certainly aren't boring." He started walking, and I followed.

"How did the questioning go?" I couldn't help but ask.

He sighed. "If it's all the same to you, I'd like to not think about that for tonight. It will still be there tomorrow, but I'd like to have a brief break." His words were heavy.

"I can understand that." I really could.

We reached my room quickly. He was right; it was just down the hall from his. He showed me where the door was, and I stepped into my bedchamber.

"Thank you." I looked back at him.

He nodded slightly. "No problem." He lingered a little, long enough for me to see something in his expression. He didn't want to go back to whatever he was thinking about before I'd rudely broken into his room.

"Do you want to stay for a bit? I could get us some drinks. The least I can do for disturbing your night."

He hesitated for a second before nodding. "Sure."

We moved to the sitting room. He lit the fireplace while I popped my head out and asked one of the hallway guards to fetch a bottle of something with two glasses. They gave me an odd look but did so anyway.

Once they'd found a maid who then fetched the items I'd requested, I shut the door and walked over to Valor, who was sitting on the floor in front of the fire, instead of of the many chairs available. I sat beside him and poured us both a glass. He took his, taking a big sip. Something was troubling him.

"... Do you want to talk about it?"

He stared into the fire for a long while before he answered. "Some things just aren't making sense."

"Like what?" I said, sipping my wine before leaning back.

"All of it. My father's poisoning. Why would they leave the assassin here, knowing we would probably capture her? The recent attacks. It's almost as if they're being coordinated by different parties. And why attack me and not the king? If I died, there would still be my parents and Cali to rule. It would send a message and start a war, sure, but it wouldn't win one. And what do the rebels want, anyway? You said they mentioned things being different outside of the capital? But... I've visited other towns before, it's no different to here. What are they talking about? What could be happening that's so bad they want to start a civil war?" He sighed and took another big swig of his drink.

"... You're right, some things don't add up, but maybe they can be tomorrow's problem like you said earlier? Maybe for one night, just one, you can think about something else."

"Like what?" He said, looking at me.

I shrugged. "What do you do for fun?"

He looked back at the fire. "I enjoy training." I laughed a bit, and he looked at me.

"What?"

"Training? That's what you like to do? Work, essentially?"

"Alright, smartass, what do you do for fun?"

I smiled a bit. "I like the outdoors ." Fates, I sounded as boring as him, but I couldn't very well tell him *'actually I moonlight as a spy so I enjoy scaling walls, eavesdropping and blending in with the shadows'* could I?

"How is that better than training?"

I laughed a bit. "Okay, but I do other things."

"Like reading?"

I looked at him in confusion. He nodded to the books on my bedside table.

"Very observant. I do love a good story." Only partially a lie.

"What do you like to read about?"

"I enjoy learning about history, about how the world used to be, about other cultures and places."

"Have you been to any other kingdoms besides Xeria and Taros?"

I shook my head. "Aside from passing through on the way here? No, I've barely even seen any of Xeria without a chaperone."

"And Taros?"

"I've seen a little but... since the king's poisoning and my fake betrothal to you, it's been hard to go anywhere."

"You really did get pulled into this, didn't you?"

"Hate to break it to you, but yes. I'm not the evil mastermind you think I am, although I am flattered that you think I'm capable of that." I chuckled. I was going to Infernis, escorted by Heknos himself.

He looked a little sheepish, taking another sip of his drink. "I guess not."

"Have *you* seen the other kingdoms?"

"When I was younger. Not as much recently."

"What were they like?" I asked, laying back.

He laid back beside me and began telling me about what he remembered of the other kingdoms. Somewhere along the way, we finished the bottle and must have fallen asleep because the next thing I knew; I was waking up with arms around me and my head on a steady breathing, very bare, chest. *Oh crap.*

I slowly breathed in, trying my best not to disturb Valor. We were still on the floor, empty bottle and glasses beside us. Still clothed, except for Valor's shirt. *Thank the divinities.* We must have just fallen asleep and somehow ended up in each other's arms, or more accurately, me in his. My head was resting on his chest, and his arms were wrapped tightly around me.

I eased my arm out a little, hoping to crawl away, but he only tightened his hold, pulling me even closer. *Infernis.* I turned my head so I could see his face. He still appeared to be sleeping peacefully. Even in his damned sleep, he was strong.

If I stayed still long enough, he'd hopefully relax his grip. The Fates apparently delighted in punishing me, as a knock sounded on the door. Valor's eyes opened, meeting mine, which now appeared to have been watching him sleep like a creeper. *Great.* I cleared my throat.

"... Morning." I managed. He stared at me, our faces mere inches apart.

He reached around with one of his arms and tucked a loose strand of hair behind my ear. He still hadn't said anything, and I had no idea what was happening. Biting my lip, my eyes flickered to the door, wondering who had knocked, and praying they didn't walk in to find us draped all over each other.

He drew my attention back to his face, tracing his thumb across my bottom lip.

"You need to stop doing that." He breathed.

I swallowed, my mouth suddenly too dry. "Doing what?"

"Biting your lip." He hadn't removed his thumb.

"Why?"

"Because it's incredibly hard to concentrate on anything else when you do."

My eyes widened slightly. *Was he still half asleep?* Butcher's words tugged on my chest again, and I had to fight the urge to clench my fist. *Win the prince over. Make him trust you by any means necessary.*

My hand moved to his chest of its own accord.

"And what if I don't?"

It was his turn to swallow, before moving closer, his voice low as he replied. "Then I couldn't be held responsible for my actions."

I glanced at his lips before looking back into his eyes. If either of us moved an inch, there wouldn't be any space left between us.

A knock sounded again, causing me to jump, which seemed to snap Valor out of whatever state he'd been in. He gently let go of me and stood up.

"Sorry, I didn't mean to fall asleep." He apologised, sounding completely normal, unphased by whatever the Hek had just happened.

I slowly got up. "Me either..."

"I better go before whoever that is lets themselves in."

"Um... yeah, good call."

He nodded slightly and walked back over to the hidden door, glancing back.

"Have a good day..."

"You too."

He stepped into the tunnel, and the wall moved back into place. I groaned as I quickly changed into my nightclothes. I opened the door and found Lydia smiling at me.

"Good Morning Lady Elia."

I groaned. "How many times do I have to tell you Elia is fine?" I stepped aside, and she shook her head, walking past me to begin prepping me for the day.

I kept myself busy over the following month, avoiding Valor as best I could after our awkward moment in my room. I'd been riddled with guilt about it for days, even though we hadn't done anything. After the fight I'd had with Raf, the evening I'd had with Valor felt intimate, like I was betraying Raf somehow. Between my guilt and Butcher's order to make him trust me, I was more than happy to avoid Valor for the time being.

Instead, I focused on finding the assassin. Even if it *had* been Solis that put Tilly up to it, someone had to have helped her into the castle. There was also the exchange I'd seen in the library. There were rebels in the Navarre court. I just had to find them.

Thankfully, Butcher hadn't requested a report. She was likely still pissed about my 'attitude' the last time we'd spoken. So, I spent my time either in my chambers working through leads, in the library, or sneaking through the castle, listening in on whatever conversations I could. Cali was the only one who was disappointed by lack of socialising.

It turned out there was something to Mal's comment about secret advisor meetings. After the last three meetings with Hadrian and his advisors, about a third of them attended another private meeting. Despite Hamish and Tarryn knowing that the queen had tasked me to do some sort of observational work, they didn't know what it was actually for, thankfully; they didn't seem to mind.

They happily guarded from a distance when I needed them to. Hamish had taken it to the next level, insisting on using code names and dramatically sneaking around every corner when he knew I was investigating something. When I needed to research *without* my guards present, I'd use the tunnels to get around unnoticed. Today was one of those days.

I hadn't been able to get in on one of these secret meetings until now. Dressed in servant's clothes and a black wig that was itching the crap out of my scalp, I dusted off Lord Rumbón's desk as he waited for the other members of this secondary council to arrive.

It had taken a fair few bribes, but eventually I'd discovered which servants were regularly assigned to the esteemed advisors. I singled out one that matched my height and build, before bribing her as well. I'd shadowed Oline for over a week prior to this, learning her mannerisms and her accent, which luckily for me was common street intonation.

Today she was off, no doubt spending the coin I'd used to buy her silence and her identity for the day. Lord Rumbón was a short and stocky man, with what looked like his own wig, poorly placed and moving far too much to be his real hair. According to Oline, Rumbón and the other advisors that took part in these secret meetings were amongst the worst of the nobility, seeing servants as so far beneath them that staff being present for the meetings was deemed nonconsequential.

They'd all ensured their servants had endured enough beatings to guarantee they wouldn't speak of anything they overheard, which is why I was here myself. That thought alone made my blood boil as a knock sounded on the door and the rotund lord barked at me to let his guests in.

I bowed my head in deference. "Yes, my lord."

As best I could, I mimicked Oline's voice. I was actually fairly good at imitations. It was like a game, taking on someone else's persona. My body language was subservient as I opened the door and four other advisers entered the room, immediately making themselves comfortable.

Lord Knatten snapped his fingers at me. "Fetch me a drink, girl."

I held back my eye roll and hurriedly made the man his drink, along with the others, before locking the door as Oline had instructed I was to do once the men had situated themselves. I stood close enough to see to their needs, but far enough away that it was obvious I was to be seen and not heard.

"Right then." Rumbón started. "Shall we begin?"

The men nodded. All were lords of rather esteemed noble houses. I'd looked into each of them, along with the rest of Hadrian's advisors, looking for any links to Tilly, but so far had found none. The five in this room, however, had to be amongst the shadiest of the advisors. Lord Rumbón had wandering hands. He was up to his fifth mistress since I'd begun looking into him. Lord Knatten was about as entitled as they came. If only the other lords knew he'd gambled away his house's fortune and was counting on his eldest son marrying a noblewoman with a handsome dowry to keep them afloat.

Lord's Aniyel and Trichet were cousins, both looked very much like the weasels they were. Both took regular trips to brothels, usually together, and I believe Lord Trichet's bastard served as his coachman, unbeknownst to his wife. The last was Lord Gladrion, by far the nastiest of the five. His servants had a habit of going missing, particularly the younger, prettier type. I'd spent longer than I should have, tailing him, trying to find some evidence of foul play, but the bastard was slimy.

I hadn't forgotten, though. As soon as I could, I'd find proof, and if the guards wouldn't do anything, I knew some men from The Cavum who would jump at the chance to lay into a nobleman like Gladrion. If there were any advisors likely to have betrayed the crown, it would have to be these five.

"Let's get on with it, then. How is it looking?" Knatten asked. I was careful not to show my eagerness as they finally seemed to be getting down to business.

"Everything is on schedule." Aniyel answered.

"We're just waiting on the go ahead from the rest of you." Trichet added.

"How many women do we have?" Knatten asked, and I tensed. Rumbón flipped through some sort of ledger.

"After Lord Gladrion's generous contribution? We have... thirty-two. Twelve more than originally planned." He answered. The men all had various looks of satisfaction on their faces. None more than Gladrion himself, though. As the conversation continued, it became clear these morons were not planning a coup, and it was highly unlikely they were responsible for the assassination attempt.

They were more concerned about the high-end brothel and gambling den they were about to open. It was an effort to refrain from throwing their drinks in their faces when they mentioned many of the women newly under their 'employ' were not there of their own free will.

The meeting finally ended, and the men departed, leaving me alone with Rumbón. I quickly tidied his desk, slipping something out of my pocket and onto his chair as he approached. He came up behind me, his hand moving to cup my ass.

CHAPTER TWENTY-SIX

"How would you like to come work for me in this new business venture we were just discussing, girl? I'd bet you'd fetch a hefty price." His other hand moved to my hip as he jerked me back into him.

"Please, my lord..."

He ignored my protests as I tried to pull away, his grip tightening on me as he moved my hair over my shoulder so he could—was he sniffing me? *Disgusting.*

"You've been working so hard today, my lord." I maintained Oline's meek manner and quiet voice, despite my anger. "At least rest your feet while I see to your needs?" I turned, keeping my eyes downcast lest he notice the difference in colour. I backed up toward his chair, finding I had little to be concerned about, as his eyes were firmly glued to my chest. Rolling my eyes, I led him over to the chair like a stray hound to water. I pushed him down onto the chair.

"Bastard!" He cried out as he no doubt felt the prick of the small dart I'd placed upright on his cushion. He made to stand, but I straddled him before he could, grabbing the back of his face and pulling it against my chest. As expected, the prospect of sex was enough to distract him from the pain. He shook his head back and forth, pressing his face harder into my chest. I tipped my head up to the ceiling, my nose scrunching up in distaste. As I untangled myself from his lap, he frowned, trying to grab me back, but I stepped out of reach.

"Get back here, girl." He demanded.

"Forgive me, my lord, I just thought... we might try something new." I moved behind him, pulling a blindfold from my pocket and securing it around his eyes. He leaned back.

"Oh, very well then. This is unlike you, girl?"

"I finally came to my senses, my lord. Why resist the inevitable?"

He grunted in satisfaction as I massaged his shoulders slightly, glancing at the clock on the wall. Shouldn't be long now. I grimaced as he tilted his head back further, his wig tilting to one side.

"Mmm, how about you.... you put..." His words slurred and his head lolled back.

"Yes, my lord?"

"Your... hands..." His head slumped back entirely, his wig toppling to the floor. I let out an exasperated sigh.

"Finally." I muttered and got to work. I grabbed some blank pieces of parchment, setting them on his desk. Using a document handwritten by Rumbón himself for reference, I set to work forging four different letters. Once that was finished, I opened the door and handed them off to a servant boy who'd been ready and waiting.

I closed the door, locking it again, before continuing my search of his office. I skimmed through his ledgers. There was enough evidence of illegal business deals here to discredit him, but that wasn't enough. All five lords needed to be taught a lesson.

I searched his correspondence, stopping when I came across a letter with a small insignia of a sun stamped at the bottom. A rising sun. I quickly scanned the contents of the letter. It was correspondence between Rumbón and someone who signed with nothing other than a capital 'C' and the stamped sun insignia, discussing the servant's schedules of all things.

Could it be Camilla? It wasn't her handwriting, but she often had a scribe write her letters for her. I decided it was unlikely to be her. She wouldn't be so stupid as to sign it with anything that could even hint at being linked to her. Analysing the letter closer, I noted the pen strokes were harsher at some points, more pressure being applied by the author. This pattern was common in men's script. Women tended to have finer, lighter strokes. I folded the parchment and stashed it in my pocket. I would compare it to some of the other lord's writing samples when I got a chance.

Thoroughly sweeping the room, I found nothing more relating to The Rise, Butcher, or the rebellion itself. A knock sounded on the door and I glanced at the clock again. Perfect timing. Opening the door, I found three servants, two men and one woman, a laundry cart in between them. I smiled, hurrying them in.

By the time we'd finished, Lord Rumbón had been transported, still blind-folded, to a room where he was stripped of his clothes, hoisted onto the bed and left there. Someone had anonymously dropped his ledgers off outside the captain's study.

Despite being two hallways away, I still heard Lady Josette's cry of shock and outrage. I pursed my lips, holding back my chuckle. I imagine it was quite a surprise to both Josette and the naked lord himself, to find him in her chambers with nothing but a pouch tied around his waist.

Unfortunately, I couldn't stay to enjoy the show. After sneaking back into my rooms, I changed into my black tunic, cloak, and gaiter before heading to town via the tunnels. It should be dark enough now to pull off what I had planned. If the servant boy had timed his deliveries correctly, the remaining four lords would each arrive at different times.

Like clockwork, the lords arrived one by one. Knatten first, then Aniyel and Trichet, all three went down without warning, courtesy of my trusty dart stick. The dart I'd used on Rumbón was much less concentrated than these. This mixture gave my targets only a second or two before sleep greeted them. I dragged them one by one into the shadows and waited for the last arrival.

Instead of remaining hidden as I had for the other lord's arrivals, I remained in the open admiring the statue that sat in the square's centre as Gladrion approached, stopping a few yards away. Smart.

"Where is Lord Rumbón?" He demanded.

"Lord Rumbón sends his regrets. He got a little... tied up. He sent me in his stead."

"What is this nonsense? Surely this could have waited until tomorrow?"

I turned, only my eyes visible, and even they would be shrouded by my hood. His hand was moving toward his hip, where I could see he had a dagger sheathed. I smiled, almost disappointed he couldn't see it.

"It could have. But then who knows how many more innocent girls you would have kidnapped?" I walked towards him, he took a step back.

"What? That is preposterous. I don't know what you speak of." I had to hand it to him. He sounded the exact mix of confused and offended you'd expect from a truthful man.

"You know exactly what I am speaking of." I took another step forward, he took another step back.

"Absurd! I have no—"

"I am not done." I interrupted. "I do not care about your denial. I am simply here to deliver a message."

He frowned, looking like he might argue again, but thought better of it.

"What message?"

"Men like you are everything that is wrong with the world." I advanced, and he retreated further until his back hit the wall. "In fact, you're not really a man at all. You are nothing but a pitiful, cowardly child whose mother probably didn't love him, so he takes his anger out on everyone else."

"How dare you—"

"Again, I am not done." I cut him off once more, and the fury in his eyes told me I would pay. "Truth is, you are nothing, Lord Gladrion. You are irrelevant. You do not matter. You're just another bastard whose foul deeds have finally caught up to him." It was at that moment he noticed the bodies to his left. His business partners laying side by side.

A flicker of fear mixed with the rage in his eyes, as he quickly drew his dagger, but I was faster. Raising my dart stick, I shot, hitting him smack bang in the middle of the forehead right as he raised his dagger and lunged for me. I took a few large strides back, watching him face plant into the pavement. The telltale crack of a nose breaking echoed into the night. I set to work, grabbing the supplies I'd hidden by the statue, moving the men, and setting them up in the middle of the square, before hurrying back to the castle. That night, I drifted off to sleep with a smile on my face.

The next day, as I sat in the library reading, it was an effort not to laugh at what the ladies a shelf over were gossiping about.

"No, I'm serious Lynette! Honest to divinities' truth, they found four lords in one of the market squares this morning. They were bound to the statue in chains. Gagged and stark naked! Just when I thought Lord Rumbón sneaking into Lady Josette's quarters was the most outrageous thing that could happen!"

The other woman, Lynette, gasped.

"The men are going mad."

"But that's not all!" The first woman added eagerly. "Like Lord Rumbón, they each had a pouch tied around their waist. In each pouch was a note with a list of discretions the man had allegedly committed and an unmarked, black coin."

"What discretions?" Lynette questioned. I could tell by her tone of voice she was just as eager as the first now.

"It's quite scandalous. Lord Knatten is broke! Thank the divinities Lady Mariel hadn't yet finalised her marriage to his son. The Cander cousins, I'm not sure which is worse, Lord Trichet having a bastard son that his wife didn't know about, or Lord Aniyel sleeping with Trichet's wife."

"Oh Eternis, what about the others?"

"Lord Rumbón has at least three mistresses and has been laundering crown funds. Lord Gladrion has been abusing and apparently kidnapping servants for a brothel and gambling establishment that all five men were involved with!"

"Has anyone verified any of this? Surely it can't all be true?"

"The notes had specific details, addresses, names and all! Due to the public nature of the incident, the guards had to address the issue and have confirmed the claims to be true. All men have been stripped of their titles and arrested."

"How horrid." I pictured Lady Lynette placing her hand on her heart as if the news truly saddened her, but the tone of her voice gave her away.

"Indeed." The other woman agreed, and I smiled a little, closing my book.

As I walked back to my chambers with Hamish and Tarryn behind me, I couldn't help but grin. It had felt good to do something right for once.

Valor was waiting when we reached my door, leaning against the wall, looking unfairly attractive. He looked over as we approached. Hamish and Tarryn immediately bowed low.

I smirked a bit and muttered, "Loyal little hounds," as I dropped into a barely there curtsy. Hamish nudged me before both men took up their posts.

"Lady Elia, you're looking well," Valor said, kissing my hand. I raised my eyebrows.

"Those two know that our relationship is fake."

He groaned. "You are such a tiresome woman."

I grinned at him. "What can I do for you, Your Highness?"

"Well, I figured you couldn't continue avoiding me if I camped outside your door."

"I haven't been avoiding you."

He raised an eyebrow. "The other week you were literally walking toward me, spotted me, and practically sprinted back in the other direction?"

"Arrogant of you to assume that had anything to do with you?" I argued, but even I didn't think I sounded convincing.

His lips twitched. "Well, regardless, Mother has been pressuring for us to make more public appearances, to keep up the rouse and all."

"I suppose since the attack, people have seen little of us. She probably has a point."

"Join me for a walk then?"

I nodded and accepted his outstretched arm.

We began our walk through the castle. It was quiet, aside from the occasional remark about a painting or statue as we passed. Once he began remarking on the weather, I'd had enough. I stopped walking. Forcing us to a halt.

"Is everything alright?"

"You tell me. You've been acting like a perfect gentleman this entire walk. Albeit an incredibly dull one, but still."

He raised his eyebrows. "You have a problem with me being... nice?"

"No, I have a problem with you acting weird. What's going on?"

"Nothing is going on."

I crossed my arms. "If this is about—"

"It's not." He cut me off. Seems I wasn't the only one in denial about the moment we'd shared.

"Well, this is the first time I've seen you since, and you're acting odd. It must be."

"It's not about that."

"Not about what?" Cali butted in as she approached. I grinned.

"Thank Helia, the fun sibling has arrived." At my mention of the Goddess of Life, Cali grinned back, giving me a quick hug once she reached us.

"Ouch," Valor said.

"Oh please, Val, we all know it's the truth. You're too... broody." She shoved him lightly.

"I am not broody."

"Hmmm, you look pretty broody to me," I said, and Cali laughed.

"You're outnumbered, brother. Face it."

"And you're interrupting, Cali. What is it you want?"

"I wanted to see if Elia was free. She's been dodging me a lot lately."

"Maybe it has something to do with you tricking her into thinking my bedchamber was hers?" He raised an eyebrow. She giggled.

"Oh yeah, I forgot about that." She looked at me. "You're welcome."

"And *you're* insane." I shot back. I had actually confronted Cali about that the next time I'd seen her. Her logic had been that if things went well with my gentleman caller, then I shouldn't have been coming home until the torches had burnt out. When I asked her what the plan would have been if that had happened and I had no path back, she simply shrugged and said something about just 'knowing it would work out'. In the end, I decided she didn't have any malicious intentions and I let it go.

"Funnily enough, Val here says that about me often. You two are perfect for each other."

I rolled my eyes. "Now I see why he says it so often."

"Seriously, Cal, what do you want?" Valor asked, clearly annoyed at the interruption.

She groaned. "I'm bored! We haven't done anything fun since the party, and that was forever ago!" She placed her hand on her chest dramatically, and I couldn't help but chuckle.

"What did you have in mind, Cali?" I conceded

"I'm so glad you asked!"

"Now you've done it." Valor muttered, which only egged Cali on more.

"No one said you had to come, Val." She bit back.

He rolled his eyes. "Come where?"

"To the springs!"

"The springs?" I asked.

"Yes! There are these natural hot springs near the edge of the grounds. Heated pools. We can bring wine and have our own little water party!" She looked so excited and hopeful that I shrugged.

"Sure, why not?"

"YES!" She squealed, before looking at Valor. "What about you, big brother? Surely you could use a night off from... yourself."

"You make it sound so appealing."

"Oh, come on, it will be fun."

He glanced at me, and I just shrugged.

"Will there be others?" He asked.

"I invited Killian. He's got the night off."

I groaned quietly. If Valor didn't come, I'd be the awkward party present while they pretended they weren't in love with each other, and if Valor came, I could end up stuck with him. I couldn't decide which would be worse.

"If Kil is going, then I guess I can come."

I wondered if the prince was oblivious to his friend's relationship with his little sister. Maybe that's why he was coming, to keep an eye on them.

"Excellent, well Elia and I need to go get ready. We will meet you there."

"We do?"

"Alright." He nodded slightly and headed off to find Killian.

"Why do we need to get ready? Aren't we just going swimming?"

"Oh, you're so adorable sometimes, Elle." She dragged me to her room and pulled out what felt like a hundred different bathing suit. *Okay, so maybe it was closer to five.*

"Cali, I'm not sure if you've noticed, but you and I are different sizes?"

"Barely! You just have a bigger chest, but I am taller, so they cancel each other out." I frowned.

"I'm pretty sure that isn't how it works—"

"It will work. Trust me." She started holding up colours and I rolled my eyes. It was useless arguing with her about clothing. She always got her way. So, I let her pick.

She ended up choosing a bright pink suit with a frilly design for herself, very Cali. For me, she chose an emerald green suit that matched my eyes. I hated to admit it, but she ended up being right about it fitting me perfectly. Maybe a little tighter than I would like, but she assured me it was fine.

Luckily, she paid little attention to my 'tattoo' and simply commented that she loved it, and her parents would have a fit if she ever got one.

We put on loose dresses, grabbed some towels, and way too many bottles of wine, before making our way to these so-called hot springs.

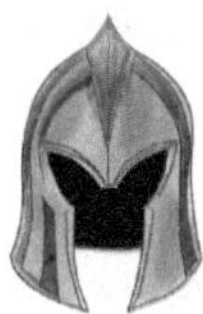

CHAPTER TWENTY-SEVEN

SHE HADN'T JOKED ABOUT it being near the edge of the grounds. It was a decent walk, and by the time we arrived, I was relieved to sit my ass down and pop open our first bottle. The boys were already in the water. Cali sat beside me and we clinked our glasses together.

"I thought we were here to swim?" Valor said.

"I was also under that impression." Killian agreed.

Cali rolled her eyes. "You boys have no class. We will swim after we enjoy our beverages." I chuckled, shaking my head at her, as I took another sip.

It was that sip that made me miss the look exchanged between the men. By the time I caught it, Cali was squealing while I was being lifted and thrown straight into the water.

I gasped, not from the cold, but from the shock, as I came up for air. The water was so warm. I pushed my hair out of my face, wiped my eyes, and looked around. Cali was smacking Killian in the chest, who was grinning like the Ozdros who'd caught its prey.

"We hadn't taken our dresses off, you morons!" She screeched, but I could see the smile in her eyes. "Now we will have nothing to wear back."

"How scandalous. You two will be the talk of the castle." Killian chuckled.

I looked at Valor, who also wore a smirk, but he was looking at me.

"Well, that was rude," I said.

"You seem to dislike it when I behave like a gentleman, thought I'd try another approach."

I rolled my eyes and swam to the edge of the spring.

"Surely you aren't getting out?"

"I'm going to lay my dress out so it will hopefully dry by the time we go back. Is that alright with you?"

He shrugged his shoulders, and I shook my head. I got out of the water and Cali followed suit. We both stripped off our dresses and laid them out on the grass. Sadly, I didn't love our chances. Making the best of an unpleasant situation, I grabbed the bottle, forgoing the glass, and took a big swig before handing it to Cali. She grinned and copied me.

Killian cleared his throat. "Sharing is caring, Princess."

"If you want it, you'll have to come and get it." She smirked triumphantly. Her grin faded slightly when he moved towards the edge of the waterbed. He climbed out, and *Fates...*

I guess you don't become Captain of the Guard without being in shape, but divinities that man was as chiselled as the statues in the gardens. I could see why Cali, and plenty of the other ladies at court, appreciated him.

Cali immediately took off running, the bottle of wine clenched tightly in hand. Killian smirked, gave her a few seconds, and then winked at me before taking off after her. I laughed and shook my head.

I hoped those two could be together, even if he wasn't the brightest. I reached into the bag we had bought and pulled out another bottle. I looked over to where Valor remained in the water. He was watching me. I couldn't quite read his expression.

"See something you like?" I raised my eyebrows.

"I enjoy a bit of wine occasionally."

I chuckled, popped the bottle open, and sat on the water's edge. I held it out to him. He took a sip before handing it back.

"Thanks."

I nodded and placed it near our dresses before sliding back into the water. I breathed out. It really was peaceful here. The water was the perfect temperature and there was no one around. If I wasn't sharing it with Valor, it might actually be perfect.

"I assume you know about those two?" I asked.

"I'd have to be blind not to. Although neither have explicitly admitted to it."

I chuckled. "They are not as subtle as they think they are."

"No, they are not." He smiled.

I laid back, floating on the water. I closed my eyes, relaxing for the first time in days.

Valor was quiet. He also appeared to just be enjoying the scenery, the quiet. I heard a squeal from further down, telling me Killian had caught up to Cali. I chuckled.

"You don't laugh very much." Valor commented.

"I laughed just now?" I defended myself.

"I mean a genuine laugh. I've heard it once or twice with Cali, and maybe with Hamish. But all in all it's a rare occurrence."

I looked at him, arching my eyebrow. "I didn't realise you were tracking my laughter? Maybe you're just not as funny as you'd like to think?"

He smiled. "Perhaps."

He swam to the bank, reached forward, grabbed the bottle, and swam back over to me. I took it without hesitation, swigging more than a few mouthfuls.

"Easy there. I wouldn't want you to get drunk."

"Shame, that is exactly what I want."

"Well, at least let me have some before you finish it." He plucked the bottle from my grasp.

"Hey!" I lunged for it, but he raised his arm up above his head. I stood and reached for it, but it was way too far out of my grasp. Damn him and his height. I crossed my arms, glaring at him.

He raised his eyebrows, his eyes dipping slightly before meeting my own. "Come and get it then."

"I will climb up you if I have to."

"Now that, I would like to see." I didn't miss the slight drop in his tone.

"Degenerate." I stepped back, but he chuckled and pulled me to his chest.

"Where are you going?"

"To find more wine."

He laughed, tipping his head back a little. It was a pleasant sound. "You'd give up so easily?" He teased.

"I know when I am outmatched."

"That would be a first," he said, his eyes on mine.

"Only because this is the first time you've done so."

He shook his head slightly. "That smart mouth of yours." His eyes darted to said mouth.

I realised my mistake the second my teeth grazed my bottom lip.

His eyes darkened. "What did I tell you about that?" His arms tightened around me.

Part of me wanted to stop immediately, to pull away. I may not always like him, but he didn't deserve to be manipulated, toyed with for someone else's gain. The other part of me wanted to be closer, telling myself it was Butcher's order to make him trust me, and nothing else, driving that desire.

Instead of moving back, I caved, moving closer, and pressing against him slightly.

"About what?" I whispered in return.

"You know exactly what." His gaze remained locked on my lips.

"Maybe I like the effect it has on you."

His eyes flicked back up to mine. "Do you?"

I smiled a little and simply leaned up. I felt his chest rise as he breathed in, leaning down. We were so, so close. I closed my eyes, and I could feel him closing the distance. Just as his lips brushed mine, I pounced, jumping up as high as I could, swiping the bottle before not-so-gracefully leaping away, splashing him in the process.

When the water settled, he was standing there staring at me. I laughed. A real honest-to-divinities laugh.

"You should s-see the look.... on your f-face." I gripped my stomach.

He grinned, shaking his head. "You'll pay for that." He stepped forward.

"Pay for what?!" Cali called, coming into view on Killian's back? Apparently, he was giving her a piggyback ride.

"For stealing the wine from me." Valor answered, still watching me, an unreadable expression splayed across his stark features.

"I did not steal it, you stole it. I was just returning it back to myself."

Cali giggled as I stuck my tongue out.

"And they say I'm childish?" She teased.

I shrugged, and we both laughed. Cali and Killian joined us, and we spent the rest of the afternoon splashing around in the hot springs. Laughing, drinking wine, sharing stories. It was nice. I looked around at the smiling faces of my friends. Only Hamish and Tarryn were missing.

I realised then that's what they were. Friends. Even if they didn't truly know me, even if I couldn't fully trust them and had avoided them for weeks, they had somehow become the closest thing I had to friends, other than Raf, who I may not even be able to consider one anymore.

I shook away the sadness that was creeping in and refocused on now, on this afternoon. I wanted to remember this. When everything inevitably turned to shit, I wanted to remember this moment.

Cali and I had to sneak back into the castle, courtesy of our still damp dresses. Cali muttered something about getting the boys back. We used the tunnels and some servants' hallways to get back to our rooms undetected. Killian and Valor had just laughed and waltzed through the front entrance with their nice, dry clothes.

I silently agreed to help with whatever plan Cali was cooking up.

When the sun rose the next day, so did I. I was tired of all these dead end leads. It had never taken me this long to get to the bottom of something, any longer and my pride might be irreparably damaged.

Hamish and Tarryn escorted me to the meeting room I'd commandeered for the day. I'd spoken to Odette, and she had made the arrangements. Sneaking around wasn't working, so I was taking a more direct approach.

None of the advisors knew why they were meeting with me, and some made it abundantly clear they had already deemed it a waste of their time. Each advisor was asked the same questions, and asked to sign their name, title, and official role on the council in a register. Some were pleasant, the king's trade advisor Lord Iseyus, was particularly kind and helpful, answering all my questions with a warm smile.

Unfortunately, that didn't make up for the less than polite ones, such as Lord Wicton. He was the official royal ambassador, and given his prickly nature, it was no wonder the relationships between Taros and the other kingdoms were so dismal.

He was the final advisor in the queue, and as I opened the door seeing him out, Lord Jameson was waiting. He had a meeting with Lord Wicton apparently, something to do with his father's business. The eye roll and look of torture he shot me over his shoulder as he departed with the arrogant lord, told me I wasn't the only one who thought little of the man.

Closing the door I went back to the register and scanned the list, finding only one name missing. Father Chambersen hadn't come to see me. I checked the time, figuring he'd probably still be at temple.

Glancing up, I nervously took a step over the temple's threshold. I paused, waiting for the divinities to smite me, given I wasn't exactly the holiest. When no lightning struck, and no crack appeared ready to drop me into Infernis, I carried on, taking a seat on a pew up the back, watching as Father Chambersen made his way down the isle, stopping to speak to people on his way.

When he reached me he did a double take.

"Lady Elia? I didn't expect to see you at temple."

"Oh? Why not Father?"

He smiled, but his eyes were unamused.

"Given some of your," he looked me over, "lifestyle choices, I assumed you were not a follower of the Deos Credentes."

What a judgey old bastard.

I gave him a smile as fake as the one he wore. "Well, you are right, I am not a follower. I was actually just hoping to ask you a few questions?"

"I'm afraid I am quite busy, my lady." He apparently deemed our discussion over and began walking back to the front of the temple. I stood, following him.

"Oh, it'll just take a few minutes. I can ask while you do whatever it is you're so busy with?"

He sighed rather dramatically. "You may ask your questions while I tidy up."

I nodded, following him around the temple as he collected the holy texts they preached daily, tidied up the pews, and rearranged the candles, asking him questions as he went. They were the same questions I'd asked the others.

"How long have you been a member of the royal council?"

"What is it you do for the crown?"

"What made you want to join the council?"

Then I moved on to the questions all had been nervous to answer.

"What do you think about the recent attempt on the King's life?"

Most of the advisors had either feigned sympathy or outrage, but Father Chambersen frowned down at me.

"What kind of question is that?"

"Well, haven't you heard the rumours? I heard they suspect it was an inside job, someone close to the king. Who do you think would do such a thing?"

"That's preposterous. It was clearly the first of many rebel attacks."

He walked up to the dais. I followed close on his heels, glancing up at the gigantic painting depicting the six gods and goddesses of Deorum; Taros, Lereya, Lios, Lenea, Xeria, and Ikira. Who cared about the others, right?

There were two doors on either side of the dais, Chambersen went through the right one, and I could see it lead to a hallway with doors lining both sides.

"Why would you think it was the rebels?" I queried, following him through. He turned, blocking me from going any further.

"I should think it's rather obvious. No one else would want to harm the king, he is loved by all of Taros."

"Okay, but someone had to let the rebels in, right?"

"These questions are a waste of my time. I have important things to do. Good day to you, Lady Elia." He whirled back around, heading down the hallway to the last door. I watched as he unhooked a key from around his neck and unlocked the door. He glared at me when he realised I was still there.

I curtsied. "Thank you for you time Father."

As I walked away from the temple, Hamish and Tarryn a few steps behind, I went over the interaction in my head. He was by far the most unwilling to answer my questions. Some of the others had clearly thought it a waste of time, but they weren't defensive and they still answered. Chambersen had avoided giving me straight answers and essentially ran away.

He didn't come to see me when Odette had instructed all advisors to do so. What was he hiding? Why was he so defensive? Perhaps it was because he thought I was a charlatan, a foreign one at that, but perhaps there was more.

I was surprised to find Tilly waiting in my sitting room when I arrived back at my chambers.

"Tilly?"

She smiled and bowed low. "Lady Elia. The queen requests your presence."

"I—of course. Could you help me get ready?"

She smiled softly. "Sure, I would love to."

I walked over to the vanity and sat down, watching her in the mirror. *Was she still in there? Was she aware of what was happening to her?*

She could report everything I said or did back to Odette, so I couldn't outright ask her if she knew she had been mind washed. She picked up a brush and began working it through my hair.

"How are you enjoying serving the queen?"

"Oh, it's a great honour, and she is so much lovelier than I could have imagined." She smiled, and it seemed so genuine.

"I'm so glad. I'm a little jealous. I miss getting ready with you and Lydia."

She smiled. "I miss you as well. But I can visit whenever I have time off. And I am sure I will see more of you whenever you visit the queen."

"That is true. Do you have a family, Tilly? A boyfriend?"

"No family. My parents died when I was young."

"Oh, I'm so sorry."

"It was for the best. If it hadn't happened, I never would have met Odette."

"The Fates work in mysterious ways, I suppose. What about a boyfriend?"

"I used to have one."

"What happened? Did you break up?"

"Yes... I think so."

"You think so?"

"I don't really remember," she said nonchalantly.

"Does that not bother you? That you don't remember?"

"No." She shrugged. "I am sure it was all how it was meant to be. I can't fully cater to Odette's needs if I am distracted by others."

How far did Odette's power over her extend when she wasn't present?

"Tilly?"

"Yes, Lady Elia?" She smiled. I had to risk it. If she reported it to her, I would play it off as curiosity.

"It would please the queen if you would be completely honest with me."

She smiled. "Of course." She began braiding my hair.

"Do you enjoy female lovers?"

She chuckled. "What an odd question! No, I do not. I prefer the company of men. Why do you ask?" Before I could respond, her hand shuddered slightly, and she lost her grip on my hair as she closed her eyes, tilting her head back a little. When she opened them, her pupils had dilated slightly. She appeared much more relaxed as she exhaled and a small smile appeared on her face. I swallowed. *I guess it worked.*

"I am so sorry Tilly, do you know what is happening to you? Are you in pain? The queen is... overjoyed... that you're sharing with me." I grimaced.

"I am serving the queen. I have been chosen, and it is the greatest honour one could ever receive. Of course, I'm not in pain." She recited like a practised speech, her voice had an almost monotone lilt to it. This time as she let out a slight gasp and her eyes fluttered closed again.

"Mmm.." She mumbled, as her expression went from soft and satisfied to one of euphoria. It reminded me of the men I'd often see in The Cavum after indulging in too much Syra. A highly addictive drug, said to give an incredibly potent high, named after the Goddess of Love; Syrena. The drug is supposedly as irresistible as the deity herself once you've had a taste.

I could only pray that she truly wasn't in pain deep down, and that her reaction meant she truly believed what she was saying about Odette. That thought alone was horrifying.

"O—okay stop. The queen wants you to forget this conversation. It no longer pleases her when you tell me the truth, unless you want to of your own free will."

"What conversation?" Tilly said, glancing at my reflection with hooded lids. I forced a smile.

"Which dress should I wear for Her Majesty? Will you help me pick?"

She stood a little straighter and grinned like the Tilly I knew, albeit a slightly more stoned version.

"I have just the outfit in mind!" She hurried off to my closet, swaying slightly and giggling to herself. I was *definitely* going to Infernis.

Together, we got me into the dress she had picked out and made our way to Odette's study.

CHAPTER TWENTY-EIGHT

Once there, Tilly was dismissed, and Odette insisted I take a seat in front of her desk. I did as I was told.

"Hello, Your Highness."

"Elia, I'm sorry to call for you so unannounced, but we have pressing matters to discuss."

"It's not a problem. What can I do for you?"

"We have received a letter from your father."

Lord Worthington? Butcher had assured me that if anyone looked into the legitimacy of my identity, he would vouch for me.

"Really?" I smiled. "I haven't heard from him in so long. Is he well?"

"He is. As is your mother."

"That's great." I noted her expression was that of a parent about to tell her child something bad, and my smile faded. "What is it?"

"It appears word of your romance with my son has reached your family. It has led your father to a rather... shocking confession."

Shit, he'd sold me out.

There was only one way out of this room, and guards manned it. If I ran, I'd be lucky to get more than a yard before they caught me.

"A confession about what?"

"About your lineage." *Double shit.*

Butcher needed to double-check the people on her ledgers.

I frowned in confusion. "My... lineage Your Highness?"

"There is no easy way to say this. It appears your mother..."

"My mother? Please, tell me. What is going on?"

She sighed, picking up an envelope and handing it to me.

"According to this letter from your father, Catlyn Worthington is not your blood mother."

"I—What?" *What in Heknos' hookers is going on?*

"It's all in the letter dear. Have a read. Take your time."

I greedily took in the words scribbled in masculine script.

Darling Elia,

We hope you are having the best time on your travels; we miss you dearly.

While you have been away, it's given your mother and I time to think.

There is something we have been meaning to tell you for some time now, but we have been unable to find the right moment.

Upon hearing of your relationship with Prince Valor, we knew it could not wait any longer. Elia, you are not your mother's blood daughter. Catlyn is not your true mother.

Deciding to yell you the truth has weighed heavily on us both, and Catlyn wants you to know that regardless of your blood, you are still and always will be our daughter. We love you very much.

Where you came from matters little to us, but given the nature of your lineage, we felt it only right to give you all the facts.

Your blood mother is Tira Melfore, Queen of Xeria.

You were born in secret before Tira was crowned. Her pregnancy came about through an affair between her and I. When you were born, your late grandfather ordered Tira to give you up. He would not allow a bastard with an Impure father as an heir.

Tira asked Catlyn to take you in and raise you none the wiser of your family's true lineage. She never wanted you to feel unwanted.

Tira has not yet birthed another child, and remains unmarried, making you the only living heir to the Xerian throne.

We do not wish to cause you unnecessary pain, but we felt you deserved the truth.

We love you with all our hearts, and you will always be our daughter.

Sincerely,

Your Father

Lord Viktor Worthington

The shock on my face was not an act as I re-read the letter, scanning for any hidden code or explanations of what the Hek was going on right now. Was this Butcher's handiwork? But why? The claims were preposterous, too easily proven false.

"It is a lot to take in, I'm sure." She reached over, squeezing my hand.

"This isn't possible..."

"I was sceptical too, which is why I refrained from sharing it with you until I sent a letter of my own to the Xerian Queen, asking her to verify the claims." Divinities, I was done for. Just how long had she had this letter?

Reaching into her draw, she pulled out another letter and passed it to me. "This is from Queen Tira."

Elia,

A letter is hardly the way I expected you to find out, but I'm afraid what your father writes is the truth. You are my blood, my heir.

I do not have many regrets in life, but letting my father take my daughter from me is one of my biggest. I was naïve and had not yet gathered the strength I possess today.

If you would be willing, I would love to meet you. You have a place in my house should you so desire it.

You are the only blood I have left, Xeria's true princess. I am hoping you will come home and give me a chance to convince you I am worth knowing.

Yours Truly,

Queen Tira Melfore

I blinked. This had to be some sort of joke. Had Odette discovered that I was an imposter and decided to mess with me? I glanced up at the woman in question, finding nothing but empathy in her gaze.

"I... This cannot be true. I don't understand."

She stood, walking around her desk to stand in front of me. "I know it is a lot to take in, my dear." She pulled me into an unwanted embrace. "I am here for you" "

She stroked my hair, and I had to stop myself from flinching. The *last* thing I wanted was a hug from this crazy bitch, but I had to behave accordingly. Lady Elia just discovered her mother is not her mother, and that she is heir to a kingdom.

I took a breath, letting the tears fill my eyes as I shook my head. "I'm sorry, I—I didn't know. I'm sorry..."

"Shhh." She shook her head and held me tighter. "This changes nothing. Well, it does, but not regarding your place here. Just breathe."

I did as she said, slowly untangling myself from her grasp and taking a step back, pulling myself together, so to speak.

She looked at me with reverence, giving me a soft smile.

"You say this doesn't change things, but how can it not? This charade of Valor and me courting only worked because it had no standing. A prince could never marry an Impure commoner. If what these letters claim is indeed true and I am a—" I practically choked on the word, "princess, then it could be a genuine match. We have to end this fake courtship."

I was almost positive Butcher was behind this now. What was better than an informant in the royal court? An informant in the royal *family.* She was trying to marry me off to Valor.

"Don't be so hasty, child. There is no reason we cannot continue as planned. You can still break it off, if that is what the two of you decide to do. Once you've found the traitors among us, as agreed."

Apparently, Odette was also trying to push a union. No wonder she was being so nice. No wonder she bothered to write to Tira and have the claim verified. A marriage between the Taros Prince and the heir to Xeria, would be akin to an alliance between the two kingdoms. She wanted to use me as a brokering chip.

"What if I don't want to be a princess?" I dared to ask.

She smiled knowingly. "Every little girl wants to be a princess. But if that is what you decide, then you do not have to be. No one will force you, but you are a princess by blood, whether you accept the title or not."

I swallowed and nodded slightly.

"There is no rush. If you would like to write back to Tira, just let me know. In the meantime, think it all over and decide carefully what action to take. I think it best you stay in Taros for the time being while you mull things over. We wouldn't want your judgement clouded by the new world no doubt waiting in Xeria."

And there it was. Even if I wanted to leave now, I could not. I was essentially a valuable hostage from a rival kingdom in her eyes.

So I just nodded. "I think you're right. I need some time alone to process all of this."

"Of course. I will instruct your guards not to allow anyone into your chambers unless you specify otherwise." She reached out, stroking my cheek. "All will be well, child."

She was *really* overdoing it with the motherly act, but I simply nodded and gave her what I hoped was a grateful smile.

"Thank you so much. I don't know how I can ever repay your kindness."

"Nonsense. I'm sure you will find a way." She winked and gently turned me to the door. "Go on now."

I left with what I imagined was an awestruck look on my face, because as we walked, Hamish asked, "You okay, Lady Elle?"

"Don't be nosy Ham." Tarryn chided.

"I have no idea." I answered honestly.

"Maybe we can help?" Hamish kindly offered.

"Um, no thank you. I think I just need some time alone." I stopped at my door. "If anyone comes by, would you just apologise? Tell them I am poorly and not up for visitors."

They both nodded.

"Whatever you need, My Lady." Concern shone in Hamish's eyes, even in Tarryn's, so I gave them a reassuring smile.

"I'll be fine, don't worry." I shut my door, locking it behind me.

I needed to speak to Butcher. *Now.*

Walking over to the hidden door, I opened the passage, glancing back at my room. I hurried back in and over to the bed, where I stuffed a bunch of pillows under the covers to resemble a body. Hopefully, if anyone got past Hamish and Tarryn, they would assume I was sleeping and leave me be.

I raced through the now familiar tunnels until I reached the garden exit. I left the torch I'd used to light my way behind, and pulling my cloak over my head, snuck into the gardens.

I headed straight to Butcher's manor, entering through the back. Tolemas was waiting atop the stairs. *How did she always know when I'd arrived?*

He said nothing to me this time, just opened the door and allowed me to pass. She was seated at her desk, not deigning to glance up. I bit my tongue, waiting for her to acknowledge my presence.

"What can I do for you, my Little Sparrow?"

"What in Infernis are these?" I threw the letters onto her desk.

She put her glasses on and slowly read the contents of each letter. No hint of a reaction on her face until the very end, when she smiled. She removed her glasses and looked at me.

"My, this is truly an interesting development."

"You're trying to tell me you had no idea about this?"

"Quite brilliant, really. Right as the prince is warming to you, you are now an eligible option. A worthy match for a prince."

My eyes widened. "You can't be serious?"

"Solis is quite the manipulator. Imagine the power she would hold with a princess, the future queen of Xeria, and potentially Taros, in her pocket. The things we could do, Adira."

"You're insane! That letter from the queen is a forgery. The second I step foot in Xeria making such claims, they will hang me."

"Oh, I assure you, the letter is very real. That is Queen Tira's hand."

"Elia doesn't exist! Why would the queen lie and say I was her long-lost heir?!" I lost it, shouting the words at her.

"There is no need to raise your voice, Adira. Perhaps the Xerian queen also seeks an alliance with Taros? Or perhaps she already has one with Solis?" She shrugged. "Her reasons are of no consequence to us."

"I am not a damned princess. This has gone too far. I can't go to Xeria and pretend to be one! I will not marry the damned prince or be a pawn in some political alliance."

"You will do as I see fit."

"NO!" Pain coursed through me. This was too much. I couldn't leave Taros, not without Sierra. I had to get out of this. I stepped back. We would run. The blood oath couldn't be enforced if I couldn't hear the orders. I turned quickly, making a run for it, but she saw it coming.

"Stop." She commanded, and I froze, my heart thudding in my chest. I couldn't move, couldn't even turn to face her.

She rose from her chair and came to stand in front of me. Panic slithered through me like a winter chill. She lashed out, striking me hard across the face. Tears stung my eyes at the contact.

"I have had quite enough of your insolence. I will punish you for your insubordination, but right now you're going to listen up, Adira. Listen and obey. You are going to not only win the prince's trust, but you will make him fall in love with you. When he asks for your hand, which he *will,* you will accept. Write back to Queen Tira, telling her you would like to get to know her and this new side of your family, but you're going to finish up the rest of your stay in Taros first. Then, you *will* go to Xeria and accept your title as princess. You will continue as planned, playing any roles we ask of you. Is that clear?"

I tried to nod, but I couldn't.

"You may speak."

"Yes." I gritted out. "I understand."

"Good. This is the last time I will repeat myself. If you disobey me again, I will take it out on darling Sierra. Now get out of my sight before I decide to pay her a visit, anyway."

I stumbled forward as my body was released, able to move again. Swallowing down my fear and rage, I hurried out. I tried to go to where I'd stashed what little coin I had so we could flee, but my legs wouldn't cooperate. I tried to go to Raf's loft to get Sierra and Raf, but I could not.

The pain in my chest grew each time I tried to take a path that inevitably lead to disobeying my orders. No matter how hard I fought, I couldn't beat it.

Tears fell as I made my way back through the tunnels and to my chambers.

Sitting on my bed and burying my face in my hands, I crumbled. I couldn't beat her, couldn't beat *them*. I didn't know how to win this game. I thought I could outsmart her, but it always came back to this damned blood oath.

I stood, knocking the contents of my bedside table onto the ground. A glass shattered, my hairbrush clanged to the floor, and the books went flying. I was so angry. I hurled anything within reach before falling to the floor in a flood of tears.

I don't know how long I wept, how long I had wallowed in defeat, but eventually, the tears had run dry and I was left sitting silently on the floor, surrounded by the destruction I'd caused. I sighed and slowly began cleaning up my mess.

I made the bed before carefully sweeping the glass into a pile. I would have to ask the maids for a dustpan. Then I picked up the books. Luckily, they appeared to be undamaged. Placing them back on the bedside table, I noticed something sticking out from one of the texts. It looked like another page, but it was not the same colour as the rest.

I opened the book and examined it properly. It wasn't a page from the book. The inside of the cover had come loose, revealing a hidden piece of parchment. I carefully peeled back the rest of the cover and looked at it. My breath caught. At the top of the page, in the centre almost as if it were the title, was another drawn symbol of the mark I carried.

The same symbol I'd seen in the book about the Giftings, the same symbol I'd seen on the hilt of the white-eyed man's dagger, except for one difference.

This one had a serpens curled along the blade. This damned symbol kept appearing, with no explanation. There was more than just the symbol this time, though. There was someone's handwritten text.

This sigil; a dripping, diagonal dagger, with a serpens coiled around it, is the mark of the seventh house. The most powerful and feared of the seven kingdoms.

I flipped the page over, searching for more, but found nothing. I lifted my top and looked at the symbol. Mine was missing the serpens, but it was the same dagger. The detailing was a perfect match. What did it mean, the seventh house? The seventh kingdom?

There had only ever been six kingdoms. Before that, the divinities ruled. There were no mortal kingdoms or lands. Is it possible the history books got it wrong? Had there been a seventh house?

Could Solis be from that house? It would explain why this mark was used. It might explain the rebellion if she thought they owed her a kingdom, if they erased hers from history. But how? How could something that big simply be forgotten? Someone must remember the seventh house if there was one?

I tucked the piece of paper back into the book and pressed the cover back into place. If there was any information on this so-called seventh kingdom, I would find it. It was a lead, a tiny, tiny thread of hope. But it was all I had. Without it, I would likely drown in self-pity. No. I would find a way out of this. Even if it meant playing their games.

CHAPTER TWENTY-NINE

AFTER PULLING MYSELF TOGETHER, I headed straight for the library. I went over all the notes I'd taken during my questioning of the advisors, before taking out the document I'd taken from Lord Rumbón's desk, and comparing the signed 'C', to the writing samples I'd stolen from all but Father Chambersen. No match.

Could it be as simple as the C standing for Chambersen? Why would he want to remove Hadrian from the throne? Was it just him, or was the entire Taros sect of Deos Credentes behind him? I had to get a writing sample. I made plans on how I might obtain one, before continuing my research into the other mystery on my mind.

I put back yet another dead end book on the history of Deorum and its kingdoms. I'd found no mention of a seventh kingdom or house. Then I had a thought. I walked over to where Hamish was standing guard, looking incredibly bored.

"Thank the divinities. You done for the day?"

"Yes, and no." He groaned, knowing me well enough by now to know that whatever I had planned, he probably wouldn't enjoy.

"What is it this time?"

"How would you feel about a quick trip to the cells?" I batted my eyelashes at him, giving him my best puppy dog eyes.

He crossed his arms and eyed me suspiciously. "Why?"

"You'll see when we get there! Pleaseee, Hamish?"

He sighed and shook his head. "It cannot be more boring than this. Let's go."

"You're such a pushover." Tarryn called from his post before joining us. I grinned.

"Shut up, you were practically asleep, Amesley."

"I certainly was not."

I laughed a little and linked my arms through theirs.

"You two argue like a married couple."

Hamish scoffed. "As if he could pull a man like me." He flexed his biceps as if to prove the point, eliciting an eye roll from Tarryn and another laugh from me.

"Alright, Casanova." I started walking, forcing them along with me.

As we reached the cells, I noted with dismay that the smell hadn't improved since I'd last been here. Hamish had a word with the guards on duty and convinced them to let me through.

Some nonsense about having to keep the noblewoman he was guarding happy, or the captain would give him night shift for the next month. In fact, it was more likely the opposite, with Killian punishing Hamish if he knew he took me down here.

Luckily, the guards bought it. I asked Hamish and Tarryn to wait a few cells down once I'd found the one I wanted. I stepped forward and squinted into the darkness. At first I thought it was empty, and I'd wasted a trip, but then I heard her.

"They have not caught the fox, interesting."

I breathed in as a figure emerged from the shadows. The old crone. Still cloaked in such a deep black that she blended into the darkness like the two were old friends. I looked to where the men stood, then back to the old woman.

"You know me?" I questioned, with absolutely no idea what I really expected to glean from her, but the fact that she was here, was a start. I was told there were no women in the cells. Odette, I could easily believe, had lied, but Hadrian? Had he lied or did he simply not know?

"As well as the moon could know the sun. Only ever glimpsed from afar, but glimpsed nonetheless."

I frowned. "You keep calling me a fox. Why?"

"Because that is what you are. Sly, cunning. An omen from the divinities themselves." She glanced up, and I found myself doing the same.

She tilted her head to the side. "But that is not the knowledge you seek from me." Here goes nothing.

"Was there a seventh kingdom?"

"Was, or is?"

"Are you saying that there was one and that it still exists?"

"What is a kingdom without a ruler?"

"... So it exists, but has no one to rule it?"

"Can one exist without the other? Hmm, what makes a ruler? Is it a crown? Land? Subjects?"

"Lady, can you just give me a straight answer?"

She made a 'tsk' sound and glanced at the ceiling again. "She is not ready, this one. Too impatient. Too naïve. Too self pitying." She began pacing and gesturing with her hands as if she were conversing with someone.

"Who are you talking to?" I asked, ignoring her insulting comments.

"Don't interrupt, girl." She shook her head and continued pacing. "I suppose she could, but only if—No. No, she's not ready. The serpens is on the move. The fox cannot see. She won't see."

This woman was insane. I sighed. This was a dumb idea. I made to step back, but before I had even blinked, the old woman was in front of me, gripping my dress and pulling me against the bars. I cried out in shock. Her eyes—she had none. There were nothing but dark holes where her eyes should have been.

"Elia?" Hamish called. "Is everything okay?" Footsteps sounded as he approached.

"See, little fox. See! The seventh kingdom will only live if you see!" She hissed. "When the river runs red, then you will know. Only then will you know. The rest will be up to you, but watch the grass, little fox, the serpens is moving. Arm yourself with allies. You must trust to win! You must!" I jerked back, stumbling a little, before I regained my footing.

"What happened? Did you see a rotmouth?" Hamish smirked. Rotmouths were foul, rodent-like little beasts. They were fairly harmless to mortals, just gross to look at and likely to devour any food it finds, leaving nothing but a putrid smell of rot in its wake.

They could grow to the same size as a hound pup, and were common in the slums, sewers, and apparently, castle dungeons.

"I wish. The old hag pulled me into the bars." I dusted myself off.

"What old hag?" He looked at me weirdly.

"That one." I pointed, looking back at the cell. My eyes widened. She was gone.

"Um.... Elle, there's no one in there?"

"She was there. I saw her." I frowned, stepping forward. "I spoke to her..?"

"Right... maybe we should get you back to your chambers?"

Was I the crazy one? No. I'd seen her. Felt her. And she knew about the seventh kingdom. It all had to mean something.

I received more looks than usual as we made our way back through the castle. When I passed, conversations turned to hushed whispers and stares. I frowned.

"Do I have something on my face?" I asked, turning to Hamish and Tarryn.

"No?" Tarryn answered quizzically.

"Then why is everyone looking at me strangely? Well, stranger than usual."

"Probably because of the new rumours—" Hamish was cut off by a swift elbow to the ribs. He grunted. "Ow?! What was that for?" He glared at Tarryn.

"What rumours?"

"Well, that depends, there are the ones about you and a certain nobleman..." I breathed a sigh of relief. The rumour about Valor and me being betrothed must have just reached more people. I could handle that. "Which, judging by the look on your face I'd say are true?"

"Hamish. Divinities." Tarryn scolded, and I smiled a little. That man had absolutely no filter, and it was one of my favourite things about him, even at times like these.

"It's alright, Tarryn. Yes, depending on what you've heard."

"So you slept with Killian Ambrosia?" Tarryn asked. I gasped, immediately coming to a halt.

"WHAT?!"

Hamish cracked up, and Tarryn smirked at me. I looked between them before crossing my arms.

"Okay, that is *not* funny. Tell me you're joking and no one thinks that?"

Hamish doubled over, gripping his stomach, and Tarryn just shrugged innocently.

"Ugh, you two are insufferable." I continued walking without them, hiding the smile tugging at my lips.

It took them only a few seconds to catch up to me. Hamish was still chuckling.

"No one thinks that no. Although, you probably could and no one would notice. Too distracted by the whole you-being-a-princess thing," Tarryn finally said.

I stopped. "What."

Tarryn smiled at me sympathetically.

"There are rumours circulating that you are the daughter of Tira Melfore, Queen of Xeria."

"Shit." I cursed. How the Hek had people found out? Had Butcher leaked it, or Odette?

"But hey, bright side, at least people don't think you're sleeping with Killian?" Hamish offered.

"Great, very reassuring."

"Although, if you *did*, it might distract from the princess thing? If you don't want to sleep with him, I could take one for the team and offer you my services?" Hamish volunteered, wiggling his eyebrows. I fake gagged before laughing a little and shaking my head.

"That is a very inappropriate thing for my guard to say."

"I agree."

I looked over to find Valor standing there, aiming a frosty glare at Hamish. Who, to his credit, quickly wiped the grin off of his face and bowed. Tarryn followed suit.

"That wasn't what it sounded like, Your Highness."

"Oh? It wasn't you propositioning Lady Elia?" I smirked slightly, enjoying the look of horror on Hamish's face for a few seconds longer than necessary as he scrambled for something to say before I stepped in.

"He was kidding, Val." I looked at Hamish and Tarryn. "The prince can walk me the rest of the way. Would you mind fetching some dinner for me from the kitchens?"

Hamish nodded, relieved. "Of course." He nodded again before heading in the opposite direction with a sniggering Tarryn.

"You shouldn't let them treat you like that," Valor said, and I looked back at him. He still looked grumpy.

"Like what, exactly?"

"Like you're just any woman they have a shot with."

"Who says they don't have a shot with me?"

He frowned. "Funny."

"Who says I am kidding? Why wouldn't I? They are both lovely, good-looking men."

He gritted his teeth. "They are guards. It would be improper."

I scoffed. "Only because snobby people like you decide so." I continued walking and, much to my disappointment, he followed.

"I am not a snob."

I sighed. "Is there something you want, Your Highness?" He looked like he wanted to say more, but he closed his eyes instead, before shaking his head and breathing out.

"No, I just spoke to my mother, and I wanted to see.... how you were doing." He opened his eyes and looked at me. That sounded like it pained him to admit.

"I was doing well until you reminded me just now." I really was not doing a good job of getting him to like me. Luckily, Butcher hadn't given me a time frame, so I wasn't technically disobeying her orders.

"Sorry..."

I sighed. "Apparently the entire castle knows, probably the whole capital by now." I came to a stop in front of my door.

"Do you want to talk about it?"

"What's there to talk about?"

"A Hek of a lot, I'd say."

"Are you here to check on my wellbeing, or to see if I'm considering the other heirs?" I said boldly, looking at him. His eyes widened, but he didn't deny the latter fast enough.

"Mmm, that's what I thought." I entered my room, figuring it wouldn't be that easy to lose him. I was right. He followed and shut the door.

"That's not fair."

"Life isn't fair."

He rolled his eyes. "That's a tad dramatic, Sunshine."

"It's Princess now, remember?" I bit back sarcastically. Something about him just brought out the anger in me so easily.

"So I've heard," he said, watching me, "I've heard a lot of things, but I would like to hear them from you."

"What difference does it make?"

"It makes all the difference," he said, "please."

I raised my eyebrows and looked at him properly. Then it clicked. He wanted to hear that I truly hadn't known, that I hadn't lied to him. He wanted to trust me, but part of him was still sceptical. I sighed.

"No Valor, I didn't know. I'm just as shocked as anyone, probably more so."

"Why didn't you tell me when you found out?"

"Why would I tell you?"

He sighed. "Come on, Elia, whatever this is between us, I know you feel it. I thought you trusted me."

"Oh, you mean like how you trust me completely?"

He sighed, running his fingers through his hair. "That's different. I'm a prince. We... I can't trust just anyone."

"Yet you expect everyone else to give theirs to you without you doing the same?"

"Not everyone. I don't care about everyone's trust."

I rolled my eyes. "Is that supposed to make me feel better?"

"Yes, it is."

"You are so entitled." I crossed my arms. "Not everything is about you, Princeling." Again, I *really* wasn't helping my situation. Anyone else I would have been able to flirt with, smile at, and lie my way into their affections, but something about this man just set me off. Worst of all, a part of me, a large part, actually *enjoyed* that about him.

He groaned. "You don't get it!"

"Oh, then please explain it to my simple-minded self, Your Highness."

"I NEED TO KNOW I CAN TRUST YOU, ELIA. I DON'T CARE ABOUT ANYONE ELSE'S TRUST. I CARE ABOUT YOURS!"

"WHY?!" I didn't even know why we were yelling.

"BECAUSE I WANT TO TRUST YOU, ELIA! But I can't let myself do that until I know for sure. It was fine *before* because you were just a lady, you weren't a viable option, but now that you're a divinity damned princess, I am struggling to find a reason to push you away!" He shouted back, his chest rising and falling, his fist clenched at his side.

I wanted to keep shouting at him. This time it wasn't because I was mad at him, it was because I wanted to protect him from me, but my chest tugged and Butcher's words echoed in my head.

You are going to not only win the Prince's trust, but you will make him fall in love with you, and when he asks for your hand, you will *accept.*

I swallowed and walked over to him, stopping in front of him.

"I'm sorry," I mumbled. "I didn't tell anyone. I needed to process it on my own. I was... overwhelmed and not ready to share it with anyone. That isn't because I don't trust you, I do." I put a hand on his chest and realised that I was telling the truth, at least about the trusting him part. "Despite trying really hard not to." Also completely true.

He breathed in as he listened, a storm brewing in his eyes as he fought a silent battle with himself.

"Elia, you being a princess changes everything..."

"It doesn't have to."

He moved his hand over mine. "But it does. If your mother decides she can use you to form an alliance with whoever she sees fit." I heard the words he didn't say. If he let himself care for me, and I was married off to someone else.

I shook my head. "A stranger will not push around me just because she is a queen. I won't be forced into anything I don't want to do." Lie.

"And what if you want to?" What if I want someone else? His words hung in the air between us.

"They wouldn't be you." I was torn. Part of me wanted him to laugh in my face and leave the room like the prince I'd met on that first day would have done. To not fall for any of this, to protect himself from me. The other part needed him to believe it, needed him to fall for it. For Butcher. For Sierra. A tiny part of me even wanted it just for me, the part I had buried the second Butcher had ordered me to gain his trust.

"I didn't want this." He muttered. I swallowed and looked down, nodding slightly.

"Right... sorry..." I made to step back, but he gripped my hand. I looked back up at him.

"But, I do."

My eyes widened slightly, and I opened my mouth to say something, but before I could, his lips were on mine.

He tasted like Spring, fresh and cool, as he pulled me against him. I wanted to stop him, to pull away and confess. But did I?

I wasn't sure if it was the stress, the heightened emotions, Butchers order, or something within myself I wasn't yet ready to acknowledge, that made me give in, but I didn't have the willpower to stop and figure out.

Make him love you.

So instead, I pressed into his hold, wrapping my arms around his neck, and I kissed him back. Apparently, that was all the encouragement he needed because the next thing I knew, he was backing me towards the bed, not breaking the kiss, not letting go.

My knees hit the bed frame, and I fell back onto the mattress. Before I could sit up, he was leaning over me, kissing my lips again, before moving to my neck. I closed my eyes, tilting my head to the side. It had been a while since I'd been with anyone other than Raf. I hadn't realised just how long until now. Until, with just a few kisses, I was coming undone. Granted, they were extremely good kisses.

My hands seemed to move on their own accord as they slid down his chest, un-tucking his shirt so they could feel along his chiselled abdomen and up his toned chest. He shivered at my touch, but didn't stop me. Rather, the opposite, as he began expertly undoing the bodice of my dress. His hands were both hot and cold. Everywhere he touched, I burned, in the best possible way. I pressed my hips up against his, eliciting a small groan from him.

"Elia..." he murmured against my ear. I ignored the traitorous part of myself that longed to hear him whisper a different name. His breath was hot against my skin.

I shook my head, one of my hands moving out of his shirt and to his belt, swiftly undoing it.

"No talking," I said and kissed his lips. I felt him tense for a second, battling whatever part of him wanted to be sensible and stop, but like me, he caved to the alternative instead.

He worked swiftly, getting the rest of my dress off, leaving me in only my undergarments. I returned the favour, practically ripping his shirt from his body before returning to his belt and pants.

He stopped me, stepping back. I looked into his eyes, their dazzling blue swirling like a storm. I could see the hunger on his face as he took me in. I swallowed, feeling exposed, but unable to stop the tingling low in my stomach as his eyes roved over my body.

He deftly removed his pants before kicking off his shoes and leaning over me again. This time, there was no restraint. His hands explored my body like a man starved of touch, as he freed me of my remaining clothing. My hands answered in kind, pushing down his undershorts. He bit my lip, eliciting a gasp from me.

CHAPTER THIRTY

APPARENTLY, THAT WAS HIS intention, because as soon as my lips parted his tongue was exploring my mouth, as eagerly as his hands were the curves of my body. My hips pressed into his, and I could feel him hard against me now. He was even less patient than me, it seemed, because his hand moved to my waist, pulling me almost roughly against him again. His other hand slid down my stomach, then kept going. *Fates.* I couldn't tell Elia's desires from Adira's as his hand reached its destination, and I couldn't care less.

My hips bucked slightly, but he'd been prepared, using his other hand still gripping my waist, he pinned me down. He watched me like a hunter watched its prey. I'd never been so glad to be the hunted. His fingers worked me like a string player would their favourite instrument. I moved my hand over his crotch, but he gently grabbed my wrist and pinned it above my head.

"No," he said, shaking his head as he met my eyes, "not until I've had my way with you."

Sweet mother of Heknos. As another wave of pleasure hit, I threw my head back. I wasn't sure how much longer I'd last, but I didn't want his hand. I wanted him.

"Please." I whimpered, breathing heavily as I once again tried to reach down. He kept my wrist pinned and smirked down at me. He leaned in, placing a trail of kisses down my neck, across my collarbone, then down to my chest, paying special attention to that area. I moaned, my legs tensing.

"Valor." I rasped frustratedly, and he chuckled softly.

"So impatient, Sunshine" He placed a kiss on my stomach before repositioning himself, and before I could tell him off, he slid his length inside me in one smooth motion. I cried out in pleasure, gripping his arm with my free hand. He grunted slightly as he adjusted himself. Starting slowly at first, as my body tightened and relaxed, moulding to his sizable asset.

Once he'd deemed it comfortable, he began thrusting. Keeping my wrist held above my head, he gripped my waist tighter. My breathing increased, and I threw my head back once again, lifting my hips in time with his as best I could. His thrusting increased.

"F-faster.." I breathed, and he responded in kind. His movements sped up as he let out his own groan of approval.

I nodded, moving with him. He let go of my wrist and cupped my breast in his now free hand, leaning down to kiss the other one as he did. Before my brain could catch up to what he was doing, his hand was on the move again. Trailing down my stomach, further and further. My eyes widened slightly as his fingers lightly hovered over me, teasing. I thrust my hips upwards, digging my nails into his skin, letting him know exactly what I thought of his tease.

He chuckled roughly and my stomach dipped at the sound, I just about lost it then and there. His eyes met mine as his fingers finally caressed me. Then I really came undone, my back arched as I jerked slightly, letting out a loud moan that was smothered by his lips on mine as I fell over the edge, taking him with me.

I wasn't sure how long we laid there in each other's arms before one of us spoke. That one of us being me because I am an idiot with a big mouth.

"Well, that was... unexpected." I grimaced. *Moron.*

He looked down at me, raising his eyebrows. "Really?"

I groaned. "I didn't know what else to say, okay?"

"How about, *oh my gosh, Val that was amazing, you're the best I've ever had! When can we do it again?*" he said, imitating my voice in a terrible, high-pitched tone.

"Okay, first of all, I don't sound like that," I said, grabbing a pillow and smacking him with it. He chuckled, stealing it from me.

"Second, it was alright. I'd shut that trap of yours if you want it to happen again." I raised my eyebrows back at him.

He smirked. "We both know it was better than alright."

I rolled my eyes. "Men. Insufferable." I rolled away, but he pulled me back and I could feel his chest vibrating in silent laughter.

"Don't move away."

I looked up at him, and he placed a hand on my cheek. "You realise this makes things a lot more complicated, right?" I once again moronically pointed out.

He nodded a bit. "I was hoping we could avoid that for a bit." I gave him a look that said something like *'yeah right, because life is that easy.'*

He smiled a bit and sighed. "Alright, fine, but I don't see how talking about it is going to help."

"What exactly do you propose we do, then?"

"Nothing."

I frowned. "Nothing?"

"What else can we do? We just have to see what happens. Neither of us can control anything until we know what the situation is."

I looked at him incredulously. "If I had known all I had to do to make you relax a bit was sleep with you, I would have done it a Hek of a lot sooner."

"Ha ha," he said, shaking his head.

"Honestly, though, it will not be that simple. Don't we need to, I don't know, discuss what just happened?"

"I'd really rather we didn't."

"Rude," I said.

"I *meant* I'd rather we just enjoyed it for a bit longer." He stroked my cheek. "We have plenty of time to discuss it." He kissed the spot where his fingers had just been. "But right now, I just want to not worry about it and simply enjoy you."

"Alright," I conceded, "But only for a little while, then it's back to reality."

"Yes, ma'am." I rolled my eyes but smiled.

"Now where was I?" He said, moving closer.

"Um." I shrugged innocently. He grinned and kissed me once more.

A *little while* turned out to be three weeks of stolen kisses, secret rendezvous, and ignoring the reality that would soon be at our doorstep. Valor was almost like a different person. He'd stopped trying to hold himself back, and so had I. I couldn't tell how much of that was because of Butcher's orders and how much was because I wanted to.

We were yet again in my bedchamber, taking some time for ourselves. Valor had been going on more and more reconnaissance trips, chasing leads on the rebel movements. Whenever we could sneak away and distract each other from our troubles, we did. Valor was doing just that as he placed a kiss on my neck. I smiled, wrapping my arms around him as a knock sounded at the door.

"Sorry to bother you, Elle, but the captain is here looking for the prince," Hamish called from the hall.

"Thanks, Hamish! Tell the captain he'll be out in a minute!"

Valor groaned silently, but rose and began grabbing his clothes. I did the same, quickly gathering mine, and slipping back into them as hastily as I could. I turned to find him standing there still stark naked, watching me with an amused smile on his face.

"What are you doing?!" I whispered. "Get dressed. If you keep him waiting, he'll think something was going on."

"Something *was* going on."

"Yeah, well, he doesn't need to know that."

He smirked. "You were loud enough that I'm sure the guards posted outside have already informed him." My eyes widened.

"*I WA*—I was not!" I whispered-shouted at him. "Just hurry up."

He chuckled but conceded and lazily put his clothes back on. I shook my head at him, checked my hair in the mirror and promptly hurried to the bathing chamber to run a comb through it. Thank Helia I'd checked, or us being dressed wouldn't have hidden what had just occurred.

I came back out once I was convinced I'd hidden all the signs.

He grinned at me. "Nice."

I stuck my tongue out before going and opening the door.

"Killian, come in."

Killian was standing, chatting with Hamish and Tarryn. I could tell they respected him, not just because he outranked them, but because he'd earned it.

He bowed his head. "Lady Elia, or is it Princess now?"

I groaned. "Not you as well."

He chuckled. "If you don't use my title, I won't use yours."

"Deal." I stepped aside.

"I actually can't stay. I just came to fetch Val. Figured he'd be here."

"You have the worst timing, Kil," Valor said, stepping out.

"Why is that?" Killian asked.

"Well, it's not the *worst* timing," he said thoughtfully. "It *definitely* could have been worse." He nodded.

I glared at his back. Shaking my head, I looked at Killian.

"Lovely seeing you, as always, Killian." I stepped back and made to shut the door.

"What about me?" Valor said, sounding offended.

"It's never lovely seeing you." I shut the door and locked it to make my point, also to hide the smile that appeared against my will.

I heard three out of the four men laugh before two of them said farewell to the others and departed. I listened at the door until I could no longer hear their footsteps, then I quickly changed into my dark tunic and cloak.

I started down the tunnel, no longer needing to light the way. I'd memorised the routes I might need, and the ones I didn't. It was actually an excellent training exercise, even if I had gotten lost for longer than I'd like to admit when I'd first tried without lantern light.

I pulled my cloak over my head and snuck out through the gardens. I kept to the side streets and avoided drawing any unnecessary attention as I made my way to Raf's loft. We needed to talk. I'd let him brood for weeks and now it was time we made up. This was one of the longest we'd gone without speaking. I hated every minute. I tried not to think about the fact that I could very well have been letting Valor distract me from missing Raf.

Relief filled me as I eyed his door. I made my way up the steps, but stopped short. The door was slightly ajar. My eyes quickly took in the surroundings. Nothing else was amiss.

I withdrew my dagger and stepped forward, slowly nudging the door open. I stiffened. Someone had trashed the front room. His furniture was in shambles. The floor was littered with shattered glass. I stepped around the broken shards, searching the other rooms. They all resembled the front room, broken and torn apart. Raf and Sierra weren't anywhere to be seen.

My blood pumped so fast I saw red. I took a breath to calm myself, but then I actually saw red. My heart stopped as I noted the blood on the ground, next to the remnants of Sierra's roller. *No.* My hands shook as I took another steadying breath. It wasn't a large amount, and there were no bodies. They had to be okay. It looked like someone put up a fight. If it had gone terribly, there would be a lot more blood.

Butcher had said she would punish me for my 'insubordination', but we had a deal. Sierra was off limits. I slid my dagger back into its sheath on my thigh. She wanted me panicked and thrown off guard. I wouldn't let her have that satisfaction.

I hurried out, shutting the door behind me, making my way across the quarter. I was about to duck into an ally that would lead me to Butcher's, when I noticed a crowd forming in the centre square, usually reserved for royal announcements. *I swear if they announced my new title to the citizens so soon.* I made my way to the edge of the crowd. It was silent. No one was chatting or really even moving much. I couldn't see over the heads of the people in front of me, so I slowly weaved in and out until I could get a closer look. I caught a few whispers as I moved through the mob. Saw a few ladies make a prayer to whatever divinities they worshipped.

"Fates forbid..."

"D'ya reckon they'll leave 'em there long?"

"Fools to get involved."

"Their poor mothers..."

I finally made my way to the front and got a good look at what they were all muttering about. What I saw made my blood run cold. Everything around me froze as I took in the scene.

The usual scaffolding, used so everyone could see and hear the announcer, had been turned into gallows. There were four bodies hanging from the wooden structure. Their eyes were wide and lifeless, swinging in the light breeze with nooses tight around their necks.

There was a blonde man who looked to be in his late twenties. Next to him was a woman with tawny hair, her hand still gripping his, frozen in time, as their limbs had no doubt seized up, but they refused to part.

Next to the woman was a boy who looked no older than ten. My heart ached to see such a small child hung up like a puppet, like a doll. What could he have possibly done to warrant such a harsh punishment? But it wasn't the lovers still clinging to each other or the child reminding me of Sierra that crippled me. It was the fourth body.

Tall, muscular, and shirtless, his blonde curly hair flowing in the wind, his lifeless blue eyes staring into the distance as if he had been searching for something, *someone*. Carved across his chest, the word *TRAITOR* was still dripping, as if it had happened only moments ago.

My knees gave way as my heart cracked open. I didn't care that everyone could see me, that a guard could think me affiliated with them and serve me the same fate. *Raf.* Raphael Morrighan. Who'd given me reasons to smile when I couldn't find any. The orphan who got out. The man who outgrew everything but his boyish grin. The one that could trick you into thinking anything was possible. The man I'd loved but never told. The boy who breathed life into me when I had needed it the most was dead, branded a traitor to his kingdom because of me.

A sob racked through me, and I didn't bother bracing my knees as I fell. But the impact never came.

Strong hands circled around me, pulling me up against a hard body. I cried, lost in my grief, let the guards drag me away for all I cared.

They led me out of the crowd and away from the centre. It wasn't until we rounded the corner and stopped in a secluded alcove that I let myself open my eyes, preparing for whatever punishment was to come. I came face to face with a familiar royal guard.

"T—Tarryn?"

He nodded solemnly. "I'm so sorry, Adira." I stiffened, pulling back.

"What?" I was struggling to keep my composure. Raf's lifeless eyes kept flashing across my mind.

"... I can explain everything, but we need to get somewhere less exposed."

"I'm not going a—anywhere with you." Another sob slipped free as I took another step back, my knees shaking.

"Adira, I wasn't the only one who noticed your reaction to the — they will come looking and if one of them recognises you, your cover will be blown."

"Is this some kind of sick joke? Have you been working for Butcher this whole time?" Even in my current state, I used her damned alias.

"No. I don't work for The Butcher."

"Bullshit!"

"Shhh!" He said and glanced around the pillar keeping us hidden from the rest of the world. "I work for The Crone, Adira. Please. I can explain everything, but not here. You have to trust me."

My chest ached, feeling like it might fracture into everlasting pieces. I couldn't comprehend what he was saying. I kept glancing back towards the centre of the square. I had to get him down. He couldn't stay like that. I tried to step around Tarryn and do just that, but he blocked my way.

I gritted my teeth. "Move."

"They put them there on purpose, Adira. To see who would collect them, who is with them. If you go anywhere near them in broad daylight, you'll join them."

"I don't care!"

"What about Sierra?" I froze and stared at him.

"What did you just say?"

"Your sister needs you..." He said, watching me.

Without thinking, and faster than I'd ever reacted, I had my dagger drawn and pressed to his throat.

"Give me one good reason I shouldn't slit your throat right now for even daring to say her name?"

"Because I am on your side! Yours and hers. Because I am trying to help you. That includes saving her. I can explain everything, but not here, and certainly not at knifepoint."

"If you want me to trust you, then leave. Walk away. I'll find you when I am ready."

"I wouldn't do whatever it is you're thinking of doing, Adira."

"What I do is none of your business. If you're serious about me being able to trust you, then prove it. Leave."

He sighed. "Don't do anything stupid, please." He held up his hands and slowly stepped back. "... I'm truly sorry about your friend."

Tears threatened to fall again, and I gripped the dagger as I lowered it. "*GO.*"

He nodded slightly, backing up further, turning, and disappearing into the crowd. I closed my eyes for a second, breathing out shakily. He was right about one thing. If I went back and took Raf down now, I would risk getting caught and not being able to save Sierra. I would have to come back under the cover of darkness, even if it killed a part of me to leave him there. Butcher would be waiting for me.

I couldn't run. I had to face her. After wiping my face and sheathing my dagger, I made my way to Butcher's. Sierra had to be my priority now. There was nothing I could do for Raf until nightfall.

CHAPTER THIRTY-ONE

I TOOK A MINUTE to steel myself before entering the manor. Tolemas was waiting atop the staircase. He looked at me with pity in his eyes. That look threatened to break me all over again, so I ignored him and simply walked into the study.

"You know better than to enter without a proper announcement, Adira," Butcher said, glancing up.

I knew I looked a mess. My eyes were still red from the tears, my cheeks likely a matching rosy colour. I was not a pretty crier.

"Why?"

"Because it is impolite."

"Why Raf?!" I demanded.

She glanced at me, her eyes showing no remorse, no emotion. She was calm and collected, which only incensed me more.

"I told you I would punish you for your insubordination. I can't physically punish you or it would jeopardise your assignment and I agreed not to harm Sierra. Honestly, I would prefer not to have to. I am quite fond of the girl and she is such a good bookkeeper. Which left only one other person you cared about. Well, two, but I doubted your anger at Tolemas's betrayal had lessened enough to really drive my point home."

My heart ached. "He was innocent... He didn't deserve that. It should have been me."

"He was, he didn't, and you are far too valuable to share his fate. I warned you, Adira, but you kept on pushing, kept fighting. You were always a smart girl, careful to never let yourself get too close to anyone, but Raphael, your childhood friend turned lover? Well, any girl would struggle to shut those pretty blue eyes out. It was an admirable effort, though."

I clenched my fist, and unable to hold in my pain any longer, a tear rolled down my cheek.

"Where is Sierra?"

"She is safe, and she will remain so, as long as you behave and stop with all of this defiance."

"*Where* is she?" I demanded once more.

"You are in no position to make demands, Adira. Make no mistake, if you misbehave again, whilst I won't enjoy it, I *will* take it out on Sierra. I promised *I* wouldn't harm her. Tolemas made no such promise."

I tensed. "Tolemas wouldn't hurt her."

"Are you willing to risk that? You once thought he would never betray you either, and yet, here we stand."

I wasn't, and she was right. I didn't know what Tolemas would really do anymore.

"Please, just let me see her. I got the message after my last visit, Camilla."

"Yes, well, we felt it prudent for you to face the consequences of your previous actions, so there are no repeats."

I closed my eyes, defeated. "I understand, please. I just need to see that she is alright."

"When I am convinced you have learned your lesson, then you may see her."

I swallowed. "How may I serve?"

She grinned. "I assume you have heard by now that Queen Tira, as well as the other Royal families, will pay us a visit to discuss the peace treaty King Hadrian has been pushing for, for years."

"What? All five kingdoms are coming? Including Xeria?"

"They haven't announced it? How interesting. Well yes, they are all coming, *especially* Xeria. In fact, Queen Tira insisted on coming early, to meet her long-lost daughter."

I stiffened. "So that's it then, you're pulling me out before I am compromised?"

She laughed, and it was cold, without humour. "Why on earth would I do that? You are in the perfect position."

"Are you insane? The second Queen Tira arrives, my cover will be blown and I'll be hung!"

"Oh, don't be so dramatic."

I couldn't believe what I was hearing. Had she *actually* lost it? She looked at my expression and rolled her eyes.

"I must confess, the last time we discussed this, I didn't give you all the information."

Not surprising in the slightest. "What do you mean?"

"The Xerian Queen knows nothing of myself or Solis, she is not an ally of ours. As far as she knows, you *are* her long-lost daughter. She did in fact have an affair with Viktor Worthington, resulting in the birth of a little girl."

I said nothing, allowing her to continue.

"As far as Queen Tira knows, you are that little girl."

My stomach dropped.

"What happened to her real daughter?"

"She was taken care of."

"How?"

"We had her killed, of course. Her alias was too perfect to pass up. It was the best way for us to get you in and keep you there. We couldn't risk someone finding her, or finding out that you are not her."

I felt sick. "But, when? How old was she when you murdered her?"

"A year after I took you in. Once I saw your potential and realised what we could make you into."

I swallowed. "She was just a child, the same age as I was? You had a seven-year-old killed?"

She rolled her eyes. "You always were so dramatic. Knowing this changes nothing, so I suggest you move on from this subject."

Closing my eyes for a second, and sending a prayer to whatever divinities might be listening, that the little girl whose name I now bore was at peace. I doubted the divinities heard, or cared, if they would let a child die like that. Opening my eyes, I refocused.

"When does she arrive? When do the other kingdoms arrive?"

"Queen Tira is leaving soon. It will take her the longest to get here. She would like to arrive before the others. So roughly six weeks, give or take a few days. The rest will take their time, make sure everything is stable in their kingdoms before departing. I expect them to arrive in a little over two months."

"And what about when they ask me to demonstrate my Gifting? If I were indeed Tira's daughter, I'd be a Para."

"You leave that to me."

"You can't be serious?"

The look she gave me was severe. "Stop with that line of questioning." My chest tugged painfully, and I sighed.

"Okay, what am I meant to do in the meantime then?"

"Continue as you are, keep earning the royals trust, keep earning the prince's affections. Although, it's worth ensuring he has a little doubt. The other kingdoms may be coming for the peace treaty, but they no doubt have also seen the same opportunity the Navarre's have."

"What opportunity?"

"A political marriage of course. You are a new royal that hasn't yet been influenced by your blood family. Any kingdom could use you to broker an alliance, figuring you'd be easy to control."

"I thought you wanted me to say yes to Valor if he proposes, now you're saying I should let myself be considered by all the kingdoms?"

She shrugged. "Yes, I think that would be beneficial to all of us."

I shook my head, not pushing her lest she order me to do exactly that. "Can I see Sierra?"

"No."

"Camilla please—"

"The answer is no. Now leave."

I turned on my heels without choice and left like the obedient mongrel she had turned me into.

My brain was struggling to process all that today had brought as I made my way back through the city, giving the centre square a wide berth. *Just breathe, Adira. Keep calm. You can't freak out here.*

I slipped back into the tunnels, leaning against the wall. In the darkness, I finally let myself think. I swallowed, closing my eyes. The other five kingdoms were coming, Raf was dead, Butcher had Sierra, Tarryn knew who I was, and apparently worked for someone called The Crone. What if the 'C' was for Crone? I was screwed. There was no other word for it. Completely, royally screwed.

I cursed The Fates for continuing to deal me such awful hands.

Once I was safely back in my chambers, I changed into 'lady appropriate' attire and began pacing, trying to wrap my mind around everything. Every time I tried to make sense of it all, I'd have to walk through the events of the day. Including finding Raf. It overwhelmed me anytime he popped into my head. My heart ached, my eyes hurt, and my body was tired. I had seen him with my own eyes, but I still couldn't comprehend that he was gone.

I thought back to the last words I'd spoken to him. *I'm sorry*. He'd told me to leave. He was hurting, and I knew it. I knew it was because of me, but I'd left, anyway. I'd just left. The only explanation I could come up with, a piss poor *'I'm sorry'*. I'd thought I'd have time to make it up to him.

I punched the wall, wincing in pain, but in truth, I barely felt it compared to the hole in my chest. *Raf was gone*. Tears fell again, and all the anger that had been building in me since Butcher's first betrayal came spilling over the edge. I punched the wall again and again, crimson staining my knuckles. I glanced at my hand, not caring about the fact that I'd have to explain this to people, not caring about the blood dripping onto the floor.

I stared at my reflection and the woman staring back was a stranger. I was not the clean Lady Elia. My ledger was dripping in red. I had more than just Raf's blood on my hands, and it would only get worse from here on out. I wouldn't allow myself to forget what I had caused. What I was yet to cause.

Whether or not I had a choice in it, this would always be me. She had won. She'd successfully moulded me into what she wanted, a monster. My ledger would always be red. There was no point pretending otherwise.

I looked out my window. Night was approaching. Soon, I'd have to sneak back out to retrieve Raf's body.

I went to the bathing chamber, washed my face and my hands, before bandaging my knuckles and stepping into the hall. As expected, Hamish and Tarryn were dutifully standing guard.

"Hamish? Would you do me a favour and fetch me a few things from the kitchen? Cali will be coming by soon."

Hamish raised his eyebrows. "Sure? What do you need?"

I gave him a list of items. A specific type of wine and some snacks. He still looked like he thought it was a weird request to make of him, but he didn't complain and he left.

Tarryn said nothing while I gave Hamish the instructions, remaining silent after he was gone.

I stepped back into my room. "Don't just stand there. I have no idea how long it will take him to find everything and get back here."

Tarryn stepped inside and closed the door. Again he said nothing, he just waited.

"Really? You're just going to stand there?"

"What else would you like me to say? You made your opinion clear. You wanted me to leave you be if I want you to trust me."

"Don't be a dick, Tarryn. You said you could explain everything. Now is your chance. I am listening."

He sighed. "I have been working for the Taros Guard for years, but my loyalty is not to them. It is to The Crone."

"Who?"

"I believe you met her in the dungeons?"

Just when I thought I couldn't be surprised by anything else today.

"I'm sorry, *what?*"

He bit his lip. "Yep. People call her The Crone, I just call her Baubo. She's looked out for me for as long as I can remember."

"Okayyy. Tell me why I should care, and why she's messing with me?"

"She's not messing with you she's... just a tad cryptic."

I gave him an incredulous glare. "A *bit?*"

"Okay, a lot, but that is just how she is. She is trying to help."

"Why?"

"She hasn't said. But I trust her. She asked me to keep an eye on you. So I got Hamish, and myself assigned to your service."

I shook my head. "So you've just been spying on me this entire time?"

He sighed. "It wasn't like that, Adira. Baubo told me I wasn't to interfere, just to protect you. I thought about telling you, but couldn't find the right time."

"Oh, and when would the right time have been? Once I trusted you, and would just stupidly believe whatever lies you spun me?"

"No. I wasn't supposed to get involved unless it was necessary. My job was to protect you. That much is true. The difference is, I know who you really are, who you really work for, and partially why you are here."

"How could you know that?"

"Baubo, she somehow just knows things, always has. When my parents died, she took me in. Half the time I had no idea what she was talking about, but she saved my life, and I've followed her ever since."

"You lost your parents?"

He nodded. "They died when I was six."

I stopped and looked at him. "How?"

"A house fire, why?" He responded, clearly unsure about the direction I was taking the conversation. I breathed in. *That can't be a coincidence.* Both of our parents died when we were six, in the same way?

"And The Crone saved you?"

He nodded. "She pulled me out, kept me safe. Then she found me a home with one of the castle guards. A kind one. Who fed, sheltered, and trained me—why do you look so freaked out?"

"Because my parents died when I was six. In an unexpected house fire. Only no one pulled me out. I pulled my sister out. We were taken in by Butcher. Fed, sheltered, and trained, but she was not kind."

"She said you were important. That we were linked, but she wouldn't tell me how. Just said that I would know in time. Maybe that's what she meant."

"Why are you so calm? This is all crazy."

He shrugged. "I used to get frustrated when she wouldn't explain things, but it never got me anywhere. She still wouldn't tell me and she is usually right in the end, so I learned to trust her methods, as strange as they are."

"Okay, so she asked you to protect me. She told you my name? Why I am here?"

He nodded. "If you're trying to figure out if I know about your blood oath, I do." I inhaled sharply, shaking my head.

"That's impossible..."

"She said you were important, that I had to protect you. She told me your real name, what you do, and why you're here. The rest I've figured out as I went along. But I trust her. So, I got myself and Hamish assigned to you."

"Does Hamish know about any of this?"

He shook his head. "He knows more than he lets on. I haven't told him anything, but he's smart enough to have figured some things out on his own. I picked him because I trust him with my life and I knew he would protect you with his. He is a good guard, but an even better man."

"He will be back soon."

He nodded again. "I should get back out there before he returns, but..."

"What?"

"I was hoping you would let me help you."

"With what?"

"Your friend." He looked at me with sympathy in his eyes, but no pity. Just sorrow and understanding. I wondered who he had lost.

I shook my head. "I need to do it alone."

"No, you don't, and before you argue again, it will be safer and easier with the two of us. With my strength. You want to honour him? The best way to do that is for us to move him gently and respectfully, then lay him to rest. You can't do that all alone. Let me help."

"Fine. Meet me in the alcove you accosted me in, at the twelfth hour."

He nodded and turned back to the door to leave, but it swung open before he could. Valor was standing there. He frowned slightly as he took in the both of us.

CHAPTER THIRTY-TWO

"Valor, have you not heard of knocking?"

Seeing him, I couldn't help but think of Raf. How the man standing in front of me was responsible for the guards that had strung them all up. The couple, the little boy, and Raf. *His* guards had carved *TRAITOR* across his chest, no doubt while I'd been in bed with their prince. My heart ached.

"There were no guards posted outside. I was worried. What's going on?"

Tarryn looked like he was about to politely explain nothing was going on, but I frowned and jumped in before he could.

"It's none of your business."

He narrowed his eyes. "It's improper for a lady of your stature to be alone with a guard in your bedchamber."

I knew him well enough to know his anger wasn't out of concern for my stature or reputation.

I scoffed. "But it's fine if it's with you?" I crossed my arms, which I realised was a mistake, as his eyes zeroed in on my bandaged hand. His gaze hardened, and he walked over.

"Who did this to you?" His body was tense and his voice was full of deadly calm as he stepped towards Tarryn. I quickly stepped in between them.

"Don't be an idiot. Tarryn had nothing to do with this." I turned to face Tarryn. "Sorry, I think it's probably best if you go back outside."

Tarryn nodded, but he hesitated. I realised it wasn't because he was afraid of Valor; it was because he was worried Valor might hurt me.

I shook my head, touching his arm to reassure him I was fine. "It's alright, Amesley," I said, hoping he would take my use of his nickname for what it was. An olive branch and a sign that I wasn't worried. "Go wait outside. We will talk later."

He gave me a look, but heeded my request and left the room, closing the door behind him. I turned back to Valor, frankly annoyed at his alpha-egotistical behaviour.

"What. Happened."

"That is also none of your business, Valor."

"Like Hek it isn't. If someone hurt you, you *will* tell me who it was."

"Is that an order, Your Highness?" I hissed.

"Does it need to be?" He countered.

I threw my hands up. "You're being ridiculous! Why are you here Valor?"

He took that as an opportunity to grab my waist and press me against the wall. I breathed in sharply, surprise temporarily overpowering my anger. I looked up at him. He looked back.

"What happened, Elle?" His voice was low, softer, but still firm.

Staring at him, the surprise and the anger shifted to pain as I thought of Raf again. I looked away from him.

"I punched a wall. Let go of me, Valor."

He tilted my chin back towards his face. "Why?"

I swallowed. "I get that this is your weird way of caring. At least I think that's what it is, but I can't do this with you right now." I moved my unwrapped hand to his chest and gave him a light push to put some distance between us.

"Can't do what, Elia?"

"Please." My voice broke, and it was a battle to keep my eyes from filling with tears again as I looked at him. His eyes were that bright icy blue, so similar to Raf's.

While I was in bed with the man in front of me, the man I should have been with was being beaten and tortured.

I took a deep breath. "I need you to leave, Valor. Now."

"If you think I'm going to leave with you like this with no explanation, then you—"

"That's not up to you! I don't have to appease you anymore and you no longer outrank me, Valor." I bit out harshly. His eyes widened at my outburst and I almost felt bad. No doubt this was confusing given our last interaction, but if I had to be this close to him for any longer, I would lose it all over again. "Get. Out."

"Elia, talk to me."

"GET OUT!!" I screamed. Seems like I'd already lost it.

He breathed in and stepped toward me, but the door opened, revealing Hamish and Tarryn, faces impassive and their eyes hard.

"Your Highness, I think it might be better if you respect the Princesses' wishes and leave," Hamish said, his eyes not leaving the prince's.

Tarryn's gaze was on me. I was breathing heavier, my nails digging into palms that had somehow become clenched without me noticing. I looked back at Tarryn and nodded slightly. He stepped forward.

Valor looked at them in shock, then back at me. There was a pause as no one in the room spoke. Valor shook his head and simply left without another word.

I closed my eyes, breathing out, slowly opening my hand. Hamish followed Valor out. Tarryn stayed only long enough to whisper that he would wait for me at the alcove if I was able, and that if I didn't show, he would ensure Raf was safely taken care of.

He closed the door and left me there in silence. It was pressing in on me until I could practically hear the tears as they slid down my cheeks and dropped to the hardwood floor.

This is all I would get. *Drip.* This small piece of quiet to grieve and to mourn. *Drop.* This sliver of silence to patch up the holes in my chest, bury the pain, and prepare for what was to come. *Drip. Drop.*

I'd considered Tarryn's offer. A selfish part of me wanted to accept. To let him handle it all so I wouldn't have to. But, I couldn't do that. I had to be the one, not just for me, but for Raphael. He deserved that much.

Tarryn was waiting for me in the shadowy alcove before the twelfth hour struck. He'd gotten hold of the guards' shift changes and pulled a few strings to ensure the changeover that was scheduled to take place in fifteen minutes took a bit longer.

"Where do you want to go after getting him down, Adira? Where would you like him to rest?" It still threw me, hearing him say my real name.

"It's just outside of town... we—" I couldn't finish that sentence. How could I explain to Tarryn that it has been our spot since we were children? How could I talk about it without breaking down again? "You don't have to go that far. You've done more than enough."

He shook his head. "I'm staying until it's done." He met my eyes and once again there wasn't any of the pity that I expected to see. There was only understanding and respect.

I nodded slightly. "Thank you..." He nodded back, and I saw him shift to work mode. He peered around the corner.

"The guards' changeover is about to happen. We will have about five minutes to get clear."

I took a breath. "I have a carriage waiting nearby. We just need to get him there unseen."

He looked at me. "Do I want to know how you got hold of a carriage?"

I shrugged. "I'll return it."

A tiny smile edged the corner of his mouth, and he shook his head before turning away to monitor the guards. I slipped my dagger out of its sheath. I had to keep my head. The effects of decay would have already started to show, having been left out in the sun all day. We had a chance of getting him out and I couldn't let whatever state he may be in interfere with that.

Tarryn nodded. "It's clear. We need to move now." I nodded, taking a steadying breath, pulling my hood up as Tarryn did the same, and stepped out of the alcove.

Sticking to the shadows, we moved quickly and silently towards the makeshift gallows. I wasn't sure if I was more impressed or concerned at the level of stealth he displayed. None of the guards I had ever interacted with had half of the skill he apparently possessed.

I mistakenly glanced at the structure before we got there, and my stomach turned. All four bodies were still strung up. They were deathly pale. They'd still had some colour when I had last seen them, but it was long gone now. The stench of rotting corpses filled the air, and there were crows perched atop the wooden structure. They had already started picking away at the little boy's body. He was missing an eye. I couldn't bring myself to look at Raf's face, for fear of what I might see, or worse, not see.

We climbed the gallows, keeping a sharp eye out as we did. *Treat this like another assignment, Adira. Get in, get out, fall apart after.* Tarryn held Raf's body as I climbed the scaffold, walking across it to the notch that Raf's noose was hooked on. I crouched and cut the rope so Tarryn could slowly lower Raf's body. He appeared all business, as if he weren't transporting a dead body. I glanced at the others.

"Adira, we need to move," Tarryn said as if he were reading my thoughts.

"We can't just leave them here, Tarryn. They have families too. They didn't deserve this."

"I agree, but we don't have time."

"I'm making time." I continued along the beam, maintaining my balance without trouble, until I reached the boy's noose. My heart ached for his family. He was so young. Did he have siblings? Was this boy supposed to grow to be his family's provider? What was his name?

"Adira! We don't have time!" Tarryn whisper-shouted at me.

"Then go, Tarryn. Get Raf to the carriage. It's waiting at Retcher Alley."

He muttered under his breath before stepping over to where the boy was hanging. I cut the rope when he nodded to me. He caught the boy and gently laid him down, before moving to the couple, the same as I did, monitoring for the guards' return. I made quick work cutting down the woman and then her lover. Tarryn caught both of them, the same way he had Raf and the little boy.

"How do you propose we move them all out of here?"

"I can carry the boy and woman. You carry the men."

"Are you sure you can manage?"

"I can manage." *I would have to.* "Just help me position them."

He looked at me like he didn't believe I could carry them. I was only five foot five, after all. But I was an aerialist, a gymnast, trained to support my entire body weight using only one arm, not to mention my additional training. If that wasn't enough, my sheer determination to not allow these people to remain here would do the rest.

I opened my mouth to tell him to hurry, but he stepped forward.

"The woman is the heaviest, so you should carry her over your shoulder, the boy in your arms." He gently picked the woman up.

I hunched forward a little as he placed her over my shoulder, and the little boy in my arms. The boy was small enough for me to support with one arm, so I held him as tightly as I dared, using my free hand to keep the woman in place.

I swallowed, breathing through my mouth, and not my nose. Tarryn bent down, carefully sliding the boy's eyelids, or what remained of them, shut. He whispered what sounded like a prayer to Helia for safe passage.

It was an effort to keep the woman balanced without the use of both hands, but not much different to when Butcher had made me walk across a log that had fallen over the Sepa River during the winter months, two full bags of grain on either shoulder and my wrists bound.

If I fell, which I did, regularly, then both the bags of grain and I received a freezing bath. The boy was not much bigger than one of those bags of grain. That thought was unsettling, but grounding. I could do this. *I had to.* I nodded to Tarryn that I was good to go, and he quickly slung Raf and the other man's body over each of his shoulders, right as the guards returned for their shift.

"HEY! YOU THERE, STOP!"

We took off running. The guards, not expecting anyone stupid enough to attempt something like this, fumbled for their swords as they hurried down the steps after us. I didn't look back as we ran, but I could hear them gaining on us. Well, me. Tarryn seemed to keep up a good pace, despite the two fully grown men on his shoulders.

I, on the other hand, had only successfully gotten across that fallen tree with precision and patience, allowing me to properly balance. I could feel the woman slipping from my shoulder. If I had any fighting skills, I could try to distract the guards long enough for Tarryn to get away, but I didn't possess enough to pose any sort of threat. I slowed, jerking my arm up, so she didn't slide to the ground.

I should leave them, I should drop their bodies and run. But I couldn't. I couldn't stop looking at them and seeing Raf. Imagining their family's grief, even stronger than my own. I couldn't leave them behind. There was so much I had no control over in the past few days, months. I would not lose control of this. I glanced behind me. The guards were close. I wouldn't be able to outrun them. Tarryn was slowing down to help me. I shook my head.

"GO!" I shouted. I heard him curse as he weighed up the situation, and the best way out, but there weren't any good options that got us both out of there. I wouldn't forgive him if he didn't get Raf's body out, or if he got himself captured trying to help me.

Thankfully, neither of those things happened, a carriage skidded to a halt in front of me, blocking me off from Tarryn who was still a good five strides ahead, causing me to almost lose both the woman's and the boy's bodies, as well as my own, to the pavement.

I thought it was a guard who'd had enough brains to cut this chase short, using a carriage instead of chasing on foot. Looking closer, it wasn't the watch guards. The carriage was the one I'd *borrowed* earlier tonight. I also recognised the driver.

Hamish. I had to bite down on my tongue to stop myself from saying his name out loud. He looked at me, and despite the seriousness of the situation, he managed his signature grin.

"I'll return it," he said, and relief washed over me. "Now get in."

He glanced at the guards behind me, not taking his eyes off them as I hurried around, throwing the bodies in and jumping in myself. There was no time to be gentle now.

As soon as I was in, Hamish flicked the reins, and the horse moved in Tarryn's direction. Tarryn met us halfway. Raf's and the unknown man's bodies joined the woman's and the boy's before Tarryn himself jumped in. Hamish spurred the horse into action before Tarryn had even landed. The horse took off in a gallop, putting some much-needed space between us and the guards, as I pulled the doors shut, keeping an eye on the bodies. Tarryn looked at me, and he gave me a small nod. I nodded back, more relief coursing through me. We'd done it.

I leaned my head out the window, shouting directions to Hamish. He nodded and once we were sure we weren't being followed; he guided the horse along the route I'd described. None of us spoke, and it wasn't long before we came to a stop.

We were just outside of the city, atop a hill that overlooked Kendelen, our place. Hamish jumped down from the cart at the same time Tarryn did. I glanced at the beautiful view, then to the bodies laid out before me and swallowed. I turned to see both men watching me. Waiting.

"We used to come here as children. This was our meeting spot when one of us had a bad day at training, or... just a bad day. As we got older, we continued to spend time together here." I glanced back out at the view. The watchtowers lit up the city. "*Look how small it all is*, he'd said when we were about eleven. *One day, I will take you out of this place, and we will see the world, Adira. You and me.*" I smiled sadly at the memory. "I'd told him he was a fool that day. Told him there was no point dreaming about a life we could never have. He simply smiled at me and said, *It's alright, Adi. I will dream for the both of us.*"

CHAPTER THIRTY-THREE

Tarryn leant over and whispered something to Hamish, who nodded in return and walked back over to the horse, unhooking it from the carriage, then mounting it.

"Where is he going?" I asked.

"To get the supplies we need." I nodded slightly in understanding. *Shovels. He meant shovels.*

"How did he know where we were? You said you didn't tell anyone."

"I didn't. But I told you, he's smart. He most likely figured out something was up and followed one of us."

"Can I trust you both? Truly?"

"I trust Hamish with my life, and I give you my word you can trust me with yours."

I bit my lip. It was a colossal risk, trusting one person, let alone two, but with everything that had happened lately, a huge part of me just wanted to give in and let someone else help. To for once, just once, not have to do it alone. I had to think about this objectively. My feelings right now aside, I had a job to do, and a little sister to protect.

Strategically, it would be useful to have other people helping me, especially people on the inside, *but* it was a risk. If one of them exposed me, it would be all over for me and for Sierra. I would allow them to help but prepare for the betrayal. I nodded and looked at Tarryn.

"I have to go back into the city."

"Now? Why, exactly?"

"To track down their families. They might want a say in what happens to their loved ones' bodies."

"That is risky, Adira. Any of them could alert the guards."

"Relax, I'll wear a mask. I need you to stay here and make sure the bodies are safe."

"I don't like it, Adira, but I will keep them hidden." He nodded, and I gave him a half-smile.

"When Hamish gets back, we will start on the graves. He will have questions." I understood what he was asking. *Could he answer them?*

I nodded. "You can tell him what you know if you're certain we can trust him with it." A part of me already knew we could. I would have picked Hamish to be the first one to help me if I hadn't been sworn to secrecy, not Tarryn. He nodded, and I glanced at Raf's body before making my way down the hill.

Sneaking back into the city, I didn't bother to conceal my face for the first stop. I steeled myself as I knocked. It took a minute, but Tolemas answered, dagger in hand. His eyes widened in surprise, quickly scanning the quiet street, before stepping back.

"Inside."

I ducked under his arm, and he shut the door, turning to face me.

"You shouldn't be here, Adira."

"Trust me, I wouldn't be here if I had another option. I just need information, then I will be on my way."

He looked like he wanted to say more, but he didn't. "If you're coming to me, you must be desperate."

"I need the names of the people that were hanged in the town square. Their names and their families' addresses."

He looked at me. "The Morrighan boy was a good kid. He grew into a decent man."

"I'm not here to discuss him, especially not with you. Can you get me the information I need or not?"

He sighed. "Everyone knows their names by now. No one is associating with any of their families until the dust settles. You'd be wise to do the same."

"The names and addresses, Tolemas."

He sighed and got out a piece of paper, writing three names and locations as I glanced around the room. I'd been here more times than I could count growing up. Sometimes for training sessions, sometimes to escape Butcher, and others just because Tolemas wanted us around.

Despite the many times I'd been in this house, this room, it felt foreign now. It looked more or less the same with its minimalistic design, coupled with splashes of colourful art and books, but now it felt like a stranger's home.

As always, his house was incredibly neat. There was a glass of ale and a novel on the table. He must have eaten already. Everything was in its place, just the way he liked it.

There was a singular rose in a glass vase on the table. It struck me as a little out of place. That's when I realised it was probably from Butcher. She loved the scent of roses and the two were clearly close. I had to force myself not to clench my fist and instead glanced at the piece of paper he was now holding out. Indigo Kole, Matias Telfor, and William Downs. He wisely left Raf's name off of the list.

"You shouldn't get involved, Little Sparrow."

"How much do I owe you?"

"Adira—"

"This should suffice." I took out a few coins and placed them in his hand. He sighed and shook his head, handing them back.

"No fee. Consider it a favour."

"I don't want any favours from you. This is business."

"You aren't business to me..."

This time it was me shaking my head, ignoring his comment as I walked to his door.

"Be careful, Adira."

I scoffed and looked at him. "That's rich advice."

"Look, forget what you think you know. I can't say much, but there's more at play than you think. There's more at stake than you know." He winced slightly, as if something had stung him. "Don't trust anyone. *Anyone*, Adira."

I watched him. "Yes, you've made it clear that anyone could betray me."

He shook his head. "No, I didn't, Adira I—" He winced again, gripping his stomach. I frowned.

"What is going on?" I stepped forward, but he shook his head.

"Go, she knows you're here, go."

"Who knows? Butcher?"

"No, not Camilla. It's never been Camilla."

I frowned again. "Who then? Solis?"

"She's not what you think. It's not what you think, Adira. You have to see. You have to see the truth!"

"What truth, Tolemas? You aren't making any sense!"

He groaned and dropped to his knees as blood trickled down his nose. "Go, Adira. Get out of here."

I fought the instinct to help him. It was difficult to ignore, but I turned and walked out, telling myself whatever was happening to him; he deserved it. I would decipher his cryptic warning later. Right now, I had to get to Indigo, Matias, and William's families. I checked the addresses, thankfully; they were all in the same neighbourhood. Unsurprisingly, it was one in the slums.

I put my gaiter on, pulling it up and making my way to the first address. Indigo had lived with her parents. I knocked and felt as if Dykos himself greeted me when the door eased open. The grief was smothering. A man I assumed was Indigo's father had an arm around a woman whose eyes were bloodshot from too many tears.

After I'd apologised for their loss and told them what I had done, she'd broken down into more tears. Her father had looked relieved and sad at the same time. He was holding it together for his wife. He asked me to leave them directions to her gravesite, so they could visit discreetly when it was safe. They didn't want to risk burying her somewhere themselves and getting caught. I nodded and wrote down the directions.

Next was Matias. He lived with his grandmother. She was not a grieving mess like Indigo's parents. This was a woman accustomed to loss, being the only one of her line remaining. I could see the relief in her eyes as she thanked me, the ease of tension knowing that her grandson could rest peacefully. She touched her necklace, a semi-circular pendant that resembled a crescent moon. The symbol of the Deos Credentes.

"Thank you for your kindness. May Taros watch over you, child." I bowed slightly, not wanting to disrespect her beliefs by telling her the divinities were probably watching and simply didn't care.

The last house was the one I dreaded the most. William's. I took a breath and knocked. A little girl answered. She couldn't be older than six. My heart ached. She shared William's eyes and hair.

"Hello there," I said, bending down, "are your parents' home?" She looked at me, not with fear as most children would if they found a cloaked and masked stranger on their doorstep, but with curiosity.

"Yes."

I smiled a bit. "Can you fetch them, please?"

"Papa said not to disturb Mama. She's sad about Will."

"Aren't you sad too?"

"I was sad, but Papa said to be strong for Mama and for Jemella. He says Will is in Eternis now, looking over us. He's lucky."

I smiled sadly and nodded a bit.

"Okay, well, I don't want you to disobey your father, so I'll tell you what," I reached into my pocket and pulled out the directions I'd scribbled out, in case they too just wanted the location like the other families, "you can just tell him that if he ever wants to visit William, he should follow the directions on this note. Can you do that for me? For your brother?"

She nodded and stood a little taller. "Yes."

"I thought so. You're tough." I handed her the note. "Thank you for being so brave." I stepped back as I heard a man's voice calling out.

"Tarina?!" She turned, hearing her name, before glancing back at me. I winked before disappearing into the shadows. I watched as her father approached, only turning away once he had shut the door. Loosing a breath, I felt better knowing their families knew where to find their loved ones' resting places. I let that thought ground me as I made my way back to the hillside, where I would say goodbye to Raf for the last time.

When I got back to Hamish and Tarryn, they had already started digging. There was a third shovel nearby. Without a word, I picked it up and joined them. By the time we finished, the sun was rising. We buried Indigo, Matias, and William, near each other, but Raf I buried at the top of the hill where we used to sit, overlooking the city, marking it with two sticks and some ribbon torn from the carriage's interior.

Tarryn and Hamish gave me some space once we were done. I pressed my hand to the freshly placed dirt and closed my eyes. I didn't know what to say. There wasn't anything I could say that would undo his death or the circumstances that led to it. So I simply sat beside his grave and watched the sunrise like we had so many times before.

I stayed as long as I could, but I could tell the men were eager to return, so we didn't encourage suspicion. I stood, glancing at the view, then back to Raf's grave. I closed my eyes and whispered softly.

"I'll dream for the both of us. May you rest, my friend."

We hurried back to the castle, taking the tunnels and servant entries to avoid being seen. We all went our respective ways before returning to where we should be. For the men, that meant guarding my chambers, for me, that meant *inside* them.

I sat in my reading chair, going over everything that had happened over the last few days. My heart was still in pieces, but I needed to keep it together if I wanted to stay alive and free Sierra. I couldn't lose sight of that. I had to do whatever it took to keep her safe and get us out of here. Whatever it took.

Whilst I'd visited the families of the deceased, Tarryn had filled Hamish in on what he knew. Why I was there, his own connection with The Crone, and now, me. Apparently, he took it well. He no doubt had a million questions, but he kept them to himself and simply stated that he was in.

I'd told him there was nothing to be 'in' on, but he'd just winked, whispering, "Right, of course."

I shook my head and Tarryn had told me he'd handle it. So, when a knock sounded at my door, I'd expected it to be Hamish, having finally cracked and needing to ask his endless questions.

"Come in," I called, and the door opened, but it wasn't Hamish, it was Cali. I was unsure how I felt about her right now. She was a part of the system responsible for Raf being hanged, and the others. Both she and Valor were party to the crimes in a way. "Cali... I wasn't expecting you."

"Well, strangely enough, my brother actually suggested I check in on you. He seemed... worried. Which is new," she said, walking over. I'd debated trusting Cali as I had with Tarryn and Hamish, not with the whole truth, but with some of it.

"... Did you hear about what happened in the town square yesterday?"

Her smile dropped, and she looked saddened. "I did..."

"And?"

"And what?"

"What do you think about it?"

"I think it is a horrible outcome, but the law is the law."

I shook my head. "The law? Exactly what crime did a ten-year-old boy commit that warranted being hanged in the town square to have his eyes pecked out by crows?"

She stiffened. "What?"

"What crimes did any of them commit that warranted that punishment? What evidence do you have? Was there a trial?"

"I... I don't know the details, Elia, but the crime must have been bad, or they wouldn't have been executed."

I shook my head. "I ask again. What crime could a ten-year-old boy commit that was *so* bad? Did he murder someone? Or was he simply Impure and poor, which was reason enough?"

Her eyes widened. "Elia! Why are you saying these things? What has gotten into you?"

"What's gotten into me is I am seeing the cracks in your family's rule, Cali. You walk around like a ball of sunshine, always smiling and cheerful. I don't know how you do it when your family is responsible for the deaths of innocent people so nonchalantly."

"That isn't true."

"Then explain yesterday! I know for a fact that one man hanged was guilty of *nothing*! Neither was that little boy, and I find it hard to believe the other man who was living and caring for his elderly grandmother, or the woman who was the child and provider of a poor but hard-working couple, was guilty of anything other than being easy, Impure, targets." I shook my head. "I'm not really up for company right now." I turned back to the window.

"Elle..."

"Please. Go."

She sighed, her reflection pleading with mine through the glass. The hurt was clear in her eyes, but she headed my request and left the room. I was harsh on her, but none of what I said was untrue.

Butcher had a hand in making sure Raf was one of the people hanged. The other three, though, who picked them? Why was there no trial after they were chosen? Why was no one else involved in the decision to take their lives? Because the system is flawed. It is unjust and caters only to a few.

If it had been a Pure accused of whatever crimes they supposedly committed, they would have simply walked away unpunished, or had a trial to determine their fate. For the first time, I understand the rebellion's motives. Being in the beast's belly had shown me there was a bigger divide than I'd felt when simply living my life as an orphaned thief.

My frustration at how unfair the system is, wasn't the only reason I'd been harsh on her. Between that and my recent arguments with Valor, it would help put the royals on edge. It lined up with the other kingdoms' visits and my so-called mother arriving soon. It would help sow unease. They would work to keep my favour over the other kingdoms' if it meant either having me marry Valor and forming an alliance, or getting Queen Tira on their side.

I changed into tights and a loose tunic, opened my door, and stepped into the hall.

"I'm ready for that lesson you promised me," I said, directing my words at Tarryn. Hamish raised his eyebrows.

"What lesson?"

"I offered to teach her to fight. Given recent events, and the events that I'm sure are to come, she should be able to defend herself properly, and attack, if need be." Tarryn answered.

"Isn't that what we are for?" Hamish countered.

"And when we aren't around? Like the attack in the dining hall?"

"Fair point. I'm in."

I groaned. "You need to stop saying that."

He just grinned. "I'm going to enjoy getting you into shape."

I stuck my tongue out.

"Alright, you two. We aren't getting anything into shape just standing here. Let's go."

CHAPTER THIRTY-FOUR

I FOLLOWED HIM TO a training room, Hamish too. Tarryn, not all that surprisingly, was a real slave driver. First, he had me warm up, run a few laps, and then complete numerous exercises to test my current fitness level, along with my reaction time and manoeuvrability.

He stood arms crossed, watching me seriously, whilst Hamish leant casually against the wall, flipping his dagger into the air and catching it, without really paying attention to it. *Show off.* He caught me glaring at him, simply winking in response, before returning to his dagger throwing. Tarryn, of course, observed our interaction and promptly forced me to do extra push-ups as punishment for getting distracted.

"First rule of any combat situation. *Never* allow yourself to get distracted."

"If I had known you were going to be such a hard bastard, I would have asked Hamish to train me."

"Trust me, Hamish is worse." That elicited a chuckle from Hamish's direction, but I knew better than to look over again.

"Alright, let's see what you've got, then. Hamish?" He nodded, beckoning him over.

Hamish sheathed his dagger, removed his weapons belt, and joined us.

"You want me to fight, Hamish? You already know I know nothing about offence."

"I didn't say fight. I said show me what you've got. You are trained in acrobatics, you're in good shape, and you know how to move stealthily. All of which are useful in any fight. If you can't fight, then you still need to find a way to avoid getting killed or injured."

"Acrobatics and fighting are two very different things."

"They aren't as different as you think. Hamish, show her a few things." He stepped back, his arms still crossed, like the hard-ass sergeant he was acting like. Hamish didn't waste any time, immediately throwing a punch. My eyes widened as I ducked, narrowly evading the blow.

"Hey! I wasn't ready!"

"Do you think you will always be prepared for an attack?" Tarryn called as Hamish threw another punch. I dodged left, only to have him sweep my legs out from under me, knocking me onto my back. I gasped slightly, and he pounced, holding an invisible knife to my throat.

"Killed ya," he said, smirking above me.

I shoved him off, sitting up. "Exactly, I am hardly trained to fight him, Amesley."

"I didn't tell you to fight him. Before learning offence, you need to learn defence. You are smart, Elia. I see you assess everything when you walk into a room. This is no different. Assess your opponent, read his movements, and react accordingly. Go again."

Like last time, Hamish didn't waste a second. I was a little more prepared and evaded him easier. Nevertheless, I was knocked down repeatedly before I could evade his attacks for any decent period. I was puffing by the time Tarryn finally called the session to an end for today. Hamish extended his hand to help me up after he'd knocked me down yet again.

"Not bad, Worthington, not bad." He grinned, pulling me upright. I groaned and rotated my shoulders, knowing I would be very sore tomorrow.

"Liar."

He chuckled. "No, seriously. You did better than most rookie guards or soldiers."

"Mmm." I stretched.

"Go bathe, you reek," Hamish said, plugging his nose.

"*Me?* You smell worse." I shoved him. "Then again, you usually do, so I don't blame you for not noticing the difference."

"That's not what the ladies tell me." He wiggled his eyebrows. "I'm told I smell delicious, taste delicious, too. You're welcome to find out for yourself. I could do worse than a princess." I gagged and shoved him harder.

"In your dreams, Hamish."

Tarryn rolled his eyes at our banter as we made our way back to my chambers, but I could see the amusement in his eyes. While he might be a stoic trainer in the practice room, outside it he was still quiet, but he saw everything as I did, and he enjoyed the little things.

I spent the next three weeks taking part in gruelling dawn training sessions, investigating who this mysterious 'C' could be, searching for any information on blood oaths and the so-called seventh kingdom, followed by more training in the afternoons.

During that time, I had made multiple attempts at getting a copy of Father Chambersen's script so I could compare it to the sample. Each attempt had proven unfruitful. He rarely wrote things down, apparently. He was the only advisor left. If the handwriting didn't match, I'd be back to square one.

This time, I waited until evening. Dressed as one would expect a truly conservative noblewoman to dress, I made my way to the temple. Hamish and Tarryn accompanied me. To anyone else, it would simply look as though I was attending temple for some private evening prayer. Unfortunately, that meant Hamish and Tarryn had to remain outside to keep up the charade.

The castle temple was never locked. People could come at all times of the day to say prayer or seek a priest for guidance. There were morning and afternoon masses, of course, which most regular members attended, but the temple was still open all hours for whoever needed it. I was hoping since there'd been an afternoon mass today, there wouldn't be many people around at this time.

Entering through the thick wooden doors, it was dimly lit, the only source of light provided by candles around the edges. The pews were thankfully empty as I silently made my way to the dais. I glanced up at the gigantic painting of The Six that I'd glimpsed the last time I was here.

It was eerie staring up at the artwork, feeling as if their eyes were staring right back. I shivered, returning to the task at hand. There were two doors on either side of the dais. I went to the right one first, the one I'd followed Chambersen through. Listening for any sounds, I carefully tried the knob; it was unlocked.

As quietly as I could, I opened the door, revealing the empty hallway. I went straight for the door at the end. The one Chambersen had needed a key to unlock. There was a gap between the door and floor, but I couldn't see any light shining out, so I took out a hairpin and picked the lock.

The door squeaked as I pushed it open, causing me to wince. It felt odd to be sneaking around without my hood or gaiter. I felt exposed, but it would have been too suspicious if I'd been seen entering the temple dressed that way.

Thankfully, the room was empty. Why was this one locked when all the others weren't? At first glance, it appeared to be a regular study, much like the others. I searched the shelves first, finding nothing of note. Mostly just religious texts. I moved to the desk, searching through the letters and parchments. Thankfully, there were more than enough documents signed by Father Chambersen, so I took out the sample and compared the scripts. It wasn't a match.

Groaning quietly in frustration, I turned to leave when movement caught my eye from the edges of my vision. I frowned, turning, and glancing at the ground where a piece of paper lay near a wastebasket. I watched it closely and—there! The piece of paper lifted slightly, as if being moved by a breeze. There were no windows, and I'd closed the door behind me. I waited for it to move again, trying to figure out the direction the draft was coming from, and was led to one of the shelves. I bent down, glancing at the floor. They were light, almost unnoticeable, but there were scuff marks.

I glanced up at the shelf. There was something behind it. I braced my shoulder against it and pushed. It slid away from the wall with ease, revealing, what a surprise, another tunnel. How many of these damned things were there? There was a candle lit on the wall and I could feel the breeze much more strongly now. I grabbed the candle and headed down the tunnel, following the wind.

The sound of chanting stopped me in my tracks. I glanced ahead, spotting the source of the sound and the breeze. There was a lone door at the end of the tunnel, left open. Placing the candle down, I kept my footfalls quiet as I slunk along the wall towards it. The chanting grew louder, and I could now make out what was being said.

"Blessed are we, for we are the Divines' tongues."

"Blessed are we, for we are the Divines' ears."

"Blessed are we, for we are the Divines' eyes."

What in Infernis? The voices sounded male. As I moved closer, only a few feet away from the open door, the chanting continued.

"We give our hands, we give our homes,"

"We give our blood, we give our bones,"

"We worship, we tithe, we forfeit our lives,"

"We yield to the divine."

Goosebumps pricked my skin as I risked peeking around the door frame.

"The Divinities chose us!" A voice I recognised boomed.

Father Chambersen stood atop a podium. He was in a pure white robe that stretched to the floor. The sleeves were so long that his hands were not visible until he raised them to remove his hood. Seventeen men knelt on the ground in a semicircle before him, with matching robes. Their hoods were raised, obscuring their faces.

The chamber they were centred in was large, with at least six other tunnel entrances spaced around the walls. None of them had doors. I'd hazard a guess that at least a few of them led outdoors, which would explain the soft breeze. The room was bare save for the podium, a very large chalice on a small stool beside it, and far too many candles lit around the room. The flames cast the chamber and its occupants into dim lighting and dancing shadows.

"We are their messengers and we are their swords. We shall strike down those that oppose us! We shall surrender those that ignore the Divinities will! We are Deos Credentes!" Chambersen said, drawing my attention back to him.

"Deos Credentes!" The men all shouted, and their voices echoed around the chamber, amplifying their words as they recited the original chant over and over. Chambersen smiled and nodded, descending the stairs of the podium, and walking over to the man on the far left of the semicircle. He reached to his side, unsheathing a dagger that his robe had concealed.

"Stand." He commanded. The room went silent. The man obeyed, standing, but keeping his head bowed. "Make your offering." He held the dagger out to the man.

The man took it without hesitation and sliced a clean cut across his palm. My eyes widened. Fates, they were mad.

"I submit." Head still bowed, he handed the knife back to Chambersen before kneeling once more. Chambersen made his way around the group. Each man repeated the first man's actions, cutting themselves, before announcing they 'submitted.'

When they'd all bled, Chambersen wore a satisfied grin on his face. His eyes were that of an excited child. I thought I might be sick.

"Those that submit shall be rewarded! Those that resist shall be persuaded! And those that refuse will be struck down!" Shouts of agreement rose as Chambersen bowed to the men, and they bowed back.

"We will rise." He muttered, almost as if to himself, before turning and heading straight toward where I was still peaking around the doorframe. *Shit.*

I scurried back as silently, but quickly as I could. Scooping up the candle, I hightailed it back to the study, placing the candle back. I slid the bookcase into place, faintly making out footsteps of not only Chambersen, but the other men heading this way. Seems they were all done with their creepy ritual bloodletting for the day.

I opened the door leading back into the hall, turning the lock before hurrying out, closing it and praying they weren't close enough to hear. I raced back into the main area of the temple. Taking an aisle seat in one of the empty pews, I clasped my hands and bowed my head.

A few minutes later, eighteen men emerged from the same door I just had, no sign of any white robes as they chatted quietly amongst themselves, passing by without a care for my presence. I didn't dare look up until a pair of white shoes came to a stop beside me.

I kept my head bowed. As far as any of them knew, my eyes were closed in prayer. Someone cleared their throat, and I glanced up.

"Oh, Father Chambersen? My apologies, I was so lost in prayer I didn't hear you approach." I smiled apologetically. He smiled back at me, his eyes still holding some of that childlike excitement I'd seen in the chamber.

"Lady Elia." He bowed his head slightly. "I thought you didn't practise?"

I flushed. "Thought I'd give it a go after our last conversation."

"I see." He watched me, and it reminded me of the stray cats that hovered when they sensed food, waiting for the perfect time to swipe it. "Well, I am glad to see you finding time to visit the divinities' place of worship. There is no better place for your prayer. No where closer to them than here." His smile was tight-lipped.

I somehow masked my grimace with a guilty but eager smile as I nodded. "Of course."

He stared at me then, saying nothing. I wanted to stare back, to let him know I saw right through him, despite the fact that his gaze was terrifying. But lady Elia, proper, devout, lady Elia, would not stare back. She would not challenge him here. So instead, I blushed, averting my eyes and shuffling slightly in discomfort.

"I should retire. It is getting late and I fear my guards may be dying of boredom outside." I stood, glancing at him after a few seconds of avoiding his eyes. He was smiling. This time an amused one that told me he knew I'd mentioned my guards to let him know I wasn't alone nor unprotected.

"Yes, ladies shouldn't be wandering the halls late at night, even with escorts. The darkness is Heknos' domain." I nodded in agreement and stepped forward to leave, but he didn't retreat as any sane person would. He remained where he was, staring down at me, with barely half a foot between us now. I met his eyes once again. He was still smiling.

"Was there something else, Father?" I said, ending the silence he seemed all too eager to extend.

His lip twitched, but he finally shook his head and took a step back.

"Good evening, Lady Elia. May the divinities watch over you."

I dipped my head, stepping around him, and exiting the temple as gracefully as I could. I could feel his eyes on me long after the doors had closed.

Hamish had given me a quizzical look when he'd seen my face, but I'd simply shaken my head.

"I'll fill you in later." Thankfully, they'd both accepted that response and walked me back to my rooms.

As I lay in the bath, I thought over the creepy interactions and the ritual I'd witnessed. None of the men appeared to be there against their will. Was what they were doing terrifying? Yes. Seven different kinds of mental? Also yes. Was it a crime what they were doing? No, but it should be. Why were a bunch of priests running around cutting themselves?

He'd mumbled, 'we will rise,' that cannot have been a coincidence. It can't have been, but I still had no hard proof either way that he had somehow planned the assassination. I needed to link them to Tilly.

Groaning in frustration, I got out of the tub and practically crawled into bed. Unsurprisingly, sleep didn't come for some time. The spine chilling chanting seemed to echo in my head, getting increasingly more terrifying every time. Eventually, though, exhaustion won the battle and sleep claimed me.

CHAPTER THIRTY-FIVE

QUEEN TIRA WAS DUE to arrive today, so Lydia and a few other maids had just arrived, ready to prepare me for the Xerian Queen. I let them work, styling my hair and face perfectly. They dressed me in Xerian colours; black and silver.

The skirt of my dress was a beautiful, black, floor length piece with slight ruching at the top, flowing into a modest slit and creating a beautiful draped effect. The top of the gown began at my mid waist, and was a beautiful sheer corset with silver stones covering anything indecent, black boning, and thin off the shoulder sleeves of the same black silk as the skirt.

My hair was mostly down. They'd braided only a small portion around the crown of my head. It was all very regal looking. I breathed out, taking one last look in the mirror, before heading out to meet Tarryn and Hamish. They were waiting in their formal guard attire. Hamish whistled when he saw me.

"Syrena's song, dress like that more often. You look like an actual lady." He practically drooled.

I rolled my eyes. "You both look rather dashing yourselves."

Tarryn chuckled slightly. "You look beautiful. Are you ready?"

"No, but that, unfortunately, is irrelevant. Let's go." He gave me a pitying look before they escorted me to the royal hall, where we would greet Queen Tira.

They seated me atop the dais, a level below where the King and Queen's thrones sat, but on the same one as Valor and Cali's. Unfortunately for me, I was placed beside Valor. It was to be just us and Queen Tira's court, before a formal welcoming party held in the grand ballroom. Cali watched me from where she sat with longing in her eyes. Her tiara glistened upon her head and she looked every bit the princess she should be, with Killian standing to her right. I should take notes.

Hadrian smiled warmly at me, but he had no doubt heard about the tensions between Cali, Valor, and myself, as he hadn't visited in the last few weeks like he usually did. Odette nodded to me and flashed me that vipers smile, before turning her attention back to the floral arrangements she was having the servants move in a final touch up of the room.

Valor ignored me, which suited me fine for now. A servant entered the room, drawing all of our attention. He stepped to the side as the double doors to the hall swung open, revealing a woman clad in—not a dress as I'd expected, but a tunic and pants. It was clearly an expensive set. Her pants were cotton, a dark silver colour paired with her tunic; black with silver trimming that practically glimmered in the light, and a belt matching her pants.

Her brown hair was braided to one side and her crown was simple but elegant, containing a singular black diamond in the centre. She looked like the Goddess of Death, Dykos, in mortal form, practically oozing confidence and grace. The glint in her piercing green eyes dared anyone to test her. Piercing, emerald green, the same shade as mine. The coincidence was unsettling.

The warriors behind her helped further the effect. They were all huge and male. With corded muscles and barely any armour on, instead, simply sporting all black outfits with the Melfore family crest; a silver bear's paw. They rarely had use for armour, I supposed. I could immediately tell they were all Virbi Pures or, at the very least, strong Virbi Paras. I figured she would have a mix of Forti and Argenti amongst her personal guard, but it was difficult to pick which was which. The servant spoke up then, but all eyes were on the woman as she entered the room, coming to a stop a few feet away from where we were seated.

"May I present, Her Majesty Tira Melfore, Queen of Xeria."

Queen Tira gave a shallow bow, more of a slight dip, and a nod of the head. As a queen in equal rank to Hadrian and Odette, no more was expected. Some rulers outright refused to bow at all, even for others of equal rank. The Xerian Queen, apparently, did so out of respect, and in turn, Hadrian bowed low in his chair. Odette's gaze was frosty as she dipped her chin, whilst Valor, Cali and I all stood, demonstrating curtsies and a bow fit for the woman standing before us. We resumed our positions in our chairs as Hadrian spoke.

"Tira, you look well. I hope your travels were uneventful?" He smiled that genuine smile I'd seen him give me and the rest of his family.

"As well as can be expected, given current events." She replied, but she wasn't looking at him, she was looking at me.

Seeming to take the hint, he stood. "You remember my wife Odette and my children, Valor and Calliope?" Calliope gave her a smile equal to her fathers, Odette remained impassive, and Valor nodded politely. "May I introduce you to Elia Worthington, or perhaps, Elia Melfore?" He finished, gesturing to me. I rose, feeling too odd sitting there like a statue as she looked at me.

"Hello, it's an honour to meet you, Your Majesty," I said politely but still reserved. This woman was a stranger to me, after all, and a queen.

"You look like your father," she said, looking me over. Her tone was neither cold nor warm. It was inquisitive. I bit my lip, unsure how to respond. Thankfully, Hadrian was a brilliant buffer.

"She also has a few of your qualities. Your eyes, for one, and I can attest that she certainly has some of your spirit." He chuckled. "You have had a long journey. I imagine you would like to freshen up before the festivities begin?"

She nodded. "Yes, that would be preferable."

"Of course, my Captain of the Guard, Killian Ambrosia, will escort you and the rest of your travelling companions to your chambers."

Killian stepped forward and bowed low. "It is an honour to meet you, Your Highness." He stepped down from the dais and moved towards her and her imposing guards. Killian was a big man, but next to the Virbi, he appeared small.

"I would like for my daughter to escort me." This woman was bold. It was clear to everyone in the room that this was a show of power. Her refusal of the King's highest ranking guard was certainly a touch disrespectful.

"If Lady Elia would like to, then of course she can. However, Killian will still join you. I am sure you understand."

She finally looked at Hadrian and nodded, a small smile tugging at her lips.

"But of course, I would expect nothing less from a gracious host such as yourself, Hadrian."

He smirked a little. Just how well did they know each other? Judging by the look on Odette's face, too well for her liking.

I was so busy watching them, I took a moment to realise they were now all waiting for me to answer.

"Oh! I'm sorry. I can escort you, of course." I made my way to where Killian was standing. He smirked slightly before his expression settled back into captain mode.

Queen Tira nodded. "Thank you, as always, for your generosity and warm welcome, Your Majesty."

She turned then and looked at Killian expectantly. He exited the room, starting in the direction of the wing that would house Queen Tira and her companions. The Virbi Queen's guards flanked us as I fell into step beside her. I noticed Hamish and Tarryn, who had been posted at the doors, falling into their ranks, one of them on either side, watching me closely. I hid my smile at their protectiveness. Not failing to notice Queen Tira watching me just as closely as they were.

"How was your journey to Taros, Your Highness?"

"Tira will do just fine. Most likely the same as yours was." She answered.

I smiled politely. "Well, yes, but I imagine your experience was a little different from mine."

"True." The corner of her mouth tilted upwards. "It was long and incredibly dull with this lot for company."

A cough that sounded an awful lot like an offended laugh sounded from one of the surrounding guards behind us. I couldn't tell which, though. Her smile grew.

"You didn't bring a friend or a lady's maid to keep you company?" I asked.

"That would be even worse than guards."

I chuckled a little, finding I agreed. "At least the scenery is enjoyable for most of the trip, especially in Reya." I lied through my teeth.

"Yes, but the endless meetings with the royals in each kingdom I had to pass through were tedious and made it difficult to enjoy the view."

"You met with the other kingdoms?"

"Only Reya and Ikira."

I nodded slightly. I suppose that would make sense. It was the respectful thing to do.

"So, are we to pretend this situation isn't extremely awkward for the entire time, or will that ruse end once we reach our destination?" She stated.

"I was not under the impression you found this situation awkward. You seem to be very composed."

"I am a queen. We are always composed. That does not mean it is not awkward."

"I suppose not. Well, I am not entirely sure what to ask first, and I would prefer we have the conversation with fewer listening in."

She smiled. "Nothing is private when you're in the house of a royal, my dear, especially the Navarre royals." I raised my eyebrows. *What did that mean?*

"You make a fair point, but that doesn't mean I need to broadcast my affairs without care."

"You are wise for your age."

"Thank you."

"Here we are, Your Majesty, Lady Elia." Killian came to a stop.

"This wing has multiple rooms. The master, of course, is reserved for you, Queen Tira. The rest of your men, and whomever else you please, can fill the rest of the rooms, or if you'd prefer for your men to stay in the guards' quarters, they can. The staff have already brought in your luggage."

"Thank you, Captain." She nodded. "That will be all."

He nodded at the dismissal, but glanced at me before making any attempt to leave. I nodded, and he stepped back before heading down the hall in the direction we had just come. I was sure Tira noted the exchange. Hamish and Tarryn did not make to leave, which she also noticed.

"Are these your personal guards?"

"They are, as well as my friends. This is Hamish Tomon and Tarryn Amesley."

Both men bowed respectfully before taking up posts on the wall facing her door.

"Friends? So you trust them then?"

"More than I'd trust your guards."

She grinned. "Well, I should hope so." She opened her door. "Will you join me?"

I nodded. "Of course." I followed her inside. All but one of her guards remained outside. The one who stayed was one of the oldest in the group. His hair was greying at the roots, but he was still in impeccable condition. He was certainly a Pure, an ancient one by the looks of it.

"This is my Captain of the Guard, Yarik."

Yarik took my hand, bowed, and placed a kiss on my fingertips. "It is an honour to meet you, Princess Elia. I will protect you with the same conviction in which I protect my Queen."

My eyes widened slightly, and Queen Tira laughed. "Oh enough, Yarik, don't scare the girl."

He grinned a little, releasing my hand and straightening. "Apologies, Princess."

"No apologies necessary..."

"Come, I'd like to sit." She inspected the rooms as we went until we found her master suite. "Ah, finally." She stepped inside and made a beeline for the sitting area. "You can wait outside, Yarik."

He nodded. "Go easy on her." He directed at me, winking before he left. I had no idea what to make of that. I glanced at Tira, who was rolling her eyes.

"Pay no mind to his antics. He loves to stir the pot. Please, have a seat."

I sat down opposite her and waited. She watched me closely, and I shifted nervously in my seat. *I guess I have to go first then.*

"Forgive me for being blunt, but I see no reason to tiptoe around this. I know I haven't been in your life and that you have a mother and father who love you, Elia. But you are my blood and I made a mistake allowing my father to take my daughter away from me. It has been my biggest regret."

"Well, since we are being blunt, I will be honest and tell you I am having a troublesome time wrapping my head around all of this. I am not a princess, and it's nearly impossible to believe that I could actually be one."

She smiled a little. "I'd say that's a valid reaction to the news. I can imagine it was quite a shock, and to learn it from a letter, no less."

"That's one way to put it."

"I imagine you have many questions, questions I am happy to answer, but I am hoping you will give me a chance to get to know you. I do not expect you to suddenly give up your life, taking on the role of princess and acting as if we are not total strangers to one another, but I hope you will give me a chance to see the type of woman you've grown into."

I swallowed. "I can try..."

She smiled. "That is all I can ask. I'll let you get ready for the festivities. I will see you at the welcome party?"

I nodded, standing. "Thank you, Your majesty." I curtsied, and she chuckled.

"You may call me Tira and don't worry about the curtsy. We are family. Such formalities are hardly necessary."

"Um, alright. Thank you, Tira."

With that I left her chambers, Hamish and Tarryn falling into step beside me. We walked quietly back to my rooms. I let them inside and shut the door. Hamish practically burst with questions once we were safely alone.

"What was she like? Does she suspect you aren't her real daughter? What's our next move?" I was grateful that, aside from that first night when I'd sworn the blood oath, Butcher hadn't forbidden me from discussing all my other interactions with her.

"Our?" I said, raising my eyebrows.

"Yes *our*! We're in this together now."

"Hamish, your loyalty is to your kingdom, not me."

He shook his head. "My loyalty is to what is right. I am not blind and I know you are important. I believe in you, Elia, so you have my loyalty. As well as Tarryn's."

Tarryn nodded in silent agreement.

"Which means this is an *'us'* situation."

I smiled a bit. "We can agree to disagree, but to answer your questions, she was very regal, very brash. She certainly acted as if this entire situation was real and that I am, in fact, her long-lost daughter. Says she wants to get to know me."

"So, you're just going to play along, then?" Tarryn chimed in.

I groaned. "Why does everything always have to be so damned complicated?"

Hamish glanced up at the ceiling. "She didn't mean that."

I frowned. "Oh, come on, did you just *apologise* to the divinities on my behalf?"

"Uh, *yes*," he said matter-of-factly, "I know you will not do it."

I scoffed. "If they are even watching, which I'm sure they have better things to do, but if they don't, I doubt they care."

"They *are* watching and they care. You never know when you might need them, Adira. Don't be so quick to overlook them." I rolled my eyes and Tarryn chuckled.

"Let him have his faith. He hasn't seen what we have." He smiled sadly. Hamish's smile faded a little, and I squeezed his arm.

"Sorry, Ham, you're right." I even forced myself to glance at the ceiling. He grinned and nudged me. I shook my head, laughing a little. I often forgot that Hamish was a man of faith. He wasn't as devoted as some of the Deos

Credentes, but he still prayed to the divinities, believing they were watching over us.

"Alright, you two better get back to your posts. I am sure there are lady's maids anxiously waiting to prepare me for the festivities." I rolled my eyes again, and both men smirked.

"I would happily take one for the team and stay to help you dress," Hamish said seriously, placing a hand over his heart. Now it was Tarryn's turn to roll his eyes.

"Out." He began pushing a laughing Hamish out the door before exiting himself.

Sure enough, a few minutes later there was a knock on the door and after I had called out for whoever it was to enter, Lydia and the other maids that had helped me earlier were swarming me again, starting on my look for the welcome party.

They wrestled my hair into an elegant updo, which I hated, but allowed. What did I care at this point? My hair was the last thing that should be on my mind. They attempted an outfit change, but I argued that was ridiculous since I'd just put this one on. Eventually they gave in, simply freshening my face a little and darkening my eyelids with more kohl. I conceded to a shoe change, though, switching to a beautiful silver pair with heels about three inches too high for my liking.

Finally, to finish the look, a beautiful flower called the Queen of Night Tulip, named for its dramatic black colouring, was tucked into my hair, matching the shade of the black jade gemstone glistening at the end of the silver chain necklace I wore. Glancing in the mirror, I looked incredibly regal.

It was an odd reflection to be staring at, and I couldn't help but prefer the Navarre's royal colours; sapphire blue and red, to the Melfore's silver and black.

"You look stunning, Elia." Lydia beamed at me, having dismissed the other maids after they'd placed the flower in my hair.

I chuckled. "Thank you, Lydia, you are a miracle worker."

She shook her head. "Nonsense, it is all you." She smiled. "Do you require anything else from me?"

"No, thank you. Go enjoy the rest of your night." She bowed and left, but for some reason, she didn't close the door.

I walked over to do so for her and found Valor standing there. He was wearing a suit in his house colours. His blue eyes popped against the red of his cape. We hadn't spoken since he'd accused Tarryn of hurting me or sleeping with me, and I had freaked out on him in the aftershock of Raf's death. Yet here he was, at my door, looking criminally good in his formal wear. I wasn't sure what to say first.

Luckily, I didn't have to figure that out because he stepped forward, meeting my eyes and said, "We need to talk."

Infernis.

CHAPTER THIRTY-SIX

"Wish I could, but I actually have plans." I made to step around him, but he blocked my path. I sighed and looked at him. "Really, Valor?"

"Yes." He grabbed me by the arms and lifted me up, moving me back into the room, kicking the door shut before putting me down. My eyes widened, and I gave him a shove.

"You can't just manhandle people when you don't get your way."

"I can when they are being ridiculous."

I groaned. "What can you possibly need to talk about so badly that it has to be right now?" As if I didn't know.

"A Hek of a lot, Elia. You've been avoiding me for weeks. You went off on Cali and now your long-lost mother is here."

"None of which is your business."

"What happened Elia? We were getting along, quite well, I'd say." He gave me a knowing look. "Then you show up with a bloody fist, way too close to your guard, and you go off on me. Then I hear you've gone off on Cali too. What are you trying to do? Cut ties so that when the other kingdoms arrive, your options are open? Is that it?"

I crossed my arms. "You're a jackass, you know that?" Even though that's exactly what I'd wanted him to think.

"Why? Because I'm telling the truth?"

"Oh, screw you, Valor."

"You already did, remember?" He looked down at me. That storm I was beginning to recognise, already brewing in his eyes.

I scoffed. "Which was clearly a mistake."

He sighed and ran a finger through his hair. Seeming to consider more carefully what to say next.

"Did I do something wrong, Elia?" He looked back to me. "Did I somehow make you uncomfortable or..." There was genuine concern in his voice.

"No, you didn't. At least not in the way you're thinking." I softened.

"In what way, then?"

I sighed. "It's not personal. I just don't think our core values align."

"What does that even mean, Elia?"

"It means we are *different*! I see things differently! You live in your gilded cage and are happy to turn a blind eye to things, but I am not."

He frowned. "What are you talking about?"

I should have kept my mouth shut. This would not help win him over and I could feel pressure building in my chest, but I just kept seeing Raf's face. The other victims' faces. Their families' faces.

I clenched my fist. "I knew one of the people that your guards executed in the square."

His eyes widened slightly. "Elia, I'm... so sorry, but they were traitors."

I scoffed. "Says who? Exactly what evidence do you have?" I shook my head. "You know what? It doesn't matter. I know for a *fact* they were not traitors. They were innocent people. But because they were Impure, no one cared. Your family acts as if they care, but when it comes down to it, they murdered those people without even an afterthought."

"Elia, that's not... you have it wrong—"

"No, *you* have it wrong." I shoved him. "You are just another entitled prince that doesn't know the true meaning of right and wrong. Cali tries not to be, but deep down, she is the same. *That* is why I have avoided you. *That* is why I went off on you. Now, if you'll excuse me, I have an event to attend." I tried to shove past him, reaching for the door, but he pulled me back again.

"Please," he begged, in a tone I hadn't heard him use before. I looked up at him, seeing the pain in his eyes. A large part of me wanted him to hurt, wanted him to feel a fraction of the pain I felt, but the other part hated seeing that look on his face. Worse, I hated that I'd put it there. I closed my eyes.

"Please what?" I finally responded.

"Don't push me away." I opened my eyes, looking at him again.

"Val..." I sighed.

"Please," he tried again, "maybe you're right, but we can talk about it, we can work through it. I am sorry. Just don't walk away..." I ignored the ache in my chest, if I was lucky, I'd be able to convince myself it was because I was almost disobeying Butcher's orders to win the prince's affections, and *not* because it hurt my heart to hear him beg me like that.

"I need some time." I conceded, turning and walking to the door. This time, he didn't stop me. I opened it and stepped out, heading toward the awaiting festivities. Hamish and Tarryn fell into step behind me. Valor didn't follow. I didn't know what I would have done if he had.

"Wanna talk about it?" Hamish asked

I shook my head. "No." He nodded and wisely kept his mouth shut.

We reached the ballroom, stopping just outside. I allowed myself to close my eyes for a second and take a steadying breath. By the time I opened my eyes, there was no trace of the anger or the pain, only a bright, hopeful smile belonging to a young lady whose dream of being a real princess had just come true. I nodded to the servant at the door and entered, Hamish and Tarryn, still on my heels. I stopped and turned to them.

"This is a party. If you two aren't on duty, go enjoy it."

"I wish. We are on duty. Especially with the Xerian visitors."

"Okay, but does that require you being right behind me the entire time?" I raised my eyebrow.

"Well, no.... but.."

"Come on, Ham, she'll be fine. We will be watching, as will all the other on-duty guards."

I smiled gratefully at Tarryn, whilst Hamish shot him a glare.

"Fine, but if anyone bothers you.."

"Yes, yes." I waved my hand, shooing him off. "Go." I smiled a bit, shaking my head.

He huffed, but took up a post on the opposite side of the room from Tarryn, crossing his arms stoically. That man was going to make someone very happy one day. I breathed out and made my way to the drinks table.

Taking a glass of champagne, and, in a genuine test of patience, I took only a small sip instead of downing the contents in one gulp like I so desperately wanted to.

"Careful, squeeze that glass any tighter and it might break." Turning, I smiled, and it was a real one this time.

"Lord Jameson." I glanced up at him. I had forgotten how tall he was. He was grinning at me, his dark green eyes shining in the light, his blonde hair slicked back.

"Lady Elia." He took my hand, bowed, and kissed my fingertips. Eliciting an eye roll from me and a chuckle from him. "You look absolutely breathtaking."

"You cannot help yourself, can you?"

"Not around beautiful ladies such as yourself, no." He smiled. "It has been a while."

"It has. How have you been?"

He shrugged. "Bored, very bored. Mostly preparing for this visit from the other kingdoms. All the high nobles, lords, and ladies, are going absolutely bonkers. All trying to figure out the best way to gain favour with the visiting royals."

"Sounds delightful."

"Mmm, something you, it seems, don't have to worry about."

"How so?"

"Many of the kingdoms have been weary of Xeria, but you would know that. Your forces are vast and your training is exceptional. An alliance with Xeria would prove fruitful for any of the five kingdoms. The easiest way to do that is through marriage to a Xerian heir, who, until now, did not exist." He titled his head to the side, "Quite unusual."

I sighed. "Yes, well, frankly, I'd rather go back to just being Lady Elia, with no royal title and whom no one wanted to marry."

"I hate to break it to you, Elle, but even without the title, I guarantee there would be a line of suitors wanting to marry you."

I chuckled and shook my head. "Shameless."

"Absolutely. Speaking of, how about you finish that drink and join me for a dance? Hopefully, this one doesn't get interrupted."

I grinned, downed the rest of my drink, and followed him out to the dance floor. He wasted no time pulling me close. I narrowed my eyes slightly, and he simply glanced around the room in feigned innocence. I couldn't help my amused smile.

We spun and danced as the music progressed, somewhere in the centre of the dancefloor. With James, everything was always much simpler and much more enjoyable. I'd distanced myself from him once Valor and I were rumoured to be engaged, to help keep up the ruse. Which was unfortunate, because he really was fun to be around.

"I heard a rumour about you recently," I said, remembering something Lydia had mentioned.

"I am sure you have heard many rumours about me."

"True, this one I found particularly... disturbing."

He raised his eyebrows. "Oooh, what scandalous act have I committed this time?"

I smiled. "Allegedly, you and a certain lady have been seen sneaking around."

"Which lady? It's hard to keep track of them all, if I'm honest." He smirked, and I rolled my eyes.

"This one, I'm sure you'd remember."

"Are you jealous, Lady Elia? Had I known you were available, I certainly would have made every effort to add you to the list."

"How romantic." I laughed as he spun me.

"I know. I am quite the charmer."

"Sadly, I have no interest in being on the same list as Lady Josette."

He groaned. "How on earth did you hear that?"

"So it's true?"

He glanced around. "Maybe."

"Oh Jameson, you can do better."

He sighed. "Hey, I'm not one to discriminate. I've had maids, noble-women, servants, market workers, you name it. I'm a giver darling. Although I can't say I've had a princess." He smirked at me and I rolled my eyes.

"Yes, the entire capital knows how much of a *giver* you are. But come on, *Josette?*" I wasn't exaggerating. It wouldn't surprise me if all of Kendelen was aware of Jameson's escapades. He was known for sharing himself around, no matter a woman's class or marital status.

"I *know.* But honestly? She is quite surprising behind closed doors."

"Ew. I don't need details."

He laughed. "Honestly, though, Val and I have known Josie a long time. She's really not so bad away from all of this."

I almost gagged at the nickname. "Mmmm, I somehow struggle to believe that."

He smiled a bit. "She was raised differently. She only knows how to compete."

"That doesn't make her attitude okay."

"You're right, but luckily for me, that isn't exactly what we are exploring. Not a lot of talking goes on during our interactions."

I pulled a face. "Again, ew."

He laughed. "How did you know, though? She was adamant about keeping our rendezvous under wraps. We have been *very* careful."

I winked. "A lady never reveals her sources." Or in my case, her *very* informed lady's maid.

He shook his head, smiling, before stopping as someone approached and tapped him on the shoulder. I peeked over, surprised to find Yarik standing there.

"Can we help you?" James said politely, but not all that friendly.

He bowed his head slightly. "I am sorry to interrupt, but I was hoping the princess would allow me the honour of a dance before I am required on duty?"

James glanced at me, and I nodded. "I'm sure I'll see you later tonight."

He sighed, smiling. "One of these days, I will get an entire dance with you, uninterrupted." He kissed my cheek before stepping away, only to be swooped on by eligible ladies. I laughed a little, then turned to Yarik. He held out his hand, and I took it.

"Out of all the people I expected to dance with tonight, you were not one of them, Captain Yarik."

"That is not surprising to hear. I hope you are not upset at the intrusion. I simply wanted a chance to chat, and of course, judge your dancing for myself. From what I hear, you are quite skilled on the dance floor and the stage?"

I chuckled a little as we moved to the music. "You've done your research."

"Of course, it's not every day the lost heir to a kingdom shows up. Let alone, in another kingdom, rumoured to be betrothed to a prince."

"Honestly, I think you'll find that I, out of everyone, was the most surprised by that revelation. It still seems like some kind of joke."

He smiled a little. "Understandable. I hope you don't think this brash of me, but I feel it is my duty to my queen to look out for her best interests."

"I would expect so." I looked at him.

He leaned in a little closer, his voice dropping. "I am sure this is all a lot for you to take in, but the queen is hopeful she can get to know you and have you be a part of her family. Of course, that all hinges on you being who we think you are."

"What do you mean?"

"She will explain. That isn't what I wanted to discuss. This court is beautiful, especially the gardens, but where there is beauty, there is also danger. There are serpens slithering in the grass, Princess. Be careful where you tread." His smile was gone, and he was looking at me seriously. Before I could ask him what he meant, the song finished, and he stepped back.

"Duty calls. Thank you for the dance, Your Highness." He bowed and disappeared into the sea of partygoers that had been surrounding us.

I was getting incredibly fed up with all these cryptic warnings. I needed another drink. I stopped a nearby serving girl, grabbed a glass and downed the contents, before putting the empty glass down and grabbing a new, full one. Turning, I assessed the room.

The party was in full swing. The Navarre King and Queen were seated on the dais, smiling and chatting with their advisors and highly esteemed nobles. Killian was close by watching them, but also someone else in the crowd. Following his line of sight, I was unsurprised to find Cali dancing and giggling, thoroughly enjoying herself.

I regretted how I'd said what I had to her, but not what I'd said. I hadn't meant to take it all out on her, but it was the truth. She might ignore it, but I couldn't. I sighed and continued surveying the room. Hamish and Tarryn were in the same positions as before. There were Xerian visitors scattered throughout the room, drawing crowds of people wanting to get any bit of gossip they could. It didn't appear that Queen Tira had arrived yet, which no doubt was another power play.

I turned, coming face to face with Valor, who was smiling at me like we were old friends. I just about turned and walked away, but he saw it coming, looped his arm around my waist, and pulled me against him.

"Don't make a scene, love," he said, voice low, "that would be embarrassing."

I ground my teeth together. "You have ten seconds to let go of me, Princeling."

"Yes, I am sure you have many painful ways to punish me when those ten seconds are up, but I am hoping it won't come to that." He looked at me and sighed. "I know you need space, and I want to give it to you. I'm only here because my mother insists we keep up this ruse of our relationship, especially with members of the Xerian court here. You are more than welcome to tell her you do not want to play along anymore, but until then, they expect us to at least appear to enjoy each other's company."

I scoffed. "Did your mother tell you why she had us pretending to be lovers?"

He shrugged. "Not entirely."

"It was so I could infiltrate the court and figure out who, amongst her trusted few, were traitors."

He raised his eyebrows. "That's why she let you come to The Cavum with us."

"Part of the reason."

"Well, did you find anyone?"

"I can't discuss that with you." Truthfully, I still didn't know who was a serious traitor to The Crown, and who was working for Butcher.

I'd been a little distracted by everything going on. Tilly was not responsible for the assassination attempt on her own, that much I knew. Even if Solis had been pulling the strings, she couldn't have acted alone, there had to be others involved, potentially true rebels in the court.

After checking the advisors, I was back to square one. I was *sure* something was going on with Father Chambersen, but I didn't know if it was related to the assassination attempt.

"You can."

"It is between your mother and I. For all I know, *you* could be a traitor." We both knew he wasn't, but the look on his face was worth the lie.

He sighed. "That's ridiculous."

"Is it? It has to be someone close to your family. Very few people knew that your poison master was travelling to Reya, let alone when. And yet, somehow, your apprentice poison master was also killed when their master was away, and right before the king. It had to be someone in your inner circle."

"No one in our inner circle would betray The Crown. They know the consequences." Just like the execution he swears wouldn't have been committed if they weren't traitors, he was so naïve.

"Consequences are irrelevant when someone is fighting for something bigger, Valor."

"Like what?" He said, watching me.

"Like freedom."

He tensed slightly. I wouldn't have noticed it if he hadn't been holding me, but I did.

"Everyone in Taros is free," he said sharply.

"Is it not possible that your definition of freedom differs from that of some of your subjects?"

His arm tightened around my waist. "We are not the monsters you seem to think we are, Elia."

Clearly, he hadn't seen his mother's party tricks. "The word monster is subjective. Not everyone fears the same things."

"I fail to see how this conversation is helping you narrow down who may be the traitor amongst the court. I could actually help you, you know? I know this court inside out. I know the advisors well, the Credentes, the Lords and Ladies."

Screw it. At this point, it couldn't hurt to ask him for some insight on things. I didn't truly believe he had anything to do with his father's attack anymore.

"What do you think of Father Chambersen?"

He raised his eyebrows. "Chambersen? He's a bit stiff, but I find most leaders in the Credentes are. As far as priests go? He's a pretty fair man. He has worked with my father for years."

"What kind of work does he do with your father?"

He shrugged. "All sorts, mostly keeping a balance between those of faith and those not. Together, they run the kingdom. Even when Chambersen disagrees with some of Father's more progressive rulings, they have worked through it. He's a good man."

"Why is he good? Because he's a man of faith?"

He chuckled. "No. Because he does good things. Like I said, many of his followers are often unhappy when the king seeks to change the ways we know, in favour of more progression and inclusivity. That aside, I've seen him feeding the homeless, volunteering in the slums. Hek, he met his wife there and went against his followers to bring her in."

"What do you mean?"

"Well, as you know, it's only been the last hundred or so years that the hunting of witches was put a stop to. The burning of anyone with deformities or markings. It outraged many of the Deos Credentes when that call was made. Chambersen's wife was born with a deformity that caused a stunt in her growth. She is barely the size of a ten-year-old. Yet he brought her in, convinced his temple to accept her, and even got her a job as a maid in the castle."

"Interesting." Chambersen's wife is a maid? Could that be the link I was missing between him and Tilly?

"Well, I'll be damned. You're useful for something, after all."

"What?"

"You just gave me an idea that's all. Surely we have danced long enough to appease your mother?" I was impressed I hadn't spilt any of my drink.

He sighed. "Maybe it's me who needs a little more appeasing?"

I looked at him then. Over the past few weeks, I'd learned how to read Valor better. It had been a struggle at first, since he always wore a mask of indifference. But once I'd spent more time with him, I learned his tells, just like I did everyone else's.

"Valor..."

"Whatever you're going to say, don't say it."

I gave him a look. "It could have been something good?"

He shook his head. "I can tell by the look on your face it wasn't." Apparently, I wasn't the only one who had been paying attention. "You were going to tell me we are too *different*, that we just see the world differently or something like that."

CHAPTER THIRTY-SEVEN

I HAD WANTED TO say that. We *were* different. It was no secret that I cared for Valor, more than I'd admit, but he saw the world through a stained glass window. He saw colour, and light, and peace, when those of us outside saw grey.

"... Do you think that statement is wrong?"

"No, but I *like* that we are different." He met my eyes. "We don't need to be the same, Elia. We just need to be there for each other, despite our differences."

I closed my eyes.

"I don't know if I can do that, Valor." I whispered, so incredibly torn. Every time I thought of my growing feelings for this man, I thought about how he was partially responsible for Raf's death, and that killed me inside. I was so angry, but I was also so sad. He made the anger at the injustice spike, but he also made that sorrow sting a little less when he was around. Not to mention the fact that they had ordered me to make him fall in love with me. I felt him lean in and rest his forehead against mine.

"Then I will do it for you. I think we have something here, Elia. Something good. So you can yell at me, you can scream at me, you can take your space. But I'm still going to be here. I'm not going to go away."

I swallowed, opening my eyes and looking into his.

"You can't get rid of me that easily, Sunshine." He stroked my cheek softly, smiling a little. I slowly nodded, breathing out.

"Okay."

His smile grew. He leaned in further, placing a soft kiss on my lips. I heard a few gasps, my eyes widening as I realised it was the first time he'd kissed me in public. I glanced around before I looked back at him, only to find a satisfied grin on his face.

"You just kissed me in public," I said like a moron.

He smirked, running his thumb across my bottom lip. "I'd very much like to do it again."

"I need a refill." I muttered, pulling back before he could stop me, and exited the dance floor, just in time for a voice to call for me from a nearby booth. Turning, I found Queen Tira smiling hopefully, and about half of the room staring at me. I hadn't even noticed her arrival.

I suppose hoping to avoid her for the entire night was an unrealistic goal.

I made my way over, the crowd parting like they would for a true royal. Odd, considering they hadn't officially named me a princess yet. I curtsied low.

"Your Majesty."

"Elia." She smiled warmly. "Will you join me for a drink?"

"Of course." *As if anyone could say no to a queen.* I sat in the seat beside her, and a servant immediately handed me a drink. I thanked them, turning back to the queen.

"Are you enjoying the festivities?"

"They are a lot more tame than the ones back home, but it is nice nonetheless."

I nodded. "That is good to hear."

"Are you enjoying yourself? You seem to be quite the sought after dance partner tonight."

I glanced at Yarik, who winked, then continued assessing the party.

"Honestly, I am glad you invited me to sit down. My feet could use the break."

"Hard to believe." She smiled. "I see the way you enjoy it, even if you don't particularly enjoy your partners at times." She glanced at Yarik herself, then back to me.

I chuckled a bit. "Yarik is a surprisingly talented dancer."

"Don't let him hear you say that. His head is big enough."

I smiled a little.

"What's on your mind?"

"It's just, I am not sure how I am supposed to act or what I am supposed to do. Or what you even want. What if I am not your daughter?"

"I want a chance to get to know you. I'd like to give you the birthright we have denied you until now. What you choose to do after that is completely up to you, but you *are* my blood, Elia. You'll just have to trust me on that."

"What if I don't want to be a princess?"

She smiled knowingly. "Whether or not you formally accept the title, you are already a princess, Elia. You have been since the day you were born. It is in your blood." I sighed. "I don't know how to be a princess." I barely know how to behave as a noblewoman.

She gave my arm a squeeze. "That is what I am here for. We can teach you the formalities. But from what I have seen and heard, you already possess the important qualities a princess should have."

"I find it hard to believe you've seen enough of me in less than a day to know that."

"You're right. But my people are very thorough. I've done my research."

"I suppose I should have expected that. I'm still new to court politics. I wasn't exactly a high standing noble back home, and here, well, this is also very new."

She nodded. "It's alright, you'll pick it up in no time, I'm sure."

"So, what happens next?"

"Formally? We will hold a ceremony to declare you the Princess of Xeria, my heir. Ideally, we would have the ceremony back in Xeria, but because of the upcoming meeting for the peace treaty being held here, there isn't time to get home and then return. So we will have the formal acknowledgment of your title here, but we will have an official crowning ceremony back home with our people."

I nodded slightly. "That makes sense. I know little about the upcoming meeting, only that all six kingdoms are coming, which hasn't been done in a long time. Is there anything I need to know?"

"There is a lot you need to know, but it would not be appropriate to discuss here. How about tomorrow morning? You can join me for breakfast?"

"That sounds lovely."

She grinned. "Now, I'd like to know how much stock the rumours regarding you and Prince Valor have?"

"So we can't discuss politics, but my love life is acceptable?" I raised my eyebrows.

"One's love life is always an acceptable topic at a party, but I doubt you want to discuss mine. That leaves yours."

I pulled a face. "You assumed correctly." I looked around, then back at her. "That depends on what rumours you've heard."

The queen nodded to Yarik, who obviously knew whatever the silent signal meant, as he nodded back and had everyone else leave the booth. With only Queen Tira, Yarik, and me, left within earshot of one another.

"Now that the vultures have gone, I have heard plenty of rumours, but I am sure you know which one I'm referring to."

"My supposed betrothal to the prince?"

She nodded. "So it's true then?"

"Not exactly."

She raised her eyebrows. "Care to elaborate?"

"We are rumoured to be betrothed, but we aren't *actually* betrothed. We never denied the claims. Although, I'd also be lying if I said our relationship was strictly platonic."

"Was that his idea or his mothers?"

Interesting. "Why would you think Queen Odette had anything to do with it?"

She rolled her eyes and leaned back. "I have known Odette for a long time, King Hadrian even longer. It isn't his style, but it's certainly hers."

"What do you mean?"

"I mean, she is smart and continually looking for ways to use people to her advantage."

"Before now, before yours and my father's letters, I'd gotten the impression that relations between Xeria and Taros were less than desirable."

She smiled a bit. "Of course you did."

"So it's true then?"

She nodded. "Relations between all six kingdoms have been tense as of late. Taros is not the only kingdom with a rebellion problem. Some of us find that to be more than a coincidence and think perhaps one or more of the other kingdoms could be responsible, using the rebellion to mask a larger intent."

"You're talking about war? You think someone is trying to destabilise other kingdoms?"

"I think the war started some time ago. It was simply quiet until now."

"And you think Taros is one of the responsible parties?"

"I think it would be out of character for Hadrian to seek war. His wife, on the other hand?" She took a sip of her drink. I couldn't disagree with her.

"Exactly how well do you know King Hadrian?"

"We were also betrothed for a time." I almost spat out my drink. Coughing, I placed my glass on the table.

"I'm sorry... You were betrothed?"

"Yes. It was arranged when we were children." She smiled a bit. Hadrian mentioned he had been to Xeria when he was younger, that it was how he knew my 'father'. Perhaps also my supposed mother.

"What happened?"

"My mother was assassinated, and my father was convinced that the Navarre family had something to do with it. Severing all ties between our families. The Navarres found a new marriage alliance for Hadrian from Lenea." *Odette*.

"Why didn't you find another fiancé as well?"

She smiled sadly. "Not long after you were born and given to your father, my own passed away. I was named queen. One after another, other members of my family began passing away, until I was the only Melfore left. One reason I did not track you down was to keep you safe. It was clear someone was targeting my family. I couldn't risk them coming after you. It left me with a kingdom to run and a target on my back. Remarrying was the last thing on my mind. By the time it was, I discovered I could not bear any more children, which was important to a lot of marriage alliances. Heirs."

My eyes widened. *Divinities*. She had been through the wringer.

"I'm sorry for all that you've had to endure, and alone nonetheless."

"I was not alone." She smiled a bit, glancing at Yarik, then back to me. "I have a loyal crew surrounding me, and now I get to know you. I have what I need."

I nodded a bit. "Do you believe the Navarre family had anything to do with your mother's death?"

"I believe it's possible. I also am smart enough to see how another kingdom who was vying for an alliance with Taros would benefit more from severing the ties between the Navarre family and my own."

"Lenea? The Krundell's?" *Odette's family.*

She nodded slightly. "The marriage, and therefore the alliance between Hadrian and myself, was practically guaranteed. Our families had been friends for years, a friendship the other kingdoms envied, given the separation between most of us. Queen Ferelia wanted her daughter to marry Hadrian, they had the most to gain. And gain they did."

"So your problem isn't exactly with the Navarre family, it's with the Krundell's."

"One of whom is on the Navarre throne, meaning they are one and the same."

That made sense. It explained why, despite the tension between the two kingdoms, neither had openly attacked the other, but they kept their distance and the relationship was strained. Hadrian and Tira were friendly when they'd met this morning. That was why. Out of respect for their shared history, neither had fully severed their ties.

"But you still came here earlier than you needed to."

"I came early for you. None of that was a lie. I wanted time to get to know you before the other kingdoms arrived. Who knows what will unfold once they do? I wanted to keep you close, protected by people I trust, people that Odette's influence cannot sway... or Hadrian's."

I nodded slightly. "Well... thank you, I guess."

She smiled a bit. "This is not proper talk for a party. I am sure you are eager to get back out and socialise with your friends. I have monopolised your company for long enough. Go enjoy the festivities."

I knew a dismissal when I heard one, and given all the information I'd just received, I would not argue with it.

I stood. "I will see you for breakfast."

"I look forward to it." She nodded, which I returned, before leaving the booth and heading outside to the gardens. Despite the warnings of serpens, I figured they weren't literal.

I sat down on one of the outdoor benches and breathed in the night air. Relaxing a little, I leaned back and thought over everything I'd learned tonight. It was going to be an absolute shit-storm when the other kingdoms arrived. Who knew what other politics were at play? I wondered if Butcher was aware of the other rebellions? Did Solis have any connections to them?

I had no idea where this Solis was even from. She might not even be from Taros, she could be from anywhere.

"A mark for your mind?"

I glanced up as Cali sat beside me. "I wouldn't even know where to start."

"Then let me. You were right."

"Cali..."

"No, let me get this out." I nodded and waited. She took a breath. "Everything you said was true. I don't agree with the way some things are, but I haven't done enough to change them either. I benefited from them unintentionally, and I am sorry. I am sorry for not doing more. That changes now, and I just wanted you to know that I heard you." She stepped back. "Sorry for disturbing you."

I sighed. "Cali, wait."

She stopped and looked at me. I dipped my chin towards the empty seat beside me. She smiled a bit and sat.

"I'm sorry for going off on you the way I did... I was just—"

"Mourning. You were mourning." She looked at me knowingly. "He was the man you had been involved with.. the one you said was complicated, wasn't he?"

My heart ached. She had no idea. I swallowed the lump in my throat and nodded slightly.

"I'm so sorry, Elle..." She squeezed my hand tightly. "I'm so, so sorry."

I breathed out. "Thank you... I... can't really talk about it right now, but thank you."

She nodded. "Of course. I just want you to know that when you are ready, I'm here."

I gave her a small smile and squeezed her hand in return. "I have some gossip for you. You probably already know, though."

"Ooooh, pray tell."

"Lady Josette and Lord Jameson."

Her eyes widened, telling me she, in fact, had not yet heard. James wasn't kidding, they really had been keeping it quiet.

"Shut up!? No way. Oh, James can do so much better." She pulled a face.

I laughed. "Obviously, this stays between us. He says they are trying to keep it under wraps for now. So if people suddenly find out, he will probably know it was me."

"Got it. Lock and key." She nodded. "But come on *Josette?*" She sighed, shaking her head. "What is the world coming to?"

I chuckled, and she joined me. I looked at her, at the happiness and openness in her eyes. She really wasn't holding my outburst against me. I was too harsh on her. She was a good person, she just didn't know better.

"So, you met your mother?"

I exhaled. "That still sounds weird to say... but yes."

"Tell me everything."

So I did. I left out the political parts and the relationship between the Navarres and the Melfores. But I told her about everything else and she listened, chiming in when she had something to add or ask. It was like the argument had never happened. I hadn't realised how much I'd missed her. Hamish and Tarryn were great, but Cali was my first friend here, and some things she just understood better than the men could.

The night breeze was starting to bite. I rubbed my arms and noticed she was also shivering a little.

"We better head back inside."

She nodded. "Thank Ades." She rubbed her hands together, standing up. She linked her arm through mine, and we made our way back down the path towards the party.

It was freezing out. I hadn't noticed it earlier, too busy enjoying Cali's antics, but I noticed now.

With cold comes quiet. All the animals seek shelter. Even the guards keep on the move or position themselves somewhere protected from the wind. Which is why, when a twig snapped nearby, I noticed.

I stopped and listened, causing Cali to stop as well. Bushes and trees surrounded us, making it hard to see beyond the path at this time of night. I could see the door to the party. The guards there were monitoring us. The bushes rustled again. Whatever was in there was getting closer. It could just be a rabbit.

"Elia?" I shook my head slightly.

"Sorry." I smiled. "Just thought I heard something." I continued walking, so she shrugged and simply started chatting again. There were only about ten yards between us and the guards. *Snap. Rustle.*

The sounds were getting louder. Brows furrowing, I let go of Cali's hand and turned, positioning myself in front of her, just in time for an arrow to whiz straight past us. I breathed in, hissing in pain as it nicked my arm.

"Cali, stay close to me, but hurry to the door."

"What?" She tried to turn, but I didn't let her, instead reaching behind me and giving her a light shove.

"*Move,* Cali, now!"

The guards shouted and hurried toward us. They'd spotted the arrow now embedded in the ground. I kept my back to Cali, so I was facing the garden. I pushed her a little to get her moving, shielding her with my body.

My eyes swept the bushes, but it was impossible to see anything in the dark. The garden was quiet again, until the almost inaudible, but recognisable, *thwack* of a drawstring release sounded.

I pushed Cali down, throwing myself on top of her. I felt the swoosh of air as another arrow flew over our heads, hitting a guard that had been running toward us. He went down quickly, the arrow protruding from his forehead; a perfect shot. Cali screamed and covered her head. The guards reached us, forming a protective barrier. The bushes rustled again, but this time, the sound was quieter. They were retreating.

CHAPTER THIRTY-EIGHT

S

OMEONE PUSHED THROUGH THE wall of guards. Two someones, actually. Valor and Killian. I sat up, moving off of Cali. Valor was in front of me immediately. He gripped my chin firmly, but gently.

"Where are you hurt?" His voice was laced with barely restrained anger. His eyes swept across my face, deeming it unharmed before they assessed the rest of me. It took him all of a second to spot the blood sliding down my arm. His jaw clenched.

"It's just a flesh wound. I'm fine."

"That's what you said last time." He examined my arm. *He had a point.*

"*Okay,* but this time I wasn't stabbed. It just nicked me, that's all."

He wasn't really listening. He turned my arm, checking for an exit wound.

"Val." I grabbed *his* chin this time, forcing him to look at me. He breathed in. "I'm *okay.* I swear."

He looked into my eyes and slowly breathed out. He nodded slightly. "Did you get a good look at them?"

I sighed and shook my head, lowering my hand. "No, I'm sorry. I tried, but I couldn't make anything out. I heard them. It only sounded like one archer, one set of movements, but there could have been more."

"That's okay. That's more than enough to go on. We already have guards searching the grounds."

I turned to ask Cali if she was alright, but she was bundled in Killian's arms. She wasn't crying, but she was clinging to him. Which, if I'm honest, was a bit out of character for her. She wasn't the type to cower, as much as she enjoyed letting people think she was. I'd say her reaction was partly relief, partly to keep up her charade as the innocent princess, and partly so she could grope the handsome captain that came to her aid. I smiled a bit.

"Alright, we need to get inside," Valor said, deeming me fit enough to walk.

I nodded and let him help me up. Cali remained close to Killian as we made our way back to the door. The circle of guards remained tightly around us. I glanced back at the fallen guard and then further along to the arrow digging into the ground. The bottom of the tip was just visible, sticking out of the grass. *Silver.*

They hadn't been targeting Cali then; they had been targeting me. Given they'd missed when they'd had the element of surprise and the time to line up a clean shot, yet had managed to hit a bullseye with the guard, it seemed unlikely their intent was to kill me. Were they testing me? Testing my Gifting, to see if I was an Argenti or a Forti, or simply trying to expose me as an Impure?

Inside was even more insane than outside. People were crowding around, trying to get a good look at what happened. The guards were trying to keep them all back. Guards surrounded Hadrian and Odette at the dais before ushering them out of the room. I could hear Hadrian protesting, but Odette was there at his side, assuring him Cali was okay, that they needed to get out of the open in case the attacker was still nearby.

In contrast to the Navarre rulers, Queen Tira was already organising the room. Ordering guards into formations, and ordering the general party goers out of the room, efficiently. She commanded with ease, and her guards swept the room, carrying out her orders.

They cleared the room within minutes, leaving only us in our circle of guards, Queen Tira, and her court. Valor remained close by, but he was watching Tira closely. No doubt noting the same thing I was. Killian was checking Cali over again, and she was swatting him away, much to his annoyance.

Queen Tira approached. She looked at the guards circling us expectantly. They glanced at Valor. He nodded, and they parted for her.

She surveyed me before deeming me unharmed.

"What happened?"

"Someone fired on us from the gardens. As far as I could tell, there was only one archer, but there could have been more."

"Who were they aiming for?"

"The first arrow grazed my arm. The second arrow would have hit me if I hadn't knocked Cali and myself down. I don't think they were aiming for her, though."

"What makes you say that?" Her question drew Valor and Killian's attention.

"The arrows were silver-tipped."

Killian cursed, Cali remained quiet beside him. She did not seem surprised. She'd noted the arrow the same way I had, and recognised what it meant.

Tira turned to Valor and Killian. "You have guards searching the grounds?"

"Yes, Your Majesty." Killian answered. "We will find the archer."

"And what about the people from the event?"

"What do you mean?" Killian asked. Valor hadn't said a word. He was simply watching and waiting.

"She means, are they being questioned? This wasn't a random attack. They can't have just been waiting in the garden hoping I would step out. I hadn't mentioned to anyone that I was going out there, only deciding to in the moment. Which means someone from the event either saw me go out and notified the archer, or they followed me out and took the shots themselves. Either way, someone that was at the party was involved."

Queen Tira raised her eyebrows, impressed at my deduction.

"Precisely."

"We have moved them to another hall. We will question them before they leave." Killian answered.

"That's if the responsible person didn't already slip out in the chaos."

"Queen Tira, would you like to simply say whatever you're implying?" Valor finally said.

"I'd like to know how someone could get into your home, with silver-tipped arrows and fire not one, but two shots at my heir and your sister."

"What response are you hoping for?" He stood taller.

"I'd like an explanation for your guards' incompetence."

I groaned. "This is not helping anyone. It also isn't undoing what has already been done. We should focus our attention on catching the archer."

"You need to get checked for that cut. Make sure there is no poison or anything we missed. Cali, You should go back to your quarters, where it's safe." Valor looked at Killian. He nodded. "I'll escort her and make sure she's protected before I update the king and queen."

"Take Tarryn." I offered. Valor looked at me. "He's a brilliant guard, and I know he isn't in any way involved in this. Best to have someone we know for sure isn't a threat guarding her, if Killian himself can't be there."

"You can't be certain of that," Valor said.

"I can, and I am."

"Relax, Val. She literally used herself as a human shield to protect me. I trust her judgement." Cali nodded to me, then looked at Killian. "Let's go."

Killian looked at me then.

"Thank you for protecting her." He was working hard to hide it, but I could read the guilt in his eyes. He felt like he'd failed her.

"Of course." I nodded, giving him a small smile. He turned and led Cali out of the room, stopping to request Tarryn join them, before they all disappeared through the doorway.

"Speaking of trustworthy guards, Elia, I'd like to assign you some of my own. Clearly, the ones here aren't capable of protecting you."

Valor tensed beside me. "Our guards are perfectly capable—"

I placed my hand on his arm, but kept my attention on Tira. "I'll accept, but only out of respect for you, and to put you at ease. Valor is right, his guards are skilled, particularly the ones I have guarding me. We were in sight of them the entire time, and as soon as there was danger, they were with us. Blaming them does no one any good. Not until we know how the archer got in."

"It would not have happened in Xeria."

"Perhaps it wouldn't have, perhaps it would have. Again, there's no point speculating. I am going to go see a medicae and have my arm inspected. Your guards are welcome to follow." I walked over to Hamish, who was waiting nearby. He gave me a reassuring smile, and we headed towards the medicae wing.

"Nicely handled." He commented, and I rolled my eyes.

"They were behaving like children."

He laughed. "Ironic."

"Ha Ha."

He grinned. It appeared Queen Tira hadn't been kidding. Two Xerian guards had joined us.

Hamish leaned in and whispered. "These guys are *huge*."

I smiled a bit. "Intimidated?"

"Pfft never." But I saw his eyes dart between the two men. I chuckled and sat down on one of the cots. A meda came over and inspected the cut on my arm.

"You're very lucky, Lady Elia." He commented

"How do you figure?"

"Well, it's only a flesh wound. I can't find any traces of poison. You said the arrowhead was silver? That can only mean you aren't an Argenti?"

"It's not appropriate for you to ask about the lady's Specialty." Hamish interjected.

I smiled a bit. "That is lucky. Thank you, Medicae. Am I fit to return to my quarters?"

He nodded. "Of course, my apologies, Lady Elia. I meant no offence."

"None taken." I stood up. "Thank you."

We headed back to my quarters, and I turned to Hamish, who had opened his mouth to say something.

"Before you even start. You have nothing to apologise for, Hamish. There were guards all around me. You couldn't have known we were going to be attacked, and you couldn't have stopped it, so don't you dare apologise."

He paused and looked at me like a stunned goldfish. "How do you do that?"

"Do what?"

"Know what I'm going to say, before I even know what I'm going to say?"

I chuckled and hugged him softly before opening my door.

"A lady never reveals her secrets, Ham." I winked and closed my door, but not before I caught the Virbi guards giving Hamish a once over, and him looking incredibly uncomfortable.

Shaking my head, I quickly got out of the ridiculously lavish dress and into a simple black nightgown. Breathing out, I poured myself a drink and sat down on the lounge. I needed to check in with Butcher soon. It sounded like Queen Tira wanted to have the official title ceremony sooner rather than later.

I took a long swig of my drink and sat back, closing my eyes. The sound of brick scraping across the floor had my eyes opening and darting to the hidden door. Valor emerged, closing it behind him.

"It's impolite to break into a lady's room, you know." I finished the glass before placing it on the coffee table beside me.

He didn't answer. He just walked over. I couldn't read the look on his face from here. The room was too dimly lit.

"If you are here to argue some more, I really am not in the mood."

"I'm not here to talk," he said when he finally reached me.

"Then why are you here—" He cut me off with his mouth on mine.

I had little chance to protest before he was laying me back on the lounge and moving over me. His hands roamed up my body, quickly, hungrily. Maybe it was the drinks, maybe it was the exhaustion, or maybe I just needed a distraction, because I didn't stop him. My arms wrapped around his neck of their own accord, and I pressed into him.

Just like the last time we'd been this intimate, everywhere he touched, I burned and, based on his reactions; it was the same for him. He did not make me wait this time. Before I knew it, we were both undressed and pressed as close to each other as we could get. He swiftly made sure I was ready for him, leaving me breathing heavily, while he looked completely unaffected. No one should be that skilled with only a few fingers.

His skin was smooth when I ran my hands across his back, tracing along it, trailing the few little scars that peppered his shoulder blade. He kissed my neck as he repositioned himself, spreading my legs. He bit down on my neck as he slid into me, causing me to gasp as I dug my nails into his arms slightly. Valor didn't seem to mind, as he kissed along my jawline and back to my lips. This time, we moved together, hard and fast.

Clearly, we were both working out our frustrations on each other. Hek, I'd be happy to resolve all our issues this way. It wasn't long before he took, or more accurately, threw me over the edge, jumping right off with me. He carefully pulled out, rolling to lie beside me.

Thank Ades the royals saw it necessary to have unorthodoxly large lounges. Catching my breath, I turned my head slightly to look at him. He was doing the same, but his eyes were on the ceiling. I didn't know what to say, what to ask. Butcher's words were echoing through my mind. *Make him fall in love with you'*

I told myself that's what made me roll over, wrapping my arms around his torso and resting my head on his chest. I felt him tense beneath me, and it took a second before he relaxed, responding in kind.

"We should not talk more often," I whispered, and I felt, more than heard, a breathy laugh escape from him.

"Of course you'd say that."

I smiled. "Hey, you started it." I looked up at him from my comfortable spot splayed across his chest.

He smiled a little in return before looking down at me. "That's true."

I bit my lip. "Why?"

"Why what?"

"Why did you come back here?"

He paused. "I just needed to touch you."

I nodded. "Did they catch the archer?"

"I'm not sure. I'm here with you," he said matter-of-factly.

"Shouldn't you be out there?"

"Yes." He confessed, and I wasn't sure why that had my stomach fluttering.

I smiled a bit and placed a kiss on his chest. His arms tightened around me.

"Don't look so smug, Sunshine."

"Or what?"

Turns out, or what meant another round of 'working things out', before moving us to the bed and going again. *Third times the charm.* I would have happily continued onto round four, but my body had other ideas and I fell asleep in his arms.

I woke the next morning to Valor, placing a tray of breakfast beside my bed. Rubbing my eyes, I looked at the food, then at him.

"Is it morning?"

"I'm pretty sure it was morning *before* you fell asleep."

"Oh. Well, good morning then." I sat up and he chuckled.

"Sorry, I didn't mean to wake you, but they had breakfast sent up."

"Who's they?"

"The staff, I guess?"

I nodded a bit before the realisation hit. "Wait. Did you answer the door? Looking like that?"

By that, I meant shirtless and wearing only his briefs.

He smirked. "I did."

I groaned. "Who saw?"

"The maid carrying the food, and the guards that were on duty."

I covered my face with my pillow. "You did that on purpose." I muttered.

"Did what?"

"Before I've even eaten, the entire castle will know you answered my door half-naked. They will all assume we... you know."

"Which we did."

"Yes, but the entire castle doesn't need to be privy to that information!"

He chuckled. "Relax." He sat beside me, prying the pillow from my fingers, before leaning down to kiss my forehead, despite the glare I was directing at him.

"Everyone already assumed we were, since I'm courting you."

I sighed. "Yes, but still…"

"Still?" He looked at me.

I shrugged. "I don't know. It's just very confusing. We are fake, almost betrothed, but then actually sleeping together, whilst also fighting every five seconds."

"You think too much."

I scoffed. "If you thought a little more, I guarantee we wouldn't have so many arguments."

He laughed. "You are rather savage in the morning."

"Wait. What time is it?"

"Just past eight-thirty. Why?"

"Shit, I need to get ready." I threw the covers off me.

"Ready for what?"

"Breakfast with Queen Tira."

"Ah, so that means I can eat this?" He gestured to the breakfast tray. I rolled my eyes.

"Knock yourself out." I got up and hurried to the bathroom.

"Or I could join you in there, and have you instead?"

I responded by simply closing the door and locking it. His laugh echoed through the bathroom door.

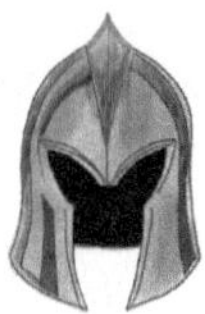

CHAPTER THIRTY-NINE

I QUICKLY SHOWERED AND braided my hair. I didn't have time to do much else with it. I slipped on my robe before leaving my bathing chamber and heading straight to my closet. Valor was spread out on my bed, enjoying the meal meant for me, no doubt dropping crumbs all over my sheets.

"Remind me why you are still here?" I started sifting through the endless amounts of dresses hanging up, finally just grabbing one of the closest ones, and then reaching down to grab some shoes. When he didn't answer me, I glanced over my shoulder to find him watching me appreciatively.

"So I wouldn't miss out on that," he said, as if it were self-explanatory. I rolled my eyes again.

"Surely someone will come knocking on *your* door soon, and you won't be there to answer it." I responded, straightening and moving over to my changing area.

It was essentially a small carpet placed in front of a beautiful full-length mirror, complete with a brief step nearby in case of a lengthy dress.

I saw Valor shrug in the mirror's reflection. "They can wait."

"You aren't staying to watch me change. Go back to your own room."

He pouted, and I shook my head, folding my arms.

He sighed dramatically. "You are absolutely no fun." He got up, though, and walked back over to the lounge, where his clothes had been strewn across the floor near mine.

"That's not what you said last night."

That got a smile out of him. "No, I suppose it's not." He dressed fairly quickly, before walking over and standing behind me. He looked at me in the mirror.

"So this breakfast..."

"She wants to discuss the ceremony, naming me princess."

He nodded a bit. "Once you are officially crowned, things are going to get a bit more complicated."

"Things are complicated already."

"You know what I mean." He met my eyes in the reflection. A thousand unsaid words were staring back at me.

"I do. We will discuss all of it soon, just not now."

He nodded a bit. "I will see you later, then."

I nodded back and watched as he left. He used the front door this time. *Bastard.*

I dressed quickly after that, before going to the door to let my guards know we would be going to see the queen. Hamish was there, along with the two Virbi guards. Tarryn must still be guarding Cali. Hamish raised his eyebrows, smirking at me.

"Good morning, Lady Elia. How was your evening?"

I shot daggers at him, ignoring his comment entirely and turning to the other two guards.

"I'm sorry. I didn't get your names last night." Both guards bowed low.

"I'm Uri, and this is Wes, Your Highness," a tall middle-aged man said. He certainly fit the picture of a soldier. His black hair was cropped short and greying a little on the sides, which only seemed to compliment his midnight kissed skin. He was insanely muscular, putting even Tolemas to shame. His companion Wes appeared younger, closer to my age, with more of a warmer bronze skin tone, and walnut coloured hair, braided back so it sat draped over his shoulder. He wasn't as muscular as Uri, but he was taller. He looked less serious than Uri, but had a look in his eyes that warned against testing him.

"It's nice to meet you both, just Elia is fine." I smiled. "I'm about to go meet the queen for breakfast. Your presence isn't necessary anymore, but you probably need to find out where you are needed, so you're welcome to escort me there."

"Queen Tira has assigned us as your personal guards, Princess," Uri said, and I could tell he would not be taking me up on my offer to use my name instead of my title anytime soon. "Not just for last night, but as long as we are able."

I raised my eyebrows. "This is the first I am hearing of it. I already have personal guards."

"We mean no disrespect, Your High—Elia." Wes chimed in. "We aren't trying to replace your current guards. I believe the queen just wanted us to become acquainted now, instead of when you return to Xeria, and you no longer already have personal guards."

That thought caused a pang in my chest, and I looked at Hamish. If I really ended up having to go to Xeria, I would have to leave Hamish and Tarryn behind. I would be alone again. Hamish smiled a little sadly, reading my thoughts, as usual.

"You don't want to be late, Elle. Are you ready to go?" He said, holding out his arm.

I took it gratefully. "Yes, thank you, Hamish." We remained arm in arm as we walked to Queen Tira's quarters. Uri and Wes followed a few feet behind us.

Once we reached her chambers, I knocked on the door and was greeted by Yarik.

"Good morning, Princess. You look lovely."

I smiled a bit. "Yarik, nice to see you."

"Glad to see you in one piece after last night's debacle."

"As am I. Is Queen Tira here?"

"She certainly is. You have impeccable timing, the food arrived just before you. Come in, child."

Yarik was an odd one to pin down. I followed him inside and to the sitting room, only to find Tira was not alone. She was smiling and chatting happily with someone sitting across from her.

"Elia, how are you feeling?" Hadrian greeted me.

"Hadrian, I'm feeling fine. Thank you for asking. How are you?"

"I'm good, all things considered."

"Have a seat, Elia. I thought it would be good for Hadrian to be here for some of this conversation, that you might feel more comfortable with someone you know better. I hope that is okay?"

Hadrian smiled warmly at me. "Of course, thank you for considering that." I sat down.

"Help yourself to breakfast. This is just an informal chat about how you want things to proceed." She took a sip of her tea. I nodded and served myself a plate.

"Okay, well, I'm new to this so you'll have to fill in the blanks..."

Hadrian chuckled. "She's talking about your naming ceremony. The sooner it happens, the better, but no one wants to rush you."

"Definitely not." Tira agreed.

"You said yesterday that regardless of whether I accept the title and have the official ceremony, I am still considered a princess if you formally acknowledge our relation, right?"

"That is correct."

"Then I guess there's not much point in refusing the title. I assume its tradition or formality that calls for a ceremony? Is there a way to accept the title without the ceremony?" I asked hopefully.

"I'm afraid not," Hadrian said, "but if you decide to accept, it will be fairly quick. We will all be there. It isn't as scary as it sounds."

"Maybe not for you." I smiled a bit. "I am not a royal. I don't know how to act or what they will expect of me. I might not be able to uphold the standards of a princess." Not that Butcher was giving me a choice, but they didn't know that.

Tira reached over and squeezed my hand. "You don't need to worry about that. All you need to do is be yourself, Elia. I expect nothing more than that, and neither will our people. Anything you need to know, we can teach you, but we don't want you to change who you are to fit the role. The role is whatever you choose to make it."

"That sounds nice, but also very hard to believe. I have seen some royal life." After glancing at Hadrian, I went back to Tira. "I know there are expectations, rules, and standards to meet."

Tira smiled a somewhat tight-lipped smile. "Every kingdom does things differently, just because some royals have certain rules. That does not mean another has the same ones."

"But there *are* still expectations and behaviours I would be required to meet as a princess?"

"To an extent, but every human being is expected to adhere to certain behaviours. Yours will only be different in that I'd encourage you to set a good example for others where you can."

"Elia, if you aren't ready for this, that is absolutely fine. If you would like to learn more first, it can wait." Hadrian added.

Tira nodded in agreement.

"No. I think I am ready for it. I just have a lot of questions." I smiled nervously. "Sorry for asking so much."

"Don't be sorry at all. We want you to be comfortable, Elia. I was going to suggest we have the ceremony tomorrow night so we can spend the remaining time that we have before the other kingdoms arrive, getting you up to speed, but we can wait."

"Tomorrow?" I swallowed.

"But as Tira said, there is no rush. It can wait." Hadrian reassured me.

I felt that tug on my chest. "No, tomorrow night is... fine." I nodded. "It's quick and easy, like you said, right?"

He laughed a bit. "Yes, it is."

"Why don't you take the day to think about it? I know this is a lot, especially first thing in the morning." Tira added.

"Thank you. I think that would be good."

"Then it's settled. No more princess talk. For now, let's enjoy our breakfast, then you can take some time. I will come and find you around lunchtime?"

I smiled gratefully and we all ate. They told me stories from when they were younger. They both laughed a *lot*. I hadn't seen Hadrian laugh like that with Odette and I hadn't seen Tira appear so carefree with anyone else yet, not even Yarik. Maybe they truly were in love back then and if her mother hadn't died, everything would be very different.

After breakfast, I left them both to continue their reminiscing. I had to speak to Butcher. I went back to my room, changed, and used the tunnels to take my usual route to her estate. When I got there, servants informed me she was at the circus. *Great.* I headed straight there, staying out of sight. Who knew what she had told them about where I was? I knew she had Mavil performing as The Masked Flyer, but the other acts would know it wasn't me. I went to her study and waited.

She eventually showed herself. Entering the room with — "Sierra?"

My little sister was in her roller, holding the circus ledgers in her lap. She used to practically live with those things before all of this. Her eyes widened, and she hesitated a second before relief filled her eyes.

"Adira…" She wheeled herself over and threw her arms around me. I hugged her back tightly, but my eyes were on Butcher.

"Hello, Adira." She walked over, taking a seat in her chair.

"What is going on? We had a deal. Sierra is to be kept out of all of this."

"Well, the deal changed when you continually tried to find a way out of it, Adira. Besides, Sierra enjoys doing the books. It gives her something to do, makes her feel useful."

I looked at Sierra. "Is that true?"

She looked down. "I'm sorry Ira. I just couldn't stay cooped up any longer. You know how much I hate that."

"I know, Sierra, but you can't work for her?"

"You are."

I looked at her in shock. "Not by *choice?*" Butcher was watching us in amusement. She leant back, clearly enjoying this.

"You are living in a castle surrounded by riches and royalty while I am here, sequestered in a room with no one for company and nothing to do but read or draw, Adira. You are more free than I am, and it isn't me that made a deal."

I couldn't believe what I was hearing. It was almost as if she were *jealous* that I was Butcher's Akros damned slave.

"What is wrong with you? I am not living it up in there, Sierra. Every day is a risk! Every move I make could get me killed. I would much rather be safe in a room where I could read and draw than in the position I am in. *Trust* me, if I had a choice, I would not be doing this."

"I'm sorry you don't have a choice, Adira, but I do. I don't want to stay cooped up in that room any longer. I am nineteen now. You're not…" she trailed off.

"I'm not what, Sierra?"

She sighed. "You're not my mother."

I breathed in, pain coursing through me. Before I could process the blow she'd just landed, Butcher conveniently stepped in.

"Now, now, children." She looked at Sierra. "Sierra sweetheart, maybe it would be best if I spoke to Adira alone? You should find Tolemas and get me the numbers from last night's fights."

She nodded slightly, glancing at me before turning and wheeling herself out of the room.

Butcher stood, walking over to the door and shutting it. "Try not to take it personally, Adira. She is young. We all have that rebellious stage."

"Some of us were too busy trying to put food on the table to afford being rebellious."

"Yes, but she is not one of them."

"I do not need familial advice from you, of all people. If I find out you are involving her in anything criminal, anything she shouldn't be doing..."

"Yes, yes. Let's skip the empty threats, shall we? Give me the update you came here to give."

Tug. I gritted my teeth and did just that. I filled her in on everything that had happened since I'd last seen her.

"They want to do the title ceremony tomorrow night."

"Excellent, the sooner the better." She grinned. It was a very pleased smile.

Soon, I would have some actual sway, and if she had her way, I would have an entire kingdom at my fingertips.

"Return to the castle then. Tell them you are ready to accept your title and are happy for the ceremony to be tomorrow." She smiled. "The next time I see you, you shall be a princess. Try to look a little happier about it."

I didn't feel a tug that time and wasn't inclined to smile. The intent behind the words mattered. The magic that bound me was too intelligent.

"Can I see Sierra again before I leave?" It killed me to even have to ask permission, but I needed to see her. Talk some sense into her.

"I think it's best if you don't. She's really come out of her shell, Adira. You would be proud. Perhaps all she needed was to be out of her big sister's shadow?"

I clenched my fist. "Please let me see her, Camilla."

"No. Now go. Return to the castle."

It took everything in me not to explode. The big pull in my chest helped. I turned and left the room, sneaking out of the circus and back to the tunnels. The entire way, all I could think about was Sierra. What had gotten into her? She occasionally rebelled a little, sure, but she wasn't stupid. I also didn't think she could be naïve enough to let Butcher manipulate her.

Could she truly not understand what I was doing here and thought I was simply enjoying myself, indulging in luxuries she couldn't even imagine? I prayed it was that. That she just misunderstood and was jealous about what she thought was going on. Every other alternative was too troubling to consider. Especially when there wasn't a damned thing I could do about it. My rage only grew as I trekked through the tunnels. I didn't head for my rooms.

Instead, I took a tunnel that led to a servants' entrance. I pulled my hood over my head and navigated my way along the worn paths until I reached the court temple. As temple goers filed out after morning mass, I remained hidden, watching and listening to their conversations.

I'd almost given up hope when a woman stopped atop the steps. Father Chambersen's wife, Kayleia, was exactly who I was looking for. Valor hadn't been exaggerating. She was tiny. I trailed her from a distance as she made her way through the castle, going about her day.

Tilly had said the woman who'd given her the poison had been very short and wore a sun symbol.

I was positive she was my missing link. She could certainly have been the robed woman Tilly described. She would have had easy access to the castle, Tilly, and to the kitchens being a lady's maid, but I still had unanswered questions.

What was her motive? Was she working for her husband or herself? Father Chambersen was creepy and certainly up to no good, but he didn't have a clear motive for removing Hadrian from the picture. Not if for years they had managed the kingdom together. He could be a rebel, but him saying 'we will rise' isn't enough evidence to prove that.

If she wasn't working for her husband, then what was *her* motive? That's what I'd hopefully discover by tailing her. She seemed to be well liked by all the servants she passed, going in and out of different noblewomen's rooms, seeing to their needs.

She held a senior lady's maid position by now and was even responsible for organising and booking things for the noblewomen. So, when she handed off a list to one of the other maids, I accidentally bumped into said maid, knocking the load of laundry she'd been carrying all over the floor.

Apologising profusely, I'd dropped to the ground and helped her collect all the garments. By the time we had picked everything up and gone our separate ways, she was none the wiser that her list had been torn at the bottom, the last few items now noted on a small piece of paper safely tucked into my pocket.

CHAPTER FORTY

I WAS PREPARING TO call it quits for the day, figuring I'd compare Kayleia's writing to the signature I was yet to find a match for, when she stopped outside the door of someone I wouldn't expect her to be serving. Lord Wicton, royal ambassador, the one who'd been the rudest of the advisors when I had questioned them all.

She knocked three times in a row, glancing around rather suspiciously. When the door opened, Wicton looked around before pulling her inside. I raised my eyebrows as the door swung shut. Was Lord Wicton was having an affair with the Head Priest's wife?

As the royal ambassador Wicton would have been one of the few people aware of the poison masters leave, he'd have known the route and how long he'd be away for. Hek, he probably organised the trip himself, corresponding with Reya to get permission to enter the kingdom.

Question is, was Wicton in on the assassination attempt or had Kayleia stolen the information from him? If she had, was it for her, her husband, or someone else entirely?

I decided I had enough evidence to take to Odette. She could do with it what she liked. I just had to head to my room first to gather the notes I'd made and compare the handwriting sample.

I took the servants' entries and tunnels to get back to my chambers undetected, and sure enough, when I opened my door, Tarryn, Wes, and Uri were standing guard outside. Hamish must be sleeping after the long shift he pulled last night and this morning.

I raised my eyebrows at the three of them. "This seems like overkill, don't you think?"

Tarryn smiled. "I'm not on duty. I'm here for your training session. Didn't think I'd let you get away with skipping, did you?"

I groaned. Having missed this morning's session thanks to the breakfast, I'd figured I'd just catch up this afternoon. Apparently not. I wanted to tell

Tarryn it had to wait. I needed to inform Odette of my theory, but I couldn't very well say that in front of Uri and Wes. I'd have to tell her later.

"Fine, give me a second." I shut the door and quickly changed into my training gear.

Reopening the door, Tarryn gave me a once over, before nodding, and heading in the practice room's direction. I fell into step beside him. I saw Wes and Uri exchange quizzical looks before following us.

Tarryn headed straight for the sparring mat. I warmed up quickly before wrapping my hands and joining him. My Virbi guards stood against the wall and watched curiously.

"You ready?"

I nodded, getting into position. I had a lot of anger that I was more than happy to beat out.

"Begin."

I didn't hesitate. I launched myself at him. Which, naturally, he saw coming from a mile away, but I kept going, kept on the offensive. I let my rage, my pain, out in the form of my hits.

"You're not controlled, Elle. Focus," Tarryn said, dodging yet another one of my attempted blows.

I'd taken to his training well. He had been right when he'd said it shouldn't be too difficult for me to learn to fight, given my background in acrobatics, stealth, and my ability to read people's movements.

I was in good shape, so it was really just a matter of learning different techniques and manoeuvres. It was just another routine to learn. I tried to do what he said, to focus. I came at him again and he easily sidestepped it, which only pissed me off more.

"You're letting your anger get the best of you. You're being sloppy, Elia."

I practically growled at him. "That's *why* we're doing this. To get rid of my anger." I attacked, he blocked.

"Yes, but you're not getting rid of it, are you? You're making it worse. You're only fuelling the anger, not using it to your advantage."

"I am using it." I struck again, landing a glancing blow to his shoulder.

"But how will you manage when someone is attacking *you*, when you're this riled up?"

"That's what we're doing."

"No, it's what you're doing. I have been strictly on the defensive."

Before I could blink, he struck, barely giving me time to dodge what would have been a painful strike. I had no time to recover before he was on me again. The blows kept coming. It took all of my concentration to try to avoid them. I was unsuccessful every time, which just made me angrier. He'd forced me into the defensive, and I was so *tired* of playing defence, tired of being helpless.

When he came for me this time, I took a breath, watching how he moved. I saw the slight change in the direction of his right foot as he struck, telling me which side he was going for. I bent, dropping to the ground in a crouch, sweeping my leg out in an effort to knock him over. He saw it coming and jumped over it, but I'd expected that too, and was already rolling to the side, out of the way of his next blow before it could hit me. I was back on my feet again, landing a kick to his side. I heard him grunt slightly and knew I was finally getting somewhere.

That was all I'd needed to help me forge that rage into a weapon I could use. Tarryn was trying to get me to control it, so I would. We traded blow for blow. Each blocking and then trying to land one on the other. It really was like a dance, as we tried to find the other person's weak spot. I was puffing by the time I landed a blow to his chin, jerking his head to the side.

I took that split second where he wasn't watching, to once again drop into a crouch, sweeping his legs out from under him. This time he wasn't fast enough, and he went down with a loud thud. He seemed almost as surprised as I was as he glanced up at me from the floor. This was the first time I'd successfully taken him down. He'd definitely gone easy on me, but still.

"Good work," he said, and I held my hand out to him.

"You went easy." He took my hand and let me attempt to pull him up. By that, I mean he mostly pulled himself up, but let me think I was helping.

"Not as easy as you think. You did well." He brushed himself off. "Grab a drink and take five. I'll set up the next exercise."

I groaned slightly. That was the thing with Tarry's training. We never covered just one thing. It was always multiple skills, no matter how hard you'd just trained on the one before. I headed over to the drink station that the servants had set up for us after we arrived, grabbed a glass and took a big swig of the water.

"He was pulling his punches." I turned to see Uri standing beside the drinks table.

"Well, yeah, he'd probably knock me unconscious if he didn't."

"Do you think your enemies will hesitate to do so?"

"No, but this is training. It isn't a battle."

"Everything is a battle."

I raised my eyebrows. "Well, I am new to fighting."

"How new?"

"Only a few weeks of combat, really."

"You're a Para. Your strength will give you an advantage. What's your Specialty?"

I shrugged. "To be completely honest with you, I don't know. I didn't even know I was a Para until I found out Queen Tira was my mother."

He frowned. "How is that possible? Children are Confirmed and Tested before they begin school?"

I couldn't very well tell him I never went to school and was therefore never Confirmed. Lady Elia supposedly had a stellar education.

"I was either never Confirmed, or it failed. My father had to keep up the ruse that I was the daughter of two noble, Impure, parents. If he'd had me tested, it would have revealed one of them was not my biological parent, and that would have raised questions that could have led back to Queen Tira."

"I suppose that makes sense. It's unusual, but we will have to do a proper Testing for you once they officially name you Queen Tira's heir."

I hid my unease at that thought. I would have to deal with that later. Instead, I just nodded.

"Are you still gossiping, or can we get back to work?!" Tarryn called out. I looked over.

Uri chuckled. "If you want to see how you'd go against someone that will not pull their punches, you just let me know." He finished his drink and walked back over to Wes.

I trudged back over to Tarryn, my body already aching from our earlier fight. His arms were crossed. He did not like wasting time.

"Sorry Tarryn. What kind of torture have you got next?"

"Cardio."

I groaned. "Seriously?"

"You know the drill. Start lapping, Worthington. I want you to beat your personal best today."

"Aw come on, Tarryn..." I begged, as he made his way over to Uri.

"Clock's ticking."

Sighing, I started my laps. One day, I would get him back for this. I don't know when or how, but I would.

By the time I finished, I had cursed Tarryn to Infernis and back countless times. Thankfully, he informed me we would in fact be skipping the afternoon session today because he and Uri were planning something different for our next session.

Not complaining at all, I headed back to my rooms and had a long hot bath to soothe my now aching muscles. After a good, long, soak, I got out and compared the C signature to the sample of Kayleia's scribble. It was a perfect match.

I quickly made myself presentable, gathered my notes, and headed to Odette's study.

"Elia, how are you dear?"

I curtsied slightly. "I'm good, thank you Your Majesty. Are you well?"

She smiled. "Always. What can I do for you?"

"I believe I know who assisted Tilly in her assassination attempt."

"Oh?" She gestured for me to explain. So I did, I told her everything I knew about Father Chambersen, Lord Wicton, Kayleia, and that they may be linked to the rebellion. She arched an eyebrow as I finished, before calling for one of her guards.

"Yes, Your Highness?"

"Fetch me Father Chambersen, his wife, and Lord Wicton, immediately."

He nodded and set off.

"As I said, they haven't confessed, but given the nature of their potential crime I thought it best I come to you with the information."

"You made the right decision child, you may go. I will handle it from here. Thank you."

"... So does this mean the ruse between your son and I can end?"

She waived her hand dismissively. "Don't be so hasty. As you said, no one has confessed yet. Carry on as you are."

I bowed my head slightly and left feeling uneasy. I couldn't pinpoint why exactly, but if they were about to be subjected to the Queen's preferred method of questioning, I certainly didn't want to be present.

The next morning, I met Tarryn in the courtyard. While I'd nearly died following his cardio routine yesterday, he and Uri had teamed up and decided they wanted to try something new today. Starting at dawn, of course.

I frowned slightly, taking in the surroundings. Someone had used sand to map out a circle in the centre of the courtyard. A sparring ring, perhaps? There were other things set up around the room that I couldn't determine a use for.

There were candles, torches, and buckets of water. Someone had somehow gotten a whole cart full of dirt and rocks in here, and more. That wasn't what had me frowning, though. It wasn't just Tarryn and Uri waiting for me. Cali, Hamish, and Wes were present, but the person I was most surprised to see was Josette.

"Um, what is this, an intervention?" I said as Tarryn approached me, Uri at his side. Tarryn smiled a bit, and Uri shook his head.

"We thought it would be a good idea to do some Specialty based training." Uri answered. I frowned again. I was going to get wrinkles.

"But I don't know what my Gifting is or how to use it, let alone my Specialty? I haven't gone through my Testing yet?"

"We're not talking about you using your Gifting. You should learn to defend and counter Gifted attacks, regardless of whether you are Impure, Pure, or Para." Tarryn explained as I stared at him.

"You're joking, right? You want me to fight Pures?" I shook my head. "You have both lost your minds. I can barely keep up with an Impure combatant, let alone a magical one."

"I guess you're in for a rough morning, then." Uri stated. "I'd warm up if I were you." He glanced at Tarryn. "Who's up first?"

"We'll start with Cali. She'll ease her into it." Tarryn suggested. Uri seemed to agree and turned, heading in Cali's direction. Crossing my arms, I glared at Tarryn.

"Who's idea was this?"

"Is that relevant?"

"Yes."

"It's not."

"Yes, it is."

"You're stalling. Go warm up."

I groaned but did as he said, dramatically plonking myself onto the ground and stretching. Tarryn's lips quirked upwards before he joined the others.

If I was lucky, maybe I'd be critically injured during this training and not have to do this naming ceremony tonight. Once I was warm enough, I made my way over to the makeshift sparring ring where Cali and Tarryn were now standing. The former grinned at me.

"Don't worry, it'll be fun!" She reassured me.

"Says the all powerful Pure," I muttered, and she chuckled.

"Don't be such a baby, Tarryn says you've progressed way faster than he expected and that you're ready for this. Trust yourself."

"Oh, did he?" I said, shooting another glare Tarryn's way. He rolled his eyes.

"Alright. This is how it's going to go. You will spar against someone from each Gifting." I raised my hand and this time it was Tarryn shooting daggers at me.

"Yes, Elia?"

"How am I going to fight someone from each Gifting when there are no Pures from Ikira, Reya, and other than you being a Tear, there's still three other Elementi Specialties missing from Lios?"

"I was getting to that. Luckily, we have Cali representing the Incrementi, Uri representing the Virbi, Josette representing the Kineti, and myself the Tear Specialty of the Elementi. Hamish and Wes are going to imitate attacks from some of the missing Giftings or Specialties. A bit of imagination will be required, but until we have someone from those kingdoms, it's the best we can do for now."

"About Josette, surely there is another Kineti available? Valor? Literally *anyone* else?"

"Valor would go far too easy on you. Josette is the best choice. She will challenge you."

"Or kill me," I muttered. Tarryn ignored that.

"Take up your positions. I'll act as a referee. The rules are simple, no fatal blows. If you are knocked out of the sparring circle you lose, however if your opponent uses objects from outside the circle, the boundary becomes void and the courtyard becomes your battlefield."

I sighed and moved to one side of the ring. Cali took up a position opposite.

"Woo-hoo! Go Elia!" Hamish shouted from across the room. I smothered the urge to flip him off.

"Tell me what you know of the Incrementi." Tarryn ordered. I didn't take my eyes off of Cali. She was flexing her fingers, readying herself. *Great.*

"Incrementi hail from Lenea. The two Specialties of Incrementi are Flori and Immuni."

"Which is more dangerous?"

"I'd say Flori?"

"Why?"

"Flori can control plant life, whereas Immuni are immune to poison. Whilst that is a very useful skill to have, I'd rather face an Immuni than a Flori in a physical fight."

"Today you're facing a Flori, what are their weaknesses?"

Cali moved closer, and I stepped to the side as we began circling.

"Umm plant toxins?" I joked, referring to a concoction used to kill off unwanted weeds.

"Do you have any handy?"

I gave him a bland look, taking my attention off of Cali, which she had clearly been waiting for. Reaching into a pouch fastened around her waist, she pulled out and threw what looked like seeds in my direction. I looked back just in time to duck. They landed behind me, and I raised my eyebrows.

"Your strategy is to pelt me with seeds?"

Cali smirked as a rustling sound started from behind me, quickly growing louder. I stepped to the side, keeping Cali in my line of sight, before turning to see what was happening.

"What in Heknos' Hellfire?" I cursed. I was staring at a replica of a mortal made up of twisted vines. A terrifying shadow with no eyes or mouth, just a body, and it *moved.* I was so busy staring at the thing that I was too slow to notice the slap coming my way until my cheek was stinging from the impact.

"Ooooh." Hamish cringed in sympathy from the sidelines. This time, I *did* flip him off.

The creepy plant-shadow thing came at me again, but this time I was ready. I blocked the blow and landed a swift kick to its stomach. The damn thing barely moved, its roots digging into the ground to keep it stable. Worse, when I tried to withdraw my foot, vines shot out from its chest, wrapping around my calf.

"Ah, Hek." I struggled to keep my balance as I ripped at the vines, losing sight of Cali, who had come up behind me and was now holding a dagger to my throat. I tensed.

"How come she gets weapons?!"

"Are you giving up?" Tarryn said.

I gritted my teeth, letting go of the vines for the time being. I'd deal with them later, a dagger I could face. It was a tad more difficult than usual, but

I reached up with my right hand, clutching her wrist and applying pressure in just the right spot. She cried out, dropping the dagger out of reflex.

I caught it in my left hand, sliding my right further up so I could grip her arm properly before bending slightly, pushing back into her and using the momentum to flip her over my shoulder, straight into her monstrous plant creation.

They both went down, but the vines were now up to my thigh. I winced as they tightened around my leg. Leaning forward and hacking them at the base of the thing's chest, I loosened its hold enough to jerk my leg free.

Cali was getting tangled in her own vines. She clenched her fist, and the thing ceased moving, decaying in front of me until it was nothing but a pile of dust and leaves on the ground. She stood dusting herself off.

"Damn Elia. When did you learn to do that?"

"I warned you not to go easy on her." Tarryn scolded, and Cali shrugged.

"Well, yeah, but I didn't think she'd be able to fend off the Hortus."

I watched her closely, not letting myself get distracted this time.

"Are you yielding, Cali?" Tarryn asked.

"Oh! Yes, sorry." She rubbed her backside, stepping out of the ring. "I can't believe you flipped me *over* you."

I raised my eyebrows. "In my defence, you had a knife to my throat?" I tossed it up like I'd seen Hamish do so many times, catching it by the blade and holding the hilt end out to her. She grinned and took it from me. "What is a Hortus?" I asked.

"It's what we call the thing you just fought. Flori have fought entire battles by sending Hortus down to fight in their place."

"An entire army of those things would be brutal." I commented, and she nodded.

"It's even worse when Immuni are involved."

"What do you mean?"

"Immuni aren't just immune to poisons. They can also create them and amplify them."

"Amplify?" I said, not sure I really wanted an answer.

She nodded.

"I could create a Hortus, and an Immuni could arm it with a deadly poison, one touch and you're dead, or working together we could make it release poisonous spores that would spread through enemy troops. Infecting anyone within range." My eyes widened.

"Divinities."

"Go grab a drink and have a quick break while we set up for the next round. Elia, you let yourself get distracted, and it cost you. You panicked when Cali used her magic. You need to remain levelheaded and be prepared for things like that." I begrudgingly agreed with him.

"Cali, you relied too strongly on your Gifting. Elia shouldn't have been able to beat you. You let your personal feelings for her soften your attack and you didn't consider the compromising position you put yourself in when you entered into close combat with her." She sighed.

"But with a little more training, you can remedy that," Tarryn added, softening his tone a little.

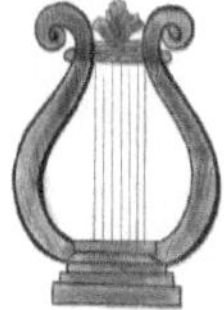

CHAPTER FORTY-ONE

SHE GAVE HIM A small smile before joining me as we made our way to the makeshift drinks station.

"How did they convince Josette to take part in this impromptu training session?"

Cali pursed her lips in response.

"What?" I said, sensing I would not like her answer.

"... She volunteered. I believe her exact words when Tarryn asked Valor and James if they could assist were 'I will gladly wipe the floor with that faux princess.'"

Rolling my eyes, I grabbed a cup of water and took a sip.

"Of course she did."

"If it helps," Cali tried, "both Val and James swiftly defended you and offered to help instead, but Tarryn argued it would be more of a realistic challenge against someone who wouldn't go easy on you."

I glanced over at the woman in question. She was flirting shamelessly with Wes, who looked torn between flattery and unease. He clearly knew who she was.

"Don't worry, Tarryn will stop her if she goes too far."

"How do you know it won't be me that Tarryn has to stop?"

Cali arched an eyebrow.

"Beating me is one thing, but Josette? She's a strong Teleki. There's a reason she would have married Valor, eventually. They'd likely produce very strong Pure children."

I pulled a face. "Gross."

Cali laughed. "My point is. Don't underestimate her. She's a bitch, yes, but she's also incredibly skilled, Elle. She can back it up."

I sighed, nodding.

"Don't worry, I know full well I wouldn't have beaten you if you hadn't been going easy on me, let alone any of the others."

Tarryn's voice interrupted Cali's attempt at disagreement.

"Tea time is over, ladies! Elia, back in the ring!"

I groaned, and Cali winked. "You got this!" She shoved me in the direction of the makeshift circle, where Uri was waiting for me. *Great.*

Stepping into the ring, Uri grinned at me and there was a glint in his eyes that wiped away any doubts that this man was a warrior through and through. I assumed all of Tira's guards were, but I hadn't expected to face off against one, even in a controlled environment like this. I swallowed. Uri's eyes tracked the movement and his grin widened.

"Tell me about the Virbi." Tarryn ordered as I watched Uri.

"The Virbi Specialties are Forti and Argenti."

"What are their strengths and weaknesses?"

"Forti have extreme strength, which sometimes means they are slower." Uri smirked at this. "Argenti have nearly impenetrable skin, but they are vulnerable to silver."

"Do you know what Uri's Specialty is?"

I assessed him.

"No. But I am going to guess he's a Forti."

"Could he be both a Forti and an Argenti?"

I frowned. "No."

"Why not?"

"Because no Pure or Para has ever been recorded capable of specialising in more than one magic. It's not possible." Uri still wore that slight smirk.

"Assuming Uri is a Forti, he is larger, taller, and stronger than you. How can you possibly beat him?"

"I can't." I shrugged. "I'm about to have my ass kicked."

"You are, if that's your attitude. How can you beat him, Elia?"

"Disarm him with my good looks and girlish charms?" I winked at Uri and he chuckled, taking a step closer. Tarryn rolled his eyes.

"Go ahead, Uri. Kick her ass."

"Shit." I muttered as Uri swung at me. I jumped back, narrowly avoiding his fist. If that had hit me, he'd have sent me flying. He advanced, coming for me again. I moved to the side, circling back away from him.

"Is your strategy to just avoid him?" Tarryn taunted.

"Running has always worked for me in the past!" I yelped as Uri charged at me again and I scrambled out of the way. He swung at me and I tried to dodge, but he'd expected that and followed me, jerking up his other arm, causing me to run straight into it.

He didn't so much as budge as I practically ricocheted off of him, thrown backwards onto my ass, as I had predicted. I gasped in pain, in need of a deep breath, one hand rubbing my neck.

Uri didn't stop though, and I slid backwards, looking for a way out. My hand hit sand, and I quickly glanced down to see that I was at the edge of the makeshift ring. My eyes darted around, looking for a solution other than tapping out.

"Remember your training, Elia. You've faced people stronger and larger than you before. Target his weaknesses." Tarryn calmly instructed. Easy for him to say when he didn't have a Virbi Forti charging at him. *Breathe, Adira, think.* I watched Uri approach. He smiled.

"You're cornered, kid."

"I'm not over the line."

He chuckled and stepped forward, moving to no doubt shove me over it. I scooped up some sand and hurled it at his face, only feeling a little bad about it since my neck was still throbbing. His eyes widened a fraction as he raised his arm to shield his eyes before clenching them shut.

I quickly slid through his legs in a very unladylike fashion before jumping to my feet and spinning to face him. He turned too, throwing another punch. I ducked, but this time I didn't back away. I stepped in close. It's dangerous to get close to a stronger assailant, but sometimes it was your only way to avoid heavy blows.

I landed one of my own punches to his stomach and was rewarded with a sore fist, but I kept going. Landing a blow to his side, then his other in quick succession.

His leg swept out to knock me over, but I jumped over it, my jaw connecting with his readied fist as I did. Stumbling back, I groaned, aching to rub my jaw but lacking the time to do so as he took the offensive again. I couldn't beat him physically. I wasn't even strong enough to block his blows, but I *was* smaller and faster. My initial 'strategy' may have been the best one. If I could avoid him for long enough, maybe I could somehow trick him into crossing the line.

I let my acrobatic training kick in, ducking and rolling out of the way of his next punch. He increased his intensity, realising I was going to remain on the defensive. He came at me hard and surprisingly fast, for someone his size, but I was faster. I flipped, rolled, ducked, jumped, and manoeuvred away from every swing, watching his movements closely to anticipate his attacks.

I was gaining some confidence. If I could keep avoiding him, maybe I could line up one solid kick or trip to get him outside of the ring. That's when I noticed the glint in Uri's eyes again. He was smiling. Why was he smiling?

He struck out, and a few seconds later, I had my answer. I bent back to avoid his fist, but then his other hand struck out. I narrowly lept to the side, realising at that moment I'd done exactly as he'd wanted. Right before I landed, Uri smashed both his fists into the ground, eliciting a massive *BOOM* as the ground shook. Hek, the whole courtyard shook.

I heard glass smash, and I was so surprised that even though I kept my balance on the shaking ground, I wasn't ready for Uri's next attack. He swept his leg out, knocking me to the ground and was on me a second later. His knee felt like it was crushing my windpipe, and I gasped for air as I pushed against his thigh. He didn't budge.

I quickly tapped the ground beside me and Uri immediately backed off, holding out his hand to help me up. I gasped slightly, closing my eyes for a second and breathing in before accepting his hand, allowing him to pull me up.

"You went easy on her," Tarryn said, and my eyes widened.

"You call that easy?!" I exclaimed. Uri just shrugged.

"I didn't want to kill the girl. It is a training exercise, after all."

I stared at them incredulously. I could tell there were bruises that were already showing.

"Yes, but you made the point that in the real world, no one is going to go easy on her." He countered.

"Excuse me." I stated. "Are you forgetting I am essentially magic-less right now? He definitely would have killed me if he'd gone any harder."

"You didn't fight like you have no magic." Uri commented, and I frowned.

"What do you mean?"

"You were incredibly fast, Elia."

"Only because you have a lot more weight to move around, and I wasn't fast enough to avoid a lot of your attacks."

"Uri is actually very quick for a Forti Elia. While it's a common, and usually correct, assumption that Forti move slower, those that hone their craft know how to use their muscle and weight to propel them faster. Think about all the muscles he has. Yes, they add weight, but he can *use* them to move as well. It's all about the right distribution. You did fairly well to avoid as many hits as you did." Tarryn praised and I stared at him, dumbfounded, before turning to Uri.

"He's right. I am fast. You were faster, which is impressive."

I rubbed my jaw. "Not fast enough."

He smiled a bit. "When you're done with the training, come see me. I purchased a few remedies from Reya on our way here. Your mother will kill me if I let you go to the naming ceremony with an enormous bruise on your face." With that, he walked over to where Hamish and Wes were standing.

"Grab a drink while we reset." Tarryn advised before going to join the other men who had grabbed some sand, presumably to fix the hole I'd made in the ring.

I did as I was told and had a drink before sitting down and watching as they continued the set up. I raised my eyebrows as the servants set up multiple common objects nearby. A few chairs, a table, a couch, and some smaller items, like plates and cups. Hamish wheeled over a barrow full of rocks and then another one full of sand. Uri redid the ring, except it was darker than the grains in Hamish's barrow, almost black. Dirt of some sort, maybe?

Tarryn waved me over, and I approached

"What is this?" I questioned.

"Honestly, even I am not really sure." Tarryn muttered and Hamish grinned.

"You ready?" Hamish asked.

"Ready for what?"

His answer was to pick up one of the little rocks from the barrow and pelt it at me. I gasped, dropping to the floor, barely avoiding it. My head jerked up.

"What the Hek?"

He simply threw another at me. I winced as it made contact, quickly rising. "Hamish!"

"What?!" He exclaimed as he threw another one. I side stepped, storming toward him. "A Turf will probably hurl entire boulders at you Elle. This is nothing." He threw another one and this time I caught it, throwing it back. He ducked, still grinning.

"Throw one more rock, Ham, and I swear..." Hamish looked at the rock in his hand, at me, then back to the rock. He paused for a second before shrugging and throwing it at me. I ducked it and ran towards him. He quickly scooped up as many rocks as he could and took off. I stopped and stared at him in disbelief.

"Really? You're going to run away?"

He once again responded by throwing a rock at me. I caught it, wincing slightly. He'd put a bit more power into that one. As I was about to throw it back, I felt something touch my head, glancing up. I had only a second to avoid the massive pile of sand that had been tipped from the balcony above.

I wasn't quite fast enough. It was an effort not to let it topple me over. I'd remained standing but was now covered in sand that I knew would be a bitch to get off. Glancing up, I saw Wes's guilty smile as he held his hands up, as if he had no say in the matter. I winced again as a rock hit my back, right in between my shoulder blades.

Spinning around, I searched for his red hair and found it sticking up from behind the couch. I was going to kick his ass, but first I needed some protection. I glanced around, my eyes landing on the table they'd set up, specifically on a formal serving tray atop it. That would have to do. I ran over, narrowly dodging a few more rocks thrown my way, grabbing the serving tray and testing its strength. It should hold up against the small rocks Hamish was armed with.

A beige speck fell onto the table in front of me, and I didn't even glance up before I jerked backwards, just as another gigantic pile of sand crashed into the table. A rock hit me in the back of the leg and I grit my teeth, giving whoever had just dumped that sand the finger, as I continued towards Hamish.

This time, his rocks met resistance in the form of my makeshift shield. I waited until I was close enough and could see him taking aim. I held off until the last second, judging his movements. Right as he raised his arm to throw another rock, I hurled the serving tray. It spun vertically through the air, much like the clay disks that the hunters used for practice, smashing into Hamish's wrist, causing him to curse and drop the rock.

I leapt over the couch and tackled him to the ground. As I was attempting to pin him down, a shadow fell over us. I glanced up to see Wes with another bucket. This time I smiled, glancing back down at Hamish.

"Paybacks a bitch." I placed a kiss on his forehead, before rolling off of him and out of the way. He opened his mouth to respond, but wound up with a gob full of sand.

I laughed, gripping my stomach as he spluttered and practically scraped at his tongue, trying to clear his mouth. I heard Wes chuckle from above, before Tarryn called out.

"Alright! I'd say that's enough Turf imitation. Back into the ring."

Smiling, I held out my hand to Hamish. He took it and let me pull him up.

"I'm going to get you back for all of that." I warned, and he just slung an arm around my shoulder.

"We'll see."

We met Tarryn in the ring, and shortly after; we were joined by Wes. I shot him a half hearted glare. He had the good sense to appear at least a little guilty. Unlike the brute still hanging over my shoulder.

"Facing a real Turf is ten times as dangerous and painful as what you just experienced. Think boulders, landslides, earthquakes. It's easy to laugh it off when it's just these two throwing pebbles and sand, but don't underestimate the real deal."

I nodded slightly, fully aware that facing off against a real Turf would likely end in me getting squished by a boulder or something.

"We won't be demonstrating the Breather Specialty, but we are going to simulate some aspects of what it might be like to face a Piro. Then you will face Josette to cover the Teleki Specialty, before facing me representing the Tear Specialty." Tarryn explained, exiting the sparring circle.

"How are we going to replicate fighting a Piro without actually having one here? Is one of you going to wave around candle sticks?" I smirked at Wes and Hamish. Hamish chuckled, removing his arm from my shoulder and walking over to the table they'd set up earlier, grabbing a torch. My smile faded a little.

"Wait, that's not really what you're going to do, is it?" I said incredulously. *Surely not?*

Hamish didn't answer, he just walked over, stopping just outside the circle. I glanced at Wes beside me, catching his brief nod to Hamish. I turned back in time to see him bend down and touch the lit torch to the black sand. Oh shit.

I realised as soon as the flame made contact that I'd been a fool to mistake it for sand or dirt. It was a compound I'd seen the soldiers and hunters use. A flammable powder used to ignite charges from a distance.

A ring of flames shot up around Wes and me. I could instantly feel the wave of heat it emitted.

"We don't have an actual Piro for you to fight, but we have actual fire, actual heat, and a rival whose fighting style you don't know. Same rules as before. First one to tap out, loses."

They were all insane. I glanced at Wes, who smiled apologetically.

"Oh, don't look at me like that. If you felt bad, you wouldn't be in here about to fight me," I said, giving him a pointed look. He chuckled softly.

"You make a good point. You've beaten Pure opponents today. I should be an easy foe at this point."

He moved forward, as did I, if only to get a reprieve from the heat. I didn't bother responding, instead I watched him, trying to gauge how he might attack. He appeared to be doing the same as we circled each other.

"I'm bored! Do something!" Hamish called from his safe, cool position *outside* this damned ring of fire. I shook my head and Wes chuckled.

To say I was both caught off guard and impressed by Wes would be an understatement. Fighting him started off as I'd expect any fight to start. Slowly, circling each other, one of us striking, and the other evading before attempting their own attack. But then, almost out of nowhere, the intensity of Wes's attacks increased tenfold. His attacks sped up and had a lot more force behind them.

We traded blow for blow, and the heat of the fire surrounding us was starting to feel smothering. More than once, I'd just about singed my hair off. I didn't have time to fret over that, though. Wes moved faster than I'd ever seen someone move. I had no time to counter his attacks and was forced into defence. Wes didn't move the same way as Hamish, Tarryn, or even Uri. His fighting style was pure grace and precision.

It was difficult not to get distracted by the abstract beauty of it. It seemed no matter which way I moved, no matter how I tried to outsmart him or feign an attack, he was ready for it. He was ready for all of them and seemed to anticipate my moves before I'd even decided to make them.

I leapt desperately, trying to avoid yet another perfectly aimed strike, but he'd already prepared and swept his leg out, throwing me off balance. I tried to correct myself, which only caused me to fall in the other direction, straight towards the flames still burning strong. My eyes widened, and I raised my hands to shield my face when Wes gripped my tunic, yanking me back just as a lick of flame met my forearm. He was fast enough that it hadn't done any serious damage, just a small, red heat mark that was already fading.

Breathing heavily, I was too shocked to notice his arm move around my neck and apply slight pressure. He leant down and whispered in my ear, a bead of sweat trickling down the side of his face.

"Tap out."

CHAPTER FORTY-TWO

I GROANED AND TAPPED his arm. I had no idea how Tarryn could even see it, but as soon as I did, water surrounded the sparring circle, enveloping the flames, and extinguishing them before sinking back into the ground. Steam rose around us and Wes removed his arm from my neck, clapping me on the back.

"Not bad Worthington. Not bad at all."

I stared at him, dumbfounded. "How in the Inferno did you do that?"

He chuckled and shrugged, slipping his hands into his pockets. All signs of that lethal elegance, gone. Replaced with the usual easy-going but imposing guard I had expected him to be.

"You have to show me how you did that! What's your Specialty?" I demanded when it became clear that he would not explain.

"Maybe sometime," he said ominously, avoiding the question.

I narrowed my eyes at him but before I could press further, Josette approached.

"That was cute." Her whiny voice drawled. I sighed, debating whether I could get away with knocking her out right now. We were inside the sparring ring. It should technically count.

"You know me, cute is practically my middle name."

"You might have everyone else fooled, Elia." She spat my name with more venom than necessary. Wes frowned and stepped forward, but I held my hand out, stopping him.

"I'm not fooling anyone, Josie." I smirked as she tensed at the nickname.

"You think you're so smart? You won't when I wipe that grin off your face in a few minutes."

"Look forward to it. If you'll excuse me, I have literally anyone else to talk to." I didn't give her a chance to respond before I simply walked away, heading for the water station near Cali, grabbing a cup, and sitting beside her.

She leant over and whispered. "If looks could kill, you'd be a dead woman."

"In a few minutes, when I have to face her in that ring, I very well might be."

She chuckled, and I watched the men reposition the objects they'd set up earlier, imagining the different methods Josette could use to pummel me with them.

Of all the ways I'd thought I might die when I'd first entered this castle, at the hands of a jealous noblewoman wasn't high on the list. However, standing opposite Josette in the centre of the circle, seeing that smug look in her eyes, and knowing that I was no match for her, it now sat at the top.

"What is Josette's Gifting?" Tarryn asked

"Kineti." I answered simply.

"And her Specialty?"

"She's a Teleki."

"How do you know?"

"Trust me, she flaunts it often enough that everyone knows."

Her fist clenched, and I smiled.

"Facing a Kineti on a battlefield, how would you identify which Specialty you're facing?"

"Well, Telepi aren't as common, and I imagine once mortal made objects start flying at you, one could assume they were facing a Teleki." If I survived, I was definitely going to pay for all my smart ass comments at our next training session. The look on Tarryn's face confirmed it.

"Okay, so you've established you're fighting a Teleki. How do you win?"

"I will let you know," I said, eyeing Josette closely. She was the one smiling now. Tarryn nodded.

"When you're ready."

Before Tarryn had even finished speaking, something smashed into the back of my head, making a cracking noise as it made impact, before clattering again as it shattered to the floor. Wincing, I touched the back of my head. My fingers came away wet. I didn't need to look to know that it had been a plate she'd smashed over my head, or that the wetness on my fingers was blood.

"Cheap shot," I said as I approached her. She was still smiling. She hadn't so much as lifted a finger. Before I could get close enough to attack, the rest of the cups and plates rose from their positions on the table nearby and flew toward us.

I raised my arms in case I couldn't roll out of the way entirely, but they didn't make contact with me. They came to a stop in front of Josette before cracking and breaking into small pieces of china and glass. *Fates.*

They didn't get immediately hurled at me, though. No, instead they started circling Josette, moving faster and faster until she was almost a blur behind the flying shrapnel. It was a shield. The only way I was getting through that was by cutting myself up.

As I was trying to come up with a way to penetrate her makeshift shield, something hard and wooden slammed into my side, knocking me over. It was a damned chair. I stood, dusting off my shirt.

"Is that the best you got?" I taunted, getting a smirk in response.

"Not even close." She replied as the couch raised into the air and moved to hover above me. I breathed in, quickly bending to scoop up a leg of the chair that had broken off when it had struck me. She laughed almost maniacally.

"You think you can stop a couch with one chair leg?"

"No." I hurled the chair leg as hard and fast as I could, right at her face. The chair leg broke through her shield but froze in place inches from her eye. The shrapnel came to a standstill as well, remaining suspended in the air. Her lip twitched, and she looked almost disappointed at my efforts.

I quickly kicked another broken bit of wood behind me as she dropped the couch from the air and it fell from directly above me. I was ready though, already launching into a back handspring, just clearing the couch before it flattened me. As I flipped out of the way she fired the shrapnel that was once her shield, in my direction.

Dropping to the ground, I used the couch as a shield of my own. Crouching down, I picked up the second bit of wood, dropped my shoulder against the couch and pushed, both me and the lounge advancing closer to Josette, who couldn't see exactly where I was thanks to her own attempt at squashing me.

I heard her huff in annoyance before the couch lifted and hurled itself across the room. I heard what might have been a yelp from Hamish as it slammed into the wall beside him, but I couldn't risk looking. Instead, I hurled the second bit of wood at Josette and this time; she wasn't ready for it. It speared her in the arm, jagged end first.

Not going too deep, but deep enough that it was now protruding from her perfect porcelain skin. She gasped, yanking it out, and throwing it on the ground. When I met her eyes this time, she was glaring daggers at me. Now she was *really* pissed.

She made a sweeping motion with her arm, as if she were knocking an invisible chess piece off an invisible board. A second later, the table that had been housing the now smashed plates and glasses barreled into me.

Only this time the furniture didn't just knock me over, it maintained its momentum, causing me to fly across the room and slam back first into the wall, the table breaking upon impact. I cried out a little as I fell to the ground, surrounded by the remnants of the table.

"Josette!" Tarryn yelled. "What in Dykos's name was that?!"

I felt someone pull me into a sitting position. Opening my eyes, I saw it was Wes.

"You alright?"

I nodded slightly and stood, wincing as I did. Shit, I was lucky nothing was broken.

"Good, then get back in there. You're fighting her all wrong. If you let her stay on the offensive, you will never be able to beat her. You need to break through her defence. She's easily riled, and she's overconfident. Use that."

"I was knocked out of the ring, though. I'm out?"

He shook his head.

"Since Josette used items outside of the ring, it rendered it void. The entire courtyard is your battlefield now." I was annoyed at myself for forgetting that loophole.

"I'm an idiot." I complained, but he just nudged me toward the centre again.

"Elia, you don't need to continue." Tarryn stated. "Josette was out of line with that hit. It could have been fatal."

"I'm good. We can continue."

Josette laughed.

"Tap out. You can't win. You don't want to miss your naming ceremony." She rolled her eyes, and I simply smiled.

"It must really rile you, huh?"

She frowned, and I went on.

"It took me all of five seconds to achieve everything you've ever dreamed of."

She scoffed. "Like I would ever be jealous of the likes of you. You're just a nobody. A lower class noble."

"That might be true, but this nobody has the man you wanted, the friends you wanted, the room, the clothes, and soon I'll have the crown too. Divinities, it must sting having spent so much time trying to seduce Valor, only for me to succeed without even having to try. How many times did you pray to Syrena begging for help?"

Her face tightened, and another chair hurled itself at me. I rolled out of the way, slowly closing the distance between us.

"How does it feel knowing that the only thing you have going for you is your Gifting? And even with that, you're still incapable of beating a practically Impure, *lower class noble?*"

"You don't know what you're talking about." She clenched her fist, the chair I'd just evaded, breaking apart and coming at me again. This time she attacked in more of a strategic form, the chair striking like a person would. It forced me to block the blows, wincing slightly at the force behind it.

"But I do." I continued to speak as I fought off a bloody chair. "Everyone knows you were supposed to marry Valor. Now that it's off the table, the truth is, I pity you. At least my purpose in life doesn't revolve around a man."

I swatted away a piece of wood, narrowly avoiding a nasty gash to the cheek.

"Regardless of what rich, stuck up nobles, like you, think of me, I know my worth. I know I have more value than the man and the money I can bring home to my family."

"Shut up." She gritted her teeth, and I moved closer, watching as she fought to contain her outburst.

"At the end of the day Josette, you are nothing but a spoiled," I took a step closer, "entitled," I took anther step, "and common, high lady." I was face to face with her now, looking her in the eyes as she practically shook with rage.

"You are no different from the rest. You are not special, and worse, you go out of your way to make others feel irrelevant. Well, I have news for you, Josie. Look around. You want to know the actual difference between you and me?" I was in her face now, and it was as if her anger had bled into me. All the anger I'd felt, all the words I'd wanted to scream at Butcher, at Josette, at Raf, at the world, came bubbling up to the surface.

"I might be a nobody, a lesser noblewoman, but you? You're nothing but a political pawn whose own family sees her as little more than a high-class whore."

I saw the moment she snapped; she lashed out, palm open, ready to smack me across the face, but I caught her wrist and landed my own blow to her jaw with my other hand. She was quick to recover, jerking her arm back and kneeing me in the stomach. I grunted slightly, but this kind of combat I could do.

We traded blow for blow, blocking and evading, landing a few hits in here and there, but mostly we were evenly matched. Josette seemed to get more and more angry as the fight continued. Eventually she slipped up, and I was waiting.

She threw a punch that I'd expected, so I sidestepped right before she made contact, striking her hard in the stomach, causing her to hunch slightly. As she did, I kicked her feet out from under her, and she went down face first. I was on her immediately, pulling her arms behind her back and keeping them there. She struggled, practically hissing at me, but my grip was firm. I applied a bit of pressure as my body kept her weighed down.

"Tap out Josette."

"Get the Hek off me!!" She shrieked, but I held on.

"Tap out." I repeated, about to say it a third time, but something tightened around my neck. My eyes widened, and I glanced down. My tunic had tightened around me and the collar was now pressing tightly into my neck. I kept hold of Josette's arms, but the material only tightened until it was choking me. I couldn't breathe.

I let go of Josette, moving off of her and sitting back on the ground as I pulled at the material. It wouldn't budge. It wouldn't move. The pressure increased, and I gasped, one hand falling to the ground, barely holding me upright.

Panic set in as everything spun. I could hear voices that sounded like they were yelling, but the sound was distorted. I tried to speak, but I couldn't get any air out. The pressure didn't stop after I tapped the ground. My arm gave way as I tapped again, falling forward. It wasn't stopping; she wasn't stopping. I clenched my eyes shut when suddenly the pressure disappeared and my clothing fell back to where it should be.

I gasped, my eyes flying open, as I struggled to take in air. My lungs felt like they were on fire and my chest heaved. I rolled onto my back, closing my eyes again, trying to slow my breathing. *Relax, Adira,* I thought to myself. *Breathe. Just breathe.*

I did. I ignored everything else and counted as I took deep breaths. Voices filtered back in, and I slowly opened my eyes to find Cali and Tarryn kneeling beside me.

"Fates, Elle! Are you alright?!" Cali exclaimed, radiating concern.

I nodded slightly.

"I'm…" I winced slightly. There were no doubt marks already showing around my neck. "Shit. I'm fine." I sat up. "I'm okay. What happened?"

"Josette strangled you with your own shirt," Tarryn said, and I could hear the anger and guilt in his voice. I rubbed my neck softly.

"Damn. I probably should have seen that coming." I glanced over to see Josette lying unconscious on the ground. My eyes widened.

"Wait, what happened to her?"

Tarryn nodded to the person standing beside Josette's now sleeping form. My eyes flicked up and met Hamish's, whose own just widened as he gave me an innocent 'what?' look.

"You knocked her out?" I questioned.

"I wouldn't say *knocked.*"

I couldn't hide my amusement. "What would you say?"

"Neutralised?" He offered, and I laughed a little, wincing at the movement.

"Is she alright?"

He nodded. "She'll be fine. I just did what she was doing to you. Well, without the magic part. I snuck up behind her. She was so focused on you, she didn't notice until I had her in a chokehold."

"You didn't have to do that, Ham."

"Actually, he did," Tarryn said.

I frowned.

"I provoked her. In all honesty, I probably went a bit too far. She was within her rights to kick my ass, as much as I hate to admit that." I meant that too. I'd been trying to rile her yes, but I let my anger, not even all of it directed at her, get the better of me.

"No Elia, he had to because she wouldn't stop."

"What do you mean?"

"You tapped out. But she didn't stop." Cali chimed in. "We all saw you tap out, and it was clear you couldn't win at that point. We all shouted at her to stop and she wouldn't. If Hamish hadn't stepped in, she might have killed you."

My eyes widened. "Shit. I didn't think she'd go *that* far."

"Neither did I, or I never would have let you face her. I'm so sorry Elle." Tarryn apologised, and I shook my head.

"It's not your fault Amesley. I'm fine. No harm done."

He gave me a look, and I put on my best 'I'm fine' smile, which he didn't buy for a second.

"Break time before I face you?" I offered, and he shook his head.

"I think that's enough training for today."

"No, come on, I've survived this long. I know you won't kill me. Besides, after I'm officially named a princess, who knows if I'll even be allowed to keep training?" I pouted, and he crossed his arms.

"You almost died."

"*But* I didn't."

He gave an exasperated sigh. "Elia. You have no self preservation."

"Untrue."

He smiled a bit, but shook his head.

"That's enough for today. We can practice with the remaining magics another time, *after* your naming ceremony."

I groaned.

"There's one more Specialty you can at least see," Uri said, walking over and I raised my eyebrows, realising I was still on the floor. I slowly stood, wincing again. Divinities, I was going to be stiff tomorrow.

"You heard Tarryn. No more fights today."

"Who said anything about fighting?" He gestured for me to follow him over to the bench. I did as instructed and sat beside him as he took out a small vial that looked as if it glowed. Not the vial, I realised, the white liquid inside.

"Um, what is that?"

"The remedy from Reya that I mentioned earlier."

"You didn't mention that it *glowed*." I pointed out, still in awe of the tiny vial. He smiled a little and handed it to me.

"Drink it."

I laughed a little.

"No way am I drinking that."

He rolled his eyes. "Do you want to know about the Healeti Specialties or not? A Remedi made this." That piqued my interest.

"What is it? Pain relief?"

He sighed. "If you stop asking questions and drink it, then you will see for yourself."

I hesitantly removed the lid and smelt it. The white liquid appeared to glow even brighter. I couldn't identify any of the aromas. I bit my lip before shrugging off my apprehension and downing the liquid. Uri watched me, shaking his head a little, as he took the vial back.

"It's not liquor. You don't have to skull it." He commented, and I grinned before freezing as a warm, tingly sensation spread through me. I glanced down at my arms and hands. He chuckled.

"Relax, it's meant to feel like that."

"What is happening?"

"You're healing."

I frowned. "I'm what—" I cut myself off as I realised he was right. I could *feel* it happening. The throbbing in my cheek from the blows I'd copped to the jaw dulled before disappearing. Reaching up and touching my neck, I could no longer feel the marks that my tunic had left during Josette's attempted assassination, and the burning in my lungs faded. Every cut, scratch, and bump, ceased hurting or closed up, and it left me feeling warm. It felt comforting, like curling up by a fire and falling asleep. I swallowed and glanced at Uri.

"How in the Hek is that possible?"

"It's difficult, but a strong Remedi can infuse their power into healing potions for a short time. It will only work on superficial wounds. It won't do anything for broken bones, fatal blows, or poisons, though. Back when territory battles were still fought, the smartest warriors would befriend Remedi, in hopes it would incline them to send a few vials of this stuff with them into battle. Like I said, doesn't help fatal wounds, but it can relieve some pain and make a bad, superficial, injury easier to withstand, buying time to get to safety. Or in your case, prevent any of us from having our asses handed to us for sending you to your naming ceremony, bloodied and bruised." He smirked.

I stared at him dumbfounded, and even a little disappointed. For a second I thought maybe, just maybe, if I could get hold of some of this stuff, I could give it to Sierra. But it likely wouldn't work on an injury as bad as hers. A thought struck me then.

"Can Morti do the same thing? Infuse their power into potions?"

Uri's smile faded a little as he nodded. "Yes, they last a little longer, too."

I bit my lip. "What does it do?"

"About what you'd expect. Think of it like a poison. If you so much as touch a drop of the stuff, it will spread through your body like a rot. Decaying every inch of you. Men have cut off limbs to prevent it from spreading and ultimately killing them." I shivered.

"Does that work?"

"If you are quick enough and can survive the blood loss." He answered, and I grimaced, praying I never had to deal with a Morti. They sounded horrifying.

"Well, this seems like a good time to interrupt." Cali announced as she joined us. "It's time to prepare for the ceremony."

I groaned. "Is it too late to ask Josette for a rematch?" I honestly might have preferred that to what was to come. Cali and Uri both rolled their eyes, and I sighed, standing.

"Fine." I looked back at Uri. "Thank you. For suggesting this and helping with it."

He just nodded in that stoic way of his, before bowing his head slightly to Cali as well, leaving to go speak with Wes.

"You know he's quite good looking in that big, protective, type of way." Cali mused, watching him walk away.

My eyes widened. "Don't you think he's a little old for you?"

She shrugged. "Probably."

I laughed and shook my head as she linked her arm through mine, giving me her own grin.

"Let's get you ready, Princess."

Once again I groaned, having little choice but to let her lead me back to my chambers and put me through another kind of torture.

CHAPTER FORTY-THREE

"You look stunning," Cali said as we both stared at my reflection in the full-length mirror.

"How on earth do you always make me look so good?"

She laughed. "You flatter me, but we both know I barely did anything. You are simply that good looking." She winked.

I rolled my eyes. "Yeah, sure."

Even I had to admit, she'd done a wonderful job. I looked good dressed once again in the Xerian colours. My gown was again black, made of a smooth material I couldn't place, with a heart-shaped neckline, with long, almost puffy sleeves. The bodice was tight-fitting, with a beautiful silver floral design covering the entirety of it.

Once it reached my hips, it fanned out, making my waist look cinched, emphasising my curves. The skirt of the dress was layered, covered in the same beautiful flower design, and there was a silver sash draped across my front, very regal looking, that matched my gloves.

Cali had made me look fresh and vibrant. My hair fell in waves, most of it flowing freely, with only a small section on top braided around the sides, leaving my face on display. A perfect resting place for the tiara that would soon be placed there.

"You're nervous." She wasn't asking. We both knew I was.

I nodded. "Absolutely terrified."

She smiled. "So was I, and they'd prepared me for mine since I could walk. I can't even imagine what it must be like for you."

I nodded a bit. "I have no idea what to expect."

"It's honestly just a bunch of formalities. All you have to do is stand there while they spout some traditional nonsense, say you accept, and then let them crown you. All you have to do is be present. It isn't as scary as it sounds."

"You better not be lying to make me feel better." I gave her a look, and she chuckled, shaking her head.

"I'm not. I'll be close by. The whole family will."

"And quite a few other people, I imagine?"

"Ignore everyone else." There was a knock on the door, signalling it was time. I breathed in.

"Don't worry, Elia, you'll be fine. Trust me." She squeezed my hand. "And afterwards, we can get very drunk and forget the whole thing ever happened."

I laughed, and we linked arms, exiting the room. Hamish, Tarryn, Uri, Wes, and Killian were all waiting for us; for me, I suppose. *Hek* if they weren't giving me a run for my money in the looks department. They were all wearing formal guards' uniforms. Hamish and Tarryn in Taros colours, red and blue, Uri and Wes matched me, and Killian also wore the colours of Taros, but trimmed in gold. I'd never seen so many attractive men in such a confined space before.

"Close your mouth, Elle. You look like a codfish." Hamish quipped, and I quickly switched from gaping to glaring.

"Sorry, it is such a shock to see you looking halfway decent, Hamish. I almost didn't recognise you."

He covered his hand in mock hurt. "You wound me, Princess."

"I'm not a princess yet."

"You will be in less than an hour." Tarryn added, smiling. "You look beautiful."

I waved off his compliment, and Cali saved me from having to respond with a clap of her hands.

"Right, well, we don't have all day. It would be very improper to be late for your own title ceremony. Chop, chop everyone." I smiled at her gratefully, and she returned it with a wink.

I caught Hamish roll his eyes before Tarryn swiftly, but subtly, elbowed him. They took their positions in front of us, Uri and Wes taking up the flank.

Killian held out both of his arms. "Ladies."

We took an arm each and made our way to the room in which they would hold the ceremony. It was an open council room of sorts, used for public decrees and debates. It was large, but not large enough to fit the entire capital, reducing the onlookers to just the higher nobles mostly, some guards, and some staff.

We entered the room, and they instructed me to stand in the middle.

Cali squeezed my arm and whispered, "You'll be fine. Just fake it until it isn't so scary anymore."

Killian escorted Cali to her seat, and I followed with my eyes. Sitting up on the dais were the royals. King Hadrian was in the centre, Queen Tira to his right and Queen Odette to his left, on a throne covered in vines. *Subtle.*

A tier down was Valor, who winked at me, giving me a reassuring smile when I met his eyes, and Cali on the other side. Everyone was so formally dressed. Cali had gotten ready with me, so I'd been prepared for her, but everyone else was still a shock. Hadrian was in an all red suit. The only blue items on him were a cape that draped behind him and matching shoes. Odette was the opposite, dressed in a light blue shimmering gown. She had on red lip stain, red earrings, and matching red jewellery, which you'd think wouldn't go together, but they did.

Tira was once again not in a dress, but in a beautiful formal tunic. The contrasting black and silver design sprawled across it was beautiful. Eye-catching, yet still simple. Valor wore a shirt with long red sleeves and a blue vest on top. It had a beautiful white design tailored down the left side, hooking onto a black cape. He'd swept his hair back. Even I could admit he looked insanely good up there.

All the royals were wearing their appropriate crowns and tiaras. They painted a breathtaking picture, one I'd love to paint if I was artistically inclined. A picture I didn't belong in.

A king with a queen on either side, one of ice and one of iron. The two heirs sat just below, waiting for their turn. To avoid staring at them too long, I cast my gaze around the room. The seats were all filled. I saw faces I recognised, and faces I did not. I saw James, who flashed me a grin, much to the dismay of Lady Josette, who sat beside him. She smiled at me, an Ozdros's smile. As if she knew something I didn't. Which, given our earlier encounter, was unsettling.

Moving on, I saw Yarik posted near Queen Tira. He wiggled his eyebrows at me and I gave a slight shake of my head, smiling a little. The guards were all at attention and the audience whispered amongst themselves. I did not like being in the centre. Surrounded like this, I felt exposed. Everyone's eyes were on me.

The atmosphere of the room was smothering, like everyone's energies were mixing, and I was picking up on it in a whirlwind of emotions. I took another steadying breath. As Hadrian stood, the room fell silent.

"It is with great pleasure we gather here today to officially welcome Lady Elia Worthington into the Melfore family. Now that we are all present, let us begin." He retook his seat, and a man dressed in priest's garb stepped forward, stopping in front of a small podium.

I couldn't help wonder if Father Chambersen was meant to be running the ceremony. I glanced at this priest's hand to see if there was a cut mark. There wasn't, which settled me a little, but not a lot. He went through the motions, going over the great honour that was being bestowed today, and the unique situation it was.

He really overplayed the whole long lost princess bit. It's not like the queen didn't know she had a daughter or where to look for her, but that apparently was not relevant here. I thanked the divinities for all the years of training I'd endured, or I would not have been able to remain standing here for so long in these heels. I suppose that was a test in itself.

"Your Majesty, Queen Tira Melfore of Xeria." Tira stood and walked over to the priest.

"Do you acknowledge Lady Elia Worthington's lineage to be true? Do you acknowledge her blood claim to your throne and name her Princess of Xeria?"

She looked at me and smiled. "I acknowledge her blood claim."

She picked up the ink pen from the podium and signed the document the priest was lording over, before placing it down and taking a step back. She remained by the priest, rather than returning to her seat.

"Before we call Lady Elia to accept her birthright and title, are there any who object to this ruling?"

I glanced around the room. Everyone was watching, looking as bored as I felt at this point. I looked back at the priest, who smiled.

"Lady Elia, come forward—"

"I object to this ruling." I turned to find Josette standing from her seat with a wide-eyed Jameson beside her, leaning as far away from her as he could when he realised what was happening.

Gasps spread through the room like wildfire. The priest appeared as shocked as the rest of the crowd. I, however, was not surprised. Leave it to Josette to cause such a spectacle, no doubt payback for this morning.

"On what grounds, Lady Josette?" Hadrian spoke, sounding as if he were dismissing a child.

"On the basis that we have no proof she is who she says she is. She weaselled her way into this court, and has done nothing but sneak around."

"No proof? We have her father's letter and her own mother," he gestured to Tira, "swearing to the court that she is who she says she is. Elia was not aware of her heritage until we told her. You are misguided, Josette."

"With all due respect, Your Majesty, she is a skilled performer, one such as her could deceive even the brightest among us. There are things she has kept from us, things that prove she is a liar."

I thought I saw Hadrian actually roll his eyes before responding. "I will hear no more of this. Take your seat, Josette—"

"Let her speak, Hadrian. What things are you referring to, Josette?" Odette chimed in, her elbow propping her chin up on the edge of her chair. She looked amused.

"You wish to allow this jealous girl to falsely accuse my heir, Odette?" Queen Tira said, stepping in.

"I merely think we should establish all the facts. Josette comes from a family loyal to the Navarre's for years, unlike some of us, and I believe that warrants us hearing what she has to say. Unless, of course, you think there is merit to some of what she says and simply do not want the truth to be out of the shadows?"

I saw Tira's fist clench as she stepped forward. I also saw the glint in Odette's eyes. She wanted a fight.

I stepped in before it came to that. "It's alright. This is why we hold these ceremonies open to the public, so everyone can be heard." I looked at Josette. "Say what you have to say, Josephine. We are listening."

Her eyes flashed in anger and I heard a few muffled laughs, no doubt from people who had witnessed the many times I just could not seem to remember her name correctly.

"You had a relationship with a commoner. A blacksmith boy."

I stiffened slightly.

"Last I checked, Josette, that was not grounds for the kinds of accusations you are making." Cali stated, looking ready to throw hands herself.

"No, but it is when that blacksmith is found to be a rebel, and she helps remove his body from the noose it belonged in."

The room went silent. All I could hear was the blood pumping in my ears. I didn't risk glancing at Tarryn or Hamish, though I could tell they were tense. I looked at Cali and Valor. Aside from my guards, they were the only two who knew of any type of connection with Raf. Cali looked angry and Valor looked shocked.

"Nonsense. What evidence do you have? I will not stand here and listen to such vulgar accusations being thrown at my blood," Tira said.

"Your daughter is a rebel sympathiser, Your Majesty."

She nodded to a guard standing at the entrance, who stepped to the side and opened the door, allowing a couple to stumble in, surrounded by her father's armed guards. The couple I recognised as Indigo's parents. The woman hanged along with Matias, William, and Raf. Indigo's father appeared battered and bruised, his wife dirty, with tear-stained cheeks.

Valour stood, frowning. "What is the meaning of this?"

Josette walked down the steps, leading the couple to where we were standing.

"This is Mr and Mrs Kole. Their daughter was hanged for crimes against Taros, for rebel involvement. Someone took down their daughter's body, along with the other criminals who should have remained to rot in punishment for their sins."

"That has nothing to do with today's proceedings, Josette. You are out of line," Cali said, standing to join her brother.

"Guards reported a woman amongst the thieves who stole the bodies, matching Lady Elia's description. Lady Elia confined herself to her room for days after the execution, in grief."

"That is mere conjecture. What proof do you have, Josette? This is all very convenient for you. We all know you were favoured to marry my brother until Elia came along. If your argument hinges on the fact that it was a woman that helped in the removal of the bodies, then you or I could be just as responsible. It sounds to me you are simply jealous, and trying to sell a lie." Cali coldly bit out.

"Mr and Mrs Kole, is this the woman that came to you and told you the whereabouts of your daughter's body?" Josette asked smugly.

Mrs Kole was sobbing. Mr Kole could barely stand upright. A guard stepped forward, and the woman flinched.

"Sh-she concealed her face. It was dark... it's h-hard to say..."

I stepped forward. I couldn't let them be punished for what I'd done, but a hand stopped me. Looking over my shoulder, Valor had moved to stand beside me and was holding my arm. He shook his head in the slightest of movements.

"But surely, if you heard her voice, you could tell us?" She glanced at me and wasn't completely able to hide her satisfied grin. She knew she had me.

How she had figured it all out, I had no idea. She may very well have just been guessing. I couldn't prove her wrong. Before Mrs Kole could speak again, Valor stepped forward.

"I will hear no more of this. Elia was with me on the night in question. She could not have committed the crime." Murmurs broke out across the room. Even though we were rumoured to be betrothed, it was still improper for a lady to spend the night in a prince's room. For it to be outrightly admitted to? That was downright scandalous, even though most people already knew.

"My Prince, you have a kind heart, but you should not lie to protect her. She—"

"*Enough!* You would question the words of your prince? You would call me a liar? I am protecting no one but you. Do you know the punishment for slander against a royal, Josette? We could consider it treason. Queen Tira is well within her rights to lock you up for the claims you've made against her daughter. Lady Elia was with me all night. I have guards that can testify to her comings and goings." He turned to the guards holding the Koles captive.

"Take Mr and Mrs Kole to a guest room where they are to be seen by a medicae, cared for, and cleaned up." The guards nodded and escorted the Koles out of the room.

Everyone was staring at Josette now, who looked shocked, but I could tell some people were buying her story. They believed the prince was lying to protect me because I had him under my spell. It was easy to believe in the world they lived in, that I had beguiled him with my good looks and my willingness to bed him.

"But she did it! How could you defend someone who would sully themselves with a street urchin?!"

I gritted my teeth and stepped forward. Enough was enough.

"You mind your tongue. You may accuse me of whatever you like, Lady Josette." I hissed her name with all the venom of a true noblewoman, letting everyone know I knew exactly what her name was. "But do not speak of things you know nothing of, regarding people you know even less of. You are nothing but a vile, jealous little brat. Those *people* you refer to as street urchins are the people that pay for your mansion, for your pretty dresses, for your privileged life. I would rather spend the rest of my days with them than to be surrounded by even one person like you."

People gasped in shock at not only my outburst but my declaration, my preference to the poor. I glimpsed Hadrian looking unsurprised, and Queen Tira looking proud. Odette looked bored.

The king cleared his throat. "Right, I think we have cleared up this accusation. May we now continue with the ceremony? I am sure we are all eager to get out of this drab chamber and enjoy the drinks and entertainment that awaits us, no?"

He smiled, and a few awkward chuckles echoed throughout the room. "Please escort Josette back to her seat, or out of the room, if she cannot remain quiet for the duration of the ceremony." He nodded to the guards, who stepped toward her.

Josette, however, was not ready to back down. "There is still no proof that she is the princess! She could be anyone! She is an Impure, she *couldn't* be Queen Tira's heir!"

A guard grabbed Josette's arm, but she struggled. "She has no Gifting! She can't be the princess!"

Odette raised her hand, halting the guards that were trying to respectfully remove Josette from the room.

"What do you mean, girl? Speak quickly. I tire of your whining."

"I am convinced she was the woman who stole the bodies. If you question the Koles, you will see what I see, but even if that is not true, she has displayed no Gifting or Specialty. I should know. I sparred against her just this morning, as did multiple others. No one has seen her use magic. She has not undergone The Confirmation, or Testing as tradition dictates. Until she has been proven, to be without a doubt, a Virbi Para, how can we allow her to become heir to a kingdom with no one else to inherit it?"

"We will complete The Testing on Xerian soil. With our own people, in our own court," Queen Tira said.

"I mean no disrespect, Your Majesty." It was clear to everyone in the room that is *exactly* what she meant. "But tradition states that a royal must be determined to be, without reasonable doubt, who they claim to be, to be given their official title. Elia needs to either show us her Gifting now or be put through The Testing before she can be named Princess."

"Josette, you are embarrassing yourself, honestly." Cali shook her head.

"That may be true, but she has a point." Odette stated. "Our tradition and our laws state a royal can only be named so, if there is no doubt of who they are."

"I have no doubt of who she is, nor do I have such laws in my kingdom," Queen Tira said.

"Ah, yes, but we are not in *your* kingdom, Tira. Since the ceremony is being held and decreed here, for the title to be legitimate, she must either demonstrate her magic or undergo The Testing. Surely Lady Elia can put everyone's minds at ease and simply show us? Unless she has a reason not to?"

"I would gladly demonstrate, Your Majesty, however, I have not been Tested, so I could not say for certain what my Gifting is."

"Because you don't have a Gifting! You are an imposter!" Josette shouted.

"If I may, Your Majesties?" The priest stepped forward, seeming to have regained his composure. Odette rolled her eyes, but nodded.

"I propose we resolve this the way the law advises by vote. The council will vote on whether they believe there to be a reasonable doubt about Elia's identity. If the majority finds there to be no doubt, we continue with the ceremony as planned. If the majority finds there to be too many inconsistencies, then Lady Elia shall undergo The Testing before she is crowned."

"This is nonsense. I will not stand for this level of disrespect. Don't bother with your vote. We shall simply return home to Xeria at once and complete the coronation there. We remained here out of respect for you Hadrian, and to make this entire situation less daunting for Elia, but clearly, the same respect is not being returned."

"Tira... perhaps we can discuss this in private? This is all being blown way out of proportion. I am sure they meant no disrespect."

"That is bullshit and you know it, Hadrian." The crowd gasped. To hear a monarch curse at another in such a formal setting. *Oh boy.*

"Do not speak to my husband that way. You are no better than Josette. Jealous that you're not the one up here beside him. It is time you got over that and moved on, Tira. It is very unbecoming of a queen."

Hadrian's face went white, in shock, and in horror, no doubt. Cali and Valor looked confused. They clearly hadn't known about his previous engagement then. Tira stepped forward, her fist clenched. She was practically radiating power. I realised it was her Virbi magic, rippling to the surface.

"Why don't you come closer, Odette, and say that to my face?"

Odette took a step forward, vines from her chair coming to life and weaving along her arms. She smirked, happy to oblige. Hadrian looked like he had no clue how to stop the two women. It was no longer about my legitimacy, but the age-old feud that existed between them. He was the last person who could talk them down.

I pulled away from Valor and moved in between the two queens of ice and iron, holding out my hands.

"STOP! I WILL TAKE THE DAMNED TEST!"

The room was dead silent. The two queens looked at me; one like a mother about to scold her child, the other like a predator having found another target.

"Elia, you do not need to do that. They have no right to ask that of you."

"Excellent!" Odette clapped, her vines retracting. "I will prepare a room now. You may want to change into something more comfortable."

"It's alright." I looked at Tira. "I would have had to do it, eventually. I would rather do it now and end this unnecessary tension, so we can all move on and enjoy the rest of our time here."

She sighed, knowing I was being diplomatic and trying to stop a full-blown war from breaking out, and nodded, placing a hand on my cheek.

"This is why I know you will make a great princess, Elia."

I smiled a bit and turned to Odette. "How much time do you need?"

"An hour maximum, just to ensure everything is properly procured and set up."

"We will do The Testing in private. I will have no more outbursts from unqualified and misled fools." Queen Tira looked at Josette, then back to Odette and Hadrian. "Only those necessary."

Hadrian nodded. "Of course. It will be simply you, Odette, myself, and the bare minimum of guards and staff required."

"Good. Elia and I will be in her chambers. You may fetch us when ready." With that, she turned, her guards falling into their ranks. I had no choice but to follow, apparently.

I moved to Tira's side, and we exited the room. I had less than an hour to find a way out of this Testing, or a way to cheat it. Otherwise, I'd be offered as a fresh new meal to the vultures scavenging at the gates. Helia save me.

CHAPTER FORTY-FOUR

MY DOOR CLOSED BEHIND Tira, locking me in my chambers with her. I turned, biting my lip, honestly unsure what to expect from her.

She looked at me. "Is what that girl said true?"

"Which part?"

"All of it."

I said nothing. She sighed, closing her eyes. "Good. Say nothing if you're asked. If anyone else asks you, come find me."

"You don't want an explanation?"

"I don't need one. I know what happened."

"How could you know what happened?"

"Because I saw the look on your face. Whoever this boy was, you loved him. I don't believe you are foolish enough to get involved with rebels. It's doubtful you'd be involved with someone that was. If they hanged one innocent person, why not four? I would have done the same if four innocents were wrongfully executed and left to rot."

I swallowed at how spot on she was. She had read me and determined that I *loved* Raf. Something I hadn't truly acknowledged myself.

"We can discuss that more at a later date." She squeezed my hand. "I am sorry for your loss, Elia, but we need to prepare you."

I nodded a bit. "How can I complete The Testing when I haven't been Confirmed?"

"The Confirmation is just used to check if you have magic. It's not actually required in order for one to complete their Testing. It's mostly so Impures don't endure the process as it can be dangerous for those without magic in their blood."

I stiffened. "What happens if an Impure undergoes The Testing?"

"You don't need to worry about that."

"But what if you're wrong about who I am? What if I'm truly not your daughter? What if I fail?"

"Elia, take a breath. You are my blood, I am sure of it. You won't fail. Ideally, I'd have more time to prepare you, but we can manage with the time we have." She sat down and gestured for me to join her.

"Has anyone ever failed?"

"Once."

"Just once? What happened to them?"

"Elia, I know you are worried, but we are wasting time."

"Tell me, please."

She sighed. "If an Impure undergoes The Testing it can be dangerous. The one failed case we know of was a very rare one, from hundreds of years ago. A prince underwent The Testing, unaware that he was not his father's child. His Para mother had an affair with an Impure man, resulting in his birth. His mother bribed the priests to lie about having passed his Confirmation, so her husband wouldn't reject her son. She was unaware of the dangers an Impure may face if they enter The Testing. They simply aren't built to withstand the magic involved. He survived, but he was not the same. Some say he lost his mind, some say he became a prophet of the divinities. No one truly knows. He and his mother fled once the king discovered his wife's infidelity and stripped the prince of his title."

I swallowed. "What if I am not your daughter, Tira? What if I truly am an Impure?"

"Elia." She grabbed both of my hands. "You *are* a Melfore. You just have to trust me, even though it doesn't sound logical. You are my blood. I am not worried about you failing, not even for a second."

I swallowed. She was nuts. She was so hopeful she had found her daughter that she was letting it blind her.

"But there's a chance you're wrong."

She shook her head. "I'm not wrong." She smiled reassuringly. "Knowing more about the process will put your mind at ease."

I breathed out. Maybe knowing more about it would give me a way to cheat. I mean, no Impure, aside from that one boy, had ever taken the test, so there's been no need for cheating. That didn't mean it wasn't possible.

"Okay. What do I need to know?"

"It's important you go in as calm as possible. If you're panicking, it's harder to control the scenario."

"What scenario?"

"They will give you a concoction containing divine herbs used only for these types of ceremonies. The herbs contain their own magic." Magic outside of the Giftings? Like the Blood Oath? Could that have been how Butcher had done it? She'd somehow gotten a hold of these herbs?

"What do they do?"

"They allow your spirit to enter Erro." She smiled a little. "Each person sees something different. It is usually someone important to you. I saw my mother, which is fairly common when you're a child going through The

Testing. For you, it could be anyone. Whoever you see acts as a guide of sorts."

"And that someone helps me figure out what my Gifting and Specilaty is?"

She nodded. "Yes, so you may return to the mortal realm and begin training in your Specialty."

I swallowed. "Okay. That doesn't sound too bad."

"For the most part, it isn't."

"For the most part?" I said, picking up on her unsaid words, "What do you mean?"

"Well, it is called The Testing for a reason. It is meant to be challenging, to prove you deserve the magic you've inherited."

"What sort of challenges?"

"It usually depends on which Gifting you have. Some are tests of strength, some of wit, some of faith. Once again, it is different for everyone. The important thing to remember is that the divinities know who you are. They will not give you anything you cannot handle."

"Unless they deem me unworthy or Impure and they smite me." I muttered.

She chuckled softly. "That will not happen. Even that horrible girl Josette went through her Testing and passed. If she can be deemed worthy, you certainly will be."

She made a good point. I'd met plenty of vile Pures. The divinities deemed them worthy? But then again, that just further proved it was not a test of morals. I needed to speak to Butcher, convince her to pull me out.

"Could I have some time alone?"

"Elia..."

"Please, Mother." I was banking on her maternal instincts making it easier for me to manipulate her. "I just... need a little time alone to prepare myself."

Her face softened. "Of course. I will come back before the hour is up, so we can go together."

I nodded. "Thank you."

She reached forward and hugged me. It took everything in me not to flinch away. I hugged back. She seemed pleased by that as she stood and left. I followed, locking the door behind her, I was running out of time. I threw off my dress and quickly changed into a tunic before hurrying through the tunnels. Butcher should be home by now. I thanked The Fates when I snuck in and found Tolemas waiting at her door.

"Is she here?"

"Yes. Are you alright? You look... scared, which is unlike you."

I didn't bother answering. I just opened the door and walked into the room.

"Pull me out or they're going to boil my brains."

She let out an exasperated sigh. "You know how to knock, Adira, and yet you choose to barge in here like a barbarian."

"I am not screwing around, Camilla."

That seemed to get her attention. "What is it?"

"They're making me do The Testing in," I looked at the clock on her desk, "about forty minutes."

"And what exactly is the problem?"

"The problem is, I am *Impure*! I will fail, and apparently failing means my brain will turn to mush!"

"You are so dramatic sometimes."

"Dramatic? How is that being dramatic? I could go insane. Please, I am no use to you if my mind doesn't work."

"Your mind will work just fine. You will pass."

"That is impossible, unless you know of a way to cheat."

"You cannot cheat."

"Then I will fail."

"No, you will not."

I groaned. "This is not a funny. Call it off. I'll get your information some other way."

"No. Solis was very clear. You are to undergo The Testing."

"So, she wants me dead, then? Tying up loose ends, is she?"

"No. She has assured me you will pass. That is all you need to know."

"That is *not* all I need to know! How? Has she rigged it?"

"You know how I feel about repeating myself, Adira."

"Camilla—"

"Enough. Return to the castle now. Complete The Testing to the best of your abilities. The plan remains unchanged."

I stiffened, digging my feet into the ground as I tried to fight her command. She watched me, amused.

"Go. *Now*."

I cried out in pain as I stood my ground. My chest felt like it might burst. I tried to fight through it, but I couldn't. The pain lessened as I quickly turned and walked out, breathing out in frustration and hopelessness. I didn't have much time left. Hurrying back through the tunnels, I made a beeline for my closet, just as someone knocked on my door.

"Just a minute!" I called.

I practically ripped off my tunic and scavenged for something appropriate. What does one wear for their last day as a sane woman? I settled on a plain tunic. A simple light blue one, with a grey robe and hood. I practically ran to the door, stopping to regain my composure before opening the door.

Tira was waiting. She looked at my outfit approvingly and nodded. "Ready?"

"No. Not in the slightest."

She smiled. "You will be fine." She took my arm and started leading me down the hall.

Uri fell into step on my other side.

"People have been making bets on what your Specialty might be, or whether you have one at all. A surprising amount of people have bought into that girl's story. She's been badgering anyone who will listen to her." He chuckled, shaking his head. "Fools."

"Yeah," I muttered. "Very foolish of them."

"Just don't pull your punches, and you'll be fine," he said.

"Alright, stop scaring the girl," Yarik said, joining our little escort.

"No one else will see what I see, will they?"

"No, it's rather boring to watch." Yarik complained, and Tira scolded him.

"It is an honour to be present for someone's Testing."

Yarik rolled his eyes, but smiled. "Of course it is."

He shook his head at me when she looked away, and I smiled a bit, appreciating what he was trying to do. We stopped in front of a room I'd never been in.

"Don't worry, Elia, you will pass. Just breathe."

I nodded, swallowing as Uri and Wes opened the doors. Tira, Yarik, and I entered, finding a cot in the middle of the space. The room looked like an apothecary. Hadrian and Odette were standing by the cot. The priest was in the corner, eyes closed. He appeared to be praying, hopefully, in my favour.

Killian was standing nearby. One guard per royal family, and then the Priest to oversee and witness. Whatever conversation Hadrian and Odette were having ceased as we approached. Odette moved to a table and began mixing different ingredients, most of which I had never seen or heard of before.

Hadrian smiled reassuringly at me. "You look prepared."

"I don't feel it."

"I am sure you will do fine."

"Yes, well, she would have a bit more confidence if your wife hadn't unnecessarily sprung this on her."

He sighed. "She meant no offence. You know the position we are in. Someone referenced the law. As rulers, we have to abide by it."

"As rulers, we have to choose when they are being used to someone's disadvantage. You could have given her more time. That wouldn't have broken any laws and still given her the opportunity to prepare."

"Tira."

"Can you guys maybe have this conversation while I'm in The Testing? Or after?"

Tira smiled apologetically. "I'm sorry, Elia, you're right. We don't want to stress you out anymore. Have a seat on the cot."

I did as she said, sitting on the cot. I watched Odette. She had combined all the ingredients and poured them into a vial. A vial that was glowing, like the remedy Uri had given me. This one was a bright green colour. I *really* did not want to ingest anything of her making. My nervousness obviously showed because Tira took my hand.

"It's safe, don't worry. We all drank the same thing before our Testings. Just try to relax."

"You keep saying that, but it doesn't make it any easier."

Hadrian chuckled softly. "No, it does not. Nothing will make it easier, so you may as well just suck it up and get it over with, kiddo."

My eyes widened at his brazenness, but he wasn't wrong. I shouldn't have, but I stuck my tongue out at him. Causing a more hearty laugh to escape from his lips. Odette chose that moment to bring over the vial.

"Here we are. Drink all of it." She handed it to me, and I took a deep breath.

Sure, fine. I will just down the contents of this magical goo, go to a realm between here and the divinities, pass some unknown tests, and come out with my mind intact. Easy peasy.

I glanced at the people surrounding me. Tira was still holding my hand and nodding encouragingly, Hadrian was smiling reassuringly, and Odette looked on eagerly, which was very off-putting. I closed my eyes and downed the contents in one gulp.

I felt someone remove the empty vial from my hand, but I couldn't see them. I felt them lay me down on the bed, but again, I couldn't see them. I couldn't see anything but darkness as I drifted off.

Voices I didn't recognise roused me from my sleep, that, and the pointy object digging into my side repeatedly.

"Is it dead?" The voice closest to me asked, as something prodded me again. It sounded like a man's voice.

"What do you mean 'it'? She's clearly a woman, and she's clearly breathing," a second man said.

"Will you two knock it off? Sig put that stick down." This time it was a woman's voice.

Finally managing to open my heavy eyelids, I glanced up at four strangers garbed in armour. Two men and two women.

"Oh look, she is alive!" The one who'd spoken first exclaimed. I guess that was who they'd called Sig, and the stick he was about to poke me with had been the pointy object I'd felt prodding me.

He was light-skinned, with a lean build, a moustache that didn't entirely suit him, cedar coloured curls, aurora grey eyes, and a thin face.

One of the women rolled her eyes, grabbing the stick and chucking it away. Sig's pouty response was almost comical.

"Who are you?" It was then that I realised she was speaking to me.

I pulled myself up into a sitting position, dragging myself back a little to put some distance between us.

"I could ask you the same thing.."

She arched an eyebrow. "You could, but considering you're trespassing in *our* territory, I'd say you'd be wise to answer us first."

She was much darker than Sig, with deep brown eyes and facial features reminding me of the islanders I sometimes saw at the docks bringing in fish for the markets. Her dark brown hair was short. One side was parted with a braid and cut so close that it was almost completely shaved. The other side was wavy and free. Her weapon of choice appeared to be short swords.

"...I'm Adira."

"And what are you doing here, Adira?" The imposing warrior of a woman asked.

"I'm supposed to be completing my Testing. Is this part of it?"

The four of them glanced around at each other, exchanging a look I couldn't decipher.

"Which divinity sent you?" The second man, the one that had clarified to Sig that I was a woman, and not an *it*, demanded.

He was tall and muscular, towering over everyone else. He had a more square face, with ashy almost white hair cut short and close. His golden skin and piercing blue eyes were difficult to look away from.

"What are you talking about? I wasn't sent by a divinity. I'm just here to do my Testing."

"Sounds like a spy to me." It was a new voice this time, the final of the four, the other woman.

She was the shortest of the group. Her onyx hair was so dark it practically glistened in the sun, going all the way to her hips. Her narrow eyes were as dark as her hair as they met mine. Her stare was cold, her voice bored.

"I'm not a spy." I responded, realising I was still on the ground. I stood, dusting myself off. "Look, I didn't mean to trespass. If someone could just point me in the right direction, I'll be on my way."

The short one chuckled, and Sig grinned. "I like her. Can we keep her?"

The others didn't acknowledge his question, but the fact that they didn't roll their eyes, or stare at him like it was a ridiculous thing to ask, was unsettling.

"We do not know of what you speak. What is a Testing?" The first woman, who I'd decided was the nicer of the two, asked.

I frowned. "You know, The Testing? For Pures and Paras to be challenged by the divinities so they can unlock their magic?"

"So the divinities *did* send you."

"No, mortals sent me. The King and Queen of Taros?"

"We do not know this Taros. Is that in Kiverian territory?"

"No." I closed my eyes in frustration. What was going on? Was this part of my Testing?

"Regardless of where she is from or who sent her, what are we going to do with her? I am tired of this interaction. We have better things to be doing." The short woman drawled.

"One of the divine must have dropped her here as punishment." The first woman pondered.

"When are they going to stop doing that?" The burly man said.

"Well, if the divinities did drop her here, then you all know the drill. Let's go. Sig, Troja, grab the girl."

Sig and the other man who I now knew was named Troja stepped towards me and I took a step back.

"Um yeah, no. Pass. I'm not going anywhere with you."

The woman smirked. "It's cute you think you have a choice."

I turned to make a run for it, but faster than I'd think possible, Sig appeared in front of me, blocking my retreat.

"I'm not going anywhere. I don't even know who any of you are! You can't just kidnap me."

"She's right. We have been quite rude," Sig said solemnly.

"Apologies Lady Adira, I am Sig. This is Troja," he gestured to the other man, who looked like he could crush my skull with one hand. Troja nodded in greeting.

"And this is Moira, and Amory." Moira was the first woman, Amory the short one. Moira looked all business. Amory still looked bored.

Wait a minute, I knew those names?

"You're The Warriors Four? Known for your skill on and off the battlefield. You are notorious in our history books. You're not divinities, but you fight like them. Mortals don't have a word for what you are. No one truly knows, but they say you have some other type of magic. You were Xeria's warriors, his personal guard."

"She's star-struck. How sweet." Sig smirked.

"Who, or what, we are doesn't matter. All you should be concerned about is convincing us to help you and not kill you," Moira said.

"Why would you kill me? I have done nothing wrong."

"Trespassing is reason enough."

"Oh relax, Moira, you know you're not going to kill her. At least not yet." Sig added. *Comforting.*

"Just hurry up. Grab her and let's go."

"Don't touch me."

"Start walking then." Moria order, before leading the way.

Amory followed her, but Sig and Troja remained watching me, ready to manhandle me if I didn't comply. I groaned and followed the women.

This had to be part of my Testing? Either that or the divinities were punishing me for doing it as an Impure. Perhaps this was my mind turning to mush.

The walk was much longer than I'd anticipated, but I wasn't sure if that was because of the actual distance, or simply all the annoying questions Sig was hurling at me while we walked.

I answered them all, figuring at this point what did it matter? I told him I was from Adysium, about Pures and Impures, and about The Great War.

"So you're saying there are no gods or goddesses left in this realm of yours?"

I shook my head. "Are you saying there *are* in your realm? In t*his* one?"

"Of course?"

"But, I don't understand. If you don't know about Adysium, about my realm and have never been there, then how come the mortals there know about you? We have history books about you guys. All four of you."

"How much do you know of the creation and the realms?" Troja asked, joining the conversation. He'd been silent the entire walk so far.

I glanced at him. "I know little to nothing about realms other than Adysium. They teach us that Adysium is the realm that homed the divinities. During creation, Adysium was formed, then the divinities, who lived in Adysium for millennia, until some left, and some stayed. Ades and Akros stayed, creating mortals and beasts?"

"You speak of Primis."

"Of what?"

"The realm you describe, home of the divinities? Where Ades and Akros created mortals, beats, monsters? We call that Primis, The First."

"The first home of the gods and goddesses, but not the only. Like you said, some divinities left Primis, seeking other realms. Well, they found them."

"But Adysium, Primis, whatever you want to call it, is the only realm with mortals, so if you are not from there, then how do we know of you?"

Sig snorted, and Troja's lips twitched into a smile.

"What? What's so funny?" I asked, and Troja continued.

"Why do you believe your realm is the only one with mortals?"

I frowned. "Because Ades is the one who created mortals, and she died at the end of The Great War, she never left Adysium?"

"She didn't, but plenty of others did. A lot of them even came and went. Xeria was one of those divinities."

"So you're saying Xeria left Adysium? That he came and went, eventually staying and taking part in The Great War?"

He nodded. "After your Great War, the divinities were all locked out of Primis, so they went back to, or found, different realms. Xeria returned to this realm, the one you're currently standing in, Novus."

My mind was reeling trying to process all of this information. Was Novus their name for what we refer to as Erro? The same as how they apparently call Adysium, Primis?

"Okayy, but that still doesn't explain how mortals got to the other realms."

"Ades may have been the first one to create mortals, but she was not the only one. Other gods and goddesses learned from her, and many left, settling in their own realms and creating life of their own; mortals, beasts, and all sorts of being once Ades had shown them it was possible. Xeria was one of those. So I imagine when he returned to Primis, prior to your Great War, he told stories of us, and others from Novus, and your scribes must have recorded them, and either not known, or left out the fact that the events occurred in different realms."

"... I guess that makes sense. So Xeria to this day resides in this realm, Novus?"

Troja smiled. "He comes and goes, but we are one of his favoured realms. This is his territory, so the other divinities do not come without his permission, unless they have malicious intent, of course."

"But that's impossible. I can't be in another *realm*. My spirit is meant to be in Erro, a place *between* realms so I can complete my Testing."

"I can assure you this place is not 'in-between' anything. It is just as much a realm as the one you have supposedly come from."

"Then how... why in Heknos' name am I here?"

Sig raised his eyebrows. "Careful now, you may be protected from the divinities in your realm, and in this Erro you speak of, but here, not so much. Heknos has a habit of smiting mortals for far less than using his name in vain."

My eyes widened, and I glanced up nervously. Sig burst out laughing.

"I'm only joking. Well, mostly."

"Mostly? That's hardly reassuring."

He shrugged. "Well, I guess you just have to assume this is all part of your Testing. Divinities have been known to drop mortals here from time to time. Either to be trained by the God of War's best, or for us to teach them a lesson. Perhaps your test is to see if you can pass our training?"

"That seems a bit farfetched."

Troja arched a brow. "That's where you draw the line at too much crazy?"

He had a point, but still. Either way, I couldn't even begin to figure out how I might leave this place, or where'd I'd go if I somehow managed to. I would just have to trust that this was part of my Testing, and try to pass.

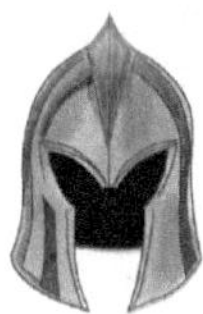

CHAPTER FORTY-FIVE

FINALLY, WE REACHED WHAT the others called, the compound. It was huge. The structure looked like something from our history books, it even had its own fighting arena.

Moira led me to what would apparently be my quarters. It was a tiny room, although still bigger than the one Sierra and I had shared. Housing a cot, a wardrobe, a small bedside table, and a little basin. It seemed more like a barrack than a bedroom.

"How long exactly do you expect me to stay here?" I questioned Moira. The others had gone to Ades knows where once we had arrived.

"As long as it takes." She simply responded.

"Uh, huh? To do what, exactly?"

"Convince us, and whoever sent you here, that you are worthy."

I sighed.

"Can I save us all some trouble? I am probably *not* worthy. If I didn't have to be here, I wouldn't be."

"Luckily for you, we make that decision. Come, we need to take you to see the armourer and then the blacksmith."

"What for?"

She rolled her eyes and just left the doorway to the small room, heading down a hall. I stared at the spot she had been standing in, seriously debating not following. I groaned under my breath before hurrying to catch her. This place was like a maze. Even I had trouble memorising the twists and turns.

We came to a stop in front of some very fancy looking double doors. I glanced at Moria, who looked at me expectantly.

"Well? In you go."

"You're not coming?"

"If you require someone to hold your hand at all times, this is going to be an endless process for all of us."

I rolled my eyes.

"Well *sorry*. I'm just not all that fond of entering situations without all the facts."

She watched me. "If you want to survive, I suggest you reevaluate that preference. We are not always given the luxury of knowing what we are about to face. That does not mean we can afford to be any less ready for it."

She made a good point, which was incredibly annoying. I sighed and pushed open the double doors. They swung open much easier than I'd expected, causing me to stumble into the room. A small man looked up from where he was sitting, sewing needle in hand, with some sort of fabric draped across his lap. He gave an exasperated sigh, before carefully putting the needle and fabric to the side. He leaned forward and squinted at me, pushing his glasses to the bridge of his nose.

"Hmm, come closer. I can't see a darned thing from this far."

I raised my eyebrows. "Sorry for interrupting you. Moira said you were expecting me?" She hadn't technically said that so much as *implied*, but still.

He nodded. "Yes yes. Come closer so I can see what I'm working with."

I stepped forward. "I'm Adira," I said, as he stood and circled me.

"Hmm, yes, I can work with this."

"Work with what, exactly?"

"Come, come, we are wasting time," he said, pulling me over to a small step.

He hadn't even given me his name.

"I'm sorry but, who in the divinities' names are you?" I finally said.

He sighed dramatically. "I am Ehsys. I will be your armourer."

I raised my eyebrows.

"As in, Goddess of Harmony, one of the Fates, Ehsys?" Every mortal in Adysium knew of The Fates, Edyna Goddess of Faith, Etheara Goddess of Fortune, and Ehsys Goddess of Harmony. Key word being *Goddess*.

This time, it was his turn to raise his eyebrows. "So typical for mortal men to rewrite history to suit their narrative. Eternis forbid a man be remembered for making clothing, even though I also made armour and battle wear. All they saw was a man playing with dresses instead of swords." He shook his head.

I bit my lip. "I'm sorry, the Goddess—God, of Harmony is a tailor?"

He fixed an unimpressed look on me. "Yes. Don't you know your history, child?"

I thought I did. "I.. guess not. Sorry, I just assumed one of the Fates would have their hands full with well, you know, fate."

"Never assume darling, you'll make an ass out of yourself quick smart if you do. If you must know, I became a tailor and then an armourer, thanks to the nature of my work *as* one of the Fates, always dealing with the thread of people's lives. This is the same thing just in a more physical form."

"Oh, well, alright then."

"Now are you done chattering?"

I nodded.

"Good, then undress, so I can get your measurements."

"Usually men have to at least take me to dinner first."

He tilted his head down, looking over the top of his glasses.

"My dear, you may be beautiful in the mortal realm, but I have laid with *actual* gods and goddesses. If you want dinner, you're going to have to do better than that."

I couldn't help but laugh. He made a fair point. I stripped down to my underclothes and allowed him to take my measurements. He was odd and very eccentric, but I found I actually enjoyed talking to him as he showed me his designs and ideas. The armour he dreamt up was not only efficient and protective but also beautiful and radiant. When he eventually finished, he shooed me out, muttering something about fetching me when the designs were done.

Moira was waiting for me when I exited the room.

"Did Ehsys get everything he needed?"

I nodded. "He sure knows how to talk."

"Why do you think I didn't come inside?" She pointed out, and I chuckled.

"It's clear now."

She nodded and started walking. I followed.

"Where to now?"

"Dhedros." I stopped walking, staring after her. It took her a few seconds to notice. When she did, she stopped and did not look pleased.

"What is it now?"

"Dhedros? Are you joking?"

"Do I look like I'm joking?" She said, deadpan.

"Well... no but—"

"It is rude to keep a divinity waiting, you know." She began walking again, and I hurried to catch up. *Bloody Hek.*

She led us outside and down a cobblestone path. It was an effort to keep moving as we approached the man standing out the front. He was working on some sort of sword. I felt the power radiating from him as he hammered the metal. The legends hadn't been exaggerating his appearance, though he looked older than I'd expected. For a god, he was rather plain looking. His features were all just a tad too close together, and he had an unkempt beard. If the history I knew was correct, he would also have a limp. He stopped hammering when we reached him.

"Dhed, how goes it?" Moira said casually, like they were old pals.

He grunted, placing his hammer down.

"Busy. What do you want now, Moira?" He said, much less friendly.

"You already know the answer to that."

He glanced at me, surveying me as Ehsys had, much less approvingly though.

"Why should I help?"

"The same reason the rest of us are."

He crossed his arms. I kept silent, which was a rarity for me these days.

Moira sighed. "It's just a weapon or two, Dhed. You have the time." My eyes widened slightly.

He looked back at me. "Do you even know how to use them?"

"I—"

"That is what we are here for. She will learn to use them, just craft them, please."

He grunted and walked back inside. I glanced at Moira.

"Well, that went well."

She smiled a bit.

"That's just Dhed. He likes to whine, but he is a softy at heart."

I raised my eyebrows.

"Dhedros, the God of Forgery, is a *softy*?"

She grinned and started walking again. It would be nice if she actually announced when we were going somewhere.

"What happens now?" I said, walking with her.

"Ehsys and Dhedros will have everything ready in the morning, so you have a night off."

I raised my eyebrows. "A night off?"

"Actually," a booming voice interrupted. I turned to see Sig and Troja grinning.

Moira crossed her arms. "No."

"Oh, come on, Moira. Don't be such a buzzkill. It's her first night." Sig complained.

"Exactly."

"Would someone like to explain to me what's going on?" I asked.

"It's a tradition to welcome a recruit properly." Sig answered.

"He means getting them wasted and making a fool of themselves." I looked over, finding Amory leaning against the doorway, picking her nails with... a dagger? Amory was the perfect picture of deadly calm. She looked incredibly bored and yet somehow, still one of the most scary looking people I'd ever seen.

"Oh well, thank you, but I will pass."

"It's adorable that you think it's a request," Sig said as he and Troja approached. Moira sighed, shaking her head.

I took a step back. "What are you doing?"

Their grins were terrifying as they each took one of my arms and lifted.

"Put me down, you brutes." I looked to Moira for help, but she just shook her head, an almost smile tugging at her lips.

"Good luck."

My eyes widened.

"Okay, wait. I can at least walk to wherever you two are taking me." I tried, to no avail.

How I went from being taken captive by two of the scariest warriors known to man, to drunkenly dancing with said warriors in the middle of an arena, was beyond me. Yet only a few hours later, here I was.

Sig and Troja could put away alcohol like no mortals I'd ever seen. I had no idea where they were putting it all. I used to pride myself on my ability to handle my liquor, having out-drank Raf and the other orphan boys on more than one occasion. Not anymore. For the first time in a long time, I was positively smashed.

Which is why, in a very similar fashion to how they had carried me *to* the tavern, they'd also carried me back to my room, where I promptly passed out.

I awoke to a loud knock on my door.

"Rise and Shine Adira!" Moira's voice called. "Solissia waits for no one."

I groaned as I rolled straight out of the bed and onto the ground with a loud thud. Judging from the chuckle sounding through my door, Moira had heard. I managed to get up and open it.

Moira let out a low whistle, causing me to wince.

"Did you try to keep up with them?"

"No, but even half of what they had—" I held up my hand before covering my mouth and hurrying over to the basin, promptly emptying the contents of my stomach.

She smirked, remaining in the doorway while I yacked my guts up. Sliding down to the floor, I closed my eyes and groaned.

"A bath will help. Just be quick." She started walking again with no verbal directions. I scrambled up and followed her. She led me to a communal bathing chamber. I raised my eyebrows.

"Not a lot of privacy here?"

"Modesty is overrated. We are, however, still civilised. The men have a different bathing room."

Well, that was something I supposed. She threw me a towel, knowing I was far too groggy to be ready for it. It smacked me in the face.

"Thanks." I muttered sarcastically through the material.

"Are you always this grumpy in the mornings or are you just too liquor-sick?"

"Both."

She chuckled. "Hurry up. We need to collect your things from Ehsys and Dhedros before you begin your training."

I was still trying to wrap my head around the fact that two of the divinities were here, and I had *met* them. I didn't know what to do with that information.

She left the bathing chamber, giving me a small amount of peace. I glanced around the vast stone chamber. Someone had taken the time to intricately decorate the walls, carving beautiful swirls and patterns. There was a section for more practical, quick bathing. There were also beautiful large spa baths that could fit multiple people, decorated with the same swirling carvings, and there were, what looked like, steamed seating sections. Thankfully, no one else was occupying the room.

As much as I wanted to climb into one of those spa baths and relax, I would likely fall asleep. So instead, I walked over to one of the more practical looking tubs, stripped down, turned the water to cold, and slipped in before I could change my mind. I let out a loud gasp as the icy water hit my skin. It was bloody freezing, but it woke me up.

I quickly washed and dried off. I glanced at the clothes pile at my feet. After the men dropped me off last night, I was apparently too drunk or too tired to change. I sighed, putting them back on before rejoining Moira. Hopefully, I could stop and change on the way.

"Ehsys first, then Dhedros," she said as she led me back to the double doors. There goes my hopes of a wardrobe change. Once again, she remained outside. I gave her a look, and she just shrugged.

"In you go."

I sighed and pushed open the double doors to find Ehsys sorting through some different fabrics. He glanced up.

"You're late," he said far too loudly. I winced yet again.

"Sorry." I walked over.

He looked me over and sighed. "Sig or Troja?"

"Both."

He laughed a little. "You poor thing. I'm surprised you're still standing. Have a seat."

He didn't need to tell me twice. He exited through a side door after I gratefully sat down. I had no idea what was back there, but when he returned, he was holding a glass containing some kind of bright orange liquid. I raised my eyebrows.

"You don't expect me to drink that?" I had drank far too many foreign liquids in the past twenty-four hours.

"If you want to make it through the day, I suggest you do," he said matter-of-factly, holding out the glass. I hesitantly took it.

"What's in it?"

He shrugged. "A little of this, a little of that. Either drink it or don't, but hurry with it."

I looked at the drink again. I sighed and downed the contents. Covering my mouth as I fought the urge to vomit it back up. I coughed slightly, placing the glass down.

"That is *vile!*"

"I never said it wasn't. Now let me show you what I've made for you. Come." He hurried behind a partition, only stretching across half of the room. I stood and followed him around it, finding rows and rows of armour on one side, dresses, tunics, and finery on the other. It was brilliant. I smiled a little, despite the lingering taste of that awful drink.

"Wow. This is…"

"Wonderful, exquisite, full of masterpieces? Yes, yes, I know. Now come." He walked over to a mannequin and I followed.

"You made this for me?" I said, running my hand along the armour displayed in front of me.

"You are going to need it if you are as unintelligent as you sound." He shook his head, and I withheld an eye roll, keeping my attention on the mannequin and what it was wearing; armour. Completely black, with incredible detailing. I once again ran my fingers down it. The suit was clearly made for a woman. It flattered the curves but still left them protected. The bottom piece was an armoured skirt.

"Just because I'm a female doesn't mean I should wear a skirt to battle." I commented.

He rolled his eyes. "Child, I'm not sure what kind of armour the people wear wherever it is you come from, but here? Men *and* women favour the *Bellator*. Which means—"

"Warrior." I translated as I looked at the pleated metal skirt. "My middle name is Bellator. After our grandfather Belamy, who was supposedly a formidable warrior, or perhaps I was actually just named after a skirt. They named me after him, and my sister after our grandmother, Tuora."

He nodded, impressed. "Both genders use the Bellator. As it allows the wearer to move more freely, unrestricted. There are layers beneath to protect from anything that slips through."

I nodded slightly. "It seems fairly lightweight. The metal armour covers all the kill points, but the rest of the suit is made from something else?"

He grinned. "Yes, this Tunicam," *Undercoat,* I translated in my head, thank the divinities I'd been forced to learn so many languages, the old tongue being one of them, "is a design of my making. It goes under the armour, covering almost your entire body. Starting at the neck, stopping at the elbows and the knees. It offers protection to the places your armour doesn't, instead of leaving those areas bare and vulnerable." I nodded slightly.

"But what is it made of? I've never seen this material?"

"No, I don't suppose you would have. I believe the creature responsible for this beautiful material is rare, possibly extinct, in your realm."

"Creature?" I frowned, looking closer at the material. It could be scales, I supposed, but no creature, beast, or monster I'd ever seen or read about had scales like this.

"They are feathers, my dear." He answered my unasked question.

I raised my eyebrows. "Feathers? You want to protect me with feathers?"

He sighed dramatically. "Not just *any* feathers. Feathers from the Ignis Avis."

I stared at him blankly.

He groaned. "The firebird. They shed regularly, but their feathers are still rare, as there is only ever one bird at a time. You are very lucky to have this commissioned for you."

I raised an eyebrow.

"These feathers are impervious to flame and incredibly durable, more so than any chain-mail or undercoats in existence. Trust me. This is something you want."

I remained sceptical as he directed me to a dressing room. I began putting the garment on, starting with the tunicam. It was nearly impossible to discern that it was made of feathers. They were woven together so tightly. It was the colour of shadows and midnight, repelling the light when it hit. I wasn't sure if it was dye or the natural colouring. It was incredibly form fitting, scandalously so. In fact, it practically melded with my body, almost as if it were learning and adjusting to my shape. *Creepy.*

Next, I donned the bellator. It fit perfectly and, if I was being honest, looked pretty intimidating. Then I put on my chest plate, shoulder guards, and arm guards, before finally slipping into my boots and metal knee guards. These again were lightweight, as all the other metal guards had been, but they still felt strong. Looking at myself in the mirror, I certainly looked like a warrior, a badass one at that. I smiled a little and stepped out. Ehsys grinned and clapped in excitement. He was quite strange.

"Oh, you look fabulous, darling. If I do say so myself."

I chuckled a bit.

"It's easier to manoeuvre in than I expected." I commented, twisting and turning around.

He nodded. "Firebird feathers. I told you. There's just one last thing left."

I raised my eyebrows. "What?"

He frowned as he glanced around before rummaging through piles of clothing and materials.

"Drat. Where did I put it?"

"Put what?"

"Ah hah!" He exclaimed, practically climbing out of a pile of dresses, holding something very shiny. I groaned when I realised what it was.

"A helmet, really?"

He gave me a look as he walked up and practically shoved it on my head.

"Yes, *really.* Do you fancy blows to the head? If so, I waste this armour on you."

I sighed.

"No, they just seem like a nuisance. Wouldn't it hinder my line of sight? And honestly, I'd probably put it down somewhere and lose it."

"First of all, if you lose my helm, I will stab you myself. Second of all, yes. When designed poorly, yes, they are a hindrance. Which is why this one protects but allows you your full range of sight. It mostly covers the back and sides of your head, but is thinner and closer framed to your face once it reaches your ears. Practically metal sideburns, if you ask me. You should be able to see everything."

He was right. I could still use my peripheral vision. Turning my head, it didn't feel loose, but it wasn't too tight. I nodded.

"Thank you." I looked at him.

He smiled a bit, almost proudly. I could tell he took pride in his work.

"Yes, well, use it wisely. I suggest you head to Dhedros. He is not a patient man."

I bit my lip. "Alright, well, thank you again, I guess?" I said, walking back over to the door.

"Adira," he said, and I stopped, looking over my shoulder. That was one of the few times I'd heard him say my name.

"Part of being a leader means making tough decisions, even when it feels like that might break you in two. The many have to come before the few," he said calmly.

I frowned slightly. "... I am not a leader. But I also disagree with that. Why should strangers, potentially even *bad* ones at that, come before the people I know and love?"

He smiled a little. "How do you know whether they are good or bad? How do you know they have less value than the ones you love? Are you a goddess, Adira? Can you tell a mortal's worth at a glance?"

I sighed. "Obviously not."

He smiled a little. "You mortals live in the how and why. That is what makes mortals so very... well, mortal. But for those like you, there is no middle ground. You will have two paths to choose from. I am so very interested in seeing which one you take."

"What does that even mean?" I said, but he simply turned away.

"*Bona Fortuna*, Child." He disappeared behind the partial wall. *Good luck.*

I sighed, squashing down the unease that cryptic message from one of the Fates themselves caused, and made my way to Dhedros's workshop. I'd luckily memorised the way yesterday, because Moira wasn't outside to escort me this time and I believed what Ehsys had said about Dhedros not being very patient.

CHAPTER FORTY-SIX

WHEN I ARRIVED, HE was once again outside working on some sort of weapon. He glanced up, grunted, placed his hammer down, and headed inside without saying a word to me. I bit my lip and glanced around. Was I supposed to follow?

"Well?" His deep voice called. "Are you going to stand out there all day or come and collect what you came for?"

I hurried inside. "Sorry." I apologised, not bothering to explain my hesitation. Glancing around, it looked like a regular blacksmith's shop, only with weapons of much larger magnitude and finer calibre than any mortal could produce. I finally laid eyes on Dhedros, who was standing with his arms crossed next to a table with multiple weapons laid out.

I walked over and glanced at them. There were different kinds, and each was beautiful, with its own little detailing. My eyes widened as I noticed the one thing they all had in common. A small carving, present on all of them. For the swords, it was on the metal blades themselves. For the daggers it was on the hilts. For the bow and arrows it was on the length of the bow and the tips of the arrows. A dagger with a drop of blood on its tip.

"What the Hek is this?" I accused angrily.

He arched a brow, amused. "They are your weapons," he said matter-of-factly.

I almost growled, picking up the dagger and gesturing to the design.

"Do you think It's funny to make me wield weapons with a symbol that is holding me captive? How did you even know about it?"

He looked at me, unflinching. "Are you done?"

I took a deep breath. "Can you explain, *please?*" I gritted out.

He smirked a bit. "I did not know you were bound, human. If you do not recognise this symbol for what it is, then perhaps you are not ready to know. That explains why the serpens is missing." He pondered, as if any of what he was saying made sense.

I frowned. "What do you mean?"

He shook his head. "It is not my place to say, but know that I meant no offence. You may take them and go. I trust The Four will show you how to use them adequately." He was definitely a no nonsense type of man.

"Actually," A shadow stepped into the doorway. Troja. I held in a groan, and he smirked at me before nodding respectfully at Dhedros. "You can leave those here. You won't need them today."

"But Moira said—" I tried to argue. Definitely not because I really wanted to play with these new weapons.

"You're with me today, not Moira. Let's go." He cut me off as he walked out. I was getting sick of trailing people around. I thanked Dhedros before following Troja.

"How's your head?" He said as I fell into step beside him. I cast a side glare his way.

"Perfectly fine." Thanks to Ehsys, I wasn't being completely dishonest. There was still a dull ache, but I no longer felt like throwing up, and was functioning well enough.

He smirked. "Good. You are going to need a clear head for this, and you can lose the armour."

"For what, exactly?"

"The others and I spoke this morning and organised a training roster. I've got you for the first month."

I stopped walking. "The first *month?* I'm supposed to be here for four months?"

He stopped, shaking his head. I breathed out in relief.

"No, you'll definitely be here longer than that."

My eyes widened. "What? I can't be here that long. I have a Testing to pass, people to get back to."

"As far as you or any of us know, this *IS* your Testing. Also, time works differently in each realm. If you are from Primus, then you do not need to worry. We could keep you here for years, and your friends would never even know you were gone for more than a day."

I breathed in sharply. "Please don't."

He smiled. "Guess it depends on how well you take to the training. Speaking of, we are wasting daylight." He began walking again and I somehow, despite my dazed state, followed him. I was still processing his words when we halted atop a grassy hill. I glanced down at the steep cement stairs leading down to what looked like a small village.

"If this is where you tell me to run up and down the stairs to get my fitness up, that's a bit cliche, isn't it?"

He smirked, and I did not like the look in his eyes.

"Not to fear Adira. No stair climbing, unless you fail, of course. Lose the armour."

I frowned and glanced down. "I would hardly call what I have on underneath this armour appropriate day wear."

He crossed his arms. "If you want to wear full armour, then by all means, but it will make your task more difficult."

I sighed and carefully stripped out of the armour, laying it down gently on the ground, leaving me in only the Tunicam. Troja made no comment. His eyes didn't wander. He looked positively unbothered. I wasn't sure if I should be offended or grateful.

"What am I doing then?"

"There are five thousand steps leading to the Katari Village. A small fishing village. Nice people," he said as he started walking down the steps.

"That's nice?" I said, following him.

He nodded, coming to a stop in front of a boulder. "It is, and they are. You have a simple task." It was ovular and about the height of your average man, with some sort of wooden stoppers propping it up. *Precarious place for a rock that size.*

"What task?" I said, coming to a stop beside him. He walked around the boulder until he was standing beneath it by a step or two.

"Stand where I am standing." He ordered, moving aside as I took his place. He was a lot more serious than he'd been last night. All business now, it seemed.

"As I said." He took a few steps until he was on the same level as the rock. "Your task is simple." He kicked out one stopper, and my eyes widened.

"Wait, what are you doing?" I made to move, but before I could, he kicked out the second stopper and the rock tipped straight toward me. I grunted as I reached out and held it in place, stopping it from squashing me.

I could hear the smile in Troja's voice. "Good reflexes. Where was I? Oh yes. Your task is to stop this rock from rolling down these steps, inevitably destroying some poor fisherman's home once it reaches the bottom."

I stared at him. "This is a joke, right? This rock weighs twice what I do!"

"Yes, it does. As will most of the opponents you could come up against? You need to build endurance. You need to last as long as possible against someone bigger and stronger than you."

I shook my head, already feeling the strain. "You can't be serious? There are easier, less dangerous ways to do endurance training!"

He shrugged. "Of course there are. But I find this the best method. It is unconventional and has the added motivation that you would not have if you were simply to run laps or do obstacle courses. You not only have your fate to think about but also the villagers and their homes. This rock isn't huge, but it is big enough to do some serious damage at a high enough speed." He took a step back up the stairs.

"Troja, this isn't funny. Where are you going?"

He took another step back. "I'll check on you every hour or so."

My eyes practically shot out of their sockets. "What?! What if I can't hold it?"

"Then you are going to have some very unhappy fishermen. If it doesn't squish you on its way down, that is." He shrugged and turned away from me, climbing back up the stairs, and disappearing from sight. Holy Heknos. Surely this was a joke, and he'd reappear any minute now to remove the rock and we would laugh about it. *Surely..?*

Apparently, it had not been a joke, and 'every hour or so' meant more like whenever he felt like it. Two hours had to have passed already, and he still hadn't come back. The sun was nearing its apex. My arms were aching, and I was sweating like a madwoman. I had tried to push the rock up at first, hoping to stabilise it or relieve some pressure, but it was too large and close for me to build up enough momentum. I ended up shifting down a few steps to put the strain on different parts of my arms before moving back up and repeating this over and over.

When Troja did finally enlighten me with his presence, he strolled down the steps with an apple in his hand. I had taken to turning away from the boulder and resting it against my shoulders and back by this point. Which is why I didn't notice him at first, just about jumping out of my skin when he took a loud bite of the apple and came to stand beside me.

"Nice. You haven't been pushed back too far."

"Damn you Troja, I am going to get squashed. Please end this."

"No can do. We need to see how long you can last so we can improve it."

I ground my teeth. "Troja."

He smiled, and I took my attention off the boulder, just for a second, but that was all it had needed. I fumbled as I tried to regain my footing, but had no luck. I fell to my knees and braced my head, preparing for impact. It never came.

Opening one of my eyes and peeking behind me, I found Troja standing there, holding the boulder back with *one* hand, still eating his apple with the other. I stared at him incredulously. As I stood, my whole body ached.

"You are *insane!*" I shouted. He didn't look bothered and simply finished the apple before he opened the satchel I now noticed he wore.

"Here. Some food and water. You can have a twenty-minute break, then it's back to it."

I laughed a bit. "And if I say no?"

He looked at me and shrugged. "Then you fail, which could mean failing your Testing and going insane or going back to your realm, with everyone knowing you're a fraud."

I glared at him as I took the food and water before sitting down. My arms were shaking badly. Once my twenty minutes were up, he made it clear I had to either retake my position or he would let it roll to the village himself. *Bastard.*

I retook my position and grunted as he let go of the boulder, leaving me straining against its inevitable descent. My arms and legs trembled in perfect rhythm. The break didn't matter. My body couldn't take it anymore. It occurred to me, as it pushed me down a few more steps, that I was losing a battle against a damned rock. Troja watched but didn't step in. I groaned as it pushed me further down again.

"Troja, I'm going to drop it. Please."

He shook his head. "You haven't dropped it yet. You have more left in you."

"Trust me, I don't!" I shouted. Something salty and wet trickled from my eyes, down my cheek and over my lips. I clenched them shut, trying to push the boulder back up. Trying to get some momentum, but it was no use. I couldn't do it. I jumped to the left, and out of the way, falling to my knees as it rolled towards the village. Guilt and pain coursed through me, but I couldn't make my body move.

I saw Troja's small smile before he stepped back, removing his shirt. I frowned. What in all that is divine? My thoughts were interrupted as wings appeared from his back, spreading out at least six feet on either side. They were dark grey, feathered, and shiny. Before I could say anything, he pushed off the ground and *flew* toward the boulder.

It had rolled a good five hundred steps before he landed in front of it, holding out his palm and ceasing its movement. He whistled, and eventually two children ran past me, down to where Troja stood, both holding the stoppers that had been used to prop it up originally.

He grinned as he propped it back up and handed both of them a coin, before scooping one up in each arm and flying them back to the top of the hill. I was practically dying on my step when he flew back down, both from pain and shock.

"It's rude to stare, Adira." He reprimanded as his wings folded back into wherever they'd come from and he put his shirt back on.

Was I hallucinating after being in the sun holding that damned boulder for so long?

"Are you — What in the...?" He apparently found my reaction very amusing, as he let out a laugh. The first one I'd heard since yesterday.

"No Adira, before you ask, I am not a god. Come on, you're done for the day. Go rest."

"I..." I stared at him like an idiot.

He chuckled and held out his hand. I slowly took it, wincing as he helped me up.

"I don't think I can get back up those steps."

"You can."

"Troja."

He looked at me. All traces of humour were gone. "When it is a matter of life or death, you may *have* to. If it is the difference between your loved ones living and dying, wouldn't you at least try with everything you had?"

I swallowed and glanced toward the top of the stairs. It seemed so far away. "I'd die trying to save the people I loved, if I had to."

"Exactly. So you *can*, Adira. I will help you." He slung my arm over his shoulder and placed his arm around my waist, hunching to match my height. "But you *will* get to the top of these stairs."

After meeting his eyes, I took a slow breath and nodded. I looked down at the step beneath my feet. I could do this. One step at a time.

That is what I kept telling myself, as every step got harder. As Troja supported more and more of my weight. My legs were burning, my eyes were tired, and I thought I might pass out from exhaustion. But I kept going. Troja remained silent unless I halted, at which point he'd stop and wait until I began again. Eventually, we got to the top, and I fell to my knees, promptly throwing up in front of us.

Troja didn't look at all surprised and just waited until I had finished before handing me some water. "We still have to get you back to your room. You can rest there."

I shook my head. "Nope... just... leave me here. I'm good here," I said, laying on the ground.

He chuckled softly. "You sure?"

I nodded, closing my eyes. "Yep."

"Alright then. I have already taken your armour back to your room, so don't worry about that. Just meet me back here at dawn tomorrow."

I groaned and could practically feel his smile through my closed lids as he walked away.

I remained sprawled there for some time before I eventually gathered myself and hauled my ass back to our shared quarters. I didn't go to my rooms, though. Instead, I headed straight to the bathing chambers and into one of the hot baths.

As the heat worked on my aching muscles, I breathed out. I could only pray that whatever we were doing tomorrow was different from today's challenge. Given the location, though, I didn't like my chances.

After nearly falling asleep in the water, I forced myself out and back to my rooms, where I fell asleep and did not wake again until dawn.

For the next two weeks, I spent my mornings trying to hold up that damned boulder before practically crawling to the bathing chambers and then passing out back in my bed. It went on and on. Any time I slipped and let the boulder roll too far, Troja would move it closer to the village. Not so close that it wouldn't do damage, actually quite the opposite. He would move it close enough that I couldn't afford to let it roll very far or it would hit the village, still gathering enough force to cause serious harm. When the day started anew, the boulder would be back in its original starting place.

Slowly but surely, I stopped slipping as much. As the days went by, the boulder remained in the spot it had been in at the start of the day. I was finally gaining some confidence in my ability to hold this damned rock, and the muscles forming on my arms showed it.

That was, until I turned up one morning, and the boulder was not where it usually was. It was, according to the two children waiting for me, at the very bottom of the steps, as was Troja. I groaned and began the long walk down. Once I got there, he nodded.

"We're changing things up today."

"Thank Ades."

His smirk told me I had spoken too soon. I sighed.

"What is it this time?"

He nodded to the rock. I hated that thing.

"Time to build some strength. Push the rock up the stairs."

I looked at him blankly. "Seriously?"

He crossed his arms. Over the past few weeks, if I'd learned anything about Troja, it was that he did not joke when it came to training. He was a hardass, even worse than Tarryn.

I sighed and glanced up at the stairs. I rolled my shoulders and moved in front of the rock that was propped on the first few steps. This wasn't the same one I realised. It was smaller and more round, about two third of my height. I rubbed my hands together, taking a breath before even attempting to push it.

"This is some bullshit." I grumbled. He ignored me. Troja was taking inspiration from Heknos himself with this unique form of punishment.

"Your aim is to get it to the top of the hill. You can stop for a break once a day for only thirty minutes. If you need to stop more than once or can no longer continue, then when you try again the next day, you will start back at the bottom of the stairs, instead of wherever you were when the session ended the previous day. Understood?" I nodded.

"Begin."

I braced myself and began pushing. It was seemingly impossible. I ended up having to push mostly from the bottom half, which then risked it rolling right back over me.

Naturally, I ended up having to stop multiple times. So when I returned the next day, the rock was back at the base of the stairs. Any progress I'd made, erased. I hated that rock almost as much as I hated the man standing beside it. But every time I wanted to quit, he would remind me of what was at stake. My sanity, and the chance to see Sierra again. If I failed, I would either lose my mind or they would behead me for being a fraud and a traitor to the crown. So I kept going. I kept pushing. Even if I didn't get very far, I kept trying.

On the thirty-first day, I walked to where I'd last gotten to, about halfway up. Miraculously, I now only needed to stop once, for less than thirty minutes. I was convinced there was some magical juju going on, strengthening me in this place, but progress was still very slow. Today was different, though, because both Troja and Moira were waiting for me.

"What's going on?"

"It's time for your training with Moira," Troja said.

"But I haven't gotten to the top?"

Moira smiled a bit and shook her head. Troja chuckled.

"What's so funny?"

"You would never have gotten it to the top, Adira. It would be impossible for someone of your size and strength, without stopping more than once. I can't believe you even got this far." Moira explained, and I looked at Troja.

"Is that true?"

He nodded.

"What the Hek, Troja?!" I said, throwing my hands up.

"Would you have tried as hard if you knew you would never succeed?" He said simply.

"What?" I groaned. "No, but that doesn't make it okay! I practically killed myself trying to achieve something I now find out was impossible, anyway?"

"Battle and war are not *easy*, Adira. You will face opponents and challenges that make you feel as if you're pushing a boulder uphill. But *now*, when you face those things, you know you can do so. Even half way is more than you *should* have been able to do. Sometimes you have to face the impossible as if it *were* possible, and sometimes you have to know when to walk away. You will be the only one who decides when to do which, but now you have the tools to at least make an informed decision."

I couldn't argue with him. He made a good point, but I was still annoyed. Which he could tell because he smiled a bit.

"You did good Adira, hopefully you don't have to use it, but if you do, I am confident you'll be able to hold your own," he said before he headed into the fishing village.

"I have never wanted to strangle someone I actually agreed with so much."

Moira chuckled. "He can have that effect. If it helps though, that was actually pretty high praise from him. Ready to use some of those beautiful weapons Dhedros made for you?"

I had no trouble believing *that* was Troja's idea of praise. The bloody hardass.

I nodded. "As long as it doesn't involve a rock, I am in."

She smiled and began walking back up the stairs, the stairs I had hated as much as the rock, but was begrudgingly grateful for now. My strength and endurance had improved more than I'd have thought possible. I felt more like myself than I had in a long time. Too long.

CHAPTER FORTY-SEVEN

M OIRA LED ME TO the arena I'd seen on my first day here. This type of training environment, one I was at least familiar with. I noticed the weapons Dhedros had constructed for me laid out on a table, along with my armour. Saying I was excited to finally wield them and be taught to do so was an understatement. I moved to approach them, but a harsh thump to the back of my legs had me struggling to remain upright as I spun around.

"Ow!" I exclaimed, finding Moira leaning casually against a tall, dark blue staff of some sort. Judging by its size and shape, and the slight grin on Moira's face, I'd say that had likely been the cause of the blow to my legs. "What was that for?"

"You think you're ready to use those weapons?"

"Isn't that what you are here for? To teach me?"

"Yes, but not foolishly. Go stand in the middle of the arena," she said, straightening. I sighed and walked to the centre. I should have known better than to expect something a little more enjoyable after Troja's gruelling methods.

"Now what?"

She smiled a little and tapped her staff on the ground. I raised my eyebrows, opening my mouth to ask what that meant when, to my surprise, a cage appeared around me. I stepped forward, touching the bars, only they weren't normal bars. They weren't wood or metal; they weren't any type of material I'd ever seen, and they *glowed*. Actually glowed. They were a deep blue colour, the same as her staff, appearing solid but flexible.

"What on Adysium is this made of?"

She shrugged. "Troja has his wings. I have this."

"What exactly is *this*?" I said, as I looked for a way out of the cage, finding none.

She smiled as she approached. "Think of it as an illusion brought to life."

"You're saying this is all in my head? That it isn't real?"

"In a way, it is in your head, but it is also real. What makes something real? If you and I can both see, feel, and touch it, can it be fake?"

"Can other people see, feel, and touch it?"

"If I choose to let them do so, then yes."

"It sounds more like you're creating or manipulating matter, rather than an illusion?" I said, watching her.

She smiled. "If I were manipulating matter, then everyone would see it, not only those that I choose."

"So it isn't real."

"My Ramus certainly felt real when it smacked the back of your legs, didn't it?" She said, twirling her staff. "You felt a solid object hit you? And yet…" The staff in her hand became pliable and bendy as she held it, before disappearing entirely. "It is no more than a very convincing illusion. One you can feel, see, and smell, but an illusion nonetheless."

I breathed in. "What are you people? You cannot be mortal."

"We are mortals. At least mostly."

I frowned. "What does that mean?"

"That is not what today's lesson is about," she said as the staff reappeared in her hand.

I groaned. "What is it about? Finding a way out of a magical cage?"

"No." She tapped her staff on the ground twice. In response, the two children I'd seen when training with Troja entered the room carefully, carrying some kind of closed hessian basket. I was ashamed to say I was beginning to hate those kids. Anytime they popped up, it was never a good sign for me. Even if they were adorable.

The little girl had blonde ringlet curls and piercing turquoise eyes that practically glowed. The little boy had the same eyes, and same blonde curls, but his were shorter, sitting around ear length. Twins. Beautiful, foreboding twins whose names I didn't know.

A door appeared in my carefully constructed cage. The twins opened it, scurrying in silently. They carefully placed the basket down before hurrying back out. The door promptly disappeared, replaced once again with bars.

"What's in the basket?"

"Why don't you open it and see?"

"I'm assuming you won't let me out of this cage until I do?"

She just smiled. I sighed and lifted the lid off of the basket. At first glance, I thought it was a rope coiled up inside. Confusion filled me until it moved. I jumped back, my eyes flying to Moira.

"Is this another illusion?" I said, refocusing on the basket as a *hiss* sounded, followed by the creature uncoiling and raising its head up out of the basket. It had shiny black scales, with a red underbelly and matching red eyes. It flared its hood.

This wasn't just any serpens. It was a Serpens Mortiss. The Serpens of Death, said to have been created by Dykos himself. A deadly creature whose venom has no antidote. If bitten, you had maybe five minutes before your organs shut down and your body failed. Unless you had a Remedi nearby, you had zero chance of survival.

"Tell me this is another illusion."

"Unfortunately not. This is very real."

"Are you mad?"

"Possibly." She mused.

"Moira."

"Take a breath, Adira. Simply avoid the creature using the skills you already possess."

"What does this have to do with wielding weapons?!" I whisper shouted, not wanting to startle the thing that had now slithered out of its little basket. I backed up.

"You'll just have to trust me." Music began playing, from where, I couldn't say. I wasn't about to take my eyes off of the mortiss long enough to find out. It was no doubt another one of Moira's illusions. One the serpens could apparently hear, as it raised itself up to almost half my height and hissed at me. It struck out, and I lept to the side, cursing loudly.

"Moira!"

"Pay attention. Anticipate its movements." I took a deep breath and watched the serpens. If I could, in fact, anticipate which direction it was going to move, figure out how fast or when it would strike, and then avoid it for long enough, maybe it would get bored.

Swallowing before quickly jumping out of the way as it struck again, I clenched my fist. I knew if I let my anger get the best of me, it may very well be the last thing I do. I could yell at Moira if I got out of this damned cage alive. Right now, I had to focus on my current opponent.

It became a dance of sorts, between the serpens and I. We both moved in harmony, and yet contradiction of the other. I kept moving, making it harder for it to establish which direction I'd go next. It was constantly swaying, keeping itself upright. I wasn't sure how much time had passed before the music stopped, but once it did, the mortiss also stopped.

Slowly, it slithered back into its basket. I didn't hesitate to drop the lid back on before stepping back. The surrounding cage disappeared, and I turned to find Moira clapping slowly.

"Not bad."

"You could have killed me," I said, finally able to express my anger as I walked over, putting a grateful distance between the serpens and myself. Moira tapped her staff twice again. The twins of doom reappeared, collecting the basket, and retreating to wherever they'd been waiting.

"The mortiss could have."

"Which *you* locked me in with!" I said, throwing my hands up.

"And yet you are fine."

"That's not the point."

"What is the point?"

"The point is, I could have died?!"

"Buy you didn't."

I groaned in frustration. It was like talking to a brick wall.

"Why are you so concerned about the past?"

"The *past?*" I said incredulously. "I would hardly call sixty seconds ago, the past."

"But it is. It is done. It has no effect on anything anymore. Except your tantrum, apparently."

My eyes widened. "Are you really trying to tell me the past has no bearing on the future?"

"I am saying *you* decide how much weight it carries and what you choose to take or learn from it. The past can be a great tool, but you cannot let it define your future."

I stared at her. "So that entire experience was just to teach me some philosophical lesson about the past, present, and future? What's next, a palm reading? Can you tell me if my future husband is handsome?" I said sarcastically. She grinned.

"No." She threw her staff at me and I caught it, frowning.

"No, he's not handsome? Can I redraw?"

She simply smiled, as another staff appeared in her hands and she took up an offensive stance.

"Show me what you learned," she said, swinging it at me.

My eyes widened again as I jumped out of the way.

"I learned nothing about fighting?"

"Didn't you?" She launched at me again, but I evaded it easily enough, much to my surprise. Her blows kept coming, but I kept dodging them, anticipating her moves. She stopped and smiled.

"If you can anticipate the moves of a creature like the Serpens Mortiss, a mortal opponent should be easy."

She wasn't wrong, but I didn't think it was entirely necessary to risk my life just to learn how to dodge.

"Now, instead of moving out of the way. Block me."

I frowned. "What?"

"Block me," she said, striking at me with her staff. I breathed in and raised my own, wincing slightly as it made contact with hers. The vibrational impact shuddered down the stick and up my arms.

"You're holding your hands too close together." She walked over and adjusted the positioning of my hands. "You don't want to hold it too tightly or you will feel too much, but too loose, and I will knock it from your hands. You need to adjust your grip according to what you are doing. And don't stand with your feet so close together. You need balance."

Focused on her instructions, I adjusted accordingly.

"Better." She nodded. "Now block."

She came at me again, and I held my staff up, blocking her blow. I still felt the impact, but it wasn't as painful and was much more controlled.

We continued like that for another hour before she called the session. I still hadn't touched my armour or the weapons Dhedros had made for me. When I'd asked what I was supposed to do with the rest of my day, she just shrugged and told me I was free to do whatever I liked.

I was tired, but there was still plenty of light left since we'd started at dawn. So, I fixed myself some food before heading down to Katari, the little fishing village I'd regularly almost destroyed with that damned boulder.

For such a small village, it certainly was busy. The markets were bustling and there were people everywhere. Selling, trading, and buying. I noted there were a fair few statues and artworks depicting the divinities throughout the village, and not just the six that were revered back in Deorum. Gods and goddesses linked to the sea were especially popular here, such as Neselia; Goddess of the tides and wife of Rhamus, the god that reigned over every sea creature and sea divinity. There was Xodella; Goddess of sea monsters, Zulphine; an ancient sea goddess, mother of all the fish in the ocean, Omlo; the god who protected sailors, fishermen, and anyone else travelling by sea, among others.

It was Rhamus's statue I was currently standing in front of. I looked up at the man, stood in the centre of a fountain, depicted with the upper body of a beautiful man, the lower body of a fish and his infamous trident in hand. The trident was said to have been forged by Dhedros, the same man, *God*, who had forged weapons for me. I still couldn't quite wrap my head around that. I took a seat on the fountain edge, staring back out at the busy village.

"You don't belong here." I looked over to see Amory leaning against a nearby alley wall, blending into the shadows.

"In this village or this realm?"

Her lips twitched at the hint of a smile. "You don't belong anywhere. You are not the same as everyone else."

I raised my eyebrows. "Trust me, I'm pretty ordinary."

She rolled her eyes. "You are a child who does not know half of what is meant for you."

"I'm not really a big believer in the whole destiny thing."

This time, she smirked. "When we are young, we call it destiny. When we are older, or perhaps wiser, we call it fate."

I looked at her. "What fate exactly are you talking about?"

"That remains to be seen," she said, pushing off of the wall.

I sighed. "Why must everyone speak in riddles?"

"Perhaps it is not everyone else that is the problem. Perhaps it is you?" Turning, she disappeared back into the shadows. I frowned. What was her problem?

I stood, trying to shake off the strange interaction, and instead wandered through the markets, talking to the locals, and admiring their crafts. Before

I knew it, the sun was setting. I had a long walk ahead of me, so I left the village and headed back to my room.

The next day, Moira once again locked me in the cage and played music that aggravated both me and the mortiss. I went through the motions of avoiding the creature; it didn't get any less scary when I was made to do it again on the third day, or the fourth, or the fifth.

Training with the staffs always followed the deathly dance. Dhedros's beautifully crafted weapons, laid out close by but unused, were a continuous tease. Close, but just out of reach. After a week of the same routine, Moira had apparently decided to change things up.

"You've spent the last seven days countering the serpens, reacting to it and then using that to block and react to me. Now I want you to be the serpens. I want you to mimic it."

I frowned. "And how will that help?"

"Less asking, more doing." She chided, and I rolled my eyes. They brought the serpens out, but this time no cage appeared around me. I raised my eyebrows and carefully removed the lid, taking a few steps back. The signature hiss I'd come to recognise as a dislike of being disturbed sounded as it poked its head out.

Music played as usual, only this was a different tune. It was melodic and soothing. Calm. I glanced at Moira, then back at the creature. It wasn't showing any of its usual signs of aggression. If anything, it appeared content, slowly swaying in time with the music.

"Um Moira? You really want me to mimic... that?"

She nodded. "Yep."

I sighed and watched, observing how it moved, how its entire body worked at once. It wasn't like a mortal that could move their arms without moving their legs; this creature relied on every muscle.

I felt ridiculous, but I knew by now that Moira would stay here all day until I did what she asked. So I took a breath and focused, my ears tuning in to the music and my eyes locking onto the mortiss. Mimicking its movements as best as I could, I ignored Moira. I was sure if I glanced over, I'd see her smirking or silently chuckling. I would be if the roles were reversed.

Much like the first time, this felt like a dance. A very different one, but a dance nonetheless. The music stopped, and the serpens returned to its basket. I put the lid back on out of habit and glanced at Moira. She was holding out a staff. I walked over and took it.

"Attack me."

I raised my eyebrows. "But you haven't taught me any offensive moves yet?"

"Have you not been watching me? Have you not been countering everything I do? Reverse what you have been doing. Offence and Defence are symbiotic. They are one and the same. You can take what you know and apply it to either. Attack."

I bit my lip and made to strike her. She blocked it easily.

"Again," she said, so I did. I struck at her repeatedly, and she repeatedly blocked them. Eventually, we built up a rhythm. We were both moving as we struck and parried, as we attacked and defended. I was sweating by the time she called it a day.

The next week was much like the first. The first half of my days spent mimicking the mortiss and attacking Moira, the second half exploring the nearby villages. Sometimes the others joined me, never Amory, though. When I'd asked the others about her, they'd shrugged and said that it was just how Amory was. Whatever that meant.

On the fifteenth day, I walked in and found Moira with lightweight armour on. I breathed in.

"Does this mean I am finally allowed to use the weapons you so *rudely* had Dhedros make, dangle in front of me, and then deny me?"

She chuckled a bit and nodded. "Yes."

"Finally!" I exclaimed, walking over to my armour. I had taken to wearing my tunicam for my training. Firstly, because I was hoping if the damned serpens bit me, it would provide a modicum of protection, and secondly because I was hoping for this opportunity.

Once I'd dressed appropriately, I met Moira at the weapons table.

"Where do we start?"

"We will start with your standard sword." She nodded and walked back to the centre of the arena. I slowly picked up my shiny new sword, testing the weight and balance of it in my hand. Moira instructed me on how to hold it and how to stand. I struggled a little more than I'd thought I would, having to adjust to wearing armour. All the fighting thus far had been without it, and whilst it wasn't too heavy, I was unaccustomed to the added weight.

We started slowly, with Moira letting me adjust to my new outfit, whilst also showing me some simple manoeuvres.

We ran through those manoeuvres and combinations on repeat until I had them perfected. Then she would add in more complex things. I found I really enjoyed it. Having spent so much time analysing that damned serpens, I realised Moira had been right. I anticipated outcomes far easier than I would have thought.

We spent a week on long swords, then a week on short swords; Moira's weapon of choice. She explained to me she didn't see them as two separate weapons, and that I should wield them as one. It took me a while to grasp that concept, but I was gaining more confidence as we progressed.

My body now woke me at dawn without quarrel. I had a good routine and was often excited about what I might learn next, but when I met Moira at the end of our short sword week, the weaponry and my armour were nowhere to be seen. Neither was the mortiss or the cage.

"No training today?"

"You'll be training, just not with me. I'll take you to your next session, but I just wanted to speak to you first."

"Sure?"

"I can see you enjoy our training. You enjoy fighting with steel, as do I, and you have picked it up quickly. You should be proud of that, of the work you've put it in. You enjoy the artform and it shows, but facing me differs greatly from facing an opponent in a proper battle. One that bleeds. One that dies. One that will make *you* bleed." She wasn't smiling like usual. She was looking at me seriously.

"If you are going to use weapons like these, you need to be prepared to wield them well and win. The cost of failing is steep."

I swallowed and nodded. "I know."

She nodded back; her smile returning. "Good. Now let's go. Sig is no doubt waiting."

"Should I be scared?" I asked, as we walked to the where grass became thick forest that encircled the compound.

She grinned. "I'm sure you'll be fine. Sig is tough, but he loves a laugh as much as the next person. Whatever work you do with him will be rewarding." She came to a halt, so I stopped as well. We were at the edge of the forest that bordered the compound.

"What now?"

"I was instructed to walk you here, then leave. Have fun." She winked and walked away. I frowned, turning back to the forest, just in time for something small, round, and hard, to come flying out, hitting me right in the forehead.

"Shit!" I cursed, rubbing my forehead.

CHAPTER FORTY-EIGHT

"THAT WAS TOO SLOW. I expected better from you, Adira," Sig said, jumping out of the tree he had apparently been hiding in, landing in front of me.

"Was that necessary?" I frowned at him. "What were you even doing up there?"

"Waiting for you. You need to be prepared for surprise attacks at all times." He glanced around dramatically, as if he were assessing threats.

I rolled my eyes. "From an acorn?" I said, glancing down at the projectile in question.

"From anything. Are you ready for the best training session yet?"

I smiled a bit. "Depends on what it is."

He reached into his pocket and pulled out another acorn. I glared at him, but it didn't stop him from hurling it at me. This time I ducked.

"Sig!"

"Still slow. Alright, for your first task, you're going to go for a walk through the forest."

I raised my eyebrows. "A walk through the forest?"

He nodded. "Yes. I will follow you, unseen, and I will throw these." He pulled another acorn from his pocket. *How many did he have in there?* "Your job is to not get hit."

"And what exactly is this supposed to improve?"

He raised his eyebrows. "Did the others explain their methods to you beforehand?"

"No, but—"

"No buts. Off you go. I'll give you a head start."

I sighed and trudged into the forest, eventually coming to a small clearing. These unorthodox training sessions were going to be the death of me. I walked for a while, listening carefully. My senses were one thing I was confident about, something Butcher had me honing from the minute she took us in.

I had exceptionally good hearing, which came in handy when spying. I had to admit, though, with the rustling leaves, the wind, the birds, and wildlife, it was difficult to pinpoint what didn't belong.

Sig was better at being quiet than I was at hearing things apparently, because I didn't hear the acorn he'd hurled, until it hit me in the back of the head. Spinning around, I scanned the forest, before looking up to see if he was hiding in the trees again.

I didn't see or hear anything until another acorn hit me in the back of the head. Groaning and turning around, I crouched lower, scanning my surroundings again. I could use the trees for cover, but he moved so inhumanly fast that I doubted I'd remain sheltered for long. Listening carefully, I heard a subtle *whoosh* of air to my left. I raised my arm and blocked the acorn.

"Ha!" I grinned, but my victory was short-lived, as more and more acorns pelted me. One after another, after another. I tried to deflect all of them but ended up just waving my arms around like a madwoman before hiding behind the closest tree. Even then, he *still* somehow hit me. I groaned.

"I surrender! This is going nowhere!"

He chuckled, and I peaked out from my hiding place to see him standing in the clearing. I sighed and stepped out.

"I suppose you enjoyed that?"

"Immensely."

"Glad to be a source of entertainment for you, but I cannot see how this will help."

"Hand to hand combat is about many things and requires many skills. Like... FAST REFLEXES!" He shouted as he threw another acorn at me. I caught this one, having been expecting it by now, and gave him a pointed look. He grinned.

"See? You're already improving."

I rolled my eyes. "So that's what we're going to do today? Throw acorns?"

"Yep. Start walking." I stared at him for a minute before groaning and setting off again, muttering a curse under my breath.

"I heard that!" He called, and I rolled my eyes.

We must have spent hours walking through the forest. I had no idea how he was remaining so quiet, or changing locations so fast, but safe to say by the time he finally called our session for the day, my skin was peppered with little red marks.

The next day, I met him back at the edge of the forest, and he walked me to the first clearing I'd come across. Thankfully, there were no acorns falling out of his pockets this time.

"I trust I made my point about reflexes well enough yesterday?"

I glared at him. "I actually have some bruises."

He smirked. "Well, you may have a few more tomorrow." He walked over and pulled out a long, thin piece of black fabric from his pocket.

"A blindfold?" I said, already not liking where this was going.

He nodded. "Turn around."

I sighed, knowing there was no point in arguing, so I did as he said and let him fasten the blindfold around eyes. He turned me back to face him.

"Can you see?"

"No." I answered before something small and round hit me in the face. By now I was intimately acquainted with the feel of an acorn, even blindfolded. "Ow." I winced. "What was that for?"

"Just checking you weren't lying."

I took a deep, calming breath. This man was infuriating. "What now?" I hesitantly asked.

"Now you stop the acorns from hitting you. This time you will be still, able to better concentrate on what you are hearing."

"Sig, I could barely block them when I *could* see."

"Then I suggest you learn fast," he said as another acorn hit me in the face. I groaned and heard him chuckle, taking a few steps back, before going silent. I couldn't hear his footsteps or his breathing. There was no sign of him. I took a breath and focused on what I *could* hear, attempting to block out the sounds I didn't need to be listening for.

Acorn after acorn hit me. Again and again. They were so small, I rarely heard them coming until they were right next to me and by that point, it was too late. Sig called the session, and we met the next day to do it all over again.

For days, I stood blindfolded in that clearing, getting pummelled by acorns. Slowly though, I improved. I realised I was listening to the wrong things. The acorns were too small to make much noise at all until they were close enough to hit me, making it a waste of time listening for the sound of the acorn. I should have been listening for the moment before they were being thrown. Sig was trying to be as quiet as possible, so I listened for the lack of sound. I listened for the gaps, and I found them.

When I noticed an unnatural quiet coming from a particular direction, I could determine roughly where the acorn would come from. Right before throwing them, Sig would make some noise. Whether it was the rustle of a tree branch or the sound of his clothing snagging as he aimed, there was always some indicator. Slowly but surely, I anticipated his throws and could move out of the way. I was still a large target, and Sig hit me more times than he didn't, but dodging eventually turned into blocking. It wasn't a perfect success rate, but it was a Hek of a lot better than I'd have thought possible.

At the end of the week and a half, I turned away to let Sig blindfold me as usual, but he stopped me.

"Now the real hard work begins." He spun me back to face him and walked me through a few manoeuvres. He explained that hand to hand combat was about anticipating your opponent's movements, and quickly at that, before using your height, weight, and speed, to counter or avoid them.

"There is no weapon here to protect you from a blow like there is with sword fighting. There is no time to prepare like there is in a strategic battle.

Hand to hand combat is about agility, speed, and strength. Troja has built up your muscle and your endurance. Moira has taught you to expect manoeuvres and counter them with weapons. Put those skills together, along with the reflex training you have been doing. Use all of what you already know and use your instincts," he said, taking out the blindfold, much to my dismay.

"I thought we were done with the acorn throwing?" I practically pouted.

"We are. No more dodging acorns, now you dodge me."

"What? You want me to block you whilst *blindfolded?*"

"And Ehsys said you weren't very bright. Look at you figuring things out." He smirked.

I glared at him. Ignoring the fact that Ehsys had told him I was dumb.

"I fail to see how this is a fair fight," I said as I let him blindfold me.

"It isn't. Newsflash Adira, the real world isn't fair."

I gasped as his fist made contact with my stomach. Not too painful, but I hadn't been expecting it.

"Divinities Sig!"

"The divine will not help you Adira," he said, as he swept my feet out from under me and I went down. Groaning, I stood. "Only you can get yourself out of this situation."

"Sig!"

This time, he swung for my face. I heard him move and felt the air shift as he did. Reaching up in anger, I blocked his fist with my arm. I breathed in sharply, preparing for his blow to still glance off my cheek, but it didn't. He lowered his hand.

"Good," he said, "use that anger, use whatever you need to, but don't let it use you. Focus Adira. You have the skills. Show me."

I took a steadying breath and did what he said. I took up a defensive stance that he had shown me and focused on my available senses. Hearing and Touch were my best defences. Since I couldn't see, taste, or smell him, I really didn't *want* to do the last two anyway, I had to either hear him coming or *feel* it. By either intuition or the slight changes in the air.

I spent the next week getting my ass handed to me daily. It was impossible for someone as inexperienced a fighter as I was to counter Sig's attacks, let alone blindfolded. But no matter how much I complained, Sig insisted I could do it, insisting that I was getting better and would have it soon. Even if I didn't, he said it was his month to train me and we'd keep doing this, regardless. *Jerk.*

I'd taken to practising after our sessions had ended. I would remain in the clearing, take the blindfold off, and practice the manoeuvres that Sig would teach me at the start of every session, before he temporarily stripped me of my sight. If I could get them to be second nature, then I could focus solely on sensing him.

Towards the end of the third week, it was like something just clicked. I'd grown confident in my movements; knowing how to block or counter, so I just had to figure out where Sig was going to attack from. He kept his attacks fairly simple for me, only using a certain number of combinations. Soon I could recognise the sounds and signs right before he would attack, and could therefore respond accordingly.

On day twenty-two, Sig took the blindfold out of his pocket and burned it. I raised my eyebrows. I'd come to realise he had a flair for dramatics.

"You don't need this as a tool anymore." He grinned. "Now's your chance to face me head on." He made a gesture with his hands, daring me to attack. "Let's see if you've learnt anything."

I grinned. I'd been waiting for a chance to fight unhindered for three weeks. He didn't need to tell me twice. I launched myself at him, using one of the offensive techniques he had shown me, and was promptly thrown onto the ground for my efforts. I groaned and closed my eyes.

"Shit."

He chuckled and held out his hand. I opened my eyes and looked at him.

"That was not a move you've shown me or used on me before."

He raised his eyebrows. "Do you think you will only ever face opponents with fighting styles you already know?"

I sighed. "No, but you know mine." I took his hand and let him pull me up.

"You were complacent. You were relying on your memory and assumptions to tell you how I was going to come at you. Instead of using what you've just learned. Anticipate what I am going to do, Adira." He took up a fighting stance. "Or perhaps you need some more sessions with the blindfold?" He smirked.

I came at him again; he was prepared and made to throw me down again, but this time I'd taken his advice and watched him closely. I saw his body turn slightly, saw his right arm tense, and I knew he was going to attack from that side. Ducking under his punch, I landed my own on his stomach.

Fates, it was as hard as a rock. Despite his lean frame, the man was clearly concealing some secret abs under that shirt. I'd still knocked him back a few steps, though. He smirked and nodded.

"Again."

So we went again, and again. By the end of the month, I felt like a well-oiled machine. I could anticipate Sig's movements easily now. He still got the better of me plenty of times, but mostly, I could counter his attacks. If I didn't know how to, I could switch to defence and fend him off.

Sig clapped me on the back as we walked back to our quarters.

"Not bad for a mortal."

I rolled my eyes. "Aren't *you* supposedly mortal?"

He grinned. "Sort of."

That's when I realised I hadn't seen him use any kind of ability like Troja's wings or Moira's illusions.

"Hey, what's your special ability?"

"My what?" He raised his eyebrows.

"Troja has crazy wings, Moira has insane illusions, I refuse to believe you and Amory don't also have some super cool powers too."

He chuckled, taking a step to the left and disappearing in front of my eyes. I gasped, staring at the spot where he'd been standing mere seconds before.

"Holy shi—" A tap on my shoulder from behind had me whirling around, only to find Sig standing there smirking.

"How did you...?" My eyes widened. "That's how you stayed so quiet when you were throwing acorns at me! No wonder I couldn't hear you moving positions. I *knew* you shouldn't have been able to change locations that quickly!"

He shrugged and disappeared again. This time he reappeared, leaning against the wall a good ten yards away from us, with a smirk on his face.

"How are you doing that?" I couldn't help but smile a bit as I walked over.

He chuckled. "I can move through what I guess you could call space and matter?"

"So you can just appear anywhere?"

"Sort of. I need to have been there before or at the very least have seen it to envision where I want to go, and there are limitations. It takes a lot of energy to go long distances."

"That is so cool," I said, and he smiled, "but how? Troja said you weren't divinities, so what are you?"

"We are like you."

"Regular mortals can't do anything like that, not even Pures can. I've seen no one with Giftings or Specialties like that. Like any of yours."

He shrugged. "Come on, Moira wants to have a family dinner tonight," he said, changing the subject and leading me to a dining hall. Troja and Moira were waiting for us.

"Is Amory joining us?" Sig asked as he sat down and immediately took a big swig of the ale that was waiting for him. I held in a chuckle.

"No, you know what she's like." Moira answered, and Sig nodded.

From what I gathered, Amory liked her solitude. The other three all lived here in the compound, but Amory had her own home on the outskirts of the forest, away from everyone else. I was not looking forward to our training tomorrow, especially given our interaction in the fishing village.

"In that case, let's dig in," Sig said, doing just that.

I glanced around at my three trainers. They were very different off the training field, but also the same. They had a bond I'd never really seen. They were a close-knit unit, even Amory. I couldn't imagine the amount of trust they had in one another. That wasn't entirely true. Their friendships reminded me of Tarryn, Hamish, and even Cali. Albeit ours was newer, but... in a perfect world, maybe we'd have ended up like these four.

"Something on your mind, Adira?" Troja asked quietly from his seat beside me. I smiled a bit. He was by far the most observant of the three, even off duty. I shook my head.

"Nope. Just admiring the food." I smiled and began eating. He gave me a knowing look, before smiling a bit and digging in as well.

We ate, drank and laughed. I felt free to just relax and enjoy myself for the first time in I didn't even know how long. Safe and included with friends surrounding me. I pushed down the guilt I felt at enjoying myself when Sierra was still stuck back home with Butcher, and just let myself have this night and this memory.

I woke the next morning, grateful I hadn't drunk as much as that first night with Sig and Troja. I was clearheaded as I made my way to Amory's home. She hadn't met me at my room. I stopped by the arena, but she wasn't there either. Her home was my only other guess.

Knocking on the door of the small cottage, I waited. No answer. Biting my lip, I knocked again.

"Amory? It's Adira. I'm here for our training?"

Still no answer. I looked around. Maybe there was a back door? I walked around the side. There was a back porch of sorts, but no yard, and she wasn't sitting outside. I frowned slightly. Could she have forgotten and just gone somewhere else? I walked up the steps, peeking in a window.

"I've shot trespassers who weren't as close as you are now." I spun to find Amory standing at the edge of the forest, bow and arrow in hand.

"Sorry, I didn't mean to snoop. I knocked, but you didn't answer, so I thought you were maybe around the back or just couldn't hear me from wherever you were."

She walked over and opened her back door.

"I'm not sure what etiquette is like in your realm, but here, if someone doesn't answer a door, that generally means they aren't home or don't wish to be disturbed." She walked inside, letting the door swing shut in my face. I pressed my lips together.

"Right, sorry. I am here for our training!" I waited for a response but didn't get one. Rubbing the back of my head, I glanced around, unsure what to do next. I made my way back down the steps with a sigh. The *click* of a door opening sounded. Glancing over my shoulder, I found Amory standing in her doorway, arms crossed.

"What are you expecting to be trained in?"

My eyes widened slightly. "Um, whatever you want to teach me? The others said—"

"I didn't ask what the others said. If you do not know what you are to learn, then why should I teach you anything at all?"

I frowned slightly. "I think we may have gotten off on the wrong foot." I tried, she scoffed.

"The wrong foot? You are nothing but a child playing games here. What are you going to do with these newfound skills? With the others' teachings. Will you use them? Or will you continue to cower in the shadows like you have thus far?"

My eyes widened. "Excuse me? I don't cower in the shadows."

"Oh, you don't?" She said, walking down the steps and approaching me. She was really getting on my nerves.

"No," I said firmly, "I don't."

"I think you do. I think you want these skills for selfish reasons. I don't think you intend to use them for anything worthy."

"You know nothing about me," I said, trying not to let my anger show. The small smirk on her face told me I hadn't succeeded.

"Go home Adira. You are wasting our time here." With that, she turned and walked back into her house, closing the door once again. I stared at it in shock. I don't care what I did to piss her off so much. Who does she think she is? I was no coward.

I stomped home angrily, practically running into Dhedros on my way. I breathed in, quickly stepping back.

"Sorry! I didn't mean to..." I trailed off. How does one apologise to a divine being? He smiled a bit, and it shocked me. I hadn't really seen him smile before.

"No trouble. You look a little... agitated?" He chose his words carefully. My eyes widened slightly.

"Oh um, just a slight disagreement with Amory. I'm sure it will work itself out."

He chuckled a bit. He truly was average looking for a god. I felt bad for even thinking it, but he was. He was known for it. Those physical differences were supposedly the reason he was outcast by his parents and many of the other divinities.

"I'm assuming she is hesitant to train you?"

"How did you know that?"

He nodded for me to walk with him. I could hardly refuse a god, even if it meant trying very hard not to stare at his leg as he limped along.

"Amory is stubborn. Once she has made up her mind, it is difficult to change it."

I sighed. "So I won't be able to convince her to train me?"

"I said difficult, not impossible."

"If she doesn't train me. I don't know if I'll be able to leave here, having passed my Testing."

"Probably not."

I frowned slightly.

"You are not very good at consoling people, are you?" I regretted the words as soon as they came out. Hek Adira, just piss everyone off, why don't you? Much to my surprise, he didn't smite me. Instead, he let out a hearty laugh as he glanced at me.

"Ah. I should apologise for my behaviour when we first met. I was in a bit of a mood that week."

I didn't know what to say. "No need to apologise. We all have bad days."

He smiled. "I suppose we do. Do you know much about my history?"

I bit my lip as we sat down on a stone bench. "I know a little. I know you are the God of Forgery. That you are the son of Dykos and Khollios," The Goddess of Death and the God of Punishment, "and that you are married to Ceari?"

He grunted at the mention of his wife, the Goddess of all Monsters.

"Yes, that is all true. I am also responsible for teaching mortals how to work a flame and for teaching art to many of them."

I hadn't known that, and wasn't sure why it surprised me so much. Talking to him now, he seemed kind and peaceful. Very at odds with the man, the *god*, I'd met at the beginning of all this.

"Why doesn't Amory want to teach you?" He asked, reeling my wandering thoughts back in.

"She says I am a coward, and that I won't use it for good." I sighed.

"Are you a coward?"

"No." I frowned.

"Are you afraid of nothing, then?"

"What? Of course I am afraid of things. That doesn't make me a coward."

"What do you intend to use these skills for?"

"She is forgetting that I did not *choose* to learn these things? I actually had no choice."

"So because you did not choose this, that means you do not have to use them for something worthwhile?"

"What am I *supposed* to do with them? I'm not sure why this is even part of my Testing. I am grateful, but I am not a warrior. I am not needed as one back home. Not like The Four are here."

"Are you not needed, or perhaps simply not willing to be?"

I looked at him in confusion. "What?"

He smiled a bit. "When you spend your life in the shadows, you do an excellent job of avoiding scenarios where people may need you. Where people might want to rely on you."

"I did not choose to live my life in the shadows. I have chosen very few things for myself."

"Then perhaps that is what Amory means, when she calls you a coward."

I thought about what he was saying. I suppose, to some, I might seem like a coward. Spies were often thought of as cowards for hiding and fighting with information, rather than fists. But I'd spent my life fighting for survival. I have done things I am not proud of, and maybe I shut myself off from everyone else's problems, in favour of protecting Sierra, but I didn't regret that. She was my responsibility.

"I do not lack courage. I just have other responsibilities."

He smiled a bit. "Amory is stubborn and brash, but she is formidable at her craft. You could learn a great deal from her. My advice? Don't give up just yet. Show her you are worth teaching."

I sighed, and he chuckled.

"Or ignore me completely. What do I know anyway? I'm just an old blacksmith." He winked and stood, leaving back the way we had come. I watched him go and mentally groaned to myself. He was most likely right. That was annoying. I'd heed his advice, but I'd give myself today to be annoyed about it. Tomorrow I would try again.

CHAPTER FORTY-NINE

TRY I DID. EVERY day for a week, I knocked on her door and every day she either ignored me or opened the door, only to close it in my face. Today was no different. I didn't even bother knocking this time, I just sat down outside her house and continued reading a book that Moira had leant me.

I eventually laid back and closed my eyes, enjoying the sun. That was until something blocked it. I opened my eyes to find Amory standing over me with her hands on her hips.

"Follow me." Without waiting, she turned and walked away at a brisk pace. My eyes widened, but I wasn't about to argue. I fumbled to my feet, leaving the book behind, I'd grab it later. I stayed quiet, not wanting to open my mouth and say something that inevitably made her change her mind. She remained silent as we walked, leading us down a path and into the forest.

I hadn't been this deep before and soon enough I heard the telltale sound of rushing water. We eventually came to a stop in front of what looked like a thick wall of vines, reminding me of the castle tunnel's exit into town. Amory parted them and stepped through.

I followed, finding a beautiful waterfall cascading down the side of a huge rock and into a stream. The surrounding greenery was practically walls of vines and flowers. They completely enveloped the hidden oasis.

"Get in the water."

I raised my eyebrows. "I'm sorry?"

"Your sorry is worthless here. Get into the water."

I took a breath and stripped down to my underclothes before wading into the water. I turned, looking at her.

"Now what?"

"Now you go through the waterfall."

I glanced over at it. "Why exactly?"

"Stop asking so many questions. You either do it or I turn around and go home."

I withheld my groan and made my way over to the wall of water, closing my eyes, and walking through it. Once I could no longer feel the water hitting my skin, I opened my eyes, realising everything had gone completely silent.

I breathed in and looked around. I was in a cave. There was nothing other than cave wall, water, and stuck to the roof of the cave were beautiful, glowing bugs? They covered the ceiling, illuminating the cave with their soft glow.

There was not a single sound, though. I couldn't even hear the water rushing anymore. Even as I watched the water fall, it made no sound. I felt as if something had trapped me in some sort of bubble that sound could not penetrate. I turned to walk back through the water, but a voice stopped me, Amory's voice. Only it wasn't coming from inside the cave, or from outside it; it was in my head.

Don't come back out.

I breathed in.

"How?" I said aloud.

That isn't relevant. You are here to learn. Are you not?

I bit my lip and nodded, before realising she couldn't see me.

I may not see you, but I know what you are doing.

I tensed.

"You can read my thoughts?"

I can.

"I'd rather you didn't."

Tough.

I groaned and could have sworn I *felt* her smile.

"Okay, go ahead then, teach."

You think too much. I watched you train with the others. For a spy, you have remarkably little focus.

"If you're just going to insult me..."

Then what, you'll leave? Making the last week you spent grovelling at my door all for nothing?

I closed my eyes. "I know how to focus. I'm actually great at it."

No, you were good at it. As soon as Camilla took your sister, she made it personal, and you've been a mess since.

I gritted my teeth. "Stay out of my memories."

Focus and I will.

"Focus on WHAT?!" I said, finally losing my patience.

On nothing.

I frowned, throwing my hands up and startling some of the little glow bugs.

"You want me to focus on nothing? That makes *no* sense!"

It does. You need to learn to clear your mind. You need to learn The Killing Calm.

"The what?"

A state I call The Killing Calm. Allowing you to focus on what needs to be done, rather than letting things like emotions, memories, or feelings get in the way.

No wonder she's so cold all the time. She doesn't have any bloody emotions.

I can assure you I have emotions. I have experienced ten lifetimes more than anything you could even dream of.

I winced, realising she could hear me. I almost apologised but thought better of it. She hadn't exactly been kind to me.

"Okay. So you want me to detach from everything? It's not possible to empty your mind completely."

Not literally, it isn't, but with enough focus and the proper techniques, you can calm yourself and focus on your objective. At least enough so that things that would normally distract or sway you cannot.

"How healthy." I muttered.

If you needed to kill someone you knew and loved, Adira, if you had to kill Sierra, could you do it?

"Of course I couldn't. She is my sister."

What if it meant saving the realm? What if it was everyone or her?

"That's a ridiculous scenario."

If you HAD to kill her, would you let the world burn or would you get the job done?

Pain coursed through me at even the thought of harming Sierra.

So you would let everyone else die?

Could I kill Sierra? I didn't think I could, even to save everyone in Deorum. Did that make me a terrible person?

No. It makes you mortal. That is the first thing to remember.

Amory answered my unspoken questions.

"What, that I am mortal? Trust me, I am *very* aware of that fact."

No. That love is a weapon. It can be wielded for or against you. Love is what's stopping you from being capable of killing your sister. In that case, it would be her or someone else wielding it.

"Can we stop with the whole 'could you kill your sister' thing?"

Okay, say someone else you loved tried to kill you. Would you be able to defend yourself against them if that meant hurting them?

"Why would someone I love try to kill me?"

Existence is chaos. People do crazy things. Stop overthinking it. If it is you or them, who do you choose?

"Well, I don't want to die, so, me?"

Alright, but it's someone you love. Do you think it's likely you might hesitate to hurt or even kill someone you love?

"Yes, I imagine I would hesitate."

Exactly. Pain, anger, love, fear — these emotions can aid you or hinder you. The Killing Calm protects you when it might hinder you. When you need to block that out and not hesitate. Not falter. Not crumble.

As much as I hated what she was saying, I understood her point.

"Then teach me." I could feel her grin. Such a strange thing.

First, we work on your breathing. I want you to go under water and hold your breath for as long as you can.

I raised my eyebrows. "Okay?"

I took a deep breath, closed my eyes and ducked under the water. I probably should have been counting, but I figured Amory would be. When I felt my lungs starving for air, I pushed back up to the surface, but something stopped me. The water above me was solid. I couldn't break through.

I shouted in my mind as I repeatedly banged against the water. I couldn't breathe. I was going to drown. That bitch had lured me here with the promise of training and then trapped me in here. What even happened if you died within The Testing? Would I go insane? Would I die in the real world or would I wake up fine?

Xeria give me strength, even when you're drowning, all you do is overthink. Those are irrelevant things.

Amory's voice pierced through my thoughts at the same time my fist crashed through the water, the liquid becoming, well, liquid, again. I shot upwards, coughing and gasping for air. I put my hands on my knees and bent forward a little as I hyperventilated, trying to feed my starved lungs. It burned my chest and up my throat.

It took a few minutes before I was breathing comfortably again and my heart rate had gone back down to a healthy pace.

Are you done?

"Are you insane?! YOU ALMOST KILLED ME?!"

I did not almost kill you, Adira. You are fine.

"FINE?! THAT'S EASY FOR YOU TO SAY! YOU DIDN'T NEARLY DROWN!"

Calm down Adira.

"No! I won't bloody calm down!" I said, clenching my fist. I was absolutely furious.

Go home. We will try again tomorrow.

I scoffed. Like Hek would I be coming back here tomorrow. I stormed back through the waterfall, as best as one could when wading through chest deep water, and back out of the stream, grabbing my clothes.

I didn't even bother to put them on. I just scooped them up and stormed straight past Amory, who was sitting on a nearby log.

She was crazy. She didn't like me and was apparently determined to kill me to prove it. I shook my head, practically stomping through our living quarters.

"Woah, what happened to you?" Sig asked as he rounded the corner and took in the sight of me.

I must have looked a right mess. Dripping wet, fury written across my features and probably still blue from being unable to breathe for so long.

"Amory."

He grimaced. "Ah, makes sense."

"That bitch."

"Okay, hey, no need for that. Let's get you dried off. You can tell me about it after," he said, walking over. I shook my head.

"She tried to bloody kill me. I'm not about to be polite."

"I mean, look, she's tried to kill all of us at least once or twice? Surely that counts for something. You're really one of us now?" He tried, hopefully. I just stared at him blankly.

"Okay, not helping. I will fetch Moira."

"I don't need Moira. I just need to get out of this Akros forsaken place and back to my home. Back to my real friends and family. This is all just a sadistic joke," I said, walking away, but not before I saw him flinch, a look of sadness filling his eyes. I was too mad to care, as I made my way to the bathing chamber.

Once there, I stripped off completely before sinking into one of the spa baths, pushing past the fear of being trapped underwater again. I wasn't about to let her take away my love of a long hot bath, too. I wasn't sure how long I stayed in there, but my skin was pruned by the time I got out. When I finally exited the chamber, I was surprised to find Dhedros waiting for me. My eyes widened slightly.

"Dhedros, hello?"

He smiled a bit. "You can call me Dhed, you know. Everyone else does."

"I don't know you as well as everyone else."

He shrugged. "Walk with me?"

I nodded slightly, falling into step beside him.

"I'm guessing you ran into Sig?"

"I did."

He nodded.

I sighed. "I didn't mean to be so harsh with him."

"Well, that's something you should speak to him about, but that isn't what I'd like to discuss."

"Oh, then what?"

"You know I am married to Ceari." He stated. It wasn't really a question, but I nodded, anyway.

"Do you know how that marriage came about?"

"Khollios arranged it?"

"That is correct. Do you know why?"

I shook my head. I hadn't really cared about who was married to who or why. Half of them slept around or killed their spouses, anyway.

"Ceari made a wager with Khollios, and she lost. My father, unsurprisingly, enjoys finding particularly creative punishments for those he bests. In this case, he saw a way to kill two birds with one stone in marrying me off to her. Claiming, since she loved her monsters so much, surely loving an ugly, deformed, beast such as me should be no problem."

My eyes widened."You're not.."

He chuckled softly. "It's alright Adira, you don't need to lie to me. I know full well what I look like and who I am. For a time, I hated that about myself, but it just made me focus on other things. Prove myself in other ways."

I bit my lip. "Good for you then, I guess?"

He smiled. "Ceari truly is one of the most beautiful beings I have ever seen. Unfortunately for my father, being married to me didn't have the desired effect he intended it to. She cared for me, but she did not love me, and she did not see a forced union as a true marriage, meaning she had no trouble finding other lovers to meet her needs. She could never quite get past the fact that I was the son of the god she despised."

I grimaced. I had read briefly about Ceari's infidelity.

"I'm sorry," I said, unsure of what else to say.

He shook his head. "I was under no illusion she would be happy with just me. My point is, once I got over what everyone else thought of me, once I started doing things for me, I became my true self. I honed my craft and became the best blacksmith in all the realms. The divinities that mocked me, now beg to have something made by me."

I nodded a bit. "That's great and all, truly. I'm just not sure why you are telling me this."

He smiled a bit and shrugged. "My story had a good ending. Not everyone is so lucky."

I looked at him.

"Amory had a more unconventional upbringing than the other warriors. Closer to your own, actually. Her parents were killed when she was very young, in front of her. An awful man took her in. For a long time, all she knew was pain, torment and suffering."

I breathed in. "I don't care what kind of sob story she has, it doesn't excuse what she did."

"I'm not excusing her actions. I am simply trying to give you some perspective. Even when Amory was free from the man, after that kind of manipulation and abuse from such a young age, for such a long time, it took her an age to find even a glimmer of happiness."

I sighed. I really didn't want to be feeling bad for Amory, of all people.

"What does that have to do with me?"

"Well, aside from the minor similarities between your upbringings, it explains a lot about why Amory is the way she is. Left alone for extended periods of time, and shown nothing but evil, she had no choice but to embrace the dark parts of herself. She saves it for the battlefield these days, but it is still a huge part of who she is. She is stubborn and brash, she is harsh and can be cruel, but she is also fiercely protective and incredibly smart. She has seen things even I shudder at the thought of."

It was hard to believe a god could be afraid of something a mortal experienced, but I didn't think he was lying to me.

"The point I am trying to make is, Amory's methods may be unorthodox, but she would not put you through something she didn't know you could handle. That she is pushing you so hard means she sees potential in you. If you no longer wish to train with her, then don't. But, if you'll forgive me for my brashness, it is my opinion that to do so, to deny yourself her teachings, would be extremely foolish of you."

I rubbed my face. "She nearly drowned me today."

"Maybe you should ask her why?"

"Is there a reason that justifies it?"

"Are you still breathing?"

"Yes, but that is besides the point."

"What is the point?" He glanced at me.

"It's the principle of the thing. You shouldn't drown people, for crying out loud."

He smiled a little. "But you didn't drown, and Amory also wasn't the only one involved."

I frowned. "What do you mean?"

"How do you think she trapped you beneath the surface?"

"I assumed it was a part of whatever Amory's abilities are?" He shook his head.

"Amory's gift is a sixth sense, if you will. It is an entirely communicative ability. She can read your thoughts and speak to you with her own. She can project her thoughts thousands of miles away and she can do the same with her real voice. Amory can influence sound. But she cannot change objects, she cannot make them go against their natural form."

"But neither can any of the others, as far as I know. Do they have multiple abilities?"

"The ability used did not make the water solidify, it just made you think it did."

I breathed in. "It was an illusion." I looked at him, and he nodded, confirming it had been Moira to help Amory.

"Son of a—" I stopped myself, even I wasn't brave enough to curse in front of a god.

He chuckled, realising we'd come to a stop in front of my room.

"My point is, you clearly don't trust Amory but you do trust Moira, correct?"

I frowned. "Well, I *did.*"

He gave me a look, and I sighed.

"Fine, yes. I trust her."

"Then if you can't trust that Amory will not let you truly be harmed, trust that Moira won't. She wouldn't have assisted Amory if she thought it could really hurt you."

I groaned slightly.

"Get some rest. Both Amory and Moira will be waiting for you back at the waterfall tomorrow, should you choose to meet them," he said and walked away.

"Dhed!" I called out, the shortened, casual version of his name tasted strange to my tongue. He turned.

"... Thank you."

He smiled and dipped his head, before continuing off to wherever he was going.

I sighed and entered my room, practically flopping onto my bed. I'd have to find Sig and apologise for my outburst. It could wait until tomorrow though, as could my decision regarding Amory's training. I closed my eyes and eventually drifted off to sleep.

CHAPTER FIFTY

I STOPPED BY SIG'S room first thing the next day, but he wasn't there. I searched for some time before finally giving up. My apology would have to wait until after the training session I'd begrudgingly convinced myself to attend.

I made my way to the waterfall, and as Dhed had said, both Amory and Moira were waiting for me. I crossed my arms. Amory looked bored and Moira smiled a little.

"Glad you made it," Moira said.

"That makes one of us." I quipped back.

"We would never have let you actually drown, Adira." She reassured me.

"Although, given her response, I'm thinking maybe we should have." Amory commented, and I clenched my fist.

Moira preemptively stepped between us.

"Hold your horses. Just give Amory a chance to explain? And Amory," she said, glancing at her, "stop being an ass."

Amory shrugged, and I took a deep breath before nodding.

"Fine. Go ahead."

Amory looked like she'd rather do anything but.

"There were two reasons I kept you under that long. First, to prove that you could last longer than you thought. Despite your dramatic ravings about drowning, you *didn't* drown. You stayed under a good minute longer than you thought you could."

I refused to acknowledge she was right.

"Second," she continued, knowing I wasn't about to respond, "to show you how much control you are giving your thoughts and emotions over you. You panicked and started thinking about nonsense."

I frowned. "I thought I was going to die. What did you expect me to do?"

"I *expected* you to do exactly what you did."

I threw my hands up in exasperation, but she fixed me with a look that said she wasn't done.

"What I am *saying* is that there was another option. If you had been calmer, if we had equipped you with the right tools, you could have tried to see if there was a point in the barrier that wasn't solid. You could have looked around for another way out or for a tool that could have helped you break through. That is what I am trying to teach you. I am sorry if you felt my methods to be too extreme, but battle is extreme. Death is extreme. Extreme situations call for extreme measures."

I wasn't sure what I was more mad at. Her answer, or that I knew she was right. I had panicked, and I had been completely useless. I sighed and nodded slightly.

"Teach me."

"It involves getting back into the water."

I looked at Moira, who nodded. "We aren't about to let you drown, Adira. Trust us."

"You, I trust," I said, glancing at Amory, "her not so much."

She grinned in response. "Even better. It will be more of a challenge for you then."

I sighed and stripped down, getting back into the water.

For the next week, the three of us met back at the waterfall, and proceeded to fake drown me. Amory would speak inside my mind, giving me guidance or ways to calm my thoughts, whilst Moira kept me trapped underwater. When they thought I was becoming too comfortable with the scenario, they would change it up.

Some kind of sea creature attacked me, and I had to beat it or escape. They pulled me along the stream, about to go over the edge of the waterfall, unless I found a way out of it. They trapped my leg underwater so I couldn't reach the surface to break it. Countless scenarios to ensure I could calm myself under any circumstances.

We continued on like that until it became easier and easier for me to slip into what Amory called her 'Killing Calm' and focus on the problems in front of me. As a bonus, I could now hold my breath underwater for an *insane* amount of time.

When I went to meet Amory and Moira back at the waterfall for our next session, only Amory was there, and she was holding my bow and arrows, crafted by Dhedros.

"Are we going hunting?"

"We are. It's time you put your new skills to the test."

I wasn't about to complain. I happily took the bow and accompanying arrows. She then handed me a quiver. I gratefully secured it on my back and placed the arrows in it, slinging the bow across my shoulder.

"You've handled a bow and arrow before," she said, more of a statement than a question, but I answered anyway.

"Yes, it was the only weapon I was allowed to learn, just in case I needed to eliminate someone while on assignment." Thankfully, I hadn't had to use my archery skills for that scenario. "My friend Raf occasionally let me hunt with him in the woods near Kendelen." I smiled sadly at the memory.

"Let's see what you've got, then." She walked into the forest and I followed. I'd thought we'd be hunting for rabbits and foxes, maybe even a deer or two. But no, apparently our prey was the mythical creature kind. The 'monsters from bedtime stories' kind. I had never seen so many vile looking things in my life.

I also, apparently, wasn't allowed to return home at the end of the day. No, this was a proper track and hunt situation. We hunted for our food and fashioned supplies from what we could find. Amory had me working on close and long range archery and I actually enjoyed it, present company and hideous monsters aside. I hadn't even realised a month had passed until Amory nudged me awake and announced that it was time to return home.

We made our way back in companionable silence. Certainly a drastic change from when we first met. When we arrived, the other three were waiting for us with smiles on their faces.

"Welcome back, strangers," Sig said, embracing us both. "Phew, you two stink."

I laughed and hugged back. "There is no soap in the forest."

He smiled. "Go get cleaned up, then we celebrate the fact that Amory didn't kill Adira!" I shot him a glare and Amory just smirked a little.

Troja nodded to me as he followed Sig, no doubt to source some liquor and food. Amory headed back to her cottage, and Moira walked with me to my room.

"How was your hunt?"

I nodded. "Different, to say the least."

She chuckled a bit. "I can only imagine."

I smiled. "You don't need to escort me, you know?"

She smiled back. "I know, I just wanted to give you a heads up."

I raised my eyebrows. "A heads up about what?"

"Tonight we celebrate. Tomorrow we all leave."

My eyes widened slightly. "I passed?"

She shook her head a little. "No, all of us will leave, including you."

"What do you mean? Where are we going then?"

"We're going to put all of your training into practice. You'll join us in what we usually do. Travel around fighting beasts, winning wars, solving conflicts and all that." She spoke casually, as if none of those things were a big deal.

I bit my lip. "You want me to fight alongside you? The Warriors Four?"

She grinned. "That is what we have trained you for. I doubt it could be considered a real challenge if you cannot put what you have learned to use in genuine conflict."

I nodded a little, suddenly very nervous.

"Okay. I don't really have much of a choice, anyway."

She smirked. "That's the spirit. I'll see you at dinner." She winked and departed, leaving me staring after her like a stunned mullet.

Something nudged my foot, threatening to disturb my much needed sleep.

"If you value your life, Sig, I suggest you stop that and let me rest. I have at least two more hours before it's my watch." I half threatened, half grumbled, my eyes remaining firmly closed as if I could pretend I'd never woken. When there was no response, I relaxed, breathing out slowly. A hand touched my cheek, and I was instantly alert. None of The Four would wake me like that.

My eyes flew open, one hand sliding under my pillow and gripping the blade I never slept without. In one fluid motion, I struck out with my fist, landing a harsh blow to the intruder's stomach, causing them to let out a low groan and hunch forward, before sweeping my leg out, knocking them over.

It was a man's grunt of pain, definitely not Sig's or Troja's. I rolled, practically straddling him as I pressed my dagger against his neck.

"Fates Adi. What are you gonna do, kill me again?" The man was frozen beneath me. I knew that voice.

"Raf?" I looked down at him in shock, the knife still firmly pressed to his neck.

"I would nod, but I'm afraid I'll slit my own throat if I do. Do you mind?" His eyes were wide as they flicked to the dagger and back to me. I quickly tossed the knife aside. It, along with the makeshift bed I'd been sleeping in, vanished as I pulled him into a tight embrace. He was tense for a second before he relaxed and hugged me back. I could feel him chuckling a little.

"You just about murdered me." He remarked when I still hadn't let go.

When I finally managed to release him, he grinned at me. That same boyish grin I'd seen a thousand times, the same grin I was sure I'd never see again. Tears stung my eyes.

"Aw don't cry, Adi. It's just me."

I swallowed. "You aren't real..."

"How do you know?"

"Because you're dead." I watched him closely. "I buried you."

"Okay, that's a fair point, *but* just because I'm here does not mean this isn't real." He reached out, stroking my cheek.

I breathed in sharply. "I can feel that."

He chuckled. "See? Seems pretty real to me."

I practically flung myself into his arms, hugging him tightly again. At that moment, I didn't care if it was real or not. I was just so grateful to be able to hold him again.

"I'm so sorry, Raf. I'm so, so sorry." The tears came spilling out like a damned waterfall.

He held me back just as tightly, moving his hand over my back.

"Shh, you have nothing to be sorry for."

"You died because of me. You died not knowing how much I..." I choked on my words. I'd never told him I loved him. I'd never let myself.

He smiled a little, pulling back to look at my face. "I did not die because of you. And I already know, Adira. I knew before even you did, I think," he said, as if he'd read my thoughts.

"What? But..."

"We don't have a lot of time. I've been looking everywhere for you. Where have you been?"

I frowned. "What do you mean, where have I been? Completing my Testing I think?"

He shook his head. "Adira, *this* is your Testing. I am your guide, meant to lead you to the answers about your magic, revealing your Gifting and Specialty."

"That... can't be right. I..." I shook my head. "Raf, I don't have a Gifting. I am Impure. I must be losing my mind. Yep, that's it. I'm going insane like the Impure prince. I imagined an entire year of my life in a fake realm. My divinities."

"Woah, slow down. Tell me what you saw?"

So, I took a slow breath and did.

It had taken me some time to process what had really happened, where I was, and what was even real. I had to stop my explanation multiple times as tried to convince myself it must have been some sort of fever dream brought on by the divine herbs. Through many tears and moments of confusion, I'd managed to explain it all to Raf, and he had listened.

"So you're telling me you spent four months' training with the infamous Warriors Four, another eight months *actually* fighting alongside them against *Infernis creatures* that were being summoned by a corrupt group of *heretics*, and then suddenly, one day without warning, you woke up back here?" Raf recapped in disbelief from his seated position in front of me.

I nodded, glancing around at the darkness that surrounded us. Raf had said this was Erro, which made sense. But if *this* was the Inbetween, where had I been this entire time, Novus? I can't truly have been in another realm?

"Well, as much as I'd like to hear more, like I said, time is running out. But at least you're one step closer to returning home."

Home. Tears stung my eyes.

"Woah hey, what's wrong? This is a good thing?"

The word held an entirely new meaning now. I'd gotten used to calling whatever campsite, tent, tavern, or inn, The Four and I had stayed at home as we travelled through the realm, dealing with the blight of under-wordly creatures that were wreaking havoc throughout the lands. The Four were my home. But Raf was also my home. As was Kendelen and Sierra. I swallowed, closing my eyes.

"I didn't get to say goodbye." I whispered.

He nodded in understanding. "I'm sorry Adira. I know you are still processing a lot, but we have to get you to where you are meant to be."

"And where is that?"

He smiled a little. "There."

He pointed to something in the distance. One second I was squinting, the next we were standing right in front of the object.

A throne, with a familiar symbol carved into the back of it. A damned dagger with a drop of blood, a serpens coiled around it. Just like the weapons Dhedros had forged for me, like my blood oath, excluding the serpens.

"What is this?" I looked at Raf.

"Take a seat and find out."

I swallowed. "Will I see you again if I do?"

He shrugged. "Possibly."

"It's not fair." I muttered, struggling to hold back tears yet again. It was a wonder I had any left.

"What's not fair?"

"You shouldn't have died so young. You'd barely lived. We could have gotten out like you'd always wanted. If I had listened to you, if I had let you take me and Sierra away, none of this would have happened."

He pulled back a little and looked at me. "That wasn't how it was meant to be. Besides," He smiled, brushing his fingers against my cheek, "we never would have worked."

"What do you mean?"

"You wouldn't have been truly happy with me, Adira. You weren't ready to settle for the life I could give you, and you shouldn't have to. You deserve someone who can give you the world." He smiled, looking into my eyes. "You always thought I was the dreamer out of the two of us, but it's really you. It's always been you. You dream of a better life for your sister, a better world for the Impure. You dream of adventure, whereas I would have been perfectly content in a four-room cottage on a plot of land that we owned and worked."

"Four?"

"A room for us, a room for your sister, if she wanted it, and rooms for our future children. Two, maybe three, kids."

A tear slid down my cheek, despite my best efforts. The future he described was beautiful, safe, and wonderful. But he was right. I wasn't ready for that. I didn't know exactly what I wanted right now, but I knew it was not that.

"I would have been lucky to share that life with you, Raf."

He ran his thumb across my bottom lip. "You would have been," He grinned, "But you deserve more than anything I could have ever given you, Adira." He leaned in and kissed me deeply. I responded in kind, wrapping my arms around his neck. He pulled back, just far enough to rest his forehead against mine.

"I can't leave you here, Raf. I can't. I don't want to go back to a world where you're not in it. I —"

He cut me off with his lips on mine again. I returned the gesture, kissing him back deeply, until I felt him chuckling against me.

"What's so funny?" I pulled back slightly.

"Now I know why you used to kiss me mid-sentence all the time, to shut me up." He nodded approvingly. "Very effective."

I laughed a bit, smacking him on the chest.

"I love you Adira Nightfell."

My lip quivered as I whispered. "I love you too, Raphael Morrighan. You huge pain in my ass."

He laughed, and the sound filled me with more joy than I could have imagined.

"Now sit *your* pretty little ass down in that throne and pass your Testing."

I swallowed, pulling back and stealing myself. I managed to let go of Raf, taking a seat. I glanced back at him, and he was smiling that same boyish grin.

He winked, and I closed my eyes to stop more tears. When I opened my eyes I was in... a bedroom?

I stood up and looked around. It looked to be a child's bedroom. The colour scheme indicated it was a boy's, but I didn't want to assume. The door opened, and I spun around in time to see a small boy walk in. He couldn't have been older than five.

Shutting the door, he plodded over to his bed and flopped down onto it. He breathed out and looked at the ceiling.

"... Uh, hello?"

He didn't respond. He just rolled over, reached under his pillow, and pulled out a book. It was old and tattered. Clearly a well-loved one.

"Can you hear me?" Again, no response. *Okay, so he can't see or hear me.*

Footsteps sounded, and the door opened again.

"Tarryn, sweetheart, dinner is almost ready. Come and wash up."

My head jerked back to the little boy. That's why he looked so familiar. Tarryn?

The little boy groaned. "But Mamma, I'm not hungry."

I heard a soft chuckle, turning I froze. *Mother?*

The woman standing in the doorway was smiling, with her arms crossed. "Yes, you are. You just want to read instead."

He shrugged. "It's the same thing."

She shook her head, slinging the tea towel over her shoulder, before taking a seat next to him on the bed.

"Okay. How about I read a few pages with you and then you come down for dinner with your Papa and me? After that, you can have the night off from chores and can continue your reading?"

The little boy's face lit up, and he nodded eagerly. "Deal."

She laughed and pulled him into her lap. At first glance, I could have sworn it was my mother standing in the doorway. But upon closer inspection, I realised there were differences. This woman was younger than I remembered my mother being.

They had the same smile and the same eyes, but this woman was slightly taller, skinnier as well. Her hair was the same colour as my mother's, but this woman's was cut to just above her shoulders. My mother's hair had been long, like mine. This woman, Tarryn's mother, was the spitting image of mine, only younger. *What was this?*

"Once upon a time," she began, and little Tarryn practically shook with excitement, "there was a beautiful kingdom called Adea, named after the Goddess of Desire, Thadea. Its people were content and its lands were prosperous. In the kingdom, lived the much loved King and Queen of Adea. They had been blessed with two daughters. As the girls grew, the king and queen noticed their magic was only growing stronger and stronger each day. They were not the only ones that noticed.

The surrounding kingdoms had noted the children's powers, and they were afraid of what it meant. Whilst the King and Queen's people loved them, and their country was in good health, the other kingdoms were weary. They did not understand the King and Queen's magic, and were concerned that if they ever waged war against the others, they would win."

"But the king and queen didn't want a war, Mamma!"

"That's right baby, they only wanted to live peacefully on their own lands. They had no interest in conquering the others. But, once word spread of their daughters' strong Giftings, the other kingdoms decided it was not worth the risk. They united to launch a devastating attack on the kingdom."

"No!" Tarryn shouted in anger. Causing his mother to smile softly and rub his back.

"Yes, sweetheart. The king and queen fought back, but the other kingdoms were stronger together. Eventually, after years of battle, they could no longer hold off the enemy armies. So they entrusted their daughters to two of their most loyal friends. They fled with the princesses. One going north, and the other going west, knowing that if they travelled together, they would likely be found."

"Did the little girls get away, Mamma?"

"Yes baby, both of the princesses escaped. The king and queen held on for as long as they could, but eventually, their defences were overrun. The other kingdoms destroyed Adea, capturing the king and queen, questioning them, and threatening them with death if they didn't reveal the location of their daughters."

"But they didn't tell them!" Tarryn exclaimed proudly, causing his mother to chuckle.

"That's right. Their love for their daughters was stronger than their enemy's swords. They would not give up their children. And so Dykos greeted them."

Tarryn looked sad as he hugged his mother tighter.

"Legend says the crimes committed by the other kingdoms, against their own kind, angered the divinities. The land the other kingdoms tried to claim from the dead king and queen, that was once plentiful and healthy, became baron and dead. Nothing would grow there. Signs that the divinities were displeased kept coming. The longer the enemy kingdoms lingered, the worse it got. Floods, earthquakes, famine, and fires. People rebelled against the other kingdoms' actions to protect themselves from the divinities' wrath. So, the remaining rulers of the other six kingdoms got together and swore none of them would take ownership of the land. That no one would be permitted to enter. They all agreed that they would never again speak of what had occurred. To make sure that no one ventured into the forbidden lands, the kings and queens united their magic, working with the most powerful Pures of their kingdoms, to erase Adea from history. All the books and ledgers were destroyed. People who knew about Adea were killed, and eventually, even the kingdoms involved in the attack, forgot the true version of history."

"But the princesses got away. What happened to them?"

She smiled softly. "No one knows. Some say they remained in hiding for fear of being found. Some say they are waiting for their chance to take their lands back. They never saw each other again, according to others. Instead, they started their own families, content to live peacefully under new names. No one truly knows, but they are out there somewhere. Out in the world. As long as they live, they will always have a claim to The Forgotten Kingdom."

Tarryn's stomach chose that second to let out a grumble. His mother laughed, scooping him up as she stood.

"Time for dinner."

He grinned. "Maybe I am a little hungry..."

She shook her head, kissing his forehead as she carried him out of the room and downstairs to what I imagine was the kitchen.

They left me standing there in shock. The Forgotten Kingdom? Had I just heard the story of the Seventh Kingdom? As a childhood fairy tale? The book.

I walked over to the bed and reached for it, but it disintegrated at my touch. As did everything else in the room. I turned and found myself standing back in the darkness. Raf was not here this time, but I also wasn't alone.

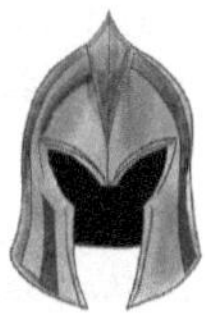

CHAPTER FIFTY-ONE

A FEW YARDS AHEAD of me sat seven thrones. Each had someone sitting in it, and there was an eighth person standing. They were all facing away from me, and they were fuzzy, dark, and difficult to make out, like a shadow.

What I could see, though, were the symbols carved into the back of each throne, and I realised they were representing The Six.

The wheat stalk was for the Goddess of the Harvest, Zalnea.

The bow and arrow was for Ikeara, Goddess of the Hunt.

The helm, for the God of War, Xeria.

The lyre was for Lereya, Goddess of Healing.

The four elements, the symbol of Elios, God of Unity.

And lastly, a balanced scale for the God of Strength, Taros.

The final throne was the one I had sat in, the serpens and dagger. Was that the symbol of the seventh kingdom? After the Goddess Thadea? It had to be.

I took a step forward, attempting to get a better look, but couldn't. Glancing down, I realised my wrists and ankles were shackled. I stiffened, tugging on them, but they would not give. I opened my mouth to demand I be released, but a man spoke.

"She is not ready."

"On the contrary. I think she is. I think we are wasting time by not revealing the truth to her." A woman's voice countered.

Others joined in, each voicing their opinions, which were apparently evenly divided. I could only assume they were talking about me, but I didn't know what I was or wasn't ready for. Frankly, it was pissing me off, all these riddles. All these people getting to test me without me knowing why or who. This was my life.

"Excuse me?" I called.

The figures all turned towards me, and I heard someone scoff. The eighth figure spoke for the first time, her voice familiar, but I couldn't quite place it.

"It is not a question of whether she is ready. She has completed The Testing just like everyone else. She either passes or fails. Make up your minds and release her from her trials."

More arguing ensued, but I couldn't make it all out. It was muffled.

"Hey!" I shouted, a lot less politely this time.

The voices went quiet, then the figures and their thrones disappeared.

I closed my eyes, sighing in frustration. When I opened them, I was staring at a mirrored image of myself. *What in the...?*

"It has been decided," my reflected self said, and I jumped back, nearly tripping over my shackles, "you are not ready for all the knowledge that you need to do as your destiny demands, but in light of your unique circumstances, you are being allowed to return to your realm."

"... So I haven't actually passed?"

"You are being allowed to return, but they shall be seeing you again."

I frowned. "What, like another Testing?"

"You may call it that." My reflection responded, looking annoyed at my questions.

"Why? What's so special about me that I have to return? Is it because I am Impure?"

My mirror image sighed in frustration. "You are not this stupid."

My eyes widened. "Excuse me?"

"If you were Impure, you would not have made it through the first minute of this Testing. But you know this."

"So, what are you saying? That I am actually a Para? One of my parents was Para or Pure?"

"You are not a Para."

"Then what am I?" I said, my frustration now matching hers.

"You know what you are."

"Aren't I supposed to be guided as to what my Gifting is? And my Specialty?"

"Typically, yes."

"But not in this case?" I was about to lose it. This was all ridiculous. They were playing games, and I'd had enough.

"Think about it, Adira. You know the truth. You just refuse to acknowledge it, because of all the other doors it opens."

"No, I *really* don't!"

"I am you. If I know, then you know."

"*Ugh!* This is ridiculous! You are not me. You are a figment of my imagination, or a drug-induced hallucination from that concoction Odette cooked up!"

"What is the *one* requirement to pass this Testing Adira?"

"You have to be a Para or a Pure."

"And I already told you, you aren't a Para."

"I can't be a Pure! I would have known if both of my parents were Gifted."

"How could be sure? You were so young when your parents passed, and you never had a Confirmation."

I shook my head. "Okay, sure, let's say I am a Pure." I rolled my eyes. "*What is my Gifting? Am I a Virbi? An Elementi? A Healeti?*"

"You do not possess any of the six Giftings you're familiar with." I never thought I'd want to punch myself in the face, but I wanted nothing more at that moment.

"What does that mean?!" I threw my hands up.

"Your magic is being blocked."

I frowned. "Blocked?"

My reflection nodded to my mid-section. At first I was confused, then my eyes widened in realisation. I quickly lifted my top. The brand. The blood oath.

"You're saying this is blocking... whatever my Gifting is?"

My reflection nodded, finally seeming a little less annoyed. "Yes, you will only have access to a small amount of your abilities when you return."

"So my Gifting would not manifest until I underwent The Testing, but because I have this... brand... even though I've gone through The Testing, I can't access it?"

She nodded. "The divinities cannot undo the binding in this realm, so you will have to do that yourself."

"How? It's impossible to break."

"Is it?"

"If it isn't, then tell me how!"

She rolled her eyes. "Think Adira. There is always a way. Perhaps you're just looking in the wrong places."

"I have looked everywhere."

"Well, you haven't, or you would know that certain types of magic, certain Giftings, have the ability to remove your binding."

I frowned. "What?"

She groaned. "Honestly, you're making us look bad. It is blood magic, right? It has infected your body and is blocking your magic. What Gifting do you know of that deals with infections?"

My eyes widened. "You're saying a Healeti, a Remedi, could break it? They could *heal* it away?"

She shrugged. "You said that, not me. Now, you will have access to just enough of your magic to pass as the Para you are posing as, with a little help, that is."

"Help from who?"

"That doesn't matter. Time is up." She leaned in, whispering something into my ear that had my blood turning cold.

"Wait."

My reflection disappeared, and I groaned loudly in frustration, yanking roughly on these damned chains.

"Woah, easy there Adira. You don't want to break those pretty little wrists of yours."

I breathed in, turning my head to see Raf coming to stand in front of me.

"Raf... You're still here?"

He smiled. "For as long as you're here, I am, too." He bent down, and with unnatural strength he shouldn't possess, he broke the chains around my ankles, then the ones on my wrists, too.

I threw my arms around him again. "I don't understand any of this."

He hugged me back. "I know, but you will. It's time to go, Love."

I shook my head profusely. "No."

I felt him grin against my hair.

"You are a force of nature, Adira Nightfell. You could shake the entire realm if you truly wanted to. Do not let anyone convince you otherwise."

I nodded slightly, still gripping on to him. I couldn't let go of him yet.

"Is this the part where you tell me to dream for the both of us?" I swallowed. He smiled softly and shook his head.

"Dream for you, love. Not for me, not even for Sierra. Dream for you." He pulled back despite my protests. He put his hands on my shoulders and met my eyes.

"No, wait. I'm not ready." My heart ached.

He dropped his hands and took a step back, shaking his head. "Yes, you are. Good luck, Adira." He winked, taking another step back. I reached for him, but he was already fading.

"No..." I whispered.

"Dream for you, Adira Nightfell!" He called, but his voice was far away.

I could only just make out his silhouette now. Just enough to see him raise his hand and wave. I could tell he wore that same boyish grin that was as good as his signature.

Taking a breath, I whispered, "I love you, Raphael Morrighan! I LOVE YOU!" My declaration fading into the darkness that now surrounded me.

Closing my eyes, I pushed down my grief, my heartbreak, and my relief at getting to have our goodbye. When I opened them, I expected to be thrown into yet another traumatic experience, but instead, the ground beneath my feet disappeared, and I fell. I let out a scream as I plummeted.

"Elia!" Someone called, shaking my shoulders.

I gasped, sitting upright, reaching for a dagger that wasn't there.

"Easy, easy. It can be a little disorientating at first. Don't rush." I recognised the voice as Hadrian's.

He was the one holding my shoulders. After taking a deep breath, I slowly calmed myself. I had to squint, adjusting to the brightness of the room, compared to the darkness I'd apparently grown accustomed to. I glanced down at myself. *Was this real?* Sitting up slowly, I held up my arms out in front of me and studied them. All the muscles I'd spent months building were gone. Had it truly all been a crazy, drug-induced dream?

"Are you alright, Elia?" Tira asked, touching my arm.

"I... don't know.."

She smiled a bit. "You should have seen me after my Testing. I was a wreck, even at five."

I nodded numbly. My brain was having trouble reconciling where I was and whether this was all just another test. How much time had passed for everyone else? I felt like I'd been gone a whole year.

Hadrian stepped back, deeming it okay to do so. Odette was watching me closely from across the room.

Tira chuckled a little at the no doubt confused look on my face. "You did well."

"How long was I in for?"

Tira looked at the only clock in the room, then back at me. "A little over two hours. Long for a Para's Testing, but not a concern."

I cursed.

"That—that's impossible." I muttered.

"Time works differently in The Testing. No one has proven for certain, but it appears whatever realm our minds enter during the experience is also in a different time." Troja mentioned the time being different there, but he'd been talking about Novus, not Erro.

"... I feel like I've been gone for a year." I breathed out shakily. Almost an entire year of my life amounted to two hours for everyone else? I was no longer the same person as when I went in, but how could I explain that to anyone if not even a day had passed for them?

The priest approached, distracting me from my inner panic.

"May I?" He requested, addressing both Tira and me apparently, because Tira nodded, then looked at me.

"May you what exactly?"

"There's just one more step left. I need to check the strength of your Gifting."

"Right." I nodded. "Go ahead."

"It's quite simple," he said, taking out a small stone. "All you have to do is hold the stone. The brightness will give us an indication of your Gifting's strength." He smiled to reassure me, but it had the opposite effect. "When you're ready, hold out your hand."

I bit my lip and did as he said. He placed the stone in my palm. It was cool to the touch at first, then it warmed. I glanced down at it, and it started to glow, pulsing between a deep purple and a lavender colour. Virbi colours.

I glanced at Tira, who grinned. The priest noted something down on a piece of parchment, reaching to take the stone back, but before he could, a sudden flare of heat shot through my hands, right as the glow exploded from a somewhat dull purple into a bright gold light. I gasped, shielding my eyes, as did everyone else. The priest actually *flinched*.

When I risked looking back at the stone, the gold light had gone, and it was back to flashing the Virbi purples. I glanced around the room. Everyone was staring at me.

"Is that normal?" I dared to ask.

"I'm sure it's just an anomaly with the stone. I probably didn't prepare it right." The priest laughed as he nervously took the stone from me.

"... Right."

"Lastly, I just need to record your Specialty, then you are free to go." He joked, and I swallowed.

"... There's no rule that says I *have* to declare my Specialty, right? I've heard of plenty of Pure's and Para's keeping their Specialties to themselves."

The priest looked surprised, glancing at Tira before looking back at me. "Well no, there's no *rule,* so to speak, but royals usually want everyone to know their Specialty and how strong they are."

"Well, I'd rather keep it to myself for now, if it's all the same to everyone." I glanced around at them all. "I'm still adjusting to not being Impure, let alone having a Gifting. I'd like to just... get through this ceremony, then deal with everything else afterwards."

"Of course. Whatever you want, Elia." Hadrian answered, and I breathed a sigh of relief as the priest backed off.

Thank Ades for paranoid Pures and Paras. If I'd been forced to declare my Specialty, I would have had to lie and say Forti or Argenti, and since I don't even know what my Gifting is, let alone my Specialty, it would only take one person asking me to prove I was whichever one I declared, to blow my cover entirely.

"Are you satisfied now, Odette?" Tira said, looking at the Queen of Taros. "May we proceed with the ceremony?"

Odette was watching me closely as she nodded. A small smile on her face. "Absolutely. Let us return to the council room."

Hadrian smiled reassuringly at me. "You have time to change while we reset the room."

I nodded slightly. "Thank you."

Tira took my arm, and we walked back to my room.

"You're very quiet, Elia. Would you like to talk about it?"

I would, very much, but I couldn't. Not with her. Even if I could, I didn't even know where to start. So I shook my head, giving her a reassuring smile. "Sorry, it's just taking me a minute to readjust. It felt like I was in there for some time."

She nodded. "It's quite crazy, isn't it? Minutes here feel like hours there. Everyone's experience is unique, but it's rare that someone wakes up unchanged."

I nodded. "I am just looking forward to this entire ordeal being over with."

She chuckled. "Rightly so. I can't believe that witch Odette entertained that jealous brat's accusations."

Right, Josette's outburst. It all felt so irrelevant now, so far removed. "At least now there's no doubt."

She nodded. "That is true, but I'll still enjoy the day we can leave this place and that awful woman behind. I will wait here while you change." I smiled a little, grateful to have a moment of privacy.

I shut my bedroom door, moving to my closet. Mind still reeling, I searched through it. *Snap out of it, Adira.* You can spiral later, just get through this ceremony. I took a few seconds to calm myself, using some of the techniques Amory had taught me and ignoring the pang in my chest at the thought of not seeing her or the others again. If I'd ever really seen them at all.

I changed into an outfit that would be considered inappropriate for the occasion, but I didn't care. Throughout my time with The Four, I hadn't once worn a dress or heels. I donned plain black pants, with knee high lace-up boots, paired with a light silver, long-sleeved shirt with a square neckline, layered under a black corset style vest top.

It felt odd wearing my hair down after almost always having it braided so it wouldn't get in the way during battle, or simply for convenience, but I couldn't muster the energy to do anything else with it. I completed the look with a bright silver, almost white, cloak that would inevitably get dirty, but what did I care at this point? Opening my bedroom door, Tira raised her eyebrows at my outfit, then grinned.

"You will definitely make a statement with that."

"They seem to enjoy causing drama with me. I may as well choose their topic of conversation for once."

She chuckled. "Well said."

I pulled the hood of my cloak up over my head as we made our way back to the council room, which had filled up with as many people as it could fit this time around. Hadrian, Odette, Valor, Cali, and Killian were in the same positions as before. Glancing around, I caught Valor appraising my outfit appreciatively, whilst Cali grinned at me and made quite a vulgar gesture to convey her own approval of my clothing choice.

I couldn't help the small smile of relief that appeared at seeing both of them. I had missed them more than I'd realised. Josette wasn't in the crowd this time, but James was still present. Shame, she should be here to see the ceremony she tried so hard to prevent. Tira remained beside me.

Hadrian stood, quieting the crowd.

"Now that everything has been cleared up, Lady Elia has undergone her Testing and passed with flying colours. Let us continue, so we can all finally enjoy the awaiting festivities."

The priest stepped forward.

"I believe we can skip most of the formalities and go straight to where we were up to before the, uh, interruption."

"Queen Tira Melfore has accepted Elia Worthington as her heir. She has passed her Testing and, if she accepts, is ready to take her place in the Melfore family, as Princess Elia Melfore. Do you accept this honour, Lady Elia?"

Like I had a choice. "Yes, I accept," I said, smiling the way I imagined a girl who actually wanted this life might.

The priest smiled. "In that case, Queen Tira, would you do the honours?"

Tira nodded. Stepping in front of me, she carefully removed the hood of my cloak. I looked at her, and in her eyes, all I saw was happiness and pride. I barely registered the guilt, feeling like I was watching the ceremony unfold from outside myself.

"Do you, Elia Melfore, swear to uphold the values of the Melfore name?"

"I do."

"And do you swear to serve your kingdom to the best of your ability for as long as you live?"

No pressure. "I do."

"And lastly, do you accept the title Princess of Xeria, heir to the throne, and future successor to Tira Melfore?" She grinned. "And everything that comes with that title, from today onwards?"

"I do."

The priest stepped forward, now holding a very fancy-looking cushion, with an even fancier item on top. Tira reached down and carefully plucked the beautiful tiara nestled safely into the pillow. I dipped my chin slightly as she placed it on my head.

"May I present to the court, from this day forth, Her Highness Elia Melfore, Princess of Xeria."

The crowd erupted in claps and cheers. Bells rang, but I barely registered the sound. Tira spun me to face everyone. They all stood and slowly dipped into their respective bows or curtsies. I swallowed and glanced at Tira.

She whispered, "You can tell them to rise."

"Oh, right." I flushed. "Please rise and make your way to the banquet hall to enjoy the festivities King Hadrian and Queen Odette have so graciously provided for us all."

They rose and began filing out of the room. I breathed out. Tira pulled me into an unexpected hug.

My eyes widened, but I returned it.

"Sorry," she said, pulling back, "I just never thought I'd get to see this."

I bit my lip. "It's okay..." I smiled a bit. "Neither did I, if I am being honest." *Boy, was that the truth?*

She laughed. "I will give you some privacy. When you are ready, Wes and Uri will be waiting outside to escort you to the festivities."

I nodded. "Thank you."

She turned and exited the room, along with most of the other occupants. I sensed someone behind me and turned to see Valor standing there.

"Val…" I trailed off, unsure of how I felt. I'd missed him more than I cared to admit, and a part of me felt like a weight had lifted. I'd been carrying so much guilt about Raf's death, about what he would think of my relationship with Valor. I felt like I'd been betraying Raf every time I let myself enjoy my time with him, but now that I'd gotten my goodbye, gotten to speak to Raf, I felt lighter. That, however, made the other part of me all the more terrified. I could use Raf as a reason to keep parts of me held back, to protect myself from falling too hard. Now that the barrier was gone, I felt exposed.

He bowed slightly. "Princess." He smirked.

I rolled my eyes. "Cut it out."

"Congratulations."

I shook my head. "Thank you for what you did for me earlier," I said, remembering how he and Cali had stood up for me.

He looked at me. "All I did was tell the truth."

"Still, it meant a lot."

"Now that you are officially a Princess…" He trailed off.

"Things are a lot more complicated." I nodded. "I know."

He smiled a bit. "Save me a dance?"

"No promises."

He chuckled, placing a kiss on my hand before leaving the room. I glanced around, noting it was only Odette and me remaining. *Great.*

She approached, saying nothing.

I dipped into a curtsey. "Your Highness."

She smiled. "I hope you harbour no ill feelings towards me for following our protocols?"

"Of course not. I understand it is your duty to follow your own laws."

"I'm glad. I hoped you'd see things that way. Now that we have named you an official heir to the Xerian throne, your rumoured betrothal to Prince Valor need not be mere rumour."

I raised my eyebrows. "You wish for me to marry your son?"

"An alliance with Xeria would be very beneficial to Taros. It could settle the strenuous ties we have currently."

"With all due respect, Your Majesty, I have been a princess for little more than a few minutes. I have no interest in a politically arranged marriage at this current point in time."

"Do not forget who welcomed you into this palace, *Princess. W*ithout us, you would not be wearing that crown on your head."

"Which I am extremely grateful for. However, this topic is not up for discussion right now. If you'll excuse me, we don't want to keep anyone waiting." I made to leave, but she gripped my arm tightly. Too tightly. I forced myself not to wince, or worse, retaliate like my instincts begged to, and instead looked back at her. She was smiling.

"Be careful where you step, Elia. You never know what lies beneath the surface."

I stared back at her. "Thank you for the advice," I said, jerking my arm free, "but I believe I can choose my own path."

I left her standing there, exiting the room to find Tarryn, Hamish, Uri, and Wes waiting for me. The doors closed behind me, but not before I heard a soft chuckle from the Queen of Ice.

CHAPTER FIFTY-TWO

AFTER EVERYTHING, THE LAST place I wanted to be was in a room full of pompous nobles, all trying to garner favour with the new princess. People who wouldn't give Elia Worthington the time of day before, now suddenly wanted to be best friends. It was ridiculous. At least there was liquor. I grabbed another glass and took a sip.

Come on Adira, you can do this. You took on literal Infernis creatures, divinity-like warriors and heretics. You can handle a little party. Or maybe I just had the fake memories and none of it had really happened at all?

I shook my head, trying to dispel those doubts and focus on the present, but I couldn't stop going over everything I'd experienced and learnt from the Testing. Or, more accurately, everything I hadn't learned. For every question I'd gotten an answer to, another three made themselves known. I was trying to work through it logically, paying more attention to the few major revelations.

If what my reflection had said was true, then I'm a Pure? Meaning my parents had to have both been Pure as well or one a Para and one a Pure. Which was insane. If I were a Pure, that damned Testing was supposed to reveal to me what my Gifting and Specialty was, but I still had absolutely no idea. I felt different, though. I couldn't quite put my finger on it. It was almost like a sixth sense, a gut feeling that I didn't recognise.

I'd also learned that a Remedi could supposedly break this blood oath. The other kingdoms were due to arrive in just under four weeks. That's how long I had to think of a way to convince a Remedi to help me.

Despite the magnitude of those revelations, they weren't what I was fixated on, what I couldn't stop replaying. No, I was stuck on the words I had whispered to myself before disappearing.

One more thing Adira. The answers you seek about your past are closer than you think. Just ask the one who calls you Little Sparrow. Ask him where he first heard that nickname. Better yet, ask yourself if he was truly the first person to call you that.

"You look like you've got the weight of the world on your shoulders," Tarryn said, as he fell into position beside me. Shit, that's another thing. The vision I saw of Tarryn and his mother. The story. It was an effort not to hug him, but since that would probably freak him out and no doubt start all kinds of rumours, I just bit my lip and asked,

"Tarryn, did your mother read you bedtime stories?"

"Whose mother didn't?" He raised his eyebrows.

"Specifically, a story about a forgotten kingdom and two lost princesses?" I said, keeping my voice low. I felt, more than I saw, him tense slightly beside me.

"Why are you asking?"

"We need to talk later, in private."

He nodded slightly. "Alright."

"May I interrupt?" I looked up to see James standing there, smiling almost sheepishly.

"That depends, is your friend with you?" Tarryn answered before I could. His arms crossed, his face impassive. We all knew he was referring to Josette.

He cleared his throat. "No. No, she is not. I haven't seen her since the ceremony."

"Hmm," Tarryn said, but didn't move. I smiled a bit, placing my hand on his arm.

"It's alright Amesley, thank you."

Tarryn nodded, ever the dutiful guard, and took a few steps back, but he didn't take his eyes off of James.

"They are very protective of you, aren't they?" He said nervously, which was an odd look for him, usually so confident.

"Well, I believe that is their job," I said, smiling a bit, "although, if Josette had been successful in her slandering, it wouldn't have been any longer."

"Yes, that's why I wanted to speak to you. I hope you know I had absolutely no idea she was going to pull something like that. If I had known, I never would have sat near her, and I would have tried to talk her out of it."

"Oh?"

"Come on, Elia, you know me. I wouldn't do that to you."

"You never truly know how people will react to certain situations, Jameson. I know you, but not as well as you are implying."

He sighed and nodded. "I just hope you'll accept my apology on her behalf, and that it doesn't affect our friendship."

"As long as you had nothing to do with her accusations, then you have nothing to apologise for."

He smiled a bit. "I didn't. I swear to you, I had no clue."

I'm not sure why, but something told me he wasn't being honest. I had to hold back my frown because I couldn't pinpoint why. It was just a feeling. I'd always been able to read people well, but this was something else. I watched him, trying to figure out what was different. I'd always had a good feeling about Jameson, until now.

He cleared his throat, no doubt growing uncomfortable under my scrutinising stare. "I don't suppose we could try to have that uninterrupted dance finally?"

Shaking off the feeling I chuckled and held out my hand. "Lead the way, my lord."

He grinned, placing a kiss on my hand before taking it. "You honour me, Your Highness," he said, putting emphasis on my new title as he led me to the dance floor. I rolled my eyes but still followed him.

We danced and laughed. Jameson glared at any man that approached if it looked like he might cut in, which only caused more laughter. He was a brilliant distraction. At the end of the dance, he bowed low.

"Thank you for the dance, Princess."

I curtsied in return. "Any time, Lord Jameson." I smiled softly and watched as he disappeared into the crowd, the odd feeling I'd had at the start of our interaction practically forgotten.

"*Finally.* I thought he'd never let you go." Turning, I found Cali rolling her eyes dramatically. I chuckled.

"Hi, Cali."

She grinned, linking her arm through mine and leading me to a booth where we sat down. "So, how was it?"

"The dance?"

"No, your Testing! No one I know has ever taken the Testing as an adult."

"Um... I don't know. I imagine it was the same as everyone else's? What was yours like?"

"Well, I saw my father, thank Taros. If it had been my mother, I probably wouldn't have passed." I could certainly understand why she'd be glad it was her father. "We went for a walk through the castle grounds, ending at the gardens. When we got there, all the flowers bloomed, the trees grew, and the plants reacted to my presence. That's when my father told me I had my mother's Gifting and Specialty. At first, I was disappointed. I wanted to be like Valor and him, a Kineti, not an Incrementi. But then he made me look around at all the beauty I would one day be able to mould and create." I smiled a bit, listening to her talk about that experience with her father. Even if it was a drug induced one, she certainly talked about it as if it were real.

"After that, he told me I had to walk through the rest of the garden on my own, which I did. As I walked, I came across different puzzles I guess you could call them. I had to solve them to move on to the next one. Once I'd solved them all, I could exit the garden, where my father was waiting for me. When I reached him, I woke up, did the whole 'touch the stone' thing with the priest, and the next day began my Flori training."

"That sounds..." *Nice? Positively pleasant compared to mine.*

"Valor said his was similar, but he saw our mother, and his challenges were a lot more physical. Who did you see?"

"I saw an old friend."

She bit her lip, clearly wanting to hear more, but trying not to push me. I smiled a bit.

"I'll tell you all about it, just not here."

She nodded. "Oh, of course." She grinned, and I could practically feel how happy she was. She'd clearly had a few drinks. Speaking of, I looked around, waving over a server. He approached with a smile and held out the tray.

"You know what," Cali said, taking hold of the tray. "You better just leave the whole thing." She smiled charmingly at him. I raised my eyebrows. His eyes widened, and he stammered, probably from being spoken to by a royal and also at her request.

"O-oh, of course, Your Highness. Your Highnesses." He bowed to us both before he quickly retreated.

"The entire tray, Cali?"

"Um, yes. That way, we don't have to go looking for more later." She handed me a glass, then picked up her own. "Cheers to you, *Princess* Elia." She grinned and clinked her glass with mine. I chuckled and had a sip.

"How do you feel? With your new title? Your new mother?"

"It feels unreal. Like someone else's life, not mine."

She smiled a bit. "You'll get used to it."

I could tell she believed that. If it were a normal situation, she would probably be right.

I looked at her. "I'm sorry I haven't given you much time lately, Cali. I haven't been a great friend to you."

"Oh, nonsense. You've had a *lot* going on."

"Yes, but that's no excuse. You were my first friend here, and you treated me the same, regardless of my status. I haven't forgotten that, and I promise to be a better friend to you. To both of you." I cast a quick glance around the room, spotting Valor, who was, as usual, surrounded by people. I smiled a bit before looking back at Cali. She was my only female friend here. The men sorely outnumbered us, we needed to stick together.

"Well, I'll drink to that," she said, downing her drink. I laughed and did the same.

I decided then to table my list of never-ending problems for just one night, to let myself enjoy what was going on around me. Surrounded by friends, and probably enemies, but for one night, I could let myself enjoy the life of Princess Elia Melfore, if only to stop me from spiralling.

It was in the early hours of the morning, by the time I stumbled drunkenly back to my room, Cali right beside me. I giggled once we reached my room.

"Are you going to be okay to get back to your room?"

"Yesss, Motherrrr." She rolled her eyes at me. "It's just around the corner. I'll be fine."

I grinned and looked at Tarryn and Hamish. They both nodded, telling me they'd make sure she got there safely. I hugged her goodnight and entered my rooms, locking the door. I kicked off my heels, breathing out in relief. *Finally.*

I made my way to my vanity, quickly undressed, and threw on the closest nightgown I could find before sitting down in front of the mirror. I grabbed a washcloth, closing my eyes and wiping my face. Something cold and hard pressed against my neck, causing me to go still. I slowly removed the cloth and looked into the mirror.

"Josette?" I frowned, now acutely aware of the blade in her hand. She had about two seconds before I shoved it somewhere no one wanted an object to be, let alone a dagger.

"Oh, now you remember my name." She snipped, pressing it more firmly against my neck. It was at that moment I remembered that my body was back to the way it had been before the Testing. What if I no longer possessed the ability to fight the same way? Josette outmatched me when we'd fought before.

"How about you put the knife down, and we can talk?" I tried keeping my voice calm. Annoyed that in my exhausted and drunken state, I'd let my guard down. Sig would have had my ass for that.

"How about you shut your mouth and listen for once?"

"You don't want to do this, Josette. My guards will check on me soon. It's not worth it."

"I will slit your throat long before a guard can reach me. That is definitely worth it." Her grip remained annoyingly solid. I'd known she was crazy, but I thought she was just the *privileged noblewoman* kind of crazy, not psychotic, attempted murderer kind of crazy.

"Okay," I said, keeping still, watching her closely and assessing the room as best I could for anything I could use. I made a mental note to get a new pillow dagger. "I am listening. What do you want?"

"I want you *gone*. Everything was perfect, we had it all arranged, until you arrived and messed it all up."

"I'm sorry if you feel that way." The hand that was in my lap clenched into a fist as I tried to keep my body loose but ready.

"Oh, shut up. You're not sorry. You did this on purpose. You took *everything* from me." Her eyes were darting around, her voice was almost shaky. She sounded really unstable.

I could practically *feel* the anger radiating off of her. I stayed quiet, figuring anything I said would likely just agitate her more.

"I have worked *so* hard. Mapped my entire life out. Everyone expected *me* to be with the prince. To one day take the throne. And then you just swoop in and rip it all away."

"Put the knife down and we can work something out." I reasoned.

"*NO!* It's too late now. Everyone just *loves* Princess Elia. Even when I *TOLD* them what you did! Even when I exposed you as the liar you are. I tried everything to get rid of you. There's only one way left." I felt the drops of blood sliding down my neck as she pressed the knife harder. *Right, so talking her down wasn't an option. Plan B then.*

"Please, Josette. You're not a killer. You don't want to do this." I tried one last time.

"Oh, yes, I very much do." I moved at the same time she did.

As she tried to swipe the knife across my neck, I threw myself backwards, knocking over the chair, along with Josette. The knife flew out of her hands, landing an arm's length away from her. I rolled to the side, quickly jumping to my feet. I landed a swift kick to her stomach and lunged for the dagger, but I'd forgotten one thing. Josette was a Teleki.

Right as I remembered that helpful fact, the chair I'd just knocked over slammed into me with force, breaking upon impact and throwing me across the room. Groaning, I quickly jumped up, going still as I noticed the knife hovering about five feet in front of me. I glanced at Josette; she was standing now, hands by her sides, fingers moving slightly, the only sign she was the one controlling the knife.

"Josette, please." I held my hands up, my eyes searching for something I could use.

She laughed, and it was an ugly sound, full of hate and rage. That's what she truly felt when she looked at me. Hatred and anger. She tilted her head to the side as the knife moved closer. I took my chance, ducking and rolling forwards to where the broken chair lay. I grabbed one of the chair legs, raising it just in time to deflect the blow meant for my face. She smirked confidently, and I jumped to my feet, backing up. The dagger attacked again, but once more I deflected it, ignoring the sense of Déjà vu.

She frowned slightly and increased the speed of her attacks. I had to hand it to her; she was good. Her technique was practically flawless and unlike me, there was no body for her to keep out of the way of my counter attacks. This would not work. I couldn't stay on the defensive. I waited, timing my next move carefully. The dagger struck, and I raised my makeshift wooden staff with as much force as I could muster, causing the dagger to imbed itself into the wood.

I didn't give her time to huff in annoyance as I hurled the chair leg, dagger still attached, at her. It didn't fly nearly as far as it should have. Damn this weak body. I would need to get back into the training ring, fast.

She held up a hand, easily stopping it midair just like the last time we'd faced off like this, but the distraction cost her. I tackled her to the ground, both of us hitting the floor with a loud thud. Landing a hard punch to her jaw, I raised my fist to strike again, when I was suddenly flung backwards by my clothing as if I were being yanked. I hit the wall with a sickening force, dropping to the ground. I groaned, thankful nothing had broken, yet.

"Everyone will think it was the same people that attacked you outside of the party the other night, which technically it was," she said as I rose to my feet again. I looked closer at the dagger that was back in her hand then. It had a silver blade.

Suddenly, it clicked. You wouldn't need to be an archer if you were a Teleki. Josette could have seen me leaving the room and walking outside. She could have easily snuck out and waited. Could have controlled the bow and arrow with her magic. She wasn't an archer, so her aim wasn't perfect, but maybe she hadn't wanted it to be. She just needed to prove I wasn't a Para Virbi, since she hadn't been able to stop my naming ceremony.

"You were the archer in the bushes." I stated rather than asked.

"A lot of good that did. No one seemed to care that you clearly aren't a Forti and yet, the silver didn't affect you at all, so you also couldn't be an Argenti. There is no way you're a Para Virbi. I should have just killed you then and there. No one suspected me. They never do."

"Your logic doesn't even make sense. A Forti doesn't need to have rippling muscles to be one!" Although it certainly helped. She was unhinged, but arguing with her bought me time as I inched towards the door.

"I am sorry Josette, I never meant to take anything from you. You can have Valor. You can have this kingdom. I will go back to Xeria." I lied.

"Oh, how kind of you to offer him to me!" She shook her head. "He doesn't want me. He wants you. So the only option left is to remove you from the equation. Permanently."

"Wait."

"I'm done waiting." Her fingers curled into a fist, and the knife flew towards me.

I leapt out of the way, but she had been prepared for that this time and the dagger curved, following me. I landed in a crouch and tried to dodge the next attack, but I wasn't fast enough. It slashed across my chest, and I jerked backwards, hissing in pain as blood trickled down my chest. I took another step back but again she was prepared and the once stationary foot stool nearby flew into my feet, tripping me over.

The dagger was shooting toward me as I fell backwards. I raised my arms defensively, turning my head away as I braced for impact and pain, but it never came. Instead, a translucent, gold shock wave erupted from my hands, throwing both the knife and Josette across the room, pinning them to the opposite wall. I slowly opened my eyes when I realised I hadn't been stabbed.

They widened in shock as I glanced from my hands to Josette, then back to my hands. Wes and Uri chose that moment to bust open the door. They took in the scene and hesitated for only a second before they exchanged a look and spurred into action. Wes quickly shut the door while Uri hurried over to me.

"Princess? What's going on?"

"I—Josette was waiting. She attacked me, do you... how much did I have to drink?" I asked, my arms still outstretched as I looked back at Josette and the dagger. Both had the same translucent gold, almost net like substance, around them, moulded to their shapes. Almost unperceivable, if it weren't for the glimmering gold colour.

"Not enough to make you see that."

"You see it too?"

He nodded. "Not sure exactly *what* I'm seeing, but yes. I see it."

I swallowed, unsure whether I should be relieved or worried.

Wes walked over to where Josette and the knife were pinned, and let out a low whistle.

"Damn," he said, glancing at me, "that's a new one."

"Grab the knife and restrain Lady Josette." Uri ordered.

Wes hesitantly reached for the knife and tried to grab it off of the wall, but it didn't budge.

"Uh, yeah, that might be a problem."

Uri looked at me. "Elia?"

I was still staring at my hands. Had I done that? It *looked* like I had, but that's not a Gifting or Specialty I'd ever heard of.

Uri stepped in front of me, grabbing my hands. "Hey, Princess. Snap out of it."

I breathed in, looking at him. The sudden contact seemed to pull me out of my shock. The gold netting disappeared, both the knife and Josette dropping to the ground.

Wes let out a curse at the unexpected movement, but quickly grabbed the knife, tucking it into his weapons belt before detaining Josette.

"Elia. I need to inform the royal guards. Will you be alright? I'll send for a medicae to check out that wound, but it doesn't look too deep."

I touched my chest, just below my collarbone. When I pulled my fingers away, they were stained red. I reached up with my other hand, touching my neck. That hand came away red too.

I nodded. "I'm fine. Go ahead."

He looked sceptical, but he quickly hurried out the door. Within a minute, Hamish and Tarryn were hurrying in asking what had happened. Wes still had a hold of Josette, who was just staring at me in shock.

"What are you?" She said. *I wish I knew.* I wanted to respond.

"Hamish, show Wes to the cells. We can hold Josette there while this gets cleared up."

Hamish nodded, leading Wes and Josette out of the room.

"Adira," Tarryn said softly, "are you okay? Let me see your wound." I tilted my head to the side a little so he could get a better look. He stepped forward and inspected it before nodding and moving on to the one on my chest.

"She got you good. I don't think it will scar, though."

"Good. Tarryn I—" someone interrupted me as they jerked Tarryn away. My eyes widened. Valor was standing there, his hair ruffled as if he'd just gotten out of bed.

"Valor?"

"What happened? Tell me what happened right now." His voice was deadly calm, but I could feel the anger radiating off of him.

"Josette attacked me."

"Josette?" He looked taken aback. "Are you sure?"

I rolled my eyes, regaining my senses. "Yes, I'm *sure*. Why would I lie?"

"No, I don't think you're lying, I just — why would she attack you?"

"Why do you think, Valor?" I gave him a look.

He frowned in confusion, before realisation hit him. "*Me*? You think she attacked you because of me?"

"I *know* she did. She told me as much whilst she had a dagger pressed to my neck."

His anger grew, and he turned to Tarryn. "Where the Hek were you? How could you let this happen?"

I frowned. "Hey, back off. He was helping your sister get to her room safely. Both he and Hamish were. Uri and Wes were guarding the door, but she was already in here when I came in. I don't know how she got past the other guards."

His eyes sparked as he realised something, which seemed to infuriate him more.

"What is it, Valor?"

"The tunnels. She knows about the tunnels." My eyes widened.

"She *what*?"

He sighed. "Elia, it's not what you think..."

"Oh? So you *didn't* tell her about the tunnels so the two of you could rendezvous in secret?" I didn't love how jealous I sounded, but I couldn't help it at this point.

"Well... okay, it is what you think, but that was before you."

I shook my head. "How many other women should I be worried about sneaking in here to slit my throat? You certainly have more than your fair share of jilted lovers, Princeling." I knew I was being irrational but after the last year, no day, I'd had, I felt like it was warranted.

"Elia."

"If she had waited until I went to sleep, I would have had no chance at fighting her off, Valor! You don't think I should have been told other people knew about the tunnels?!" I didn't know why I was getting so mad at him, it's not like he knew Josette was going to attack me but once again, I couldn't stop myself.

"I didn't think she'd use them for this! No one else knows. It's only her, James, my family, and you."

I shook my head. "You can go, Valor."

"Elle…"

"Please, just go. Your face is really not one I want to be seeing right now."

Valor stepped towards me, but Tarryn moved faster. He stepped between Valor and me.

"She said no, Your Highness."

Valor's eyes widened slightly at Tarryn's nerve. I held my breath. Valor could easily order him hanged for that, but he didn't. He simply stepped back, turned, and walked out of the room. No doubt to question Josette himself.

I sighed.

"Well, there's never a dull moment guarding you," Tarryn said half-heartedly, trying to lighten the situation.

He wasn't wrong. It's a miracle he and Hamish hadn't quit by now. Josette knew about the tunnels. *That's* how she knew I was truly involved with Raf, and maybe how she knew I had taken the bodies. She could have followed me. I was careful, but I'd clearly underestimated her. She could have a lot more information than she's shared. *Crap.*

"We need to find out how much Josette knows."

Tarryn looked at me. "Hamish will make sure she says nothing she shouldn't. The medicae will be here soon, probably Queen Tira, and maybe the Navarre king and queen as well. You can't leave."

I closed my eyes, praying that if she knew more than she'd let on, that our altercation was enough to keep her mouth shut for the time being.

CHAPTER FIFTY-THREE

Tarryn had been right. Within minutes, my room was full of people. Tira was standing close by, watching the scene unfold. Odette didn't make an appearance, thank Ades. Hadrian, however, did.

He looked like he'd just gotten out of bed and immediately rushed over, which I would laugh at if it weren't for the circumstances. His eyes swept the room, finally landing on me. Relief filled his features as he walked over, pulling me into a hug.

"Elia, are you alright?"

I noticed Tira raise her eyebrows in surprise from the corner of my eye. I nodded and hugged him back. "Really, I'm fine."

He stepped back and looked at me. "Has someone looked at those cuts?" He glanced at my neck.

"Not yet. They've sent for a meda. I'm sure they'll be here soon."

He looked around. "Clear the room, please."

By now, Hamish, Tarryn, Uri, and Wes were close by. Tira's personal guards, including Yarik, were present, as well as the King's guard. Some were inspecting the room, trying to establish what happened, and others were waiting for orders. Tira nodded at her guards. All but Yarik stepped out of the room.

"Uri and Wes should stay. They were the ones that found us and apprehended Josette," I said.

Hadrian nodded before glancing at Hamish and Tarryn.

"As her personal guards, I believe we should be present for this conversation," Tarryn said.

Hadrian glanced at me then, obviously leaving it up to me. I nodded.

"Of course, I'd appreciate that."

Hamish closed the door. I took the opportunity to sit down.

"What happened?" Hadrian asked, and I sighed. I'd already had to go over it with Tira, then the guard who would have to report the incident, but I guess we were about to go again.

"That girl you let slander my daughter in front of your entire court, broke in here and attacked her. That's what happened."

Hadrian let out a tired sigh. "I was asking Elia."

"Well, yeah, pretty much what she said." I bit my lip. "Josette must have slipped into my room on the shift change when everyone was still at the council room or the party. Probably right after she left the ceremony." I didn't mentioned the tunnels, I couldn't risk them being closed up or having guards posted there.

"When I came back to my room, I was preparing for bed at my vanity," I nodded to it, "it was dark and I may have had one or two drinks, so I didn't notice her until she was right behind me with a knife."

"Did she say anything to you?"

"She was angry. I apparently have everything she has always wanted, and she was angry. She's worried Valor will marry me, and not her. She's spent her whole life in this court with things expected of her. And I suppose she just... snapped."

He closed his eyes. "I should have paid closer attention. The ladies of the court were always Odette's forte, but I should have noticed her behaviour sooner."

"Hadrian, it's not your fault. It's no one's fault but Josette's."

"I beg to differ." Tira commented, and I groaned slightly. "If you had that girl locked up after her initial outburst, like you *should* have, then this wouldn't have happened."

"Tira—" I tried to interject.

"It's fine, Elia. Your mother is right. It was a bad call. I was trying to find a compromise for everyone. Josette had a right to object, but when she carried on and displayed the behaviour she did, I should have had her removed and watched. I'm sorry for my part in that."

I shook my head. "None of that matters. I am fine."

"You're not fine, Elia. I have been here less than a week and someone has attacked you twice. Clearly, this castle's security is severely lacking."

Oh, shit. They didn't know Josette was responsible for both attacks.

"Those were not typical circumstances, Tira. Our security is fine."

"Well, obviously, it's not fine. Have you found the archer?"

Hadrian looked defeated. I felt like a child whose parents were having an argument, which was ridiculous, since neither of them were my parents, nor were they together. A quick glance at the amusement on Hamish's face, the knowing look on Yarik's, and Uri, Wes and Tarryn looking like they'd prefer to be anywhere else, told me they all were thinking the same thing.

"Stop, both of you. Josette was responsible for the attack at the party, too."

That got their attention. "What?" Tira said.

"I forgot in the chaos of everything. Josette admitted it was her. Which explains how she got around the guards, and why the archer hadn't been found. It explains the aim as well."

"She said that? She admitted she was the one that fired the arrow? I didn't know she had any archery training."

"I don't think she has much, but she used her Gifting. All she needed to do was aim."

Tira shook her head. "You realise attacking my heir could be considered an attack against Xeria itself? Kingdoms have gone to war over less."

My eyes widened. "War? Okay, everyone calm down. Tira, it is not Hadrian or Taros's fault that Josette is unhinged. She is locked up now, and I am sure they will deal with her." I tried to diffuse the situation.

Hadrian nodded. "I assure you, we will."

"Let's focus on the positives. There's no real security breach. There's no one trying to attack you through me. It was all just Josette." I continued.

Tira sighed. "We can discuss this more later." *Oh, goody.*

"Josette, while not a trained archer, is a strong Teleki. She used to train with Valor and Jameson until her other duties took up more of her time. If she caught you off guard, how on earth did you fight her off?" Hadrian asked.

Excellent question. I noted Tira paying close attention. "I..." I trailed off. How did I explain that I'd possibly undergone a year of warrior training, or whatever I'd just used to pin Josette to the wall?

"Does it have something to do with your Testing?" Tira guessed and I glanced at her, nodding slightly.

"I think so, but I'm not entirely sure."

"Care to elaborate?" Her words were gentle, undemanding. I looked around the room, wondering if I could really trust everyone here with the details of my Testing, with my concerns. Obviously, I couldn't tell them all the details, but I had to know if what I had experienced was in any way real.

"Elia, we can step outside if you'd like to talk to Tira and Hadrian in private?" Tarryn offered. I smiled a little and shook my head. I had no issue with him or Hamish hearing this. Uri and Wes I was a little unsure about, but something told me I could trust them. Yarik was an unknown, as was Tira. Hadrian, I knew I could trust with some parts.

"No, that's okay. I'm just having trouble adjusting back to this life? If that makes sense. The timeline of it all has me confused." I finally conceded. Everyone in the room wore similar looks of understanding and patience.

"Ah," Hadrian said, "I take it your tests went for what felt like an extended period of time?"

"You could say that." I muttered.

"How long?" He asked. It was a risk. Telling him the truth could give away that my Testing was different in more ways than one. However, if I didn't tell him, I couldn't really explain my behaviour or get some reassurance that I wasn't completely insane.

"About a year." I finally confessed.

Tarryn let out a low whistle as Hadrian arched a brow.

"Well, no wonder you were so disorientated." He smiled reassuringly.

"Is that... normal?"

"No two Testings are alike. They are all unique to the individual. Obviously, some things are the same, but time is one thing that consistently varies."

"He means," Tira added, shooting Hadrian an exasperated look, "some people come out of their Testing feeling as if no time has passed. Some feel as if they've been in there for hours, days, or even months. The longest a person has claimed to have experienced, that we have a record of at least, is three years."

My eyes widened.

"Three years?" I repeated in shock.

"A year is certainly longer than we'd typically expect for a Para but it isn't cause for concern. Those that take their Testing later in life tend to feel as if more time has passed. Something to do with the mind being more developed and therefore more sceptical throughout the process." Hadrian reassured again.

"But I don't understand. If I was in there for that long, yet only two hours passed for all of you, was I actually there or was it all just a dream? Was what I experienced real?" I couldn't hide the confusion or the slight panic as I voiced my concerns. Hadrian nodded at Tira, clearly deciding she was better equipped to deal with my borderline hysteria.

"Elia." She took my hand. "As you know, there is a lot we cannot explain about the Testing, but I'm afraid you went in more unprepared than most. If we'd had time, I would have explained that out of all the unknowns surrounding the process, one thing we know is that what you experienced was, in most senses, real."

"But how can that be possible when I saw..." She gave my hand a small squeeze.

"Saw what?"

"... I saw someone that is dead. It can't truly have been them?"

"Ah. That is a question many have asked. Since we often see someone close to us, more often than not, those people are still alive, so how could it possibly be real?"

"So it isn't real? It's just what, a mirage made up of my memories?"

"The simple answer is we do not know. Most believe the guide is not real in the sense that we wish them to be. But, there have been too many cases where a guide has revealed things to the testee that only the guide themselves could have known, leading us to believe the guides aren't just memory based. We don't know if the divinities convene with the spirit of the guide prior to the Testing, if the spirit can enter Erro the same way ours do and therefore it truly is them, or if our minds are simply giving us answers to things we weren't able to process in our realm, but can in the Inbetween.

Ultimately, we cannot explain how it works, some things only the divinities can answer."

"But what about those whose guides are still alive? That obviously isn't them, so it can't be real?"

"We believe that the realm we enter during our Testing, which is very real, exists somewhere between here and the afterlife, Eternis. A place where our physical bodies cannot travel, but our spirits can. It stands to reason that the guide's spirits could also travel there. However, it doesn't explain why *we* remember everything from our Testing, but the guide does not. So, in most cases, we assume they are simply conjured by our memories or connection to them and are not really who we are seeing."

She clearly expected my next question from the look of utter confusion on my face, as she added.

"Long story short," Tira finished, "Whoever you saw, alive or dead, you saw for a reason. If you have reason to believe it was really their spirit, I cannot tell you it was not because we do not know. We don't know the true power of the divinities, but personally, I do like to think, at the very least, the essence of our guides is real. The thing that makes them important, and makes them who we cared for, is real."

"... Okay." I would try to untangle the web of confusion that explanation had created in my mind later. "What about the way time works? I still don't see how it could be so different."

She smiled a little and shrugged.

"I don't have an answer as to how it's possible, or even how it truly works. We do not know if everyone's Testing takes place in the same timeline. We don't know if it's possible for two people to come across each other if they both undergo the Testing at the same time. Scholars have pondered these questions for years, but there are simply some things only the divinities can answer."

"But," Hadrian said, joining back in, "they have proven that what a person experiences during their Testing, follows through when they wake. There are cases where people come out of their Testing with skills they previously didn't have, knowledge they hadn't possessed before. In rare, unfortunate cases, particularly when older Pures and Paras undergo their Testing late, much like yourself, there are even accounts of people so dramatically changed that they wake an entirely different person. Some people have woken and mourned as if their Testing was where they truly belonged. Some claim to have fallen in love during a trial and returned home to a partner they no longer care for. However, as we usually undergo the Testing before the age of six, those cases are uncommon."

The second last thing he said hit a little too close to home. I'd finally felt like I fit somewhere during my time with The Four. If it weren't for Sierra, I could have easily become one of those people mourning a life they wished they'd had instead. I swallowed and nodded.

"So we don't know how, but skills are transferable from the time spent in Erro, back to our real lives?"

Both Tira and Hadrian nodded.

"I will happily teach you what we know about the whole process when you are up for it." Tira offered, and I nodded.

"Sorry, you asked me how I fought off Josette and I forced us all onto a tangent." I apologised, but Hadrian shook his head.

"Nonsense, you've been through quite the ordeal in the last twenty-four hours. I'd say it's fairly warranted."

I smiled a little. "To answer your question, I fought her off using skills I picked up during my Testing. I spent a lot of time... training, during my test, and I guess it paid off because I was able to fend her off until Uri and Wes burst in and handled the rest."

No need to mention the unexpected golden explosion that apparently came from me.

Hadrian watched me and nodded. "It's lucky you had your Testing when you did, then. I am looking forward to hearing about it and seeing you in action." He smiled a bit.

I gave what I hoped was a reciprocating smile. "Absolutely."

A knock sounded on the door. A guard called out,

"Your Majesties, the medicae is here to tend to the Princess."

Hadrian stood. "I will make sure Josette is secure. I am truly sorry this happened, Elia. I hope you can forgive me."

I shook my head. "There's nothing to forgive. Don't worry about it."

He gave me a half-smile. "Yes, it looks like it's not your forgiveness I need to earn," he said, glancing at Tira, who just folded her arms. I bit my lip.

"I'll see you soon, Hadrian. Thank you for coming to check on me."

"Of course." He left, and the meda came in, finally giving me a minute to once again try to process everything that had occurred. He cleaned up both wounds, using some sort of herbal concoction to prevent any infection, before bandaging both.

"The cut on your neck is fairly superficial. You can remove the dressing after a day. The one on your chest is deep, but not deep enough that you require stitches. Just change your dressing daily, keep it clean. The herbs should stop any infection."

I nodded. "Thank you, Medicae."

He nodded. "Is there anything else you require?"

I shook my head. "No, that's everything. Thank you."

He bowed to Tira, and then me, before exiting my room. Which was still pretty crowded with Hamish, Tarryn, Uri, Wes, Yarik, and Tira.

"So, are we going to talk about what really happened tonight?" Tira asked.

"What do you mean? I told you what happened."

She sighed and turned to Uri and Wes, raising her eyebrows.

Uri looked at me. "I have to tell her, but if you'd prefer for the others to leave while I do...?"

I shook my head. "They may as well stay. I trust Hamish and Tarryn more than anyone else here. Wes saw what you saw and I am sure you will inform Yarik either way."

Hamish and Tarryn exchanged looks. I didn't miss how they subtly moved closer to me. Yarik didn't miss it either, and he half-smirked.

Uri sighed and turned to Tira. "We heard a loud thud. The door was locked, so we kicked it down. We found the princess with her hands out-stretched, standing over there." He pointed. "Lady Josette and the dagger were pinned against the opposite wall. There was some kind of golden layer of magic holding them suspended there."

Hamish frowned. "Sorry, what? Like a magical net?"

"Not a net per se... more of a barrier? Moulded to the shapes it was hold-ing. It was almost invisible. If it weren't for the gold colouring it would have just looked like they were floating against the wall." Wes offered.

Tarryn's eyes flew to mine. I averted my gaze. The last thing I needed was someone to realise there was something else going on. I flicked my gaze to Tira, who was watching me closely. Her arms still crossed. I couldn't read her expression.

"Hamish and Tarryn, please leave the room."

I frowned. "Why?"

"Because what I have to say can only be said around those we can ir-refutably trust."

"I trust Hamish and Tarryn with my life. More than I trust, frankly, a single one of you. Anything you have to say, you can say in front of them." Hamish and Tarryn wisely stayed silent, not budging from my side.

"Elia—"

"No. They are not leaving. Regardless of what you order them to do. They don't answer to you, they answer to the Navarre family, and therefore, me." I hoped they didn't mind the faked authority. I never enjoyed thinking of them having to answer to anyone.

She was quiet for a moment before she sighed, letting her arms drop to her sides, running her fingers through her hair.

"Okay. Just remember, I tried to keep it between us." She looked at Tarryn and Hamish. "You've obviously earned Elia's trust, but you haven't earned mine. If either of you even attempt to breathe a word to anyone outside of this room about what you hear today, and I *will* know if you try, you will be dead before you finish your sentence." She looked each of them in the eyes, without a hint of hesitation on her face.

A queen well prepared to follow through on her threat. To their credit, neither of them flinched. They simply nodded. She seemed satisfied with whatever she saw in their expressions, because she sat down opposite me and visibly deflated a little. She placed her hands in her lap and stared at them. It was quiet for a solid minute before she mustered the courage to say what she wanted to say.

She finally took a deep breath and met my eyes. "... I am not your mother."

Of all the things I was expecting her to say, that was not one of them. *How long has she known? Did Butcher or Solis reach out to her?* I glanced at Hamish and Tarryn before looking back at Tira.

"What?"

She sighed. "I am not your mother. My daughter died. I know for a fact she died."

"Then why would you say that I was? Why would you go through with the ceremony? Fates, you didn't just play along, you officially named me your heir."

"Because I made a promise to an old friend."

I frowned. "What are you talking about?"

She groaned. "I'm not explaining this well. Bear with me. I'm not sure how much you know of my family history, but let me explain. Did you know my father was not meant to inherit the Xerian throne?"

"What do you mean? Who was?"

"He had an older sister, my Aunt Gwyndelen. She was supposed to inherit the throne."

"Why didn't she?"

"Well, as I've mentioned, my father was a traditionalist. It's why I had to give my daughter up. He got that from my grandfather. When Gwyndelen declared she had fallen in love with an Impure, grandfather tried to persuade her to leave the man, but she would not. He had raised a stubborn daughter. When she refused to marry anyone else, and then fell pregnant, it was the final straw. He stripped her of her official title and gave the throne to her little brother, my father."

I raised my eyebrows. "Oh, that seems..."

"Harsh? Yes. The Melfore family is not known for its kind-heartedness. With some persuasion from my father, my grandfather allowed Gwyndelen to remain on the royal grounds, along with her soon to be husband, Diomedes. Gwyn was like a second mother to me. She was very close with my own mother, so when I was growing up, I'd often spend time with her and Uncle Dio." She smiled softly.

"Where are they now?"

"You remember me saying shortly after my mother died, many more Melfores died unexpectedly or were killed? They were among those casualties."

"I'm sorry to hear that, but I am still unsure what this has to do with me, or why you'd claim to be my mother."

"Diomedes was not from Xeria. They always just said he was a nomad from one of the other kingdoms, but never really said which one. Soon enough, they had their baby, a little boy, Zoron."

I tensed. My father's name was Zoron. It wasn't a common name, but it had to be a coincidence. Tira was watching me closely, but she carried on.

"Zoron and I grew up together. One day, I was at Gwyn and Dio's house playing with Zoron, when a man who looked like Uncle Dio showed up at the door. He had a little girl with him around my age. I think she was eight? The adults put all three of us in the playroom, before moving to Gwyn's study to talk where we couldn't hear them. The girl was quiet. We tried to play with her, but she just sat down by herself. Zoron thought she was weird."

"I'm still not sure where this is going." I had a feeling I might, but my brain refused to entertain that possibility.

"Well, when the adults came back, they explained to us that the man was Uncle Dio's brother, and he needed some help, so they were going to look after the little girl for a while. The little girl screamed and cried when the man tried to leave, but Uncle Dio held her back until the man left. The strange man had a look on his face that I will never forget. I think it was the first time I had seen someone look so pained. I was a child who had experienced no loss or hurt. But he left, and days turned to months, and months eventually turned to years. It took time, but the little girl ended up warming to us. She and I became good friends." She smiled reminiscently. "Very good friends."

"What was her name?" I dared to ask.

"Her name was Leigha." I froze. *Leigha.* My mother's name was Leigha. Zoron and Leigha Nightfell.

CHAPTER FIFTY-FOUR

Tira reached out to take my hand, but I pulled back. She swallowed.

"Uncle Dio's full name was Diomedes Nightfell. My aunt Gwyn became Gwyndelen Nightfell when they married. Their son—"

"Zoron Nightfell. You're—you're saying that your Aunt and Uncle were my grandparents? Zoron was your cousin?"

She nodded solemnly. "Yes. I was there when you were born, and your sister. I couldn't visit often, I had a kingdom to run, but I made it to your births. Your parents were like the siblings I never had."

I stood, shaking my head. "That makes no sense."

She stood with me. "Zoron and Leigha insisted on moving around, on travelling. They said they wanted to see the world and were never in the same place for long. It wasn't until you were born that I found out that wasn't the whole truth."

"What do you mean?"

"We were all told the reason my grandfather disapproved of, and ultimately disowned, my aunt was because Diomedes was Impure. That's what everyone was told. When you were born, I found out my father did truly think he was an Impure, but that was not the truth."

"He was Pure, wasn't he?"

Tira nodded. "He was. And Gwyn was a Pure Virbi."

I breathed in. "That's how I passed The Testing? My... you're saying my father was Pure?"

She nodded again. "Not just your father. Your mother was also Pure. I wasn't supposed to find out. I only did because I was there for your birth. It's rare, but sometimes when a powerful Pure baby is born, there are signs. Some say they are a blessing from the divinities. They take different forms, but they are unmistakable. As your mother went into labour, those signs became apparent. I thought it was an earthquake at first, but when I looked outside, nowhere else was affected. It was only their house. I turned and saw the panic in Leigha's eyes as she shared a look with Zoron. He kissed her hand, glancing at me standing there in the doorway, before stepping back from Leigha and closing his eyes. He extended his hands in front of him, and I watched in shock as a gold, translucent substance appeared out of nowhere, covering the inside of the room. It was like they were wrapped in a bubble. The shaking and the noise stopped affecting the rest of the house. I couldn't hear it, or them, anymore, but I could see them, I could see their furniture shaking, I could see Leigha's mouth moving, but I couldn't hear her words. They were all contained inside this golden orb. I'd seen nothing like it."

I glanced at Wes and Uri, who were staring in shock. Clearly, they hadn't heard this story either. Yarik, on the other hand, didn't look surprised.

"Once you were delivered, Zoron dropped his hands and the golden bubble disappeared. They sat me down and told me the truth. Uncle Diomedes hailed from a kingdom I'd never even heard of. It didn't exist. He possessed a Gifting I also hadn't heard of, which Zoron inherited. It was how he'd created that golden orb. Leigha then explained that she was also a Pure from this unknown place."

"Wait, they were related?" I said, feeling sick. Tira laughed a little and shook her head.

"No, of course not. She explained she was the descendent of a forgotten royal bloodline, one that the Nightfell family, Dio's family, had served for centuries. The strange man that had delivered her to my Aunt's doorstep, Diomedes' brother, was a royal guard from this forgotten kingdom, tasked with keeping Leigha safe. He grew concerned that he was being followed. So, he hid Leigha with Gwyn and Dio, while he led whoever was on his tail, as far away as he could. Leigha and Zoron weren't blood related, but their families were from the same place. Zoron came from a family of high-standing warriors, Leigha, from a family of royalty."

My hands were shaking. This made no sense, and yet it made perfect sense. Everything I'd been slowly piecing together, everything I'd learned during my Testing. But if all of that was true, then that meant? I turned to Tarryn. He shook his head, looking as dumbfounded as me.

"I inherited my father's Gifting." He answered my unasked question. He clearly had his own dots to connect and had realised the same thing I had.

Tira turned to Tarryn and frowned slightly. "What?"

I sat back down, afraid I might actually faint if I didn't.

"During my Testing, I saw a memory, a vision maybe? I don't know, but it was Tarryn as a little boy." I looked at Tarryn. "We haven't had a chance to properly talk about this, but it's how I knew about the story your mother told you."

His eyes widened. "You saw me and my mother?"

I nodded. "She was telling you a bedtime story about a forgotten kingdom. A king and queen who had two daughters, and—"

"The other kingdoms feared their power, so they attacked and eventually overthrew them, but not before trusted guards smuggled the two little princesses out, split up, and went in different directions." He finished. I swallowed and nodded.

"One going north and the other going west." I looked at him. "Tarryn, what is your Gifting?" Tira practically demanded.

"I am a Tear."

Tira watched us. "The only place Lios is north of is Taros. Xeria is to the west."

"You're saying the lost kingdom *is* Taros?"

Tira frowned and shook her head. "No, that wouldn't make sense, given the difference between your parents magic and the Kineti Giftings."

"Then what are you saying?"

"Oh, shit!" Hamish exclaimed, surprising everyone.

We looked over to him. His eyes were wide, and he had a look of amazement on his face. He looked at us and rubbed the back of his neck sheepishly.

"Sorry, I didn't mean to interrupt. Taros is one of the largest kingdoms on the continent, *but* only half of it is livable. The other half..."

"The Wastes," Tarryn said as if it had clicked into place for him.

"You're saying we come from The Wastes?" I question incredulously. He just shrugged.

"It's the only thing that logically makes sense," Hamish said as if it were simple.

"But, it's not inhabitable?"

"Look, before all of this I might have agreed with you and written it off, but the theory that we came from The Wastes is the least crazy thing I've heard today," Tarryn said.

"It makes sense. What better place to hide than right next door?" Tira said, glancing between us, before settling back on me.

"I am not your mother, but we are related. Technically, I am your father's cousin. And if your mother was Leigha's sister Tarryn, then the two of you are also cousins." She looked at Tarryn, then at me. "I promised your parents I'd always look out for you and Sierra. That if anything happened to either of them, I would step in. When your parents died, I sent people to look for you, some never returned, others came back empty-handed. You were already gone."

"How did you know I was here, or who I was? I was going by a different name. There was no known connection to my parents."

"I didn't. I had planned on coming here to expose whoever was behind this impersonation of my daughter. It wouldn't have been pretty, especially if I'd found Hadrian and Odette had something to do with it. I had planned on investigating, then I saw you. You look just like your mother... but I had to be sure, which is why I assigned Wes and Uri to watch you."

I narrowed my eyes at them. Wes looked at me guiltily, Uri just shrugged unapologetically.

"If it helps, they barely told me anything, much to my distaste." She reassured.

"Okay then, how did you know for sure?"

She sighed. "You probably won't believe me, but I dreamt about it. In my dream, there was an old woman, dressed in a midnight cloak, guiding me through my memories of Zoron and Leigha. Through my memory of their first daughter's birth, her name. Adira *Elia* Bellator Nightfell. Then she showed me a young woman with Zoron's eyes, you, standing in front of an army, your arms outstretched, and a tremendous wave of gold shooting out from them. Just like I'd seen Zoron do in that house, the day you were born."

Tarryn and I locked gazes.

"Baubao."

"The Crone." We both said at the same time.

Tira raised her eyebrows. "What?"

I shook my head. "That's a story for another time."

"Alright, well, I woke up, and I knew. You were the woman in the dream, and the resemblance to your parents was undeniable. As I said before, you are the spitting image of your mother, but your eyes, you have your father's eyes."

I swallowed. "Really?"

She smiled a bit and nodded. "Yes, your facial features, your hair colour, all from your mother, but you have the Melfore eyes."

"This is all insane."

She nodded. "It only confirmed my suspicions during your Testing. When they checked the strength of your Gifting, the bright flash. It just confirmed what I knew. Although I have no idea how you made it dim again."

I bit my lip. After everything that had been revealed today, I wasn't sure it was the best time to bring up Butcher and the blood oath and well, everything. That's if I could even find a way to tell her.

"I—"

"It's not important right now. We have plenty of time to discuss those types of things," she said, clearly sensing how overwhelmed I was. "I just want you to know that me offering you my kingdom was not a strategy or a manipulation. Your parents were my best friends and my family. I couldn't save them and I couldn't find you soon enough. This is me keeping my promise to them. I have no children of my own, nor will I ever. I cannot think of anyone I'd rather have to take over from me than the daughter of Zoron and Leigha Nightfell. My only living blood." She smiled softly.

I swallowed back the emotions coursing through me. There was so much. Disbelief, confusion, heartache, sorrow, surprise, relief. Glancing around the room, I thought I might burst into tears at the sheer volume of the situation, but I kept it together long enough to look back to Queen Tira. Not my mother, but still blood-related. Family.

"Thank you..."

After we'd all taken the time to mull over what we'd just learned, and filled in a few blanks, Tira asked to speak to me and Tarryn alone. The others left the room, and Tarryn joined me on the lounge.

"I never met your mother Tarryn, but if she was anything like Leigha, then she must have been an exceptional woman."

Tarryn gave her a small smile. "Thank you."

I looked at him. "Are we sure that our parents were siblings? We don't have any concrete proof."

"Well, if what you saw is true, Adira," It was strange to hear her call me by my real name, "the memory of Tarryn and his mother, then yes, your mothers were surely sisters."

"So, not only are we cousins, but we are royalty?" I glanced at Tarryn.

"Well, thanks to Queen Tira, you're already royalty." He smirked.

I rolled my eyes. "By that logic, we are still related, so you are *also* already royal by association."

He chuckled and shook his head.

"Yes, if your court were ever re-established, either of you could rule it."

My eyes widened. "Dibs not." Now it was his turn to roll his eyes.

Tira smiled a bit. "That's actually why I wanted to speak to the two of you alone."

"What do you mean?"

"When your parents were killed, Adira, I tried to find out as much as possible about why and how. As well as anything I could regarding what little Leigha had told me about their kingdom."

I nodded a bit. "According to the story from Tarryn's mother, the rulers from the other six kingdoms united and erased Thadea. That's what it was called, right?"

Tira nodded. "From what I have learned over the years, yes. The Kingdom of Thadea. Named after the Goddess of Desire. Home of the Potenti."

"The what?"

She smiled a bit. "The Potenti, that is your Gifting, Adira. It translates roughly to power or powerful. I am sure you can see why the other kingdoms were wary of this ability."

"Yes, but what actually is it?"

"It has been difficult to find information on the Potenti magic. As you said, they erased almost all traces of it from the world."

"How did they do that? No one has a Gifting that could erase people's memories." Tarryn pointed out.

Tira nodded. "I had the same question for Leigha. The most she could tell me was that they supposedly used something that was blessed by Thadea herself. They then took turns imbuing the... object with each of their Giftings, creating something of unrivalled power. Whoever wielded it was said to be capable of nearly anything."

"What happened to the object?" I asked.

"No one knows. Some say the kingdoms took turns passing it around, so it was never with one ruler for too long. But, over time, as ties grew strenuous and alliances changed, it was no longer agreeable for any one kingdom to have it on their own. They say it was hidden, never to be found."

"That's ominous," Tarryn said, and I nodded in agreement.

"Yes, but the fact is, somehow the world forgot about Thadea. I think only those who lived there, or perhaps only those with the Potenti Gifting, retained the memory, and the other kingdoms wiped out anyone they found with the Gifting or knowledge."

I shook my head. "An entire people wiped out because other kingdoms were scared? They were peaceful. They didn't attack anyone? The other six massacred an entire kingdom of innocent people." The anger was clear in my words, rage that had been building in me since all of this began.

Tarryn looked at me, and I could see the understanding and mirrored anger in his eyes.

"I know it's an unkind history, and you have every right to be mad about what they did to your people and your families, but don't let that anger cloud your judgement," Tira said.

"You were explaining what exactly the Potenti Gifting was?" I said, looking at her.

She nodded. "Sort of. Not a lot is known. I have never met another Potenti, other than your mother and father."

"What do you know?"

"I know that golden force your father could wield is different from what your mother could do."

"What do you mean?"

"I can only surmise that Potenti are the same as the other Gifted, with at least two Specialties. Two or more potential abilities a Potenti could wield. Your mother and father must simply have had different Specialties. It makes sense since they were from different families, different bloodlines."

"And by that logic, the Potenti would also be like all the other Pure bloodlines, in that you would only specialise in one thing?" I wasn't sure what compelled me to ask that. Clearly, I'd inherited my father's ability, but I felt as if I was missing something.

"It has been hard to get any concrete facts, but everything I have found points to it being the same as any other Gifting, so yes. I don't believe your mother could wield the golden power your father could."

"Okay, so one Specialty involves this golden magic, or whatever it is. What is the other ability?"

"I don't know. Neither of them would ever tell me. Whenever I pushed, they would tell me it was safer if I did not know. So perhaps it was not your father's ability that had scared the other kingdoms into action, but your mothers."

"I suppose that makes sense." I muttered, trying to wrap my head around it all.

She nodded. "Tarryn, your father was Elementi?"

He nodded. "Yes, a similar story to Diomedes, just without the royalty tied to it. I was told that my mother was Impure. It wasn't until my parents' deaths that Baubo found me, and I learned a little more. It wasn't until my Testing that I found out I was Pure."

"Adira, how did you make the stone dim itself after your Testing?" Tira asked. I glanced at Tarryn and he shrugged.

"It's your call."

I sighed. She knew everything else. I stood, and that's when I realised I was still in quite a scandalous nightgown. Divinities, I had hugged Hadrian in this.

"Tarryn, turn around."

He rolled his eyes. "We are related, Adira. I don't think that's something you need to worry about."

I shrugged and lifted my nightgown. At which point, Tarryn rethought his comment.

"Okay, on second thought, this feels more weird." He turned away.

I laughed a bit and lifted it high enough on one side to give Tira a view of my brand. I wasn't breaking my oath by revealing my brand to Tira. I was bound not to speak of my blood oath to anyone, but if she recognised the marking for what it was, I wouldn't have to.

Tira gasped and leaned in closer. "What is that?"

"It's a blood oath." Tarryn answered, much to my relief. I had never explicitly told Tarryn about the oath. I'd chalked it up to yet another thing The Crone shouldn't have known, but did, and had passed on to him.

"We have not used blood oaths for millennia..."

"That is what I thought." I winced in pain as I tried to add, *'Until I got branded with one'*, but I couldn't.

"Who did this to you?" Tira said, watching me carefully.

"The woman who took them in." Tarryn once again filled in the gaps I could not. Anger flared in Tira's eyes.

"I've searched for ways one might break a blood oath, but had no luck until my Testing." I lowered my dress. I was sworn not to speak of *my* blood oath. They said nothing about being forbidden from discussing blood oaths in general. "You can look again, Tarryn."

He turned around and smiled gratefully at me. "Thanks."

"Your Testing?" Tira asked.

I nodded. "I was told that blood oaths were essentially just magical diseases. Ergo, a Remedi should be able to remove one, like they would another disease."

"That is good. We can find one to help."

"It's not that simple."

"Why not?"

I tensed as I tried to get the words out, but couldn't. As I strained harder, the pain increased. I held my stomach, falling to one knee. Tarryn was at my side in a heartbeat, helping me up.

"The woman who bound her. She has Sierra."

"What?" Tira said.

"The only reason she took the oath was because The Butcher threatened to kill Sierra," he said, and I swallowed. "They forced her into it, and she still has her."

I looked at Tarryn. "I never told you any of that Tarryn, how could you know so much?"

He gave me a knowing look, confirming my earlier assumption, and I groaned.

"The Crone?"

He shrugged. Tira raised her eyebrows but shook her head.

"Then we go get her. I am a queen, Adira. I can send an entire legion to her door if I need to."

I shook my head. "You don't understand. I can't fight." That was all I could manage without more pain ensuing. I had to be vague and nonspecific.

"If I kill her, then she can't make any commands."

"She isn't working alone." I managed.

She frowned. "Who is she working with?"

"Solis." I said, sworn not to discuss the oath, but nothing stopped me from discussing Butcher's alliances.

Tira cursed. "The damned Rise."

"You know about the Rise?" Tarryn asked.

"Yes, the rebellion is not just here in Taros. The Rise has become a problem all across the continent. No one has identified the true ringleader. Every time we catch a potential, another one takes their place, and they never talk. The only thing we know is that *whoever* is in charge goes by Solis." Tira's eyes simmered with rage.

"That's why all the kingdoms are coming, isn't it? Because they are all having the same problem. One that's finally big enough to get them all in the same room, willing to consider a treaty," I said, finally able to speak of at least this.

She nodded. "Yes, so you are right. Attacking this Butcher will not help us. Our best chance is getting a Remedi to remove the binding when they come for the meeting. Queen Yelara owes me a favour."

I raised my eyebrows. "Care to elaborate?"

"I would also like to hear that story." Tarryn chimed in.

"Nope," Tira said, standing up. "I better check on your attacker. Make sure they really have her secured, and that she has said nothing."

"I would appreciate that. I am exhausted." *Understatement of the year.*

"Of course. You get some sleep. Frankly, I'm not sure how you are still conscious."

I smiled a bit, and Tarryn stood, joining Tira. "I'll be outside if you need anything."

"No, you need to go back to your rooms and process all of this too, Tarryn," I said firmly.

"I'm fine." He insisted.

"I agree with Adira. My guards can cover while you take some time."

"And Hamish will be with them. Do I have to order you?" I smirked.

He sighed. "Fine."

I grinned. "Thank you."

He rolled his eyes, and Tira winked at me on their way out. Locking my door, I closed my eyes and breathed out.

CHAPTER FIFTY-FIVE

DIVINITIES. MY MIND WAS overloaded with information. I needed sleep. I walked back to my bed and practically crawled in. Within minutes, I was out. It was one of the deepest sleeps I'd had in quite some time. Clearly, I was truly exhausted and for once; I was grateful.

It was early evening by the time I finally woke. Before I'd even opened my eyes, something felt off. The bed was too soft. I jerked upright, reaching under the pillow for my dagger, but came up empty-handed. I breathed in, looking around in the darkness. I realised I wasn't back at camp with The Four. For a second I expected to find Raf, but then my eyes adjusted to the dark. I made out the surrounding objects. A familiar closet, vanity, and bed. I glanced down at myself before laying back and breathing out. *You're back in Taros Adira. Your Testing is over.*

Shaking my head, I got up and lit the lanterns around the room. The darkness made it too easy to forget where I was. I still wasn't sure if this was real. I walked to the floor-length mirror and glanced at my reflection. Thankfully, this one didn't talk or move unexpectedly.

Reaching up to my neck and then to my chest, I touched each dressing. The events of yesterday flooded back in. Waking up from my Testing, being crowned princess, being attacked by Josette, and finding out I am not only Pure, but I possess a Gifting that shouldn't exist, descend from a royal blood-line that also shouldn't exist, and I am related to Tarryn and Tira by blood.

Despite knowing all of that had happened, I felt detached, almost numb. My mind was foggy. It cleared just enough to remind me I should change my dressing and maybe have a bath. I grabbed the bag the meda left for me and went to the bathroom. Taking off my bandage and undressing, I stepped into the tub. Closing my eyes, I took what felt like the first calm breath I'd taken in days.

It didn't last long, as everything I'd learned slowly started filling my head again. I didn't even know where to start. I needed to see Sierra, given how our last interaction went. But that meant seeing Butcher, and I risked exposing what I knew to her if I did that. If she forced me to answer, it would be dangerous for everyone. I was better off staying away. Even if it killed me a little more each day that I had to spend away from her, especially when I felt as if I'd been gone a year. I wanted to tell her about our parents, our family, and apparently, our people.

Sighing, I got out, dried off, and applied new dressings. The castle probably already knew about the attack and no doubt was going crazy over the juicy gossip. I got dressed, needing some air. After spending so much time in the open outdoors with The Four, I felt suffocated in here, despite the spacious rooms. Opening my door, I found Hamish and Wes standing guard.

I raised my eyebrows. "Well, this is an odd pairing."

Hamish grinned and held out his hand. Wes groaned, took out a few marks, and handed them to Hamish.

"What was that about?"

"I bet Wes that you would comment on it. He bet you wouldn't care who was guarding you."

I smiled a bit, shaking my head. "That's a stupid bet."

"Yes, well, fool me once," Wes said.

Hamish chuckled. "Where are we going, Princess?" He said, and I shot him a glare at the use of my title.

"For a walk, outside. I am suffocating in here."

He nodded. "Excellent, I could use some air."

I smiled. Hamish just had a way of putting me at ease. We made our way out to the castle grounds. I closed my eyes and breathed in. Even before all of this, I'd spent every spare minute I wasn't working outside. Raf and I would go to our spot on the hill. My heart still panged at the thought of him, but the pain was a little less since the Testing. Real or not, I felt like I'd gotten my goodbye, and the closure I'd needed. I opened my eyes, looking up at the stars, letting myself smile a little, thinking of him.

"Can we go up to the towers?"

"I don't see why not," Hamish said.

He led us to the huge stone wall that encircled the castle, where he chatted with some guards at the bottom of the stairs and they nodded, waving us through. Hamish and Wes hung back a few yards once we were at the top. I walked to the edge and looked out at the view. The towers were lit, their reflections shining along the Sineti River.

I couldn't help but glance toward The Wastes, where nothing but a never ending wall made of thick, black fog, stretched for as far as the eye could see. Could that really be where my family was from? I couldn't help but want to go there. If what they say is true and it really is wasteland, there could be nothing, but now that I knew about it, I felt a pull I couldn't explain.

"You feel it too, don't you?" I jumped in shock, gripping the wall.

"Don't do that!" I said to the smiling old woman that had just appeared out of thin air.

"Sorry. Bad habit. Hard to break."

I shook my head and looked over at Hamish and Wes.

"They can't see me, so if I were you, I would go back to looking out at the view, so you don't look like a crazy lady."

"I think that ship has sailed." I turned back to the view anyway, leaning against the wall. "Feel what too?"

"The pull to home."

I looked at her. "Home?"

She smiled. "Yes, home."

"You're from Thadea?"

"I am."

"Why didn't you tell Tarryn?"

"That was not my place. Tarryn has his own path. He will come to know what he needs to know, when he needs to know it."

My head spun, trying to follow that sentence, but it somehow made sense.

"Right, so, it's just me you get to torment?"

"That isn't how I would put it."

"I don't think I want to know how you would put it."

She smiled at me. "I have to go away for a while, so you won't be seeing me."

I looked at her, partly relieved. "Where are you going?"

"To commune with the divine." She smirked. She looked like she was joking, but I could never tell with her.

So I scoffed. "Tell them we could use a hand."

"From what I heard, you told them yourself and didn't get very far in that argument?"

My eyes widened slightly. "How could you possib—" *Holy Hek.* "You were there! The eighth voice was yours!" The voice had been familiar, but it was muffled and I had never considered... I can't believe I didn't place it sooner.

She grinned, taking a step back.

"How? How were you there?"

She shrugged. "I didn't come to say goodbye. I came with a warning."

Oh, great. "A warning about what? More serpens?"

She shook her head. "A storm is brewing, Adira."

"Tell me something I don't know."

Her smile faded. "You will all be tested. These walls will not protect you from the true enemy. There are many factions at play. Don't forget that."

"Are you talking about the other kingdoms? Their visit?"

She shook her head. "Listen to what you do not hear."

I frowned. "I keep getting told that, but it makes no sense."

"It is up to you to make the sense, make sense."

I groaned. "Please give me something I can actually understand?"

She took another step back. "When the water runs red, you will know the storm has begun. Be careful."

"Be careful of what?"

But she was already gone. I groaned, closing my eyes. *Excellent. What's one more thing to add to the list?* I opened my eyes and glanced up at the sky.

"Bet you think this is all very amusing." I whispered, and I could have sworn the stars twinkled a little brighter in response. I shook my head, making my way back over to Hamish and Wes.

"I'm ready to go back in."

After heading back inside, I went to see Cali. I'd meant what I said to her after the ceremony. I wanted to make more time for her. Knocking on her door, I heard some rustling before she popped her head out. Her hair was a little frizzy, and she looked a tad dishevelled.

"Oh, Elle! Hey." She grinned.

I raised my eyebrows. "Is this a bad time?"

"No! No, of course not." She bit her lip. "Give me... five minutes?"

I laughed a bit. "Are you sure?"

"Absolutely. Just wait right there."

I nodded. "Okay." I stepped back from the doorway as she shut it.

I waited, and a few minutes later, the door opened. It wasn't Cali who stepped out, though.

"Killian." I smirked slightly. "Nice to see you."

He nodded. "Princess Elia, Cali said to let yourself in." He rubbed the back of his head a little.

I nodded, leaning in as I passed him. "You have something on your neck." I grinned, turning to shut the door. His eyes widened as he tried to get a look at the love bite Cali had no doubt intentionally left on him before giving up, taking his hair out of its bun, and using it to conceal the mark. I chuckled to myself as I shut the door.

"That was cruel," Cali said, and I turned to face her. Her eyes were lit up in amusement.

"Cruel was giving him that mark in such an obvious place."

She shrugged. "Accidents happen." She batted her eyelashes at me innocently. I grinned, walked over, and hugged her.

She squeezed me back tightly. "How are you? I heard what happened with Josette. That is *insane.*"

"We can talk about that later. I want to hear about what just went on with you and the captain." I wiggled my eyebrows.

She blushed and shrugged. "I think you know what happened."

"Yes, but when? I thought you decided since you couldn't be together, there was no point getting properly involved. Save yourselves from more pain and all that?"

She sighed and pulled me over to her bed. It was even bigger than mine. We both fell back onto the mattress.

"It happened after the attack. I mean, the tension has been there since that day we all went to the hot springs."

"No kidding." I rolled my eyes.

She whacked me with a pillow. "Do you want to hear about it or not?"

I laughed. "Okay! Okay, shutting up now. Go ahead."

She smiled. "So, as I was *saying*. Things have been simmering since then. It's been getting harder and harder to keep things platonic. And then after the attack, when he took me back to my room, it just... happened."

I raised my eyebrows. "Oh?"

She groaned and nodded. "Yes! It wasn't planned. He walked me to my door, checked my room to make sure no one was lurking." She rolled her eyes. "I kept trying to assure him I was fine, but he just wouldn't hear me. So, to stop him, I just sort of kissed him." She bit her lip.

I laughed. "Oh, I bet that shut him up *real* fast."

She giggled and nodded. "It did. I only intended to shut him up, but once we kissed, it just—he kissed back and..." She shrugged. "Since then, it's been hard to keep our hands off each other."

I pulled a face. "Gross."

This time I blocked the pillow that came flying at my face and laughed. "I'm happy for you, Cali. You two deserve to be happy."

She sighed. "Yeah, well, we are just prolonging the inevitable. Neither of us has spoken about the future, and I'm not going to until I absolutely have to. I've decided to just enjoy the moment."

I nodded. "If I had a drink, I would toast to that."

"I've missed you." She smiled. "What about you and my brother? He's been all sorts of moody lately."

I sighed. "I don't know. At first, it was the same reason I was avoiding you. I had a really hard time with Raf's death. I couldn't look at you two and not see the guards standing there while his body was hanging from a noose." I swallowed. Cali reached out and took my hand, giving me time to get myself together. I breathed out. "Then it was a bit confusing because of the whole Princess of Xeria thing and everyone was talking about the betrothal being real or about other kingdoms' heirs wanting a betrothal, and that Queen Tira might facilitate that for an alliance."

She groaned. "Oh, the joys of being a princess, right?"

I smiled a bit and nodded. "Yeah, I just—I don't know what I want. When I'm with Valor, it's intense, in a good way, but it feels like those are just stolen moments? When we are alone, we get lost in each other and it is amazing, but then reality sets in and we end up fighting or getting on each other's nerves. I don't know, it sounds stupid."

"No, it's not stupid. I get what you're saying."

"What did you hear about Josette?"

"I heard she snuck into your room and attacked you with a knife, but you fought her off like a badass!" She held up her hand. I laughed and humoured her, slapping my palm against hers.

"Yeah, what everyone else wasn't told is how she snuck in."

"What do you mean?"

"She got in through the tunnels, the same ones she would use to rendezvous with Valor."

Her eyes widened. "Oh, shit."

I nodded. "Yeah. That's just, I don't know. It turned me off big time. It made me think about how many other girls he's used those tunnels with and I know it's not fair, but..." I shook my head.

She bit her lip. "Well, I couldn't say for sure, but I think it's only Josette and James who know about *that* portion of the tunnels. She knew they existed from when we were kids."

I shrugged. "I know. I'm probably being irrational. I don't know. I'm probably using it as an excuse to not take things further because I don't know what's happening. There's so much going on."

"Girl, I think you're being perfectly rational."

I smiled a bit. "Thanks." I breathed out. "This is so nice, just having a conversation with a girl. Don't get me wrong, the boys are splendid, but it's just different." Amory and Moira were great, but they weren't exactly the type of friends you could have 'girl talk' with.

She nodded. "I completely agree. Even the other ladies at court aren't as easy to talk to as you are."

I chuckled and nodded. "I wouldn't know. The other ladies didn't talk to me until I was named princess."

"Yeah, well, trust me, you aren't missing anything. But what else have I missed? Fill me in."

So much. "Nothing really, just getting to know Tira, dodging attacks left right and centre, and trying to look convincing as a princess."

She chuckled. "Well, I can help with the princess lessons, on one condition."

I raised my eyebrows. "What condition is that?"

"You let me train with you and those hot guards of yours in those morning sessions you do."

I raised my eyebrows. "You want to train?"

"Yep." She simply shrugged. "So, do we have a deal?"

I laughed a bit. "I'd have to ask them, but I'm sure they wouldn't mind. I should warn you, they are hard asses." I needed to get back into condition as soon as possible.

"Good. My trainer is a 'traditionalist.' He's all about only knowing how to fight so I can use it as a last resort. Plus, he treats me like a doll."

I chuckled. "Well, Tarryn and Hamish will *not* treat you like a doll, unless it's the punching dummy kind."

She grinned. "Excellent. I teach you princess etiquette, and you teach me proper fighting skills."

We shook on it to make it official.

I smiled. "Can you teach me more about the other kingdoms' royals as well? They will be here soon, and I feel like I need to prepare."

She nodded quickly. "Absolutely. Why don't we start now?"

"Oh, we don't have to start now. That's okay."

"Well, Killian is gone, so what else am I going to do?"

I laughed and shrugged. "Okay then."

We spent well into the late evening going over all the royal families that would be visiting. Who they were, what their Giftings were, who their kids were, what they were like. Cali knew *everything* about *everyone*. It was quite impressive.

I eventually found myself yawning far too often, and so did Cali, so we called it a night. She hugged me tightly as I left.

Thankfully, it was an uneventful walk back to my room, where I ate dinner and went to sleep. No more attacks, or creepy old ladies showing up, or men busting into my room. I didn't even know what a normal night was anymore, but I imagine it's close to this. A nice evening walk, catching up with a friend, a quiet meal, and then off to sleep.

CHAPTER FIFTY-SIX

THE REST OF THE week was thankfully uneventful. I was having two training sessions a day. It was incredibly depressing that all my hard work, all the muscle I'd built, had been erased, and I had to start over. Cali and I spent a lot of time together as she continued my royal etiquette lessons. Things with Valor had also been strangely fine. We hadn't talked about what had happened the night of the attack, but we were definitely friendlier than we had been as of late.

I woke to Lydia politely placing my breakfast beside me.

"Good morning, Princess. I'm sorry to wake you, but the queen has requested your presence after your training session."

I rubbed my eyes sitting up, "Mmm that's okay, which queen?"

"Odette."

I groaned, and she smiled but kept her mouth shut, moving to tidy the other rooms. I grabbed the tray of food and started eating it right there in bed.

"What would you like to wear today?" Lydia called out.

"Whatever you think is best, Lydia!" I responded, "Surprise me!" As I ate, something occurred to me. "Hey Lydia?"

"Yes, Princess?" She poked her head around the door, ignoring my glare.

"... Are you a member of the Deos Credentes?" She raised her eyebrows. "No? Why do you ask?"

"Was Tilly..?" She paused, stepping into the room.

"She was." Neither of us had discussed the elephant in the room that was Tilly. The crown had made no announcement about the assassination attempt. As far as everyone else knew, the assassin was still at large. Lydia, however, was smart enough to put two and two together. I looked at her.

".... Why would she do it, Lydia?"

"She wouldn't Elia. I know her. She didn't do it." I held back my sigh. There was a reason I hadn't asked Lydia sooner. Multiple actually. Mainly in case she was also involved, but also because Tilly was her friend.

"And if I told you she'd confessed?"

"What? That can't be right. Elia, Tilly didn't even like hurting the spiders we'd have to remove when cleaning. It was her belief that no living thing should be harmed."

"Can you think of any reason she would confess, then? Anyone she might protect?"

Lydia shook her head, a look of concern in her eyes.

"... Is she—is she even still alive?"

She'd be better off if she weren't.

"Yes. I think I've found the people she was working for, but I still can't figure out why. If you know anything, Lydia, anything at all..."

Lydia bit her lip.

"I honestly can't think of any reason she would do such a thing. She doesn't have a family, she has a boyfriend? Maybe someone threatened him." I nodded slightly.

"Thanks Lydia, I'll look into that." She gave me a small nod before exiting the room to continue her morning duties.

I'd already looked into the boyfriend and ruled him out. He was cute, but not the brightest. He'd apparently been heartbroken when Tilly had ended things with him out of the blue. My best bet was still the Deos Credentes, Chambersen's wife. But was Tilly's faith really so strong that it could make her do something like this?

I tabled those thoughts as Lydia announced it was time for me to go to training or I'd be late to meet the queen. Apparently, she had taken my outfit request literally, because what she chose was a pink summer gown. *Pink.* I gave her a look, and she just grinned with a *'you told me to choose'* look on her face.

I rolled my eyes, put on my training gear, praying she'd have changed her mind by the time I got back. I stopped by Cali's room. She would finally join me for training. It took some shaking to rouse her from sleep. She was not accustomed to waking this early. But she got up, got changed, and we made our way to the courtyard with Tarryn and Uri. Conveniently, they were guarding me this morning. I wasn't sure why they weren't paired with their usual partners. Tarryn bowed to both Cali and me. I rolled my eyes.

"Oh, don't get polite now, just because Cali is here."

Cali grinned. "What she said."

Tarryn smiled a bit. "Alright, you know the drill. I'm sure you can enlighten Cali."

I sighed and nodded. "We start with cardio."

Cali nodded, and we ran Tarryn's instructed amount of laps before we got into some stretches. After that, we taught Cali the basics. Then we split up.

Tarryn with Cali, and Uri with me. I can't say I was excited about going up against him again, but it would be good to see just how different I was after my Testing.

Uri picked up on my excitement and smirked. "Confident are we?"

"Do you always talk this much?"

I grinned, and that was all the invitation he needed. He launched himself at me. He was expecting the untrained version of me he'd seen before. The girl who'd only just begun to learn. But in my mind at least, I'd had four months of intensive training with The Warriors Four and another eight months of putting it into practice. The memories were still there, lost muscles aside.

A thrill shot through me at the look of surprise on his face, when I ducked and rolled, springing back to my feet and immediately switching to the offensive. This time, it was me launching myself at him. We traded blow for blow. Deflecting and dodging. Both of us moved in sync as we each tried to get the upper hand. It was a blur as we attacked and countered. Uri obviously wasn't using his full force, but he landed fewer blows than both of us expected. Eventually, Uri called time. Both of us were panting. I had to give it to him; I was suffering much more than he was. He was a brilliant fighter and definitely had the most wins during our fight, but still. I was proud I even kept up.

I turned to see Tarryn and Cali sitting on a stone bench, watching us with wide eyes. They also weren't alone. At some point, Valor, Killian, and a few of their nobleman friends had joined them. Plus, the guards that came with them. All of whom were staring in even more shock than Tarryn. They'd probably never seen a noblewoman fight. Not here in Taros. It wasn't done.

Tarryn grinned as he stood, snapping out of it first, then Cali.

"WOOO!" She started clapping and practically bounced up and down. I laughed, waving her off. I wiped my face on the cloth provided and headed over.

"Girl! That. Was. *Amazing.* You totally kicked his ass!"

"I wouldn't go *that* far," Uri said, coming to stand beside me.

I smiled. "Neither would I."

"Even so. That was impressive." He acknowledged.

"Yeah, I'd like to know just how you learned those manoeuvres practically overnight?" Cali asked.

I shrugged. "I may have had a little help."

She glanced at Valor and Killian, whose shock was wearing off.

Killian shook his head. "Don't look at me." He glanced at Valor, who also shook his head.

"Wasn't me? If I had known she was that dangerous, I might have been a little nicer."

Cali smirked. "Can you train me, Elia?"

I laughed. "No. Trust me, you want Tarryn as your trainer," I said, putting my hand on his arm.

Valor's eyes harden slightly at the gesture, but I ignored it.

"Well, either way, that was awesome," Cali said.

"Thanks. I actually can't hang around. Your mother has summoned me."

"Oh, poor you."

"I know." I smiled. "But I'll see you later?"

She nodded. "Of course. Tell mother dearest I said hello."

"Will do." I looked at Tarryn. "If you want to stay here and go over some things with Cali, I am sure Uri can escort me to the queen."

"If the princess wants to, and Uri is alright with that, then sure."

"It couldn't hurt. If I want to beat you, I need all the extra training I can get." She agreed.

"How come you've never asked me to train you?" Killian said, looking almost as jealous as I knew he was inside.

"You never offered." She answered matter-of-factly.

"And that's my cue." I smiled, nodded to Uri, and we exited the courtyard.

I could feel Valor's, and a few of the other noble's, eyes still on me as I left. I returned to my room and quickly bathed, pouting for a few seconds at the fact that Lydia hadn't changed her mind about the pink dress, before letting her help me into the damned thing.

I met Odette in a tearoom, thank Ades. I did not want to be meeting in her private quarters again. I walked over and curtsied.

"Your Highness."

She smiled. "Elia, have a seat, child."

I nodded and took a seat. "Thank you."

"Tea?" She asked.

I nodded. "Yes, please."

She snapped her fingers, and I had to hold back my grimace at the gesture. A servant stepped forward and poured me a cup. I thanked them before returning my attention to Odette.

"How are you, dear? After all the nastiness with Josette?" She shook her head in distaste.

"I am doing well. Thank you for asking."

"Good, good, and how was your Testing? I know I was there, but we haven't discussed it in depth."

"It was a lot to take in, honestly. I am still processing a lot."

She nodded. "I can imagine." She took a sip of her tea.

"How is Tilly?" I risked asking.

"Matilda? Oh, she is doing great." She smiled. "Really thriving, to be honest. Serving her sentence well."

I nodded slightly, taking a sip of my drink to help keep me grounded. "I haven't really seen her around."

"Oh, well, she doesn't leave her cell unless she is serving me. It wouldn't be a punishment otherwise, would it?"

"No, I suppose it wouldn't." I had to free her.

She nodded. "But enough of that. What I really want to discuss is my son."

I coughed slightly. "Your son?"

"It's no secret that he is infatuated with you. I'm not sure even *he* realises just how much you have struck him." She smiled. "And who can blame him?"

"Um, thank you."

"I think it's time we started discussing the wedding."

My eyes widened. "Who's wedding?"

"Why, yours and Valor's, of course!"

"I'm sorry?" She obviously hadn't gotten the message after my coronation.

"Oh, I know he hasn't given you a ring yet, but you know what men are like." She flicked her wrist in what was supposed to be a *'you know how they can be'* type of gesture.

"Uh, Your Highness, I thought I made it clear last week? I have no interest in being betrothed to *anyone* right now. The fake arrangement with Valor was only so I could gather information for you."

"Of course, but now that you are a princess, it doesn't need to be a ruse. It is the perfect coupling. I can see you two have chemistry. My son would be willing. And the good relationship it could foster with Xeria is a bonus. We need something to unite us. You could be that something. Isn't that great?" She smiled brightly. *This woman had multiple personalities, I swear.*

"That is a pleasant notion, but as I said after my naming ceremony, I am not looking to tie myself to anyone right now."

"Every woman is looking to tie herself to someone. Most aren't lucky enough to get a man like my son."

"Your son is no doubt a desirable suitor for any woman—"

"Good, so we agree then."

"No, we don't. Valor and I are not betrothed, Odette. Nor will we be anytime soon. We aren't even courting." I shook my head slightly, not entirely sure if that was true, but she didn't need to know that. "I'm sorry, but I am not the solution to your ally problems."

"If this is because you think there might be a better offer from one of the other kingdoms, there won't be," she said, sitting back, "they *only* want you for your title. Here, you could be a part of the family. You practically already are. Hadrian loves you, my daughter considers you a good friend, even Valor, despite trying not to, has warmed to you. Look at all we have already given you."

I frowned slightly. "I am thankful for your family's generosity and for welcoming me into your home, but that does not mean I am going to marry your son. It's not about the other kingdoms and what they may offer. Right now, I am not interested in a betrothal to anyone." I repeated, standing. "I have a few things I need to attend to. Thank you for the tea."

"I think you will change your mind."

"Respectfully, I will not."

"If you are wise," she said, and her eyes hardened slightly, her smile turning cold, "you will."

"Enjoy the rest of your day, Your Highness." I turned and made for the exit as hastily as I could, without looking like I was running away. Even though that's exactly what I was doing.

"That was one of the most polite and yet terrifying conversations I've ever seen." Uri commented as we walked away from the tearoom.

I looked at him. "No way you heard us from where you were standing?"

He shook his head. "No, I didn't. But I could read your body language, and hers. You were smiling at each other, but there was nothing friendly about that interaction. Am I wrong?"

"No, you're not."

"What did she want?"

"She wants me to marry her son."

"Ah, the prince. And you *don't* want to?"

I rolled my eyes. "Oh, because who wouldn't want to marry someone solely for other people, and not because they're in love?"

He chuckled. "I don't know who you do or don't love. For all I know, you could be in love with the guy. He seems alright, for a Kineti."

I scoffed. "For a Kineti?" Ignoring the fact that my heart sped up on that last part.

"The Virbi and Kineti don't have the best history. It's interesting they would want to match their son with you. No offence."

"None taken. Honestly, Hadrian is a good man. It is Odette that is the issue. She hates Tira, so I can't think of a good enough reason she would want the daughter of a woman she despises, a woman who used to be betrothed to her husband, to marry her son."

"Tensions have been brewing for years between Taros and Xeria. Perhaps she sees the marriage as a way to ease them? To prevent a war?"

"Do you really think it could come to that?"

He shrugged. "Honestly, I don't know. Things have been tense with all six kingdoms of late. With the rebels stirring trouble, old wounds are resurfacing."

"Even so, Hadrian is the one that wants peace? He would be the one to seek an alliance, not Odette."

"Okay, so then what is her motive?"

"Maybe she's simply doing it to spite Tira? To get a foothold into Xeria through me?" I sighed. I couldn't shake the feeling that I was missing something. *Why* would Odette want this union? It made no sense.

"Well, it seems like you don't want the marriage, so does it really matter?"

"I just have a bad feeling."

He nodded. "I've seen the way you interact with people. The way you analyse them. If you have a gut feeling, I'd say you'd be wise to listen to it."

"The problem is, I don't know what it's trying to tell me."

"I'm sure it will come to you."

I rolled my eyes. "I appreciate the misplaced faith."

He winked. "Anytime, Princess."

I shook my head.

"Maybe she's heard the rumours, and thinks she can get back at Tira through you."

I raised my eyebrows. "What rumours?"

"The ones about Hadrian and Tira."

I frowned. "What about them?"

"You really haven't heard?"

"No. So spit it out, Uri."

"You know," he glanced around, lowering his voice, "the rumours that he and Tira are having an affair?"

My eyes widened. "What?"

He nodded. "I've heard whispers."

"That's ridiculous. They aren't having an affair."

He shrugged. "I didn't say I thought they were, but it could have something to do with Odette's behaviour. I don't know."

I shook my head. An affair? That's insane. People would make up the most ridiculous things. Although, even I could admit Hadrian and Tira would make a much better pair than Odette and Hadrian.

"Does Tira know about the rumours?"

"No clue. If she does, she has said nothing to me."

"Fates," I said, still in disbelief.

"So, are we going anywhere in particular?"

We were going in the general direction of the gates. I glanced at them. I really wanted to see Sierra, but I couldn't without risking Butcher ordering me to give her an honest update. Who knows what I might reveal? I could, however, see Tolemas. He could tell me how she was, and I could confront him about what I learned in my Testing.

I glanced at Uri. "How do you feel about a trip into town?"

He grinned. "Better than wandering around this place, but you need more guards than just me."

I sighed. "No, I don't."

"I don't care how well you did in training. You're a princess now."

"But it's so much harder to go undetected with an entourage of guards trailing me." I said, sounding like a whiny child.

"Too bad."

I sighed. "Fine."

He gave me a look. "I'm not leaving you alone to go get them. You can come with me to the guards' quarters."

I groaned. "Lead the way, then."

He smirked a bit, and we turned left instead of going straight to the gates. I realised, a little too late, that women rarely come down to this area of the castle, let alone princesses. There were men everywhere, in all various stages of undress. Some were in their full guards' uniforms, some were in training uniforms, some were in casual wear, some had no shirts on, *plenty* had no shirts on actually, and some were walking around in barely a towel. We made our way through what I suppose you could describe as barracks. A lot of the guards lived here rather than in town. Much closer, and given the hours they had to work, it made the most sense.

There was a mixture of expressions as we passed them by. Some looked shocked, some looked embarrassed, but the majority were raising their eyebrows or smirking slightly. There were even a few catcalls.

"Alright, what is going on?" Killian stepped into the hallway, no doubt to investigate what had gotten his guards so boisterous. When his eyes landed on me, understanding filled them.

"I can't say I was expecting to see you here, Princess."

I glanced at the spot on his neck. Conveniently, he still wore his hair down "This counts as the second time we've unexpectedly run into each other, Captain. I'd say that makes us even, wouldn't you?"

He smiled a bit. "I suppose it would. How about we step inside?" He said, glancing at the guards still watching us.

I nodded. "I'd appreciate that." I stepped past him and into his centre of command. Uri followed.

"Alright, enough gawking! Get back to whatever you were all doing unless you want to wind up on a double." I heard a few groans and a few chuckles. I smiled and glanced around the room.

It was neater than I'd expected it to be. Although his desk was littered with documents and maps.

Killian stepped inside, closing the door behind him. "So, what brings you all the way down here, Elle?"

"Uri insisted that if I wanted to go to town, I had to bring an entire entourage." I rolled my eyes.

"Uri would be correct." He agreed matter-of-factly.

I sighed. "You don't have to have babysitters with you at all times?"

"I am not a princess, nor am I prone to as much drama as you are."

"I am not *prone* to drama."

He gave me a look. "No? Shall I go through the list of dramatic events that have occurred since you showed up at our gates, Princess Elia?"

Okay, he may have a point there, but most of those things were not my fault.

I crossed my arms. "Just assign some guards, and I'll be on my way."

He smirked and looked at Uri. "I assume you have some in mind?"

Uri nodded. "A few, yes."

"Okay, well, take some Taros guards as well. Tarryn would have been joining you two anyway, so take him and Jenkins. Then, however many of your men you want to add." Uri nodded and suggested some guards he thought would be suitable.

While they were talking, I walked the length of the small room and looked at the papers scattered on nearly every surface. I stopped in front of a mantle. I could see the corner of a map sticking out from under a document about guard rotations. My curiosity got the better of me, and I slid the map out.

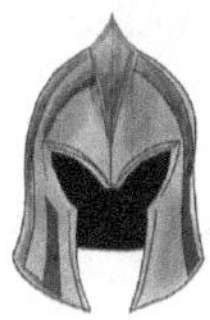

CHAPTER FIFTY-SEVEN

Unsurprisingly, it was a map of Taros. It displayed everything in great detail until it hit The Wastes. Just like every other map of Taros, nothing was marked there. There was only a name and a lot of space. No, wait. I leaned in closer. There was one landmark noted. Falcon's Head. It was towards the southeast part of the area. I could see why it was named that. It was an inlet of sorts, by the looks of it, maybe a harbour? Where the water came inland, it formed a shape that, from this view, resembled that of a bird. I guess you could call it a Falcon. How was it marked on a map, when supposedly no one who went into The Wastes ever returned?

"Snooping, are we?" Killian's voice pulled me back to reality, and I glanced over to find both men had stopped talking and were watching me.

"Where did you get this map?"

"Which map?" He asked, walking over. Glancing down, recognition filled him. "Ah, that map."

"Well? Where is it from?"

"A travelling pedlar. I picked it up at the markets in town a few years ago. The merchant was passing through. Why?"

"It's the only map I've ever seen with any landmark beyond the border of The Wastes themselves."

He frowned. "What do you mean?" He leaned closer, looking at the map.

"Falcon's Head?" I answered, pointing to where the name was scrawled across the parchment.

"I mean, I guess you could say that inlet looks like a bird? But I don't think you could class that as a noted landmark?"

"What? No, it's the actual writing that makes it a noted landmark? What are you talking about?"

"Elia, there's no writing? There's nothing there but land. I can see the shape you're seeing, but I am not sure where you got Falcon's Head from."

Was he messing with me?

"Uri, you see it, right?"

He walked over and peered at the map. All three of us were staring at it now.

"What am I looking for?" He glanced down at it.

"Someone has marked 'Falcons Head' on this map. It's pinpointed right *here*," I said, pointing to it.

Uri squinted and then shrugged. "I'm with the captain on this one. I only see the landmass."

What in the name of Akros was going on? I frowned.

"I bought this map because Taros was so detailed. The cartography work is that of a skilled map maker. It was hard to find maps of such fine detail and quality at the time. I didn't even look at The Wastes really, since we have no way of knowing what's there. You can have it."

I looked at him. "Are you sure?"

He nodded, and then shrugged. "I have plenty of other maps of the same quality now. Knock yourself out."

I bit my lip. "Alright, thank you." I rolled it up.

"Here, I'll carry it for you." Uri offered.

"A guard and a servant all in one? Isn't this my lucky day?"

"I can retract the offer," he said dryly. I handed him the map.

"No take-backs. Have you two decided on who my chaperones will be?"

Killian nodded. "I will send Tarryn and Jenkins to meet you at the gates. Uri will grab his men when you head out."

I nodded. "Alright then, always a pleasure, Captain."

"Likewise, Princess." He opened the door for us, Uri stepped out first, and I made to follow, but Killian stopped me.

"You should give Valor a chance, you know."

I looked at Killian. "I'm sorry?"

"Give the poor guy a chance. I haven't seen him open up around any woman the way he has around you."

"It's not that simple, Killian, you know that."

"Take all the politics, titles, and responsibilities out of it. If you were just a woman, and he was just a man, would you give him the time of day?"

Based on his behaviour when we first met? No. But the way he acted now? The things I felt when I was around him? Probably.

My silence seemed to be answer enough for Killian, because he smiled. "Just consider it." He nodded towards Uri. "Uri is waiting."

I headed over to Uri without bothering to answer. He knew I would.

"You alright?" Uri asked, and I nodded.

"Yep, let's get these babysitters, and get on the road."

He chuckled. "You are the only one referring to them as babysitters, which is really only insulting yourself."

"Well, it feels like I am a child whom everyone thinks needs to be watched at all times."

"You do. You have already been attacked multiple times. You are a princess now, so suck it up."

"I didn't ask to be a princess."

"Most princesses don't have a say. They are born into it."

"What's your point?"

"My point is, you complain too much." He increased his pace, forcing me to double mine to keep up. I didn't deign to respond to him.

We picked up two of his recommended guards. One looked to be another Virbi, and the other I had a feeling was Impure. I'm not sure why that surprised me so much, but it did. Perhaps because the Virbi are a warrior people, with their Giftings, you would think they'd have no need for Impure guards. It was a pleasant surprise that I had thought wrong.

True to Killian's word, Tarryn and a man I assumed was Jenkins were waiting for us when we reached the gates, along with a carriage.

"Is the carriage necessary? Can't we just walk, or ride?"

"You'd be too much of an open target, Elia," Tarryn said, and Uri nodded his agreement.

"She's been fighting me on the security precautions the entire time. I'm not riding in the carriage with her."

"Fine, but on the way back, we swap." Tarryn countered.

Uri nodded. "Fair."

"Excuse me? Standing right here! I can hear you."

They both looked at me as if I had just stated the obvious.

"How about neither of you ride with me?" I stepped into the carriage, shutting the door.

I heard the men chuckle and snicker. The door opened, and I turned, prepared to tell them where they could shove it, but it wasn't Tarryn or Uri standing there. It was Valor.

"Valor, what are you doing here?"

"Killian mentioned you were taking a trip into town. I was hoping I might join you."

Of course he did. I made a mental note to scold him later. I shrugged a bit. "Suit yourself."

He smiled, stepping inside. He had to duck. It would be amusing seeing such a large man in such a small space if it didn't mean we were in even closer proximity to one another.

He pulled the door shut and sat opposite me. A few minutes later, the carriage started toward the centre of Kendelen.

"You were very impressive in your training session today. I had no idea you were such a fast learner." A poor attempt at filling the silence.

"There are many things you don't know about me."

"Like what?"

I looked at him and realised I'd fallen straight into his trap. I shrugged. "Nothing worth noting."

"I find that very hard to believe," he said, and I shrugged again. He sighed, clearly not as patient as he wished to be. Instead of continuing that line of conversation, he moved, so he was sitting next to me. He placed his hand on my leg, and my eyes widened slightly at the sudden closeness and the nerve of this man.

"What, exactly, are you doing?"

"Well, it seems like the only time I get anywhere with you," he said, leaning closer and tucking a strand of hair behind my ear, "is when I am touching you."

I breathed in slightly. "You have some nerve, Princeling."

He grinned, and his hand slid up a little further. "Is this what you prefer from me? Less talking?"

He was trying to get a rise out of me. I turned my head towards him. Our faces were now much closer than before. I looked into his eyes.

"I would prefer many things over the sound of your voice, Valor."

"What things would you prefer?" He asked, his eyes watching mine.

My eyes darted to his lips before meeting his eyes again. He didn't miss the movement.

"Oh, I don't know, perhaps another day spent in the cell you so courteously threw me in shortly after my arrival here?"

"That was a low blow, Sunshine." His thumb traced circles where it rested on my upper leg. "I apologised for that."

"Did you?"

"If you didn't hear my apology, then perhaps I need to show you just how sincere I am."

His hand trailed up further. It was resting on my inner thigh. If his fingers slid an inch or two to the right, we would be in dangerous territory.

I bit my lip. "That would be quite unnecessary."

This time, it was his eyes darting to my lips. Only they didn't revert to my eyes. They stayed firmly fixed on my mouth.

"What have I told you about biting that lip?"

I realised my mistake when I saw that familiar storm swirling in his eyes. "Valor..."

I made to move back, but his hand tightened on my leg. His other hand moved to clasp the back of my neck, and before I could stop him, his lips were on mine. My eyes widened, and I tensed. *Damn, he was a good kisser.*

It really was not fair for someone to be *that* good at it. I pulled my face back a little. As much as I didn't want to further complicate my life, by getting more involved with Valor, anticipation thrummed through me. He tried to hide it from his expression, but I could practically feel the thumping of his heart in his chest. Or perhaps that was mine.

He finally dragged his gaze back to my eyes. "Surely, you could use this just as much as I could right now."

I swallowed. I could use it, but I shouldn't.

Valor knew I was about to object, so he cut me off before I could. "Stop overthinking. Just enjoy the moment, Elle."

His thumb stroked my neck, and I shivered involuntarily. I closed my eyes, trying to sort through my thoughts. He took that as an invitation. He kissed me again. This time it was deeper, hungrier. I don't know if it was the confined space, or the need practically pulsating from him, but something had me throwing caution to the wind because I kissed him back.

That was all it took to break both of our restraints. In the same movement, I was wrapping my arms around his neck as he pulled me into his lap, my legs straddling him on either side. I pressed against his chest, just wanting to be closer to him. His hands slid up my waist, pulling me even tighter against him.

Valor wasn't entirely wrong earlier. We seemed to fight when we were around each other, but then when we weren't fighting we were doing something like this, and *divinities* did it get better every time. We explored each other in time to the swaying carriage. I stopped worrying about all the reasons we shouldn't, and just let myself enjoy the fact that we were. I'd deal with the consequences later.

One of us must have had enough awareness to know we should remain dressed, because, in all our exploring, we hadn't lost any clothing. I wasn't sure how much longer I could follow that rule. Luckily, or perhaps unluckily for me, the carriage came to a stop. Were we in town already? Surely not. How much time had passed?

I looked to the carriage door, trying to listen for any sounds that might give away where we were. Valor trailed kisses up my neck, which made it very difficult to hear anything. I was, however, able to make out the sound of someone landing on the ground, dismounting, followed by approaching footsteps.

My eyes widened as I realised they could catch us in a very compromising position. I jumped off of Valor, hurrying to straighten my dress. He frowned in disappointment and made to pull me back to him when the carriage door opened, and Uri popped his head in. He took in the both of us with raised brows. A hint of a smirk graced his features.

"In case you weren't already aware, we have arrived. Whenever you two are ready to join us." Now it was a full smirk on display. I shot him a glare as he retreated, closing the door again.

Valor smiled a bit sheepishly. "Sorry."

I glanced at him and bit my lip. "Well, that wasn't entirely your fault. I suppose I should share in some of the blame."

His eyes zeroed in on my lips again. I pursed them, quickly moving to stand, as much as one could stand with such a low roof.

Ever the gentleman, he moved faster, opening the door and getting out. Then he turned and held out a hand to help me exit the carriage.

I hesitantly took it and stepped out. I glanced around to find Tarryn and Uri watching us with amused expressions on their faces, while the other guards attempted looks of disinterest, but failed.

This was going to be a fun outing.

I ignored all of them and simply stepped onto the busy streets, heading into the centre. It was odd, the stares and whispers that followed when I walked. In the castle, people still stared, but they weren't so obvious or shocked. People moved out of the way. Some even bowed or curtsied. It was not something I would ever get used to. It didn't help to have five burly guards and a prince behind me, but they wisely gave me space.

I made my way to the city square. The markets were in full swing, there were stalls set up with merchants peddling their goods. I had to figure out a way to get to Tolemas with these guards and everyone else watching my every move. He wouldn't appreciate half the town wondering why the Princess of Xeria was visiting him. Maybe I'd have to just sneak out again tonight. That seemed like the best option. Either way, it was nice to be out of the castle, back on familiar ground, around people I understood.

Once the initial shock wore off, the vendors were all vying for my attention. Hoping to sell me their wears at completely inflated prices, as they always tried to do when they saw a rich market goer, an easy mark. A familiar head of black hair caught my eye as I wandered along the cobblestone.

I turned, shocked to find Sierra in front of a stall that sold flowers and gardening supplies. I tried to appear calm as I made my way over. She never ventured into town. She hated it because of her roller, usually needing me there to help her navigate rougher terrain. Stopping beside her, I leaned forward, smelling the closest bouquet, making a show of browsing. Luckily, the seller was busy bartering with another customer.

Sierra glanced at me then, and her eyes widened.

"Adi—" I quickly cut her off.

"Please, call me Elia," I said.

Realisation filled her features, along with embarrassment, as she glanced around, noting the people still staring and the guards close by. She dipped into a curtsey as best she could while seated.

"Princess."

"What brings you to the markets?"

"I'm buying supplies for my garden."

"Your garden?"

She nodded. "Camilla has allowed me to use a bit of her garden as my own. She had it completely cleared so I could start fresh." She grinned, excitement in her eyes.

"As in the woman that is holding you hostage against your will? Sierra, she's trying to bribe you into behaving."

Sierra rolled her eyes at me. "She isn't bribing me. And honestly, A—Elia. She's not keeping me hostage. I can come and go as I please. More so than when it was just you and me. You were the one that kept me locked up."

My eyes widened. "What? That is not true. I always encouraged you to get out and explore. I brought you with me every chance that I got."

She shook her head. "And treated me like an invalid."

I frowned. "I have never seen you as an invalid, Sierra."

"Of course you have. You've spent your whole life trying to *fix* me." She glanced at her roller.

I breathed in. Where was this was coming from? Sierra wanted to walk. We'd had so many conversations about this. That is what she asked me for as a gift, almost every winter solstice when we were younger. I'd promised her I would do everything I could to make it happen while reassuring her I didn't care whether she walked or rolled. She was going to be my sister either way.

I just wanted her to be happy. Over the years, she'd lost hope of it becoming a reality, but she'd never said she didn't want to walk anymore. She always just said it was a faraway dream that was unlikely to be achieved. Which was okay, I could believe enough for the both of us.

"I *never* saw it as 'fixing' you, Sierra. You are perfect the way you are, but you wanted to walk? So I've done everything I can to make that possible for you. And we are so much closer now. Butcher betraying us complicated things but—"

"If you had just agreed to the job she asked of you, then all the drama could have been avoided. You spend your life spying and thieving, but you draw the line on that one?"

I frowned. "I spent my life doing those things to keep us alive!" I took a breath, lowering my voice. "Because that's what Butcher forced me to do?"

"Camilla didn't force you to do anything. She trained you, gave you valuable skills. You continued to use them for criminal activity, rather than earning an honest living. That's on you."

I couldn't believe what I was hearing. She can't seriously think that? I know she didn't see the things Butcher had made me do, but she saw the aftermath. Too many times I'd returned bruised and bloodied, with broken bones, ripped clothes, or just traumatised from something I'd had to do. Did I hide too much of it from her in order to protect her childhood, her innocence?

"That is a lie. I had *no* choice. I had no childhood. She took that away from me, and I did everything I could to make sure she didn't do the same to you."

"No, you did everything you could to make sure you were her favourite."

"Her *favourite?*"

"You are pissed that I'm in town, buying things for a garden she's given me because you're jealous. You can't handle that you're not the centre of attention anymore. When you said no to her for a simple job, you blew it. That isn't my fault, so don't take it out on me."

My eyes widened. "You aren't this stupid, Sierra. Whatever lies she has been spinning, you need to get them out of your head."

To Infernis with this. I was bringing Sierra back with me. Tira would keep her safe, even if Butcher calls on me.

"Come on, we're getting out of here." I placed my hands on the handles of her roller.

"What are you talking about?"

"Butcher is manipulating you. You can come back to the castle with me, where you'll be safe."

She gripped the wheels, preventing me from moving her. "Sierra, what are you doing?"

"I'm not going anywhere. I am happy here. I'm finally getting a life of my own. Camilla treats me like an adult, not a child."

"You're only *nineteen* Sierra! You're not a child, but you're certainly acting like one. *She* is not your family. I am, listen to me."

"You aren't my mother!"

I stiffened and looked at her. She knew she'd struck a chord. I saw it in her eyes, but she persisted anyway.

"You pulled me from that fire and saved my life, but it is Camilla that has kept *both* of us alive. Not you. She is family, too."

"She is *not* family. Sierra, there's so much you don't know. Come back to the castle with me. I can tell you everything about our parents, our home, who we really are. What Butcher is really involved in."

She frowned. "What do you mean by our parents and our home?"

I glanced around quickly before leaning in and whispering. "Our parents weren't who we thought they were, Sierra. They were Pures, both of them."

Her eyes widened, and she looked at me. "What are you talking about?"

"Come with me to the castle, Sierra, and I can explain everything."

"What about Camilla? The blood oath?" She looked to where she knew I was branded.

I shook my head. "I'll deal with it. I've found a way to have it removed. I just need to get you somewhere safe first."

Her eyes widened, and she hesitated before finally shaking her head. "No."

"What do you mean, no?"

"I mean, no, I'm not coming with you. Our parents are dead. It doesn't matter what they were."

I looked at her in disbelief. "Yes, it does? And there's so much more you need to know. I'm not arguing about this anymore. You're coming."

I tried to forcefully pull her back, but she only gripped the wheels tighter. "No. I'm not. You don't control me anymore. I can make my own choices. You made yours, and this is me making mine. Now let go before I cause a scene."

"Sierra, what is going on? I'm your sister. Why won't you trust me?"

"Because we *aren't* all we have. I have Camilla, and Tolemas, and the circus. I have a good life here. It is you that is unsatisfied. Not me. If you want more, then go find it, but don't use me as an excuse to justify your actions." She turned on her roller and wheeled away.

CHAPTER FIFTY-EIGHT

I WAS TOO SHOCKED to stop her, and even if I wasn't, people were staring now. I watched as she made her way through the crowd, eventually disappearing down a street, no doubt leading back to Butcher's manor.

Valor stepped up beside me. "What was that about?"

I swallowed. "That's none of your concern." I straightened. "I'm ready to go back to the castle."

I turned and started walking back in the carriage's direction. Much to my dismay, Valor easily caught up.

"Who was that girl?"

"I don't know."

"Did she say something to upset you?"

I sighed. "What part of none of your concern don't you understand, Valor?"

"All of it when you look like someone just punched you in the gut. You knew her. Was she friends with you and..." He was trying to figure out what to call Raf.

"His name was Raf. And yes, fine, she knew him too."

"What did she say to you?"

"It's personal, Valor. Can we just leave it at that?"

He sighed. "You are so very hard to deal with. I try to be nice to you, and it gets me nowhere. If I'm an ass, it does better *sometimes*, but most of the time, the same results. It gets me nowhere."

"Then maybe you should stop bothering."

"You're worth the trouble."

I stopped and looked at him.

"Well, I'll be damned. She has nothing to say back?" He smiled a bit.

I shook my head slightly and continued walking. He chuckled softly, once again catching up with me. He kept quiet this time, thankfully. The carriage ride back was awkward, but I didn't care enough to make small talk. I was too busy going over everything Sierra had said to me. *Was part of what she'd said true? Did I really make her feel less than?*

My heart ached. I'd never wanted her to feel that way. I'd spent my life trying to make her feel the opposite. I could tell Valor was itching to say more. He could read the hurt in my features, but didn't know how to fix it.

He opened his mouth, having apparently decided on what to say, when the carriage came to an abrupt halt. I practically fell on top of him. His arms immediately wrapped around me.

"Are you okay?"

I tried to move off of him, but he still had a firm grip. I cleared my throat. "I would be better if you'd let go."

He chuckled softly before finally releasing me.

I sat up. "Why did we stop?"

"I'm not sure." He moved towards the door, but before he got there, it swung open. Tarryn was standing there, his sword drawn. He was covered in blood.

"We're under attack."

Valor's smile vanished, and he immediately went into soldier mode. "How many?"

"Unsure. They got Jenkins with an arrow. He was sitting next to me. I tried to stop the bleeding, but they hit an artery." I could see it pained him not to have been able to save his fellow guard, but he knew he couldn't dwell.

"Another two arrows, straight into the horse's eyes. I cut it loose before it fell, toppling the carriage along with it. Uri sent one of his guards on foot to call for aid."

I glanced over Tarryn's shoulder to see Uri and the other Virbi guard he'd brought standing with him, covering Tarryn's back. Both were armed and in fighting stances.

"Any visuals on the attackers?"

Tarryn shook his head. "No."

Valor looked at me. "Stay here."

"But—"

"No buts. *Stay. Here.*" His tone left no room for argument and now wasn't the time to start a fight with him, so I nodded. I'd reassess once he was gone.

Tarryn stepped out, and Valor followed. Turning to me, he said, "Do not leave this carriage," before shutting the door.

I heard him bark orders. The four of them each took a corner of the carriage, instructed to keep an eye open, and signal if they spotted anything. It went quiet. I could just make out their breathing. I didn't risk peeking out of the curtained window. It was quiet for too long. You don't just shoot a man and a horse, then run away. *What were the attackers waiting for?* I got my answer a second later, as if the fates had heard my question and taken it as a dare.

Suddenly, footfalls sounded followed by Uri shouting, "Incoming!"

The sound of metal clashing against metal rang out into the air. Blade against blade. If there were more archers, they were not firing. I couldn't tell how many there were, but it sounded like they'd attacked from the right.

I pulled my dagger from my thigh sheath. If whoever this was had the numbers, then I should be out there helping, not hiding in this damned carriage. I wasn't helpless anymore, or at least I didn't think I was after my Testing. The only thing that held me back was knowing I'd be a distraction to Valor if I was out there.

The sound of fighting increased. I heard Uri curse. *Screw it.* I eased the curtain aside a fraction so I could get a look at what was going on. I could see Uri a few yards away fighting against three masked attackers. A few yards to the right, the other Virbi guard, whose name I hadn't even learnt, was fighting off his own onslaught as more soldiers appeared from the woods. I couldn't see Valor or Tarryn. I could only assume they were on the other side of the carriage, fighting off another assault.

I tried to establish who was attacking us. They were in black outfits with orange masks on. Looking closer, I saw the masks had a distinct, familiar design. A damned rising sun. *The Rise.* It was the same uniforms the rebels wore when they'd attacked Valor in the dining hall. Were they here for him, or me? If Solis was in charge of them, then it shouldn't be me, which only caused my concern to grow. Valor was a sitting duck out there. He should be the one hiding in the damned carriage.

Suddenly, a masked face popped up right in front of me. I jerked back. The masked figure ripped the curtains from their hooks and looked as if he might try to climb through the window. But a large hand gripped his neck, followed by a loud, unmistakable cracking sound. I saw the life fade from the masked man's eyes as the Virbi guard dropped him to the ground.

Glancing up, my eyes widened. "Look out!"

He spun as another masked soldier launched himself at him. The guard quickly blocked the blow with his *arm*. I gasped in horror, knowing what a blow like that meant, before realisation struck; he must be an Argenti. The metal blade bounced right off him. I was pulled from my stupor when an arrow whizzed straight past my head, embedding itself in the carriage's wall. *Shit.* I quickly ducked away from the window, but depending on where the archer was, they may still have a shot. I looked at the arrow embedded in the wood and stiffened. *Silver.*

"They have silver arrows!!" I screamed out, standing up to make sure the Argenti guard heard me.

I was too late. The nameless guard had his back to the window. He was fighting off two Rise soldiers when an arrow came from the right, slicing straight through his neck and poking out the other side. I tensed as I watched him jerk slightly before falling to the ground. Both of his eyes were still wide open in shock. Uri cursed and began backing towards us, but he was being swarmed. He had eight soldiers surrounding him and more approaching. *Where were they all coming from? Where were Tarryn and Valor?*

"Don't come this way!" I shouted at Uri. "Find shelter! We still can't see the archers!" He grunted, parrying off another attack. If he were a normal man, he would have been down already.

"Wait!" He called, no doubt guessing my next move.

The two soldiers that had been aiming for my now fallen guard were heading towards me. I wasn't about to be trapped in here. Hurrying to the other side of the carriage, I swung the door open, almost stumbling at what I saw.

There was practically an entire platoon surrounding Valor and Tarryn. How had they gone unnoticed this close to the castle? There had to be over thirty masked attackers. It looked like they'd only had two squads attack the other side. On this side, they had three or four. No doubt because Valor was on this side, or maybe the door to the carriage. But that wasn't what had me nearly falling over. It was Tarryn and Valor. They were standing back to back in the middle of the attack, both men using their Giftings.

Tarryn had opened a large flask attached to his hip, and he was pulling water from it. Tiny droplets slowly froze over and were being shot at the enemy soldiers trying to attack from the side. Those in front of him were being kept back by a whip of water. It looked like it packed a mean punch. Behind him, Valor was no less impressive. He was fighting off a few soldiers directly in front of him, sword in hand. There were also the swords from, I assume, fallen men, floating in the air on either of his sides, battling with other soldiers. I'd seen a lot of fantastical things during my Testing, but this was different. My hesitation cost me, as the closest soldier who'd been approaching the window reached in, clearly possessing longer arms than I'd thought.

He grabbed my hair and jerked me backwards. As I hit the ground, he began dragging me towards the window. I struggled against him, gripping my dagger tightly. I just needed to get close enough. The soldier actually chuckled as he pulled me closer.

"What have we here?"

I waited until the last second, before grabbing the wrist that was dragging me, twisting and with my other hand, driving the dagger straight into his neck. He gasped, dropping me instantly. Blood squirted from his neck all over me. I quickly closed my mouth, not having forgotten that there were two soldiers earlier, and more could have joined. I quickly got to my feet and took a deep breath, thinking back to what Amory had taught me.

I swallowed, closing my eyes for a second. I couldn't let myself be distracted by Valor, Tarryn, or Uri. *The Killing Calm,* she'd called it. I understood why, now that it was an actual situation with people I cared for. I opened my eyes. The soldier that had attacked me was stuck half in the carriage and half out the window, blocking his allies from reaching me. I removed my outer skirt, grateful I was wearing the proper undergarments today. I grabbed the sword that was sheathed on the soldier's side, shoved him out the window, then carefully looked out.

Luckily for me, the other soldiers that had been heading toward the carriage had gotten distracted by Uri. He looked beyond pissed now. He was practically throwing men away, but they kept coming. I threw the sword out the window, grabbed hold of the curtain railing, which was thankfully sturdy, and used it to hoist myself out of the carriage.

I quickly picked the sword back up and looked around at our options. We were outnumbered, but my travelling companions seemed to be doing a good job of keeping them at bay. It was the archers I was worried about. Scanning the surroundings, I frustratingly couldn't determine the archers' positions. I needed higher ground.

I hurried to the nearest tree, jerking back as I narrowly avoided a sword to the neck. Spinning, I faced two soldiers that were no longer distracted. The two of them took up positions on either side of me, but their relaxed stances told me they didn't consider me a threat. I smiled at them. The man to my right arched a brow. He died first.

As I'd expected, it hadn't been difficult. Men could be downright stupid when they were facing a woman in a dress, or in my case, in various stages of undress. I wasted no time attacking the second man. He was quicker to react than his friend, and he was well trained. He had excellent technique and was stronger than me, but I was faster. Our swords clashed as I blocked his blow. He swung again, but I ducked, thrusting my sword forward, aiming for his gut.

He jerked backwards, my weapon just catching his shirt and ripping a hole in it. I raised my arm, slashing down at him, but he met the blow with his own blade, each of us gripping the other's sword holding wrist. He smiled, knowing he had the advantage with his strength as he prepared to shove me back and deliver a killing blow.

However, instead of that, I felt him tense as I released his wrist, reaching down and gripping the now familiar hilt of my dagger before I plunged it into his throat. I yanked it back out, and he froze, his eyes wide as he stumbled back, falling to his knees. Re-sheathing the dagger, I turned away as he bled out on the ground, staining the green grass crimson.

Uri had cut down half of his attackers and was holding off the rest with ease, but there were arrows digging out of the ground nearby. The archer was still close.

I returned to the tree I'd been aiming for and hoisted myself up onto the highest branch I could reach. It was difficult climbing with a sword, but I might need it, so I couldn't risk leaving it behind. I pulled myself up to a high enough vantage point that I could see the ongoing fights. Rise soldiers surrounded all three of our men. Where was the other guard that Uri sent to get help? Surely reinforcements would be here by now if he'd made it there?

Focus. You're up here to find the archers. I scanned the trees and the forest below, looking for any signs of life, anything that didn't belong. I couldn't see anything, but I *knew* they were here. I glanced in the direction I knew, for certain, someone had fired shots from. They could have easily moved positions since then, but I had to start somewhere. I closed my eyes, frustration vibrating through me. That's when I felt it. What, exactly? I had no idea, but I sensed something. I opened my eyes and looked around for the source. Still, I found nothing. Frowning, I closed my eyes again and listened.

I heard nothing, but I definitely *felt* something. Anticipation? Adrenaline? Fear? But they weren't my emotions? I focused on those feelings, slowing my breathing and turning my head slightly. It was stronger to the left. I opened my eyes, but this time instead of seeing an empty forest, I zeroed in on a tree branch, sheltered by another thickly leaf covered branch above it.

It looked ordinary at first, but there was something there. I knew there was. I squinted, trying to get a better look, but I was too far away. *Dammit.* A memory came back to me, multiple actually. Specifically, words I'd been told. *'Listen to what you do not hear, Adira.'* Is this what they were talking about?

I focused on the emotions I'd felt earlier, latching on to the last one: fear. I focused on that one; it was the strongest out of the three. I tried to get a lock on where it was coming from. It felt like pulling on a thread that I couldn't see, only I wasn't sure if I should pull or push. Pulling seemed to give me a stronger indication of where it was, but pushing? I hadn't tried that.

How do you push away an invisible object? Mentally laughing at myself for considering it, I tried to picture that thread and push it away. The feelings disappeared. I couldn't feel them anymore. I groaned under my breath. I wasn't sure what was going on, or if this damned blood oath limited it, but I felt like it was *right* there. Just out of reach.

Shaking my head, I climbed back down, keeping low and heading in the direction of the tree I'd fixated on earlier. Moving carefully, so as not to alert anyone to my presence, I ducked behind a bush and glanced at the branch. From down here, I could see a person's foot carefully balancing on the branch, moving anytime the wind blew the leaves that they were using for cover.

I grabbed my dagger. I could see them now. They had a bow, which they were drawing back, preparing to fire. I looked in the direction they were aiming. *Uri.* I tensed, gripping the dagger by its blade. I took aim, hurling my weapon. It whistled as it flew; the archer heard it and looked down just in time for it to embed itself in their forehead.

They weren't wearing a mask, probably so they could see clearly as they aimed. They fell out of the tree, landing with a loud *thud.* I hurried over to make sure they were truly dead, and immediately wished I hadn't. I could tell right away that the emotions I'd felt had somehow been coming from whoever this was. It was a boy. He looked no older than sixteen. I swallowed.

I'd killed a kid. No wonder he'd felt so much fear. He was practically a child. I pulled the dagger out of his forehead and closed his eyes. I quickly wiped the blood on my shirt, not wanting a reminder of what I'd done. *He is the enemy, Adira. This is no time for guilt.* I had to check for additional archers.

Turning away from the body, I focused on reaching out as I'd accidentally done earlier. I couldn't feel anything immediately close to me. My senses were open as I moved through the forest. I didn't see or feel anything else. The boy must have been the only archer on this side. I made my way back towards the fighting, to find we had gained the upper hand now. The Rise soldiers were dwindling, and they'd obviously realised they were fighting a losing battle because one of them called out.

"Retreat! Fall back!"

Slowly, they all pulled themselves back from the fighting. They had been on the offensive until now. Now that Valor, Tarryn, and Uri had taken down enough of their men to switch tactics, they were running. The ones closest to the three were not so lucky, copping the brunt of their attack, whilst the rest of their comrades disappeared into the forest. I saw Valor turn to the carriage. He stiffened and ran over. I'd left the carriage door open. He looked inside and turned around with a panicked look in his eyes.

"Where is Elia?!" He looked at Tarryn and Uri, who had moved to join him.

"Shit," Tarryn said, looking around.

"She climbed out the window. I couldn't get to her. I saw her take down two guards, but I don't know where she went after that."

Valor grabbed Uri by the shirt. "You let her run off?! They all came from the forest. One of them could have gotten her!"

Uri tensed. "The only reason you aren't on your ass right now is because you're a prince, but if you don't take your hands off me now, title or no title, I will put you there." Okay, I should probably step in. I was about to when a fallen Rise soldier grabbed my ankle. My gaze darted down to see that three of the fallen enemy soldiers were, in fact, not so dead.

"Oh, come on." I muttered as I planted my boot into the first guard's face. He cursed as the other two jumped up, taking on positions a few feet to either side of me. I sighed.

"I would run." I suggested, bending slightly, keeping my eyes on the two standing guards, but never losing sight of the guard cupping his bleeding nose on the ground beside me.

The one to my right sneered. "You'll be dead before they stop bickering and notice us." I grinned.

"I meant you should run from me Hot Shot." He didn't have time to scoff as I unsheathed my dagger, slicing it across the grounded guard's neck, before hurling it at the one to my left, nailing him right in the eye. Leaving only Mr Hot Shot, and I left standing.

His eyes widened, first in shock, then in anger, as he lunged at me. I easily sidestepped him, which only infuriated him more. He slashed his sword down, but I raised mine, blocking the blow as I lifted my foot, kicking him in the groin.

He grunted as he stumbled back, but he didn't fall. I switched to the offensive, and I had to give it to the man, he blocked my blows better than I'd have expected. He was still angry, but he'd gotten control of himself and was thinking more clearly now. Growing bored with the back of forth, I prepared to disarm him. Better we take him alive and question him.

Before I could, a sword thrust through Hot Shot's back, poking out of his stomach. His eyes widened as he dropped his weapon, glancing at his torso and falling to his knees. I frowned, just as surprised, when there was no attacker standing behind him holding said sword. The blade, as if it were sentient, jerked itself out of his back and flew in the direction Tarryn, Uri, and Valor had been arguing.

Turning, I saw Valor catch the sword without so much as glancing at it. No, his gaze was fixed firmly on me. All three men were staring at me in shock. I lowered my sword.

"What did you do that for?!" I called out to Valor as I stepped completely out of the forest. Glancing at the three of them, I added. "Divinities, fighting off an entire company wasn't enough. You had to fight each other, too?" I said, walking over.

Tarryn snapped out of it first, chuckling, but I could see the relief clear in his eyes.

Valor stepped back from Uri, storming over to me. "I told you to stay in the carriage."

"Yeah, well, I don't always do as I'm told." I replied, crossing my arms. "Also, you never answered my question. We could have interrogated him. Why did you kill him?"

He shook his head, finally reaching me.

"He was trying to kill you? He would have killed you, which is why I told you to stay in the carriage."

I rolled my eyes at his lack of faith in me. "Look, Princeling, I know you are used to people obeying your orders. And you're also used to women who can't defend themselves, but I'll have you know —"

His lips cut me off as they slammed into mine. I nearly fell over. It was that forceful. My eyes widened as he pulled me against him. He pulled back, resting his forehead against mine. His eyes were closed.

"You could have died..." He whispered this time. The quiet fear in his voice had me softening and placing my hand on his chest to reassure him I was alright.

CHAPTER FIFTY-NINE

SOMEONE CLEARING THEIR THROAT interrupted us. I glanced over Valor's shoulder to see a man on horseback. Not only that, but he seemed to have a very large, very armed, travelling party with him. Including a very royal looking carriage with a flame on the side of it. I felt Valor tense up before turning to face our new guest.

"Sorry to interrupt," the man said.

But from the grin on his face, he didn't appear sorry at all. He was tall, even on horseback. He had honey blonde hair and olive skin. His eyes were a striking amber colour, with darker specks thrown in, making them look alight. I could see the end of a tattoo snaking up his neck. He was perhaps the most attractive man I'd ever seen.

"You're early." Valor practically groaned out.

"And you are very rude to not introduce me to your companion, Val," he said, dismounting and walking over.

He sighed. "Elle this is—"

"Adonis." He interrupted, flashing me a brilliant smile. "Adonis Jandar. Pleased to make your acquaintance. I must say, you fighting off those soldiers was as impressive as you are breathtaking." His voice was deep, and smooth. Like a fine whiskey. He held out his hand, which I did not take. Hot or not, something else was obviously going on here, which elicited a smile from Valor.

"As I was saying, this is Adonis. Prince of Lios."

My eyes widened slightly. *The Flame of Lios*, the Elementi prince.

"Do you speak?" He asked me.

I arched an eyebrow.

"You'll regret asking her that," Tarryn said, and Adonis turned.

"Amesley?! Holy Heknos, fancy seeing you here my brother." He walked over and they embraced, clapping each other on the back.

"I could say the same to you. We weren't expecting you for another three weeks?"

"Yes, well, I like to arrive early and suss everything out before the other vultures arrive. Apparently, I didn't come early enough though," he said, glancing around at the carnage. "It appears I missed quite a fight."

"Very convenient." Valor muttered, but Adonis heard, and his attention returned to us.

"Well, it looks like you could use a ride. You can tell me all about it on the way back." He smiled, then looked at me.

"You can travel with me, love."

I smiled. "I'd rather walk." I moved away from Valor and started doing just that, heading in the castle's direction.

"Feisty." I heard him say.

Followed by, "You have no idea." Tarryn grinned and jogged to catch up with me.

"Brother?" I asked.

"We aren't related, just a term of endearment for an old friend."

"Hmm, seems like a jackass."

He laughed. "Oh, I cannot *wait* to see the two of you interact properly." *Oh, joy.*

Despite my words about preferring to walk, I was relieved when Adonis simply smirked and offered us our own horses. We rode back to the castle. On the way, we found the guard we'd sent for help, or, more accurately, we found his body. An arrow through the neck. That must have been why there was such a big gap between the archer's shots during the attack. He went after our guard. Guilt shot through me when I thought about the child archer, but I pushed it back.

We caused quite the commotion when we entered through the main gates. Uri, Tarryn, Valor, and I, were covered in blood. I think Tarryn and I looked the worst, both of us having been sprayed by a close-range shot or stab. The guards sounded an alarm when they saw the state of us, alerting whoever needed to know that there was a problem. This would not help me prove I was not the cause of any drama.

Killian met us as we unmounted. "What in Ades' name happened?"

"Rebels ambushed us," Tarryn said.

"And you wanted to take no guards," Killian said in an *'I told you so'* fashion.

"Pretty sure if I'd taken no guards, they wouldn't have even known to attack."

He shook his head. "You don't know that. Are you alright?" He said, looking pointedly at my blood-soaked clothes and level of undress.

"Yes, I'm fine. None of the blood is mine."

He looked at me. "That doesn't mean you're okay." He hit the nail on the head, but I just gave him a small smile.

"I'm better than others. We lost good men today."

"How many?" He asked, glancing around.

Uri stepped forward. "Jenkins, Taggs, and Yohan."

I saw the sadness in Killian's eyes. It never gets easier losing men, but it gets easier to hide the pain.

"We ran into some friends along the way."

Killian nodded. "The sentries informed me you arrived with an Elementi escort. Who came?"

"Adonis, the King and Queen, and Princess Alina. I had a gate guard take them to the stables before escorting them to their rooms. Mother will greet them there." Valor stepped in.

Tira, Wes, and Hamish approached.

"Divinities." Tira gasped when she got a look at the four of us.

I bit my lip, not sure how she would react. She was already on edge about the security here in Taros.

"We're alright, Tira."

"I would hardly classify that as alright," she said, giving me a look.

I rolled my eyes before a crushing hug from Hamish blindsided me.

"Can't. Breathe." I uttered.

"Don't care, you could have died." He responded, still squeezing the life out of me.

"It would be an awful shame for me to have gone through all the trouble of staying alive out there, only to be suffocated right here."

He groaned and pulled away, before moving to hug Tarryn, who promptly pointed his sword at him.

"Touch me, and you'll get a nice little jab."

Hamish pouted, but I could see the relief in his eyes that Tarryn was in okay spirits.

"We need a debrief of the attack," Killian said.

"Surely they can get cleaned up first?" Tira said.

"The sooner the better. That way, the details are still fresh." I appreciated Killians no nonsense attitude, and that he treated me the same way he treated the men, regardless of attire or the amount of blood.

"It's fine, Tira," I said, touching her arm, "what's another thirty minutes?"

She sighed and conceded. "I would like to be present."

Killian nodded and looked at Valor. "Your father is waiting in the briefing room."

"Best not keep him waiting, then." He replied and led us to the so-called briefing room.

There was a large circular table in the middle. We all took a seat. Killian, Valor, Tarryn, Uri, Tira, and Hadrian. Hamish and Wes remained standing by the door.

"I'm glad to see you're all okay," Hadrian said.

"Not all of us." I pointed out. Hadrian looked at me and nodded solemnly.

"A terrible loss. We will honour them tomorrow morning when we hold a service for them and their families."

I nodded slightly.

"What happened?"

We each explained our version of events. Tarryn went first, as he was the first person to see the attack. We explained the ambush. It was Valor who suggested The Rise soldiers could have used a nearby cave system from the old mine that bordered The Wastes. It's the only way anyone could think of that would explain them getting so close to the castle undetected. Hadrian agreed we should investigate it, and that he would send some scouts tomorrow.

"I would like to go." I added.

"No."

"Nope."

"That is not a good idea."

A chorus of nos echoed around the room, namely from Valor, Killian, and Hadrian.

I rolled my eyes. "Why, because I'm a woman?"

"Yes," Valor said.

At the same time as Hadrian said, "No, of course not."

I raised my eyebrows.

"What we are trying to say," Killian said, "*Is,* it would be unwise for a princess to go on a scouting mission. You'd be an ideal hostage."

"Oh? Will Valor be going?"

"Probably."

"Then your logic is flawed because Valor is a prince. The Prince of *Taros,* the current kingdom that is being targeted, would make a much better hostage, and therefore, a higher risk to take."

I saw Tarryn smile a bit from his seat on the other side of the table.

"I say she should be allowed to come if she wants to." Uri put in. I gave him a grateful smile.

"I agree. Elia has proven multiple times she can handle herself," Tarryn said.

"That is ridiculous. It's too big of a risk." Valor argued.

"Really? Because I saved you, and I also saved you," I said, addressing Valor and Hadrian, "both of which I did before I'd had any training."

"She is more than adequate in combat, thanks to whatever went on during her Testing." Uri agreed.

"She's proven herself capable in our regular trainings, and even during today's attack." Tarryn added.

My heart swelled a little at their support.

"Fact is, this matter doesn't concern you, Elia. It is a Taros problem." Valor tried.

Anger filled me. It was times like these that reminded me why things with Valor were so undecided. One minute everything was great between us, the next he'd open his damned mouth and say something stupid like that.

"So, because I am not from Taros, I can't care? Screw you Valor. If I was a man, you would have no issue with me helping. How dare you?" Valor opened his mouth to respond, but Hadrian interjected.

"You're awfully quiet, Tira?" He tried directing the conversation toward someone else.

"As much as I don't like the idea of my heir being in harm's way, it seems she can take care of herself. The only reason she is being denied is because she is a woman. Being a woman myself, I can hardly side with you all based on that reasoning."

I nodded slightly in thanks.

Hadrian looked around the room and sighed. "Elia is the one that has been most impacted by these attacks, in all honesty. So, I don't like it, but if you all deem her capable of handling herself and she is set on going, I will not order otherwise."

"You can't be serious! Would you send Cali out there?" Valor said.

I shook my head and stood up. "This is a ridiculous argument and, honestly, quite offensive. If we are done with the briefing, I am going to get cleaned up," I said, ignoring Valor and looking at Hadrian.

He nodded. "Of course. Thank you for what you did today, Elia. Go get some rest." He glanced around the table. "I think we've got all the relevant information. You should all do the same."

I nodded back and walked out of the room. *The nerve of those damned men.* I was so preoccupied with my anger at male stupidity that I almost ran into someone in the hall.

"Woah, easy there," a silky male voice said, as I came to a stop. Glancing up, I saw it was Prince Adonis. Up close, his eyes were even more intense, appearing as if flames were dancing around his irises.

"Sorry," I said rather insincerely, as I made to step around him. He matched my step, blocking my path.

"I'm sure you can make it up to me," he said, giving me what I am sure he thought was a charming grin.

I rolled my eyes. "I retract the apology. You can move now." I looked at him impatiently.

He laughed a bit. "Feisty."

"You have no idea."

He stepped closer; he smelt like burning wood in the winter. I suppose that made sense since he was a Piro.

"I'd be more than willing for you to enlighten me, Elle, was it?"

"In your dreams."

"Oh, that I can guarantee."

"Ugh, men like you are the problem with society." Apparently, I was directing my anger towards all men.

He arched an eyebrow. "Who pissed in your porridge?"

"Charming," I said, stepping to the other side again, which he mirrored. I let out an exasperated sigh.

"How about we go back to your room, and I can show you just how charming I can be?"

"Not if you were the last man in all of Deorum."

"Ohhh." He nodded. "You're not into men. That makes sense now that I think about it. Very progressive of you." He nodded again, surveying me from head to toe, and finally, to my relief, stepped aside to let me pass.

My eyes widened. "A woman tells you she's not interested in you, and your immediate conclusion is she must prefer the same gender? How very predictable from someone so arrogant."

He chuckled. It was deep and low. He was all smiles and jokes, but there was a darkness to him I couldn't quite place.

"You are more than welcome to prove me wrong, love."

"I'd rather the women, thanks." With that, I walked past him and I didn't look back.

I could feel his eyes on me until I rounded a corner. I finally returned to my room, where I jumped straight into a cold bath and scrubbed the blood off of me. After that, I emptied the water before running another very hot bath and sinking into it. A sigh of relief escaped my lips, and I relaxed for what felt like the first time all day.

I closed my eyes, but I kept seeing that boy soldier's face. His wide eyes. I kept remembering the fear that was emanating from him. Fear that should have kept him out of this rebellion. How could they arm and send out a child like him? Were they so desperate in their cause? I still didn't even really know what their cause was. What were they truly fighting for? Their attacks didn't make a large impact, other than probably annoying the Navarre family. If they were trying to remove them from power, they should hit places that would hurt.

My thoughts moved on to Sierra. I couldn't believe the things she had said, the way she was acting. Butcher was getting into her head. There's only one person who might give me some answers. I got out of the bath and quickly dried off. Changing into my black tunic and cloak, I opened the hidden door and made my way through the tunnels. That reminded me, I really should find out exactly what Josette knew.

The walk to Tolemas' place was uneventful. I stuck to the shadows; it was quiet tonight. News had probably spread of the attack, and people were keeping to their homes. I knocked on his door. A minute passed before he opened it.

"You shouldn't be here," he said, glancing around.

"Where did you first hear the nickname Little Sparrow?"

His eyes widened slightly, and he stepped aside. I entered, going straight to where I knew he kept his liquor. I poured myself a drink and took a long swig, glancing around the room. It looked the same as always, aside from the fresh flowers on his table, like the last time I'd been here. Another gift from Butcher, no doubt.

He closed the door and gave me an annoyed look. "By all means, help yourself."

"Well?" I said, getting straight to the point.

"How did you find out?"

He assumed I knew, so I was better off playing along, then maybe I'd learn something useful.

"I want to hear you say it, Tolemas." Venom coated my words as I said his name.

He breathed in before walking over to me and pouring himself a drink. "Your father. He'd call you his Little Sparrow, and Sierra his Little Spark."

I stiffened, ignoring the sting of memories resurfacing. "You knew my father?"

He nodded. "Zoron was a good man."

"How did you know him?"

"I worked with your father before he and your mother went into hiding."

"When they left Xeria?"

He nodded. "Then how did you know where we were?"

"... I was sent to track you and Sierra down after your parents' deaths."

"By Queen Tira?"

He looked surprised I knew so much, but then must have remembered she was here, in Taros, and probably told me herself.

"Yes. Tira sent me, and others, to find you and bring you home to Xeria."

Anger filled me. "Yet when you found us, you didn't bring us back. Why?"

"I don't know."

I frowned. "What?"

He sighed. "I don't know, Adira. By the time I'd found you, Butcher had taken you in and when I went to take you both, I... I don't know. I can't explain it. I just... I didn't think I should take you. I thought I should stay. We should all stay."

My face was practically scrunched up at this point. "What? That makes no sense. Why?"

He closed his eyes. "I can't say."

"Can't, or won't?"

"Can't."

"Why not?"

"I can't tell you that either, Adira. How did you find out?"

"I completed The Testing."

His eyes widened. "You what?"

"Yep. Thanks for the heads up on that one. Let me guess, you *couldn't* tell me about us being Pures either?"

He nodded slightly.

I sighed and shook my head. "I can't believe I'm saying this, but everything regarding my parents can wait. We need to talk about Sierra."

"What about Sierra?"

"Butcher is brainwashing her. I saw her today. She was like a different person."

"I can't talk to you about Sierra."

"Surely there's a loophole around whatever hold she has on you. I've found workarounds."

"That is something we need to remedy." Butcher stepped out from the shadows of Tolemas' bedroom.

I quickly stood, taking a step back. My eyes darted to the exit.

"Uh, uh, uh. Do not leave this room."

I winced at the tug and stopped my retreat.

She sighed. "You always were such a stubborn child. No matter how hard I tried to drill it out of you."

I looked at Tolemas, who appeared pained. He didn't meet my eyes. I shook my head.

"So, you knew? That's how you knew I'd pass." I looked at her.

"I knew your parents were Pure, and so I knew you'd pass. I don't, however, know what your Gifting allows you to do. Your parents never trusted Tolemas enough with that secret."

"Apparently they were right not to."

She shrugged. "Not that it matters now that you've gone through The Testing, you can simply tell me yourself."

"No," I said, and she chuckled.

"It's cute of you to think that was a request."

"Why are you doing all of this, Camilla? What's the real reason? It's more than just because you're a horrible person working with the rebels. Who, by the way, need to stop trying to kill me if you want me to be of any use to you."

"That's quite a long story."

"Well, since I'm unable to leave, I find I have a fair bit of time."

She smiled. "Very well." She walked over and sat beside Tolemas.

"Do you know where I am from, Adira?"

"I assume Kendelen, given that you run the criminal underground here. Which implies you've been here a long time."

"You're right, I have been here a long time, but Pures age differently."

I frowned. "You're not a Pure? I've never seen you exhibit magic, nor have you ever implied you have any. I don't know a single Pure that doesn't brag about their powers every chance they get."

"I am from Lenea." I stiffened. "My married name is Stakov, but my maiden name is Camilla Krundell." I shook my head in disbelief.

"No."

She chuckled, glancing over at the flowers I'd noticed earlier. Before our eyes, they went from vibrant and fresh to withering and lilting.

"I assume my cousin has already shown her power to you, probably in a very obnoxious way?"

I swallowed. "I don't understand."

"Odette is my cousin. We were raised together in Lenea, but it wasn't exactly a typical upbringing, actually you may find some similarities to your own. Yours was a walk in the park compared to ours, though. Our family has a long history of seclusion, as I'm sure you know. Part of that is because the Krundell's are one of the few families who disagreed with the regular moving around of the Kamara, the object used to wipe Thadea off of the map."

"You know about Thadea?"

She nodded. "Of course. For centuries, my family has been a part of a secret order within Lenea. All members' children are trained in subversion, espionage, destabilising governments, and prepared for deep undercover operations. Over the years, we have been responsible for countless assassinations, arranged marriages, and falling outs between kingdoms who were previously allies." Could they have been responsible for the Melfore's being practically wiped out? For the failed alliance with Xeria? Could this secret sect be the real mastermind behind the rebellion?

"How does Solis fit into things?"

"Solis has her own agenda, but we share some similar goals, so we work together."

"So, you're not responsible for the start of the rebellion?"

"Not really, no. We aid it, but The Order prefers to work in the shadows. It is the most efficient way to gain control, after all."

If Butcher could do what Odette could, that would explain how she's been controlling Tolemas. It could be what's going on with Sierra as well.

"But why me? Why us?"

"Well, The Ordo Veritatis—" The Order of Truth, I mentally translated. "—dates back to before Thadea was overthrown. In fact, it dates back as early as the first few years after The Blessing. After the divinities disappeared, some of the Lenean elders felt they needed to prepare in case they ever returned, and so they created The Ordo Veritatis. Thousands of years later, after the Kamara was used to wipe Thadea from existence, The Ordo Veritatis went mostly inactive. Until an elder of the order recovered records. Records containing knowledge that the rest of the world had forgotten thanks to the Kamara or simply time. Realising the unique opportunity and advantage this posed, The Ordo Veritatis was reimagined and reformed. Now we simply go by The Order, and have a vast network of members all throughout Deorum."

CHAPTER SIXTY

I STARED AT HER in disbelief. I had no idea what this Kamara was, but it must have been how the other Kingdoms erased Thadea and its people from the world. She continued, apparently not finished.

"We have improved on the original founder's ideals. They were quite small minded, really. Unable to see past their need to prevent war, instead of seeing the bigger picture. A completely underground network with strategically placed people of power is capable of almost anything. So, The Order has spent the last few centuries planning, preparing, and infiltrating. Finding or buying assets," she met my eyes and smiled, "and putting them to use."

I shook my head. This sounded like a fictional tale.

"We knew about the two lost princesses of Thadea, and we knew the threat they could pose if they ever discovered how to reverse the Kamara's effects. It was simply a matter of finding them and ending their line. We thought we had succeeded. Two different strikes on the same night, sixteen years ago. Only somehow, the children of both couples survived. We could not find your cousin, but we found you and your sister. Collectively, we realised we had an opportunity, if you had inherited the Potenti Gifting. If we had you on our side, we would have a weapon no one else would see coming. So, I took you and Sierra in. Her accident made her a poor candidate for certain things, just as your attitude made you a poor candidate for others. Try as I might to get you to be loyal and obedient as a child, you never quite gave in. *So,* I had to find other means of controlling you." *The blood oath.*

"But *why*? What is your end goal?"

"What is anyone's end goal, Adira? What does your training tell you I am after?"

"Power. It's always about power."

She smiled. "Very good. Whoever holds the most power has the most control. The Incrementi have convinced the other kingdoms that they have grown weak over the years, using their magic for mere agriculture and parlour tricks. Instead of using it as intended, as a weapon of war, we have allowed the others to believe us unthreatening, so they focus on each other instead. All the while, we have been gaining power behind their backs, in their own homes, until we are ready to take what we want. You, my dear child, are the perfect ticket to ensure we succeed."

"This is unbelievable. You're completely unhinged. You and Odette." I shook my head.

"That is not a very nice thing to say."

"You're insane!"

She smiled. "Sanity is overrated. Now that you are informed, I have some places to be, so let's speed things along."

"Speed what along?"

"My cousin informs me you are being quite stubborn. I tried to warn her about that, but she thought she'd be able to manipulate you like she did that dim-witted girl Josette. I trained you better than that." I tensed.

"So, here's what is going to happen. Listen closely and obey. Do not speak of what I've told you tonight to *anyone*."

I winced at the tug that ensued.

"Apologise to Odette. She is quite pissy about your constant rejections. So whatever she deems necessary to earn her forgiveness, you will do."

I clenched my fist. "No, stop."

She smiled. "Do whatever she says is necessary. But she only has a limited amount of time with you. Hmm, let's say an hour? We don't want her getting too greedy and forgetting that you are my asset, not hers."

"I am no one's asset. Go to Infernis."

She sighed. "You really should know when to keep your mouth shut. Go, now. Straight to Odette's quarters and beg her forgiveness. She is expecting you. After the other kingdoms have arrived, and you have gathered information from them all, report back to me with a full update."

My feet moved on their own accord, out of Tolemas' house. Butcher walked to the doorway and waved.

"Get home safely, honey!"

Bitch.

My mind raced. This entire time, Butcher and Odette had been behind everything? Them and this mysterious Order. My parents' deaths, Tarryn's parents, Raf's death. Everything they'd had me doing was to stop me from connecting the dots. I still didn't know why they were working with the rebels. My guess was the chaos Solis created only aided The Order in expanding their reach. Tilly had been an example to make me fear Odette and again keep me at bay. The engagement to Valor was no doubt just another distraction. Odette had manipulated Josette into attacking me and trying to expose me, but why would she do that if she were working with Butcher? If I was an 'asset,' Odette's insistence on a genuine betrothal to Valor made sense now.

The Order would then have control over multiple power players. The Taros queen, The Butcher of The Cavum, who clearly has strong ties to Solis and The Rise and, if I married Valor, the Xerian Princess also set to inherit the Taros throne. Who knew how many order members had infiltrated the other kingdoms? I still couldn't figure out the rebellion's true motivations, but my brain was already struggling to process everything else. I couldn't unravel that now. The rest would have to wait.

Despite how hard I fought, I couldn't stop myself from going to Odette's quarters and knocking on her door.

Tilly opened the door, in nothing but a completely sheer and very short undergarment. I averted my eyes.

She smiled. "Princess Elia. The queen has been looking forward to your visit all afternoon. This way," she said, and made her way down the hall.

I followed, and much to my growing discomfort, we seemed to pass all the sitting and entertaining rooms, heading for the bedchamber.

She stopped and knocked. "Your Majesty, your guest has arrived." *More like hostage.*

"Enter." Odette called, and Tilly walked in with me behind her.

The queen was sitting in her bed, reading glasses perched on the end of her nose. She looked over, closed her book, and smiled.

"That will be all, Matilda." Tilly smiled, bowed, and left the room, closing the doors on the way out.

I swallowed and looked at Odette.

"Please, Adira. Have a seat."

Panic finally set in. Hearing her say my real name, confirming everything Butcher said, was true. She knew who I truly was this entire time. I had no choice but to walk over and sit on the edge of her bed.

"I've been waiting for this conversation for some time."

"I owe you an apology. I am so sorry for my behaviour. I shouldn't have been so rude. Please forgive me?" I forced out as sincerely as I could manage, fighting with every bone in my body not to drop to my knees and beg as Butcher had commanded.

"How long did Camilla order you to be here for?"

I sighed. "An hour."

She smiled a bit. She had an odd look in her eyes. One I hadn't seen before. If I didn't know any better, I'd say it was a mixture of pity and kindness.

"We have little time then. There is a lot you won't understand right now, but I'm hoping it will eventually become clear."

"What are you talking about?"

"You are going to agree to marry my son."

"Odette, please."

She shook her head. "I will tell him tomorrow that I have proposed a genuine marriage. When he comes to you about it, say yes. If you do that, and anything else I tell you to do for the rest of our time, then I will forgive you."

"Please don't make me do this." It didn't go unnoticed that this request was much more sincere than my apology had been.

"You need to trust that it is in the best interest for both of you. Now, lay down."

I tensed, trying to fight the command, which only elicited a groan from me, as my intestines felt like they might rip themselves from my stomach. As I finally conceded, laying down, she stood, and I wasn't sure if that was more concerning or relieving.

"An hour is not a lot of time. But I will do the best I can."

"Do what? Please, don't. Please Odette."

"Take off your shirt."

Panic shot through me. I was helpless. I lifted my shirt and removed it. Swallowing, I tried again.

"Please, Odette! Please, don't." I begged.

She sat beside me, closed her eyes, and took a deep breath. Her hand moved over my stomach before it opened to reveal a seed. I immediately sat up, trying to leave the bed. The room. The damned city.

"Stop. Lay down, be still and don't struggle."

My heart was racing. She was going to turn me into Tilly.

"No, no, please." I begged as I lay back down, my body going still. Tears pricked my eyes as she placed the seed on my stomach.

"P-please, Odette."

She placed her hand over the seed, palm flat against my stomach as it took on a soft glow. This was my worst nightmare. I couldn't move. I couldn't stop this.

"Look at me." She ordered, and I fought with every ounce of my being not to. I prayed to whoever was listening, and whoever wasn't, but once blood started trickling down my nose and I felt like blood vessels were bursting, I had no choice but to meet her eyes.

"Relax." I obeyed. My breathing slowed and my muscles relaxed, but it didn't stop the panic inside. The small smile that appeared on her lips as she watched me told me she could tell. Her fingers reached out to brush my cheek, and I flinched back.

"Not just your body, your mind as well. Relax your mind. Do not worry."

My eyes widened in fear, but then suddenly, I couldn't remember why I was trying to resist. As my thoughts calmed, I breathed out. I remembered the panicked feeling I'd had just moments ago, but I couldn't really determine why I'd felt that way. I had nothing to worry about.

Meeting Odette's eyes again, she smiled a little more and the look in her eyes should have been concerning, but it wasn't, really. She looked conflicted as she shivered and closed her eyes, her fingers hovering near my cheek.

She took a moment before she opened her eyes and muttered something unintelligible.

"What?"

"... The voices. The voices say it would be so easy to just...." Her fingers brushed my cheek before she quickly snatched her hand back and took a breath. "No. Not today, not today. I am wasting time. Time is wasting." She sounded unhinged as she shook her head, seeming to refocus.

"What do you mean—"

"Shh." She mumbled.

I closed my mouth, a little frustrated. *What was going on?*

"Okay, okay. Where was I?" She glanced at her hand. "Oh! Yes. Relax your body and mind. Trust me completely and do as I say. All is well."

I didn't think it was possible to relax any further, but as she told me to trust her, I realised it was. The apprehension I didn't know I was feeling disappeared, and any doubt I had about the situation I'd found myself in drifted away, leaving me feeling calmer and more content than I had in months. *Why hadn't I trusted Odette sooner?* I smiled a little and nodded.

"All is well." I repeated. She nodded quickly, that familiar look of insanity flickering in her gaze.

"Good, now... now..." She seemed confused as her nose scrunched up slightly and she glanced at my torso. A distant part of me whispered that should have made me anxious, but I trusted Odette. What's the worst that could happen? "Just lay there, don't think about what I'm doing. Just comply and don't think about anything." She nodded again, and I wasn't sure if she was nodding to herself or to me. Happy to oblige anyway, I — *What was I meant to be doing again?* I stilled as things went fuzzy. All thoughts dissipated as my gaze fixed on a random spot on the... on the... what was it called? I found it didn't matter as my thoughts flittered away and I laid there, my mind full of fog. Fog so dense that any thoughts that formed slipped away before I could grasp them.

I vaguely felt something move as little vines crawled along my skin, wrapping around my torso.

"I'm afraid this will be quite painful. Bite down on this." She handed me a rolled-up towelette with her free hand. My mouth seemed to understand the command, even if my mind didn't, as it slowly opened and then clamped down once she had placed something in it.

She placed her free hand atop the one pressed to my stomach. Both were glowing now. One minute, it was a tickling sensation, the next, a pain I'd never imagined possible shot through me. I screamed, involuntarily biting down on the towelette as the vines dug into my skin. I wanted to thrash and struggle and fight, but I couldn't. Tears streamed down my face. I felt like I was being torn apart from the inside as the vines moved through my body like a parasite, searching for Taros only knew what.

"This seed is from the Fanalia plant, a divine flower native to Reya, revered for its healing properties."

I barely registered what she'd said, as my mind fought between pain and nothingness. I screamed again, as the vines all seemed to converge in one place.

"It will be over soon. Everything will be alright," she said in a soothing voice. I believed her, I trusted her.

All was well.

But then why was I in so much pain?

It didn't matter.

What didn't matter?

Her hands moved over the dagger branded on my torso.

"I'm sorry," she said as the pain increased tenfold.

I screamed again. I felt like I was on fire, like there was sandpaper under my skin. The pain was so severe it broke through the haze in my mind as horror set in. This was going to kill me. I would not end up like Tilly, because I'd be dead. No one could survive this pain.

I clenched my eyes shut as the vines ceased their movements. I sensed a brighter glow, but didn't open my eyes. The pain stopped for a second and everything went quiet. I could hear my heart thudding in my chest. Opening my eyes, I hesitantly looked down to where Odette had her hands covering my tattoo.

She glanced at me. "This is the worst part."

I managed a slight shake of my head, but she ignored it. Her hands were glowing as bright as a lantern now, and I braced myself. I had a few seconds pain free before all Infernis broke loose.

Despite her command not to struggle and to relax, my body apparently outranked my mind, because it jerked at what felt like a hot iron being poked through my stomach at an unbelievable speed, repeatedly. I screamed and screamed, until I couldn't anymore, my voice becoming hoarse. But the pain kept coming.

I wasn't sure when I lost consciousness, but I must have, because the next thing I knew, I was waking up in my bed. I slowly sat up, my mind foggy and my thoughts jumbled. It took me a few minutes to figure out where I was and how I'd gotten here. Things were still hazy, and I was having trouble remembering. As memories and broken thoughts came back to me, I quickly sat up and looked around, expecting Odette to be standing, waiting to make me her slave, just like she had Tilly. But there was no one else here.

How had I gotten back to my room? Guards would have been on my door and surely asked questions if someone had carried me in here unconscious. I walked to my window, trying to figure out what the time was. It looked to be just past dawn. I swallowed and walked over to the mirror, lifting my top, only to find my waist bandaged up. I was afraid to look any further.

I reached for the bandage, taking a steadying breath as I unwrapped it. Naturally, I just about jumped out of my skin when Lydia walked in.

"Oh, I'm sorry! I was coming to wake you," she said when she spotted me.

I quickly tucked the bandage in and lowered my shirt. "It's alright, you just startled me." My voice sounded husky and raw.

"Are you getting sick? I'll make you some tea. I just came because I thought you may wish to attend the service for the fallen guards this morning."

I nodded, grateful she had thought to fetch me. "I would, thank you. While you fetch the tea, I'll change. I must be coming down with something."

She nodded. "I'll be right back." She hurried out.

I breathed out. Looks like I'd have to wait to see what sort of damage the crazy bitch had done to my body, and pray I didn't run into her in the meantime. I quickly changed into a respectable black dress, nothing fancy. A funeral was no time to be showing off. Lydia returned a few minutes later with the tea.

"I had the nurses make it. They used some herbal tea that is supposed to help you recover faster."

I smiled gratefully. "Thank you." Gosh, my voice sounded horrible. I took a sip.

"When does the service start?"

"Soon, we should go when you're ready. But..." She bit her lip, unsure how to say whatever she had on her mind.

"What is it, Lydia?"

"I feel I should warn you, usually women do not attend the guards' service as it's run by the Deos Credentes. I'm sure you're aware the temple's views on women attending ceremonies such as this are... more traditional? The male family members may be there, but the women are required to wait until the burial."

My fist clenched. I knew The Credentes still had backwards views, especially when it comes to foreigners and women. It had been a sore point between Hadrian and the priests. From what I understood, Hadrian had been pushing for them to abandon their less inclusive 'traditions', but the old faithful priests weren't having a bar of it. You'd think, as the king, he could simply order them, but apparently being divine servants afforded the temple leaders a certain amount of immunity to the laws the rest of us had to abide by.

My anger from the day before at the men in that briefing room returned. But today wasn't about that. I was going to be there to show respect to the guards who died protecting me and the others. Traditions and rules be damned. I'd like to see one of those creepy old priests stop me.

"Thank you. I appreciate the warning." I finished my tea. "Let's go."

She smiled a bit, clearly having expected my response. We left the room. It was Hamish and Wes on guard duty today. I assumed because Tarryn and

Uri would be at the service. Wes groaned slightly and Hamish held out his hand.

"Well, talk about Déjà vu," I said, raising my eyebrows at them. "What was it this time?"

Wes sighed, placing a coin in Hamish's hand. "Hamish said you'd go to the service. I said you wouldn't. In Xeria, anyone can attend regardless of what they've got downstairs, but here and some of the other kingdoms, I know it's not considered appropriate."

"To which I told him you are the least appropriate woman I know." Hamish added.

"Rude," I said.

"If it helps, he meant it as a compliment." Wes offered.

I smiled a bit and shook my head. "Are you going to stop me from going?"

"Hek no," Hamish said. "I, for one, cannot wait to see the looks on those bigot's faces."

"Seconded. As well as the looks on the other guard's faces," Wes said.

"Well then, let's stop dilly dallying and get going." I started down the hall, Lydia walking beside me, and the men falling into step behind us.

Hamish was right. When I reached the temple, I saw a few old lords' eyes practically pop out of their heads. Their disapproval was obvious, but it would be rude to make a scene, so they kept their mouths shut. The priests were attending to things at the front of the room, meaning they hadn't spotted me yet.

CHAPTER SIXTY-ONE

LYDIA REMAINED OUTSIDE, NOT wanting to garner their wrath. Luckily, I didn't have that problem. I went to take a seat at the back, so I wouldn't distract more than necessary, but a hand on my arm drew my attention. It was Uri. He was dressed in his formal guard uniform. Tarryn stood just behind him.

"You should sit with us at the front."

"I don't want to cause more of a scene than I already have. I just wanted to pay my respects by being present. It's okay, I can sit here."

He shook his head. "You fought like the rest of us. If you were a man, you would be praised and honoured. You will sit with us."

I glanced at Tarryn, who gave me a small smile and nodded.

I bit my lip. "Alright."

Uri stepped back, allowing me into the walkway. He and Tarryn fell into step on either side of me as we walked down the pews, Hamish and Wes following behind.

I heard a few whispers. Glancing around, I expected to see more glares or disapproving looks, but was surprised to find that most of the room was filled with guards, and they were looking at me in surprise, but also... respect? Maybe even gratitude? The priests went into an absolute tizzy when they spotted me. One even tilted his head back and prayed for the divinities to forgive this sin. What a drama queen.

The priest holding the ceremony approached, not even deigning to meet my eyes, and instead addressed Uri and Tarryn.

"This is highly inappropriate. The divine will be displeased and you risk the guards we came here to honour, being denied entry into Eternis as retribution." Father Thindwell, I recognised the man as Chambersen's right hand, scolded. "She must leave at once." As if I didn't even have a name. I opened my mouth to tell the good father something truly inappropriate, but Uri beat me to it.

"Father Thindwell, I am sure the last thing you want right now is to make a scene, so I suggest you get back to why we are all here and do your job."

His eyes widened. "Who do you think you are to tell me—"

"—Princess Elia fought alongside these fallen men, and she has just as much right to be here as I do, certainly more than you. If that isn't enough, then perhaps the fact that she is the Heir of Xeria, an honoured guest of the Navarre court and, if rumour is to be believed, the potential future Queen of Taros, is? No? Then, by all means, father, remove her from the room." He stepped back.

"I think you'll be hard pressed to find a guard willing to obey that order, and even more hard pressed to find one actually capable of dragging her out. But if you want to cause a scene, incur the wrath of King Hadrian, Queen Tira, and even worse, the Princess's herself, then go ahead." He folded his arms, holding the man's gaze.

The priest stuttered as his gaze flicked between Uri and me. He glanced at the guards closest to us. They all simply shook their head and remained where they were. Looks like he'd have to roll up the sleeves of his dusty old robe and drag me out himself if he wanted me gone. He muttered something about the divinities smiting the three of us before huffing and heading back to his podium.

I looked at Uri. "Thank you."

"Don't thank me. These rules are ridiculous."

I smiled a little and took my seat in between him and Tarryn. We were in the front row to the left of the podium. To the right were the fallen guards' families, the male members. Only Jenkins' family members were present, as the other two guards had been from Xeria, but Hadrian, Valor, Killian, and Yarik were seated there in place of the foreign guards' families.

Father Thindwell stepped up to the podium, silencing the room. He glanced around with a sombre smile. A smile that faltered when his gaze snagged mine. He recovered quickly, though, and cleared his throat.

"Thank you all for coming to show your respects on this sad day. We gather to lay Timothee Jenkins, Isiah Wilkins, and Jeremiah Carter to rest."

I knew I wouldn't forget their names or faces, along with the face of the unknown archer boy I'd killed. His face would stay with me for a long time.

The ceremony was rather formal. They gave all three guards an award for bravery, a lot of good that would do them when they were six feet under. But I suppose it was nice for their families to see that they died heroes.

Hadrian stepped up to complete the ceremony, before they would be buried in the guards' cemetery, alongside countless other fallen guards and soldiers.

"It is always a terrible day when we lose even one man, let alone three. But these three men gave their lives in honour of their kingdom. They faced impossible odds and whilst they fell, they protected my son, they protected the Princess of Xeria, and they protected their fellow guards. They journey to Eternis to join the land of the divine now, and we will no doubt see them again when our own time comes. May they live on in spirit to help guide their friends and loved ones, and may they finally rest in paradise." He finished, stepping back.

"May they rest." The occupants of the room all repeated the prayer.

"May they rest," I said, before whispering an additional, "may you finally rest fear-free." In honour of the boy archer.

Tarryn glanced at me, apparently having heard me. He stood with Uri, Hamish, and Wes, along with five other guards. Yarik, Killian, and Valor also stood. But Uri walked over to one of the five guards and muttered something. They raised their eyebrows, but nodded and sat back down. I wasn't sure what Uri was doing when he approached me.

"Will you honour the fallen guards, and everyone else here, by acting as a pallbearer with the rest of us?" My eyes widened.

Thindwell stepped in. "Sir, this is outrageous. A lady simply cannot be permitted so close to the dead."

"The Princess," he said, putting emphasis on my title, "isn't that much of a lady, so you don't need to worry." He looked back at me and I shot him a half hearted glare. "I am getting quite fed up with your nonsense, Father Thindwell, so kindly step aside or I will throw you out of your own temple." Uri's face was impassive and there wasn't a hint of a smile on his face now. He was serious. Thindwell took a hesitant step back, which seemed to satisfy Uri as he turned back to me.

"Well, Princess?"

I glanced around at the other guards who had stepped forward to be pallbearers. They slowly nodded one by one as I met each of their gazes. I swallowed and looked back at Uri.

"I would be honoured." I stood and approached the three coffins.

Uri directed me to the middle coffin, belonging to Jeremiah Carter. He stood on the left, and I took my position on the right. Wes and one more guard joined behind us, one on either side.

Valor and Killian took up the front positions for Timothee Jenkins, while Hamish and Tarryn took the front positions for Isiah Wilkins. The remaining guards filled the last spots. Hadrian signalled for everyone else to stand, and for the pianist to play. Once the music began, we all lifted the coffins, making our way down the pews and out of the temple. We carried them all the way to the cemetery, their families, women included, joining us along the way.

We placed the caskets into their rightful places, then we lowered them into the ground. Jenkins' family was the first to approach and sprinkle dirt into the grave of their son. A woman that must have been Jenkins' mother was sobbing into a handkerchief. Women were only permitted after the ceremony, and after the body had been lowered into its grave. Her husband had his arm wrapped tightly around her and looked as if he, too, were barely holding it together.

Next to them was a young man, maybe eighteen, staring at the grave and holding his little sister's hand. He must be the middle child, now the oldest. He would become responsible for taking care of his family when his father couldn't. They may very well have relied on Jenkins' soldier salary. I made another mental note to check on that afterwards.

Yarik was next, casting his into the Virbi guard, Jeremiah's grave. Then Uri, for the last one, Isiah Wilkins, the Impure Xerian guard. Then the guards that had carried the caskets, including Killian and Valor, picked up shovels. I did the same. Improper or not, at this point, what was one more infraction? It was silent as we all filled in the graves. I could still hear the piano from where we were, but that and Jenkins' mother's sobs were the only sounds other than the shovelling of dirt.

Once we had finished the burials, people dispersed. I remained, as did Uri and Tarryn. I looked over at the Jenkins family before slowly approaching them. The eighteen-year-old boy was the first one to notice. He immediately dipped into a bow.

"Your Highness," he said, tugging on his little sister's hand, who made to copy his movement.

I quickly shook my head, bending down to her level and gently stopping her.

"What is your name?"

Her eyes were wide and weary. She was too young to really understand what was going on.

"B-Bria," she stammered, gripping her brother's hand, "and this—this is my brother, Tobias."

I nodded, giving a small smile to Tobias before looking back at the small girl.

"Well, Bria, my name is Elia and today, you do not need to bow or curtsey for anyone, okay?"

She nodded, biting her lip. I saw her mother's hand move to her chest as she watched us interact.

I glanced at them and stood. "I am terribly sorry for your loss."

His father nodded. "Thank you, Your Highness."

His wife sniffled.

I shook my head. "I can only imagine the pain you must be experiencing. A parent should not outlive their children. Jenkins was a good man. You should be proud." I hoped the divinities didn't mind me assuming the character of a dead man, since it was to offer some peace to his family.

"I, and the others that were on that road, owe him our sincerest gratitude. If there is anything, anything at all that you need, please ask a guard or a servant to send for me and I will come." I said, holding out my hand.

Jenkins' father looked at me in surprise, but he slowly nodded and took my hand, shaking it.

"Thank you, Princess. That's... very kind of you."

I nodded slightly and then turned to his wife, who wrapped her arms around me in a tight hug.

Her husband looked mortified. After all, it was very improper to touch a royal without permission, let alone hug them. I smiled reassuringly at him and hugged her back.

"Thank you." She whispered, before slowly pulling back. I nodded, squeezing her arms.

"You have nothing to thank me for." I stepped back, waving to Bria, before leaving the family to their grief. Hoping they would take me up on my offer should they need it. If I was still around. I headed back over to Uri and Tarryn.

"You did good, kid," Uri said, smiling.

"You don't look *that* much older," I said pointedly.

He simply shrugged. "I look excellent for my age."

I rolled my eyes and glanced around. There were a few guards left, those that must have been closest to the deceased.

"I'm ready to go whenever you guys are, but by all means, take your time."

Tarryn nodded. "I can escort you back. I've paid my respects."

"I need to speak with Yarik. Hamish, are you fine to guard with Tarryn? Wes should come with me." Uri asked.

Hamish nodded, stepping forward. "Of course."

Uri looked at me. "Will you and Tarryn be training later?"

I looked at Tarryn, who shook his head. "I figured we'd give it a miss today if you're serious about coming on the scouting mission to the mines."

Uri nodded. "Alright, I will see you then."

"Thanks, Uri." I smiled a bit, and he nodded, before heading off to find Yarik and Wes.

Hamish, Tarryn, and I left the cemetery and were on our way back into the castle.

"Looks like the gang's back together," Hamish said, and Tarryn rolled his eyes.

"Don't call us a gang."

"No? The dream team?"

"That's so much worse."

I laughed a bit at the two of them. It has been a while since all three of us were together without something insane going on. Which, once again, the fates had apparently taken as a dare, because my name was called and I turned around to see Valor making his way over. *Oh, Hek.* I prayed he hadn't spoken to his mother already.

Hamish leaned in and whispered. "You could fake pass out? I'll catch you, of course, then you can avoid him for whatever reason you look like you want to. At least for a bit while you 'recover' in the medicae wing."

Tarryn muttered. "She's probably worried he's going to kiss her again."

"Oooh, when did this happen?"

"After the ambush, the man practically launched himself at her."

I groaned. "Tarryn."

"Oh, I need more details," Hamish said eagerly, right as Valor approached.

"Details about what?" He said, and Tarryn snorted.

"Nothing important." I quickly said before Hamish could say something even worse. "Is there something you need, Valor?"

"I was hoping we could talk…"

I saw Hamish mouth the word *'talk'* in finger quotations to Tarryn with a wink who, to his credit, only rolled his eyes.

"Can it wait? I actually have breakfast plans with Cali."

"I'm sure my sister won't mind a slight delay," he said, looking at me, "please, Elle?"

I mentally groaned and nodded. "Okay, sure. Walk with me, then?"

"I was actually hoping we could speak somewhere a bit more private. We could go to my study since it's close?"

I shrugged. *Better than his bedroom.* "Sure. Lead the way."

He did just that, with Hamish and Tarryn following.

"That was nice, what you did in speaking to Jenkins' family. Hek, it was nice of you to come to the service at all. You were not expected to."

"It seems women aren't 'expected' to do much at all around here."

"I just meant—" He groaned. "Nevermind."

I was being harsh. None of this was his fault. "No, I'm sorry. Thank you for saying so."

He nodded. "How are you holding up after yesterday? It was quite gruesome."

"It was—I'm okay. I was prepared."

"Prepared by who?"

I smiled a bit, thinking of The Four. "That's a story for another time."

"I look forward to hearing that one. Regardless, though, you can prepare for years. It is still different seeing it up close."

"You're right. I'm probably in for a few sleepless nights, but I am alright." I had killed beasts, creatures, and enemy soldiers with The Four, but other people, a child? That was different. He watched me and nodded.

"I'm fairly familiar with sleepless nights myself. Perhaps we can spend them together occasionally?"

I looked at him and thankfully; we had reached his study.

"So, what was it you wanted to discuss?"

He let my lack of acknowledgement drop and opened the door.

"I spoke to my mother this morning. There are some things we need to discuss."

I stepped into the study, and Valor shut the door behind us. He walked over to the lounge and sat down, gesturing to the spot beside him.

"Okay?" I sat beside him.

"My mother think it's time I marry. I knew it would be soon, but apparently soon is… sooner than I thought."

"Oh, is that something you want?"

"I've always known it was my duty. Marriage is not the romantic notion that it is to others when you are heir to a throne. My parents wanted me to choose someone, but I never found anyone that seemed good enough, so I ignored it and focused on other things."

"Right." I needed to get out of here.

"Now mother has decided its time. I assumed with the way everything is between the other kingdoms right now, she would try to arrange a marriage with a daughter from one of them. Not an heir, because they would need to run their own kingdom, not give that up to move to Taros. I suspected Alina from Lios, which explains why they arrived early."

I raised my eyebrows. Maybe I could convince him to marry her instead. Why did that thought make me feel ill? "I haven't met Alina. Is she nice?"

"She's fierce, her and Cali get along really well. Unfortunately, I know her brother better," he said disappointedly.

"Adonis?"

He nodded. "Mmm."

"Okay, so, you're going to marry Alina?"

"Well, my mother actually suggested someone else."

Dammit.

"Surely Alina is the best choice?"

"You don't want to know who?"

No. Not even a little. I shrugged. "It's not really my business."

"Well, actually..."

Infernis. "It's alright, Valor. I really don't need to know."

"It's you, Elia. She wants me to marry you."

I closed my eyes. *Shit.*

"Me?" I said, opening my eyes. "She doesn't even like me."

"No, but she's convinced I do, and given the tension between Xeria and Taros, she thinks it will be a good political union."

"I'm too young to consider marriage."

He nodded a bit. "I get that. You weren't raised a princess and this must all seem so fast, but I—"

"Valor..." I tried cutting him off.

"Please let me say this?"

I swallowed and nodded. Odette must not have known that Butcher had already ordered me some time ago to say yes if Valor proposed to me. I've been fighting the *'make him fall in love with you' command* as much as I could, but when moments like this came up and there were two clear, opposite options, I was screwed.

"I know it hasn't been long, and I know that you're new to court politics, but I also know you feel something, just like I do. I've met a lot of women, Elia, and none of them have ever had the effect you do."

I kept my mouth shut, not trusting what might come out if I did. As long as he didn't ask, I might be able to avoid saying yes.

"We could agree to the betrothal to keep both our parents and our people happy. We could have a long engagement, and just see how things go. It doesn't have to be set in stone." He rested his hand on my leg. "What do you think?"

"Valor I—" I stopped myself, taking a breath. "Of course I feel something for you, but things haven't exactly been perfect between us? We are so different, maybe too different. I don't know if I could marry someone who doesn't support me."

"I will support you."

"Supporting me means supporting the things I care about or believe in, Valor. We have drastically different views on some pretty important things."

"That's true, but I can work on supporting you more. I like that we are different. If everyone was the same, then no one would think of anything new. I love that you make me see things differently sometimes."

I closed my eyes.

"I'm not saying we should be the same. I am just saying, I mean come on Val, we drive each other mad half the time? You said yourself that we get along better when we aren't talking. It's not healthy."

"I know. That's because I put up a wall between us, and you keep chipping away at it. Sometimes I let you before I realise what I'm doing, and as soon as I notice, I slam it back up and lash out. That's not fair to you, but I was trying to protect both of us." He met my eyes, and I swallowed. I'd done the same thing.

"I didn't think I could have you, Elia. I sure as Hek didn't think I deserved you. So I tried not to want you. I tried to push you away, but it didn't work. I have never felt the way I feel about you. Even knowing you weren't an option, thinking I'd be married off to a random princess I didn't know, I couldn't stay away." He tucked a strand of hair behind my ear. "I promise to let you in and to support you. Just give me a chance to prove it?"

"I don't know what to say." *Not anything that would get me out of this situation, anyway.*

"Say yes."

I bit my lip to keep it shut. As long as he didn't phrase it...

"I think there's something worthwhile here. More than I could have hoped for. I will make a good partner and a good husband, if that's what you choose. Marry me, Elia?"

Shit.

I looked at him. "Yes." *Double shit.*

His eyes widened. "Wait, what?"

"Yes," I repeated, "BUT we will see how things go? I don't want to rush anything." I added, trying to do damage control.

He nodded quickly. "Yes, exactly. Sorry, I just didn't think you would say yes so easily."

If only I'd had a choice. I shrugged slightly. "I can happily take it back..."

"No!" He blurted, and I raised my eyebrows. "I mean, no, that isn't what I meant."

I smiled a bit. "You're nervous."

"I'm not." He mumbled.

I chuckled a bit. "You can take on rebel soldiers, but you can't ask me a simple question?"

"In all honesty, a bunch of soldiers are a lot less scary than you are."

"Rude."

He smiled a bit and took my hand. "Sorry."

"You realise, regardless of this betrothal, I am still going on this scouting mission, right?"

He sighed. "Elia."

"Nope. No arguments. I am going."

"I know. Even though I still think it is a bad idea."

"I should prepare. We leave soon, right?"

He nodded. "Yes, but there's one more thing." *Fates, what more could there possibly be?*

"Oh?" I said, looking at him

This time, he bit his lip. He moved off of the lounge, falling on one knee. My eyes widened.

"Traditionally, I believe one is supposed to kneel and ask in a much more collected manner than I just did. So, will you do me the honour of becoming my wife?" He said as he pulled a box out of his pocket, opening it and revealing a beautiful ring.

It looked like he'd taken it straight from the royal vault. It had a gold band with a beautiful sapphire gemstone in the centre, and what looked like two smaller diamonds on either side.

"I thought you might like something a little more interesting to wear."

I swallowed. "It's beautiful." And it really was.

He nodded, watching me. "As are you."

I looked at his face. Did he truly want this? The traitorous part of my heart had swelled at his words, his promises, not wanting to believe he was being manipulated, or worse, that he was lying. That part of me wanted to give in, to accept that he was a good man underneath it all.

I slowly held out my hand, and he slipped the ring onto my finger. "Yes," I said again. I was beginning to hate that word.

He grinned, standing up, pulling me with him, and kissing me. I kissed back a little. Thankfully, he didn't take it further.

"You're right, we should get ready."

I nodded. "I'll see you when we're preparing to leave."

He nodded and opened the door for me.

"Thank you," I said and left, heading straight for my room.

CHAPTER SIXTY-TWO

HAMISH AND TARRYN WALKED with me. I knew they noticed the ring, but thankfully, they said nothing. Entering my room, I shut the door and closed my eyes. How in the Inferno was I going to get out of this?

"Is this a bad time?" I squealed, my eyes flying open to find Tira sitting on my couch.

"It's as good as any, I suppose. Sorry, I didn't notice you there."

"I could see that," she said, standing up. "What's wrong?"

Without thinking, I went to tell her about what happened with Butcher, expecting an immediate and painful pull to stop me from saying anything, but it never came. I frowned.

"Okay, you're concerning me." She walked over. "What is it?"

"I saw Butcher last night." My eyes widened. What the Hek?

"What happened? Did she make you do something?"

"This doesn't make sense. I'm not supposed to tell *anyone? S*he ordered me. I—"

"Okay, hang on. Come sit, and then we can start at the beginning." She led me over to the couch, and I sat down.

"I went to see Tolemas last night. I had to get answers from him."

"Who is Tolemas?"

"He a Para Forti, practically raised me after he joined the circus. He was the closest thing I had to a second father."

She frowned slightly. "Not Tolemas Sullu?"

I looked at her. "The very one."

"Son of a —" She seemed to catch herself, shaking her head. "He is one of the warriors I sent to find you and bring you home. One that never returned. I thought him dead. What happened last night?"

"I went to his house to confront him, about something I learned in my Testing. I found out he knew my parents and he told me you sent him to find me, but Butcher was there and she..."

I explained everything. Who Butcher really was, her relationship to Odette, her plans as far as I knew, and then the event with Odette this morning. Tira listened without interruption.

"I don't know how I'm able to tell you this. She ordered me not to."

"Maybe whatever Odette did has somehow undone the oath? You said she told you that seed was known for its healing properties? If what you learned during your Testing is true, and a blood oath is like a disease that can be healed, then maybe that's what happened?"

I lifted my top and undid my bandages, finally getting a good look at my torso. Glancing at the brand, the surrounding skin was irritated and red. I looked closer. It almost appeared as if someone had *redone* it. As if someone had gone over it with ink again, and it was now healing.

"Divinities, what if she somehow rewired it so she has control?"

"There's no point panicking until we know. Queen Yelara will be here in less than a month. She can tell us for sure. Until then, we lie low. Stay away from Odette and Camilla when you can."

I breathed out, nodding slowly. "Okay, good plan."

"So I take it you saw Valor this morning?" She stated, looking at my hand. I glanced at the ring and groaned.

"I am such an idiot. I was so convinced I'd be forced to say yes, I didn't even try to say the word no. Do you think I could have?"

"Possibly. You can still say no."

"Dammit, this is all so complicated. If Odette knew her orders wouldn't stick, why would she do whatever she did to the oath, before I'd said yes to him?"

"Honestly, it all seems very out of character for her. Something just doesn't quite make sense. But, Adira, you can say no. We can leave. If you really want to, we can get Sierra and leave right now. We can stop in Reya on the way and have your blood oath properly checked."

I swallowed. "There's so much at stake, Tira. I thought at the first opportunity, I could grab Sierra and run, but I've gotten to know these people. Now that I know what Butcher is doing, her involvement with this damned Order and The Rise, I'm not sure if I can just walk away." I finally voiced what I'd been thinking for a while now, and I hated myself for it.

Sierra was my family. She is the only person I was supposed to be looking out for, and here I was, trying to figure out a way to help everyone, not just her. Exactly the thing Amory had encouraged me to do and feared that I wouldn't. She taught me what she did so I could do more than just protect Sierra.

Tira smiled a little. "Do you remember when I said ruling is hard if you are a certain type of person?"

I nodded slightly.

"You are that type of person. You have a good heart. Those like you struggle to sacrifice anyone."

"That is unrealistic. I can't save everyone."

"No, but that doesn't mean you won't try," she said knowingly.

I sighed. "This is all insane."

She nodded. "It is. Maybe you should stay here and process, instead of joining the scouting party."

I gave her a look. "Nice try."

She smiled a bit. "You better get ready, then."

I nodded, hesitating for a second, but then decided to Hek with it. I reached over and hugged her.

"Thanks, Aunt Tira." I didn't really know what to call my father's cousin, but Aunt felt right.

I practically felt her smile brighten as she hugged me back. "Of course."

I pulled away, walking to my closet.

"I'll make sure you have a decent horse prepared," she said, standing.

"Thank you." She left the room.

After re-bandaging my waist, I changed my clothing. I tried to wear colours I knew would blend with the terrain. Settling on a tight-fitting training tunic with a cloak over the top, hiding exactly how form fitting it was and finding myself missing Ehsys's beautifully designed tunicam. I attached my dagger to my thigh and headed down to the stables, where we had agreed to meet.

Uri waved me over. "Hey," I said.

"Come with me."

I raised my eyebrows. He really wasn't a beat around the bush type of guy. "Okay?" I followed him towards the guards' quarters. "What are we doing?"

"I realised you've got no weapons of your own, other than that cute little dagger you carry around."

I narrowed my eyes. "My dagger is not *cute*."

He smirked. "It is very cute. But the point is, that is not enough. When we get back, I will arrange for some custom weapons to be made for you, but for this trip, you can't go in with just a dagger, so..." He finished opening the door to a room that was full of weapons. Covered wall to wall.

"Woah, awesome," I said, and he chuckled.

"Not the usual response from a Taros noblewoman, but not in the slightest bit surprising from you."

"Hey, this was your idea."

"It was, so pick your poison."

I walked through the room, looking at all the weapons. Each one brought back a distinct memory from my time with The Four. I naturally gravitated towards the short swords. Making me think of the weapons training I'd done with Moira. I grabbed a pair of twin short swords, as well as a strap for them to sit in. One that went across my back for easy access. Then I went to the daggers section. Grabbing a weapons belt, I fastened it around my waist. I carefully chose a dagger that was larger than the one on my thigh, as well as three small throwing knives. None of these compared to the weapons Dhedros had crafted, but they would have to do. I sheathed them all and walked back over to Uri. Who was standing with his arms crossed, and eyebrows raised.

"I *really* need to hear more about this training. Do you even know how to use half of those?"

I grinned. "If you're nice. And yes."

He rolled his eyes. "Got everything you need, then?"

"Yep."

We walked back to the stables. Tira was holding a black mare that I assumed was for me. Valor, Killian, Tarryn, and Hamish were all geared up and standing beside their own mounts, making our riding party six in total. We couldn't afford anymore, or we risked drawing too much attention. We would station some guards nearby in case we needed to signal for help, but they would keep their distance.

Hamish whistled. "Damn girl, you can murder me any day." Tarryn chuckled, and I rolled my eyes.

Uri mounted his horse. "Is everyone ready?"

There was a mixture of nods and *'yeses'* from all of us as we mounted.

Tira stepped back. "Be careful, and remember, this is a *scouting* mission. No one is to engage."

I nodded. "We will. We'll see you soon." I smiled.

With that, we were off. We rode hard for the first part of the trip so we could make good time and not get back too late. Everyone made small talk as we rode. Killian and Uri took point. Valor rode next to me, much to my conflicting excitement and discomfort, while Hamish and Tarryn took up the rear. We stopped once we were close enough to the mines and tied the horses off the main track, with good tree coverage.

"We walk from here," Uri said, "avoid the main road in case they're using it for transport."

We all nodded.

"We need to be on our guard, keep the talking to a minimum and keep your eyes open. Uri and I will scout further ahead and signal if there are any issues." Killian ordered.

We set off on foot in the mine's direction. I didn't fail to notice Valor, Tarryn, and Hamish had conveniently positioned themselves in a protective triangle around me, whilst trying to look like that wasn't what they were doing. *Ugh, men.*

Once we got close enough, we stopped and waited for Killian and Uri to give the all-clear. They circled back and nodded.

"It looks like Valor was right. Come see for yourselves."

We all approached, keeping low, using the trees and bushes for cover.

"What makes you think they're using this place?" I asked, "How long has it been deserted for?"

"It was used for slave labour a long time ago. They shut it down when slavery was ruled illegal in Taros, hasn't been active since." Valor responded.

"At a first glance it looks abandoned, but if you look closer, there are fresh crates. They are storing things here or transporting things."

I nodded. "Okay, so we should split and go check around the site."

"Right, Valor and Elia, Hamish and Tarryn, Killian and myself. Meet back here. No more than an hour."

We all nodded before splitting up. Hamish and Tarryn were going to take the furthermost point, basically the opposite side of the mine to where we currently were. Killian and Uri went to explore the eastern side, leaving the western side to Valor and me. After we'd gone far enough, and seen nothing, we stopped near what looked like the main entrance and waited to see if there was any movement.

Time passed, and we'd still seen nothing. It was clearly being used, but that was not enough intel for us to realistically do anything with. We needed a closer look. I made to leave the safety of the trees, but Valor grabbed my arm.

"What in Adysium are you doing?"

"We need more information than this. It doesn't look like anyone is here, so we need a better look."

"Like Heknos. You are not going in there."

"You're right, *I'm* not. *We* are."

He groaned. "No, Elia, we are not."

I gave him a look. "Okay then, I stand corrected. *I* am going in. You can stay here." I pulled my arm away.

"You're being ridiculous."

"These people have attacked us *multiple* times! People have died, Valor. Innocent people, good people. Who knows what else they are doing? The reason you have such a huge issue with the rebels here is that none of you took it seriously, and now that you are, you have *no* information. This is our best shot at getting something usable." I was probably projecting my frustration at recent events onto this situation, but I really was sick of the rebel attacks, of Solis having the upper hand, of being useless. We had to do *something*.

He shook his head. "It's too dangerous."

"Too damned bad. You'll have to throw me over your shoulder if you want me to stay here, and I really wouldn't recommend that." I looked at him before making my way out of the forest.

I heard him mutter something along the lines of *'Taros help me with this woman'* before he carefully followed me.

I quickly made my way to the entrance, listening for a few seconds before ducking inside and keeping to the wall. Valor joined me a few seconds later. I felt along the wall as I moved further in. We were approaching what looked like a T-section. I stopped when I heard footsteps. I pressed against the wall, keeping to the shadows. Valor gripped my arm, readying to pull me behind him. *Idiot.*

I could see the light getting closer. Two men in Rise uniforms walked into view. They hadn't glanced our way yet, but they had stopped. We could see them clearly, but the shadows and the darkness should keep us hidden.

"How much longer d'you think we'll be down here?" The one closest to us asked.

"Hard to say, since we don't even know what we're s'pposed to be looking for."

"Yeah, I'm gettin' sick of being kept in the dark. And I ain't just talking 'bout this damned mine. We are told nothin' and are stuck down here like a bunch of ragrots."

"I agree, but ya gotta think bigger picture. We signed up for a reason. We don't deserve to be treated as less than because some noble pricks with Giftings think they're superior."

His friend sighed and nodded. "It just feels like we ain't doing nothin'. We ain't doing any serious damage."

"I know, but you 'eard what the Cap said. We need to be smart. Revolutions take time. We strike when the time is right. If we play our cards right, the rulers of all six kingdoms will be here in Taros. We can take out multiple, if not all of 'em, at once. Hit 'em where it hurts." He grinned and the other man joined him before they continued on.

How in the inferno did they know the other kingdoms were visiting? Hadrian said no one was told. Eventually, people would know when they all arrived, but they shouldn't have known before then. Butcher must have clued Solis in. I looked at Valor, signalling for us to retreat. We'd gotten information and knew they had soldiers stationed here. He nodded and turned to leave. Suddenly, the ground shook and a barrier of rock shot up in front of him. My eyes widened as I pulled him back so it didn't crush him.

"Well, well. What do we have 'ere?" A voice said from behind us.

I turned to see the two guards grinning at us.

"We were just leaving." I smiled.

They looked at each other in surprise for a second before shaking their heads.

"I don't think so," the one on the left said.

"See, honey? I told you this was a bad idea." Valor put his arm around me and shook his head at the guards. "Women, am I right? I *told* her it wasn't a good idea to come down here, that we'd probably get into trouble. But she just *had* to see the cave, thought it might be an exciting place to... you know?" He rolled his eyes.

The one on the right chuckled a bit. "Typical." The one on the left elbowed him in the ribs.

"Idiot, look at their clothes. They ain't just a couple of dumb kids looking for somewhere to get busy."

"Good job," I said to Valor, "way to make me sound like a common whore, and a dumb one at that."

He shrugged. "It was worth a try."

He made eye contact and, with the slightest incline of his head, gestured to my throwing knives. I nodded slightly, looking back at the guards.

"Look, I don't suppose there's any way we can convince you to let us go? We really are not worth the trouble."

The one on the left smirked. "No chance, sweetheart, but if you're looking for somewhere to do the deed, I'd be happy to show ya a place."

Gag. Well, I'd tried to be polite. I quickly grabbed two of my knives, tossing both of them at the guards before drawing one of the short swords. Valor ran towards the men, in case I missed. *Insulting.*

I didn't miss. I hit the one on the left, right in between the legs. He wouldn't be doing the deed with anyone anytime soon. I hit the one on the right in just the right spot to pin him to the wall by the collar of his shirt. Valor, like me, clearly decided the guard on the left hadn't suffered enough, as he socked him in the jaw, knocking him out cold.

Punching him was quicker than using his Gifting, but I think Valor had wanted to use his fists for this one, regardless. Which, in all honesty, was a mercy, based on the sounds he'd been making after my knife had hit its mark. The one on the right saw an opening while Valor was going for his friend, but I beat him to it. My sword was at his throat before he could reach for his. He groaned and held his hands up in surrender.

I glanced at Valor. "Feel better?"

"A little," he said and began frisking the guard.

"What are you looking for?"

"They must have some sort of key or something that they used to trigger the wall. We need it to get out."

I looked at the still conscious guard. "Now would be a good time to cooperate."

"Oh, it wasn't a key," he said, smiling.

Before I could ask what he was grinning about, when I had a literal sword to his throat, a rock detached itself from the cave wall and flew straight into Valor's head, knocking him out just as quickly as he'd knocked the other guard out. My eyes widened, and I moved to slit the guard's throat, but I'd lost my advantage when I'd glanced at Valor.

Another rock slammed into my wrist, forcing me to drop my weapon and step back. I reached for it, but suddenly, I couldn't move. Dirt had wrapped around my feet and was holding me in place.

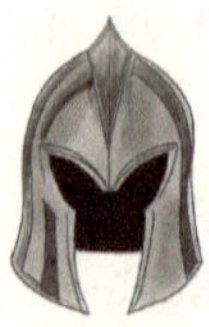

CHAPTER SIXTY-THREE

OH, HEK.

I glanced at the guard. Not just a guard. He was a Turf. An Elementi earth manipulator. *Were the Elementi working with the rebels, or was this just a coincidence right as they arrived in Taros?* I shouldn't be thinking about this now.

"Stay here," he said, chuckling at his own joke. He left, and I quickly tried to pull myself free. *Shit.*

"Valor!" I called to him. He'd been hit pretty hard. "Dammit. *VALOR WAKE UP!*"

He didn't move. I couldn't tell from here if he was breathing or not. I prayed he was. That was how the wall had come out of nowhere. We'd stupidly assumed because of how they'd talked about the Pures, that they were Impure themselves. I leant as far forward as I could, grabbing my dropped sword and sheathing it back with the other. Grabbing my dagger, I tried to chip away at the dirt. But whatever I cut away was just replaced by more dirt. I put my dagger away and looked around for anything I could use. There was nothing. I heard a set of footsteps approach, and the same guard returned.

"Cap wants to see ya for himself. Should be here in a few minutes. Don't mind waiting, do ya?" He smirked.

"Not at all." I replied, still searching for something I could use.

'Listen for what you do not hear, Adira.' This time it was The Crone's words in my head, as if she had spoken directly to me. *Was she telling me to do what I'd done in the forest?*

I calmed my breathing and tried to open myself up to whatever sense I'd picked up on before. When I imagined it as a thread last time, it had been easier. I looked at the guard and pictured a thread leading from him to me. To my shock, a dull red thread actually appeared between us. I glanced at his face to see if he'd noticed, but he looked none the wiser.

"This was a good shirt." He complained, inspecting the hole my throwing knife had created when it pinned him to the wall.

"Let me go and I'll buy you a new one?" I offered, and he scoffed.

Okay, Adira, what did you do last time? I'd imagined pulling on the thread? I did just that and it came much easier this time since I had a visual to focus on. I mentally pulled and suddenly was flooded with emotions. *Mild irritation. Excitement. Pride.* I pulled harder and it was almost as if I was getting a closer look at each emotion.

I felt like I could just about reach out and touch it. Which is exactly what I did. I reached out mentally and touched the first emotion I'd felt. *Irritation.* As soon as I touched it, the thread vibrated, pulsing toward the guard. He tensed, the thread becoming a brighter red as the pulse hit him. He looked at me and he looked... angry. Before he'd mostly looked bored. I was suddenly flooded with anger, too. The dirt around my ankles tightened.

"Maybe I shouldn't wait for the Cap. I should just deal with ya myself," he said, walking over. The dirt began crawling up my legs, compressing as it did. *Shit.*

"Um, no. I think you should wait for your captain."

He struck me across the face, hard enough that my head snapped to the side. I spat out blood. Had I somehow *increased* his anger? Did that mean I could decrease it? If I could make myself feel his emotions, then... could I make him feel mine?

I took a breath and focused on the thread again. This time, I thought of a happy memory. One that gave me joy. A memory of playing with my mother when I was a little girl. I clung to that memory and the emotion that it brought. This time, instead of pulling from him, I imagined pulling from me.

I pulled as hard as I could on the thread, and it morphed from red to purple. Once again, the string vibrated, a small rhythmic pulse travelling down the thread from my chest to his.

I watched the guard, and suddenly, the anger left his features entirely. He smiled at me. A bright, cheerful smile. I swallowed. *What in Akros' name was going on?* He whistled a cheery tune as he looked around the room. There had to be a way I could use this to my advantage.

I quickly thought back to the books on the mortal mind that I'd been forced to study as a part of my training when learning to read people and how to manipulate them. They trained me on how to enthral people with my looks, my behaviour. How to manipulate them. Which, at its core, was simply using certain techniques to make them feel a certain way, right? Evoking certain emotions or a combination of emotions, could manipulate someone into doing or feeling what you wanted.

I focused on the guard. Slowly, I pulled out the only emotion I could think of that I might manipulate. I didn't have time to deliver a cocktail of feelings, hoping it would work. So I concentrated, focusing on a specific feeling, and drawing from countless memories, I pulled an emotion I knew helped women manipulate men all the time; lust.

I saw the moment it hit him, the thread now pulsating a deep pink. His eyes darkened. The dirt retracted, stopping back at my ankles. Presumably, so he could appraise my body properly.

"Hey, my friend is waking up," I said, which should have made him to look over and either restrain him or knock him out again, but his focus was on me.

He walked over, and I tried not to flinch. I gave what I hoped was a charming smile. He looked at my lips before his hands reached out, roaming freely down my body. I clenched my eyes shut for a second as I pushed again.

He groaned slightly. "Syrena, you are something." He muttered and leaned in to kiss my neck. *Gross.*

"Mmm... if you let me loose, then I could definitely show you something," I said, dropping my voice into a huskier tone. I pressed into him a little, despite being absolutely disgusted.

He squeezed my breasts. "I think you can show me plenty from right here."

His hand slid down my side, moving to the waistband of my pants. This was not working. I heard footsteps. Multiple sets, coming this way. *Shit.* I was running out of time. *Okay, new tactic.* I pulled back the lust back and sent through a different emotion I was familiar with; fear. His hold on me loosened, and he stumbled back, staring up at me in fright.

I swallowed, drawing on all the times I'd felt afraid and useless in my life, too many times to count, pulling all of that out of me and into him.

He practically whimpered, tripping over his feet and dragging himself backward.

"You're going to let me go. NOW. Or it will be the last thing you do."

He was shaking now, his eyes wide. The dirt immediately dispersed from my feet. I could move.

I stepped towards him, and he flinched back. "P-please..." He held up a hand as if that would protect him.

I hurried over to Valor, praying he was still breathing, and began dragging him. The footsteps were getting closer. He was too heavy to drag fast enough.

"Lower the wall or... else." I said, frowning slightly at my lack of a proper threat, but my words didn't matter. He was terrified. He lowered his shaking hand, and the wall of rock blocking our exit sank back into the ground. Taking a deep breath, I focused on the other foreign feeling I'd recognised inside me since my Testing. It felt like a well that hadn't existed before. It wasn't empty.

I pulled on whatever had been building since I'd woken on that cot, and it responded. Golden light poured from my hands, pooling on the ground beneath Valor like liquid, before solidifying and becoming the same, nearly translucent substance that had pinned Josette to the wall.

"What is going on here?" A male voice said, and he sounded pissed.

I cursed, praying to Ehsys, Dhedros, Ades, and anyone that might be listening for this to work. I raised my hand, and thank the divinities, it did. The gold... force... acted as a stretcher, responding to my will as it lifted Valor from the ground.

I wasted no more time, hoping it held as I took off, pushing the magical carrier in front of me.

"What the Hek?!" The male voice cursed. "Soldier, what are you doing?! Get off the ground you fool."

I didn't look back; I ran out of there as fast as I could, but I couldn't shake the feeling that there was still something down there that I needed to see. Valor was still out cold as we reached the cave entrance. Once I'd put enough distance between us, reaching the cover of the trees, I gently pushed the stretcher down, and it lowered to the ground before dissipating like mist.

How long had we been down there? I put my thumb and my pointer finger in my mouth and whistled, praying one of the others was close enough to hear it.

A whistle sounded back, and relief filled me. I whistled again so they could pinpoint where I was. A few seconds later, Tarryn and Hamish appeared. Their eyes widened when they saw the state Valor was in, and they hurried over.

"What happened?" Tarryn said.

"No time for that. There are guards, or soldiers, or whatever in there. We need to go," I said.

Tarryn and Hamish hoisted Valor up in between them, and we hurried to the meeting point. Uri and Killian were waiting.

"Shit, is he alive?" Uri said.

I glanced over, relieved to see he was breathing. I nodded. "But we need to go. We were spotted."

No one asked any more questions. We all just hurried back to the horses. Valor was practically slung onto Killian's horse, so Killian could make sure he didn't fall off. Uri took the reins of Valor's horse. We all mounted and raced the Hek out of there. Once we were far enough away, Uri and Hamish backtracked to be sure they didn't follow us. We all waited in silence for them to return. Once they did and had deemed the coast clear, we all collectively relaxed.

"What happened, Elia?" Killian asked, and everyone glanced at me.

"It's my fault. We'd found nothing useful, so I suggested we look in the cave. We can't just keep playing defensive. Valor disagreed, but I went in any way, so he followed. We came across two guards. It didn't look like they'd seen us, and we got some valuable intel, but they spotted us and attacked. We had it under control, had knocked one out and disarmed the other, but that one turned out to be a Turf. We weren't expecting it. A rock knocked Valor out. I was closest to the guard, so I was able to knock him out, but before I did, he called out, sounding the alarm. They came looking to see what was happening, and I dragged Valor out. I don't know how much they saw, but the two guards that attacked us had no idea who we were."

"Val is going to be so pissed when he wakes up," Killian said, and I groaned.

"Yeah, I know."

"Not to mention you comprised the mission, Elia," Uri said sternly. "If they think we have made them, they will move their operation, and we will have lost our opportunity to strike."

I bit my lip. He was right; I had screwed up big time. I looked down.

"You're right. I'm sorry. I wasn't thinking straight."

"However," Tarryn said, "We could use this. If they move, we can now track them. We don't know how many are down there, but it can't be their entire operation or Elia and Valor wouldn't have been able to escape having only faced two guards. I can go back and monitor for any movement, and track wherever they move if they do."

I was grateful for the loyalty Tarryn continuously showed, even when I did not deserve it. This was one of those times.

"We wait for Valor to wake up, then we report that we all decided it was worth the risk if they could get more intel. Luckily, they got away, but the rebels may now be on alert or may move their base of operations," Killian said.

"You guys, it's alright. I messed up. We can tell them it was my idea. I will face the consequences."

"We don't need to give anyone reason to regret sending you on the mission Elia, it doesn't benefit anyone in this situation. The fact is, it happened. Now, we just have to make the best of it," Killian said.

I looked at Uri, who still looked disappointed, but he nodded. "Someone better wake the prince up, then. I'll keep a lookout." He disappeared into the trees, and I felt like a child who'd let someone down.

"I'll go with Hamish to monitor the mine and make sure they don't change locations. Send more guards to change shifts once you've updated Hadrian and Tira," Tarryn said before he and Hamish mounted their horses again and made their way back to the mine. I sighed and headed in the direction Uri had gone. He leant against a tree, monitoring the surrounding forest.

"I fought for you to come on this trip. Now I'm thinking that might have been a mistake." He looked at me as if he somehow knew I hadn't been entirely honest with my recap.

"I'm sorry, Uri. I didn't mean to disappoint you. I just thought it was our best chance at getting information. I overestimated myself. I'm sorry."

"Never overestimate yourself, or underestimate others, Adira. You could have gotten Valor, or yourself, killed."

"I know. It won't happen again."

"It better not," he said, before finally sighing and unfolding his arms. "I'm glad you're okay. Walk me through the intel you said you got before the attack."

Just like that, he was back to his usual self. The disappointment was gone. Men are so odd. But right now, I was grateful.

I smiled a bit and told him what we had overhead. "Do you think the Elementi could be involved?" I asked.

"No way to know for sure. It could have just been the one man who happened to be one. But if the royal family is involved, it would explain how the rebels knew all five of the other kingdoms would be in Taros."

"That is concerning."

He nodded. "We will see what Hadrian wants to do with the information. But I imagine he, and the rulers of Lios, will have a long discussion about this." He glanced at me. "You should have waited for us before making the call to enter the caves. You can't be running in alone or without backup. I know you took Valor, but you had us here. We could have helped."

I nodded, averting my gaze. He was right. I was too used to doing things on my own, or working in sync with The Four. If one of us branched out, the others would cover or join instinctively.

"But," he continued, "if you hadn't, we might not have this insight."

I bit my lip. That was as much praise as I would get for my actions today, and I was totally okay with that.

A groan sounded from the direction I'd left Valor and Killian. He must be waking up.

Uri nodded. "Go, check on your betrothed."

My eyes widened. "How did you know?"

"Are you kidding? That rock is the size of something I could have pulled out of that mine back there. Doesn't take a genius to figure it out."

I sighed. "I suppose not."

"Why you would choose to be betrothed to someone you clearly do not want to be betrothed to is something I haven't yet figured out, but I am sure I will."

I shook my head. It was easy to forget how observant Uri was. I didn't respond, and just headed back to Killian and Valor for the inevitable '*I told you so.*'

I stepped into the clearing, only to find Killian practically holding Valor down.

"She'll be back in a second, man. Calm down."

I pursed my lips, trying not to smile at the scene. Valor looked worried, and judging by Killian's words, he was worried about me.

"I'm here and I'm fine, unlike some of us."

Valor's head jerked in my direction, and relief filled his features.

Killian stepped back. "See? She's fine, just like I said. Stay seated, you moron."

I chuckled and walked over to the two of them.

"He was a Turf?" Valor asked, still assessing me as if an injury would suddenly reveal itself.

I nodded. "How's your head?" I gently brushed my fingers along his forehead. He winced a little.

"Could be better. How did you get us out?"

"A lot of luck. The Turf wasn't expecting me to be so fast. As soon as he attacked you, I took him out, then dragged you out of the tunnel. I'm so sorry. It was my idea to go in there. I screwed up, and you got punished for it."

He shook his head. "Should I have thrown you over my shoulder, as you suggested? Probably. But we both went in there. I knew the risks. It's not only your fault." He kissed my hand, and I smiled a bit, despite the rising shock and panic as the reality of what I'd just done, the magic I had used, sank in.

"Gross." Killian muttered, and I laughed, linking my fingers through Valor's.

"When you're feeling up to it, we should get back and update our parents. The sooner the better, then someone can relieve Tarryn and Hamish."

Valor nodded. "I'm good to go now." He sat up.

"Easy, you got hit really hard," I said, looking at the lump on his head. "That's going to be a nasty bruise."

"Might even make him better looking." Killian quipped, and Valor rolled his eyes.

"I'm good, don't worry." He slowly stood, and I gave him a look that said I didn't believe him for a second.

"Good, let's go then," Uri said, joining us in the clearing.

We all mounted and rode back to the castle, everyone accepting my lie about how I'd gotten us out without question, much to my never-ending guilt and confusion.

We met Hadrian and Tira in one of the briefing rooms and explained the *slightly* abridged version of what happened. It went over smoothly. They suspected nothing.

They sent other guards to relieve Hamish and Tarryn, as well as sending out more scouts to cover the area and watch for any movements.

"What are the chances that Lios is involved in this? Could it really be a coincidence?"

"I have known Rahmor for a long time. He is brash and unfiltered. He has always been very adamant about caring for his people first, but this would be a stretch," Hadrian said.

Tira nodded. "I agree. We shouldn't rule it out, but I believe the best approach is to simply ask him and Elsbeth, and see what we can learn."

"What about their children? Could they be going behind their parents' backs?"

"Adonis certainly could," Valor said, and Hadrian gave him a look.

"Are you sure your history isn't clouding your opinion, son?"

He frowned. "Of course not."

"What history?" I asked.

"There's no history. The guy is just an arrogant ass, so I wouldn't put it past him."

"He isn't the only child, though, right?"

"Not even close," Tira said, "given the structure of their kingdom, it's common for the ruling family to have many children, so they have an heir from each element. You've met Adonis. Alina is also here. Leaving Aimee, Ansel, Ambrose, and Avery back in Lios."

My eyes widened. "Uh, what is with the 'A' names? Also, that's a lot of kids."

Tira smiled a bit. "Apparently, Elsbeth has a thing for the letter A."

"Clearly," I said, "well, I'd like to be present when you ask them. I can explain what happened."

Hadrian looked at me. "You are quite invested in this situation, Elia."

"Aren't you? These people have caused enough chaos. People have died. You might not take it seriously, Your Majesty, but I do. So do the people of Kendelen who will be hit first. If we simply sit here and wait, next time it will be more than a few lives that are lost."

Valor's eyes widened slightly, and I caught Tira hiding a smile.

Hadrian arched an eyebrow at me. "I'll ignore the insulting part of that statement. I simply meant it is good to see you so invested."

I nodded slightly. "I meant no offence. This could have huge ramifications for all of us, especially the people in the lesser neighbourhoods that have no protection. I'd rather we stop the problem before it reaches them."

"As would I. You can sit in on the meeting if you like, but I would advise against such... honest... feedback in the presence of the Lios King and Queen."

I smiled a bit. "I can't make any promises, but I will certainly try."

He chuckled a little and shook his head, glancing at Valor. "This is whom you gave my mother's ring to? It's not too late to take it back," he said light-heartedly. I could hear the affection in his voice for both Valor and me. Shock filled me. He'd given me his grandmother's ring?

Valor smiled a bit. "Keeps things interesting."

"Mmm, I bet. I haven't congratulated the two of you." He continued, smiling. "We should have an engagement party."

"Oh, no," I said, "I'm not all that keen on making a spectacle of things."

"Nonsense," Hadrian said. "It is worth the celebration. Even if it is just with close friends and family. Perhaps a dinner?"

"Perhaps now isn't the best time to discuss this. We can talk about it after we have dealt with the current threat?" Valor suggested.

Hadrian nodded at the same time I said, "That would be good."

"Alright, now that we've sorted that out, I'd say now is as good a time as any to speak to the Jandars." Tira changed the subject, and I shot her a grateful smile.

"I will send for them to meet us, but I suggest a change of scenery. One of the private tea rooms?" Hadrian offered.

Tira nodded. "Will Odette be joining us?"

"No, unfortunately, she is a little under the weather," Hadrian said.

"Oh, nothing too serious, I hope?" Tira asked conversationally.

He smiled a bit. "She will be just fine. Shall we?" He stood and the rest of us followed suit.

She is probably recovering from the excessive amount of power she would have exerted in doing whatever the Hek she did to me. *Good.* Hopefully, that means I can avoid her for as long as possible.

Hadrian sent a servant to collect the Jandar family, and we all made our way to a tearoom reserved for royal use. It was private, but also much less formal than a meeting room. Servants brought in drinks and snacks, as we all got comfortable. Tira thought it might go over better if we limited the audience, so it was only Hadrian, Valor, Tira, and me.

CHAPTER SIXTY-FOUR

HADRIAN AND VALOR WERE sitting on a couch, Tira and I on the other. Leaving two more free in case the Jandars bought their children. It wasn't long before the servants opened the doors and our guests arrived. We all stood. Royal etiquette was so strange. Why must everyone stand when a royal walks into the room, rather than when they approach?

"Rahmor, Elsbeth." Hadrian greeted. Walking over, he shook King Rahmor's hand and kissed Queen Elsbeth's. "Thank you for coming."

"Your servant made it out to be quite urgent," Rahmor said. He was a stocky man. Clearly, he had relaxed on the training over the years, however, you could see he would have been attractive in his youth. He was a traditional man, known for his no nonsense attitude and somewhat outdated beliefs.

"I'm afraid it is," Tira said, approaching. "It's been a long time." She allowed Rahmor to kiss her hand before she briefly embraced Elsbeth.

Tira and Elsbeth could not be more opposite. Queen Elsbeth was a petite woman, with perfectly kempt mahogany coloured hair. She was the perfect picture of what I imagined a perfect noble wife to look like. I couldn't quite explain why. She was the depiction of soft and feminine, whereas Tira projected strength and power.

"Too long." Elsbeth responded with a smile on her face.

"What is so urgent?" Rahmor asked, getting straight to the point.

"Come, sit. We can discuss it over a drink." Hadrian walked back over to where we still stood. "You remember my son Valor?"

Valor bowed his head. "Your Majesty, Your Highness." He greeted.

Rahmor nodded, seeming more interested in the drink Hadrian was pouring.

Elsbeth smiled. "It's lovely to see you again, Valor."

He smiled. "Likewise. I'd like to introduce you to my fiance, Princess Elia Melfore."

I almost stumbled at the word 'fiance' as I stepped forward and curtsied. "It's nice to meet you both."

They seemed interested now. Rahmor looked me up and down.

"So, this is who all the fuss is about?" He said and Elsbeth nudged him.

"Likewise, Princess. Our son mentioned he ran into you on the road. It's good to see you are faring well after such a terrible ordeal."

I nodded. "Thank you. That is actually relevant to what we have to discuss with you today."

Rahmor took the drink Hadrian offered. "Well, out with it then." He sat down, as did the rest of us.

"Elia, would you fill the Jandars in on today's scouting mission?"

I could see Rahmor would have preferred practically anyone else to be explaining, but I ignored that and explained.

"This is all very well, but what exactly is the relevance to us, Hadrian?"

"The relevance is, an Elementi attacked my heir, as well as the Prince of Taros. Coincidentally, around the same time you arrived. We'd like to know what you make of that." Tira explained, clearly having had enough of his attitude.

He smiled a bit. Clearly, he enjoyed antagonising people. "What do I make of it?"

"What Tira means to say is, is it just a big coincidence? Is it possible someone in your travelling party is involved with the rebel movement?" I interjected.

"No, it is not possible. None of my people would be involved with that ramshackle rebellion." Rahmor answered.

"How can you be so sure?" I asked, and he turned to me, looking at me like one might look at the dirt on their shoe.

"My word should be enough," he said.

"Perhaps it is for those that know you, but I haven't had that luxury, so why don't you humour me?" I said, and I saw Hadrian practically grimace.

Valor pursed his lips, and I couldn't quite tell if he was trying not to laugh, or to cringe like his father.

"Oh, leave the girl be, Rahmor," Elsbeth said, touching his arm and facing me. "What he means is, our people are loyal. If any of them are involved, well, it is unlikely. However, we can see if anyone knows anything. You said it was a Turf who attacked you?"

I nodded. "Yes, it was, and that would be appreciated."

She nodded. Rahmor took a sip of his drink and looked back to Hadrian.

"What is being done about the rebels here in Taros? Or are you still trying to play the peaceful monarch?"

"Why would I not want peace in my kingdom?" Hadrian answered.

"You can have peace without being weak, Hadrian. If there are no consequences, then things like this are bound to happen."

"As far as I was aware, Lios has its own rebel problem?"

"Ones we are dealing with actively and efficiently. We do not wait for them to make the first move, and we do not sneak around. We use force to eliminate the threat."

"Without gathering information, how can you be so sure you are eliminating the right people?" I asked.

Rahmor sighed. "Girl, unless you have something valuable to add, I suggest you stick to drinking your tea and let the adults talk." *What a horse's ass.*

"I would advise you to be careful of how you speak to my betrothed in our own home, Rahmor. King or no," Valor said, stepping in.

Rahmor raised his eyebrows at Valor. "So, he speaks. For a minute there, I thought you enjoyed letting your woman speak for you."

I frowned, glancing at Elsbeth to see if this was regular behaviour. She had a slight frown on her face, but she did not look surprised, nor did she interrupt. Honestly, Rahmor was an enigma to me. His kingdom was one of the strongest, with both male and female warriors of the highest calibre. Yet the way he speaks of women doesn't suggest he values females at all. Was it all women or just those who he didn't see as warriors like his wife and myself?

"She is perfectly capable of speaking for herself."

He scoffed slightly. "I'm sure she is." He sipped his drink.

"Okay," Hadrian said, standing up, "I believe we have covered what we came here to discuss. If your people have any information that may help, that would be greatly appreciated. Rahmor, how about you and I enjoy a drink in my study? I have a fresh bottle my brewers have been working on, and I would love your opinion."

"Very well," he said standing, "lead the way."

Hadrian nodded and left the room, not bothering to facilitate a goodbye. Tira looked pissed, Valor looked annoyed, and I was about ready to throw the dagger strapped to my thigh at the king's pompous head. Rahmor didn't even say goodbye to his wife as he left.

I glanced back to find her watching me. "I apologise for my husband's behaviour."

"You are not the one that should apologise," I said.

She sighed. "He can be difficult at times, but the rebels are a sensitive topic for him. As much as he may like for you to believe otherwise. Whilst what he says is true, that we fight our own rebel problem with force, he neglected to mention they fight back with equal force. It is causing a big issue in Lios, and they appear to be a lot more violent than what you have experienced here."

"Why wouldn't he just say that?"

"Would you tell a room with the rulers of two other kingdoms present? As well as two heirs you do not know? My husband is many things. A prideful man is one of them."

I nodded. "I suppose not."

"I think the men had the right idea," Tira said. "Elsbeth, I want to hear about everything I've missed since I last saw you. Would you join me for a more casual tea, perhaps in the atrium?"

"That sounds nice." She stood, glancing back at me. "You might try speaking to my children. They may have a more unique insight. My daughter Alina is the general of our army, and Adonis knows practically every person in the kingdom, or he knows someone who knows someone." I found it hard to believe a man like Rahmor would allow his daughter to run his army, but there was still a lot I didn't know about the family.

I gave her a small smile. "Thank you."

She nodded before exiting with Tira, leaving me alone with Valor. I turned to him and he was giving me a look.

"What?! He started it," I said.

He shook his head, but I could see the smile in his eyes as he wrapped his arms around my waist and pulled me to him. I gripped his arms a little in surprise.

"You have a knack for pissing people off."

"Do not."

"You pissed me off when we first met."

"And yet, you asked me to marry you, so I can't be all that aggravating."

"Oh, you are. But you are also incredibly fascinating."

I rolled my eyes. "So I'm an experiment?"

He shrugged, placing a soft kiss on my lips. "I didn't say that."

I kissed back. "Mhmm, may as well have."

He grinned and kissed my forehead. "Can we skip Adonis and just go see Alina?"

"Why don't you like Adonis? Unless, of course, he's like his father, in which case, I completely understand."

He sighed. "Does it matter?"

"I'm thinking it does."

"We've known each other since we were young. Being the same age, we were always pretty competitive. When one of us would visit the other, we used to train together. Long story short, we had a bet. Whoever won our next training competition, got to take Lorielle Parkwell to the upcoming noble ball." So Adonis is twenty-nine.

I raised my eyebrows. "And what, you lost?"

"No, I won."

"Then what's the problem?"

"I took Lori to the ball, but he is the one that took her home."

I looked at him incredulously. "You hate him because he stole a girl?"

He groaned. "When you say it like that, it sounds ridiculous."

"It *is* ridiculous."

"It wasn't just that! He always had to make everything a competition. He is so arrogant. I don't hate him. I just don't love the guy. He also just gives off a bad feeling. I can't explain it, but he just... I don't trust him." He looked at me. "You think it's because of the girl, don't you?"

I pursed my lips. "No..."

He rolled his eyes. "You're a terrible liar."

If only, I thought. The familiar feeling of guilt crept in. "Regardless of your feelings towards him, we do still need to talk to him. We can do it now, or after Alina."

He sighed. "Let's see Alina first, then maybe we won't need to speak to him."

"Alright, do you know where we might find her?"

"I'd say she'd be in the guards' quarters or the Lios soldiers' barracks."

I raised my eyebrows. "Really?"

"She takes her role pretty seriously."

"Alright, well, let's go then."

He nodded, and we made our way to the guards' quarters. Sure enough, Alina was running drills in the training yard.

Valor waved her over. She approached. "Hey, Vally boy, you look good," she said, grinning.

He chuckled. "As do you, I hope we aren't interrupting anything important."

"Just normal training drills. I don't like for my soldiers to get too comfortable when we are away from home."

He nodded. "Have you met Princess Elia?"

"I haven't, but I've heard a lot about her." She smiled and held out her hand to me. "Nice to meet you. You can call me Ali."

I raised my eyebrows and shook her hand. "All good things, I hope."

"Oh, absolutely not." She smirked, "Which is why I think you and I will get along just fine."

I heard Valor groan beside me. "I should have thought this through." He muttered.

I smiled. "If you have a minute, we were hoping you might help with something?"

"How about you fill me in whilst we spar?"

"Alina, we aren't kids anymore. I will not spar with you."

"I wasn't talking to you, Vally boy," she said, looking at me.

My eyes widened slightly. "You want to spar with me?"

"Like I said, I've heard things. So have my soldiers. I'd like to see for myself how much is true. Spar with me, and I'll answer your questions."

"Elle, you don't have to—"

"Sure, why not?" I said, and Valor's eyes widened slightly, whilst Alina lit up with excitement.

"Brilliant." She walked over to a spare training ring that had been marked out with pegs. She took off her coat.

Luckily, I was still in the same clothing I'd worn on the scouting mission. I took off my cloak and handed it to Valor.

"Elia, I'm not so sure this is a good idea…" Valor tried.

"Why not? It's just a little sparring. I spar with Uri and Tarryn all the time."

"Alina is different."

"Why?"

"She won't hold back."

"Are we doing this or what?!" Alina called.

I sighed. "You will pay for that comment later," I said, walking over to join Alina.

"Ready when you are," I said, repositioning my feet.

She smirked. "Excellent."

Before she'd even finished getting the word out, a gust of wind knocked me on my ass.

My eyes widened, and I looked up to see a ball of air floating above her outstretched hand. She was a Breather. *Okay then.*

I got up, dusting myself off a little. Noting that the guards and soldiers who had been training stopped to watch.

I smiled a bit, planting my feet. "Is that all you got?" I taunted.

She laughed a bit. "Not even a little."

She extended her hand towards me, flicking her wrist as she did, sending the ball of air flying straight for me. This time, however, I was prepared. I rolled to the side, wasting no time in standing, and launched myself at Alina. She blocked my strike and attempted to land her own blow.

We traded off like that for some time. I knew I had to keep her busy so she wouldn't attempt any more Breather attacks. I moved swiftly, but she countered as well as I did. She wasn't backing down, even though I was on the offensive. We both took a step back, breathing increased as we reassessed. If we continued this way, it would simply be an endurance contest and where was the fun in that?

"Not bad, Melfore. Not bad," she said as she circled me. There were a good few yards between us now, "but do you really think you can win? A Virbi is no match for an Elementi, especially not a Virbi Para."

I smiled. "Sure, if you rely only on your Gifting."

She raised an eyebrow. "Come on then. Let's see what else you've got."

She sent a gust of wind my way. I pulled from my training not only with The Four and Tarryn, but from the circus. I ran towards the wave of air. When she ducked as I'd expected, I increased my speed, launching into a cartwheel to avoid her air attack. Rotating my body slightly, so I landed with my back to Alina, I bent my knees and pushed forcefully off the ground.

I used that momentum to flip backwards over Alina's head, landing directly behind her after a perfect round-off tuck. Just like I'd done a thousand times as The Masked Flyer. Wasting no time, I struck her in the lower back twice, then once more in the spot between her shoulder and her neck. She grunted as I drove my knee into the weak spot at the back of her calf, just behind her own knee. The pressure caused her leg to give way as she fell to the ground on one knee. I reached over, wrapping my arm around her neck and squeezing a bit.

"Tap out," I said, as she struggled to break free.

I had a good grip. If she didn't tap out, she would pass out. Suddenly, it was like someone had sucked all the air out of my chest. I gasped, letting go of her to grab at my neck. I couldn't breathe in. Air was being forced from my throat.

I looked over to see Alina standing and rubbing her neck with one hand, whilst the other looked as if it were cupping something and twisting it. She was literally sucking the air out of my body with her Gifting. I gasped again. This time it was me falling to my knees.

"Alina! That's enough!" I distantly heard Valor call.

"She hasn't tapped out." Alina responded.

I probably would have if it didn't feel like the oxygen was being cut off from my brain and I'd forgotten how to speak.

"Because she can't speak. Stop, Alina!" Valor demanded, as if he'd read my mind. His voice sounded closer now.

I could hear the panic in his voice. No, I could feel it. He was panicking. I could feel his fear, his anger, and his worry. It was seeping into me, making me panic. I couldn't shut it off, couldn't get any words out. Couldn't tell the difference between Valor's emotions and my own.

"Tap out Elia?" Alina said, sounding surprised I hadn't already. Somewhere in the back of my mind, I noticed she'd eased up a little, but she was still sucking the air out of me and I was still being overwhelmed by emotions that weren't my own. "Tap out."

I could feel something building inside me, drawing from that new well of power, like a dam ready to explode. Fates, my Gifting couldn't come out now. Not in front of all these people. My fist clenched. I tried to tap out, but I couldn't. My body had gone into self-preservation mode.

Suddenly, a wave of heat blasted me. The air that had previously been cut off was suddenly breathable again. Choking slightly, I gasped, trying to inhale, trying to steady my breathing. Opening my eyes, there was now a wall of flames between Alina and me. She cursed. I closed my eyes and just focused on breathing. I felt arms around my waist, pulling me up.

"Elia, are you okay? Elle?" Valor asked.

"Just... catching... my breath." I rasped out, regretfully opening my eyes again, only to see Valor looking at me, concerned. Swallowing, I managed a soft, "I'm alright."

He breathed out, closing his own eyes for a second before opening them and looking at me. "Don't do that again. Why the Hek didn't you tap out?"

"Because she knows the importance of not backing down," a deep voice said.

I looked over to see Adonis standing by Alina. That had been the source of the fire. He'd cut off Alina's hold on me with a literal wall of flames.

I breathed out, confident I would not suffocate. I looked at Alina.

"Rematch?" I said jokingly, and she laughed, looking a little relieved.

Valor groaned. "No way on Adysium."

"You had me for a while there, Melfore." Alina nodded. "If you were anything other than a Virbi, you may have actually won," she said, and I chuckled.

"We're just going to breeze over the fact that Alina just about killed you?" Valor asked incredulously.

"Well, she wouldn't have if you had stopped it sooner." Adonis retorted.

Valor frowned at him. "I don't recall anyone asking for your input."

"If I hadn't given my input, we'd be having a very different conversation right now." He glanced at me, then back to Valor.

"Oh piss off, Adonis."

Alina looked at me and rolled her eyes, before turning to the still gathered crowd of soldiers that had watched me epically fail in that fight. "Alright, you lot, back to training. Unless any of you would like to see if you can do what the princess couldn't?" She gestured for anyone brave enough to approach.

They all went back to what they had been doing prior to our spectacle, and quickly, might I add. Meanwhile, Valor had let go of me, and was staring off with Adonis, who had also gotten a lot closer.

"What's the matter, Val? Afraid there will be a repeat?"

I saw Valor clench his fist. *Men were so stupid.* "Luckily, my choice of women has improved since we were young. I wouldn't associate with anyone stupid enough to enjoy your company."

"Oh?" Adonis taunted, with a challenging smile on his face.

CHAPTER SIXTY-FIVE

I CLEARED MY THROAT, stepping in between the two of them. They were close enough that either could easily throw a punch and that's the last thing we needed.

"Alright, you two can fight later. We actually came because we needed to ask Alina some questions, which she promised to answer if I sparred with her." I looked at her, and she nodded. "Since you're here, Adonis, you may also help shed some light on the situation. Alina, perhaps we could take this conversation to wherever you've set yourself up?"

"Sure, follow me." She started walking, but Valor and Adonis didn't move. They were both still looking at each other. I suppose, compared to their towering forms, my height made it easy for them to ignore the fact that I was between them. I sighed, placing a hand on both of their chests and shoved. They barely moved, but Adonis glanced down at me in slight amusement, a knowing look in his eyes that had me tensing slightly with a feeling I couldn't pinpoint.

I shook my head. "Fine. You two enjoy your little pissing contest. Don't bother joining us unless you've sorted through your issues." I walked away, ignoring their protests, and joined Alina, leaving them to themselves.

"Men are ridiculous," I said, falling into step beside her.

"Why do you think I prefer women?" She responded.

I raised my eyebrows. "I wasn't aware that you did."

"Well, that explains a lot."

"What do you mean?" I asked, confused.

"Not all kingdoms support non-traditional unions," she said. "Taros has never been a supporter."

My eyes widened. "I don't think Hadrian would have any issue with it."

She shook her head. "No, but his father did, and the Deos Credentes have enormous influence here. The members of faith are slow to change at times. This is one of those times, despite Hadrian's efforts."

I bit my lip. "Well, I am not a Credentes, and even if I were, I would not have a problem with it."

She chuckled, looking at me. "You fought well out there."

"You still won." I commented, not completely able to hide the disappointment in my voice.

"Because I used magic. From what I hear, you've only known you had a Gifting for less than a month?" I nodded. "I have been training my entire life as an Elementi. Not to brag, but I am not the general of my father's armies just because I am his daughter. That you held your own, even in hand to hand combat, was impressive. I also understand why you didn't tap out. It is the same reason I didn't stop before you did. Valor doesn't get it. Most men do not understand that we have a lot more to prove as a woman in this world. They don't even realise the prejudices they have." She nodded at me in what looked like respect, and I smiled.

"I appreciate that. Next time I plan on beating you, though."

She grinned back. "I look forward to it."

We reached her makeshift study and sat down. "It doesn't look like the boys are coming, so what did you want to know?"

I told her the same thing we had told her parents. She was frowning by the end. "That is awfully convenient timing. What my father said is true though, loyalty is a huge part of not only our kingdom's values, but our army's. That doesn't mean one of them might not have chosen a different path and gotten involved with someone they shouldn't have. Can you give me a description? I'll talk to my men and see if anyone recognises him. As well as if any of them have heard anything."

"How likely are they to actually tell you, though? If they are involved with the rebels?" I asked.

"Do you have a better idea?"

"If I could accompany you, I am fairly good at reading people. I might catch something if you miss it."

If I could figure out how to tap into whatever was going on with my Gifting, I had a feeling I could tell if someone was hiding something.

She shrugged. "Couldn't hurt. Would you like to start now?"

"If you're free, then we may as well. Best not to waste time."

She nodded and stood. We went to one of her lieutenants first.

"Lieutenant Umbrah." She greeted, as he saluted her. "At ease."

He nodded, relaxing his stance. "General, what can I do for you?" I found it interesting that they addressed her simply as General, not Princess.

"This is Princess Elia of Xeria."

Umbrah's eyes widened slightly, and he bowed. "Apologies, Your Highness, I didn't recognise you in..." His eyes swept over my clothes, and I chuckled.

"Don't worry about it. I am aware I do not look very 'princess-like' at the moment. It's nice to meet you."

"Lieutenant Umbrah is head of the Turf division of our army. If there is something to be reported, it would be to him." I nodded, and Umbrah raised his eyebrows.

"What exactly are you looking for, General?"

"Rebels amongst our troops, Lieutenant."

His eyes widened. "Rebels? There aren't any rebels in my ranks. Why would you think that?" He appeared genuinely surprised, perhaps even a little offended.

"We have it on good authority that a Turf was involved in a rebel attack here in Taros. That's all you need to know right now. Have you heard any rumours? Noticed any unrest?"

He shook his head. "The only talks I've heard to do with rebels is when the troops are complaining about them."

"Would you mind if we spoke to some of your troops?" I asked, and he shrugged.

"Sure, I don't think you'll get much of use, but go ahead."

Alina nodded, and we followed him to where most of his unit was. We took our time speaking to them all. Nothing odd came up. I got no sense that anyone was being deceptive or even nervous, beyond the normal amount of nerves you would expect from a soldier facing their general and a foreign princess. Eventually, we called it quits and headed back to the castle.

"I'm sorry we didn't gain any new information on the attacker. I'll keep looking," Alina said, and I shook my head.

"Don't be. Like you said, we'll keep digging. If there is a link, we will find it. What are you doing now?"

"Now?" She shrugged. "I will probably get something to eat and then, I don't know, maybe go have a drink with some of the troops. Good for morale and all that. Why?"

"How well do you know Cali?"

She smiled a bit. "Pretty well. Why do you ask?"

"Well, you seem to be one of the few women I can tolerate in this castle, Cali being another. I thought perhaps we could all do something? I wouldn't be opposed to a few drinks myself."

"Sounds like a great idea. Cali is an excellent gossip, and it has been far too long since I let her talk my ear off."

I laughed, and we made our way to Cali's room. I knocked, and she opened the door. When she took in the two of us, she squealed. I winced, and Alina blocked her ears.

"Divinities woman. I like my eardrums intact, thank you." Alina commented.

"I *knew* you two would hit it off!" She exclaimed, hugging us both. "Come in, come in!" She stepped aside.

With all the serious things that had been going on lately, I'd forgotten how hyperactive and energetic Cali could be. I stepped inside and so did Alina.

"So, what are we doing?" She asked excitedly. Alina and I looked at each other. Apparently, we'd both forgotten how astute Cali was.

"We were thinking, something involving liquor?" I offered, and Cali clapped.

"Count me in! Oh, I know just the place. James has just opened a new tavern. It has an upstairs private area where the Gifted can relax. I've been dying to go, but Killian hates those kinds of establishments, and Valor is boring."

"Sounds kind of elitist?" I commented, and Alina nodded.

"Oh, no, it's not like... segregated... anyone can go! It's just more marketed as a place where the Gifted can relax and be themselves, and use their magic without being gawked at." I noted she refrained from saying Impures and Pures.

"Sounds interesting." Alina said before she shrugged. "I'm down."

"Alright," I said, "as long as it's not a snobby place."

"It's not, I promise! If it is, we will just go somewhere else. I am so excited! We can get ready together."

I groaned, and Alina winked at me. "Okay, but you have to do my hair. You know I'm useless at it."

Cali's entire face lit up, and she practically threw Alina into a chair before rushing to grab a hairbrush. Alina and I both laughed. It looked like we were all in for a good night.

Cali fussed over all of us, herself included. She *insisted* on finding the perfect outfits, which took some time.

For herself, she went with a forest green dress. Unlike the usual gowns she wore, it was tight-fitting and figure-hugging. It had one strap that sat just off the shoulder, and her hair was up in a beautiful bun with loose curls framing her face. She was really rocking the nature look.

She gave Alina a beautiful sky blue outfit. The top of the bodice was corset-like, with no straps, and the bottom of her outfit was a matching pair of beautiful silk pants. Her hair had been curled with hot rocks and pushed back a little, giving it a naturally windswept look.

My outfit took the longest for her to find, and despite my protests, both Alina and Cali made it clear it was not optional. They insisted on a bright red dress, way too bright, if you ask me. When I voiced my concerns to Cali, she just waved her hand and said something about red symbolising strength. The bottom half of the dress hugged my body, with a slit running far too high to be considered at all appropriate for a princess to be wearing. So high, in fact, that I had to switch my dagger to my other thigh so it wouldn't be on display.

Where the dress reached my hips, it clung in a way that even I could admit was flattering, coupled with the way the top cinched in at my waist. The top was long-sleeved, and had a 'V-shaped' neckline, revealing much more cleavage than I was comfortable with, but again, I was overruled. Unlike the other two, they left my hair out.

"With a dress like that, you need a simple hairstyle that won't pull attention away from your killer curves." Cali had explained. I simply rolled my eyes at her before letting her have her way.

When we were finally done, and standing in front of her enormous mirror, I had to admit; we looked pretty damned good. Cali practically glowed in her provocative green dress, looking every bit the Incrementi princess that she was. Alina looked breathtaking, which was ironic, given what she had done to me earlier today. It was in contrast to the badass persona she gave off, and yet it still worked. She looked beautiful.

My reflection was the hardest one to come to grips with. Standing here in the brightest colour of the three, I looked... I looked powerful. That was the only word I could use to describe it. I looked powerful and confident, even though I felt anything but. Cali really was a miracle worker, which she had stated herself multiple times during the getting ready process.

"Alright, we are all ready? Let's go."

Alina leant forward and whispered to me as Cali exited first. "This isn't the type of drink I had planned, but I gotta say, she has a real gift." I laughed a little and nodded.

Cali led us down to the courtyard, where a carriage was waiting. I thought back to the last time I'd been in a carriage. Or, the last two times, I guess you could say. The first was when Valor and I had—well, we hadn't done much, but it still brought a slight flush to my cheeks thinking about it. That flush disappeared the second I thought about the return trip and the boy whose face I couldn't forget.

"Are you coming, Elle?" Cali called, popping her head out.

When she saw my face she must have realised, because her own expression paled.

"Oh, Hek I'm so sorry, Elia! I didn't even think. We don't have to take a carriage." She made to step out, and I quickly shook my head.

"No, no. It's fine. I'm fine." I smiled a bit, stepping in. "Just needed a second. I'm good."

"Are you sure?" She asked, concerned.

"Positive." I smiled. "Shove over."

She smiled a little, moving over for me. I hadn't seen James since the Josette incident and our shared dance, where something had felt off with him. I wondered if he would be there tonight.

There was a queue when we arrived. I made for the end of the line, but Cali grabbed my hand.

"Where are you going?"

"To line up?" I responded, confused.

She put a hand to her heart. "Honestly, you're so cute sometimes, Elle."

She started walking to the front, pulling me with her. I caught Alina smirking at me.

"What's so funny?"

"Cute isn't a word I'd use to describe you." I made a vulgar gesture at her, which just caused her to laugh.

We reached the front of the line. Many stared and whispered as we passed. The guard at the door didn't say a word. He simply bowed his head slightly and stepped aside. Cali grinned thankfully at him and we all walked in.

The establishment looked like any high end tavern upon first glance. High end being the key word. There were lavish booths, plenty of tables, and a bar that no doubt served only fine quality drinks. Cali grinned, looking around.

"Let's go straight upstairs?" She suggested. Alina and I both shrugged.

We moved towards a nondescript door at the back of the Tavern. Cali knocked, and a guard opened it, crossing his arms. "Do you have the pass phrase?"

I raised my eyebrows. "There's a pass phrase?"

Cali giggled. "Yes, isn't it cool?"

The guard cleared his throat impatiently. Either he didn't know who Cali was, or he just didn't care. It had to be the latter. Everyone knew who Cali was.

"Sorry! The pass phrase is…" She leaned in, dropping her voice to a whisper, and I chuckled softly. She would not be good in covert operations. Judging by the smirk on Alina's face, she was having the same thought as me. "Jameson is the best-looking lord in Taros."

I coughed slightly, looking at her. "That is *not* the pass phrase?"

The guard smirked and stepped aside. "Enjoy your evening, ladies."

Cali grinned and headed upstairs. Alina and I exchanged looks before shaking our heads and following her. Typical of James to have something so conceited as an entry requirement.

My thoughts were interrupted when we got to the top of the stairs and took in the room. It was a massive open area. There appeared to be not only private booths, but private rooms all along one side of the wall. Raised platforms housed dancers and performers. Patrons filled the dancefloor, but what had me staring was the open use of magic. If the floating drinks were any indication, the bartender was a Teleki. I could see what must have been a Piro soldier from Lios, impressing a few women with flames dancing along his fingers, creating shapes.

The music that I'd expected to be drowned out, coming from the corner where a live orchestra played, was audible from the opposite side of the room. It shouldn't have been loud enough, especially with all the additional noise, but it was. That's when I noticed someone standing next to the band, focusing on multiple horns placed in each corner of the room, used to amplify sounds to a small degree. Her fingers moved similarly to how Alina's had during our sparring match today. I glanced at Alina, and she nodded.

"She's a Breather. She's using her powers to amplify the sound."

Damn. "I have never seen so many Pures using their abilities in a noncombat situation before."

She gave me an odd look. "What exactly did you do when you still thought you were a lord's daughter staying in town?"

I shrugged. "I never really fit in with the nobles. I didn't go to things like this. Plus, I know the kingdoms don't all get along, so I didn't expect foreign visitors to stay here."

"You're not wrong. I think there are definitely more here because of the upcoming visit. A fair few of the Pures and Paras here tonight travelled with us. The others are Kineti. But there are still Pures from other kingdoms that live here. Just mostly high class nobility." I nodded. That made sense.

"Let's get some drinks!" Cali half-shouted as the music seemed to grow louder.

We both half-shouted back in agreement and made our way to the bar. They served us quickly. We should have more Teleki bartenders, they were very efficient. It was odd seeing a Pure doing such a menial job, but honestly, it made so much more sense.

Thinking about it, they wasted the Giftings on most of the Pures that weren't soldiers. They were just nobles, not using them for anything worthwhile. No wonder the rebels were so committed to their cause. We downed some kind of burning amber liquid in short glasses, which tasted terrible, before we grabbed regular drinks I recognised.

The night went by pretty quickly after that. I lost count of how many drinks we'd had, which was not good. We danced, we laughed, we drank. Cali seemed to know everyone in the damned room, or be determined to meet them, so we were constantly being introduced to new people. I kept getting handed drinks, which I graciously accepted, as did Alina.

We were all on the dance floor now. People naturally surrounded Cali. Alina was dancing with a very attractive woman. I couldn't tell if she was Pure or not. I felt hands on my waist before they spun me around. My head spun a little too, thanks to my now empty glass. I reached over, placing it on a nearby table before looking to see who had rudely accosted me.

Adonis was standing there with an amused look on his face. "Having a good time I see, Princess."

I rolled my eyes. "Gross. When did you get here?"

His laugh was deep. "Is that really how you greet someone who saved your life?"

"Pfft. You did not. I was fine."

"Sure, if you don't mind asphyxiation being written on your headstone."

"Nuh-uh." *Wow, my responses were really eloquent right now.* "Valor would have saved me if I was in real danger."

He rolled his eyes. "Really? Because when I got there, he was just standing there, uselessly asking Alina to stop."

"Exactly. He knows I don't need anyone to fight my battles for me. He was respecting me."

He scoffed and sipped his drink before stepping closer. "You think you need a man that will respect your boundaries, and let you do your thing because you're an 'independent woman'?" He asked, looking down at me.

I frowned up at him, crossing my arms and meeting his stare. "Yes."

He took another sip of his drink. "Even if it means letting you die?"

"I wasn't going to die."

"No, because I stepped in. I think you're wrong about what you need."

"Oh, I'm wrong? About my own needs?"

"Yep. If that's what you needed, you wouldn't be with Valor. From what I have heard, he chooses when you're allowed to fight your own battles, and that is not regularly." I tensed at what he was insinuating, partly because it was offensive, and partly because there was some truth to it.

"You don't know what you're talking about." I argued, and he shrugged.

"Maybe not. But you know what I think? I think you need someone who doesn't simply respect you when it suits him." He stepped closer again. His chest was practically touching my arms. "You need someone that will respect your right to choose and act, no matter the circumstance. Someone that will still step in when you inevitably put that perky little ass of yours in danger without undermining you."

I breathed in at our proximity. His eyes hadn't left mine. His tone was intense, yet his body language was relaxed.

"Valor respects me," I said, having no idea how else to respond, if I was honest. Who did this guy think he was? Acting as if he knew me.

He smiled a bit and leaned down, whispering in my ear, and eliciting an involuntary shiver from me, "Whatever you say, Princess." With that, he was gone.

He just walked away, making his way through the crowd. *What the Hek was that?* I shook my head. *Jackass.* I went to the bar to grab another drink.

CHAPTER SIXTY-SIX

"Now what's a girl like you doing in a place like this?" A familiar voice questioned from my left.

I turned. "James!" I shouted, before practically tackling him in a hug.

His eyes widened, and he took a step to steady us both, but he caught me. "Um hey, Elia? Had a few free drinks tonight, huh?"

I shrugged. "I lost count."

He chuckled. "Well, what's one more then?" He signalled to the bartender and someone immediately floated two drinks over.

"Man, that is *so* cool."

He raised his eyebrows. "What is?"

"Pures doing regular jobs!"

"It's not super common, but it happens. You don't have places like this back in Xeria?"

"How would I know?"

He frowned in confusion. "Uh, because it's where you're from?"

Shit. "I mean, I didn't go to places like this! Plus, the Virbi Specialties aren't exactly easily demonstrated, aside from lifting a tree or something. I wasn't a super high standing noble."

He seemed satisfied by my answer, and he chuckled. "Well, I'm glad you find my establishment entertaining."

I nodded, sipping my drink. "What are all those rooms for?" I asked, gesturing to the rooms I'd seen people coming and going from. Usually couples, sometimes entire groups of people.

He smirked. "I can take you and show you if you like?" He suggested, wiggling his eyebrows.

I smacked his arm. "Pervert. I'm engaged to your best friend."

He glanced at my hand and smiled a bit. "Yes, you are. Congratulations are in order, I suppose? It's not too late to change your mind, though." He winked, and I shook my head, smiling.

"You are shameless."

"I certainly am. Are your friends having a good time?"

I glanced over to find Alina now making out with the woman from the dancefloor, and Cali laying on a table letting some guy do a shot from her chest. My eyes widened.

"Oh, divinities..."

James laughed. "When she drinks and lets loose, Cali's alter ego comes out. A liquor loving, flirtatious little party animal."

"Shouldn't I stop her?"

"Not unless you want her to scold you."

I bit my lip. "I'm still going to check that she's fine."

He nodded, smiling a bit. "You're a good friend. Before you go, Elia, I wanted to apologise again for everything that happened with Josette."

I looked at him and saw the smile had left his eyes. He seemed genuinely sad, with guilt written all over his face, so why did I feel like he was being completely insincere?

I shook my head, chalking it up to the liquor, and hugged him. "You have nothing to apologise for, James. You didn't know."

"I should have, though. I should have seen it coming." He shook his head.

"No one saw it coming." Probably not even Josette, now that I knew they had manipulated her. A part of me almost felt bad for her.

"Still. I am really sorry, Elia."

"It's alright. Honestly, it is all fine," I said, letting go and looking at him, "please don't feel guilty, or I'll feel bad. And then that will ruin my night. You don't want to ruin my night, do you now, Jameson?" I raised my eyebrows at him.

He smiled a bit and shook his head. "Absolutely not."

"Exactly, so come help me make sure Cali hasn't completely lost her mind and isn't about to take her dress off or something." I didn't wait for his response, but I felt him follow me as I went over to Cali.

"Eliaaaa!" She called out when she saw me. Her words were even more slurred than mine.

I chuckled. "Hey, Cal, are you doing okay?"

She sat up from the table and grinned. "I am doing positively brilliant! Where is Alina!?"

"Right here," she said, coming to join us. I raised my eyebrows.

"You've got a little something—"

"You go girl!!" Cali shouted, cutting me off before I could point out the lip stain mark on Alina's neck.

She glanced down at herself though and when I pointed to her neck; she wiped it off, and I chuckled.

"Jamie! This place is greaaaat!" Cali said, hugging Jameson.

I raised my eyebrows. "Jamie?"

He groaned. "I think that is a sign for you to get this one home before she has everyone calling me that."

Cali giggled. "Probably."

I smiled and looked at Alina, who nodded. "I'm ready to go if you are?"

"One on either side, then?" I suggested, and she nodded, taking up a position on Cali's right while I took the left.

James put one of Cali's arms around each of us and helped us carve a path through the packed room, as we had to practically carry her out. Turns out, she'd been laying down for so long she'd forgotten how to walk. Together, we all got her into the waiting carriage. We said goodbye to James and promised to come back soon, congratulating him on his establishment.

We had to stop the carriage ride twice so Cali could get out and throw up. She would not feel good in the morning. Once we got back to the castle, I had to cover Cali's mouth with my hand to stop her from making so much noise. We got her into bed, placed a bucket beside her, and made sure she had plenty of water nearby. She fell asleep the second her head hit the pillow. I chuckled softly as I shut the door and looked at Alina.

"She's going to have a headache tomorrow," she said.

"I'm not convinced I won't have one myself."

She nodded. "Well, thanks for suggesting this. I had a great time."

"Oh, I saw." I smirked at the spot on her neck, which was missing the lip stain, but starting to bruise from what looked like a love bite. She laughed a bit.

"I had a great night too," I said.

It must have been the alcohol, because I stepped forward and hugged her. I *never* hugged strangers. Alina looked surprised, but she hugged back. It was at that moment, we both realised how awkward the interaction was.

"Nope. Too weird." I pulled back, shaking my head.

She nodded in agreement, stepping back. "Yep. I'll see you tomorrow," she said and left for her own rooms.

I chuckled a little to myself. Alina was no more the hugging type than I was. I made my way back to my rooms, well aware of the guards watching my every step. When I got there, Hamish and Wes were standing outside my door, on guard.

Hamish's eyes widened when he saw me. "Damn, Elia. You should dress like that more often."

I stuck my tongue out at him, and he laughed, opening the door for me.

"Hey," I said, looking at Wes, "you didn't pay up?"

Wes groaned and handed Hamish a mark, who was looking very proud of himself.

"What was it this time?"

"I bet you wouldn't notice we didn't have a bet tonight, and he said you would." Wes explained.

I laughed and shook my head. I entered my chambers, and went straight for my bed, falling onto it and passing out.

I woke the next morning to a pounding in my head and what felt like someone poking me in the arm.

I groaned. "What the Hek?" I mumbled.

"Rise and shine. It's time for training. We've missed too many sessions, and now that I know you've apparently picked up some weapons knowledge, I want to see it in action," Tarryn said matter-of-factly.

"Nooo. I am sleeping."

"I will flip this mattress, princess or not."

"You wouldn't."

"Try me," he said, crossing his arms.

I squinted up at him, attempting a glare, but I must have looked a mess and not at all menacing because he grinned.

"You have thirty minutes to get ready. I'll be outside." With that, he walked out, closing the door behind him.

I had half a mind to just go back to sleep, but if I knew Tarryn, he would follow through on his threat. Sighing, I got up and trudged my way to the bathroom. I needed a bath, or even better, some of Ehsys's mysterious liquor-sick remedy.

I ran myself a bath, quickly discarding the red dress and letting the hot water attempt to wash away the seedy feeling. It only partially worked. Getting out and dressed, still half asleep, I threw my hair up in a messy bun and yawned. I looked at the breakfast that had been left on my table and shook my head. Unless I wanted it to come right back up, that was not a good idea right now. There was a knock on my door.

"I hope you're decent and ready Elia, because I'm coming in," Tarryn said, before he entered. He looked impressed that I was actually up, clearly having expected me to still be in bed. I glared at him properly this time, and he smiled.

"Let's go."

I sighed and followed him to the training room. Unsurprisingly, Cali was not there. I doubted I'd be seeing her before noon. Uri was there, however. He smirked when he saw me.

"Oh, this is going to be fun." He commented, and I flipped him off.

"You know the drill. Get going, Elia," Tarryn said, and I sighed before beginning my laps.

I may or may not have been cursing both of them to Khollios. The training session was gruesome. I was sluggish, and I was almost sick more than a few times, but by the end, I was actually feeling better. I sat down, having a drink.

"I hope you don't make a habit of nights like that," Tarryn said.

"You could use one, I reckon, Amesley. Loosen you up a bit."

He rolled his eyes. "I loosen up plenty."

"Ha! Since when?" I teased, and he shook his head.

"I heard about your fight with Alina yesterday."

I groaned. "Yeah, yeah, I know. I lost."

He shook his head. "That's not what I was going to say. I heard about it from some of the Lios soldiers. They said they hadn't seen anything like it. They are lucky to last sixty seconds against Alina. You fought well, they said. And if it were a no Giftings fight, they'd back you to win. Which is high praise from an Elementi soldier. They are a warrior kingdom. Alina is especially ruthless and known for her battle skills. Good job."

I blinked. "Tarryn, are you unwell? Am I still drunk or did you just give me a compliment?"

He rolled his eyes, standing up. "And we're done for the morning. Go torment someone else." He joked.

I laughed a bit and stood. "I wouldn't have had a chance of beating her without you."

He smiled a bit. "You would have." I shrugged. "Now. Let's see just how well you wield a sword." He walked over to the weapons table I'd been trying, and failing, to not get distracted by since I'd spotted it.

I couldn't hold back my grin as he handed me a sword, before grabbing one of his own.

The rest of the week passed by rather quickly. Alina and I continued looking into the possible Elementi involvement with the rebels. Valor and Adonis still argued whenever they were in the same room, which was good for me because it kept Valor's attention off of me and talk of our wedding. Hadrian kept trying to organise an engagement party, and Odette was still under the weather.

Which is why my stomach sank when I received a summons to the cells, courtesy of the Taros queen herself. I considered my options as I made my way to the all too familiar cells. Safe to say I was not exactly in her good books, given that the last time we'd interacted, she had confirmed she was working with Butcher and forced me into an engagement.

But then, she'd also left me be since. She could have made me do anything she'd wanted during the hour Butcher had me bound to her. But she'd only ordered me to say yes to Valor, and to lie still while she tortured me. I'd been racking my brain trying to decide if she knew she had partially removed the blood oath. Surely she didn't know? Not if she was working with Butcher. I forced myself to stop the mental rambling as a guard, waiting at the entry to the cells, bowed and stepped aside.

"Your highness, her majesty is waiting for you." *Oh joy.*

Letting out a sigh, I made my way down the steps, greeted by the potent smell that seemed to seep from the walls themselves. I glanced around, seeing only guards, no Odette. I frowned a little as I walked down the hallway that seemed to go on forever, careful not to look into any of the cells for too long.

"Elia. We've been waiting." Odette's distinct voice called from a few cells down. I took a breath and approached, stopping before the bars and taking in the scene in front of me. Odette was standing in the cell. She looked paler than usual, but was no less intimidating. There was someone cowering on the ground, backed up into the corner. I squinted, trying to see past the darkness.

"There you are. Come inside, child."

"No, thank you. I am okay here." Heknos himself couldn't get me to enter that cell. My gut was screaming at me to run. The atmosphere was tense, feeling as if the entire dungeon was holding its breath. Odette simply grinned and turned back to the cowering figure.

"Kayleia was just about to finish telling me why she betrayed the family that has been nothing but kind to her and her husband for decades." My eyes widened slightly as I got a proper look at the woman. This couldn't be Kayleia Chambersen? This woman was too frail, too old, and too sickly looking. And yet, when I looked at her face, it was her eyes that shone back at me.

"... What happened to her?" I dared to ask.

Odette smiled, her teeth practically shining in contrast to the darkness that filled the cells.

"It pays to have a Morti on your ledger." Her eyes darted to someone behind me, and I spun around. A guard was leaning against the wall with his arms crossed, watching us stoically. He looked like a regular guard, but if what Odette said was true, he was a Healeti, and not just any Healeti at that. Morti were rare and generally thought poorly of. Imagine being born into a family of healers, only to discover you couldn't give life, only take it. I swallowed and turned back to Odette, taking a step to the side, so I could at least pick up any movements he made from the corner of my eye.

"A Morti did this?" I looked back at Kayleia.

"Yes. Much like the full capabilities of the Incrementi, people don't talk about the true extent of a Morti's abilities. It isn't all death. Morti can drain a person's life essence entirely, yes, but they can also choose how much to take. Adding years or taking them. They can do more than just destroy. They can decay slowly." Looking at Kayleia now, I could see that was exactly what had happened to her. She appeared years older, truly looking as if someone had drained some of the life out of her. I'd only ever heard that used as an expression, usually by men when complaining about their wives.

"My patience is wearing thin, Kayleia. Unless you would like Potrelli here to finish what he started, I suggest you give me something worth sparing you for." I mentally noted the Morti's name, or rather last name.

"I've—told you—everything... I didn't... I'm innocent." The frail woman stammered out, her eyes connecting with mine. I swallowed at what I saw there. The desperate, pleading look. She *had* betrayed her kingdom. I was positive, but that didn't mean she deserved this kind of torture.

"Odette," I figured we'd passed formalities, at least in private. "Is this not a little extreme? If not, I really don't need to be present for this."

"Oh, but I think you do, Adira." I tensed at the use of my real name, looking at Potrelli and Kayleia. Oddette just smirked.

"He won't talk," she said, nodding to Potrelli.

"How can you be so sure?"

Her grin somehow became even more wicked.

"Potrelli." It was clearly an order, but to do what?

He sighed, rolling his eyes slightly, before glancing at me and opening his mouth. My eyes widened slightly.

"You cut out his tongue?" I said in disbelief.

"Not me personally, no."

I closed my eyes. He'd been muted, a barbaric practice. One Butcher favoured. Guess it ran in the family.

"And what about Kayleia?"

"She won't be alive for much longer, so I wouldn't worry."

"Then I will be leaving. I want no part in this." I turned to leave, not missing Odette's brief nod to Potrelli. He promptly stepped forward and grabbed for my shoulder. He was quicker than I'd thought, but I'd expected him. Before he could clamp down, I spun to his left, unsheathing my dagger, shrugging off his grip, and pressing it to his neck in one fluid movement. Facing him now, I caught the look of surprise and excitement in his eyes. He certainly hadn't expected that.

"I'd advise against that." I stated simply, my voice low.

Odette chuckled. "Careful, Adira. What makes you think he needs to be touching you to use his magic?" I didn't let my unease at her comment show, nor did I lower my dagger.

She sighed. "This is a lesson you need to learn. You have two options. The first, I continue my torturing of poor Kayleia. It *will* be slow and painful. As you know, I like to take my time with these things."

I didn't take my eyes off of Potrelli when I responded.

"And option two?"

"You take that pretty dagger of yours and put her out of her misery."

"I'm not doing that."

"No? You'd rather her suffer?" My eyes flicked over to the servant woman before moving back to Potrelli. He was smiling. *Jackass.*

"I'd rather none of this. I am not responsible for her life."

"Well, you *were* the one that turned her in? I'd say that makes you very responsible."

"I was doing my job."

"So was she." I frowned.

"That's not the same thing. My job doesn't involve assassinating people."

"But it could. If they ordered you to kill someone, you would have no choice, would you? How is this different? You don't know what position she is in."

"We are *not* the same." I gritted out.

"Why not?"

"I have no choice! You damned well know that."

"What makes you think she had a choice?" She looked back at Kayleia.

I shook my head. I would not let her manipulate this situation.

"I will not kill her, Odette."

She shrugged.

"Very well. Potrelli, you may resume."

He stepped back from my blade and entered the cell as Odette stepped out. He bent down, placing a hand on Kayleia's forehead.

"No! Please no! I've told you everything! Please!" She begged, but it was no use. The Morti's hands glowed black as what looked like spider webbed, dark grey veins appeared on her skin, where Potrelli was touching her, and began to spread.

"I'm not watching this." I stepped back, but before I could take a second step, vines shot up through the cracks of the floor and wrapped themselves around my ankles. They only tightened when I tried to pull myself free.

"Let me go, Odette."

"You can tell yourself this isn't your fault all you like. You can justify it however you want. But this woman is here, partially because of you, and even if she wasn't. I am telling you, it is now your choice what happens to her."

"It's not my choice. I won't choose either of those options."

"Ah, but when you don't pick one, you are still making a choice—" A piercing scream cut her lecture off. I looked back into the cell. Kayleia was on the ground now. The dark veins spread faster. I could see her body wasting away in real time.

"Why are you doing this?" I stupidly asked, clenching my fist.

"You need to learn, Adira. It's not possible to save everyone. You cannot remain on the fence, on the sidelines. You need to make choices and deal with the consequences."

"This wasn't my choice!"

"But it is now. What will you do, Adira? Let Potrelli continue to torture the woman you turned in? Put her out of her misery with mercy? Or do nothing, in which case she suffers all the same."

I shook my head. "Enough."

She smiled. "Fine, but you're not leaving until she is dead. You choose how quickly that happens. Look at her."

Against my better judgement, I glanced over. Her skin had gone a pale grey, her eyes were now sunken in, and she appeared to have barely any strength left. She was boney and frail, covered in spider-webbed veins.

I swallowed. I'd told myself she deserved to be here, that she'd made her bed. But Odette was right. Who's saying she had any more of a choice than I did? It doesn't make what she'd done, of her own free will or not, any better, any less permanent. But who was I to decide what happened to her? I was hardly qualified.

I closed my eyes, trying to drown out the screams and groans, until they halted. I opened my eyes to find Kayleia practically nothing but a skeleton now, her breathing slow and ragged. Surely, she would take her last breath any second and be out of this misery.

Potrelli's eyes met mine, and he smirked as his hands glowed a dark green colour this time. It took me longer than it should have to realise what was happening. He was reversing it, giving Kayleia back her life essence. I could tell by the looks on both Odette and the Morti's face's, it would not stop there. They would keep doing it. Keep bringing her painfully to the brink of death, only to pull her back and repeat.

This time, when I tried to step forward, the vines did not stop me. I walked into the cell and over to Potrelli and Kayleia. She looked up at me, pain and defeat in her eyes. She gave me the slightest of nods. I glanced at Potrelli; he was smirking at me. Daring me. Doubting me.

I took a breath, and before I could second guess myself, drove my dagger into the side of her neck. The woman barely winced. A dagger is nothing compared to someone stealing your life essence, I supposed. Pulling the dagger out, I turned and left the cell, not stopping, not saying another word. I continued down the hall, more than ready to get out of this damned nightmare.

"It's time you got off the sidelines, Adira!" Odette called. "You can't play the victim forever." She chuckled, and I clenched my fist.

Wiping the bloody dagger on my skirt and sheathing it, I hurried back to my chambers.

CHAPTER SIXTY-SEVEN

I IMMEDIATELY RAN A bath and sank into it. I'd thrown my dress straight into the bin as soon as I'd gotten the damned thing off.

I ducked below the water, trying to calm myself. Resurfacing, I glanced at my hands. Speckles of red stained them. It wasn't like this was the first time I'd had blood on my hands, literally or metaphorically. I scrubbed them, and the rest of me, until I was red raw. Wrapping myself in a towel, I sat on the end of the bed.

A knock sounded on my door, I looked over at it but did not move.

"Elle?" Hamish's voice called.

I closed my eyes. "Come in." I managed, I wasn't sure I'd been loud enough, but I must have been because the door quietly opened. Hamish and Tarryn shuffled inside, closing it behind them.

"What's going on?" Tarryn asked first. I tried to respond but was instead crushed into a tight hug from Hamish.

"Just thought you could use one. You look like shit." He muttered into my hair. I laughed a little, smacking him on the shoulder before hugging back. He smiled and let me go.

"But what Amesley said. What *is* going on?"

I looked at them both, realising I had a choice now. I *could* tell them everything. The same way I had with Tira. So, I told them what had happened in the cells with Odette, Potrelli and Kayleia. Both men remained quiet as they listened. After I'd told them what had happened, I also filled them in on Odette having accidentally removed some part of the blood oath. That one had their eyes widening slightly. When I'd finished explaining, it was quiet for a minute.

"Well, strike me with lightning and call me Nava," Hamish exclaimed, referencing the Goddess of the Sky, "that is insane. A Morti?" He whistled. Tarryn shook his head.

"Have you told Valor anything?"

I shook my head.

"But now that I'm not bound..."

"You can't tell him Adira," Tarryn said.

I looked at him. "Why not?"

"He is Odette's son. We can't trust him. He could go straight to her."

"I can trust him."

He shook his head. "You're letting your feelings cloud your judgement, Adira. If there's even a chance that he could turn you in, you can't tell him. If your own safety isn't enough of a reason, then what about Sierra's? What happens to her if you're hanged?"

I looked at Hamish, hoping he might side with me on this, but he smiled sadly and shook his head.

"I'm with Tarryn on this, Adira. I'm sorry, but it's too big a risk right now."

I swallowed, closing my eyes. Maybe they were right. There was still so much I didn't know about Valor, but deep down I knew I trusted him, despite not wanting to. I was more worried about the pain the truth may cause him than the potential betrayal.

But the secrets weren't only mine anymore. Hamish and Tarryn would be exposed. Tarryn had just as much of a say regarding who gets to know about our heritage. After all, the last time people were aware of the Potenti, they erased them from history, so they probably had a point.

Sighing, I nodded. "Okay, I won't tell him yet, but at some point, I will have to."

Both of the men nodded.

"We know," Tarryn said. "No training for the rest of the week, take some time off."

I frowned. "What?"

"You've been through a Hek of a lot in the last few months, Adira. You deserve at least a few nights off."

I shook my head. "I appreciate what you're trying to do, but if I'm left alone with nothing but my thoughts..." I shook my head. "I need to keep busy."

"You *need* to process all of this Adira. You can't keep pushing it down."

"It's worked so far." I mumbled, and he gave me a look.

"You can keep training, but just make sure you take time for yourself." He stepped back, apparently deciding the conversation was over. I looked at Hamish, who was staring at Tarryn in surprise.

"Damn Amesley, you've got me agreeing with you twice in one day? You're finally learning." He slung his arm around Tarryn's shoulder. Tarryn arched an eyebrow, moving his hand to the hilt of his sword. Hamish groaned and removed his arm, holding both his hands up in surrender.

"You are such a killjoy." I couldn't help but chuckle.

I spent the next five days trying to take Tarryn and Hamish's advice. It was easier said than done, but Valor was a brilliant distraction. We spent a lot of time in each other's beds, but also just enjoying each other's company. Taking walks around the estate, trading our favourite stories, having dinners by the fireplace.

Valor turned out to be a surprisingly wonderful cook. Things had never felt as easy between the two of us as they had over the last week. I'd also made time for Cali and Alina, finding their company almost as good at keeping my thoughts from straying to all my problems for once.

I'd also attempted drawing from that new well of power within me, trying to manifest either the golden substance, or the coloured threads, but hadn't been successful. It seemed they only appeared when I was in high-stress situations.

Sadly, before I knew it, I was standing back in the castle foyer, with Valor on my left, Cali and Killian next to him. On my right were Alina and Adonis. We were slightly to the right of King Hadrian, Queen Tira, King Rahmor and Queen Elsbeth, who were standing at the head of the room, awaiting the entry of the remaining three kingdoms. They had arrived early.

It was all very formal. The other three kingdoms had arrived at essentially the same time. The first to enter was a man, a king. He certainly had the swagger of one. He looked to be about Hadrian's age, but you never knew with Pures.

Despite being older, even I could admit the man was incredibly good looking. He had chestnut brown hair, dark brown eyes, and his skin looked like it had been kissed by the night. I'd guessed this was the ruler of Ikira, home to the Animi, which explained the swagger. King Percius was known for his many children to many women. He was the bachelor of the royal world, and I could see why. He was quite beautiful.

Hadrian smiled and approached first, embracing him like one would a brother.

"Perci, good to see you."

"Likewise, old friend." He responded. "Where's that beautiful wife of yours?"

"Under the weather, I'm afraid. She sends her regards."

"What a shame. Nothing serious, I hope?" He shook his head.

"No, no. She's fine. Just not up for a big greeting. Did you bring anyone with you?"

"Two of my sons will be along shortly."

I remembered Cali telling me he had multiple children, but his eldest were twin sons.

"Great. Well, I'll let you get acquainted with the others."

Perci smiled and turned to Tira. "Hello, Tira darling." He greeted, kissing both of her cheeks. "You are looking as beautiful as ever. My offer to get hitched still stands, you know."

She rolled her eyes but smiled. "That ship sailed a long time ago, Percius."

"Ah, well, can't fault a man for trying." He winked. "I can't wait to meet this daughter of yours."

"She's far too young for you."

"Oh, get your mind out of the sewers, woman." He chuckled before greeting the Lios rulers.

"Rahmor, Elsbeth." He nodded to them both in a much more formal greeting.

They responded in kind. There was no trading off of remarks. Luckily, there wasn't time for the silence to become awkward as the next arrivals entered the room. I knew immediately who they were. King Eli and Queen Yelara of Reya, home of the Healeti.

Both were dressed conservatively. King Eli was showing barely any skin, in a finely detailed tunic and a high collar. Queen Yelara was showing even less. She even had a sheer veil on. Standing behind them were six girls of varying ages. I'd heard Yelara only had daughters. The youngest looked to be about five years old, the oldest maybe in her late twenties. Apparently, Yelara didn't go anywhere without all of her daughters.

Tira stepped forward, the first to greet Yelara. "Yelara, it's been years. Are you well?"

Again, much more formal than Percius's greeting. Whilst Yelara and Tira chatted, Hadrian greeted Eli and struck up a conversation. Percius was next. He greeted Yelara warmly, Eli not so much, which was interesting as they were neighbours. Their kingdoms were right next to each other.

Rahmor and Elsbeth said nothing, even though they were also neighbours of Reya.

Two men, looking a few years older than me, stepped into the room quietly. They had to be Percius' sons. I couldn't tell them apart at first glance. They were the spitting image of their father, only younger. Valor nodded to them as they approached, standing beside Adonis and Alina, who also smiled in greeting. Yelara's daughters stood on the other side, next to Cali and Killian.

It was an odd sight. All the rulers were at the front of the room, their children silently standing off to the side. The room went quiet when the last kingdom arrived. Lenea. King Harris and Queen Ferelia entered, looking like they would rather be anywhere else. Odette's parents. There was a younger man and woman with them. They looked similar enough to be Odette's siblings. Hadrian was the first one to speak, moving to greet his in-laws.

"King Harris, Queen Ferelia. I'm so pleased you were both able to make it. I trust your journey was fair?"

"A waste of a journey if you ask me," Ferelia responded, and Harris smiled almost apologetically, but not quite.

"The journey was fine. Where is our daughter?"

"She is a touch unwell. She's waiting in our chambers if you would like to see her first."

"Why is she unwell? Have you been looking after her?" Ferelia said accusingly.

I heard Percius mutter to Tira. "They're always so pleasant, aren't they?" Tira bit back a smile.

"Of course I have, Ferelia. I'm sure it's just a passing ailment. Come, I will show you to her." He turned to Tira. "Would you mind showing the other guests to the dining hall where they can sit and relax?"

"Of course." She smiled and began leading the others out of the room.

I couldn't help but notice how easily, and well, Tira and Hadrian worked together. Much smoother than I'd ever seen him and Odette coordinate. Hadrian left with Ferelia and Harris, whilst Tira took the rest of the group out another door. Leaving all the princes and princesses in a room together. *How awkward.*

Valor stepped forward. "My father thought it best if the 'grown ups' spoke without us, so we can all socialise in a more casual setting if you'd like?"

"Hard pass." The man who must have been Odette's younger brother said before leaving the room. His sister trailed off after him.

"Ignore them," Alina said to me, "they don't socialise with us lowly peasants." A laugh sounded as the twins approached.

"You are quite right," one of them said, smiling at both of us, "Alina, you look great."

"We've been over this, Seb. You don't possess the right attributes."

He pouted before turning to me.

"She's unavailable." Valor cut off whatever he might have said, arching an eyebrow in invitation for him to challenge that.

Seb sighed. "Disappointing. Nonetheless, I am Sebastian or Seb, and this is my brother Liam." He took my hand and kissed it.

"Nice to meet you. I am Elia." I smiled.

"Oh, we know," Sebastian said, grinning. "So, where is this more casual setting?"

Valor chuckled. "This way." He led the rest of us to a sitting room. Luckily, there was a bar. I had a feeling some of us would need it.

"I hope my brother doesn't offend you," Liam said, directing his words to me, "he is a little too much like our father, unfortunately."

"I still don't see how that is a bad thing, brother?" Seb said, making his way over to the Reyan princesses. Liam groaned quietly, and I chuckled.

"I'm not offended, don't worry."

"Well, I am glad to hear that. Unfortunately, I think some of the ladies he's now talking to may be. Please excuse me." I nodded, and he left to go stop his brother from hassling anyone else.

Their dynamic was very interesting. It was hard to say if any of the girls were offended, as they all wore semi-sheer veils like their mother. I looked around and noticed that Cali had gone over to the Steadmere sisters as well.

Seb, Liam, and Cali were all making conversation with at least one of the girls.

There was no sign of Isiah and Penelophe Krundell, I thought, finally, remembering their names. That left Alina, Adonis, Killian, Valor and me standing in close proximity, making small talk. I smiled a bit and went to get a drink. There was a tug on my dress. I glanced down to find the youngest of the Steadmere princesses staring up at me with wide eyes. I raised my eyebrows.

"Hello," I said, bending down, "what's your name?"

"Lizelle..." She bit her lip, wringing her skirt nervously.

I smiled softly. "That's a beautiful name. I am Elia, but my friends call me Elle."

She nodded a little.

"Can I get you something?"

"Can—Can you ask if they have any juice?"

I grinned. "I certainly can." I stood ordering a juice for Lizelle and a glass of wine for myself.

I looked down at her. "Would you like to come and sit with me?"

She nodded excitedly and followed me over to one of the couches. I handed the small girl her drink.

"Thank you," she said politely.

"You're very welcome. How old are you, Lizelle?"

"I am six years old." She held up five fingers.

"Oh, my goodness. Have you been to Taros before?"

She shook her head. "No! I've never left Reya!"

"Wow. Did you know this is my first visit to Taros as well?"

"Really?" She said, and I nodded. "Maybe we can explore together, then?" She suggested, getting a little shy.

I chuckled and nodded. "That sounds like a great idea to me."

"There you are," a woman said, approaching. The oldest of the Steadmeres. "Are you bothering Princess Elia, Lizelle?"

"No! I just asked for juice!" She exclaimed.

"I hope you asked politely," she said sternly, but I could see her trying not to smile.

"Yessss." She sighed exasperatedly.

"She did." I confirmed, smiling. "I'm Elia."

"I'm Isabella. It's nice to meet you."

I nodded. "Likewise."

"I hope you don't think me rude, but I need to take Lizelle to get settled in."

"No, of course. Go right ahead."

Lizelle hopped off the couch and took her sister's hand. "I can ask Mummy if we can go on a tour together?" Lizelle suggested hopefully, and I grinned.

"I would love that."

Her face lit up, and Isabella smiled gratefully at me, heading back over to her sisters before they all departed. Understandably wanting to get settled into their quarters.

"Well, it looks like only the fun ones remain. Oh, and Liam." Seb announced. I glanced over.

Seb, Liam, Valor, Killian, Cali, Adonis, and Alina remained.

"I actually have to get back to the troops," Alina said. "I'll see you all later." She smiled at me and Cali before leaving.

"I should go check if the Hadrian needs anything, and make sure none of them are trying to kill each other," Killian said, mostly directing that at Cali, who nodded, smiling softly at him.

"Have fun." She teased, and he rolled his eyes before he, too, left.

"And then there were five," Seb said, rubbing his hands together. "What is there to do around here?"

"Depends on what you like to do," Valor said.

"You shouldn't have asked that." Liam commented and Seb smirked.

Adonis slung an arm around Seb's shoulder. "I think I have just the thing, mate." He led Seb out of the room.

"So, Liam, how was the journey here?" I asked, feeling like the guy probably gets left out a lot with a brother like Seb.

"It was fairly uneventful but still interesting."

"How so?"

He smiled a bit. "How much do you know about Animi?"

I bit my lip. "Not a crazy amount? I know you can communicate with animals, but I don't really know how in-depth."

He smiled a bit. "It's not as much a conversation as you and I are having right now. It's more that we can... understand an animal's needs or wants, and we can also allow them to understand ours."

"Oh, okay, that makes more sense."

"The strongest of us can influence an animal's needs or wants, effectively controlling them."

"I doubt the animals appreciate that?"

"Animi are peaceful by nature. They believe in a symbiotic relationship between mortals and animals. It's rare for any Animi to force their will on a creature, even if they are an Orati." Cali chimed in.

Liam grinned at her, and I could see right away the interest in his eyes. The poor guy. Cali had absolutely no clue. Typical.

"Calliope is right. We don't think it's moral to control animals just because we may possess the ability."

"That is... very noble."

He shrugged. "I think it is simply common decency."

I chuckled. He was quite literal. "I agree with you."

Lydia entered the room and approached us. She curtsied.

"I'm so sorry to interrupt, Your Highnesses, but, Princess Elia, your mother asked me to send for you."

"Oh?" I nodded. "Sure," I looked back at Liam. "I hope we can pick up this conversation later?"

He nodded. "Of course."

"It was lovely to meet you." I hugged Cali and whispered. "Go easy on the man." She looked at me innocently, and I shook my head.

Valor came over and kissed me softly. "Have dinner with me tonight? I miss you."

I smiled and was only a little surprised to find it was genuine. *Boy, was I screwed.* "You had me to yourself all week?"

"So? I can still miss you." He tucked a strand of hair behind my ear.

I chuckled. "Dinner sounds lovely. Fetch me when you're ready?"

He nodded, and I followed Lydia. We ended up outside a room I hadn't been to before. It was in the medicae wing of the castle, quite far removed from everything else.

"Did Tira say what this was about?"

"No, she didn't, I'm sorry."

"Don't be. Who doesn't like a good surprise?" *I hated surprises.*

Lydia smiled a bit, no doubt seeing straight through me. Opening the door, she stepped aside. I entered, finding Tira and Queen Yelara having, what appeared to be, quite a serious conversation next to a cot. They stopped when the door opened, looking over. I raised my eyebrows.

"Um... hi?"

Lydia closed the door, Tira walked over and locked it. "Elia, this is Queen Yelara."

I nodded and curtsied. "It's an honour to meet you, Your Majesty."

She smiled softly. "Likewise, although I wish it were under better circumstances."

"What circumstances exactly are we talking about?"

"Yelara is here to look at your blood oath, Elia."

I swallowed. *Right. That was fast.*

I nodded slightly. "Oh, do you think you can help?"

"I've only ever read about blood oaths, but from the information your mother has given me, I believe I should be able to help. Would you come and lie down?"

I looked at Tira, who nodded encouragingly. I obliged, laying down on the cot.

"Do you mind if I lift your top?"

Yes. "No," I said instead.

So she did. She lifted my top up, examining my tattoo. It had healed now. It just looked thicker than it had before, darker. She frowned as she traced along it. I'd never seen a Remedi work. She was very focused and had a soothing sort of aura about her.

"Interesting."

"What is?" Tira asked, watching, appearing more nervous than I was.

"This is very intricate magic. I've seen nothing like it. But, it's not at full capacity. It's been drained."

"What do you mean, drained?" I asked.

"Someone has removed or altered some of the magic." She looked at me.

"Odette. She must have."

"Odette? A Flori." She considered. "I suppose if she used the right combination of herbs and plants, it is possible, but it would have taken a lot out of her. No wonder Hadrian said she was under the weather. I offered to see her, but he politely declined."

"So Odette removed some of the magic, but not all of it?" Tira asked.

Yelara nodded. "Possibly. I couldn't say for certain, but it appears as if she removed at least some of the magic binding your mind, but not the magic binding your body."

"My body?" I asked. *Divinities, what was wrong with my body?*

"Your magic, your Gifting, is being blocked by the rest of this blood oath. I can feel it under your skin. It's been pushing to get out, but could not break through the barrier completely."

"Can you break it?" Tira asked.

"As I said, this is very intricate magic. Powerful and ancient. But I can certainly try." She answered, determined, rolling up her sleeves. I grabbed her arm.

"Wait."

"What's wrong, Elia?" Tira said.

"You said that Yelara owed you a favour, and that is why she would help? I—if she owes you a favour, I don't want to use it on this..."

She frowned. "What are you talking about? Of course we should use it on this. If you're about to say it is a waste, it is not."

I shook my head. "No, I want the oath removed, trust me, but... there's something I want more." I looked back at Yelara. "My—I have a friend. She's practically family. She was injured in a house collapse when she was three and she can't walk. We've been saving our whole lives to get to Reya. I was going to take her to The Sana before all of this happened. She needs a Remedi. The best. You are the best. If you would heal her, I could pay you. You don't have to worry about my blood oath. I will ask nothing of you again. Just, please, would you help her?"

"Elia—" Tira started, but I shook my head.

"I've made my decision. I can live with the blood oath. It's not forever. But it is forever for Sierra. This is all I've ever wanted."

Yelara watched us. "I can certainly try to heal your friend, but depending on the extent of the damage, it may not be possible, or it may take longer than I have here."

I shook my head. "Anything you can do, anything at all, would mean the world to me."

She nodded, smiling a bit. "Very well. Have her brought to the castle tomorrow and I will see what can be done."

I breathed out in relief, tears stinging my eyes. I was so grateful I couldn't believe it. "Thank you."

CHAPTER SIXTY-EIGHT

After Yelara left, Tira gave me a look.

I sighed. "I don't want to hear it. I've made my decision."

I could tell she didn't agree with it, but she nodded anyway.

"I've learned more about the Potenti Specialties," she said, shocking me.

"What? How?"

"I had another dream last night. With the same old woman from last time."

I groaned. How were these dreams always so conveniently timed? "The Crone?"

"The who?"

I shook my head. "Nevermind. What was the dream about?"

"It was—I was sitting in a child's classroom. I didn't recognise anyone. They were learning the history of The Blessing and all the Giftings received. At first, it was the same as the history you and I know, until they named the seventh Gifting."

"You learnt about the Potenti in a dream?"

She nodded. "Yep."

"Well, what did you learn?"

"They said the seventh Gifting, from the Kingdom of Thadea, was the Potenti Gifting. There are two Specialties of Potenti."

I nodded, and she went on. "The first specialty is Senti. A Senti can experience and feel emotions, as well as influence and create them."

"I've been doing that," I said, realisation smacking me firmly in the face. "It's how I sensed the archer and... It's happened a few other times since then." I didn't think now was the time to bring up exactly how I'd gotten away from the Turf in the mine.

"What is the second one?" I asked.

"Cogni"

"What can a Cogni do?"

She opened her mouth to answer, but then stopped, frowning. "I can't remember."

I raised my eyebrows. "You don't remember?"

She shook her head, and I could *feel* her confusion. Not that I could explain how, I just knew that's what I was feeling. "I swear I knew five seconds ago. I have no idea why I can't grasp it now."

"It's alright. We'll figure it out. Did the dream say anything about my other ability then? The golden magic?" I was definitely a Senti, I could feel it, but that didn't explain the golden force of magic I could also wield.

"Yes, and no."

"What does that even mean?"

"You won't like it."

"Shocking. What is it?"

"There is no mention of the ability you displayed relating to the Potenti Gifting."

I frowned. "How is that possible?"

"This ability you have, they have recorded it only once before. Not by a Potenti, or any of the other Giftings we know of."

"What? When?"

"At the end of The Great War. The divinities that fought on the human's side blessed one man with potent abilities. A soldier. Tasked with delivering the final blow necessary to win the war. History doesn't tell us what the man had to do. He supposedly sacrificed his life to deliver the final blow, the power too much for a mortal to contain for long, but he won us the war."

"Okay, but what does that have to do with my power?"

"The only account we have of the power that the divinities bestowed upon the man describes the man emerging, outlined in gold. When he walked, he emitted a force that no one had ever seen the likes of before. He was said to wield the golden magic like a weapon, but no one could determine what it was. They called it the Donum Omnium Donorum. *The Gifting of all Giftings,* or Donum Aureum. The Golden Gifting."

"So, you're telling me I am descended from this man? And have somehow, against all the rules of magic, ended up with the Potenti Gifting *and* the Donum Aureum?"

"Not exactly."

I groaned. "Not exactly?"

"The Donum Aureum is not a normal Gifting. The other seven were given by only one divinity each. The Donum Aureum was a combination of all seven divinities' powers, not just one. And it clearly isn't just passed down through the bloodlines, or we would have had more cases."

"So, if it isn't an eighth Gifting, what is it?"

"I think it's a sign the divine have chosen you for something, just like that soldier."

I blinked, and then laughed. "You've got to be kidding."

"I wish I was."

I looked at her. "No, you can't be serious? I am not *chosen* by the divine! I am a twenty-two-year-old street urchin."

"You are much more than that, and you know it, Adira."

I shook my head. *This was all insane. Had the world flipped upside down while I'd slept?*

"Shit."

She nodded. "But we will figure it all out." She squeezed my hand. "You aren't alone in this."

I swallowed and nodded.

"Did you and Hadrian warn the others that the rebels talked about attacking when they all arrived?" I asked, needing a distraction.

She nodded. "Yes. The Jandars said to let them. They are apparently itching for a fight." She shook her head. "Yelena is concerned about casualties. Perci is being cautious and has his travelling party on high alert. Harris and Ferelia refuse to acknowledge it."

"So, if the rebels do attack, they'd have a solid chance of doing damage?"

She half nodded. "If we remain divided, yes. Hadrian is working on it as we speak. There's been no movement at the mines. We are hoping they have decided against attacking now that they have lost the element of surprise. Thanks to you. Who knows what would have happened if we did not know?"

I nodded a bit. "Thank you for using your favour to have the blood oath removed, Tira."

She looked at me incredulously. "Of course. I said I would?"

"I know, I know. Thank you. I just meant... It means a lot to me." I stood up and hugged her.

She hugged back just as tightly. "Anytime honey."

I breathed out. "Valor wants to have dinner, so I better get back to my room in case he comes early, and to be honest, I could use some time to process. I am sure Hadrian could use you in that room, helping convince the other kingdoms to play nice."

She chuckled. "Yes, Probably. Well, take your time. I hope you have a nice evening. You deserve that."

I nodded, getting up. "I hope yours isn't as terrible as it sounds like it will be."

"Before you go. This thing with Valor..." She started, pursing her lips.

I looked at her. "What about it?"

"Is it the real deal for you?"

I hesitated before sighing and nodding. "As much as I tried not to let it be. I think it is, or at least it could be, if I gave it a real chance." I swallowed. "I wouldn't say I'd want to marry him so fast if they hadn't made me say yes, but I care about him." *More than I would admit to her.* "It's real." The fear of saying that out loud to someone was overwhelming.

She smiled a bit. "It's okay to love, Adira."

I smiled sadly. "Not in my experience."

"Well, that was before. This is now. All I want is for you to find that happiness and that comfort you've never had. It sounds like Valor is giving that to you."

I nodded a bit. "I feel safe with him." I realised I really did. He infuriated the Hek out of me sometimes, and his over protectiveness drove me mad, but I always felt safe with him around. Safety was not a feeling I'd ever allowed myself the luxury of experiencing until now, apparently.

She smiled. "Then go have dinner with him and enjoy yourself. You have to. You never know how many chances you'll get."

I hugged her again before heading back to my room. Tarryn and Hamish were waiting outside the room when I came out. They escorted me to my chambers. After getting changed, I laid down and thought over what I'd learned, and what Yelara had agreed to do for me, for Sierra. I must have been at it for a while, because a knock sounded on the door, and when I opened it, I found Valor standing there smiling with a bouquet of roses.

"Ready for dinner?" He grinned.

I smiled. "It's dinnertime already?"

He raised his eyebrows. "What time did you think it was?"

I shook my head and shrugged. "Are those for me?" I gestured to the flowers.

"Well, I was going to give them to Hamish, but he said he was too manly for flowers." I laughed, shaking my head. Both at his joke and that it was so unbelievable. Hamish would *never* turn down flowers.

He grinned and held them out. "So you may as well have them."

I grinned and kissed his cheek. "They are beautiful, thank you." I placed them in a vase and returned to the door. "So, where are we going?"

"It's a surprise." I groaned. "Yes, I know you hate surprises, but this one will be worth it."

I sighed. "Fine," I smiled as he took my hand. "Lead the way then."

He grinned and led me through the castle, out the back, and then further along the grounds. I recognised where we were going.

"The hot springs?" I asked.

He chuckled. "You're so impatient."

I bit my lip. "Sorry."

"Don't bite your lip like that, or we will not get through dinner."

I quickly stopped, smiling to myself.

"Alright, now you have to cover your eyes."

I gave him a look. "Seriously?"

He returned the look. "Yep, and no peeking."

I sighed and covered my eyes with my hand. "How do I know you won't walk me into a tree or something?"

"Have a little faith in me, Sunshine."

He led me by my other hand. "I better not regret this."

"Okay, okay, open."

I opened my eyes and gasped. We were, in fact, at the hot springs. But there was a beautiful table set up, lit by candlelight. The meal was there, ready to eat, and there were two glasses of wine. There were some towels and a blanket nearby for a potential swim. There were flower petals scattered around, and it was beautiful. I looked at Valor in shock.

"Val... this is..."

He smiled a bit. "This is one of the first times I realised how hard I was falling for you. Right here, in these hot springs." I swallowed. "So, I thought it a fitting spot for you and me to just *be* for a little while." He pulled out a chair and gestured for me to sit.

I hugged him tightly before taking my seat. "This is beautiful Valor, very thoughtful, thank you."

He smiled and sat down. We ate, drank, and laughed. I took Tira's advice and enjoyed myself.

After dinner, we both stripped down and jumped into the hot springs. They were just as amazing as last time. I smiled as Valor pulled me close to him.

"You are gorgeous," he said, watching me, and I blushed.

"You aren't so bad yourself," I said in return, kissing him softly.

He smiled. "Thank you."

I laughed. "You're welcome?"

"No, I mean thank you for just—thank you for giving me a chance. I know I didn't make it easy on you at first."

"Val, stop."

"I'm serious, Elia. I'd given up on finding something like this before I met you. But you just have this way with everyone and everything around you. You are so compassionate, yet so strong. You win over everyone that you meet. Even my mother seems to be coming around to you, which is a miracle."

Guilt flooded me at his proclamation. He didn't know the full story. I'd been unable to tell him before, but now that I could, I was intentionally keeping it from him.

"So, thank you. Thank you for letting me be a part of your life." He squeezed my hand. "I love you, Elia Melfore."

Slowly, I took my hand away. I couldn't let him confess all of this without knowing the truth. I understood Hamish and Tarryn's concerns, but I couldn't keep lying to him. I just had to hope they would understand, and that Tarryn could be okay with it. Valor's smile faded a little.

"What's wrong?" I took a deep breath. "I... there's something I need to tell you. It—it's big. But before I do, I want you to know that," I steadied myself, meeting his eyes, "I love you too. I tried really hard not to, but you just made it impossible."

For once, I was telling the truth. After I'd returned to my chambers, the initial shock of everything had worn off. I'd realised I was no longer bound to make Valor fall in love with me, and the idea of him not loving me made my chest ache. I realised I'd been so adamant that I not care for him, because I *knew* I wouldn't be able to be honest with him, because I *knew* I would use him. So I'd lied to myself. I'd told myself I didn't care. In doing so, I hid my true feelings not just from Butcher, or from Valor, but from myself. I was a damned idiot.

He smiled a bit. "Elle, whatever it is, I'm sure it's not as big of a deal as you think it is."

I shook my head. *If only. How did I even begin?* I got out of the water, and he followed me.

"Valor, I'm not who you think I am."

He frowned slightly. "I know who you are, Elia."

I shook my head again. "My name is not Elia..."

He stopped and looked at me. "What?"

"My name," I took a deep breath, "my name is not Elia Melfore or Worthington. My name is Adira Nightfell and I am not from Xeria. I'm from Taros. Kendelen, to be precise." *Way to ease into it, Adira.*

He looked at me, moving his hand away. "What are you talking about?"

My heart ached, not only at the look on his face, but from what I could feel from him. He was confused, disbelieving, and sadness was creeping its way in.

"I was born in Taros. My parents died when I was little. A woman named Camilla took me in. She trained me to be her spy, her thief. I have a sister." I swallowed. "Camilla wanted me to infiltrate your family's court and report back. She kidnapped my sister and threatened to kill her if I said no. She forced me to do what she wanted..."

I was making a mess of this.

Realisation filled his eyes. "You're a spy."

I shook my head. "N—no. I *was*, but I'm not really."

"This whole time." He shook his head. "I was right. I was right to accuse you back then. You've been playing all of us."

"No, Valor, it wasn't like that." I could feel his hurt being overpowered by his anger.

"It's exactly like that! So what, you work for the rebels?"

"*No!* I would never do that."

"Did she tell you to make me fall for you?"

"Valor, it's not like that."

"Did she, or did she not?"

"Y-yes. Yes, she did. But I really fell for you, Valor. It's all been real. I fought it at first, because I didn't want to fall for you, but I did. Everything we've been through has been real." I stood and reached for him, but he jerked away.

"No. You've been lying this *entire* time. *How* could it possibly be real?"

Tears stung my eyes. "That's why I am telling you now. Even though I'm risking everything. There's so much more I need to tell you, Valor. It will make sense. Just let me explain."

"You betrayed all of us! You betrayed me!" His voice broke at the end, and that broke me.

"Val."

He shook his head. "You are nothing but a lying, manipulating serpens, just like the rest of them." He wiped away a tear before it could fall. "I knew I couldn't trust you. Everything in me was telling me you were hiding something. Jokes on me, huh? I was right, and yet I still fell for it." He laughed bitterly.

"Valor, please... just let me explain."

"I'm done listening to anything you have to say. Clearly, it's all just false truths and manipulations."

I stepped forward again, trying to touch him, trying to get him to hear me. To see me. If he would just let me explain, he would understand. I know he would when he got the full story.

"Don't!" He yelled, and the table launched itself into the air, smashing against a tree.

Glass shattered, leftovers flew everywhere. I flinched back. He looked at me and there was so much pain and anguish in his eyes. I didn't need to be a Senti to know how badly I'd hurt him.

"Just. Don't," he said before he shook his head and walked away, back towards the castle.

As he got further and further away, I just stood and watched. I wanted to run after him. I wanted to scream at him and make him understand, but I couldn't. He needed time. I owed him that. I just had to trust that what he felt for me was real enough that he wouldn't go to Hadrian until he'd heard the full story.

Wrapping my arms around myself, I closed my eyes, letting the same tears Valor had been holding back fall freely. I sat down on the grass and cried. I cried for the loss of my parents, who would have known how to comfort me. I cried over the death of Raf, over the deaths of Indigo, William, and Matias, over the betrayal of Tolemas, of Camilla.

I cried over the way my relationship was with Sierra right now. I cried for the boy archer I had killed, for Jenkins, Wilkins, and Carter. And I cried for the pain I had caused Valor, and the pain I'd caused myself. I cried and cried, feeling every emotion at full force, until I couldn't anymore.

I was numb by the time I rose, dressed, and pulled myself together. This would not be the end of Valor and me. I didn't waste all this time fighting my feelings just to lose him now. I took a breath and walked back to the castle. If he needed time, I would give him time. But I wouldn't give up.

I looked up to the stars, and I liked to think I felt Raf nudging me forward. I'll dream for me, and I choose to dream of me and Val.

When I got back to my room, I let Hamish and Tarryn in, updating them on everything they'd missed.

"Man, do you want me to kick his ass? 'Cos I will. I don't care if he's a prince. And by the way, he did NOT offer me those flowers and I would never say something as outlandish as I'm too manly for flowers. No one is too manly for flowers. I love flowers," Hamish said seriously.

Tarryn rolled his eyes. "That's what you got out of everything she just told us?"

I smiled a bit. "I appreciate that Hamish, but no thank you. He isn't in the wrong here."

"But neither are you. None of this is your fault."

"In his eyes it is."

"Well, his eyes are stupid."

I smiled a bit and looked at Tarryn.

"Don't look at me," he said. "I'm with Hamish, but I didn't feel like I needed to point it out."

I laughed a bit. "Thank you, guys. And thank you for understanding why I had to tell him."

They both nodded and stayed with me a little longer before returning to their guard post outside my door, and I got into bed. Sleep didn't come for a long time that night. The only thing that helped was thinking about seeing Sierra tomorrow and finally getting her the Remedi I promised her. It was that thought that eventually allowed me to sleep.

I woke first thing, had breakfast, and let Lydia dress me in a random gown I barely noted before rushing into town. Hamish, Tarryn, Uri, and Wes all accompanied me, and I didn't care about the spectacle I was no doubt making. I knew she would be at the circus, so I went straight there. Butcher exited her study, smiling and laughing with Sierra. She raised her eyebrows when she saw me.

"Can we help you?"

"Sure. Sierra, you're coming with me."

"Ad—" She glanced at my companions.

"It's okay. They all know the truth."

I saw her eyes widen in surprise, as Butcher's brow furrowed slightly.

"What's going on, Adira?"

"We are finally getting out of here. That's what's happening." I walked over.

"I don't think so," Butcher said, as if she were talking to a child.

"I don't really give a damn what you think, Camilla."

She looked at me in disbelief. "Stop this nonsense, Adira."

There was no pull following her command. I grinned.

"Do you know what? I don't think I will."

I punched her hard, right in the nose, a part of me delighting at the distinct sound of cracking bone. She cried out, gripping her face.

Sierra gasped. "Adira! Are you insane!?"

"I know you and I haven't seen eye to eye lately, Sierra, and I am sorry. I am sorry I haven't been here. I am sorry you felt unheard. I have a Remedi waiting back at the castle to heal you, if that is what you want. If it isn't, then fine. We will just get out from under Butcher's thumb. You can decide what you want to do with your life, but I will not let it involve her. That is where I draw the line. I love you and I care about you. Please, *just* trust me?"

I looked at her, and she looked back at me. She was silent for a minute before she nodded.

"Okay... okay. I trust you."

Relief filled me, and I hugged her tightly. She hugged back. Hamish walked over, moving behind Sierra's roller.

"It is a pleasure to meet you, Lady Sierra. May I assist you?"

She blushed and nodded a bit. "Sure."

I smiled a bit.

"No. That isn't possible. The year isn't up." Camilla practically wailed.

"Listen closely, Camilla. If you come near me, Sierra, or anyone I care about ever again, make no mistake. I *will* kill you." I looked into her eyes, letting every ounce of seriousness and determination seep into my voice.

She wisely took a slight step back. "This isn't over, Adira..."

"We're done here."

Hamish wheeled Sierra out, and I followed. Once we were all in the privacy of our carriage and I breathed out.

"Would you really kill her?" Sierra asked quietly.

I looked at her. "Yes."

She swallowed. "You're different..."

I nodded a bit. "So are you, but we are still us. We're still family." I squeezed her hand. "I love you."

She smiled a little. "I'm sorry about what I said the last time we—"

I shook my head. "It's alright. I'm sorry too. We can put it behind us."

"Do you really have a Remedi?"

"I have the *Queen* of the Healeti."

Her eyes widened. "What? But—how?"

"Friends in very high places." I chuckled a bit. "I will explain it all soon. For now, let's focus on you."

She swallowed. "What if she can't heal me?"

I squeezed her hand again. "Then we will deal with that. Like you said, you don't need fixing. You are perfectly fine the way you are."

She nodded slightly. "Right."

When we reached the castle, Hamish remained close, making it his personal duty to get Sierra around, much to her delight. She looked around in awe, especially at the gardens on the way in.

"I will take you on a grand tour later, I promise."

She smiled. "I'd like that."

CHAPTER SIXTY-NINE

I took her to my rooms, where Tira and Yelara were waiting.

"Sierra, this is Queen Yelara of Reya and Queen Tira of Xeria."

Sierra's eyes went wide, and she quickly bowed in her roller. "I—it's an honour to meet both of you, Your Majesties."

Yelara smiled and nodded at her. Tira shook her head and embraced Sierra, who looked like she might spontaneously combust.

"We don't need formalities. We are family."

"Um, family?"

I laughed a little. "She means literally. Tira, well, it is a long story," I said, wary of Yelara's presence.

Sierra breathed out. "I feel like I'll be hearing that response a lot from you."

I nodded. "Probably."

"Sierra, do you mind if I examine your legs? It's fine if you stay in your roller for now." Yelara stepped forward.

Sierra swallowed and nodded. "Okay."

Yelara bent down and examined her legs. She ran her hands up the lengths of them and tested their motion. "Can you feel any sensation?"

Sierra shook her head.

Yelara nodded. "Okay, for the next part, it would be easier if you were laying down, would you mind?"

Sierra shook her head and wheeled herself to my bed. She pulled herself up out of her roller and onto the bed like she's been doing her whole life.

"Damn girl, you have powerful arms." Hamish commented, and she blushed.

I rolled my eyes. "Right, all men present, out you go."

Hamish pouted as Tarryn dragged him out. Wes and Uri politely left like the adults they were.

Yelara walked over. "You may feel warmth when I check for the source of the paralysis, but it shouldn't be unpleasant."

Sierra nodded. I took her hand, and she smiled gratefully at me.

Yelara's hands glowed pink, and she hovered them over Sierra's body. Sierra gasped, but other than that, said nothing.

"Sierra, is it okay if we roll you over? I just want to check your spine."

Sierra nodded, and we carefully rolled her over. Yelara repeated what she had just done, but on her other side.

"Alright, you can return to your back." We rolled her back over, and I looked at Yelara. "Well?"

"It isn't as bad as expected. There is no spinal damage. It looks like the paralysis is simply from multiple terrible breaks that weren't set properly, and some nerve damage. This should be fixable. The most troublesome part will be to reverse the dystrophy that has occurred due to lack of movement. It will probably take me most of today."

My eyes widened, and I said far too quickly, "That's fine. If you have the time, that would mean the world to me. Whatever the cost, I'll pay it." Tira put a hand on my shoulder, clearly telling me to shut up.

Yelara had an amused look on her face. "Calm down, I made sure my schedule was free, just in case. I am happy to start now, if Sierra is."

We all looked at Sierra. "You—you really think I could walk?"

Yelara smiled softly. "I know it's hard to believe, and not just any Remedi could help you, but I have healed injuries worse than yours. If someone had set and treated your injuries earlier, you would have been able to walk again within six months of the incident."

Camilla could have gotten her the help, but she chose not to. Easier to control that way. I pushed down my anger.

Tears stung her eyes. "Th-thank you..."

"Happy to help."

And with that, she began the healing. It was honestly very boring to watch. I couldn't see much happening externally, other than the faint pink glow. Yelara worked quietly, only stopping so we could all eat a bit. She explained as she worked. The first step was resetting and healing the broken bones.

That part should have been excruciating for Sierra, because Yelara had to re-break all the bones, set them properly, and then heal them. However, because of the nerve damage, Sierra felt none of it. Then Yelara went to work repairing the nerves.

I will never forget the moment Sierra felt something below her waist for the first time since she was three years old. A full breakdown followed the look of shock and disbelief on her face. Yelara and Tira had to step out so I could console her. It took a while, rightly so, but once she was okay again, Yelara went back to work.

She went from being grateful to cursing all of us for it because feeling meant pain. Once the nerve damage was repaired, Yelara started on the areas of her muscles and legs that were affected by the dystrophy. It was difficult to watch. She cried and even begged to stop at some points. We would stop for a while, then begin again. It was gruesome. I could only imagine how exhausted Yelara must be. Finally, she stopped.

"That should be it."

I sat up straight in my chair. "You're finished?" She had to have been at it for at least nine hours. Something told me it would have taken a regular Remedi days.

Yelara nodded. "Sierra, you need to take it easy. Your body needs to get used to having full motion again and you will need to build up the muscles more than I have today. But you should have full movement."

Sierra nodded slightly. She looked like she was in shock. Yelara looked at Tira.

"Are you going to the meeting tonight to discuss the rebel threat?"

Tira nodded. "Absolutely. Thank you, Yelara. I will see you there. Although, I am sure everyone will understand if you need to rest after this."

Yelara smiled a bit. "I will see how I go." Yelara stood and walked out.

I looked at Sierra. "Si, do you want to stand?"

Sierra was staring at her legs. She nodded slightly. "Y-yeah... I do."

I smiled as she sat up and slowly swung her legs over the side of the bed. She breathed out shakily.

I moved to her side. "I'm right here."

"Maybe we should call that good-looking guard back in to catch me?"

I laughed. "Don't let him hear you call him handsome. I think I can manage. Go on, I'm right here."

She bit her lip, placing her feet on the floor. Her toes wiggled and tears stung both of our eyes. She slowly took hold of my arm and pulled herself up. Tira was nearby in case we needed her help.

"That's it, you've got this."

Sierra pulled herself up into a standing position. She gripped my arm, more out of fear than the need for support. Sierra was standing, *actually* standing. I couldn't believe it. Judging by the look on her face, neither could she. She took a shaky step, then another. I followed her, right by her side the entire time. She was doing it. She was walking.

She burst into tears, letting go of my arm to cover her mouth. I swallowed, trying to hold back my own tears.

"You did it, Squirt. You did it."

She hugged me tightly and cried into my shoulder. I couldn't explain the relief and joy I felt at that moment. It was another feeling I would never forget. We both cried and laughed before sitting back down to give her legs a rest. As Yelara said, we didn't want to overdo it.

Tira watched us and smiled quietly. "I will leave you two to it. I have to meet Hadrian to go over things before this meeting." I nodded to her. "Thank you, Tira."

She nodded and left us alone. I breathed out. I couldn't believe it. I'd done it, I'd kept my promise. Now Sierra could do whatever she wanted and I... I was free to do the same. For the first time in our lives, we were both free.

"I think this calls for a celebration," I said, and Sierra laughed, nodding.

I had Lydia bring us dinner and some champagne. I gave Sierra a look. Even though she wasn't quite of legal drinking age yet, she was close enough to twenty that I figured I could allow it on this occasion.

She giggled, and together, we indulged in far too much champagne and junk food before collapsing on my bed.

"The world is at your feet now, Sierra, literally. We can do anything we want. We are finally free." I breathed out.

She smiled, sitting up. "Thank you, Adira."

"You don't need to thank me, Sierra. You would do the same for me."

"I wouldn't."

I laughed a bit. "Of course you would. You think too little of yourself."

"No, I don't. I just know I wouldn't." She said matter-of-factly.

I looked at her, a little confused. "What?"

"Honestly, I'm impressed. I didn't think you'd actually follow through and find a Remedi. I'm glad you did, but it does speed up the timeline. You always knew how to complicate things."

"What do you mean? What's complicated?"

"I grew up in your shadow, but what people never realised is I *chose* to be there. People overlook you when you make yourself small, when they pity you, when they think you are the lesser sibling."

I frowned. "I never saw you as lesser than."

"No, you didn't. Which was your problem. You were *so* focused on helping me and looking after me, you didn't see what was happening right under your nose."

I sat up, now completely confused. "What are you talking about, Sierra?"

"Camilla told you she's known who we were since she found us, right? She told you about The Order?"

I nodded. "She told you?"

"She did. I mean, I was four at the time, so I didn't completely understand it, but I came to, as I got older."

I stiffened slightly. "You knew? This whole time?"

"Of course I did. You would have too, if Camilla had trusted you."

"Trusted me?" I couldn't believe what I was hearing. "I did everything she asked of me. Time and time again, I proved myself worthy of her trust."

"Yes, very impressive, really. No matter how hard I made the tests, you continually passed them. You never broke. You were so determined to get through it so you could get us to Reya."

How hard *she* made the tests? Had she lost it?

"No, I haven't lost it. Quite the opposite."

My eyes widened. Had I said that out loud?

"No, you didn't say it out loud."

I breathed in.

"You're a Senti," she said, dragging out the words. "Do you know what Senti can do, Adira?" I said nothing. She smiled and continued.

"Senti, like you, can influence people's emotions. Cogni, like me, can influence people's thoughts. So when Camilla had me complete my Testing at aged five, she really thought I would be the easier one to control out of the two of us. She was wrong. She should have tested you." She chuckled. "She set out to be the one in control. I can't take all the credit for your training. She certainly started it, but as I got older, smarter, I realised I didn't particularly care for her leadership, so she ended up being the one controlled."

Sierra could manipulate thoughts. It was like a puzzle clicking together in my mind. One I didn't even know I was trying to solve. People had always gravitated towards Sierra. Everyone loved her, but she never seemed to notice. The roses... I'd never seen Camilla taking time to garden. She was too busy running The Cavum and the circus, so her rose perfume and her regular displays of flowers never made sense. Sierra *loved* gardening. The flowers in Tolemas' house weren't from Camilla, they were from *Sierra*.

All the warnings I'd gotten. *Beware of the serpens in the garden.* The Potenti sigil, the serpens, and the dagger. *Listen to what you cannot hear.* Thoughts. This entire time Sierra had been pulling the strings, but she's only nineteen? How could she have done all this?

She was watching me, smiling. "You grow up quickly when you gain the ability to read people's thoughts at age five. My childhood ended the day of my Testing."

"Stop that. Get out of my head."

"I can only hear your thoughts because you are letting me. Potenti can pick up on other Potenti's thoughts or emotions if they don't have their walls up, but they can't influence other Potenti. We are immune in that sense, unfortunately."

Oh, Ades no. "Raf—he figured it out, didn't he?"

She sighed. "Poor Raphael. He wouldn't leave well enough alone. I never intended for him to be caught in the crossfire, but he watched too closely. He wanted to look out for me like you asked, then he started digging, investigating the rebels." She shook her head. "He was in the way."

Tears filled my eyes as I stood up. "Why? Why would you do all of this?"

"Haven't you been paying attention? I grew up Pure in an Impure world. I went through The Testing and learned what they did to our family." She shook her head. "All because they feared our power. They were right to fear it. I vowed after my Testing to make them pay for what they did. They brought down our empire, so I am going to bring down theirs."

"But how did you get involved with the rebellion? You couldn't walk, for Heknos sake?"

She laughed, and the sound was lifeless, nothing like the Sierra I knew.

"You're right, I couldn't walk. Makes it difficult to really get things done. Camilla could, though. After years of planting thoughts in her head, she's really fairly easy to control, even if I'm not close by at all times."

"So what, you sent Camilla out to correspond with the rebels?"

"Not exactly."

I waited for her to continue.

"I was never truly involved with the rebels, nor was Camilla."

"But Solis?"

"There is no Solis Adira. I made her up. She is me."

I frowned, and she sighed exasperatedly at my confusion.

"The Rise is a very real rebellion, but do you really think their leader would broadcast themselves like Solis? Without actually stating their agenda?" She shook her head. "No. But it was a very convenient front for me, and The Order to hide behind. You were so focused on Solis, you didn't put the pieces together."

What she said made sense. It explained why I kept getting attacked, why I thought it was strange that Solis would make certain moves when they had me inside the castle gathering intel for them. They didn't need to be so aggressive. The attacks were the real rebellion.

"So Solis was just a name you picked to keep me and others from looking in the right direction? You just picked a name that sounded related to The Rise?"

"Well, it wasn't so simple. I certainly had to influence a lot of peoples' thoughts and have Camilla do a lot of networking to ensure the alias appeared legitimate."

"... You can't have done all that."

"You were simply too easy to manipulate, Adira. All it really took was Raf's death, and you soon turned on your new royal friends. You were practically a radicalised rebel yourself with the way you saw the Pure. If it was that easy for me to manipulate you into being angry at the crown, without the use of any magic, how hard do you think it was for me and Camilla to convince a few influential people?"

"Sierra... I—you—Tell me this is all some sick joke? That Camilla has bound you as well or *something?*"

"Nope. It's all true. I hadn't planned to reveal it this way, but I couldn't resist a chance at being healed by the Reyan Queen herself."

"Sierra, the Pures today are not the same ones that wiped out our kingdom. They are innocent."

"They are *not* innocent," she said. Her voice had hardened, and there was an unhinged look in her eyes.

"Sierra—"

"Their ancestors massacred ours! They have blood on their hands, whether they like it or not! They don't deserve the power they were given."

I swallowed. "Sierra, we can talk about this."

"It's too late, Adira."

She had actually gone insane. All the thoughts, and Camilla's psychotic influence, had driven her insane, and I'd missed it. I should have seen this.

"It's not too late. We can still fix this."

She rolled her eyes. "You're a spy. We trained you in espionage. How would *you* take down a government?" Horror filled me as more pieces clicked into place.

"Sow the seeds of rebellion and take down their leaders, but no rebels are breaking into this castle. We have reinforced it and are prepared for any attack the rebels could throw. We have made all the rulers aware."

She nodded. "Yes, yes, you warned them that the rebels were going to attack. There is more than one way to assassinate someone, Adira. You, of all people, should know that. Especially when you can, oh I don't know, control the thoughts and will of anyone? Do you know I don't need to see a person to influence their thoughts? My range is really quite impressive, and I passed sooo many people on our way here. Servants, lords, ladies, your precious guards, none of them had mental shields."

I tensed. "What are you saying?"

"I'm saying, by now, anyone that was in that meeting to 'discuss' the rebels should already be dead. Courtesy of the King's finest wine. Everyone will blame The Rise, as if those fools are capable of something like that."

I shook my head. "No. You're bluffing."

"Am I?" She giggled and shrugged.

I hurried to the door. She had to be messing with me.

"Oh also, you may want to check on our dear old 'aunt'. I don't believe she made it to the meeting. It's too late for the other rulers, but you might still save her."

I looked back to see her walking towards the hidden tunnel door. She opened it, and I was torn. Did I stop her, calling her bluff about Tira and the others? Or did I let her go and try to save them when it could truly be a rouse to escape?

"Tick-Tock, sister."

I breathed in and decided, practically flinging my door open. I took off down the hall, shouting back at Hamish and Tarryn. "The royals might all be in danger! Get to them, now!"

I sprinted towards Hadrian's chambers, not looking back to see if they had listened. There were no guards posted outside, as there should be. I barged in.

"Hadrian?! Tira?!" I called. No answer. I hurriedly checked every room, finding nothing.

"In here, Adira!" I stiffened, hearing Camilla's voice from the direction of the master bedroom.

I slowly opened the door and froze, not knowing where to look first. There was blood everywhere, splattered all across the room. Camilla was standing at the end of the bed. I moved closer, and time slowed. Hadrian and Tira were barely recognisable. They were both lying next to each other.

Hadrian's eyes were wide open, staring at nothing, his face frozen in horror. Tira didn't look much better. Their bodies were sliced open. Hek, there was so much blood.

But then Tira's chest rose, and I breathed in. "Tira?!"

I tried to go to her, but Camilla stepped in front of me.

"Oh, you didn't think I'd let you get away with breaking my nose, did you?" She flipped the bloodied sword in her hand, holding it out to me.

"Let me pass."

She smiled, stepping aside, and I rushed over, checking both of their pulses. I couldn't find one for Hadrian, and Tira's was weak.

"Tira, stay with me." I placed my hands over her stomach where she'd been slashed, no doubt by Camilla. Tira's blood coated my hands, my clothes, the metallic scent of it filling the air.

"Oh Adira, poor, stupid, Adira. Despite all your years of training, you couldn't figure out what was right under your nose this whole time. Your sister is quite diabolical, isn't she?"

"I will kill you for this."

Her smile only grew. "Take the sword, Adira."

"What? Why would I..." I trailed off as I stood, removing my hands from Tira's wound, and approaching Camilla. I reached out, taking the sword from her. I tensed.

"No..."

"Now hold it to your throat." Pain coursed through me as my body obeyed her command, holding the blade to my neck.

"But... no. Odette removed the part of the blood oath that bound me to you. How are you doing this? Stop."

"Oh, did she?" She chuckled. "Do you really think she would do that? My own cousin?"

"But I was able to disobey your orders?"

"Because we *let* you, Adira." She shook her head. "It's not your fault. I can understand your confusion. Having your memory wiped will do that to a person. I suppose we should restore it no? Remember Adira. Remember what you were commanded to forget."

I breathed in as it all came rushing back.

I'd woken shortly after passing out from the pain of Odette's torture. Camilla was there. Both Odette and Camilla were standing there watching me. I shot upright, trying to get out of bed, but Camilla ordered me to stop, so I did. Before I could get a word out, she spoke.

"Do not run, do not speak, do not fight Adira. Listen closely and obey."

I waited, pain and anger coursing through me. Odette was watching with an unreadable expression.

Camilla smiled. "You will believe everything I am about to tell you. Do you understand?"

I nodded, clenching my fists.

"The blood oath has been broken, at least the part that binds you to me. The part that forces you to obey. You are free. Odette must have freed you from it unknowingly. You believe the blood oath has been broken, and you will continue believing it until you and I are back in this room, and I give you an order. Now forget this conversation. Return to your rooms, and speak to no one. Simply return to your room, get into bed, and sleep. Remember nothing after you passed out from the pain Odette put you through."

And so I did. As I left, I saw Camilla open a door to the tunnel system. I walked back to my room, past the guards, into bed, and went straight to sleep.

I stared at Camilla in horror. "No..." I whispered, unwilling to believe what my mind knew to be true. It made sense, though. I couldn't figure out how Odette had gotten me back to my rooms without someone noticing. It was because I'd walked myself back there. It made little sense that only part of the oath had been removed. Why not the whole thing? Because it had never been removed in the first place.

Shaking my head in disbelief when Camilla said, "I'm afraid you will have to spiral later. We have very little time left. So be a dear and finish the job. Take that sword and plunge it into your aunt's chest." She smiled sweetly at me and I went rigid all over.

"No! STOP!!"

She shook her head. "Always so defiant. *Do it.*"

My feet moved on their own, moving towards where Tira lay prone in the bed beside Hadrian's lifeless body. Her eyes were open now, her breathing ragged, and tears spiked my eyes as they met hers.

She gave me a sad smile and managed a weak, "It's alright Adira. Do not blame yourself."

I raised the sword, both hands on the hilt, holding it above her chest. I shook my head.

"Please no. P—please don't make me do this." I looked back at Camilla, begging.

"Straight through the heart. You know where it is."

My shaky hands moved. The sword lined up perfectly with where her heart would be. Tears were streaming now, and I fought with every bone, every fibre of my body. I looked at Tira again and she reached out, touching my side.

"It's alright. Just close your eyes."

I shook my head violently.

"NOW Adira." Camilla ordered, and I could feel my hold on my body loosening. I couldn't fight her.

"Close your eyes, hon. I forgive you."

"I'm sorry." I whispered, clenching my eyes shut and slamming the sword down into her chest.

CHAPTER SEVENTY

SHE GASPED IN PAIN, and I opened my eyes in time to watch the life drain from her eyes. I dropped to my knees, tears blinding me as I pulled the sword out.

"Elia?! Father?!" Valor's voice called.

My head jerked toward the door. The distraction cost me. I turned back to Camilla just in time to see her take off into the tunnels, using the door she'd made me forget.

I stood as Valor stepped through the doorway. His eyes widened as he took in the same scene I just had, only this time it was me holding the weapon. Pain filled his features when his eyes landed on his father. His dead father, lying next to my dead aunt.

"Valor..." I stood.

His eyes flew to me, to the sword in my hand and the blood on my dress. The pain and hatred that hit me was so strong it knocked me back a step. It was a pure rage I'd never experienced, a physical force. It took me a second to realise it was directed at me.

"Guards!" Valor called. Killian and some of the other royal guards hurried in. Mixed reactions of gasps and curses filled the room. "Arrest her for the murder of King Hadrian and Queen Tira."

My eyes widened. "What? No! It wasn't me...I—" But it was me. I had murdered Tira. I looked at the sword in my hand and quickly dropped it. "Valor, wait..."

"Everything you've told me has been a lie. This is no different. Arrest her, now."

I backed up as the guards approached. "V—Val, I didn't do this willingly. I—I could never do this. She's getting away, please you have to listen!"

"Arrest her!" He wouldn't give me a chance to explain. He was too caught up in his rage and despair.

The guards lunged for me, but I was faster. Sprinting into the tunnels, I ran as fast as I could. The guards gave chase, but they didn't know the tunnels as well as I did. I figured Camilla would have gone out the same exit I normally used and could have set a trap. So I followed the only other path that I knew led outside.

I came to a halt on the small cliff face. There were remnants of an old grate or fence that I guessed was used to protect people from falling. I looked over the edge, the Sineti River running below. I swallowed. The fall could kill me. Footsteps sounded even closer. I spun around to find Killian and Valor standing there.

"Valor, Killian *please*. I did not do this. You have to listen."

"We don't have to do anything." Valor spat. He was overcome with grief now. I could feel it. I tried to lessen it. I tried to make him see things clearer, but I couldn't keep a grip on it.

"Elia, just let us take you in. Don't make this harder." Killian was in disbelief, but he was hesitant. He didn't want to hurt me.

I swallowed. "Killian. You know me."

"Then prove it. Let us take you in."

Taking a deep breath, I nodded slightly. I had to show them they could trust me. I took a step away from the edge.

"You should have taken the other tunnel," Valor said, his voice broken and unrecognisable, "this is for my father."

I looked in time to see him lift his hand. A piece of metal from the old grate flew into me, knocking me backwards and over the edge. I screamed, as my gaze locked on Valor's. A stranger stared back at me. Killian lunged to catch me, but he wasn't fast enough. I fell.

The water was dark and ice cold at this time of night. Pain shot through me as I crashed into the river, smacking my head on a rock. I fought my way to the top, gasping for air. I was struggling to keep my head above water and my eyes open. My head was spinning. I tried to look around and get my bearings, but I couldn't make sense of anything. My eyes grew heavy. As they closed, I noticed I was bleeding. From where, I didn't know, but I could see it floating in the water. As my eyes closed completely, and I sank below the surface, I remembered The Crone's words from the wall. *'When the river runs red, you will know.'*

She had known about Sierra the whole time, and now, so did I. That was what went through my mind as I drifted, then everything went black.

Warmth flooded me and my eyes shot open as I gasped, rolling to the side and vomiting up the river water I'd inhaled. Coughing and spluttering, I glanced around and found possibly the two people I least expected to see.

"Breathe Adira," Queen Yelara said.

I swallowed, doing as she said, closing my eyes for a second. When I opened them, I was glaring over Yelara's shoulder.

"What in Infernis are you doing here?"

Josette scowled. "Trust me, I'd rather be anywhere else."

"Great. Go do that. See you never."

"Ladies. Now is not the time. Josette, keep watch, please. Adira, I need to remove your oath before the others find you."

I tore my attention away from Josette at her words.

"What? But you.. I used your favour on..." My heart panged at the thought of Sierra.

She smiled knowingly. "You used Tira's favour on your sister. Consider this one a favour from me, that you can repay at a later date.. Something tells me having you owe me a favour is worth it."

I nodded slightly, not about to argue. "Thank you."

She nodded in return.

"This may hurt. Think of blood magic as a living thing. It will not take kindly to me trying to remove it."

"Ready when you are," I said, forcing a smile.

She saw right through it, but she said nothing as she placed her hands over the spot where my brand was covered by torn material.

At first all I felt was warmth, then excruciating pain like I'd never felt. I screamed, and Josette hurried over, clamping her hands over my mouth.

"Divinities, do you want the whole realm to know our location? Shut up," she whisper shouted at me and I was tempted to bite her hand, but I was soon distracted by the pain again.

Suddenly, it was gone. I was breathing heavily when Yelara lifted her hands away. I looked down at what I could see through the tears in my dress. The brand was still there, but it looked like a normal tattoo now. It was thinner, more delicate, with only one major difference. Now, coiled around the blade of the dagger, was a serpens. I breathed in.

"Unfortunately, I can't remove the mark. That is permanent, but I was able to remove the magic contained within it." She wiped her forehead.

"Thank you so much—" I gasped, arching my back as what felt like a jolt of lightning shot through me.

Golden light practically exploded from my body, shooting in different directions. Yelara and Josette were flung back. My eyes rolled back into my head slightly. I was bombarded with emotions. I couldn't tell which were mine and what weren't. I gripped my head. It was all so loud, and I couldn't make it stop. The ground shook as birds fled from the trees surrounding us.

I heard someone curse, but I couldn't tell who. The shaking got worse. *What a poor time for a divinity damned earthquake.*

A slap to the face shocked me out of my stupor as my head snapped in the direction of Josette.

"Get a grip. Now is *not* the time for a magical meltdown."

As much as I wanted to punch her, she was right. So, I closed my eyes and focused. I thought back to Amory's teachings. *Breathe Adira.*

The shaking lessened, then stopped completely as I calmed my racing heartbeat and opened my eyes.

"You have to go, Adira. Your friends will be waiting around the river bend. Go."

I stood. "What about you? How did you even find me?"

"That's not important. Go now, both of you." She nodded at Josette.

My eyes widened. "Oh Hek no. There is *no* way I am taking her with me."

"Oh, because you're such a joy?" She scoffed.

"You're a madwoman! You tried to kill me?" I clenched my fist, stepping toward her. Josette looked ready for the fight.

"ENOUGH." Yelara demanded in the voice of a true queen, and we both stilled. "You two may not like it, but you are *both* enemies of the crown right now. Josette, this is your best option unless you want to go back to rotting in that cell Odette put you in. And Adira, you are going to need all the help you can get if you want to get out of this alive. So both of you grow up and act like the mature women you are. Table your bullshit. You can deal with it later."

We both stared at her in shock and a little bit of shame.

"Now go. Follow the river for half a mile that way and you'll find your friends."

"What about you?"

"Don't worry about me. You'll see me again when I claim the debt you owe me." She smiled a little, giving both Josette and me a little shove.

It felt wrong to leave her, but I knew they'd most likely have guards searching for me. So reluctantly, I headed in the direction she had pointed. Josette, unfortunately, followed.

Yelara had been right; at what had to be almost exactly half a mile, we came across Hamish and Tarryn.

I flung my arms around the two of them, unable to stop the tears from stinging my eyes.

They both hugged me back tightly, shooting surprised looks Josette's way.

"Are you hurt, Adira?" Tarryn asked, and I shook my head.

"Yelara healed any injuries I had."

Tarryn looked at me quizzically, but before he could ask, Hamish jumped in.

"We need to go. Everyone thinks you killed—well, everyone," he said.

"What?" I asked, looking at him, and Tarryn sighed.

"Way to break it to her gently, Hamish."

He looked at me guiltily. "Sorry..."

"What do you mean? Who else is dead, aside from Hadrian and Tira?" My heart ached thinking about them.

"King Eli, King Rahmor, Queen Elsbeth and King Percius."

I breathed in. Sierra wasn't bluffing at all. She'd really done it. She'd taken out most of the rulers.

"I have to go back. If I can explain—"

Tarryn shook his head. "Adira, Valor has given the order to bring you in... dead or alive..."

"Dead or alive?" I swallowed, and Tarryn nodded.

"Okay then—then we go to Xeria and regroup."

"The rebels have taken Xeria and Reya." Hamish explained, and my eyes widened.

"What? When?"

"Word came in just before we found you."

"How did you find me?"

Hamish and Tarryn looked at each other, and I groaned. "If you say a dream or something, I swear to Helia."

Tarryn smiled a bit and shook his head. "Close..."

"The Crone?"

He nodded.

"Where is that old witch? I have some choice words for her."

"She isn't here. I just—heard her tell me to check by this stretch of the river as we were hurrying out. Some guards spotted you drifting in the river and reported it to Valor. We heard them talking about it on their way to find him. It's how we got here first, but they have to be close behind. We picked up Uri and Wes on the way and by the time we got to the gates, the order to bring you in dead or alive had already been given. Guards and soldiers were gearing up as we snuck out."

"Well, I appreciate you coming for me."

"Of course," Hamish said, as if it were ridiculous to suggest otherwise, "you, however, we didn't expect to find." He arched an eyebrow at Josette.

She held up her palms. "I don't want to be here either. But some creepy old woman unlocked my cell and told me I was needed for something. The next thing I know, I'm searching the river with Queen Yelara for your body," she said, her gaze flicking to me. "Much to my dismay, Yelara insisted on saving you."

I rolled my eyes. "I'm sure that was really hard for you."

Tarryn shook his head. "We can get a debrief later. Right now, we really need to move. They won't be far."

I nodded. "But where? If we can't go to Xeria, we aren't safe in Taros, and all the other kingdoms think I assassinated their rulers, where could we possibly go?"

"We go home," Tarryn responded.

My eyes widened. "You want us to go to The Wastes?"

"Ooooh wicked," Hamish said.

Tarryn rolled his eyes at Hamish, but nodded at me. "Thadea. We go home to Thadea, find somewhere safe, and figure out the rest as we go." A twig snapped and all four of us jumped to attention. I surveyed our surroundings. We waited, there were no more sounds. No shouts and no attack.

"It was probably a scout, no doubt off to report our location to the search party. We need to move." Tarryn urged.

I nodded slightly. "Okay." I glanced around again. We were still on the Kendelen side of the river. "We need to cross the bridge. From there it's a straight shot to The Wastes."

"Uri and Wes are keeping watch. If you're ready to move, we should go."

I nodded, and we made our way to where Uri and Wes were keeping guard. I hugged them both as well. I wasn't sure what surprised them more, finding Josette with us, or my embrace. We kept to the edges of the trees as we made our way along the riverbank. When we got to the bridge, it was clear. There were, thankfully, no guards. Hamish and Tarryn insisted on going first, with me and Josette in the middle, Uri and Wes behind me. We made our way across the bridge.

"We have company!" Uri called out, and I turned just as Valor came into view with Alina and an entire company of armed soldiers behind them.

"Turn yourself in, Adira! This is your only chance!" He shouted, and I tensed.

Hamish and Tarryn immediately moved to my side. Uri and Wes remained in front.

"I can't do that Valor! You won't listen!"

He shook his head. "Suit Yourself!"

He nodded to Alina, who stepped forward, raising both her hands. Her hair practically floated along with the rest of her damned body as she rose into the air. She can bloody fly? *For the love of Adysium.*

She extended her hands in our direction, and a tremendous gust of wind shot towards us. I braced myself for impact, but it never came. Instead, a wave of water shot out from the river, meeting the force of wind halfway and creating a wall between us and it.

"Run, Adira." Tarryn commanded, standing beside me, focusing on keeping the wall up.

"No way in Hek." I responded. Josette apparently didn't have any trouble following Tarryn's order, and she took off.

Tarryn groaned, stepping onto the wave, letting it raise him into the sky, so he could see Alina.

"Can everyone fly but me?!" I said incredulously.

"Not me!" Hamish said, raising his hand.

I smiled a bit, and we both joined Uri and Wes as they took up fighting stances. Valor held up his hand and then dropped it. Apparently signalling for the soldiers to make their move. They ran straight for us. I didn't miss the anticipatory grin on Uri's face. *Psychopath.*

The soldiers reached us, and all Infernis broke loose. Uri and Wes were practically throwing guards off of the bridge, left, right, and centre. Hamish and I fought side by side, taking on anyone that got close enough.

Glancing up, I could see Alina and Tarryn both countering each other's attacks. Where air struck, water blocked, and vice versa.

Valor was watching from the end of the bridge. I could feel his agitation and his impatience. He was sick of waiting. Finally, he appeared to have had enough. He stepped forward and clenched his fist. I heard the distinct groaning of metal. He was bringing down the bridge. My eyes widened. His own soldiers, and Alina's, were on this bridge. If he brought it down, it wasn't just me that could die.

The soldiers seemed to have the same thought because they glanced up in confusion. I breathed in.

"Run!" I shouted, backing towards the end of the bridge.

Hamish was right there with me. Uri and Wes were still locked in battle, but they began backing up as well. Surely he wouldn't take down the entire bridge? Steel fell and bricks separated. *Apparently, he would.*

Wes and Uri were still too close to Valor's side. I stepped towards them, but Hamish grabbed my arm.

"We have to help them!"

"Look at the ground, Adira. It's falling apart!"

I glanced over just in time to see Valor smirk slightly and spread his arms apart. Cracks splintered across the brick floor of the bridge. It was going to cave in. Wes and Uri finally broke free and sprinted towards us. That's when Valor started throwing the rubble at us. *Shit.* I stepped forward, calming my breathing. I could do this.

I focused on the bricks and bits of metal flying towards all of us. I raised my hand, calling on the power I'd felt inside me since my Testing, that well that had expanded beyond measure after Yelara removed my blood oath. Golden light shot from my hand, knocking a brick away. I gasped, but didn't waste time. I went to work blocking everything Valor was throwing at us. His eyes widened in shock, and all the soldiers stopped to watch.

Sure, the two flying Pures above their heads were nothing, but me blocking a few bricks? Mind-blowing. Valor grew impatient. He smashed his fist into the ground, and the bridge fell away under everyone's feet. I directed my hands towards Hamish and Wes, and the golden light slammed into them, practically throwing them to the other side, off the bridge, and to safety on solid ground.

I turned to do the same to Uri, but the ground gave way beneath me and I fell. I gasped, with nothing to grip onto to stop my fall. A hand suddenly reached out and grabbed mine. Uri groaned slightly. He was gripping a loose railing with one arm, and me with the other. I gripped onto him in return. The metal railing lifted into the air. Valor was holding it suspended there.

"Adira! When I say so, let go of me!" He said, and began swinging me. My eyes widened.

"No! I'm not going to just leave you hanging here!"

"I will be fine! Just *do it!*"

I breathed in. He had the strength to throw me to the other side, then I could use the Donum Aureum to catch him. I met his eyes and nodded. He nodded in return and began swinging me further.

"Three... two... one! Let go!" He yelled, and I did.

I let go just as he flung me with all the momentum he had. I flew to the other side, wincing as I hit the ground. No broken bones, but I was definitely bleeding and would have some nasty bruises tomorrow. I stood up just in time to see Uri's grip finally slip from the railing, and he fell. My hands shot forward and a golden platform appeared beneath him. He stood, looking down at the platform, then back at me. He raised his eyebrows and smiled at me.

"Bet you couldn't have done that if I'd let you throw your punches!" He called and despite myself, I laughed.

I began retreating, glancing back to ensure my footing was steady as the platform floated towards me. I glanced back at Uri, but something was wrong. He wasn't smiling anymore. His eyes were wide in shock and his hands were frozen in a reach toward his neck. I glanced at his neck, spotting a thin, red line that shouldn't be there. He fell to his knees, and his head toppled from his shoulders. A sharp blade hovered nearby.

I screamed, dropping to my knees as the platform below him disintegrated. He fell into the water in two pieces. The blade sang through the air, landing back in Valor's hand. Tears stung my eyes as I made eye contact with him.

I felt it then. I felt the hole inside him; the darkness forming there. He was full of hatred. At the world, at the rebels, but mostly at me. He was so blinded by his rage that he would sacrifice even his own morals to make me pay for what I'd done to him. Well, two could play that game. I stood up, clenching my fists, feeling my power rising and rising. I put everything I had into dragging up every ounce of strength.

"Adira!" Wes called, and I turned to see him holding Hamish up. Hamish had his hand pressed to his stomach. He was bleeding. I glanced up to see Tarryn take a critical hit to the head with a solid ball of air. The soldiers were regrouping on the other side. I could see Valor take in the scene. He didn't need a bridge to get the soldiers to us. He could simply lift them himself. We were outnumbered and injured. I might survive, but Wes, Tarryn, and Hamish might not be so lucky.

I nodded, backing up. "Tarryn! Fall back!"

He didn't risk glancing at me, but I saw him nod and back up as he continued to fight Alina. I glanced at her. She thought I'd murdered her family, too. I didn't want to hurt her. I closed my eyes, directing both my hands toward the centre of the bridge. Slowly, a gold, almost translucent barrier formed. Similar to the golden netting that had pinned Josette to the wall.

I quickened my pace until a wall stretched from the water to an unseen distance in the sky, right in between Tarryn and Alina. In between us and them. Valor threw everything he could at the wall. So did Alina. She tried to break it apart with her wind, but she couldn't. I could feel it weakening, but it would hold for the time we needed. Tarryn joined us back on the ground, puffing. He moved to support Hamish on his other side.

"We need to move, Adira, *now*."

I nodded, glancing back at Alina, praying she could read my face, praying she could see past her rage, even when Valor couldn't. I looked at him next. He was angry. He had stopped throwing things and was watching me with determination in his eyes. But he was still the man I loved. Swallowing, I turned away. I would make this right. I had to.

We took off toward The Wastes. I heard Valor battering my wall again with whatever material he could find. I heard the howling of wind as Alina tried to force it to break with her own power. They would succeed, but we would be gone by the time they did.

We reached the border that separated The Wastes from Kendelen. It was impossible to miss; clouded with thick, black mist. I looked at the men who had followed me. Pushing the people that didn't make it to the back of my mind. Movement had me spinning, ready to fight off whoever had breached my barrier.

Josette held up her hands again, and I was about to tell her to piss off when Hamish's groan of pain drew my attention.

"Hamish, are you alright?"

"Peachy." His smile was forced.

"Are you sure you all want to do this? We don't know what's on the other side of this. They say it's inhabitable for a reason."

"What's life without a little adventure, huh?" Hamish said, albeit weakly, as he leaned on both Wes and Tarryn.

He'd lost a lot of blood. I ripped my already torn and tattered dress, heavy from the water, stained red and brown from the blood and dirt, and wrapped it around his torso. We needed to look at his wound, but we didn't have time right now. I just prayed it was more superficial than anything else.

"Josette, we don't know if we are going to survive this. So if you're coming, I expect you to keep the bitchy comments to yourself."

She looked at us. "You are all seriously going to go into The Wastes? That's a death sentence."

"Then don't come."

I looked at Wes, who nodded. "Wherever you go, I go."

I gave him a sad smile and turned finally to Tarryn. "You could go back to Lios. I know for a fact they could use you."

He simply shook his head and held out his hand to me.

I swallowed and took his outstretched hand. I heard Josette sigh, before moving to stand beside Wes, muttering something under her breath about being far too beautiful to die so young.

I glanced at the three men, my friends against all odds. Wes held Hamish up on his right, with Josette standing begrudgingly to his left. Hamish's arms were slung around Wes and Tarryn's shoulders. Tarryn supported Hamish and kept hold of my hand.

I met Tarryn's eyes, and he smiled. "Lead us home, Adira."

I took a deep breath, as all five of us stepped into the thick fog, and everything went black.

Acknowledgments

Thank you to everyone who helped make this book happen.

I feel like I should get the cliches out of the way nice and early by thanking my parents for always encouraging me to be creative and always supporting me.

Thank you to all the friends I coerced into beta reading my book and answering my endless questions.

A special thanks to Stephen. Thank you for continuing to read, discuss, and give me notes, even after I cornered you countless times at work asking for updates.

Thank you to my partner Ben. Thank you for being the first person to read my writing, as it was happening. Literally, one chapter at a time like a Netflix show with weekly episodes, only not as good. From the very first, poorly written chapter one, you have been nothing but supportive. You made me want to keep writing. I love you.

And finally, a big thank you in advance to anyone who has bought, and preferably finished, my book!

Thank you for your time and support.

Divinity	Sigil & Gifting	Specialties	Kingdom
Elios God of Unity	Elementi	Breather = manipulates air Piro = manipulates fire Tear = manipulates water Turf = manipulates earth	Lios
Taros God of Strength	Kineti	Teleki = moves object with their mind Telepi = communicates within minds	Taros
Lereya Goddess of Healing	Healeti	Morti = kills and decays Remedi = heals and gives life	Reya
Ikeara Goddess of the Hunt	Animi	Imperi = communicates with animals Orati = controls an animals will	Ikira
Zalnea Goddess of the Harvest	Incrementi	Flori = controls plant life Immuni = immune to poisons	Lenea
Xeria God of War	Virbi	Argenti = skin invulnerable to all materials other than silver Forti = possesses extreme strength	Xeria
Thadea Goddess of Desire	Potenti	Cogni = influences and controls thoughts Senti = influences and controls emotions	Thadea

PRONUNCIATION GUIDE

Names

Adira	uh-DEER-uh
Adonis	uh-DON-uhs
Alina	uh-LEE-nuh
Calliope	kuh-LIE-UH-pee
Camilla	kuh-MILL-uh
Elia	ELLE-ee-uh
Hadrian	had-REE-uhn
Hamish	HAY-mish
Killian	KILL-ee-uhn
Odette	OH-deht
Raphael	raf-EYE-el
Sierra	See-air-uh
Tarryn	Ta-RUHN
Tira	TEER-uh
Tolemas	TOLL-muhs
Uri	YUR-ee
Wesley	WEHS-lee
Valor	Va-LUH

Places

Deorum	DEE-or-um
Ikira	ICK-uh-RUH
Lenea	luh-NEE-uh
Lios	LEE-oss
Reya	RAY-uh
Taros	TA-ross
Thadea	THAD-ee-uh
Xeria	ZEER-EE-uh

Giftings

Animi	AN-UH-my
Element	ELLE-UH-men-tie
Healeti	HEAL-UH-tie
Incrementi	IN-CRUH-men-tie
Kineti	KIN-UH-tie
Potenti	DO-TEN-tie
Virbi	VURB-eye

PRONUNCIATION GUIDE

Specialties

Argenti	aar-GEN-tie
Breather	BREE-ther
Cogni	COG-NYE
Flori	FLOOR-EYE
Forti	FOR-TIE
Immuni	Imm-YOON-eye
Imperi	Im-PEER-eye
Morti	MORE-tie
Orati	OR-UH-tie
Piro	PIE-ROW
Remedi	REM-UH-die
Senti	SEN-TIE
Tear	TEER
Teleki	TELL-UH-kye
Telepi	TELL-UH-pie
Turf	TERE